About the Author

Nina Dufort spent her childhood split between the Kent countryside and The Lebanon. After spending many years employed in diverse travels and occupations and bringing up two daughters, she became a successful painter. At present, Nina Dufort lives with her husband on Romney Marsh and spends her time writing and painting.

Praise for Nina Dufort:

'Gripping, elegant, sharply funny . . . Nina Dufort has written a stunning first novel and I wolfed it down like a box of Belgian truffles' Joanna Lumley

'In her first novel, Nina Dufort has achieved a gripping and sharply funny tale' *Prizes Galore*

'Funny and perceptive . . . hard to put down' *Home & Country Magazine*

'a lively, romantic novel full of wry wit and sparkling characters' *Prima*

'A charming first novel of some note . . . A lovely warm read' *Portsmouth News*

'A beguiling romance' *Marie Claire*

Defrosting Edmund
Painting Out Oscar

Nina Dufort

FLAME
Hodder & Stoughton

First published as two separate volumes:
Defrosting Edmund © 1998 Nina Dufort
First published in 1998 by Hodder and Stoughton
A division of Hodder Headline
A Sceptre Book

Painting Out Oscar © 1999 Nina Dufort
First published in 1999 by Hodder and Stoughton
A division of Hodder Headline
First published in paperback in 1999 by Hodder and Stoughton
A Flame paperback

This paperback omnibus edition, 2000

The right of Nina Dufort to be identified as the Author of the Work
has been asserted by her in accordance with the Copyright, Designs
and Patents Act 1988.

10 9 8 7 6 5 4 3 2 1

ISBN 0 340 79426 7

Printed and bound in Great Britain by
Clays Ltd, St Ives plc

Hodder and Stoughton
A division of Hodder Headline
338 Euston Road
London NW1 3BH

DEFROSTING EDMUND

To Sophie and Isobel

'Tis very warm weather when one's in bed.

Jonathan Swift

Upstairs in her Kent farmhouse, Xenia Whitby unfolded a pillowcase and sharply shook out its crisp folds before seizing a feather pillow and stuffing it vigorously inside. Having just telephoned her brother Edmund to invite him down from London for the weekend, she was preparing the spare bedroom for the poor betrayed darling.

Outside the window was the dark expanse of Romney Marsh, a view which she found uninteresting and sparse, preferring the tree-covered hills behind the house, where the land rose up billowing from the levels. Tonight a thin moon shone through a narrow gap in the curtains and she twitched them together to shut it out. The curtains were thick and white, and heavily lace-edged, which infuriated the more discriminating guests as they fumbled through the flounces to lean and stare at that mysterious chequerboard flatness, a world invented for the Red Queen and Alice to run across, leaping ditches and windblown hawthorn hedges in an effort to stay in the same place. Bed and cushions were smothered with pristine antique cutwork, crisp broderie anglaise and embroidered net, so that guests were frequently entrapped by button or heel and cursed the prettiness as they fought their way free from the lacy entanglements, and were deeply worried when drips from early-morning tea spattered brown spots on the arctic white sheets. However the pink sofa was comfortable and the bookcase well-stocked, surprisingly so since Xenia had no reading habit. Her husband Johnnie, together with Edmund, had unfortunately something to do with its catholic contents, ranging from Kipling to Karl Popper, via Mungo Park, Rose Macaulay and Julian Barnes. Knowing that Xenia never examined the shelves and giggling tipsily one evening prior to a visit by Johnnie's censorious and stuffy Aunt Bea, they had inserted various volumes of light pornography. Aunt Bea had breakfasted on Sunday morning with a very guarded look on her face, and the hint of a rose-coloured blush on her weatherbeaten cheeks; the books were forgotten after the childish joke and had remained unnoticed on the shelves for years.

Sniffing appreciatively, Xenia adjusted a small vase of *Viburnum farreri* and then left the room, pausing on the landing to straighten a watercolour which she had bought not long after her marriage to Johnnie. It had at first been hung in the drawing room but had been relegated to the upstairs after she had discovered that there were a great number of versions of Rhee Almshouses in the Snow by the same artist in many other people's houses. As she started down the stairs she heard the click of the telephone receiver being replaced and through the banisters could see Johnnie standing motionless on the flagstones beside the oak table where the telephone stood. He had his hands deep in his pockets and his shoulders were hunched. From her height she could see, as he turned and retreated to the drawing room, the small bald patch in the otherwise thick grey hair, and felt a rush of both suspicion and love. Her lips narrowed for an instant before she proceeded down the stairs and followed him with a cheerful smile firmly attached to her face.

She folded herself into her conventionally small armchair opposite Johnnie who sat, apparently immersed in his father's old Sussex cattle stock record book, snug in the vasty deeps of his father's huge battered shed of an armchair. Xenia was a tall woman, and the smallness of her chair exaggerated her length and long slim legs sloping out across the silky Turkish hearthrug, almost meeting Johnnie's on the other side of the fire.

'I've just been getting poor Edmund's room ready,' she said.

Johnnie looked up at the apparently calm, regularly beautiful face.

'Why do you always refer to him as "poor" Edmund? His book business is going along very nicely now he's got that Charlie Parrott fellow in on the antiquarian side, and he seems to have completely recovered from the Sylvestra debacle.'

'Of course he hasn't got over Sylvestra!' she almost snapped, startling him. 'How could he, so quickly? She was his entire life!'

'Well, he never shows his distress to me,' replied Johnnie, who privately thought that three years was quite long enough to get over someone like Sylvestra. 'He seems perfectly well balanced and in control of his affairs.'

'He hasn't had any affairs since Sylvestra!' she replied indignantly. Johnnie looked hard at her again, wondering if she was wilfully misunderstanding him, or whether he needed to explain what he meant. In either case, she was mistaken.

'I hope he won't be bored this weekend. Apart from the bonfire tomorrow night, I've nothing in particular for him to do, though I thought we might perhaps go over and have a drink at the Eeldyke pub, Sunday lunchtime.'

As far as Xenia was concerned, drinks at Sunday lunchtime meant a late, probably spoiled lunch. It had never occurred to her to shift the time of the meal so that she did not have to wait irritably for the men, trying to prevent pheasants from overcooking and parsnips from being blackened to charcoal. As she hid her irritation so successfully, they repeated the offence time and time again.

'But isn't that the awful pub where the police arrested all those druggies?'

'No, it certainly isn't. You're thinking of the Bell and Hatchet in Fingle,' said Johnnie shortly.

'Well, I'm sure it's not poor Edmund's sort of place,' she replied lamely.

'Let me be the judge of that. I think he'll enjoy the Eeldyke Inn.'

She waited until he had started reading again, and then said: 'Phil Johnson is dropping off the chair and trunk I bought in the auction up at Hilary's last week.'

'That's very good of him,' replied Johnnie patiently. 'It seems an awful long way for him to come just to deliver a bit of furniture.'

'He was coming anyway. He has a girlfriend near Fingle, apparently.'

'It's time for bed, I think,' said Johnnie, shutting up the book. He leant forward to nudge her foot with his. 'Come along, my old darling.' He held out his hand and pulled her to her feet. 'Where are all these bits of furniture to go, then?' he asked.

'I thought the trunk would be good for Rupert's room, beneath the window, to keep all his old toys in. All the rubbish he simply will not throw away. Don't forget he's out on exeat the weekend after next.'

She went to the kitchen to make some hot chocolate and he to his ritual door-locking and alarm-setting. He had just completed this when he discovered one of the farm cats crouching craftily beneath a chair, so he had to unbolt to put her out, relock and reset the alarm. The cat stared at him with great wide-apart pale eyes: like Xenia's, he thought briefly, before consigning it gently to the chilly dark. They stared at him with a strange lack of contact, as if focusing on the space between his own eyes.

Once in bed he picked up an old paperback copy of *Poets in a Landscape* by Gilbert Highet and amused himself with Catullus while Xenia fiddled with face-cream and brushed her streaked tawny bob. She took a long time so he put the book down and watched her uptilted face in the mirror, remembering her mother, who was about the same age when he had first met her as Xenia was now. The same deep voice, the same startling slanted blue eyes. But what a difference in personality! He had wondered sometimes if he had not been dazzled and confused by the mother, Sofia; bewitched, no less, into marrying the equally beautiful long-legged daughter.

Xenia's father had met her half-French, half-Russian mother in 1938 in Paris, when she was in her late teens, and had fallen in love, only to lose contact during the war. At the Liberation he had gone immediately to the flat where she had lived with her mother and elder brother before the war, hoping against hope that she might still be there. She was, and Xenia's family tradition had it that Sofia had calmly asked him: 'Darlink, what kept you so long?' Sofia had packed herself up and together with her *maman* had returned to England with him, marrying him a year later after they had had time to pick up the pieces.

Sofia had been delightful, supercharged company, Johnnie remembered fondly. She still was, but Xenia had always found her mother a hard act to follow and had retreated into as conventional a style as she had been allowed. Xenia had regaled Johnnie with the embarrassments she had suffered in her childhood when her mother had essayed to be the perfect parent visiting her at boarding school. She had turned up on Sports Day in trousers. 'Darlink, I thought you said it was picnic and games?' she had said, as she stared dumbfounded at the array of hats and pretty flowery dresses *de rigueur* for such an occasion. The school concert had also produced a sartorial misunderstanding. Sofia had worn an elegant black silk dress, proudly surmounted by her grandmother's diamonds. 'So lucky we were to 'ave saved them!' she had said, glancing curiously at the assembled neat blouses and tweed suits decorated with safe little regimental brooches on their lapels. She had not made the same mistakes again, but Xenia had been perpetually terrified of further examples of inapt behaviour and had mistaken for censure her schoolfriends' lively and eager inquisition about this glamorous parent.

Xenia had at last finished the remedial work on her face and neck and slipped into bed beside him in her white lace nightdress. Johnnie was suddenly aware of her tense boniness, which he found emotionally touching but, that night, also physically unsettling. He smiled at her as he put out the light, knowing that he was able to cure the tension, at least temporarily, but was unwilling.

Outside a deep and penetrating frost had begun to bite into the soft leaves of the remaining annual weeds, destroying their tissue so that they drooped, wilting on their stalks.

Edmund Yearne was mugged by the smell of his flat as he unlocked the door and, stooping down to retrieve the box of books with which he had staggered upstairs, nudged the light switch expertly with his chin. The major participants in the olfactory party were soot, engine-oil, orange peel and something near-indefinable which reminded him vaguely of old ladies' face powder. In spite of having had the carpets and curtains cleaned when he first moved in three years ago, the smell still lingered, annoying him each time he returned home. He dumped the books on a table, threw his keys into a chipped china bowl full of fluffy pocket jetsam and eased himself into the microscopic kitchen to make tea.

Once back in the sitting room he sorted through his haul, the result of a house sale in an unpromising part of Hackney where he had discovered a number of saleable books, although nothing too exciting. A first edition, in torn dust-wrapper, of Graham Greene's *Ministry of Fear*, 1943, very nice copy, he noted as he listed them. A first edition of Iris Murdoch's *Under the Net*, 1954. William Boyd's *An Ice-Cream War*, slightly fly-spotted dust-wrapper, and a brown paperback uncorrected proof copy of Elizabeth Jennings's poetry collection *Recoveries*, 1964. He paused with his pencil in mid-air. The titles of the first books to come from the box were disturbingly coincidental to the steps down which he and Sylvestra had slipped towards the death of their marriage, a series of events he had yet again been giving a mental dusting that afternoon while waiting to make a bid. He had not quite reached the 'recovery' stage. He rose and went to draw the curtains, shutting out the November night. Lukewarm air filtered upwards behind the dusty beige Dralon and escaped through the thin panes into the dark.

'There should be a proper tea-tray, with a teapot and a plate of crumpets,' he thought moodily, knowing that his own laziness had prevented him from getting the two former items out of the cupboard and forgetfulness had stopped him buying the latter on the way home from work. The unfinished mug of tea had cooled so he padded back to the kitchen for a refill; the kettle was the same grubby shade of cream as the mug, with identical sad brown flowers printed on it. He knew that scarlet, green and blue kettles were available and he liked strong colours, but it had not occurred to him to buy one for his own pleasure. He hadn't made the slightest attempt to change the rented flat which had most probably last been redecorated while Elizabeth Jennings was writing *Recoveries*. The wall lights were in themselves period pieces now: lacquered brass torches with white glass shades, etched with flame designs and backed with irrationally-shaped pieces of dirty teak.

He finished his list, repacked the books, ate an unappealing plate of fried black pudding for supper and then sat down to a recently discovered method of keeping unwanted thoughts at bay: having spent several years dealing in books he had decided it was time he wrote one himself and had started haphazardly to write a novel. The plot had been easy but when it had come to fleshing out the narrative he had found himself irritatingly sidetracked by details and this evening was held back by a search for a name for a minor character. Nimrod Bolt was the most recent favourite but was a touch too unbelievable even for a work of fiction. Another contender was Wisley Drizzel, but this too was out of bounds since it was not only too Dickensian but the name of one of his regular bookshop customers.

He was almost immediately interrupted by the telephone's ephemeral bleating and in reaching out for it knocked the flimsy apparatus to the floor from where he could hear his sister's fruity voice beaming up from beneath the table.

'Hello? Hello? Edmund? Whatever are you doing?'

'Xenia! I was on the point of calling you.' He lied glibly – he really had been meaning to, over the last six weeks.

Xenia was two years his senior and, since his divorce, had taken him over in a proprietorial manner, and been very kind indeed. Far too kind, in fact, and Edmund had occasionally been forced to fight off her good intentions with a metaphorical baseball bat.

Her name had been imposed by their mother, Sofia, who had refused to countenance either the Jane or Susannah suggested by their English father. The poor man had gamely fought and retired hurt, but rallied and won the second round with Edmund. Their mother had added a touch of surrealism to their otherwise conventional country child-hood in Hertfordshire, sparkling dangerously at Sunday lunchtime drinks parties and meeting her husband off the six thirty train in her grandmother's floor-length wolfskin coat.

'Come down and see us, darling,' commanded Xenia. 'You've not visited for weeks and weeks.'

Edmund was suddenly aware that he needed to get out of London for a bit quite urgently, more particularly out of the flat.

'I'd love to. I can't get away till tomorrow lunchtime though . . . If I turned up at about two thirty? Would that be all right?'

'That'll be perfect,' Xenia replied, pleased by his alacrity. 'We're having pike for supper tomorrow.'

'Sounds wonderful. Sort of deep, dark and muddy.'

'Actually, it's delicate, white, and you won't even think of mud when you taste it. See you tomorrow.'

''Bye, Xenia, and thanks.'

He was temporarily cheered by the thought of leaving London for the comfortable country time-warp in which the Whitbys lived and he returned to the novel, having to resort to the back pages of Chambers' Dictionary where, between Musical Terms and the Greek Alphabet, was an entry entitled 'Some English Personal Names'. Running his finger down the lists and marvelling at the unlikeli-hood of ever meeting anyone named Adalbert, Eusebius or Oughtred, he finally settled for Crispin Hemp, which suggested the required scratchy roughness for the character that was slowly forming in his head. He finally achieved two short-but-perfectly-formed sentences before becoming entangled in the difficulties of arranging a realistic meeting between Hemp and heroine in Pollock's toyshop.

By ten o'clock he was ready for bed. The bed in question was a lumpy double divan with both casters missing on one side and therefore propped up on book-club copies of those evergreen inhabitants of charity bookshop shelves, Pearl S. Buck and Dennis Wheatley. He had not shared the bed, or anyone else's, for some time now. His wife Sylvestra had left both him and London to go and live with a coracle-maker in Somerset, and after a lot of confabulation his two teenage children had gone with her.

Xenia had been deeply shocked by the divorce, being a person who saw other people and events only in terms of good or evil, black or white with no soft pigeon-backed shades of grey or beigy-fawn allowed existence. The word 'perhaps' rarely came to her lips. She also prided herself on her ability to judge character, which was why, Edmund thought, she was so very shocked.

'I simply do not understand!' she had kept on repeating. 'What nightmares for you, poor Edmund.'

Edmund had understood only too well. Sylvestra, having what was once termed a 'flighty' temperament, had ceased to love him and started to love someone else. She had gone, and had eventually been awarded half his assets. He had been lucky, he thought, as he pulled his jersey over his head together with his shirt, that he had been able to find a partner to buy into the business and had been able to continue with the shop at all. He was on 'good terms' with Sylvestra, that often hypocritical euphemism which meant merely that there was a polite refusal on his part to admit to any resentment.

The figure that was reflected in the wall mirror as it bent and stretched over the bed, twitching an extra blanket into position, was slim but solid, and just below average height, though not in any way out of proportion. A dark furred triangle on his chest was echoed by an arrow of dark hair which sped down his stomach as if determined to draw attention to his genitals. He was not much interested in his own appearance but imagined it to be average for his age, forty-eight, and he knew, but did not care, that grey hairs were beginning to appear in the thick, straight, brown hair, though he had recently been startled while shaving by the appearance of an enormous white hair emerging like a rocket from his left eyebrow. The clear, pale blue eyes slanted very slightly upwards. His nose was composed by genes with a penchant for architecture and was now a trifle pinched, giving a look of gentle austerity.

Edmund had got out of the way of seeking specifically female company, though he was not at all unpleased when it occurred in the natural course of his work, but he rarely now followed up any promising beginnings. There had been one or two modest attempts to kick-start his love life a year or so ago, with women who had eventually sensed his confusion and lack of real commitment and who had shrugged their shoulders philosophically, put aside their hoes and ceased scratching for those pent-up emotions which they had expected to uncover with ease and assuage with a great deal of self-congratulation.

He draped his jeans over the arm of the chair and got into bed with a sigh of relief, having become suddenly very low.

'All our bodies are made up of similar chemicals,' he thought. 'All our bodies, all over the world. And all our lives,' leaning over to turn out the light, 'all our lives are filled, all over the world, with the same events. There's a sameness to our condition which defies us to find any interest in it at all. It's only the little details that are different – and the little details are really similar to other little details all over the world, just doled out in different proportions.'

With this somewhat muddled and unoriginal thought he fell asleep suddenly and without warning before he was able to depress himself any further by the effort of thinking. The room grew cooler, and a draught from the window whistled softly in his ear, so that in his sleep he pulled the bedclothes over his head and dreamed he was in a dark and stuffy cave with wolves staring at him with their bright close-together eyes.

Edmund awoke, sharply aware of the cold. His legs had been bicycling subconsciously for some time in an effort to keep warm and he leant from the bed to feel the heater. Stone cold. Cursing a little, he rolled over the other way and reached for his jersey and jeans. His last dressing gown had started to shed little tufts of green towelling on the carpet, and then had abruptly fallen apart in despairing shreds. The smell was there again in the mornings, as it always was, but his nostrils were anaesthetized by the cold and it seemed fainter than usual. 'Jesus!' he swore as the stiff denim slid icy-cold over his thighs. The lights did not work either. A power cut. He lit the gas stove and put on three saucepans of water, for coffee and washing. The sky was clearing and brightening as he stood with his fingers tucked into his armpits, watching the tiny bubbles form and steam begin to rise from the pans.

Outside the car roofs were whitened and he looked across to the small garden in Paddington Street, a long-since ex-graveyard with the tombstones now neatly lined up against the low walls, where in the summer children played, lovers picnicked with Persian rugs and white wine, and other alcoholics sat muttering in dark brown groups in the evening, drinking cider. The grass was also white with frost. Surely it was unreasonably cold for November? A man walked slowly down the road with his hands deep in the pockets of his black leather jacket, his breath puffing out in front of him. His head was shaved and he appeared to be wearing some sort of narrow yellow hat. Edmund leant closer to the glass and stared hard to confirm what his eyes were telling his numb brain. The man had a banana stuck lengthwise, fore-and-aft, to his skull. Edmund grinned, then started to laugh hopelessly and immoderately, infinitely cheered by the utterly flamboyant ridiculousness of the gesture. What the concept behind it was he had no inkling, but the idea of getting out a tube of glue, carefully reading the instructions for gumming bananas to brain, and then proceeding to do so, gave him enormous pleasure. He was not alone. Two young women in thin jackets, hunched with the sudden cold, stopped and gaped as banana-man passed, then doubled up screeching and nudging each other.

Edmund intended to spend the morning in the shop before returning to collect his things and his car and running for the country. Searching in a dusty carrier bag he discovered a scarlet cashmere scarf which Sylvestra had once given him for Christmas, and a pair of over-large leather gloves which he had borrowed from Johnnie and forgotten to return. Encasing himself in his long black winter coat he set off for Baker Street station, carrying his box of books and whistling a marching phrase of 'The British Grenadiers' over and over again in time with his steps up Luxborough Street.

The glass door of the shop was newly painted with neat gold lettering, very upmarket, Edmund thought. 'Parrot and Yearne' above, 'Antiquarian and Modern First Editions' written smaller beneath. As he shouldered open the door, he experienced a tiny twinge of regret that he should have to share what had once been his own little kingdom which he had fought and sweated to establish, but the sight of his partner Charlie already behind his desk, wrapping up a parcel, immediately made him feel guilty.

'Morning, Eddie!' said Charlie, siting the address label neatly in the centre and rubber-stamping the shop's name and address across one corner.

'Morning, Charlie. Why are you doing parcels? Where's our Treasure?'

'Treasure has another bloody hangover. I've sent him out,

out of kindness, to buy the coffee and get some fresh air. He looks a bit ill so we'd better keep him in the back room this morning, with a bucket and towel handy, so he doesn't frighten anyone off.'

Tom Treasure was a student at London University, reading Russian. He was very impoverished and very useful, working generally Wednesday afternoons and all day Saturday. He dealt with mail-orders and the computer, effortlessly dealing with a system that had taken Edmund many painstaking hours of familiarization. Tom's abilities had lightened the workload considerably and Edmund and Charlie were prepared to put up with his occasional binges and frequently anarchic demeanour for the sake of his competence between times.

Edmund peered over Charlie's shoulder at the parcel.

'Ah-ha! Your erotic-sounding New Yorker, who thinks she's Helene Hanff.'

'Yes, except that she's no poor struggling writer, is she? These are very hard to come by, copies of Murgatroyd's *Waking Dreams*.'

'He seems to have done rather a lot of daydreaming. How many books in the parcel?'

'Four vols, half-calf, fifty pounds each,' said Charlie, cheerfully patting the parcel. 'I can't imagine that she really wants to read them.'

Charlie was tall, slim and dressed like a less confident version of one of those romantic-looking male models who so casually dispose themselves across the pages of *Vogue* as accessories to girls of aching thinness with hard-child faces. He was however quite hopeless with women, becoming idiotically tongue-tied in their presence, and the more he fancied them the worse he was at talking.

Treasure struggled through the door carrying three polystyrene beakers of coffee. His face was grey and his fingers puce with cold. 'She's only ordering those books to impress you. It must be lust, no one could possibly want to read them,' said Treasure.

'You are feeling a bit better, I take it?' replied Charlie. 'You're just jealous of my superior physical attractions, you burnt-out dissolute.'

'I've got to leave at twelve thirty,' announced Edmund, starting to sift through the mail. 'I'm off to the comforts of Kent.'

'Your sister?' asked Charlie.

'Yes. I've been neglecting her a bit recently.'

Edmund had once been lyrical about Xenia's cooking, which had caused Charlie to develop a curiosity about Edmund's private life that had surprisingly not been deadened by the odd visit to Edmund's Marylebone flat.

The morning passed busily enough with more browsers than usual, refugees from the cold, and enough buyers to keep the till bleeping regularly. Two or three people came in with books to sell. Edmund stayed till Charlie returned from a swift lunch at the pub round the corner and then re-scarved and coated himself, and set off back to the flat to collect his overnight bag. His car, a green Volkswagen estate in the evening of its life, was a mess inside. Dog-eared catalogues with muddy footprints on them and rolling tins of WD-40 littered the floor and a nest of discarded unlucky scratchcards occupied the glove compartment. Edmund drove off in the best mood he had been in for some time. It was odd, he thought, how the lethargic miasma occasionally lifted, enabling him to see, albeit temporarily, far into the distance, once more a man with keen sight and an appetite for life.

The traffic was heavy, and Christmas decorations were already, worryingly, in the shops. He did not wish to think about Christmas yet, and switched on the radio, but had to negotiate a right turn and left it for a minute on a country and western station while trying to cross the oncoming traffic. The songs seemed a procession of repetitions of a singularly small vocabulary, endlessly rearranged around one emotion to melodies indistinguishable from one another.

> 'My pore ol' heart's a-breakin',
> 'Cos my sweet lurve . . . went away-ay-ay . . .'

He tuned to another station but was already thinking about Sylvestra. Bugger it all, he thought. How does one stop going on and on about it? How does one stop examining one's behaviour for causes, mourning the effects? Edmund had not dammed Sylvestra's torrential temperament, nor thrown buckets of cold water over the pyrotechnical displays of rage; he was now unable to turn off the memory of the tiny blonde Fury, shrieking and throwing teacups and tomatoes at him. She had found their children less than fulfilling, and he couldn't stop himself from grinning momentarily when remembering her annoyance when they decided to go with her to Somerset. At some point in their life together he had ceased, perhaps through overuse of his exiguous faculty for enjoying high drama, to automatically believe all she said. His responses had become deadened, and he had been unable, for instance, to realize that her desire to leave London was urgent and real.

Via punk revival and Euro-pop he achieved some calming Brahms and managed to switch his attention to his novel. He interviewed himself, set an exam paper on the subject.

> Q. Why are you writing it in the first place?
> A. Something to do? To see if I can?
> Q. I see. Not because you have anything to say?
> A. I won't know if I've got anything to say till I've said it.
> Q. Is it about ideas, or behaviour?

A. Hadn't thought.
Q. Stop wasting time then, and think.

He paused in a minor traffic jam near Brixton. A red-haired woman in a Metro next to him was staring, and he realized that he had been talking aloud.

Q. Are you happy?
A. I don't think so. I'm not very unhappy at the moment though, which seems like a great advance to me. I even laughed aloud when I was on my own.
Q. Did you turn the gas off?
A. Don't spoil everything!

He tuned in to a talk on the invasion of Britain by the Romans, which interested him enough not to notice the miles, and suddenly found himself turning off the motorway at Parden, an unlovely sprawl of business parks, out-of-town superstores and warehousing. There were miles of interlocking by-passes weaving around builders' housing estates designed, in an attempt to relieve the monotony, to look as if each house came from a different part of the country: toy-houses with a muddle of red brick and gables, pink or yellow rendering, blue-grey slate roofs, tiled roofs, round windows, square windows, mock-Tudor beams and Georgian porticoes. Sometimes an ancient farmhouse stood suffocating amongst its brasher neighbours. Around all this was poor, marshy-looking land with little clumps of rushes and the occasional skinny pony grazing sadly beside redundant or broken stock-bridges.

'I wonder if the Celts thought the Romans' new buildings looked so hideous?' thought Edmund, circling a roundabout twice in an effort to find the right exit. 'Were they seduced by the plumbing and warm floors, delighted by the sparkling white and gold of the new temples in the new town centres? Did the Cantii feel diminished by the stone roads searing across their own ancient trackways, flattening sacred groves on their way to newly important towns?' He imagined, in cartoon-form, two Celts standing doubtfully beside a new road.

'It's a great wonder, Beric. It's what they call progress,' said one.

'It's just going to increase the number of carts and chariots,' said the other. 'More and more congestion. And we'll be inundated with tourists from Gaul.'

Another twenty minutes and he was into rural surroundings, pulling off a B road into a narrow lane running south through ancient coppiced woodland, at the end of which was the Whitbys' farm. Preferring to arrive at the back of the house rather than the chillingly elegant Georgian front, he turned through the iron farm gates with the brick cowsheds and modern barns to his left and rattled up a narrow track over a cattle grid to the back. This was considerably older than the front and had an organic look to it, as if it had heaved itself out of the ground, sprouted without any human help. The low afternoon sun shone on the brickwork, turning it pinky-gold and highlighting the tortuously twisted branches of the weeping ash beside it. There were unthawed patches of frost in the shade of the wash-house wall, where Meg and Flit the sheepdogs now slept. Edmund opened the heavy green-painted kitchen door, entered the back hall with its brick floor, muddy boots, dog leads, and derelict jackets that Johnnie wore around the farm. Hearing noises from the kitchen beyond, he called out, gingerly patting the ancient labrador that rose off its blanket in the corner and came to sniff him, farting and tail-waving.

'Edmund? Is that you? I'm in the kitchen!' Xenia called. 'Why do you always come round the back?'

It was wonderfully warm in the kitchen and Edmund put his bag down on a chair and gave his sister a hug.

'I like to surprise you. Is there anything left to eat?'

'I'll make you some lamb and lettuce sandwiches in a moment, and there's some choccy pud. I was just going to take the coffee into the drawing room. Johnnie's in there, but he has to go out soon to help set up the fireworks at Holy Hill.'

'Of course. I'd forgotten, it's Guy Fawkes.'

Xenia sliced neatly at the remains of a small leg of lamb while the kettle boiled, dabbing redcurrant jelly on to the slices before tucking them up between crisp lettuce sheets in thick brown bread.

'Here, you take this, and I'll take the coffee.' She picked up the tray and led the way, saying over her shoulder: 'As soon as Johnnie's gone we can sit by the fire and have a nice chat.' Edmund knew that a nice chat was code for a serious interrogation about his social activities since she had last seen him, and he began rapidly to invent a list of interesting events to keep her happy. In the hall they had to skirt round a large elm seaman's chest and chair placed in the middle of the flagstones.

'What are these doing here? Are they new?'

'Just been delivered. I've been naughty and gone mad at an auction.'

Edmund, knowing that money was rarely one of Xenia's problems, smiled to himself at her fake concern at her own extravagance and, not for the first time, found himself wondering why she was five feet eleven inches tall and he was only five feet eight.

Johnnie put down his newspaper and grinned at him with enthusiasm. 'Very good to see you!' He smacked the sofa beside him, inviting Edmund to sit down, and raising a puff of dust which mortified Xenia. She had not been allowed to rearrange the room at all, Johnnie being deeply wounded whenever she suggested refurbishments, and apart from one or two new chaircovers and cushions and a coat of paint, it was very much as it had been when his father had lived there, full of ancient and battered furniture and books. Edmund sank into the sofa beside Johnnie, eating his sandwiches in the light and warmth of the great log fire while Xenia poured coffee, stirring sugar into Johnnie's with concentrated devotion.

'Steady on, darling! You'll wear the pattern off the bottom,' Johnnie said.

'Xenia says you're on bonfire duty this afternoon. When's it to be lit?' asked Edmund.

'Oh, around six thirty. We like an early kick-off because of people not wanting to keep the small children out too late. It looks as if it will be a cold evening. Very clear sky again. Bound to be a sharp frost.'

'I don't think I'll come,' said Xenia, 'I'm going to cook the pike and watch a rerun of *Inspector Morse*. I've been to too many bonfire nights with the boys, and it really is getting slightly out of hand now, rather rough. I don't want to get cold feet – standing about.'

Edmund had never attended the Holy Hill bonfire rite through simply never having been staying at the house at the right time. He knew Johnnie considered it a chore, but was himself quite excited by the prospect of flames against the dark sky, loud explosions and the smell of smoke.

As soon as Johnnie had left the house Xenia started her questioning, hopeful for signs of improvement in his social life, but he fended her off admirably. No, he hadn't been eating takeaways. Yes, he had seen the Portley-Talls, and had taken Mary Portley-Tall's sister out to dinner at a Japanese restaurant in Fulham. He had eaten last Sunday lunch with old friends Seb and Fennel and had telephoned Uncle Serge in Paris. This last was true. He had, he said, his inventions gathering speed, been to a good party in

Islington, but as he saw her expression change from gentle concern to dissatisfaction at her own recent lack of social stimuli, he decided not to over-egg the cake.

'Well, you do appear to have been very busy. I'm so glad you are beginning to cheer up, and take notice of people again. Johnnie and I have been very dull these last few weeks. Everyone is holding fire till Christmas. Johnnie is always so busy with the farm, and with the boys away . . . and . . .' Her voice tailed away, almost suggestively, as if he should enquire further.

'And?'

'Well, he seems to find every excuse to go off on his own these days.'

Edmund sensed trouble. Xenia so rarely confided in him, but she had once or twice hinted that she suspected Johnnie was, well, not being faithful to her. There had once been an unfortunate affair with a farm secretary. That was long in the past, but Xenia had remained continuously and sharply suspicious. Edmund thought it unlikely that Johnnie would be straying again, although he could not entirely dismiss the idea out of hand. He tried to reassure her.

'But, Edmund, I'm sure he is up to something.'

'I doubt it. I'm sure that's all in the past. He's not really that sort of person.'

'You're all that sort of person, aren't you?' she said, hoping to provoke confessions.

'Nonsense. I resent being lumped in with everyone else in that sweeping way. And besides, both Johnnie and I are getting old and grey, and the luscious ladies we both so frequently meet behind every hedge are appalled by our old-fashioned clothes and fat tums.'

Xenia frowned.

'I suppose you think I'm past it too?'

'You, darling Xen, definitely don't look your age, and you certainly haven't got a fat tum.'

'Neither have you.'

'Well, Johnnie has, a bit, and I'm sure you're letting your imagination run amok.' Edmund hated the idea of discord between his sister and brother-in-law, the thought of friction in what he had come, since the divorce, to think of as his own family home too.

'It's just something Rosy Pressing said last week . . .'

Edmund got up and stood in front of the fire, warming his behind and selfishly trying to forestall any further confidences.

'Let's go and get that furniture out of the way. Where did you want the chest?'

'It's for Rupert's room. Johnnie helped bring it in, and said it was rather heavy.'

'Perhaps we could manage it between us.'

They went out into the hall and Xenia lifted the lid, giving a moan of annoyance.

'Oh what a nuisance! It's full of rubbish. No wonder it was so heavy. I'll fetch a bin-bag and we'll get rid of it.'

Edmund knelt on the stone flags and rifled through the contents. There was a layer of grubby newspapers dating from the year before, interleaved with plastic carrier bags, and beneath that a single layer of children's paperback books, two large Jiffy bags stuffed with odd sheets of paper, some covered in handwriting, others typed. Then there was a battered flat Kodak box, bright yellow and filled with old photographs and some drawings.

'I hope whoever sold the chest intended to part with these. It all looks as if it's been put away carefully, on purpose.'

Xenia waved the open mouth of the black plastic sack.

'Tough. They should be more careful. Come on. Start filling up.'

'I suppose they may be dead. I can't see any names anywhere, nor an address.' The bulging Jiffy bags were newish and previously unused. 'Don't you think we ought to check . . .' he started, but Xenia had already commenced whisking papers into the bag.

'They're only children's things. Do come on. We'll never get this upstairs if you start to read it all now.'

She dragged the bag out and left it in the back hall, where the contents sidled and settled, rustling the plastic and making the dog raise its muzzle and stare with a flicker of interest.

Together they lifted the chest and manoeuvred it up the stairs, past Henry's room, empty since he was at university, to Rupert's, empty because he was at school. Edmund noticed that although it had been untenanted for several weeks, it still had that smell of dirty socks and pubescent sweat that lingers even when the owner of the socks is far away. A large black and white pop poster was stuck to the sloping ceiling with red-topped pins. It showed three posturing young men with shaven heads and inexpertly applied eye makeup, waving their rudely gesturing Struwelpeter hands. Thick black lettering announced them as 'The Dark Entry'. Xenia saw his glance.

'Grim, aren't they? They were all in the sixth form with Henry when Rupert started there, and the whole school is besotted with them. I think they're what's called an "indie" band.'

Outside the sky was already darkening and the soft mist of condensation on the windows was like the bloom on a plum. They heard the back door slam, followed by rattling in the kitchen.

'Johnnie's back. I'd better go and start the tea.'

Johnnie had already put on the huge kettle and was ferreting in a tin, searching for cake. Edmund went back to the drawing room and stoked up the fire, making flurries of sparks fly up the chimney. Tea was substantial, with buttered toast and thick, juicy fruitcake. Edmund gave a little sigh of pleasure as he bit into the toast. Johnnie watched him with amusement.

'You'll need to be properly stoked up before going out. I'm collecting the Ovenden children and Freda on the way. Lucky's already over there, setting up rockets.'

Lucky was Johnnie's cowman and lived half a mile down the lane in one of the new cottages that had been built by his father in a burst of altruism in the 1960s.

Hunting for warm clothes in the back hall, Edmund chanced upon an old black fedora hat hanging dustily on a wooden peg by the door, and happily slapped it on his head, an ancient friend which he had left behind and forgotten about some years before. They set out in the Land Rover to collect the Ovendens, three of whom were already hopping and bouncing about at their front gate in a frenzy of anticipation, kitted out in identical red knitted woolly hats and reminding Edmund of a gang of garden gnomes up to no good. They tumbled into the back of the Land Rover squeaking and yapping like puppies, and Freda came out of the house carrying a fourth small person; calling for order, she settled them down on plastic fertilizer sacks.

Other groups of people were converging on the meeting point as the Ovenden-Whitby contingent arrived. They came on foot, by bicycle and by car from all directions and the pub yard was already tightly packed with people milling about an old tractor and flat farm cart on which two stools and a couple of chairs were placed. Johnnie had to park some way past the pub, so they all got out and walked back, the Ovendens melting away into the throng. Yet more people came, torches flashing, swarming down the hill from the houses round Rhee church, and a welcoming roar went up as the pub door opened and four elderly men tumbled out carrying brass instruments and a huge drum. They were heaved on to the cart with a great deal of teasing and good-natured complaints, and settled down on their seats. The drum started to thump regularly, its beat signalling the lighting of oily rags wound round staves, held, Edmund saw, by a group of hairy giants in bikers' leathers, to whose massive beer-bellied frames the harsh flaring light gave the grotesque appearance of Norse berserkers intent on setting the village afire.

'That's the local chapter of Hell's Angels,' remarked Johnnie. 'It was their turn to organize it this year.'

The trumpets tootled and the Hell's Angels surged forwards in a disorderly column, the cart lurching along behind the chugging and backfiring tractor, and following them came the crowd, their breath steaming, their boots crunching along the road. It was an impressive sight, Edmund thought, as he followed Johnnie to the bonfire field. The short walk was enlivened by an inebriated torch-bearer stumbling and setting fire to the hair of his brother-in-arms ahead of him. There were shrieks of laughter and howls of fright as he was rolled in the grass verge and extinguished, dusted down and set on his feet again, unharmed. The procession turned into a field where those without torches tripped on frozen ruts and stumbled over anthills and Edmund saw they were in that part of the land where the hills ceased to undulate downwards and became the Marsh, and that straight ahead in the flatness one lone irrational conical hill stood, a last outpost of the higher land, at the base of which was piled the most massive bonfire he had ever seen. It was the size of a house, composed of uprooted thorn hedgerow, an entire hut, old shed doors, pallets and a broken chicken coop. Surmounting it was a superb Guy which, as they got closer, Edmund saw was wearing what appeared to be a rather good pinstripe suit. Its face had been painted with skill, a monstrously malevolent expression on its mask. They pressed forwards, torches were tossed into the pile and flames started to crackle. 'There she goes!'

The flames caught hold and raced up into the night air,

roaring and hissing, and Edmund was jostled and pushed from behind, the crowd fanning out over the grass, long shadows leaping and jiggling. He lost sight of Johnnie and could now feel the immense heat from the flames on his face, see fountains of sparks rising up. The crowd quietened, absorbed in communal atavistic homage; then the Guy, burning fiercely, slipped downwards as the ropes which bound it to the stake were consumed and another shout went up: 'There he goes!'

Two boys alongside him, their faces shiny pork-pink in the firelight, unzipped their jackets and brought out bottles, swigging from them enthusiastically, their heads tilting right back, the light flickering across their gulping throats. A man in front of Edmund slid his arm round his companion, twisting his hand into the thick ginger hair that streamed down her back.

Was this still really a celebration of the discovery of the Gunpowder Plot? Of Guy Fawkes' agonizing death? Of the vanquishing of the threat of popery? Edmund wondered if it might not be some deep communal remembrance of ritual sacrifice and his skin crept into goose-pimples as he imagined the realities of being burnt alive. Surely he could smell burning flesh? Torches were now flashing up the side of Holy Hill, lighting from beneath the branches of the single tree which stood on its summit, and picking out three gallows-like constructions beside it.

Smoke from the fire drifted round the base of the hill, mingling with the greasy steam from a barbecue taking place across the field, at which a queue was already forming. The smell explained, the hairs on Edmund's arms subsided and he returned to gazing up the hill. His feet were numb and he took his gloves off to blow on his fingers.

The firebrands had been extinguished and ghostly figures flitted back and forth on the summit. Up there somewhere was Lucky Ovenden, waiting for the fire to die down a little more before he set light to the fuse and started off the display with a giant rocket.

It burst with a shattering bang that startled Edmund in spite of his anticipation. He was feeling distinctly disorientated and was wondering if he had not slipped back a few hundred years. The huge symmetrical cloud of golden stars which had been released drifted gracefully down, sparkling and twisting, some even hovering, caught in the massive updraught of heat from the fire at the base of the hill. Three more rockets were loosed to deliver their screaming, corkscrewing squibs into the atmosphere, wailing like tormented souls in hell. Someone nudged him on the arm and he looked aside to see a pale woman's face, with immense dark eyes, her hair lit with an aureole of gold flecks from behind.

'Edmund Yearne?'

'Yes?'

'Johnnie sent me over with this.' She held out a hip flask, which he took gratefully.

'It's brandy,' she said. 'He's down by the fire, watching out for any idiots who may have brought their own bangers.' She smiled, turned and slipped away before he could thank her.

The crowd had spread out across the grass and up the lower slopes. Three huge Catherine wheels now spun on their wooden uprights, a Crucifixion scene. Edmund sipped the brandy. It occurred to him that the woman might just possibly be the cause of Xenia's little misgivings. How had she discovered him in this mêlée? His neck was becoming stiff with staring upwards, and the show was flashing its way to a climax. An incongruous tank was now outlined in fireworks, spitting blue sparks from its gun, a final set-piece. One more earth-shaking explosion from a rocket and it was all over.

The fire still burnt fiercely at the centre, and was surrounded by people seeking its warmth after standing so still watching the fireworks. Duffel coats, windcheaters, Barbours, bright synthetic ski-jackets, old tweed coats. Children wove in and out of the crowd screaming and shedding bits of burger and bun, their faces streaked bloodily with tomato sauce. Edmund remembered taking his own children, Hatty and Jerome, to bonfires when they were small and held a picture of them in his mind, of their straight little figures outlined against the light, jerkily waving sparklers. Although he saw a few faces he knew from visits going back over the years, and smiled back at the nods and greetings he received, he was feeling lonely and not part of the crowd. He'd been disturbed by the clarity of his recollection of the children.

The row of willow trees which marked the boundary of the field was uplit, bare branches highlighted with gold streaming upwards into the night. A group of youths, stripped down to sweatshirts, had linked arms and were dancing a rowdy can-can, circling the fire and kicking at its outer rim, sending embers spinning red-hot into its fierce heart. Edmund had been exhilarated by the anarchic quality of the evening and wondered if the more ordered civic events, where people were so herded, guarded and taped off in an understandable desire to avert accidents, were, by denying the common need to experience the occasional exposure to danger, also denying the next generation the love and understanding of the power of fire, along with any feeling of actual participation.

Johnnie suddenly loomed up beside him, his fine, rather Roman features decorated with smuts.

'Sorry we got parted. Good show, wasn't it?'

'Very, very impressive.' Edmund waved the hip flask. 'Thanks for the brandy. It was very welcome, but I'm at a loss to understand how your messenger found me?'

'I told her to look out for the Guy Fawkes hat and red scarf,' said Johnnie, 'but I didn't think she'd find you. She wanted to go home early and said she'd deliver it on her way out if she saw anyone answering your description.'

'Who is she?'

'Amelia Sailor.' Johnnie's voice had a trace of feeling in it that made Edmund wonder if his surmise was correct. 'Lovely woman,' Johnnie continued. 'She made the Guy.'

Amelia Sailor's husband, Nick, had jumped off Beachy Head, leaving a note on the first page of a shiny new red notebook. 'I've become boring. Time to go.' This had been read out at the inquest, and there had been an inadvertently amused murmur at the Coroner's Court. Sympathy was extended more generously than it might have been had the note been more self-indulgent.

Amelia always preferred to say that he had 'killed himself' rather than that he had 'committed suicide', since the former had more immediacy than the ritualistic, considered connotations of the latter. During the first year of the eighteen months since it had happened she had endured mourning 'in the English style', when some people had looked consideringly at her as if wondering whether it was her fault, or considerately left her to herself in order for her to 'grieve in peace', 'to give her time to get over it'. She found that it was she who crossed the road to save them from embarrassment and would rather have been surrounded by wailing women in black, would rather have beaten her breast and put ashes on her head and have had it all over with a funeral the next day. Her marriage had been volatile, and, at times, worrying, since Nick had an unstable streak, but it had not been unloving and she had initially felt more anger than grief that he should leave her so flippantly. There had been months of wrangling with banks, solicitors, insurance and house-agents, leaving her in the end homeless and with a very small income from her work as a jeweller. There had been a few real friends who had not let her run away from them, who had sat with her in the evenings, brought her bottles of wine but seen to it that she didn't drink too much, who had put her to bed, taken her shopping and who had helped comfort not only her but her daughter Josie, who cried, and cried, and cried.

The house and land sold, leaving her a ridiculously tiny amount of capital, she and Josie had moved into a series of rented houses and cottages, all on short leases until this last one, which had been promised for three years. It stood in a lane between Eeldyke and Rhee, and there was an outhouse that she had contrived to turn into a jeweller's workshop where she'd worked furiously with great speed and concentration once she had settled in. Josie was still at school and unable to contribute much to the finances except in the holidays when she managed to get much-sought-after jobs picking raspberries, sorting potatoes, waitressing in pubs.

One autumn evening, running short of tobacco, Amelia had gone to the Eeldyke pub and Johnnie Whitby had been standing at the bar in his dirty work overalls, having a quiet pint. He greeted her in such a friendly and courteous way that her rather grim mood had melted. They sat far apart in the window under the eye of the landlord Seth, and chatted at first of commonplaces and then, discovering mutual interests and concerns, most enjoyably. She took great care to keep her distance however, and although she found him both likeable and attractive, and although she was mourning no longer, was very careful indeed not to appear to flirt or try to be too interesting. A couple of farmworkers and the mechanic who serviced her ancient

Peugeot were sitting in the corner. She could feel the odd glance from their direction, although they appeared to be deeply involved in talk of tractors and sprockets. One could not hiccup on the Marsh without its being reported.

When she had previously met him, casually at drinks parties in the past, he'd seemed a man of great calm and confidence, and a little unapproachable. She had also noticed and, on occasions, spoken to his elegant wife, who had never ceased to watch her husband, making sure that he didn't talk too long to any one person, particularly if they were female, and Amelia had found her overbearing and cool.

She met Johnnie several times by accident after the first drink in the pub, and he had lent her a biography of William Blake which she had enjoyed and returned after reading with a note of thanks, via Seth. The next time she had visited the pub there was another book waiting for her and slipped into the rubber band about its cover was an open note: 'We need a Guy for Bonfire Night. Could you possibly help out?'

Amelia was grateful to him for trying to draw her into local activities and set about the task assiduously, making a huge and lifelike body and a splendid head, well-stuffed with straw and newspaper. Josie had donated an armful of laddered black tights and they had made an extravagant wig from them, and stuffed old pigskin gloves for his hands. The face had been painted with an over-dramatic expression, to make an impression at a distance. Having consulted Josie first, and feeling rather strange about it, she forced the body into Nick's last surviving suit, one she had always hated but which had somehow escaped all the trips to Oxfam with his other clothes. They had been stern with themselves about these, keeping only really useful things like socks and jerseys which they could wear themselves, and the odd shirt.

'I don't think I want to come tomorrow,' Josie said.

'But why not, sweetheart? We've been before, and it's always such a good evening.' Amelia wondered if it might have something to do with the suit.

'Ruffles wants me to go out with her, to go to a gig. We've got a lift from her house into Parden.'

'And what about getting back?'

'Ruffles' Pa says he'll collect us. They're going out to dinner in Parden anyway and'll meet us outside the club.'

'Well, I suppose that's all right then. What time will you be back?'

'Oh, midnightish I should think. Don't *worry*, Mum. I'll be safe, it's door-to-door service!'

Parden being the only source of bright lights and incipient danger available, Amelia had occasionally to concede requests of this sort, in order not to seem overprotective. She was quite certain that as soon as her back was turned Josie would leap into a rundown car full of boys called Spliff, Kite and Spud and disappear into the roughest pub they could find. She was sure because that was what she had done when she was the same age as Josie.

Later that evening Johnnie had called to ask if she'd been able to make the Guy.

'Yes, I have indeed! It's been fun. What shall I do with him? Come early on the night, or do you want him before then?'

'Best if you could bring him around, say about three o'clock tomorrow afternoon? Is that OK, or would you like me to fetch him?'

Amelia didn't want him to see the inside of her house, squashed and cramped as they still were with too much large furniture and unopened packing cases. She didn't want him so close.

'No, don't worry, I'll bring him over. See you then.'

*   *   *

Amelia took the Guy over the next afternoon, putting him in the front seat and fastening a seat belt about him. Josie sat in the back, picking nail polish from her fingernails and wondering what to wear that evening. She didn't really have much choice. She could either go as herself, in jeans or leggings and a T-shirt, or dress up in her only party gear and high heels; she didn't have much in between. Or she could wear her scarlet party dress over her leggings and wear trainers . . .

They stood in the cold sunshine watching as a young man shinned up a ladder with the Guy over his shoulder, both silently judging the breadth of shoulder under the quilted checked shirt, the narrowness of hip, the mop of black hair. Johnnie pulled up in a Land Rover and trailer bringing a load of old fenceposts and pallets to add to the pile.

'Hey, that is a masterpiece! Many thanks, Amelia.'

'I think the whole thing is barbaric,' said Josie.

'Well, I suppose it is. Sometimes our civilization has a very thin skin,' said Johnnie, watching as the Guy was made fast to its stake.

'I *always* think it has a thin skin,' said Amelia. 'Perhaps there being too many people stretches it.'

Josie shivered. 'I'm getting cold.'

'Not surprising. You've never got enough clothes on. Winter's coming,' said Amelia automatically, finding that she sounded exactly like her own mother.

'Anyway, do you think we could go soon? I've got to get ready.'

Getting ready, Amelia knew, could take up to two hours and Josie was due at Ruffles' house by six.

'I'll see you tonight, then?' said Johnnie hopefully. 'I'm bringing my brother-in-law – Xenia doesn't want to come.'

As soon as they got out of earshot and had got in the car, Josie said, in a teasing, mock-whiny schoolgirl voice: 'Mr Whitby likes you, Mum.'

'Yes, I believe he does. And I like him too. Only not in the way you're insinuating, you sordid little beast!'

Josie tossed her head, flicking her goldy-red hair over her shoulder and out of her eyes and giggling. 'I was only teasing!'

'Well stop it at once. I hate being made to feel I ought to blush.'

Later, having delivered Josie, Amelia drove back to the cottage through the lane where her old house stood. She had not done this intentionally and automatically indicated left and turned into the drive, almost immediately realizing her mistake and braking. Through the leafless trees which surrounded it she could see that the study shutters had not been fastened and that the room was now painted a bright yellow; a large gilt-framed mirror hung over the fireplace. Upstairs, where their bedroom had been, the curtains were drawn, but she could see the silhouette of a figure walking to and fro. A wave of regret rose up in her throat like heartburn and suddenly she was dripping tears. Reversing sharply, driving down the road out on to the Marsh, she pulled up with a jerk on the verge beside a dyke, in whose black water was reflected a fingernail-paring of new moon. Amelia felt in her pocket for a handkerchief – she loathed paper tissues – and blotted her face with the thin cotton. She sat quietly and rolled a cigarette, leaning back, puffing, staring at the moon and trying to regain control of herself.

'You will go back to the cottage,' she ordered, 'and you will tidy your face. You will then go to the bonfire.' She took a long, last drag on the cigarette. 'That house was once my peaceable kingdom. Well, peaceable some of the time. I've been cast out of Eden, and although it wasn't all my fault, I've got to get on with things.'

She drove on to the cottage, grabbed a cold sausage from

the fridge and made up her eyes sketchily, leaving for Holy
Hill too late to catch the procession but just in time to see
the fire lit. 'There's a new bogeyman for the end of the
century – the man in a suit,' she said to herself as the
flames licked round the bottoms of the Guy's trousers,
having become more aware since Nick's death of obstructive
officialdom and soulless managements. 'Bonfire – bone fire
– no smoke without fire . . .' Her nose was scorching and
her back freezing, but she had seen Mary Beaton who had
been one of her chief comforters and suppliers of wine and
friendship when she had been grieving, and started to push
her way through the crowd to say hello. A loud explosion
close by made everyone jump – there followed a bit of a
scuffle and some swearing before she heard Johnnie's voice
raised, demanding a young boy turn out his pockets.

'Give me that banger. Thank you. We don't want any
silly accidents here.' Amelia saw him, and saw the boy
slink off, muttering brave retreating abuse. 'We can't let
them start doing that now while there are so many small
children about.' He stood by her, watching the furnace with
an expression of satisfaction. Then he turned to her. 'You
look a bit . . . well, um . . . a bit down,' he said.

'No, not really,' she assured him, then suddenly: 'That
was one of my husband's old suits, on the Guy.'

'Oh God! Was it a case of getting it out of sight, or an act
of revenge?'

She was surprised by his directness, and looked sharply
at him. 'A bit of both, in a way.'

'How does it feel?'

'Flat, actually.'

'Here, have a nip of this,' he said, diving inside his coat
and producing a hip flask. She took off her glove to undo the
stopper and had a sip, then another, and coughed a bit.

'Thanks. I can feel it going all the way down.' He noticed
her neat long-fingered hand and found himself wondering

who it was she reminded him of – perhaps a very small Queen Elizabeth the First?

'Don't get too close to the fire, you might self-ignite! Look, I've got to hang around here, wander around the fire, trouble-shooting, sort of. Could you take the flask and see if you can find my brother-in-law? His name's Edmund Yearne and he's a small man in a big black hat and red scarf.'

'Oh, I see. Very easy. There's only about five hundred people here. Well, I'll try, though I can't see how in this crowd . . . and I want to go straight after the fireworks.'

'You won't join us for a drink then, afterwards?'

'No, I'd like to go home, but thanks for the offer.'

'Well, you might see him on your way out. If you don't, you can keep on sipping, and give the flask back to me some other time.' He instantly felt silly, like a man being caught playing on his own with a toy car. But she appeared not to have noticed his spur-of-the-moment ruse, intended to engineer another meeting, and went, picking her way through the illuminated faces and dark, swaddled bodies, stepping gracefully in her long black skirt and boots over a comatose Hell's Angel who had been drinking all afternoon and was not even awakened by the first of the rockets. Contrary to Johnnie's expectations, Amelia miraculously found the owner of the hat who, with his red scarf, brought to mind the Lautrec poster of Aristide Bruant so popular in kitchens in the early 1960s, delivered the brandy and left the scene.

A police car cruised by, the last rocket scorched to its zenith and exploded, leaving a brief pink and green afterglow as its stick drifted quivering down through the dark air, landing on the back of, and startling, a Suffolk ram put in amongst a flock of Kent ewes that evening to start his duties.

Amelia caught the ice-green marbles of the cat's eyes in

the beam of the torch as it turned to lope ahead, racing
her up the path to the back door. A little owl called out
sharp and ringing, 'Qui-ick, qui-ick!' She struggled with
the key, cursing, and the cat lost patience and reluctantly
used the catflap. Her kitchen ran the length of the house
beneath the catslide peg-tiled roof. Ancient Rayburn at one
end, sink awkwardly placed at the other, and in between,
ranged against the wall, there was a long row of modern
cupboards – 'units' the agent had called them while showing
her disdainfully around the place, trying to find something
about which to be enthusiastic in a house which had already
been spurned by other would-be renters, in spite of the
shortage of available properties.

Amelia went straight to the far left-hand cupboard and
took out her last bottle of the previous year's sloe gin; she
shut the cupboard doors firmly, since they had an eerie
knack of springing open by themselves when her back was
turned, making her jump. There was no central heating,
no washing machine or dryer, no lack of mould, blackly
spreading across the bathroom ceiling, and she had found
on her first day there the skeleton of a cat in the coal shed,
beside something which she had taken at first in the dim
light to be a sheep's blackened, decapitated head, but which
resolved itself, after being poked with a stick, into an old
bicycle saddle coated in dust.

She poured herself a generous splash of gin, and leant up
against the stove warming her thighs, easing off her boots.
This year's sloes were seeping precious juices out into the
gin in two bottles in the wash-house. The sloes had been
picked only two days before, and the gin would not be
drinkable until the end of January at the earliest. Only
two bottles this year. She admired the rich amethyst-ruby
colour, the plum-almond scent, the winter taste. She also
noticed that her socks, Nick's socks, had holes in them, and
that there was a small acid burn hole on her skirt where she

had carelessly splattered spirits of salt while working on a gold ring. She must not let herself become too scruffy and careless of her apppearance; that would send out signals of defeat, or even signs of an insouciance she did not possess. She wondered if the thought had come to her because she was aware that someone fancied her, and that she could have fancied him back, had he not been married. She vividly remembered Nick had once been obsessed with a terrible little trollop of a waitress. If she were herself to indulge in adultery, the wife in question would refer to her as a terrible little trollop, and she would find that distasteful, nor would she like to upset anyone, even Johnnie's icy spouse, for the sake of her own satisfaction although she was increasingly feeling the need for male company. She preferred the term strumpet to trollop, she thought, taking another sip of the gin: strumpet sounded ringing and brassy, like a besmirched angel; trollop sounded lollopy and bosomy, like those overcooked kitchen wenches at pseudo-mediaeval dinners, with their tits hanging out of anachronistic white blouses and corsets. She finished the gin, stoked up the coal stove and boiled a kettle to make herself a hot-water bottle, then leaving the light on to guide Josie in, she went up to bed.

Her bedroom was the best room in the house, although it was on the lane side which meant she was often woken early in the mornings by tractors and lorries off on their day's work. The thin door had a delicately cut eighteenth-century iron latch and the rooms had a higher ceiling than those downstairs. It had a large sash window and in the late summer, when they had moved in, it had been light and airy with a view across acres of sunny wheat, flat greenness dotted with sheep, and sky, sky and more sky. It was also on the leeward side of the house, calmer and less buffeted by the prevailing southwesterly winds. Josie's room was to the windward, and in September they had hung out of her window watching approaching storms, the vast cumulo-nimbus clouds boiling and bursting like giant cauliflowers on the horizon, waiting till the last minute before slamming down the sash as the sky darkened and the first fierce raindrops dashed against their faces. Amelia enjoyed the weather and its inescapable inevitability on the Marsh, where there was no shelter and she felt at one with the elements and could take and love whatever they threw at her. As winter had come in, she had piled on the blankets, lit the paraffin stove and listened snugly while the rain pattered on the Kent peg tiles above and gurgled in the gutters, and the nights had become longer and longer.

She slipped off her skirt, then, good intentions thwarted by the cold, removed only her tights and knickers, tucking her long and rather grubby cotton petticoat around her pale legs as she leapt into bed wearing the two jerseys in which she had attended the bonfire. She could smell the smoke in them as she huddled under the bedclothes, waiting for her body heat and the hot-water bottle to make a bubble of warm air. Tomorrow was Sunday, so she could stay in bed as long as she liked, but in practice would get up and go out to her shed to get some work done, having a batch of silver earrings to make for a craft gallery in Canterbury.

She drifted off to sleep while planning the next morning's work, only to reawaken almost immediately, her subconscious ear hearing the click of a door being quietly closed as Josie crept in at one a.m. She was now unable to get back to sleep, and lay there stirring the immortal soup of worries and frets common to those awake at that time of the morning.

'This is the wrong way round,' she thought crossly, 'I should have stayed awake worrying because she wasn't yet back, not woken up and started worrying because she was.' She proceeded to fret about having enough sheet silver in hand to complete the job, and whether her stock of saw blades needed replenishing, and the risks involved in liking Johnnie, and who was Aristide Bruant, and what shall I do, what shall I do?

Even though orders had picked up a bit over the last two months, things looked a bit bleak. Last month, after having paid off all the bills and allowed for food and extras like firewood, she had had only ten pounds spare. The woodman had brought the logs too big. She would have to split them all. 'I'll get Josie a black velvet hat for Christmas. But there's nothing now, till Christmas. Halloween, Bonfire Night over. Just approaching winter and Advent, and that's a period of mourning. They take all the flowers out of churches in Advent. A silver, reusable Advent calendar would be fun to make, like a Russian icon, covered with small silver doors to open, with tiny bolts, and inside each a golden thing, apple, rabbit, bird, something different for each day . . .'

She slept again, the fat little cat curled up in the small of her back. Outside the water in the dykes started to solidify around the reeds, an icy skin spreading across the dark surfaces.

Three miles away, up beyond the half-moon of old degenerated cliff-face that rims the inside edge of the Marsh, Johnnie poured out three brandies, toasting Xenia's successful pike with *beurre blanc,* and put on John Lee Hooker while they settled down to roast themselves by the fire and play a round or two of cribbage. They retired to bed at eleven, Edmund relaxing into the warmth of his bed, cup of tea at elbow and book in hand, reading only a paragraph or two before slipping away on a tide of comfort and security. But he awoke during the night, his book having dropped to the floor with a thud. He was a light sleeper and he had left the bedside light on. It was three a.m. and he felt thirsty –

too much wine at dinner – and also surprisingly peckish. A navy towelling dressing gown hung on the back of the door, so he slipped it on and tiptoed out on to the landing and down the stairs to search out a biscuit or two, or perhaps a bowl of cereal. The kitchen was warm, but intimidating, having been the subject of one of Xenia's recent improving sessions. Beautiful deep cupboards, drawers that slid in and out like silk, all paint-stained a soft bluey-green. Immaculately tidy lists and neatly marked calendars hung on the wall beside the vast new refrigerator. A dark green bowl was filled with eggs, to remove one of which would have destroyed the impossible symmetry of their arrangement. The black and white tiled floor was spotless and all the supper dishes were neatly stacked in the dishwasher. It seemed quite difficult to know where to look for anything edible, but Edmund remembered the cake tin, took a plate from the wooden drainer above the sink, and cut himself a slice, careful not to leave crumbs all over the table. Too tidy, he thought as he looked about, inhumanly tidy. He appreciated order, but liked to be able to see the things that had been ordered. There was not a cup or a wooden spoon in sight. He was still not sleepy, so he searched for hot-chocolate powder, but couldn't find any. At least the milk was in the fridge and he warmed a cupful, added some sugar and sat thinking. The dog sighed in its sleep in the back hall, and Edmund remembered the sack of papers they had taken from the chest that afternoon and went in search of it. The house was immensely silent, so quiet that he could only hear the soft hum of the fridge and himself and the dog breathing.

He rootled through the sack, pleased that it hadn't yet been put out to be burnt, found the things he was looking for and returned to the kitchen table, opening up the yellow photographic paper box. On top lay a child's wax crayon drawing, much creased. It showed a boy sitting on a swing, with a girl standing behind him, her hands on her hips, looking unmistakably cross. At the bottom was written, in young child's writing, 'My trun naw' and beneath this, in sprawling capitals, IMIM. The tree from which the swing was suspended was a child's tree, but drawn with knowledge of trees and the way their branches sprang from the trunk, sloping upwards and away, not stuck on like horizontal afterthoughts. The leaves were real leaves, amongst which was a plum. The children's bodies, although square with legs and arms at each corner, had the appearance of volume. It seemed almost the work of an adult trying to be naive, but Edmund knew it wasn't.

Beneath this, a pile of black and white snapshots of picnics in rocky places, some beside the sea, and a larger photograph of a girl in a dark swimsuit, her head held self-consciously as if staring at her outstretched feet, her face almost obscured by a panama hat. Then there was a scruffy watercolour painting of cyclamen leaves, their marbled surfaces delicately but loosely done, a professional piece of work. On the back was a shopping list. 'Bread, bacon, biscuits. Cabbages and Kings. Deodorant, loo paper, toothbrush. Something for supper. Kippers? Ring Percy and get him to sort out the hedge.' This was followed by a doodle of a flower in a jug. Next came three or four letters on thin airmail paper, with no envelopes, from school friends, he thought, as he read the neat round English handwriting.

Dear Imim,

I hope you are well and having a lovely time. How is your new school? Do you have to speak French all the time how gharstly. Chooky is well and the farrier has just been to do his new shoes Mummy says I'm getting too big for him and we will have to get a new pony next year. Can you do any riding in Lebanon?

There followed more in the same vein. 'What a boring child!' thought Edmund, putting the letter down. 'But at least I know they once lived in Lebanon.' The letter was dated 1957. He felt it was probably addressed to a girl, little boys not writing letters to each other much. The other letters were much the same, except the last which came from a child with a livelier mind, detailing a birthday party and a visit to Cornwall. There was a PS: 'I've found out all about you know what and it's all revolting.' It was signed Helen, with an exaggerated amount of kisses round it.

Imim was a strange name, but perhaps it was Lebanese, though the drawing appeared to show essentially English children, the boy in long grey shorts and socks, the girl in a Fair Isle jersey. He turned to the exercise books, one of which had a name on the thin foreign cover. Beneath the black printed picture of Minerva, surrounded by a classically scrolled border, was written 'M. A. Anderson', and beneath that, less confidently, 'M. A. Fleury'. He opened the first one and found it to be a book of poetry, each poem carefully copied out on the right-hand page, while a drawing in crayons illustrated it on the left.

'Automne' par Victor Hugo
L'aube est moins claire, l'air moins chaud, le ciel moins pure . . .

Here a scarlet pen had ferociously underlined the final 'e'.

Le soir brumeux ternit les astres de l'azure . . .

Again the energetic pen had underlined the 'e' of azure.

Les longs jours sont passés, les mois charmants finissent
Hélàs! déjà les arbres qui jaunissent!

There were two or three more verses and at the end the red pen had admonished: *Vu. A récopier en écrivant mieux.*

The writing was indeed poor, sloping this way and that, the writer struggling to come to terms with all the French curlicues and flowerinesses. The drawing opposite was of a path through a wood, the influence of Arthur Rackham strongly felt, though clumsily applied. The trees bearing yellow leaves encircled a lone figure in the centre of the path, struggling with an umbrella while a positive whirlwind of yellow leaves whipped round her.

More poems, Anne de Noailles, Verlaine, Valéry. Other drawings all done with a delightful careless energy and feeling of movement. The red pen had been at it again, more approving of the drawings. *'Très bien'* was written large across the bottom of most of them. Hard to guess how old the artist was – perhaps nine or ten?

He ploughed on. He pulled out the contents of one of the Jiffy bags. Miss Anderson/Fleury had been a prolific note-maker and writer. It was full of mismatched sheets of paper, some pages torn from different exercise books, some brown-edged sheets of typing paper held together with rusty staples, some in manuscript, some typed on what had probably been an old-fashioned portable typewriter. The clock on the wall of Xenia's kitchen said four a.m, but he read on, picking out a couple of sheets at random.

I saw someone murdered once, when we lived abroad with my stepfather. The sun was hot and hard as I left school, so I put my satchel on my head to protect it, carrying it as I'd seen the Kurdish women carrying their bundles down the hill, over the stony ground where the bare rock poked through the reddish earth and scraggy goats grazed, their bells tinkling softly in the heat haze. I needed both hands free to eat the bag of green almonds sprinkled with coarse salt that I'd bought at the school gates. A tall, friendly Sudanese stood there every day at lunchtime, when we were sent home for the rest of the day, it being too hot for schoolwork. He sold almonds, and little crescents of hollow bread, which he would open and sprinkle with dried thyme and more salt. He only had one hand. I knew that this was because he had been caught stealing in his own country and had it chopped off as a punishment.

My mother would not be at home since she had a bridge morning at the St George's Club, and would stay for lunch afterwards. Georges, my stepfather, was away in Jordan on business. Nadia, the maid, would be at home in the fourth-floor apartment, and would have lunch ready. But there was a shop in rue Hamra, only four minutes or so past our apartment, which sold American comics, and I decided to pay a visit there for a quick browse before going home. The comics were frowned on by my mother. Ice-cream was also forbidden on health grounds, as was playing with the concierge's little boy, Nabil, because Georges said he had TB. Rue Hamra was noisy and dusty with traffic: mule-carts, buses, Mercedes taxis, larger American cars, pedestrians walking slowly, slowly in the 100° F humid air, on their way home to lunch and the afternoon sleep. Gently dripping with sweat and just about to turn into the cool, dark newspaper shop, I saw two men leaving the building two doors ahead. They wore unremarkable white shirts and light drill trousers, sunglasses, and both carried black briefcases, and were arguing nervously. A black car screamed to a halt just past me and suddenly from the rear side window came cracks and flashes. One man threw himself to the ground, but the other, as the car roared off, had leapt backwards against the white wall, slowly sliding down the cement, leaving a snail's trail of scarlet behind him. He lay on the ground, jerking horribly, and then was still, with a red pool slowly spreading beside him.

There was pandemonium. Jabbering, shrieking people closed around me. I was incapable of moving, legs jelly-like, stomach heaving. The proprietor of the shop which sold the American comics, the reason for my presence there, grabbed me by the shoulders, gave me a little shake before turning me round the other way and giving a little push.

'*Va*! *Va chez ta mère. Yallah*!' I fought my way back through the crowd, the heavy satchel banging against my legs.

Up in the lift, unlocking the door with my own key, I subsided on to the cool stone floor in the hall. Nadia came out of the kitchen. '*Qu'est-ce-que tu as, ma petite? Tu es malade?*' I told her it was just the heat. She fetched a glass of water and put her hand to my head. 'Come and have your lunch. I've made *sambousek* for you.' Out on the balcony, at the cool green marble table in the shade, I listened to the ice-cubes tinkling in the glass as I put it to my lips, heard a faraway hubbub of shouting and hooting cars. Beyond the red-roofed houses and tall apartment blocks the sun shone on the brilliant sea with a malicious sparkle. I ate the *sambousek*, peeled a peach and ate that too, then went to my room to tackle the grammar, the metric system, and learn by heart the weekly paragraph of French history which had to be recited aloud every Friday.

My mother looked in later, a beading of sweat curdling her face powder and dark blood-red Elizabeth Arden lipstick.

'All right, my sweet? Doing your prep? I'm just going off for my rest. So, so hot today.'

I waited, hearing her high-heeled shoes ticking across the stone-floored hall, her door shutting. I waited still, until quite sure she was asleep, then crept out into the sitting room to telephone Eugenie, who was the daughter of an official at the Russian Embassy, and who lived in the next street.

'Can you come over, after you've finished your homework?'

'I'll ask Papa. He's just off for his snooze.' There was rapid conversation in Russian, then: 'Yes, it's OK. I'll see you in half an hour. Watch for me from the balcony. I don't want to ring the doorbell and wake your parents.'

She came in due course, still wearing her blue school overall with its little white collar. Her hair was tied up in complicated pigtails finished with crisp bows of white nylon ribbon. She beamed at me and flopped down on the bed, her chin held in her hand in what she imagined to be a sophisticated manner.

'You'll never guess what! I've a secret! Shall I tell you?' said Eugenie.

'If you like.'

'Well, I've found out all about sex from Samia! Listen, this is what men and women do when they go to bed . . .' There followed a highly imaginative, and to me totally unbelievably ridiculous account, and we sat there shaking with laughter at the preposterousness of it, certain that we would never submit to such an idiotic chain of actions in order to have babies. But I was also doubtful.

'Are you sure she's telling the truth?' I asked suspiciously. Samia, their maid, was only fifteen, and a renowned fibber.

'But yes! She says she has seen grown-ups doing it when she was younger, and they thought she was asleep!'

Outside, the sun was on its downward path. Soon the world, the adult world, would wake up again, and return to work as the air cooled and the frangipani smells from the gardens grew stronger. I never told anyone what I had seen that day, in the street, and it was for a long time muddled in my mind with Eugenie's hilarious story of men with their trousers down, bouncing up and down on top of women.

Edmund was quite transfixed by this. Amused, horrified and interested all at once, he wondered if this was a fragment of an autobiography, or just a single reminiscence. He flipped through the pile of papers and found there appeared to be some order to them. First a few pages torn from an exercise book, probably used as a diary and written in immature handwriting. Then perhaps a letter or two, and then a typewritten account, then again more handwritten diary-like jottings, again followed by a rewriting in more adult language. It was as if someone had sorted through their diaries, discarding much of the material, and then reassessed, making a précis, in an effort to make sense of their life, a tidying up of the past.

He stuffed all the pages back and took everything up to his room. He was truly tired now, and would look at the rest when he returned to his flat. He slept, his ruffled dark hair and incipient stubble incongruous on the white lace-edged pillow.

'Xen? Where did that chest come from?' Edmund tried to get her attention as she fried eggs and turned rashers of bacon. She was neatly dressed that morning in clean, new-looking jeans and a navy guernsey, and was concentrating on getting the eggs just perfect.

'I told you. At an auction.'

'But where? Down here? In London?'

'Norfolk. I went to stay with Hilary. We drove over to an auction in a place called Bolt.'

'Could you give me the address of the auctioneers?'

'I've got the catalogue somewhere. Try the hall table. Why all the fuss?'

'You know those papers we found? I rescued them. I'm quite sure they were put away, hoarded on purpose. I thought I'd try to trace the owner.' He hadn't really thought of it, until that moment. 'It's just that I don't think they were *meant* to be thrown away. They are really quite interesting. There's a name on one of the exercise books. M. A. Anderson. She writes very well.'

He went off to look for the catalogue.

'Can I keep this?'

'Yes, of course. Now here's your breakfast, fusspot. *Do* get started.'

Johnnie was sitting at the table, reading the newspaper, but folded it up crisply and stretched. He had finished his breakfast before Edmund had come downstairs.

'I've got to go and talk to Lucky.'

'All right, Johnnie. Edmund and I are going to the beach.'

'Then as I'm busy all morning, I suggest Edmund and I meet up at the Eeldyke pub for a drink before lunch.'

Edmund wasn't keen on the idea of the beach, thinking that he would probably die of hypothermia, and anyway, Xenia hadn't asked him if he wanted to go, but he liked the idea of a drink before lunch.

'Don't look so miserable, Edmund. The beach will do you good. Then I can drop you off at this awful Eeldyke hole and I can get on with the lunch. I've got this wonderful lamb dish to try out.'

Being treated like a child had a curiously comforting effect on Edmund, who did as he was told, ate up his breakfast, happy enough not to have to think what to do, although he would have liked to sit and sift through the papers they had found. But it was too much to hope that Xenia would let him do anything he wanted.

Later they took the old labrador, smelly and grinning

in the back of the car, and drove to Jury's Gap, where they drove up a steep slope on to the sea wall, just past the army firing ranges. The tide was far out and the only soul in sight was a solitary shrimper, pushing his net across the still-receding tide. It was a little warmer here than it had been inland and they scrambled down the shingle past the high-tide line of jumbled seaweed and gulls' feathers, down on to the miles of scoured clean, shining wet sand, with its little runnels and channels and flocks of sparkling white birds, standing all facing one way, admiring their own reflections in the shallows. Edmund thought this must be one of the best beaches in Europe, and was instantly off, searching for something interesting . . . a stone with a hole in it, a perfect cockleshell. Xenia watched the neat, self-contained shape, hair flopping about as he stooped and examined first this, then that. She thought he really should get married again. In the year after Sylvestra had left she had often asked lone women to lunch whenever he came to stay, with the result that he came less frequently. These women had found him attractive, but puzzling. He had either had too much to drink and talked maniacally about matters which confused them, or had smiled benignly and hardly spoken at all. She had given up, at last, after he had patiently explained to her that he was not on the market for the highest bidder to snap up like some slightly scratched Regency table. He had said that he came down to see her and Johnnie, to get briefly away from work, and to wallow in her wonderful food. He had not added that the women she fished up out of her pool of acquaintances, the acquaintances of acquaintances, neither the tough Sloanes with their thin lips and thinner legs, nor the soft, fumbly women with ill-defined features and frilly shirts, were not in any way his type. Most of them were too young, in any case. He had no intention of being trapped into another family. But Xenia, who hated untidy ends hanging out all over the place, had been hard to convince. She would prefer to see him tied up, a neat package of brown paper and string, firmly sealed at both ends with emotional and physical responsibilities.

Xenia tied a scarf round her head to prevent herself from getting earache in the cold wind and bent to unleash the dog. He plodded over to the nearest pool and stood there, hoping he wasn't required to frisk about. She stepped out after Edmund, now a speck on the shoreline. When she had caught up they walked in quite comfortable silence in the direction of Rye for a while, passing a small fishing boat beached in the earlier autumn storms and already smothered in weed as it lay askew on the sand. This was the beach they had come to when their children were small, picnicking beside one of the wooden groins, and Xenia had busied herself pouring out coffees and orange squashes, setting out plates on sandy rugs, drying their damp swimming costumes on the wooden bars of the groin, and running after the children, joining in their games in an effort to avoid talking to Sylvestra, who kept on asking her what she thought of such and such a book, which she had not read, or whether she had liked a particular performance in a film she had not seen. Xenia preferred to talk about real people, their triumphs and misdeeds, and to pass judgement on their ways of bringing up children. Once Johnnie had said that she really must drag herself out of the Jane Austen era, and she had spent a whole week trying to read *Mansfield Park*, to see what he meant. She often pulled the conversation away from things that she knew nothing about, or which might be controversial. She skillfully prevented Sylvestra from talking politics to Johnnie, Edmund from arguing with Sylvestra over the rightness or wrongness of positive discrimination.

She'd so much been his guardian angel when they were children that it had taken Edmund some time to realize her chief fault was mental laziness. He preferred to think it was laziness rather than a real deficiency. She had been his champion when their father had ranted at him about leaving university, his English degree only one-third completed, and he had gratefully hidden behind her then, for the last time. He hadn't cared for academic life at all, wanting to be out and doing, earning money, not sitting endlessly pulling apart what seemed to him perfectly made novels, looking for the signs of prejudice and influence that his tutors always ferreted out, to his own amazement. He had then hated the drastic surgical operations carried out upon poetry, snipping and slicing at it so that it fell apart in his head, cut to tatters and worthless, all the immediate pleasure in reading it dissipated.

He had also become involved with the daughter of a Labour politician, whose very name was anathema to his father, not because of his politics but because of his personal offensiveness. He had, under her wing, joined in student protests, in the days when students actually did such things. Xenia, by then already married, had seemed glamorously adult, and their father had been bulldozed into acquiescence as she pleaded, night and day, for his reinstatement in their father's good books. But the poor man was already weighing up the con of Edmund abandoning his degree with the pro of his being parted from the undesirable acquaintance to whom he seemed in danger of becoming seriously attached.

Edmund had in fact only been attached by lust. Carrie had been a gorgeous girl, with beautiful breasts which she flaunted, un-bra'd in the fashion of the time, at every opportunity. He'd rarely been able to drag his eyes up to her face, with its petulant expression as if permanently waiting for an overdue compliment. She had treated him kindly enough when he was with her, but he had eventually tumbled to the fact that he was one amongst many. She explained her sudden disappearances as party commitments, but he had dismally discovered the truth one afternoon when he had been due to meet her at a friend's flat, had arrived too eagerly early and, the door being on the latch, had walked straight into the sitting room at high speed almost falling over Carrie, rolling stark naked on the floor with the friend. Her eyes were so hazed by overindulgence in Lebanese Gold that she barely recognized him and lay there giggling. Betrayed, he had lashed out at the friend unnecessarily hard, and had been told coldly, once she had recovered her clothes and senses, that jealousy was deeply uncool. He often caught sight of Carrie on the television where she presented a pretentious late-night chat show with great poise and considerably more weight than she had carried in her Cambridge days. She still looked gorgeous, and petulant.

Xenia was now complaining about cold toes, and Edmund had had enough fresh air blown into him to last till the end of the century. They turned their backs to the wind and went back to the car, driving to the Eeldyke Inn where they had arranged to meet Johnnie. They drew up amidst a bevy of motorbikes, pick-up trucks and cars ranging from a new scarlet Saab to a Morris Minor held together with baler twine. Xenia agreed reluctantly to come and have a quick drink with them before going back to get lunch ready, stepped inside with a disdainful smile on her face and was almost instantly knocked sideways as a large man, with an equally large ginger beard, lurched towards the door, belching as he went. Seth's wife, Phylly, was looking somewhat distracted behind the bar.

'You go on off home now!' she called out after the weaving giant. 'I'm not serving you again today!' She turned to Edmund. 'He's been drunk for three days now. Sorry, what would you like?'

Edmund bought Xenia a gin and tonic and himself a

pint of Goachers, nearly spilling the beer as a cream cat pranced and wove in and out among the bottles of brightly coloured squashes and cordials and jars of pickled eggs and onions. Several men had now followed the flatulent giant outside and were clapping his helmet on his head, manhandling him on to the bike and pointing it in the right direction. He rode off, sitting very upright and glassy-eyed, the bike presumably knowing its own way home.

'I'd like some ice,' said Xenia curtly.

'I've got no ice,' said Phylly, bending down to draw a pint from the barrel behind her. The cream cat leapt on to her back and she let out a screech, whereupon it jumped casually on to the shelf above her head and knocked down a glass.

'Ooh! That cat! He's getting downright familiar!'

Xenia's face was now frozen in disbelief. In the back room the piano was being played and a group of noisy young men were playing toad-in-the-hole, an ancient game of skill in which brass weights are pitched on to a low, lead-topped table with a hole in the middle. Land the brass flat on the table top and you score a point. Getting it to slither down the central hole, whereupon it rings a bell in the drawer beneath, earns you two points. Great fun for the very young or very inebriated. The ringing of the bell was accompanied by cheering and a lot of back-slapping.

It was Johnnie playing the piano, sitting in a haze of cigarette smoke which eddied about as he stood up to greet them. A woodstove pumped out a comforting heat and at a table nearby two couples sat with a baby gurgling and gurning in a basket between them. Xenia was appalled and had to be restrained from making loud remarks about health hazards and the NSPCC. Edmund was relieved to find a pub which did not smell of fried onion rings and chip fat and that had no music other than that provided by the customers. He had been shaken out of his rather frosty

London persona by the frequent changes of scene over the weekend and was considerably more relaxed, finding that he was not dreading the return to London as he usually did by Sunday lunchtime, when the thought of the dreary mess he had made of his life usually loomed up at him like an attack of indigestion. He had his work, the novel, and now there were the papers to explore, the author to uncover.

Xenia interrupted his train of thought by announcing that she had finished her drink and no longer wanted to stay in this hell-hole. Lunch would be ready at one thirty. Would they please not be late. She pushed and shoved her way to the door, her head grazing the nicotine-stained ceiling. She narrowly missed being mown down by a shaven-headed young man with seven earrings who was ruthlessly rolling a barrel through the customers to set it up behind the bar. Two young women sat chatting nearby, inexpertly smoking, drawing in too long and puffing out noisily, sliding aggressive glances about them as they spoke as if waiting to be reprimanded. 'Still at school,' thought Edmund. The barrel-roller leant over to them.

'Have a good time last night, Josie?'

'Ooh yes! Dark Entry's a really great band. You should have come.'

'Nah, couldn't get away. We had our bonfire do here, see?'

Johnnie stopped playing the piano, to expressions of regret from an elderly couple squashed into the corner.

'Good pub, isn't it? I never came here till a few months ago, and now I drop in fairly regularly for a pint after work.'

Xenia suddenly reappeared and fought her way back to the bar.

'I think you should know,' she said officiously, as if getting her own back for the lack of ice, 'that there is a toad under the washbasin in the Ladies'.' Her deep voice bounced off the ceiling, silencing the nearest customers.

'I know,' said Phylly calmly. 'Isn't he a pet? He's been there two or three days. I'll get round to putting him out this afternoon.'

Xenia left again, and Edmund and Johnnie, once they had stopped laughing, got into conversation with a professor of classics and her husband, were then joined by a farmer whose land adjoined Johnnie's, and his wife, and then by a friend of the wife's, who was a singer with the National Opera.

They noticed the time and had to make an emergency exit in order not to be late for Xenia's lamb and parsnip stew, her apple pie with cheese pastry. Amelia and her friend Mary Beaton were just arriving on the back of Mary's motorbike as they were leaving, and Johnnie paused, his hand on the roof of the car, watching Amelia's bright hair bounce back into place as she removed her helmet, and Mary's black hair slide shining out of hers. Amelia smiled at Johnnie. Johnnie felt he was beginning to slip on the oilslick of middle-aged concupiscence, but could not forbear asking her if she had enjoyed the book he'd lent her.

'I'm afraid I haven't finished it yet,' she said politely, shoving her gloves into the borrowed helmet, undoing her jacket at the neck and trying to avoid his too-fond gaze with some embarrassment. The man with him was staring at her too, with interest. Recognizing him, she thought he looked less forbidding without his hat.

'We'd better get inside – see you soon,' she said, more warmly than she intended. They entered the pub, Amelia acutely conscious of Johnnie's eyes following her, eating her up, she thought crossly. Perhaps someone was right when they said that true friendship between a man and a woman was only possible if there was a certain mutual physical antipathy.

They found a space to sit just by the door.

'So, Mr God-Almighty Whitby has the hots for you?' said Mary.

'Keep your damn voice down, you idiot! Yes, I've got a problem. But I'm not sure how to sort it out, if I want to even, just yet.'

'You've got to, you're crucifying the poor man.'

'Nonsense. We only met a few weeks ago, and *nothing* other than a little book-lending, a couple of quiet drinks, and a lot of good conversation has been going on,' said Amelia defensively.

'All right, I believe you!' said Mary. 'You may have started off with the purest of motives, but he definitely yearns for you.'

'That was the other man's name,' said Amelia. 'His brother-in-law.'

'What?'

'Yearne. Edmund Yearne.'

'Then he must be Xenia's brother. She's an airhead, seriously stunning for her age though.'

'I know, I've met her once or twice at parties. She seemed overprotective, bullying even. But he is very fond of her.'

'I'm sure he is. That doesn't mean that he isn't on the look-out, however subtly. He had a salty look to me.'

'Don't be ridiculous,' said Amelia, 'And please don't let's go on talking about it in here. Even the chairs have ears.'

'I can hardly hear you myself. Didn't you say Josie would be here?'

'Yes, she was going to walk down here to meet her friend Ruffles, so they can post-mortemize last night's gig.'

'I expect she's in the back, chatting up Mikey.'

'Oh Lord. I knew she was up to something,' said Amelia, looking around anxiously.

'You can't keep her in purdah. Life's different for both of you now. Get what happiness you can.'

'Do you seriously see me as Johnnie Whitby's bit on the side?' asked Amelia, put out by the prospect.

'No. Not really. You're not mistress material. You're too honest. Think how tiresome it would be, all that secrecy, and covering up tracks, notes in haystacks and screwing in barns.' Mary doubled up laughing.

'You're quite right.' Amelia had to laugh too, and made up her mind at last that she would allow it to go no further.

'I'll nip it in the bud,' she said, 'but it has been nice, being fancied. It's so long since that happened.'

'What about Eric?'

Amelia managed to blush and look smug at the same time. Eric had come to buy her bantams when she was selling up the house, an energetic and friendly young man who had tracked her down six months later, ostensibly to ask her advice about broody hens. He had, quite unbelievably to Amelia now, stayed the night, and come on other nights for the next month. She had been ridiculously easily seduced and, briefly, very happy, knowing that it must somehow be short-term, like a visit to a magical theatre, and it had indeed died a sudden death, as things do sometimes when they flare up too fast. She had discovered that he had a wife, and a small baby, at his smallholding near Hythe, and ended the affair at once. She frequently warmed her hands on remembrances of the physical conflagration, and had no regrets at all. She sipped her strong cider.

'Yes. That was fun. I never thought I would do anything like that.'

'I don't know why you are so shy. You've got a very strong physical presence.'

'Do you mean I smell, or that I'm an obese weight-lifter?'

'Neither! Don't be silly. I'm serious. I've seen men watching you, but because you aren't a big-chested dumbo, they don't understand why they are watching you.'

'Well, I'm so flattered and boosted by that assessment, but I've never noticed all this attention you think I attract.'

'Did you notice the brother-in-law, though? Now he had what I call physical presence, too, although he's not much taller than you.'

'Yes, I noticed him. A comfortable-in-his-own-skin sort of man,' said Amelia.

Josie appeared with Ruffles in tow, emerging from the back room. Ruffles had dark rings of slipped eye makeup, giving her a panda-like appearance.

'May Ruffles come and have lunch with us?'

'Of course you can. I hope you like mince on toast, because that's all we've got.'

Ruffles indicated that she was very happy with mince on toast, not keen to have lunch at home because her father was on the warpath about her smoking, her lack of enthusiasm for her A levels and her and Josie not being standing waiting outside the club last night on the dot of midnight.

3

Edmund went back to London late that evening, the 'boring old rubbish', as Xenia had called it, in a Peter Jones carrier bag on the passenger seat. Peter Jones, he recalled, had been Xenia's spiritual home when she first married. 'I'm going to try and visit Peter Jones,' she'd declare at breakfast, as if announcing a treacherously difficult journey to Westminster Abbey.

His flat greeted him drably, seeming even bleaker than when he had left it on Saturday. Johnnie had pressed a brace of pheasants on him when he had left and their copper-coloured plumage looked exotically out of place lying on the brawn-jelly patterned Formica surface of the kitchen worktop. They were already well hung and he fetched a bin-bag, switched on the radio and started plucking. The feathers drifted to the floor, floated up to the ceiling, got into the cupboards and clung to his eyebrows. The long barred tail-feathers he stuck in a jug like a bunch of flowers and, holding his breath, he cleaned the birds, avoiding touching their stretched scaly feet and legs which stuck out pathetically like bunches of tiny lizards.

That done, he hoovered up the remaining fluffy bits and put the birds in the fridge, and should have gone to bed, but went to sit, sifting through the papers in the Jiffy bags till well after one o'clock. He felt a twinge of guilt at his curiosity, prurience even. There were things here that weren't meant to be read by other people. Or were they? Why write down all these adolescent miseries, why edit them, keep them, if you don't want them to be read, eventually? He thought of Oscar Wilde's young lady who kept a diary in order to have something sensational to read on journeys and the guilt vanished. He read:

I was bereft in the convent's parlour amongst the ugly Edwardian furniture and lace mats. The clothes which I had felt quite proud of that morning were stiffly new and uncomfortable. Once on, they had looked laughable, as if I had been sent back two or three years and become a little girl again. Apparently it was not permitted to wear stockings until the lower fifth form and the fawn kneesocks considred suitable for twelve-year-olds were held up by elastic garters, which bit into the skin beneath the knees.

My mother had just left and now I was unable to stop crying. An elderly nun came to collect me and take me to the dormitory, and was too gentle, too understanding for me to cope with and I howled hopelessly under the weight of her kindness. The building was old, with large early-Victorian additions, and a well-preserved Victorian garden with giant yew trees and terraces, walled hide-aways, orchards and surrounding woodland. Florid yellow roses climbed over archways, releasing showers of hoarded raindrops and petals down one's neck. There were long, brown corridors, rooms named after saints and biblical places. There were lawns on which only the sixth formers were allowed, and the nuns whisked about the place in their greenish-grey habits and black veils, seemingly intent on catching one out in yet another forbidden area. It was cold that first term, and we were only allowed to light the gas fires for one hour on hair-washing days, Tuesdays and Fridays, in order to dry our hair, and we knelt, three at a time, in front of the hissing flames, our heads hanging down in a row: curly ginger, tangled black, sleekit mouse. Baths were also twice a week, with a nun on hand to check the hot water level with a ruler before we undressed and got in. What she would have done if they had been overfilled I can't imagine, since to let it out would have also been a waste, and waste was one of the greatest offences.

In the mornings a nun stood ringing a bell, bed by bed, waiting till each occupant showed signs of life. 'God bless you, my darlings. Time to get washed and dressed.' We were belled to breakfast, clappered out of classes to lunch. The chapel bell tolled continuously, it seemed to me, and for this we had to wear thin white cotton veils, tied with grubby white tapes on the napes of our necks.

I was given Latin coaching by an unctuous chaplain in swishing black soutane, who sat too close and left the convent not long after I had arrived, 'under a cloud'. I was unsure what 'under a cloud' meant, but took it to mean that he had gone to Hell, since in Heaven one was allegedly permitted to sit on them.

I waited for letters like a vigilant sparrow-hawk, alert for the thin, red-white-and-blue-edged airmail envelopes hiding amongst the fat, white, crisp English ones. But there were many other girls with parents abroad, so I had to search hard for my weekly epistle from my mother, who, amongst loving enquiries as to my health and progress, and much love and kisses, often simply listed things they had been doing, never describing them. There had been a riot, they had been over to Amman, they had lunched with so-and-so, been to a party at the Embassy, the Royal Navy was in port. But why there had been a riot, what they had eaten for lunch, was rarely mentioned, which was odd because she sometimes had stories published in magazines.

I suffered, as did many other children, from loneliness and dreadful homesickness. Homesickness is a wasting, falling disease, when one seems to be lost deep inside one's head and the eyes take in nothing, the ears do not hear and every smell is alien. No matter how kind and interesting other people are, one cannot let go the ache and join in. I grieved for my hot, dry, habitual landscape, missing out on the beauty of the surrounding thick woodlands and lush greenness that covered the clayey soil. When I had last left England, it had been from the flinty East Anglian countryside, flat and wide open to the sky. I had been to so many schools, this being the eighth, that I had lost the knack of making friends, not bothering too much, knowing that I would soon be moved on and the effort would be wasted.

Eventually, feigning a more jolly personality than I possessed, I joined in the summer evening games of cricket on the sloping lawn beneath the terraces, did handstands against the wall with the others, our striped dresses hanging limply over our heads, vests and navy knickers exposed. I wept water-marks over algebra, loved history and tolerated the rest. Toleration crept up gradually, to the point where the homesickness eased and I rediscovered my early habit of pretending to be someone else. The place had its romantic aspects, after all, and it was quite enjoyable to sit melancholic under an apple tree in the nuns' graveyard, a pre-Raphaelite prisoner, Rapunzel in her tower or the Lady of Shalott, and mope mum along the passages with my hair hanging down my back and a moody pout on my lips, looking completely idiotic. I ignored the laughter and rock and roll coming from the common room on Saturday evenings after Chapel, and hung out of the windows, brushing my hair in the twilight. But in the end I fitted in somehow. We all did, misfits all.

Edmund read the description of homesickness with a sinking sensation in the pit of his stomach, feeling a twinge of the loss he had felt at being left for the first time at prep school when he was nine. He searched for a torn-out exercise-book page he had seen earlier, which seemed to have been written at the time described, in a definite development of the sloping French script he'd noticed in the poems.

Today is the worst day this term. Uncle Theo was supposed to come and take me out as it's visiting day, but I sat all morning in the hall by the window and he never came. I suppose he must have forgotten. I checked his letter and it did say Saturday the 21st, and all the others were fetched and I wasn't. I hate him! They've all forgotten I'm here. Sister Madeleine came and made me spend the afternoon tidying up the art room to take my mind off it, she said, but it wasn't much fun compared to being taken out to lunch in Hastings. She speaks French to me in a funny accent. She says she comes from Yorkshire. She let me do some painting after I'd finished all the drawers and shelves, and washed out all the paint pots. We have to use poster paints here, and they make one's fingers feel scratchy and dry, like touching flowerpots. There is a new gardener and Carol nearly fell out of the window trying to look at him, but he's not even good-looking.

There followed three signatures, all slightly different as if she'd been practising them, and the address of the school:

Mimi Anderson   M.A. Anderson   Mimi Anderson

St Cecilia's Convent
Hatton Hoo
Hastings
Sussex

So, there she was, back in England and having difficulty in adapting to English boarding school life. The name Imim, he could see now, was merely a childish aberration, mirror-writing taken up as a nickname, and she appeared to have dropped the use of the name Fleury. She didn't sound too seriously unhappy, and he liked the slightly wistful, mocking tone of the typewritten piece. He yawned. In the morning he would telephone the auctioneers in Norfolk and get her address. Unpacking his bag his thoughts turned back to the uncertain undercurrents he had sensed between Xenia and Johnnie. All did not seem quite as it should be and he imagined he had picked up a certain pent-up frustration in Johnnie, particularly after they'd met the two women outside the Eeldyke pub. The fair-haired one, Amelia the brandy-bearer, hadn't seemed more than lightly friendly, so if something was going on between them, she was a very good actress. He had a natural brotherly interest in Xenia's welfare, but didn't see how he could interfere and supposed hopefully that it would all blow over.

'I'm afraid we cannot disclose the identity of the vendor,' said the business-like voice of the woman speaking for the auction house.

'But I'd really like to return these papers. I'm certain they were left in the trunk by accident,' pleaded Edmund.

'If you give me the lot number, and the description of the item, I can find the name and address, and if you would care to write to us, explaining the situation, we will forward it to her. Then she'll be at liberty to contact you if she wants the papers returned.'

This seemed reasonable, if tortuously slow.

'OK,' he said, reluctantly, rapidly flipping through the pages of the catalogue till he found a Biro mark against one of the entries. 'Here it is. Antique elm seaman's chest. Rope handles. Lot Number 231.'

'Thank you, sir, and your name please?'

He spelled out Yearne and told the woman to await a letter.

'Dear Madam,' he wrote on his firm's headed writing paper, 'I have accidentally come into possession of some papers which were, I feel sure, inadvertently left in the seaman's chest you sent for auction a few weeks ago. The only names I have managed to discover are on an exercise book and are M. A. Anderson and M. A. Fleury. I would very much like to send . . .' he crossed out 'send' and wrote 'deliver them to you . . . as they appear to be of a personal nature. Perhaps you would care to get in touch with me, and we could arrange the transfer?' He added his home address and phone number, and signed it, wondering if he could justify a business trip to Norfolk.

Charlie Parrott looked at him suspiciously.

'What are you up to?'

Edmund explained the story as best he could, and Charlie's face registered exaggerated disappointment.

'Oh, I thought you'd found something really exciting, like long-lost love letters from Lytton Strachey to Nancy Mitford.'

'You oaf! No, nothing like that. But these letters are sort of intriguing. Odd, and it's rather interesting, being inside the mind of a thirteen-year-old girl. She seems to have had a rather bizarre life.'

* * *

In the hiatus which followed the despatch of his letter, Edmund grew increasingly anxious, thinking that maybe the auctioneers had not passed on his letter, or perhaps had not even received it. He would have to write again. He tried to trace the Sussex convent but it had closed down, been turned into a retreat or nursing home of some sort and all the nuns who might have known Mimi were, he was told, either dead or gaga. He had made this call from his flat, not wanting to let Charlie know that he was becoming just a little obsessed and fidgety. He tried to keep his mind off the girl, about whom he was beginning to feel possessive, busying himself buying and selling, listing, answering queries, consulting catalogues, searching for elusive first editions of first novels by long-forgotten authors and matching bare volumes to near-pristine original dust-wrappers. He was on the verge of abandoning hope when the letter came, with a London postmark and an address in Camden, but the contents were deeply disappointing.

Dear Mr Yearne,

Thank you for the letter which Manson and West have passed on to me. I'm afraid I don't know anyone of the name Anderson or Fleury. The trunk belonged to my aunt, Helen Strood, and after she died in a road accident in September I, as her heir, had to clear out all her possessions and put her house on the market. There was a lot of muddle at the time, and I didn't realize there was anything in the trunk when I sent it to auction. I don't actually remember having seen it on previous visits to my aunt, but perhaps she had recently bought it herself? I'm sorry not to be able to help further.

Yours sincerely,
Marianne Strood

Edmund worked that morning in a mood of frustration,

barking needlessly at Tom Treasure and causing him to sulk
mutinously in the back room, thinking up seriously funny
and biting ripostes which it was too late for him to use.

After shutting up shop he took Charlie for a drink at the
French pub as an apology for his foul mood.

'I'm sorry. It's just these papers. I didn't get the response
to my letter that I'd been hoping for.' He outlined the problem, adding, 'I don't see how I can trace her now, at all.'

'Perhaps the aunt had an address book. It might be
possible to ring up all her friends and see if they knew
anyone called Mimi Anderson. You did say she'd lived in
East Anglia as a child?'

'Yes, she mentions it.'

'Well, try that then. I don't really know why you're so
keen on returning them.'

'Nor do I, but I just feel I have to make an effort of some
sort. I've become quite attached to the writer. She was a
funny, almost sombre little person as a child. She must be
about the same age as me.'

'She might very well be dead.'

'I know you think I'm one-hundred-and-one. Yes, I
suppose she might be. But you're right. I'll see if Miss
Marianne Strood has her address book.'

They turned to talk of other things, being joined by a
mutual friend who was waiting for his girlfriend to turn
up for a pre-theatre drink, but, five minutes to curtain-up,
she had still not put in an appearance.

'Sod it. I'm not wasting these tickets. Charlie, do you
fancy the spare?'

Charlie was agreeable, having nothing better to do that
evening, and they left Edmund to break the news to the
girlfriend, should she arrive. At a quarter to eight, there
being no sign of anyone answering her description, he
finished his pint and set off home on foot, eager to telephone
Marianne Strood and see if an address book existed. He'd

recalled that one of the early children's letters had been signed 'Helen'. It was just possible that the childhood friend might be Aunt Helen.

The printed letter-heading of Marianne Strood's letter included a telephone number, and he rang, sitting on the sofa, pulling his ear nervously. He was answered by someone with a young, rather breathy voice.

'Um, yes. I'm sure there is one. But I've had huge bonfires of all her letters and things. I did bring the business ones back, in case of having to sort out anything serious. But I was going to write to her friends, to tell them of her death, only my mother put it in *The Times* and the *Telegraph*, and said I needn't bother. Would you like me to see if I can find the address book for you? Only I can't look now, I'm expecting friends for supper in a few minutes.'

'That would be very kind. I really do want to get to the bottom of it. Sorry to be such a nuisance – can I ask one more thing? How old was your aunt when she died?'

'About forty-six or forty-seven,' the girl replied, with a slight impatience in her tone, so he thanked her again and rang off, going straight back to the papers for further delving into Mimi's childhood and adolescent years.

I've been told over and over again that being shy is a way of drawing attention to oneself. This is unfair, and untrue, in my case anyway. I'm *not* shy, but I am a bit nervous of making a fool of myself by saying the wrong thing and being laughed at. But I do wish people would leave me alone and stop trying to 'draw one out' as my mother puts it, making it sound as if I'm a thorn in the sole of her foot. There's nothing to draw out, I'm just not given enough time on my own to sit and think. At school we were hardly ever alone and I thought it would be wonderful to leave, to be allowed just to *sit*, or paint, on one's own. But Mum keeps dragging me out to lunches, and drinks parties, which are horrible things where no one listens to anyone else, and they all gabble at the same time about absolutely nothing. I hoped they were going to talk about interesting, grown-up, important things, but they just bore on about what jolly times their daughters are having being skivvies in Switzerland, or learning Italian in Florence. They only ever ask me what parties I've been to and if I have lots of interesting young men hanging around me. (No – not one. I don't actually seem to have met any interesting young men.) I suppose I'll have something to talk about when I go up to London to art school in September.

Poor child, Edmund thought sympathetically, wondering if his Hatty suffered from the same problem. He could remember with agony those parties where one was paraded, in one's best grey flannel suit, and expected to fall into line, say all the right things to complete strangers, not to put one's foot in one's mouth and to suddenly appear to be an adult without having had enough practice. Mimi's mother was back in England but where was the stepfather Georges Fleury? The next handwritten diary entry made it clear that they were back in Norfolk – he looked up Salthouse and found it was not far from Bolt, where Xenia had bought the trunk, and was presumably close to where Aunt Helen lived.

I've met one interesting man at last. But he's quite old. He's up here birdwatching, but he's writing a book about a man whose wife keeps on having babies and they can't use contraception because they're Roman Catholics. I can't see how one could write a whole book about that, but he made it seem very funny. At least I laughed because I knew it was funny, but felt I ought not to, because I haven't a clue about contraception. I think

I must be the only person that doesn't. Helen laughed at me when I asked her, but I believe *she* doesn't know either. She came over this afternoon and we went by bus to Salthouse and wandered about the beach, watching the terns dipping and hovering over the seashore. I was looking for amber, but didn't find any. Helen says it needs a good storm to bring it up, churned up from the sea-bottom. We did find some fossils, belemnites, which people call thunderbolts. We also found a dead coypu which had tangerine-coloured front teeth and stank terribly. That's where we met the man, sitting on a bank with a notebook and binoculars, and Helen asked him if he had seen anything rare, and we got chatting. Helen's like that. She doesn't have any problems talking to people. Then it turned out that he was staying with friends of Helen's parents nearby, and we went and had tea with them. Afterwards he drove us home to save us the bus fare. I wouldn't have talked to him, of course, if I'd been on my own. I think he may have thought we were older than we were. He asked me what I was reading at the moment and I said *Lolita*, and he laughed and laughed. Helen is staying on at school to do A levels, then going to university to do Eng. Lit. I do wish I hadn't been to so many different schools. I've done the Norman Conquest five times, once in French which was a quite different story. I do read a lot but Helen says I'm reading all the wrong books. I don't really choose them though, I just read whatever comes to hand. It's a habit and I panic when I've nothing to read when I'm waiting for something to happen or am going on a journey. I found the copy of *Lolita* on the bus coming home from Norwich. It had been left on the seat with a purple chocolate wrapper as a bookmark.

Edmund was entranced by this child, and the adult self that

was beginning to emerge, but he was abruptly disturbed by consecutive letters in the pile, from a man signing himself Phillip. Starting to read them, he felt his hackles rise and then a sense of shame. The cheap writing paper almost ignited in his hands – they were full of deranged hate, paradoxically sprinkled with adoration, devotion, intentions to marry her and make her his forever. They were also the written equivalent of what he imagined an obscene phone-call to contain. They detailed what this Phillip would do to her next time he met her, what he would like to do, now, sitting thinking about her in the next room. Insanity leapt from the pages, dancing in front of his eyes. He felt sick, imagining his Hatty being the recipient of such hideous letters. His picture of a funny little schoolgirl evaporated. But why had she kept such filth? The answer was in her own cool reassessment of the situation, a sad hindsight.

I settled in the small room in Oakley Street with enormous enthusiasm. Liberation at last! Upstairs were a couple with a small baby who cried a lot, and beneath me a couple of merry lesbians, who dressed up in kimonos and gave rowdy parties on Saturdays, playing a song called 'The Seventh Son' over and over again, and a lot of Rachmaninov. On the same floor as me was another room, and a bathroom between us, but I hardly ever saw the occupant. We occasionally met on the landing, both moving to the same side to let each other pass, dancing from side to side in that English way as if terrified of touching each other. He had a long, thin body and well-structured face and greeny-blue eyes with a slight tic beneath his left eye, as if he was perpetually nervous, or very tired. I was deep in my first year at art school, and although I was feeling my work didn't fit in with current conceptions, too figurative and academic for the time, I was happy, having abandoned a lot of the alleged shyness and made friends, dredged London for all that was fun and free, and there was a lot going on. I wore high black vinyl boots and very short skirts. We drank, when any of us had any money, in King's Road pubs and sat endlessly in coffee houses, talking, talking, talking. We travelled in gangs to each other's lodgings, drank bad red wine and smoked a lot. I started to meet my neighbour on the stairs more and more frequently. Now I can see that he was waiting to hear the front door open and came out when he thought it was me, pretending to be going somewhere.

Coming up the stairs one evening after having been to the pub with two friends, we were just about to go into my room to continue the session when he came up the stairs behind us, looking rather sad, so we asked him to come and join us. He sat on the floor by the gas fire, and seemed nice enough, told us he was writing a thesis on gnosticism, which I had to go and look up in the dictionary. He was erudite, good company and laughed a great deal at all our bad jokes. From then on, he latched on to me. I was flattered at first. He was considerably older than us. I won't say I fancied him because I was still a virgin, and curious, not knowing who or what I did fancy then, because I was unaware of what was on offer. The main reason most women sleep with their first man seems to be just plain curiosity, which explains why they often go to bed with people who their friends think are complete creeps. His name was Phillip, and he took to knocking on my door, standing there looking lanky and eager, and began to take up time I hadn't got to give him.

One night I let him in after he had arrived clutching a bottle of wine and explaining that he had finished his thesis and wanted someone to celebrate with. I made a disastrous mistake, since I drank too much wine and went to bed with him, in a sleepwalking sort of way, and was horribly disappointed. His bones stuck into me and I felt absolutely nothing but pain, and afterwards got up immediately, feeling dizzy, shaking and distressed, but stone-cold sober. There had been something about him which had revolted me when it was too late to stop. I think it was his hands which felt rough, scaly and cold, like a lizard. I wanted him to go. It was a mistake, I told him, but he ignored me, kept telling me how lovely I was, came after me, forced me back. I felt hot, sticky and filthy and he lay there on my sheets, with an overturned ashtray beside his arm, laughing at me. I was in a fog of anger, almost speechless with rage, but managed to get him to leave, protesting his undying love, carrying his horrible shoes in his scaly hand, saying he'd see me tomorrow when I'd calmed down, was less upset.

'No, not tomorrow. Not ever again!' I squawked at him and slammed the door, bolting it.

Out of embarrassment I didn't dare leave the room all next morning till I heard him go downstairs, and then ran to the window to make sure he had really left. I bathed, cleaned up my room in a frenzy of distaste and sat there wondering what on earth had possessed me. I mean possessed literally, since he had had a distinctly sinister feel to him. But that night he stood outside the door, knocking, rattling the door handle, swearing. I had so little experience, no knowledge of excuses, gentle dismissals. The telephone was in the hall downstairs, unreachable without going past his door. A letter was poked under the door. I was terribly shocked by it, and stayed in my room all the next day, terrified. The next night was the same, and the next, and the next. But then I watched him leave the house and I managed to get myself out to the art school, where I was asked why I looked so grey and frightened. I couldn't say, since it all seemed such an unlikely night-mare.

He was waiting on the landing when I returned at six that evening, blocking the way, his eyes quite manic. I turned and fled to the telephone at the end of the road, gibbering with fright, and managed to explain roughly what was happening to a friend who promised to be round with reinforcements in twenty minutes, telling me to wait by the telephone box. She arrived with two hefty male colleagues who escorted me back to the house and up the stairs where Phillip bounced out of his room again.

'Get into your room,' said Nails (as in 'hard as'). 'I'll deal with this.'

Once inside I couldn't hear what was being said, at first, but then there was a great deal of shouting and pushing. Phillip was screeching that he loved me: 'She's mine, I tell you, mine! I know you're going in there to screw her. She's mine.' I don't know quite what happened, but someone had fetched the landlady, the police were mentioned, and the boys sat with me all night listening to him crashing about in his room. In the morning he left. I never saw him again, but it took weeks of his absence before I could sleep properly, so frightened was I by the ugliness of what I'd brought to the surface by my own fault. I had merely been curious, and drunk, but felt that one of my nine lives had gone.

Edmund searched his past anxiously, wondering if he had ever caused such a storm of revulsion in any of his one-night stands in the sixties. He did hope not, but could see how such a thing might happen, particularly with a young girl involved with a near-psychopath. The man obviously had a severe mental problem as well as scaly hands. He hoped she had got over it and gone on to better nights with better men – but he couldn't understand why she had hung on to the repellent letters. As a warning to herself perhaps, or as proof of some sort in case he approached her again? In the sixties few people would have done other than blame her for getting into the situation in the first place, but she'd been so young, so obviously inexperienced. Sleepwalking, she had called it. Sad, very sad. But she had not really been asking for sympathy, just telling the story. An exorcism of some sort. He went on reading, looking for evidence that she had recovered herself and her physical integrity, and her pleasure in being an art student in the big city, but he was haunted by the image of the scaly, pheasant-foot hands.

4 ♪

The ice on the Royal Military Canal began to melt reluctantly, the wind blowing ripples on the newly exposed watery stretches. The sky was grey and heavy and a pair of fieldfares hung about in a hawthorn bush, flashing their pale wingpits. Amelia lit the woodstove in her workshop and set about the latest batch of earrings with the electric polisher before finishing them off with a cloth and fitting the long gold hooks for pierced ears. She checked her order book and neatly packaged them up in green tissue paper. They were very pretty, gold hoops with small jade or amethyst birds hanging in their centres as if on swings. Not particularly original, but very saleable. Six silver bangles of intricately twisted and knotted silver strands, five gold rings set with moonstones . . . '. . . and a partridge in a pear tree . . .' she sang, wrapping them up in red tissue this time, pleased with the Christmassy effect. She slipped them into little silver boxes of various sizes, each having her name printed on the lid. She wrote out a delivery note, having to stop and start all over again after having noticed that she had put 'five pears' instead of 'five rings'. They were to be delivered to Rye that afternoon, and with any luck the shop would have a cheque ready for last month's sales, enough to start off the Christmas shopping by buying Josie's hat. But she knew she had to go easy with the cash, although there was other money due in soon. It was very difficult to budget for anything with such a haphazard income.

The window darkened for an instant as a figure passed by, coming to knock on the door of the shed, making her jump nervously before she realized that it was Johnnie with a brace of pheasants in his hand. She was perpetually on the look-out for strangers, having to keep a certain amount of gold and silver on the premises; she always took it up to bed with her at night. She went to the door and he stood there, almost sheepishly, holding out the birds.

'I've brought you a present.'

'But how wonderful! That's very kind of you.'

Her resolve not to take advantage of his now rather obvious taking for her wavered. She could not churlishly refuse pheasants and make them both look ridiculous. She would have to ask him in.

'I've finished for the morning. Can I make you a cup of coffee?' she said.

'That would be very nice.'

She locked up the shed and he followed her across the yard, watching her skirt twitch from side to side, as hopelessly enthralled as a Victorian gentleman at the sight of pale stocking above a neat kid boot.

In the long kitchen the cat sat rocking and nodding in front of the old Rayburn stove and they sat on either side with their mugs, sipping, and sliding in their intentions. He noticed the poor state of the ceiling, the basket of vegetables on the floor, the brown paper sack of potatoes and the ancient, moulting piece of cut-up carpet on which the cat sat yawning and washing itself.

There was a framed painting on the wall between the windows which attracted his attention. It showed a walled garden with a woman standing naked in a bower, looking modestly surprised and covering herself inadequately with a small book. Johnnie got up to take a closer look. There was a man seated on a stool on the grass, also naked, looking across his shoulder at the viewer, holding out a book as if he had just been interrupted between lines. A lush fig tree filled in the background below a golden sky – in fact the whole picture was executed in golden tones – like a late afternoon in London, hazy with dust.

'Mr and Mrs William Blake?' he asked, delighted to have found out the subject matter without having to be told.

'. . . in their garden in Lambeth, surprised by a visitor while re-enacting a scene from Milton! Rather a long title for such a little painting,' she said, very pleased that he had recognized it.

'It's a lovely little painting.' He bent closer to look at the fine detail of the plants, the soft blue shadows on the skin. 'You painted this?'

'Yes. A long time ago, when I had more time – that's why I so enjoyed the Blake biography – I've been fascinated by him for as long as I can remember.'

He sat down again. He hoped that she had not found the pheasant present patronizing, but she was a sensible woman and surely wouldn't take such a small gift amiss, however independent she had had to become, and he hoped . . . He watched as she leant back in her basket chair and stretched her legs out, putting her feet up on the stove, her normal way of warming them up. She had not intended it as a provocative gesture, but she saw as soon as she had done it that it could be interpreted as such, implying complete ease and familiarity with his company, and cursed herself. Her skirt was long, and he could still see no more than her worn red shoes. A clock ticked on the dresser.

'I hadn't realized you had such a professional set-up, out there.' He nodded in the direction of the shed, intrigued by what he had seen behind her as she stood at the door. The glimpse of tools neatly hanging up, the gas bottles and burner, the appearance of a miniature blacksmith's forge with tiny anvils set in vices and what looked suspiciously like a dentist's drill hanging from the wall.

'I have to be particularly professional now.'

'Yes, I'm sure you do. But you enjoy it?'

'Oh yes! I love it. It only gets a bit boring when I have to do a large amount of one thing for an order. Then one has to grit one's teeth to get through all the repetitions.'

'And where do you sell them, or is it all on commission?'

'Oh, craft galleries, enlightened jewellers, craft fairs, that sort of thing.'

Johnnie thought it was odd that he met so few professional women. Most of his acquaintances' wives either did nothing or were immersed in charity work. Of the few that had trained for a particular occupation, even fewer seemed to take it up again once they had children. Of course none of them needed to work, or showed any burning desire to do so. Need was something he knew he had been buttressed against all his life. His financial problems, such as they were, were caused by the stock market, the EC and CAP, and were as nothing compared with the daily counting of pennies, the carefully rationed drink and tobacco with which Amelia wrestled. He did not feel guilt, since such matters were in the lap of the gods, he felt; but he was, in the best sense, a charitable man, and certainly put his money generously and willingly where he felt it would do most good, whether collecting boxes or into more practical and close-to-home ventures such as making sure that a certain amount of money was spent each week at the village shop. He tried to employ the maximum amount of people consistent with modern farming practices, but his father had employed seven regular farmhands, and he could find work for only two, with extra part-timers when needed. His mother had employed both cook and cleaner and two gardeners. Xenia made do with a cleaning woman two days a week. Amelia had nothing to fall back on . . . To fall back on . . . to throw up one's arms in surrender and lean back into the comforting embrace of a massive insurance policy, or yet another legacy. Insured up to the hilt, the other upper-middle-classes of his age, who believed in their own existence even if nobody else did, were mostly still as snug and smug at the end of the twentieth century as they had been at its start. There were of course exceptions to this, he remembered. Two or three people he knew had been severely discommoded by the Lloyd's disaster and sent their children to state schools, pretending that the accents they proceeded to develop for reasons of protective colouring were rather fun, really, and kept quiet that their clothes now frequently originated in charity shops. Amelia looked as if she had never been able to shop anywhere else.

'Would you care for a few more pheasants? We seem to have a glut this year.'

'Yes, indeed I would. But I have no freezer, so not until we've eaten these.'

'No, of course. I was wondering. Would you take a small commission from me?'

'Yes. What is it? Cufflinks?'

'No, I want . . .' he struggled to think of something relatively expensive, but not too obviously over the top, '. . . a bracelet for Xenia. Like the one you're wearing, or something like it. In gold.'

Amelia gulped. A small commission indeed! She wore a solid silver bangle, square in section but tapering to a gap at the back, the top flat surface covered in a writhing gold thread pattern, with golden beads set in between. It made him think of drifting seaweed, with gilded bubbles caught up in it.

'Well, yes, certainly. Is it for Christmas? I'll work out a price for you and telephone . . . no, you call me, tomorrow afternoon perhaps? What colour gold, and what carat?'

He looked at her helplessly. Did gold come in different colours?

'There's red gold, yellow, white, and nine carat, or eighteen carat. Nine would be best for a bangle, I think, and cheaper.'

'How about yellow gold, with the beady bits in another colour?'

'Yes. Well that's settled then,' she laughed. It had been a good day so far, even if it had started to rain. Work completed, new work coming in. Outside a car went past, slowed as if the occupant was looking in at the gate, then speeded up again with a great spray, soaking a young man walking his deerhound up the lane.

They relapsed into silence and the cat settled closer to the stove, assuming a meringue shape.

'I've got to deliver some work to Rye, this afternoon,' she said.

'Well, I mustn't hold you up – thanks for the coffee.' He stood up reluctantly and hit his head on a beam. He noticed a small pile of her business cards on the table.

'Can I have one of these?'

'Of course.'

He wondered if he could risk a kiss on the cheek, or even both cheeks, but decided against it.

''Bye.'

After he had left, she accused herself, unnecessarily, of rudeness. But how to cope with this enormously tall man who had turned suddenly into a jumpy schoolboy once in her house? She was as aware of his thoughts as she was aware of his height, and didn't know what to do with either of them, and had failed to send out the negative signals she had intended to. Now he had seen the scruffy interior of the cottage and would feel sorry for her. However, it was nice to be given pheasants and she was grateful for both them and the commission. If the pheasants had been shot at the weekend, they'd be ready for eating by the next, and she went to hang them in the icy pantry at the end of the kitchen. She quite often came by game, occasionally potting a rabbit out of the upstairs back window of the cottage with Nick's old four-ten. Mary had given her a hare a couple of weeks ago, which she had accidentally run over in a lane near Fingle. 'Waste not, want not,' she had said to herself as, having discovered it was not damaged, she threw it into the back of her car. 'He just leapt across in front of me,' she said sorrowfully, handing Amelia the poor, draggle-furred corpse. 'It's rather sickening, but he will make a good stew – he's not at all squashed.'

Mary was a GP with a local group practice in Rhee. She was a few years younger than Amelia, and had ripped through an inheritance and two husbands before taking a serious look at her life, whereupon she decided to become a doctor at the age of thirty-two. The years of study, examinations and training she had taken in her stride like an acrobat rushing towards a paper hoop, bursting out the other side triumphantly with a whoop and a bow. She rarely moaned about stress, and was ecstatically happy about her work, tending colds and cancer victims with equal devotion.

Amelia thought about the hare, and grinned to herself. She fetched the remains of an apple pie from the fridge, poured brown sugar and milk on it and sat down by the stove again, the plate on her lap, with a battered copy of the *Ingoldsby Legends*. Johnnie had told her that the author, Richard Harris Barham, had lived in the area in the 1820s and that there were several local stories in it. 'Try "The Knight and the Lady",' he had suggested. 'It's surprisingly risqué for the period.' She had at first found the jocular verse form irritating but soon got used to it, and enjoyed the fun-poking at contemporary enthusiasms. The illustrations by Leech and Cruikshank were rather dull, she thought, but those by Tenniel were excellent, outshining the stories themselves. 'The Knight and the Lady' was a tale of a wife with a wandering eye, left alone for too long while her elderly husband went out bug-hunting and botanizing, and who was not unnaturally soon comforted by a nice young man. The husband disappeared into a pond and was discovered dead some days afterwards, his coat-pockets full of eels. His wife had the eels cooked for supper, and ordered her husband's body be popped 'again in the pond – Poor dear – He'll catch us some more.'

Amelia rather enjoyed this, and was just starting on 'The Witches' Frolic' When she noticed that time was pressing on her and she ought to set out for Rye to deliver the jewellery. She marked the page with a jay's feather, made a shopping list, collected her stock and business cards and went off to town, taking the zig-zagging Military Road, splashing through puddles and humming a song. A heron flew up in the drifting rain, heading for Holy Hill, its neck tucked in and legs trailing, great wings slowly beating, as compact and heavy in flight as it was ethereally tall and spiky-thin on the ground. Like lapwings, thought Amelia, so elegant and slim on the fields but once in the air plunging club-winged about the sky – it being hard to imagine that they were the same bird.

Having delivered her treasure, collected and banked a cheque, she spent some time in a bookshop and there met Mary, who was chatting to a boy with dreadlocks, admonishing him jokily about not having a coat.

'Hello! I was just ticking off Steve. He's just got over pleurisy, and there he is, wandering about in the rain without a coat. What are you up to?'

'I've just been paid, and thought I'd get Josie's Christmas present – she hankers after a black velvet hat.'

'Oh great! Can I come too? I've got an hour before surgery

starts. We can try things on. It's what our mothers used to do, isn't it? Try on hats to cheer themselves up?'

'Are you down, then? What's up?'

'Not a lot, really. That's the problem. I suddenly felt an attack of winter coming on. Let's go and find these hats of yours.'

They went down one of the cobbled lanes which run between the High Street and Cinq Port Street, with a fine mizzle of rain blowing down their necks, and entered a small shop which sold, apart from velvet hats, swishing skirts in dark-dyed jewel colours, cheap embroidered bags from Chile, indigo shirts from China, and peacock-patchwork jackets from God-knows-where, all to the accompaniment of loud music. Mary thrust one of the hats on her head and posed in front of the mirror, her face a mockery of her mother, thoughtful and considering, cheeks sucked in, eyes half-shut, head turned this way and that a fraction. '*Wonderful.* I want it! She took it off and tried on another in pink, and poutingly applied imaginary lipstick. 'Listen, they're playing that song that Josie likes – "Liquid Lady, Shady Lady." Do I look like a shady lady?'

'Nothing on earth would make you look like a shady lady!' said Amelia, trying on first the black one, then the green. Mary had an open, clear-complexioned face, with wide light hazel eyes and a lightly freckled nose.

'That's my trouble, I think. I look like one of the children from the Secret Seven. Tuck your hair in under that, there. That's good.'

'I know for Josie it has to be the black one. It's just that the green looks better with my hair, and hers is the same colour as mine, only, I suppose, more so. I feel rather faded beside her.'

'Dye it then,' said Mary, looking back over her shoulder to take in the side view. 'I've been dyeing mine for years.'

She pulled off the pink hat and shook her dark locks. 'I'm really mouse, or perhaps, at a pinch, rich rat.'

'I've got to get back soon – I like to be there when Josie comes home,' said Amelia, paying for the black hat. 'And I've got to get out of here before I buy something for myself.'

Xenia caught sight of them through the window as she passed on her way to the hairdresser's, saw them giggling like children and was annoyed by the sight.

'What *do* they think they look like!' she thought patronizingly, having spotted Amelia's worn old corduroy coat, her head tipped back laughing at the sight of Dr Beaton in biker's leathers, sucking in her cheeks and pulling faces. A tiny pulse beat in her forehead, suppressed rage, which was not soothed by the process of having her hair washed, snipped and blow-dried. Emerging an hour later, neck muscles taut, she went into an expensive clothes shop and bought herself a little scarlet wool jacket with Tyrolean buttons. When she got back to the farm, Rosy Pressing was in the kitchen, ironing. A little appeased by her purchase, and the clean smell of freshly pressed shirts, she made a cup of tea for them both, and watched Rosy for a moment or two, recalling what Rosy had said a few weeks ago: 'I've just passed Mr Johnnie when I was bicycling up here. He was helping Mrs Sailor with a bag of coal. Poor lady. She's had a rough old time of it these past few months.' Xenia had seen his Land Rover outside Amelia's cottage that morning. How often, she wondered, did Johnnie help poor Mrs Sailor with her coal? Perhaps he helped her to do other things as well. He had never mentioned Amelia to her, which was in itself suspicious, wasn't it?

'If anything is going on, I'm not going to be the last to know this time. I'll have to keep a close eye on him, like watching a kettle to stop it boiling.' Her grasp of proverbs, as with so many other things, was inexact.

She admired her haircut in the hall looking-glass and ran her hand over her forehead. Her skin was getting rather dry, which in turn would lead to wrinkles. Johnnie could not have been at Amelia's house for long, because he had returned soon after her, but he had gone out again immediately after lunch with Fred Turtle to start work on the fencing at Hoppits Shaw. But was that where he still was? She picked up a magazine and flicked through it, then put her coat on again, and her Wellington boots and a hat to keep her hair from being ruined. 'Come on, Fatty.' She waved the lead enticingly in front of the old labrador. 'We're going for a walk.'

It was still drizzling steadily when she left the house, slamming the door behind her. They walked up the garden, through the white iron gate into a little spinney behind the house, following a path that in the spring would be thick with bluebells, but was now muddy and smelt of rotting leaves and fruity fungus. Amelia Sailor, stupid bloody name. Arty-farty, scruffy, and so irritatingly composed. She drew herself up and stalked along, elegant and worried. The labrador plodded behind her, hating the wet and wondering why, after several days in the warm, he was being dragged out in this appalling weather. He was her only excuse for walking up there in the rain, with her hair just done, should Johnnie see her.

She approached the edge of the wood and looked across the field that adjoined it, to where Johnnie and Fred should have been repairing the fence. She could see Fred in the distance, bending over a roll of wire. Of Johnnie she could see no sign, nor could she see the Land Rover. She watched for a few minutes more, the rain beginning to drip from the edge of her waxed cotton hat, bedraggling the feathers in the band, and then, jerking away, called the dog and set off back to the farm, where she dumped the dog and took the car, driving down past Amelia's cottage slowly. She could see Amelia's car tucked into the little driveway, but not Johnnie's Land Rover, so she speeded up and went on to the village shop at Rhee where she got out and bought a newspaper. She turned the car round too fast and Josie, who had got off the school bus at the shop so she could buy a packet of ten cigarettes, had to leap for her life.

Xenia drove back more carefully, ashamed of herself. The Land Rover was just turning into the drive ahead of her as she arrived.

'And where have you been?' she asked Johnnie peremptorily.

'Oh, just had to go and fetch some more wire. There was more to do than we thought, so I left Fred up there doing the posts. It'll be dark soon, I'd better go and fetch him and the tools. What's up?'

'Nothing. Nothing at all.'

He noticed the *Telegraph* tucked under her arm. 'We've already got the paper, I was looking at it this morning.'

'I couldn't find it.'

'Well, tea would be nice. I'll just fetch Fred.' He drove off up the rutted miry track to Hoppits Shaw, wondering if she'd gone soft in the head.

She felt deeply silly. But the suspicion still nagged at her, through tea, the six o'clock news, and supper, which was a dish of lambs' tongues cooked with apricots. After supper she sat rifling through her address book, making out a list of guests for a Boxing Day lunchtime drinks party. She hemmed a skirt, put buttons on a shirt, lost her thimble, fidgeted and then was finally unable to stop herself from asking Johnnie if he thought they should invite Amelia Sailor. She did this purely to see his reaction.

'Invite her to what?' he said cautiously.

'Invite her to the Boxing Day party, I was just talking to you about it.'

'If you like, darling.'

No reaction at all, not even a flicker.

She put the needle and thread back into the faded red velvet needlecase that had been her grandmother's, found the thimble where it had rolled up against the fender, folded up the shirt so neatly that it looked as if it had come straight from a shop. Johnnie sat there reading, as he usually did after supper, a look of calm innocence on his face.

'Well, perhaps not. After all, she won't know anyone, will she?' she said.

'I thought that was the whole idea of a party, meeting people one didn't know?' said Johnnie, looking at her with irritation. 'Anyway, she'll know lots of them. I've seen both her and her husband at the Emsleys on several occasions in the past, and at the Appletons, and she's friends with Dr Beaton. Being widowed doesn't mean she has to be avoided like a dangerous predator escaped from the zoo.'

Xenia's thermal imaging equipment picked up on the warmth of his reply.

'I wasn't thinking of asking Mary Beaton either.'

'Well you certainly should. I will, if you won't.'

Xenia found all these unattached women floating around unsettling, and she unwisely continued. 'I wonder what made Amelia's husband commit suicide? Perhaps she was playing around . . .'

'Xenia, you must not speculate like that! There are other reasons for killing oneself. Depression, loss of dignity . . . the poor man had lost his job, had no income. And he had a reputation for being a bit unsteady. Bill Emsley says he once heard that Nick was involved with a barmaid from the Bell and Hatchet. Kept on seeing them together.'

'Now who's speculating?' she pounced. 'I swear men are worse gossips than women.'

'Probably. But we're not so malicious.'

'I'm not being malicious! I will invite Amelia if you want me to.'

'I didn't say you were malicious. I was speaking generally – and can I please finish this chapter before bedtime?' He could think of one or two other reasons for suicide after this conversation. Perhaps he had defended Amelia too overtly, for Xenia appeared annoyed at being lectured and got up, sharply unfolding herself from her chair and picked up the mending, saying stiffly that she would go up to bed.

'All right, I'll be up in a minute or two. I'll bring you some tea, if you'd like it?'

'I expect I shall be asleep by then,' she said fractiously, and loped out of the room.

Johnnie immediately got up and stood in front of the fire, hands in pockets. Xenia was like a borzoi in pursuit of . . . whatever it was borzois pursued. She was definitely sniffing about, but he was damned if he could see how she had picked it up. He had not been indiscreet in any way. For God's sake, nothing *was* going on, except in his imagination, and that was a faded faculty nowadays. But he was annoyed with Xenia, unfairly so, for finding his bone before he had had time to bury it safely. *If* she had found it. Perhaps these were just scaring-off tactics; she had a habit of wheeling people around and away from whatever it was they fancied, sometimes before they knew they fancied it, in case the satisfaction of the fancy affected her adversely. He retrieved his book and settled down again, not to read to the end of the chapter but to finish the whole book.

Edmund daily expected the Strood address book to arrive
in the post, but five days had elapsed since he had spoken to Marianne, and he was dealing with a call from a
woman enquiring whether he stocked first editions of any
of Barbara Cartland's *oeuvres* when a striking-looking girl
pushed open the glass door of the shop and wandered in
confidently, glancing first at Charlie, then at him. Edmund
looked up and smiled and she quietly waited for him
to finish talking, glancing about the shop without much
curiosity.

'I'll be with you in a minute,' he promised, his hand
momentarily covering the receiver. 'No, I'm afraid we don't
have any in stock – yes, perhaps we should, yes, we
do deal in modern literature.' He raised his eyebrows in
conspiratorial mock-annoyance at the girl. 'Well, not quite
all. Romantic fiction isn't one of our specialities. Yes, I'd
be delighted to try . . . yes, yes, now which titles . . . I
see . . . and your name and address? Thank you. We'll
be in touch as soon as I can locate them. Goodbye.' He
turned back to her. 'Sorry to keep you waiting – can
I help?'

She opened her bag and produced a small packet. 'Mr
Yearne?'

He nodded.

'I've been meaning to post this for the last three days. I thought I'd bring it round in my lunch hour.'

'Aunt Helen's address book? Oh wonderful, wonderful!' He was beaming at her. At last he might be able to achieve a result. She passed it over. Her face had the neat, almost featureless perfection of a photographic model, her eyelids heavy with soft grey eyeshadow, artfully ruffled short shiny haircut; Edmund could feel Tom Treasure's eyes boring into the back of his head through the glass window from the back room, and could also sense a certain interest from the other desk, where Charlie stood, having stopped whatever it was he had been doing; now he stared in their direction in a most unprofessional fashion.

'It's very kind of you to have gone to this trouble. No Andersons or Fleurys in it, I suppose?'

'I did look, but no. It's quite exciting, this Find the Lady game you're playing, isn't it?'

Edmund could detect no signs of excitement in her face.

'Well, it would be if I could get anywhere with this. I'm sure that your aunt was at least a childhood friend of the person I'm looking for. She certainly visited, or lived in, that part of Norfolk in her teens.'

Tom Treasure popped up beside him like a glove-puppet, and Edmund took pity on him, leaving him to search for some imaginary pen on the desk for a moment, before giving him the Barbara Cartland enquiry to deal with. Tom took it, but lingered, ostentatiously dusting the shelf nearest to him with his elbow.

'I'm going up to Norfolk in a week or so – I have to see the house-agents and clear up one or two more things. Let me know if there's anything I can find out for you, up there.' She smiled her perfect little smile at Edmund, turned and swung out of the shop, mission accomplished, all long legs and little flame-coloured jacket. Tom Treasure let out a moan and clutched himself.

'Don't make a nuisance of yourself, Treasure,' said Charlie in a threatening whisper. 'Go back to your cell if you can't behave. We do have other customers in here, you know.'

These other customers, a man in a long mac with grey hair in a ponytail and a diminutive Dr Crippen look-alike, had both halted in their leisurely grazing of the shelves, and had turned, gazing dreamily after the girl.

'What very well-stocked shelves,' said Tom, forcing Charlie to giggle childishly.

Edmund was already turning over the pages of the address book, which had an unpromising soppy puppy on the cover. It looked almost new, and inside were few crossings out, no addresses changed. He would start telephoning at once. No, better wait till he got home. Aunt Helen appeared to have known a vast number of people and it was going to take a very long time if he had to go through all of them. He hoped he struck lucky before getting to C.

On his way home that evening, Edmund bought a bottle of Irish whiskey and a selection of packeted sandwiches from a Croatian-run supermarket in Marylebone High Street, preparing for a lengthy session. He made a crib sheet: 'Good evening. I'm sorry to bother you [how apologetic he always sounded] but I believe you were a friend of Helen Strood? I'm trying to trace another friend of hers called Mimi Anderson, or Fleury. I've come by some papers of hers which should be returned. Marianne, Helen's niece, gave me your address.' He poured himself a whiskey and got dialling.

Half an hour later he'd got halfway through the A's, had three no-replies which he noted down to try again later, poured himself another drink and opened a packet of sandwiches which turned out to be curried chicken. By nine o'clock he was at the end of C, and rather drunk. Feeling he might start slurring his speech, and rather disheartened, he decided to call it a day. He'd got so used to hearing 'Sorry,

No, Sorry, Can't help you, How interesting, So sorry', that he no longer knew how to spell the word sorry, felt that it was an alien word, probably from some Balinese dialect, and that it meant absolutely nothing. He ate the last half of a salami sandwich and lay back on the sofa, staring at the ceiling.

'I am undoubtedly mad, have almost lost my voice and will certainly have a huge phone bill. All in order to give back these wretched papers, which I feel are mine now anyway.' 'But,' said his quiz-master voice, 'it's no longer just returning them, is it? You want to *meet* the woman, admit it. She may be a female orang-outan married to a circus strongman for all you know. Have you thought of that? You feel attracted to her, and every simple sentence of hers you turn over, examine, pick at like a vulture. You think you know her, but you only know what she chose to let you know. You're guilty of reading other people's letters, which is a heinous crime. You're guilty of secretly opening wardrobes and examining their clothes, pawing over their mental underwear like a miserable pervert.' He was bemused by this tirade from his alter ego, but delighted with the idea of mental underwear, starting to imagine the intellectual underclothes of various people he knew. Charlie Parrott, for instance, would wear shiny black plastic boxer shorts. Tom Treasure, a leopardskin posing pouch, with a grubby, cigarette-burn-covered singlet. Xenia would have a boned corset of prejudicial steel, and long lace-edged Victorian drawers. He was entranced by this variant on the old game, poured another drink and had A.S. Byatt in a dark green and scarlet tapestry liberty bodice made by Vivienne Westwood, and Albert Einstein in graph-paper-patterned long combinations.

He went to run himself a bath, pouring an ancient and unused bottle of Floris aftershave into the steaming water. 'That'll drown the smell, if nothing else,' he muttered, getting in and lying there, wallowing. The soap flew through his fingers and he could not be bothered to retrieve it, lay there gazing at the little black hairs on his big toes.

> 'Albert Einstein,
> Had a fine time,
> In the jungle with a chimpanzee,
> Who taught him all there was to know,
> About their relativitee!'

He chuckled at this a little, but wasn't it Albert Schweitzer who had sat in the jungle in Africa? He dozed off for a minute or so and awoke with a jerk as he slid down in the water, his foot connecting sharply with the cold tap. Splashing, he heaved himself out and rubbed down with a hideous towel covered with orange parrots. Sylvestra had left him all the nastiest towels. He was slightly dizzy, and a little cross with himself for having drunk so much. He wrapped the towel about his waist and headed for the kitchen where he made himself, with great precision, a proper pot of coffee, found a blue and white cup with a saucer that matched and returned crookedly to the sofa, picking up his black hat from a chair and stuffing it on his head on the way. His brain was slowly clearing, so he started where he had left off the night before, with a couple of Mimi's handwritten sheets from the pile on his table.

He came round to the flat this evening, but I was so busy with some new designs I had to make him wait. If they weren't finished they would weigh on the mind all over Christmas, and they had to be got in to Franks the day after Boxing Day. He sat very patiently, reading *Magister Ludi*, and didn't lose my page marker. I had to keep turning round to look at him – he's so beautiful and has these long fingers, like Lytton Strachey in the Carrington portrait. I finished at nine o'clock and changed fast into red dress, but it's very cold, so had to put on old coat over it which spoilt the effect rather. We went off to the Queen's Elm where we'd arranged to meet R., and the RCA crowd. R. is celebrating not only Christmas Eve, but the fact that he hasn't touched a drop since starting his new book, and feels he can be allowed a break now he's reached Chapter Five. He was wearing his Mr Freedom satin jacket and was pissed already when we arrived, bellowing out funny stories, lighting one fag after another, so that he sometimes had three burning in the ashtray all at once, and one in his hand as well. But since he never gets belligerent when drunk, or, miraculously, boring, and everyone else was pretty much the same way, it didn't matter. I hope this book does as well as the last; he must surely have eaten up all his advance already? Sean came in saying that it was snowing and everyone rushed out to see, very excited as everyone is when it first snows; one can almost smell the change of mood, the pleasure at the initial sight of it. We left with R., he to his bed, and us to search out a church in which to go to Midnight Mass, to make sure it really was Christmas. R. fell over a cat on the way out, hugged us hugely and said he'd catch up with us on Boxing Day. There were some old Polo mints in the pocket of my coat which we sucked to take away the beery smell, sitting close together in a back pew. We needn't have worried. There were a lot of old gentlemen wearing black velvet-collared overcoats, snoring their way through the service, and you could almost see cartoon brandy fumes rising up into the air. I got an attack of morbid religiosity and felt I shouldn't take communion as I was living in sin, sort of.

'I thought you were living in Kensington, sort of.' He was convulsed at his own old joke. We fairly bellowed out 'Hark the Herald Angels' and there was an excellent choir, beautiful descants. Christmas again. I got quite choked, red-nosed with tears flinging themselves from my eyes. I know it's cheap emotion, but can't help it. When we got out it was quite white everywhere and still snowing. Quite quiet, footsteps muffled. Even the congregation coming out of church sounded snuffed out as they wished each other happy Christmas. We ran, skidding and slipping, all the way back to the flat, and wrote our names huge in the snow outside the front door. I suddenly felt I was acting in a film and nearly spoilt the moment.

There was another half-sheet stapled to this, which read:

R. was found dead in his flat yesterday afternoon. Boxing Day. I simply cannot believe that we won't see him again, *ever*. We were going to meet in the pub that night. They think it may have been a heart attack, but he was only thirty-six – not so very old, and he didn't take dope or LSD, ever. We both feel shattered and cannot let go of each other for long, reassuring each other that we are still here, I suppose. Tonight there will be a wake for him at the Q.E. It's what he would have liked – such a shame that he'll miss it. The funeral isn't for some time because there has to be a post-mortem. I remember his great width, both physical and mental; his cracking smile, his tremendous interest in everyone and everything about him, and his constant encouragement. 'Go on, my love, do it now, before you're too old to enjoy it.' Everyone who knew him loved him.

Edmund almost burst into tears himself, still sitting there in the orange parrot towel and hat. Cars slooshed past in the street, and he shivered, sobering up fast. His girl was with someone she loved, even if he did make poor jokes in church. It was most odd that she didn't mention his name, had in fact carefully avoided doing so; her intentional concealment pointing perhaps to the fact that she was no longer with that person when she wrote or rewrote the entry? As usual, no dates, no nothing.

He marked the name where he had finished phoning that night, and went to bed after drinking a precautionary pint of water. He lay there imagining himself arriving at Mimi's front door, ringing the bell and it being opened by : . . the imagining ceased to be imagining and he dreamed . . . a woman wearing a red dress, with Marianne Strood's beautiful impersonal little face, stood on the step. 'Yes,' she said. 'I am Mimi Anderson. But the papers are not mine. I never wrote them. But you are expected to stay for dinner.' He followed her into the house, whose walls were all painted yellow, with a black and white tiled floor, decorated with an armoury of swords. She turned to him, and said: 'We often do a little fencing after pudding.' And he replied: 'I'm afraid I didn't bring mine,' and the consequence was that all the other guests challenged him to a duel after dinner. Dinner was only baked beans, served on dirty cream plates with chips and cracks, and he told the faceless people that he had only come to deliver some papers, but they said he was a wimp, and made him stand on the table, flicking beans at him from the tips of their knives. 'Where are the papers?' they chanted, 'Where are the papers?', subjecting him to a cannonade of beans. He didn't know where they were but he was sure he had them when he arrived. Had he left them on the bus? Panic seized him and he was suddenly out in the street, running, miraculously not covered in tomato sauce as he'd feared. He shouted out 'My God! My God! They're persecuting me!' and he was followed by a rabble singing 'Hark the Herald Angels Sing', chasing him into Baker Street Underground station, waving machetes and kukris, hatchets and halberds. Then Marianne Strood appeared beside him at the ticket machine and bought him a ticket, but started to kiss him goodbye, which was quite exciting. She wrapped a long black leg around him, rubbed her foot on the back of his knee and he felt, well, very excited indeed, and then he woke up with the inevitable consequences.

'I really am too old for this,' he said crossly, padding off to the bathroom. He had not let the water out of the bath earlier, and he watched the soapy soup flowing sluggishly away, leaving a light tidemark behind it. He felt compelled to get the bath cleaner out and scrub.

'Here I am, cleaning the bath at two a.m. Here I am having wet dreams at the thought of an unknown woman. It's Mimi I want, not Marianne. Although I know a lot about her past, she knows nothing of me whatsoever and cares not a jot. She probably doesn't even know she's lost the damn writing anyway.' At which point the doorbell rang, so he tied the hideous towel around him again and went cautiously to see who it was, almost expecting a host of vengeful dinner party guests in evening dress.

His son, Jerome, stood there, looking both hopeful and apologetic. 'Hello, Dad. I'm sorry it's so late, and I know I've woken you up, but I wondered if you could put me up for a couple of nights?' He stepped inside, eyeing the towel with distaste, putting his knapsack down on the sofa. 'You see, I was supposed to go to a party tonight, but the train from Manchester was delayed because of the snow, and now it's too late. The others went off to somewhere in Shepherd's Bush, but I thought I'd try here.'

'Snow?' said Edmund, trying to clear his aching head.

'Yeah. It's been snowing all day up there, and got really hard just as we were about to jump on the nine o'clock train. We've been held up for hours and hours. I was quite surprised to find there wasn't any snow here.'

'Well, it's good to see you, even at this time of the

morning. I was awake anyway, just had a nightmare. How about something hot to drink?'

'Great, that'd be really good. I'll make it, shall I?' Jerome dived into the kitchen and rattled about, chatting. 'Is there any bread? I haven't eaten much since lunch. Ah, here it is. Marmite? Jam? That'll do. How's Aunt Xenia and Uncle Johnnie? Have you been down to see them recently? I've hardly seen anything of Stuffy Henry in Manchester.'

He came out of the kitchen with two cups of hot chocolate and half a loaf of bread smothered in Xenia's best raspberry jam, sat down beside his father and tucked in. He resembled Edmund not at all, except in height, for which Edmund was grateful. He had golden curls like a pre-Raphaelite angel, a small sharply turned-up nose and a chin with a cleft in it. Both girls and boys thought him rather pretty, and he was a popular member of his archaeology course.

'How's your mother?' asked Edmund.

'Oh, fine, fine. She's "doing" American Indians, at the moment.'

'Oh, I thought it was carpentry.'

'No, that was the last enthusiasm. She made a wonderful dining table, but when we tried to have lunch on it, it sort of lurched sideways and we had to take evasive action as it all slid to the floor.'

He chuckled engagingly, and polished off the bread and jam. 'Well, I suppose you'd like to get back to bed. Have you got a couple of spare blankets?'

Edmund felt delicate the next morning but arranged to meet Jerome for a drink and a meal after shutting up shop. Jerome fancied dim sum, which was handy as Chinatown was close by. He was lyrical about his first term at university and his archaeology course.

'You'll never guess what,' he said, his mouth full of sticky rice, 'we're doing a field trip at Easter, a dig near Holy Hill! Isn't that a coincidence? The field-walk round the base turned up quite a bit of first-century Roman stuff, sherds, bits of mortars. They think it's possible there might have been an army post there, and a small settlement.'

'You could stay with Uncle Johnnie. I'm sure he'd be glad to put you up.'

'Well, I'd rather do whatever the rest of the gang are doing, really. I mean I don't want to miss out on anything.'

'No, I suppose not. But it'd be useful for the odd hot bath to wash off all the mud and I daresay one of Xenia's suppers wouldn't come amiss, either.'

'Oh, yes, that'd be great.' Jerome paused. 'Pass those little cakey things, please. Stuffy Henry will be there, too, I suppose.'

'Why? Don't you two get along so well now?'

Jerome and Stuffy Henry, so named because of the prim expression on his face when teased as a small boy, had been friendly as children, in the way that cousins are when thrown together because of their parents' relationship rather than through choice, but when Jerome had moved to Somerset with Hatty and their mother, their interests and outlook had diverged naturally, and Henry had gone up to university the year before Jerome.

'He's got some very odd friends in Manchester.'

'What do you mean, odd?' asked Edmund, pouring himself another glass of beer.

'Well, I'm not sure. It's just that I thought I'd see quite a lot of him. I know he's a second-year and all that, but he wanders around looking as if he's on something. You wouldn't recognize him from last year. He was still very much the rich farmer's son then. You know, like all checked Viyella shirts and moleskin trousers? The last few times I've seen him, he looked as if he'd spent three nights on the trot raving.'

'What! Henry at a rave? Are you sure?' Edmund recalled

the boy, pink-cheeked and shining with health, as with sleeves rolled up he helped Johnnie dose the sheep. More "Hireling Shepherd" than "Death of Chatterton".

'No. I mean I don't know. I was exaggerating. But he definitely isn't the same person at all. He looks a bit pasty and out of it. Definitely going downhill. Can I finish these too? You're sure you've had enough?'

'Go ahead. Is this something I should pass on to Johnnie?'

'Good Lord, no! It's not that serious. He'll see for himself when Henry comes down.'

'Well, I'm terribly glad to see *you* so cheerful. You've obviously made the right decision about what course to take.'

'Oh yes. I am absolutely sure. It's *the* most interesting thing.'

'Lucky you, then. Now let's have a cup of green tea and then go back to the flat. I really must get an early night.' Edmund tried unsuccessfully to attract the attention of a waiter who was leaning against the wall, gazing into infinity with the appearance of a monk meditating on a mantra.

Jerome left the next morning for Somerset, with a birthday card for Hatty from Edmund tucked into his pack. 'Tell her not to forget to visit me when she's up in London next time.'

'As if,' said Jerome, giving his father a hug. 'We'll be up quite soon, before Christmas. I'll ring you.'

They were alert, friendly and demonstrative children, thought Edmund, gratefully, although he realized they were not children any longer.

'And *you* are OK, Dad?' asked Jerome, giving a final look round the dingy flat. 'Perhaps Hatt and I could give this a coat of paint, in the summer vac?'

'That would be wonderful. I've been very lazy about it and it *is* a bit grubby.'

'Speak to you soon then, Dad, and love to Uncle J. and Aunt Xenia.'

Edmund was very pleased to have been visited. He enjoyed his children's company very much and was glad that they enjoyed his enough to make contact regularly out of their own choice. Edmund had, in the early days of the divorce, been careful never to criticize their mother or stepfather, left them out of battles and always tried to consider their opinions but it had been hard work never to appear miserable or hurt in front of them and to strike the right emotional balance when in their company. They had seen straight through his well-meant dissimulations, he had found out later, when the dust had settled, but they seemed to him to have come to terms with the split-up in an unusually well-balanced fashion. Jerome had a strong practical streak in him. All for the best, in the best of all possible worlds, he thought, a trifle bitterly.

That evening he eschewed the whiskey and telephoned from C to F and struck lucky with a Mr Fuller from Sheringham, who thought the name Anderson rang a bell. 'I don't think I ever *met* anyone called either Fleury or Anderson, but interestingly I bought some books from Marianne, Helen's niece. I spent some time with the ink-eradicator on the fly-leaves. There were certainly some volumes of Napoleonic history with the name Fleury in them. If you'd care to hold on, I'll go and check.'

Edmund held his breath.

When he returned, Mr Fuller announced that two of the books were signed G. Fleury, and that the address was still faintly visible, despite his efforts with the eradicator. 'No 6, rue Flaubert, Annecy. Then there are two more, *Le Procès Verbal* by le Clézio, and an anthology of French fairy tales. The first is inscribed "Syrie Anderson", and the second "M.A. Anderson, The Flower House, Kettleham". Kettleham, by the way, is just a few miles from here.'

'That's very helpful indeed,' said Edmund, writing down

the address in excitement. 'I'm very grateful to you. Did you know Helen Strood well?'

'She wrote articles on ornithology in the parish magazine,' said Mr Fuller. 'We used to go birdwatching as part of a group. She'd give me lifts sometimes, in her beautiful car. I was very sorry to hear about her accident. She was knocked down by a truck, I believe.'

Edmund thanked him again, profusely, and felt that he was at last getting somewhere. Someone, a neighbour perhaps, must know of the Andersons, and a visit to Norfolk was now imperative. He triumphantly telephoned Marianne Strood.

'Guess what? I've got an address from a Mr Fuller. You sold him your aunt's books? Well, one of them had M. A. Anderson on the fly-leaf, and an address. It's in Kettleham, apparently quite near Bolt.'

'Yes, just down the road from there. I was going up on Saturday. I've this lovely car, courtesy of my aunt, and I quite fancy a long drive in it. Why don't you come up with me, and you can go and see if there's any sign of the Andersons?' She sounded friendly, more interested than when he'd last met her.

'That would be an excellent idea.' The thought of being driven up to Norfolk by Marianne was quite attractive, ego-boosting even.

'Where do you live?' she asked. 'Ah, yes . . . well, I may as well pick you up then. How about seven thirty, or is that too early?'

'That'll be fine. I'll be ready.'

'OK, I just hope it isn't a wild goose chase for you.'

He couldn't resist telling Charlie of his success, and his arrangements with Marianne, when he went in to work on Thursday morning.

'I don't believe it. You jammy dodger!'

'What a very strange expression. Yes, I'm quite looking forward to the experience. Driving with her, I mean.' Edmund recalled his dream rather uneasily. She couldn't be much older than Jerome. He picked up an order and went into the back room to do some work on his new section on illustrators' books, there being a lot of cross-referencing to be done. An hour later he had got as far as PEAKE, Mervyn, and entered the brothers Grimm's *Household Tales*, black and white and some colour, 1946, and Lewis Carroll's *The Hunting of the Snark*.

Charlie called out to him: 'Edmund, as you're already there, could you run a check to see if we've got anything illustrated by Tenniel, apart from the two *Alice*'s? I've a customer here who is interested.'

Edmund did so, but found nothing in stock. He glanced through the little window into the shop, but Charlie's desk was half-hidden by a jutting shelving unit. He came out into the shop and came face to face with a person, a woman, who seemed oddly familiar to him, but was, for an instant, nameless.

'Hello!' he said, confident that the name would come to him in a second or two.

'Hello!' she replied, also momentarily perplexed. They were both out of their contexts, London life and country visits being in separate compartments of Edmund's brain; Amelia, having no idea of his profession, was certainly not expecting to find him there.

'Amelia,' he said at last, making the connection.

'Yes. How clever of you, and you're Edmund, only minus the hat.' She stared at him, still fazed by the coincidence. 'I didn't know this is what you worked at,' she continued, suddenly confused, hoping he didn't think she had sought him out on purpose, which she had not. She had been to visit a bullion dealer a couple of streets away, and now had a small packet safely stowed in her bag. Nine carat red gold, a piece of eighteen carat yellow, and several ounces of sheet silver. Having completed this part of her business, she was filling in time before an appointment with the Victoria and Albert Museum's craft shop. If she could get her work on display and on sale there, she would begin to do very nicely indeed. Her samples and a book of designs and photographs were in a little black briefcase tucked under her arm. She'd just been wandering around the area, looking in at shop windows. She had been intrigued by the strength of the Tenniel illustrations when reading the *Ingoldsby Legends* and had idly wondered what else, apart from *Alice* was illustrated by him, and thought a smart antiquarian bookshop was just the place to ask.

Edmund introduced her to Charlie, who was beginning to wonder what on earth there was about Edmund that brought a succession of desirable women to his desk. What was it that women fell for? He'd once read the result of a survey in a tabloid newspaper, searching for the qualities that women find most desirable in a man, and seemed to remember that the result was a six-footer with a tight bum, huge bank balance and an improbably large penis. He could discern none of these qualities in Edmund, yet in a short space of time two very pullable women had entered the shop to search him out. This one was a lot older than the delectable Miss Strood, definitely forty, but she had something sexy about her, in spite of her rather tired clothes. The face was fine, pointed, pretty. He glanced at her neck, that being where age usually first makes an appearance, but it was swathed in a green silk scarf, wound round several times. He couldn't see the rest of her, since she was enveloped in a coat, but she looked as if she might be rather shapely beneath it. And the hair, a waving mass of dark gold, neither short nor long, nor apparently styled in any way. Lively hair . . .

He gave up, shot Edmund a suspicious glance and went

back to his catalogues. Edmund was coming to the same conclusions as Charlie as he chatted to Amelia, wondering if he could offer her a lunchtime drink. He looked at the clock on the wall behind Charlie's desk. Nearly midday. Charlie wanted a late lunch.

'I'm on the point of popping out for a pint and a sandwich. Would you care to join me, if you have the time?'

'Yes, I'd like that. I've got an appointment at two o'clock and nothing much to do in between, although I was going to have a look in the Portrait Gallery, as it's not far from here.'

'You could do both. I've got to be back by one.' He fetched his coat, leaving Amelia a moment to stand and take in the terracotta walls and the sheer weight of books lining them: the ancient leather-bound, the newer cloth, the brightly jacketed volumes of knowledge both empirical and ideological, novels imaginative, novels pretentious, learned and self-indulgent. The many millions of words poured out in the English language, most to no great effect, in the centuries since printing was invented.

'See you at one, Charlie.'

'Sure. Don't be late though, will you? I'm lunching with Rich Uncle.'

No one had ever seen Charlie's Rich Uncle, but he indubitably existed since he had, Edmund learnt, been the backer when Charlie bought into the business.

Out in the street an icy wind whipped up scrumpled chocolate wrappers and bus tickets, and a McDonald's carton flew snapping at Edmund's ankles.

'There's quite a good place just round the corner. It's full of thespians and porn-merchants, but does a decent ham sandwich.' He steered Amelia, hand beneath her elbow, through the etched glass door and to a round table by the window.

'What would you like to drink?'

'I'll have a Jameson's please, if they've got it.' Edmund was pleased she shared his taste in whiskey, and went off to get it and order sandwiches.

Amelia, her briefcase and bag tightly wedged between her ankles beneath the table, watched him with interest. He had no trouble getting the barman's attention immediately, in spite of the already busy bar. He certainly did have physical presence, but now, instead of Aristide Bruant, she saw that a slimmer, slightly taller version of Napoleon Bonaparte was nearer the mark.

He returned, bearing the drinks, which he carefully set down on the sticky brown table-top. 'They'll bring the food in a minute. So, now tell me. What's the interest in Tenniel?'

'I came across some illustrations in a book your brother-in-law lent me. One of them was of two horsemen going over a cliff – one of the horses is a ghost horse and has amazing, car-headlight eyes and glows in the dark. I was intrigued by the composition and force of it. The story's quite good, too. I found out the origin of the expression "A flash in the pan". Shall I tell you, or do you know?'

'I thought it came from those photographers with their old plate cameras, holding up magnesium flashes.'

'No, it's earlier than that. The smuggler is being chased by an exciseman and draws a pistol . . . Oh, thank you . . . what lovely thick sandwiches . . . . a horse pistol, whatever that is, and fires a shot at the exciseman's horse, which is the ghost horse, and only flame, not blood, jets out of the hole in the horse! Then he fires again, this time at the rider, but the horse pistol "flashed in the pan". I suppose what we'd call a misfire.'

She set about her ham and mustard sandwich with gusto, searching in his face for resemblances to the Xenia she had met. Just the eyes perhaps, that rather piercing light blue, and the slight slant upwards.

Edmund was delighted with her company, and could see that Johnnie, if he was indeed interested in her, had reason to be so.

'I think the *Ingoldsby Legends* were published around the 1830s,' he said.

'So you know the book! Have you actually read it?'

'Yes, but ages ago, when I was a child. I think the story you described is called "The Smuggler's Leap", am I right? I may have read the copy you've been lent, because I can remember the picture! My father had a copy. I believe they were incredibly popular to start off with. Every-house-had-one sort of popular. But later Victorians thought some of them, well, perhaps not quite the sort of thing young ladies should read in the drawing room. The moral climate started to change quite fast after the end of the Regency period.'

'Yes, I've only read a few of them so far, and I can imagine that infidelity and boredom with one's aged husband would be considered unsuitable for Victorian misses, however amusingly described.'

'Isn't it a pity that more modern novels aren't illustrated?', Edmund said, thinking of his growing collection of books illustrated by Rex Whistler, whose Rococo pastiches delighted him.

'Yes, I suppose it is. But on the other hand, illustrations do stop people using their imaginations. I used to get so cross when I came across the first illustration of the hero with quite a different face to the one I had envisaged. And now we have the "film of the book" to help out those with no visual imagination – but that can be irritating too, for the same reasons.'

'What did you like to read, as a child?'

'Everything I could get hold of. When I was quite young I loved Kipling, and C.S. Lewis of course, and all those historical novels by Rosemary Sutcliffe about Roman Britain. At school I read a lot of old children's books, the kind our parents read. Henty, D.K.Broster, John Buchan, Saki, Conan Doyle . . . then came Jane Austen and Charlotte Brontë and Dickens. Then Lawrence Durrell, William Golding. I remember a book we weren't allowed to read at school, in fact there were lots of books we weren't allowed to read at school, but this particular one had a supposedly over-explicit description of childbirth in it. So of course we read it, but remained none the wiser about how the heroine had got herself into that condition in the first place.'

The buzz of the crowd around them, the warmth and the alcohol loosened their tongues, and they carried on, and on, discovering similarities in adult reading and discrepancies and dislikes, pet hates and loves. Amelia admitted that she had got so desperate once on holiday in Greece, bookless, that she had been reduced to reading the back of a detergent packet, followed by the instructions on a roll of Kodak film, and started to teach herself Greek by translating the advertising in a local newspaper and the bilingual instructions on a bottle of shampoo.

'I've got to get back', said Edmund, suddenly remembering the Rich Uncle. It was five to one.

'Oh, goodness, yes. And I've got to get over to Kensington.'

'We'll meet again, perhaps, next time I come down to stay with Xenia?'

'I'll search you out – and we can carry on the conversation,' she promised.

They went their different ways, Amelia to the Victoria and Albert, and Edmund in some haste back to the shop. He felt warm, well nourished and philanthropic. He bought an *Evening Standard* from the bad-tempered newspaper seller on the corner, next door to whom, in a doorway, was a large cardboard box, from which a pair of boots protruded. This was unusual, since Edmund walked past that way every morning and the owner of the boots was usually rolling up his blanket and flat-packing his box at that time of the day. It was lunchtime and yet he had not got up and gone off on his rounds. Edmund paused.

'Do you think he's all right?' he asked the newspaper seller, who huddled himself deeper into his dandruff-covered, greasy duffel coat, sucking in his cheeks and blowing out steaming, malodorous breath.

'Don't see why not,' he said.

'Well, usually he's up and about by now, isn't he, by lunchtime?' said Edmund. He turned and tapped on the box. 'You all right, in there?' The boots did not stir and Edmund had a sudden sinking sensation. He bent down and shouted into the box. 'Come on! I just want to know if you're OK.'

'He's probably pissed,' said the newspaperman, flipping a newspaper neatly in half with a flick of his wrist and holding it out to a customer, palm upwards ready for the money.

'What's wrong?' said a man in a pinstripe suit and expensive camel-hair overcoat.

'I think he may be ill. I pass every day, and he's usually up and about by now, or at least sitting there begging. I've never seen him asleep at this time of day.'

The man looked about him, as if searching for help, then twitched his trouser legs up an inch and squatted beside Edmund. 'His legs are stone cold,' he said, removing his hand from the ankle above the boot. They looked at each other uncertainly but a girl came up, a girl whose clothes, face and hair were all uniformly grey.

'What's up with Gareth?'

'We don't know. We think he might be ill.'

'Pissed,' said the newspaperman, selling another newspaper.

'Gareth? Gareth!' shouted the girl, tugging at his feet.

It was awkward, trying to get him out of the box. Edmund and Pinstripe had to haul from one end, while the girl pulled at the box from the other, gradually exposing the rest of the man called Gareth. His arms were tightly folded over his chest, the hands stuck in his armpits, and he was stiff. He was quite definitely dead, and the putty-coloured face stared up into their own, unconcerned, no longer there.

'You've been selling newspapers for the past hour, standing next door to a corpse!' said Edmund heatedly to the newspaper vendor.

'Serve him bloody well right. Put off the customers, he did. You going to get someone to come for the stiff, then?'

A teenage police constable appeared, pimples standing out scarlet on his pinched face. The girl sat, stone-faced, beside the body. An ambulance was called and Pinstripe and Edmund drifted discreetly away.

Charlie, already in his overcoat, was pacing up and down behind his desk.

'You rat! I'm going to be bloody late!'

'A man died in the street,' said Edmund.

'Did you have to stay and bury him? No, I'm sorry, I'll get off. See you later.'

Edmund had been shaken out of his previous convivial mood. He'd got used to the man in the box over the past few weeks; they'd even started to greet one another.

'Morning.'

'Morning, mate, spare a fiver?'

Now he was extinguished: by the cold, disease, alcohol? He did not know. The man had had a set routine. The blanket was always placed just so on top of the flattened box. Routine keeps one going when things are bad, Edmund was aware. He'd once been obsessed with it for a short period just after he'd moved into the Marylebone flat. He'd followed a strict formula, as if that would prevent any further bouts of disaster; his talismanic behaviour including counting the steps up to his flat, placing his things in exact preordained places, and always leaving the place at eight fifteen a.m.

exactly, not a moment before or later, standing by the door staring at his watch as if waiting for a supernatural command to lift off. He had walked up the same side of the street each day, drunk one pint of beer standing in exactly the same spot of worn carpet at the bar of his local pub, and become distressed and fretful if anyone else happened to be standing there when he wished to avail himself of its particular prophylactic properties. It had all sorted itself out, eventually, when his depersonalized mind had decided for itself that this type of behaviour was a nail no longer needed to hold itself together.

He heard the ambulance coming, and went to the door, staring down the street. Then he got on with his work. The head of cheerfulness which had built up while sitting in the warm pub with the pretty, intelligent Amelia had been dissipated. Life was short, life was sweet, and he'd better get on with living it. He helped a customer with a query, sold two first-edition copies of a 1930s novel which had recently been televised, and typed up stock cards. He rearranged a shelf, made lists and was serving another customer when Charlie returned, glowing with alcohol and red meat.

'He was late too, I just beat him to it. I'm sorry about your brush with death. Now who was that incandescent lady?'

'She's from the darkest depths of Romney Marsh. I don't know what she does, or who she is really, except that my sister thinks her husband is chasing after her.'

'Don't blame him. So you didn't find out anything about her over lunch? Whatever did you talk about?'

'Oh, books, and things.' Edmund was suddenly irritated by Charlie's curiosity.

Charlie raised his eyebrows to heaven.

Later on that afternoon he received a call from Xenia, who rarely rang him at work, and who appeared to desire his company yet again for the following weekend.

'Xenia, I can't. I'm off to Norfolk this weekend. I've

got a lead on Mimi Anderson at last, and I've got to follow it up.'

'Mimi?'

'You remember! I've told you all about her. The papers in the seaman's chest?'

'Oh, that rubbish. Yes. You're getting very boring about her.'

'Well I'm sorry – but I could come down the week-end after, if you'd like, only that's getting very close to Christmas. You do still want me to come for Christmas?'

'Of course, darling Edmund. Where else would you go? I just need to . . . it's Johnnie, again. I want you to talk to him.'

'Oh, Xen! I do think you should ask him yourself, out-right, if you're so worried – I really do think you may have got things out of proportion. But I will be there the weekend after next, I promise. Take care of yourself.'

He put the phone down, anxious. She had sounded a little shrill, unbalanced even, and that was unusual.

Edmund was washed, shaved and dressed by seven o'clock on Saturday morning. He packed Mimi's exercise books and writings into a carrier bag, just in case he might be lucky enough to be directed straight to her, although he was not too hopeful of this, having checked out through directory enquiries that there were no Andersons in Kettleham. Judging by the negative response from Helen Strood's friends – he had got no further than Mr Fuller – she had most probably left the area a long time ago. A fiendishly icy east wind sliced through the cracks and gaps in the window frames, the sky was an indeterminate grey; he shoved an extra sweater into the bag.

Marianne rang the bell at seven thirty precisely, causing him to gulp down the rest of his coffee and sending him tumbling downstairs and into the street like a Jack Russell after a rabbit. The car was a complete surprise – a long, mean, navy-blue Bristol 401, and Marianne, dressed in a black leather jacket and trousers, a white cashmere shawl draped round her shoulders, looked set to raise a few eyebrows in Bolt. Her face was a beautifully painted little mask, with a small neat smile. He settled back in the red leather seat, feeling for the belt.

'There aren't any, I'm afraid. There's nothing strong enough to bolt them to. As it's a classic car, it's exempt.

You'll just have to trust me. Right? Off we go.'

The engine hummed throatily as they slid through London on their way to the M11. It was a car that was much stared at, and Edmund covertly watched Marianne enjoying the attention. She was a good driver and he relaxed sufficiently to start chatting to her, interested in the car, asking her about her job. She was pleased by his eagerness and enthusiasm, being more accustomed to dispiriting young men who were acutely, self-consciously laid-back, determined to remain unimpressed by anything in case they should seem naive. Edmund discovered that she worked for an independent TV production company, that she was twenty-five, older than he had supposed. She lived alone, she said, but had a man, which last fact she divulged without being asked, as if it were a much-practised warning. She called the man her 'partner', an expression which still jarred on Edmund. A partner, to him, was someone with whom one worked in business, an equal shareholder, or someone with whom one played tennis. He must be careful how he introduced Charlie in future.

They stopped at a service station just before joining the motorway and Edmund went halves with the petrol and bought a large bar of plain chocolate which seemed to please Marianne, who ate most of it, holding out her left hand for another piece every five minutes or so, like a child. The sun had come through the cloud and hung low in the sky like a blood orange over a landscape browned and silvered by wind and frost. Marianne did a little questioning too, in between mouthfuls of chocolate, asking about the bookshop and Charlie Parrott's place in it, and he asked her more about Helen Strood. Had she been married? No, she had not. Would Marianne's father perhaps remember some of his sister's friends? He had died, quite a few years ago, she said, which was why she had inherited the house, and the car, which had originally been her grandfather's.

Had she kept any of the private letters belonging to her aunt, he asked hopefully. She replied that she'd had an enormous bonfire of everything like that. He thought it lucky that she had not discovered Mimi's outpourings, or they would certainly have met the same fate.

They turned off and headed for Newmarket, where they eventually stopped for a short break, to stretch their legs and have a cup of coffee. Edmund had been rather aware of her legs as they drove, their leather encasements alternately creasing and straining over her kneecaps as she changed gear. When they came out of the coffee-shop, a few flakes of snow were floating down, which caused Marianne to look slightly anxiously at the yellowing sky. It was the first hint of any emotion on her face that Edmund had seen.

'That could be a real drag,' she said, getting back into the car. 'The windscreen wipers aren't exactly brilliant and the windscreen itself is a bit difficult to see through.' Edmund had noticed that it was small, and in two parts, with a central bar, but the snow seemed light enough as they drove on, more sedately. But soon there were increasingly heavy flurries, causing Marianne to lean forward in her seat, straining to see. They passed through Swaffham, then Fakenham. 'Bolt's next,' said Marianne, with relief in her voice.

On reaching Bolt, a red-brick and flint townlet, they drew up outside a pub where they had a beer and a lager, pâté, with not quite enough toast, served with a garnish of rock-hard onion rings, cress, leather-skinned tomato and the tasteless ribs of an iceberg lettuce. Marianne followed this up with a chocolate fudge pudding, which, she said, made up for the awful pâté. Edmund was now finding it harder to find subjects for conversation. She was quite hard work, he decided, as he wandered about while she did her business with the house-agents.

The snow was beginning to settle on the pavements and

the inhabitants hastened their steps as they went about their Saturday business. A tiny woman in a yellow headscarf crossed the road towards him as he loitered in front of the church, her arms overflowing with a great sheaf of funeral lilies and florist's greenery. Edmund tried to be patient, but Marianne seemed to be taking an inordinate amount of time. He stamped his boots in the snow, batting his arms up and down to try and keep warm, nearly decapitating an ancient gentleman coming up behind him in macintosh and beret, head down and semi-blinded by the snow.

She emerged at last, and leaving the car where it was they walked down a side street to Aunt Helen's house. This was also of porridgy flint, with red-brick quoins and a range of green-doored outbuildings inside a low flint wall. A black and white cat was sitting alone in the garden surrounded by clumps of blackened dead chrysanthemums and upturned flowerpots; it opened its pink mouth and miaowed silently, picking its way over the snow-dusted dark earth towards them.

'That's Tache, Aunt Helen's cat,' said Marianne. 'Don't let him get in as I unlock the door. He's got a new home now, next door with the Watkinses.'

There was a pile of letters on the floor inside, which Marianne bent to retrieve and, putting her gloves and shoulder bag on the nearest chair, started to look through.

'I have to arrange with the Watkinses to readdress the post for me, and to come and check the heating's going on and off all right. I'm worried about burst pipes.' Edmund looked round the sparsely furnished room, low-ceilinged, long, with its two Ercol chairs and pine coffee table on a great expanse of pale grey carpet, like three lonely peas on a plate. 'Most of her things are sold. I just keep the basics here, plus bedlinen and pots and pans.' Marianne sat down and started to open the letters, throwing junk mail and circulars to the floor beside her. 'So much for putting her death in the paper. There seems to be a vast amount of people who didn't see it. Look!' She held out a handful of Christmas cards. 'I'll have to get her address book back as soon as you've finished with it, and try to sort out who they are all from. Pity people only put their Christian names in cards. How am I supposed to know who Hilary and Siegfried are?'

Edmund was standing by the window, a determined figure who looked as if he were plotting to escape from Elba. Uncharacteristic impatience rising, unable to help himself, he asked when they might think of setting out for Kettleham?

'Soon,' said Marianne, opening another card and reading it before slipping it back in its envelope and putting it with the others. She joined him at the window and Tache leapt for the sill, skidding in the snow and scrabbling at the glass, his paws leaving dirty streaks. 'Of course. Kettleham and your mysterious Mimi. I'll just check everything is OK upstairs, go and visit the Watkinses and we'll be off. There's coffee and longlife milk in the kitchen if you'd like some.'

While she was away he sat in the chair by the empty hearth, sniffing the cold and musty air and wishing he had a book to read. The shelves had been emptied, leaving dark tidemarks on their cream paint. There were a few red drawing-pins stuck into the beam above his head, and by the door. Relics perhaps of long-ago Christmas decorations. A dead geranium in a cracked terracotta pot. One watercolour, of an ancient building in the snow, which somehow looked familiar. There was a little cupboard beside the fireplace, with a brass handle. He bent and looked inside it. A chessboard and box of men, a Monopoly set and a book, *Card Tricks for Beginners*, a dog-eared and sticky pack of cards. He shut the door again and leant back in the chair. There was something about Marianne that he could not quite put his finger on. She was undoubtedly remarkable visually, seemed intelligent enough, had hardly been unfriendly, in fact very pleasant . . . the outside door slammed.

'Hi, I'm back. Shall we go off then?'

In Kettleham, which consisted of only a dozen houses, they knocked on a door at random. Edmund had ready his prepared questions and explanations, but the woman who came to the door, all tightly curled mauve hair and velvety pink tracksuit, was brusque, shivering meaningfully on her door step.

'I've only recently retired here with my husband. But the Flower House is first right, a hundred yards up the lane on the left.' She whipped back inside and the door slammed behind her.

They found it immediately, and Edmund stood staring at it, his hand on the gate, his hopes shattered. It was an upright, red-brick doll's house, with Dutch gables. Its door hung from its hinges and the windows were blind, boarded up.

'Oh, shit!' said Edmund. His imagination had run away with him on the way between Bolt and Kettleham – he thought he might meet, if not Mimi herself, then at least people who knew of her, would direct him to her.

'Cheer up!' said Marianne, her teeth chattering. 'We'll go back to the other houses and knock on all the doors till we get somewhere.' She went back to the car, leant into the back seat and opened the boot by means of a button hidden beneath the armrest. She produced a pair of impossibly shiny clean Wellingtons, and Edmund discovered what it was that worried him most about her – she was too perfect, too neat, too clean and tidy. He had an overwhelming desire to roll her in the snow.

'The only problem is', she said, brushing snow out of her plucked eyebrows, 'that in this area most of the cottages are owned by weekenders, which means they are only occupied for a week or two a year. A lot of the villages round here are ghost-towns in the winter.'

The first two cottages seemed to prove her point, there being no reply from either of them. They saw a man in a flat cap, splitting logs in his front garden further down the road, a cape of snowflakes across the shoulders of his jacket, and approached him. He remembered Mrs Anderson and her daughter.

'That'll be a good while ago,' he said. 'You'd best ask the old vicar, he's retired now. Yes, the old boy'll remember.' He directed them to a white house across the road. By this time they were getting very cold indeed, the snow falling even thicker, getting down their necks. Edmund began to worry about the possibility of not being able to get back to London that night.

The vicar was at home and listened politely to Edmund's by now thoroughly confused explanation, delivered through clenched teeth, of the reason for their arrival on his doorstep, unscrambled it and invited them in. They were begged to take seats in his study, beside a coal fire which fairly belched out heat.

'Now I think I might be able to help you a little.' Edmund sighed with relief. 'I do indeed remember the Andersons. She was a *very* charming woman, but I don't know what happened to the daughter, after she married.'

'Married?' asked Edmund.

'Yes. I had the pleasure of officiating. I could find out her married name if that would help?'

It would not, unless it was something incredibly unusual, like Wisley Drizzel, but Edmund nodded enthusiastically.

'Then I'll go and and put the kettle on as you're both obviously near frozen to death, and I'll telephone the present incumbent. He's got the parish registers since nineteen fifty in his study. There's too much vandalism about to keep them in the church.'

He disappeared and they heard him using the telephone in the hall.

The warmth began to rush agonizingly back into Edmund's fingers and he watched Marianne sitting there quietly, snow melting off her boots on to the hearthrug. Her cheeks were pinker now, and she appeared a little less made-up, less immaculate than she had earlier. The window was darkened by falling snow, hypnotizing as it drifted past the panes. Out of professional interest he turned his eyes to the bookshelves, but they were overflowing with heavy theological works, aged green Penguin crime novels and learned volumes on the correct pruning of fruit trees. There was an ivory crucifix on an ebony stand on the cluttered desk, beside a shockingly flippant pink cyclamen in a pot. Edmund felt his eyes begin to close in the stuffy warmth.

The vicar returned with a rattling tea-tray on which was a motley collection of cups and saucers, placing it at his elbow on a shaky little table. He was a small, thin man, with a large Adam's apple that shot up and down in his wrinkly, mottled throat as he spoke.

'I've remembered one or two things about the Andersons while making the tea. They came here from the Middle East, although I believe they lived in Suffolk before they went out there. They rented the Flower House for a long time. Have you seen the state it's been allowed to get into? So sad, such a waste when there are such housing problems everywhere. I know two families who'd give their eye-teeth to get in there.'

He poured out the tea and handed Marianne a blue and white Spode cup, trembling in a red and gold Derby saucer, and Edmund caught the smoky smell of Lapsang Souchong.

'The child, Mimi, was an attractive little baggage. I can remember the wedding because the bridegroom wore such an astonishing velvet suit. But then it was in the nineteen seventies. I've contacted the present vicar and he will ring back shortly, as soon as he finds the entry. Poor man, so much busier than I used to be. He cares for four parishes now. Do have a biscuit.' He passed Edmund a little pink plate with a few soggy gingernuts on it, and Edmund gratefully took one and put it in his turquoise blue-rimmed Minton saucer. His cup, he noticed, was probably stolen from a railway café. Thick, white and heavy.

'My wife, who sadly died twelve years ago,' continued the vicar, dipping his biscuit in his tea, 'used to keep in touch with Mrs Anderson after she went back to London. Syrie, her name was, I think. She was some sort of journalist. It's all coming back to me now. Syrie was the daughter of the writer, Connaught Marvel.'

The telephone rang in the hall and he rose to answer it before Edmund could express surprise at such an eminent grandparent for Mimi. When he returned he handed Edmund a piece of paper with the details of Mimi's marriage on it, written in pale, wavering pencil.

Taylor – Anderson – Nicholas Charles to Miranda Amélie. June 27th 1974 – witnesses were Syrie Anderson, J. McGinnis and Helen Strood. 'I do hope that that is of assistance to you? You could perhaps look up their marriage certificate in London, which will give you their addresses at the time of their marriage. I seem to remember they came down from London for the wedding.'

The old man was so courteous, so kind, that they didn't rush immediately away, Edmund shooting Marianne a pleading glance as she started to rise from her chair, making her subside. They finished their tea, discussed Connaught Marvel, had another cup of tea and another biscuit. Edmund then thanked him profusely. 'We must, however, be getting back. We've got to return to London tonight.'

'I think that might be foolhardy,' said the vicar, waving at the window, 'it seems to be what they call a white-out.'

It was indeed a proper blizzard when they left.

'Christ! Are you going to be able to drive in this?' said Edmund, trying to wipe some of the snow off the windscreen, then going round to the sloping rear of the car.

'I'll manage. It's not dark yet . . . we'll have to go back to Bolt, and then I'll ring the AA to find out what the roads are like.'

'It's pretty obvious what they're like here. I feel I ought to be walking in front of the car with a flaming torch,' said Edmund, as they crawled forwards, the heavy car slithering. The flakes came towards them like speeding grey sparks and the wretched little windscreen wipers moaned and whined, unable to cope with the onslaught.

'I haven't a fucking clue where we are,' said Marianne. 'Could you stick your head out of the window, and see if I'm still on any sort of road?'

'I'll try.' Edmund removed his hat and leant out into the whiteness. 'Right a bit, right a bit more, that looks OK. I think there's a stop sign coming up.'

'That'll be the main road then. Thank God! I turn left there, and then we're back in Bolt.'

Edmund withdrew his head, banging his chin on the lower edge of the window. Marianne looked at him and smiled.

'Do keep your eyes on the road!' he implored.

'I can't actually see the road. I'm just guessing anyway. You look like Father Christmas.'

'I think I've got frostbite,' said Edmund, his teeth clattering together. The car chasséed round the corner and they then turned into the side street at the bottom of which was Aunt Helen's house.

'I won't try to get it into the garage – I might not be able to get it out again. There's a little supermarket just up the street. Shall we go and get in some supplies, do you think?'

They filled a wire basket with emergency rations: bread, bacon, butter and biscuits, more milk and two tins of Baxter's game soup and some marmalade which Marianne said she couldn't face life without, and a bottle of Jameson's. When they returned to the house, Tache flew through the door and sat down in front of the empty fireplace, looking huffy. Marianne flopped down in a chair and threw her head back, her once-perfect shiny hair now rats'-tailed and wild. Edmund felt that he should take charge of the evening; she'd been driving all day and must be tired.

'We'll get a fire going, that is if there's any wood?'

'Yes, there's a whole shedful.' She showed no signs of moving.

'Well, you see if you can get the heating going, override the time-switch or whatever, and get down some blankets. I'll go out and get the wood.'

'You'll need a key. It's the second shed. Here, it's on the ring with the Yale.' She passed it to him, and he made his sortie into the horizontally blowing snow. The shed was indeed full of logs, and dry kindling, and there was also a log-basket, covered in cobwebs. He made two trips across the garden with this on his back, feeling like King Wenceslas, taking enough to last the whole evening, or the night if things got worse. The night . . . he really did not want to get snowed in with Marianne. He'd run out of things to say to her. It might of course stop snowing, at any time, and he would telephone the AA at once. But he must check in the address book for any Taylors. Marianne was still sitting in the chair when he returned with the second load, looking very glum.

'What's the matter?' he asked, feeling he should be looking after her.

'No electricity, so the boiler won't fire. And there's no way you can do it manually. There are no lights, no nothing. I've tried. Power cut.'

'Well, never mind. The cooker's gas, isn't it? I'll soon get the fire going. Go on. Go and get those blankets, and then you can wrap yourself up in a rug and tell me your life story.'

She gave him an odd, almost pathetic look, but went upstairs, where he could hear her footsteps, cupboards opening, floorboards creaking.

He tore and scrumpled up the junk mail, overlaid his kindling and set a match to it. Mercifully it took flame at once, and he sat back on his heels, ready with some small pieces of ashwood to build it up. Tache rubbed his head up and down on his knee, as if scent-marking him as an appreciated piece of personal property. Edmund was relieved, there being only one thing more destructive to the male ego than failure with fire, or indeed, being obviously disliked by other people's pets. Marianne returned, wrapped in a pink paisley eiderdown, with four blankets and another blue eiderdown in her arms.

'Have we got any candles?' asked Edmund.

'Yes, a whole boxful. I'll get them.' She fetched them from the kitchen and stuck them in a line across the chimneypiece and Edmund put one in a little green enamel chamberstick he'd found in the downstairs lavatory.

'Shall we light them? I can hardly see what I'm doing.' It was dark now, and Marianne drew the curtains and struck a match, lighting the candles with some awkwardness and a lot of 'ouches', her fingers cold and stiff. The fire started to give out a breath of heat, and the room became less severely empty, all light focused around the fireplace, their shadows curtseying and bowing up the bare walls.

Edmund rang the AA, who expected the snow to ease off by midnight but meanwhile would advise everyone not to drive unless it was absolutely necessary. He relayed this message to Marianne, who had taken off her damp socks and was holding out her bare feet to the fire, her face inscrutable. He also removed his boots, hoping his socks didn't smell, and set them to dry by the fire. There was a tension between them; neither knew what to do or say next. He peered through the curtains and could dimly see a few flickering lights in windows and imagined other people digging out camping stoves, and Tilly lamps, bemoaning the lack of television. He had not got a television at home in his flat and so did not miss it, but could see how useful they were when one didn't have anything to say to one's companion.

'What about a game of chess?' he suggested. There didn't appear to be a book in the house.

She leant forward, clutching the eiderdown closer around her, and opened the fireside cupboard, pulling out the board and box.

'You've obviously looked in here – there are cards as well, if you'd rather?'

'I think I prefer chess. I'm not very good at it though. How about you?'

'I'm not too good at it either.'

'That's OK then.'

They pulled the little table closer to the fire and sat down cross-legged on either side of it. Edmund stoked up the fire, and they set out the chessmen. The pieces were tacky to the touch, lightly mottled with mildew, and they played rather cautiously at first till she, gaining confidence, started to skate about the board with a bishop with such success that Edmund decided it needed to be unfrocked immediately before it did any more damage. It took him a long time to checkmate her, and they had a cup of coffee before playing a return match. There were no sounds except the infinitely soft flutterings of the driven snow on the windows.

'There's no traffic at all, had you noticed?' she said.

'I thought I heard a tractor a little while ago.'

'My hands are still cold.' She looked at him, then held them out, tentatively. He took them, equally uncertainly, and rubbed the icy fingers, unwillingly at first, as if the familiarity might be dangerous.

'There,' he said, giving them back to her. 'I'll get us some whiskey. You can tell me about your Aunt Helen.' He returned with the bottle and a couple of tumblers and watched her as she set out the chessmen again.

'I'm white, this time. What about Aunt Helen?'

'Well, tell me what she did, what she looked like, how well you knew her . . . that sort of thing,' he said, taking a gulp of his drink, and moving a pawn in response to her opening.

'She was very clever. She read endlessly, and she took a lot of trouble with me. But I used to be made to come and stay by my parents, whenever they wanted to go off abroad, which was quite often. I think she thought I wasn't being properly educated because she kept on giving me books to read. I hate reading. I'd rather be doing something practical. And concerts, she took me to concerts whenever I stayed, driving down to Norwich or wherever, in the Bristol. She thought I was musical, but I'm not. I'd just learnt to play the piano very easily. I didn't know what I was supposed to feel about the music, how to emphasize the right bits. I just played, accurately, what was written down. I'd rather have sneaked off to a rock band.' She suddenly shifted a knight in a move which Edmund had prayed she would miss, wrecking his rather short-term strategy. She was beginning to play better and better, as if slowly rediscovering the possibilities.

'What else?' asked Edmund, who, having got her talking, was determined to keep her at it.

'She was mad about birds. She had her own income, but taught at the local grammar school, English. She was tallish, slim, quite a good figure really. But she never took any trouble with her hair or face, and had absolutely no taste in clothes or anything. No eye. I used to shop with her in Norwich, hoping to brighten her up a bit, but it was no good. We always came back with a replica of whatever it was we had gone out to replace. She was the same age as my mother, but she looked older. She made friends easily, Mother said. Very talkative. She was supposed to have had this long affair with a writer, but when it ended she never looked at anyone else. I think she put a lot of her affection into me, which was rather overpowering. It suited my parents because of their travelling. It was nice for them not to always have me tagging along.'

Edmund felt pity for her immediately, although her voice had not suggested she felt any for herself.

'How odd, then, if she was so interested in birds, that she should keep a cat.'

'Yes, I suppose it was. But she was more of an out-and-about, long-walks-and-binoculars sort of birdwatcher. And she always swore that Tache was too fat and lazy to catch any. Hey! What are you doing?'

'I'm castling.'

'Well, I don't know how to do that. It's not fair.'

He showed her the principle, and found himself, ten minutes later, to be checkmated.

'That's one-all. Shall we go and visit the pub? It's seven o'clock. Have you got a torch?'

'No. Don't let's go out again, not into all that miserable cold. I've just got nice and warm. We've got everything we need here.' She poured herself another drink, and threw another log on the fire, which by now was sending out real heat, having built up a good base of embers. 'Let's play one more game,' she suggested, 'and then we can start on the card tricks.'

Edmund was already beginning to feel fuddled, and Marianne seemed to have speeded up, not taking so long over her moves, annihilating his pawns and sending his bishops scuttling for cover whenever they dared to stick out their episcopal noses. However, he rallied and adroitly tempted her queen into danger, giving a whoop of delight as she fell into the clutches of one of his knights.

They sat back and surveyed each other in the flickering, guttering candlelight. She seemed to Edmund immensely more human, less of the supermodel. She pushed the table back towards the middle of the room, and moved closer to him, still enveloped in the pink paisley eiderdown.

'I'm bored with chess,' she said, putting her hand on his thigh.

Curious, curious, very, very curious. He could hear his own heart beating, surprised at being moved on so swiftly, surprised at his own physical response. Something was definitely stirring. A beat was missed, a lurch as he felt her body pressing closely into his, put his arms round her, feeling. He stared into her expressionless, inky-grey eyes, which had closed as he started to remove her jacket. Oh, hell! He jerked himself away, and her eyes opened sharply, read his thoughts with speed, and smiled.

'Don't worry, I've got some. Here.' She fumbled in the pocket of her jacket. So she had come prepared? The thought that she had planned this, had wilfully conjured up a snowstorm in order to entrap him fled across his mind, but he was unable to arrest it. He was not of the 'women are whores or madonnas' mentality, although he occasionally had sneaking suspicions that a great many of them were witches and possibly dangerous. They removed from each other whatever else seemed reasonable under the circumstances. She was thin, but definitely not unattractively so, very white, and seemed to know what she was doing. Yes, she did indeed. After a while he sank into her with a little gasp, instantly back into the dream of a few nights past. Any minute now a ravening horde would hammer down the door and demand his blood. He was determined to finish what he had started before he was caught and hacked to death. Her face was still, sensuously serious, and she made small encouraging sounds, her long legs wrapped about him.

'How long since . . . ?' she asked, her eyes open again, each reflecting a tiny candle.

'A very long time.'

'I thought so. Me too.'

'Why not?'

'I just haven't wanted to.'

'You said you had a man – a partner?' he said, lying back on the blue eiderdown, his arm beneath her neck, uncomfortably, his feet on the fender.

'I lied then. It was just in case you pounced and I didn't want you to. But I did want you to, and you didn't, so I had to pounce instead.'

'Oh, I see.'

She sat up and retrieved a pawn from the hearth. She was staring at him, taking in the compactness of his body, the slightly puzzled expression in his eyes, the tangled thatch of dark hair, greying near the ears, and smaller details, such as the small scar on his shoulder where he had been hit by an airgun pellet as a child, the already burgeoning dark stubble round his jaw, the lines round his eyes. He felt her scrutiny, felt as if he were being assessed for signs of age, and did not care. He also felt hungry.

'This is all very peculiar,' he said.

'Isn't it just.'

They were on neutral ground, equally balanced, and there was no more between them than that. Yellow and pink light flittered across the walls and their faces. She got up suddenly and went to her bag, taking out a green envelope which had the words 'Happy Birthday Marianne' written across it in white marker.

'Today? It's your birthday today?'

'Yes. But I had my party last night, after work. Someone gave me this as a present.' She had opened the envelope and taken out a tiny plastic packet.

'Have you ever tried it?' She poured the contents out in a neat line on the table top, made a small tube with a piece of the envelope and looked up at him. 'Want some?' He shook his head, vaguely appalled.

'No, no. It's not my sort of thing. I'll stick to the alcohol, if you don't mind. You seem rather expert at it.'

'No. I've never touched it before. I've seen others do it, of course.'

He wondered. Had he led such a sheltered life that he had never come across a nest of coke-sniffers before? No, not a nest . . . what would the collective noun be, for such a gathering? A snort, a sniffle?

She bent forward and drew it up, sneezed and wiped her nose, smiling. 'I always try everything once. Don't you?'

'Well no, not everything. How do you feel?'

'It's better than pudding.'

She eased her way back across to him, scattering chess-men.

'Supercharged. My turn now.' She pushed him gently in the chest, back into the blankets. 'We probably won't meet again, will we? We might as well make the most of it.' She laughed, rather high-pitched and clear, and talked, and talked, asking questions, which Edmund, considering his position and an almost total lack of breath, found hard to answer. He was convinced he was lying on the white king and queen, felt he was perhaps going through a mirror, as in the opening pages of *Alice Through the Looking Glass*.

'I'm so glad you bought the marmalade . . .' she said, 'I'm miserable in the morning without marmalade.'

'That's . . . that's a nice . . . oah . . . alliteration.'

'Oh, one of them. Like Caroline being continuously contented with cunnilingus?'

'Yes, I suppose so.'

He rolled, exhausted, into a blanket and watched her while she sat up and swept the chess pieces that remained upright to the floor. She pulled out the cards and set about playing clock patience, her movements fast and precise.

'Aren't you cold?'

'No, not at all.'

This, he thought, is a fairy tale without a point, without a moral. Certainly without a moral.

'Beautiful girl kisses frog. I'm afraid I'm still a frog.'

'And you can't have three wishes either,' she said, shuffling the pack with card-sharper's skill. 'It's a shame – isn't it? But I do feel as if I'd woken up,' he said.

Edmund felt starvingly hungry and rose, found his trousers and went into the cold kitchen where he opened a tin of soup and made some toast bringing it back to the fireside on a tray. She drank some of the soup, but left half of it for Tache, who had sat quietly by the fire throughout, only occasionally having to take evasive action from the flying feet and arms.

They made a makeshift bed, restacked the fire, and pinched out the candles. She tucked herself tidily up against him and they fell, both of them, into silence; warm, fairly comfortable, but somehow uncomforted, and from thence into an unsettled sleep. The snow slackened, the wind dropped, and all outside was quiet as the grave.

Not having slept on the floor for a good many years, Edmund woke that morning a bundle of bad-tempered cramps and aches, some of which he suspected had little to do with the hardness of the floor. A cold white lightness came through a crack in the curtains and Marianne was kneeling, fully dressed, by the fire, blowing hopefully on some kindling, raising a cloud of ash. She stood up when she saw he was awake.

'I've made us some breakfast – I'll bring it in. The power's back on again.'

Edmund found his clothes and tidied up the bedding. They were back to their polite communications of the day before, all possibility of anything more seemingly removed from the agenda. He felt that he had been one of those birthday presents women give to themselves in case no one else buys them what they want. 'A rather seedy, second-hand birthday present,' he thought on seeing himself in the bathroom mirror, unshaven and hair on end, with bags beneath his eyes. He rubbed a bruise on his elbow. The light was mercilessly hard. His alter ego suddenly kicked in: 'You ungrateful, self-pitying old has-been,' it said, 'you had a very nice time indeed. She's half your age and you are extremely lucky that she even looked at you.'

She returned with a tray piled with toast, coffee and marmalade. She had remade her face – it had returned to the blank geisha-girl mask, the 'I-speak-no-English' face that had so disconcerted him yesterday, held him back from searching for a definition of the person behind it. Someone was there, he was sure, but not his kind of someone, any more than he was hers.

'The road's been snow-ploughed and gritted. The Watkinses say it's not too bad at all to Swaffham, and almost clear after that. I think we should go soon.'

'You must have been awake for a long time.'

'I didn't sleep much. The cat kept shoving his whiskers into my face. I think he's starved of affection.'

'Like you and me, for instance?' he said, watching her eyes slide away from him. Edmund was confused by his own behaviour. Her motives seemed obscure and he was not sure that he wished to uncover them.

They drove back to London without incident and without any more than lightly general conversation, stopping as before in Newmarket. She treated the incident as never having occurred, which he thought was for the best. The further they travelled south, the less snow there was, and by the time they reached London there was none at all, which inclined him to think that he had invented the whole thing, so distanced did he feel from the previous night. Marianne dropped him off at his flat, offering her cheek to be kissed, which he did, thanking her for her help. He gave her a hopeless sort of hug.

'Good-bye, Marianne.'

She put her hand in her pocket and pulled out an envelope which he assumed was a Christmas card.

'You might like this.' He took it and waved, idiotically, as she drove away.

He let himself into his flat, still carrying his precious cargo of manuscripts, mission unaccomplished and aware that his trail had gone almost cold. The happenings of last night were a blurred fantasy which he had conjured up as one conjures up a fire, from tinderwood and dead twigs; all the accumulated desiccated matter that had hung around in his brain gone in one cleansing act of arson. In spite of a lingering hangover and in spite of the smell of the flat, which had risen rapturously to greet him on his arrival, he felt fresher, cleaner mentally. He pulled the card from his pocket, but saw that it had already been opened, and was addressed to Helen Strood. He sat down, winded with excitement. The writing bore a strong resemblance to Mimi's. He tore the card from its envelope and read:

Dearest Helen,

So sorry not have been in touch for so many months. The move went smoothly, and we are quite settled here now. Will see you very soon, I hope, and will relieve you of all my junk. Happy Christmas, lots of love, Mimi.

There was a PS: 'Here is the new address: Jarvis Cottage, Eeldyke, Romney Marsh, Kent' and a telephone number. 'I've lots to tell you, saving it for long letter in the New Year.'

He turned the card over, in amazement. It was hand-drawn in pen and ink, a gloriously triumphant little angel sitting in a tree, blowing a trumpet, delicately washed with blue and yellow watercolours.

Edmund did not call the number. He sat on the sofa, and, as if suddenly released from a sandbar by the turn of the tide, mentally sprinted for dry land. The sense of relief was dampened by a little splash of disappointment and he realized he had been enjoying the search itself. He needed to think hard before acting. If he rang the number, he might be told to put the papers in the post, and that would be that. Best to arrive on the doorstep.

That she lived barely four miles away from Johnnie and Xenia was a ludicrous coincidence. That she said in the card *'we're* quite settled' implied she was with someone, a husband probably, children most likely. He had always known she might have one – but he had to admit that he had been harbouring a sneaking, hackneyed Romantic vision of this woman, seeing himself arriving at her house as a knight errant, pulling up with a flourish and restoring her lost papers – she would of course have received him with loving gratitude.

It would be best to avoid involving Xenia, she had always shown impatience and boredom with the subject, and Johnnie too had not been interested in the slightest. He would keep the whole thing to himself from now on. He would be there on Friday night and could surely absent himself from the farm for an hour or two, for a long walk, or some other excuse, find her on his own and hand over the parcel.

He took out the yellow box of photographs again, and looked at the girl in the panama hat. She was what he wanted to remember about this odd phase of his life, not some greying, fatly-happy wife. Of course the photograph could be of Aunt Helen, although from Marianne's description he could not imagine that she would wear such a distinctly rakish panama; he imagined she would wear one of the garishly coloured coolie hats worn by the cardboard cut-out pin-up models advertising photographic film in chemists' shops in the 1950s.

Marianne rose up in his mind like a bubble. The card had obviously been amongst the others on the doormat, so why hadn't she given it to him at once? Perhaps she *had* planned to kidnap him for the night? He hadn't been good kidnapping material. He resolved to put his nose to the grindstone again, attend the scheduled book sales in Oxford on Tuesday, Tunbridge Wells on Thursday, assiduously hunt for desirable volumes in houses in Hampstead and try not to think of, nor read any more of, Mimi Anderson, or Fleury, or Taylor. He remembered her name was Miranda on the marriage lines in the parish register, Imim in her earliest persona. How many more names had she got? Unless Helen knew two people by the name of Mimi, but no, the handwriting had emphatically been the same on the card as on the papers. It was as if she had set out to cause confusion as soon as she was old enough to put pen to paper. And her mother, Syrie Anderson, Connaught Marvel's daughter. She had been a writer of short stories under the pen-name of McGinnis – one of those writers of great promise who had sunk into obscurity in the 1960s.

While Edmund was trying so hard to rein in his imagination and put all his energies into his work, Xenia was in a fury of suspicion. She camouflaged this under a heavy battery of smiles, force-feeding Johnnie enormous and delicious meals, polishing all his father's furniture into a state of shock. She kept up an unsubtle surveillance operation, asking aloud, while folding sheets with Rosy Pressing, where on earth Johnnie could have got to, he'd been so late for lunch, so long at the fair, so held up at the market, and Rosy's lack of response to these questionings she had taken as an admission of knowledge followed by dumb insolence. Rosy had been unfooled by the apparent casualness of the interrogation, and of course sussed that something was up; which suspicion she passed on to her brother's sister-in-law in the village shop.

On finding Johnnie's work-gloves on the kitchen table after he'd left to go and check on the sitting of a new footbridge over a dyke, she had made a special trip, trailing the labrador along with her, to where he had said he would be. He had been astonished to see her coming bravely through the drenching rain, a good mile from the house, and even more astounded by her errand.

'But darling, how kind of you. But I keep another pair in the Land Rover.'

'Oh, I just thought you might need them, and anyway, the dog and I both needed a walk. He's getting very fat.'

Lucky Ovenden had observed her at an upstairs window, peering through binoculars, and wondered uneasily if she were checking up on him, although he had merely been standing in the yard with the vet, having an invigorating exchange of views about badgers.

When Johnnie attended his annual get-together with fellow-golfers at an hotel in Parden, she had telephoned reception, asking him to ring her back over an unbelievably minor problem that could perfectly well have waited until he returned.

She patrolled the wintry lanes, particularly past Amelia's

cottage, and one late morning appeared in the Eeldyke pub, having spotted the Land Rover outside. She found Johnnie sitting quietly in the window seat with his pint, alone, apart from Phylly, who was furiously knitting a pink teddy-bear for her grandchild.

'I saw you through the window,' she announced, perching nonchalantly on a stool. 'I really felt like a drink, and thought how nice it would be to join you.'

He was a little amazed, particularly when she knocked back the gin and tonic he bought her and announced that they had both better be getting back for lunch. As it was only twelve fifteen and lunch was always at one, he felt a bit miffed. He liked to sit on his own, passing the time of day with Seth or Phylly, or just thinking about things . . . Amelia in particular.

In spite of not getting so much as a whiff of anything untoward, she was not reassured. On Wednesday morning she drove into Canterbury to complete her Christmas shopping, hoping her toes would not start hurting and hating to abandon Johnnie to his own devices, which freedom she was convinced would be abused. Avoiding groups of noisy French teenagers ganging up and down St Peter's Street and disregarding the charming group of musicians playing carols in the Buttermarket, she bought Johnnie two exorbitantly expensive jerseys, which he did not need, and a Liberty's red and blue silk dressing gown. Each Christmas they usually wrote out modest lists of things they would like for Christmas, exchanged the lists and then chose things from them for each other. This ensured little excitement on Christmas Day, but no nasty surprises either. After she had bought the dressing gown, she suddenly remembered the list in her bag, and bought him the new pair of secateurs that he wanted. Feeling a little calmer at having disposed of so much money, she headed for Marks and Spencer to buy her niece Hatty a pretty silky nightdress.

*   *   *

'Hello! Xenia!'

She looked up from the stand where hung sheaves of sugared-almond coloured nightdresses, and there stood Allie Snodland, arms festooned with artificial satin slips and lacy knickers.

'Allie! I haven't seen you for ages.' The standard greeting, whether one had met three months or three weeks before, signifying neglect on the part of the one addressed.

'Shall we pay for these and go and have a little something together? Or have you had lunch?' asked Allie. 'That is, if you've finished your shopping?'

Xenia felt quite tired, and the idea was tempting. She needed to talk to someone. They queued to pay and then headed for a small café round behind the Cathedral precincts which served delicious little fruit tartlets.

'No smoking here, I see,' said Allie crossly, replacing her packet and gold lighter in a tiny leather bag. 'Oh well! I shall just have to have two cakes instead of one. I'm sure that's why they ban smoking in these places – it makes one eat twice as much.' She ran her fingers through her faded blonde hair with a gesture of mock-resignation. She had not aged nearly so well as Xenia, was over-plump and had let her hands get quite coarse with fanatical gardening; the nails, haphazardly decorated with bright red polish, were split and stained. She sipped her coffee and looked at Xenia with an expression of affection, while thinking that she looked a bit peaky and anxious. She leant forward, bulging out of the small green velvet-seated chair.

'Now tell me all the news, Xen darling. You weren't at Smudgie's birthday luncheon last week – I was so disappointed. I was sure you'd be there?'

'I was . . .' said Xenia, desperately trying to think how she could have missed the lunch – she must telephone Smudgie and apologize – '. . . dreadfully busy – shooting lunches two weekends running, Christmas coming – you know how it is. It must have gone clean out of my mind.'

Allie knew that to Xenia a shooting lunch was like preparing a picnic for a couple of toddlers, and raised her eyebrows. Xenia really did look rattled. Allie probed and prised, poured more coffee, extracting the cause as a dentist draws a tooth. She had much experience in men's inability to control themselves and sensed that a soothing hand was needed.

'But you poor thing . . . of course, you must be worried sick.' She put one earth-stained hand on top of Xenia's immaculately manicured fingers and with the other forked up her second fruit tart. 'But are you really certain? Amelia Sailor isn't exactly the glamour-puss, is she? Hardly Johnnie's type, I would have thought. But of course, there was all that scandal about her husband Nick . . . I used to get along with her well enough at school, but she never struck *me* as being a femme fatale, although I did hear rumours that she was mixed up with some young man . . . not long after Nick died as a matter of fact.' She looked smug, having neatly contradicted her previous soothing words.

'I can't bear it! Poor Edmund says he's met her, and he's sure there's nothing in it – but you know how they all stick together. He's been off on some ridiculous romantic hunt for some woman called Mimi Anderson or something. All the way up to Norfolk to find her. It's been Mimi this, Mimi that for weeks . . . very boring, and he simply doesn't understand how much I need his support . . .' Xenia broke off as part of Allie's announcement sank in. She stared at Allie, dumbstruck. 'You were at school with Amelia?'

'Yes, at St Cecilia's. But Xenia, Mimi . . .'

Xenia interrupted. 'No, tell me all about this Amelia!'

Allie forgot what it was she had been going to say, and put her mind to recalling her days at St Cecilia's.

'Well, she was quite pretty, I suppose, and rather vague.

Her parents were abroad, I think, like so many of us. Daddy was in the Army and we kept on moving about, so I got sent back. It's a convent you know, such sweet nuns . . .'

'About Amelia?' reminded Xenia irritably. 'Know thine enemy' said a little voice in her head, though how school reminiscences would help her to de-escalate Johnnie's interest in the woman, she had no idea.

'I can't remember that much. She was good at art, used to do all the posters for plays and things. Oh, and she was one of those irritating people who never get caught. She used to get the gardener to buy her fags, and smoke in the woods, and go into Hastings by bus to see films we weren't allowed to see. That sort of thing.'

Xenia sat and digested all this unwelcome news. Allie continued: 'But, I was going to tell you before. Xenia, Amelia Sailor *is* Mimi Anderson. That's what she was called at school. I don't know when she dropped the silly nickname.'

Xenia let out a growl of rage and despair. Both the men in her life after the same woman! But Edmund could not know that it was the same person – or he wouldn't have had to chase off up to Norfolk. Did Johnnie know that Edmund was after her too? Perhaps they were already sharing her? She couldn't take in the implications of this. The horrible little trollop was obviously after anything in trousers. And the wretched woman had been invited to her Boxing Day party!

'I do wish I hadn't told you,' she said to Allie, 'I didn't mean to bore you with all this.'

Allie was not the least bit bored, she was riveted. And so were the other customers sitting near by. Xenia and Allie both had loud voices, and even their whispers had a penetrating audibility at the next table. Poor Xenia, it did not occur to her to use Edmund's interest in Mimi-Amelia to head off Johnnie's infatuation. And sadly it never occurred to her either to confront Johnnie with her suspicions. She had nothing in the way of evidence to confront him with. Allie was getting very interested indeed. Xenia, so elegant, so in control of her life, so slim, sitting white and angry in front of her, her coffee half drunk, her dear little cake uneaten . . . 'May I? Oh thanks. I do get so hungry when I'm shopping, and there was no time for a proper lunch . . . but darling Xen, I'm sure all this will blow over. Johnnie would never be so blatant and unfeeling.'

'It happened once before,' said Xenia doggedly, 'only I never actually caught him. It was going on though. I know it was . . .' She stopped.

Allie was unable to winkle out of her with whom and when, and gave up, thinking wistfully of her comfortable drawing room at her house in Chillingden, where she could put her feet up, and perhaps have one or two of those chocolate Bath Olivers which she had intended to keep for Christmas. Anyway, Xenia had been delightfully indiscreet, quite uncharacteristically so. Their younger sons both being at the same school, she would probably see Xenia at the end of term carol service on Friday. Then she could inspect Johnnie for herself to see if he bore the marks of an adulterer.

'Don't breathe a word, will you?' said Xenia again as they left the café together, causing some annoyance as crackling carrier bags bumped and jostled the other seated customers, their shoulder bags swinging indiscriminately and scattering little packets of sugar and teaspoons as they went.

Xenia drove home too fast, shooting a red light, and worrying for at least five miles that she could hear police sirens wailing after her. The road dipped down, running for a while beside the River Stour, past flooded water meadows, old water mills and ancient moated farmsteads, but she was not looking at the scenery. She was excruciatingly aware that she should never have disclosed her problem to Allie. But Allie had never appeared indiscreet, or had she? They'd not seen so much of each other since their children were older, but they frequented the same dinner party circuit, the same lunches, joined up parties for Glyndebourne. Was it Allie who had whispered to her once that something was going on between Jim Pierce-Hadstock and that sly-looking Anna Strachan? Oh God! She feared it was. What had she done? She slowed down on the outskirts of Parden, stopping to go to the supermarket. Aware of her overspending on the Christmas presents for Johnnie, she stuck rigidly to her list, not being tempted to right or left as she passed up and down the aisles with a wayward trolley, all wheels bent on going round and round in circles.

Once at home she hid her presents away in the bottom of the landing cupboard, where she had always hidden them and where everyone knew they were secreted. She took a paracetamol tablet and lay down on her bed, her head throbbing. She could think no further than trying to keep her men away from Amelia. Edmund would hardly be likely to bump into her while he stayed with them over this weekend, but he would see her at the drinks party. She could however keep him pretty busy handing around drinks and food, could make sure he was introduced to other people, led away from her. She tried to remember what else was happening this weekend that she had to take care of. Rupert's carol service, then bringing him home for the holidays. Henry back on Monday from Manchester. She had to prevent Edmund and Johnnie going down to the pub together, they might meet Amelia. She looked like the sort of woman who spent time in pubs, undoubtedly ensnaring other unsuspecting married men. She must plan carefully. And where *was* Johnnie at this moment? There had been no sign of his having come in to lunch when she'd looked in at the kitchen. And she'd left him such a dear little pigeon casserole.

She couldn't lie here forever. She got up and changed her skirt and went down to the drawing room to light the fire, pausing to rearrange the Christmas cards on the scarlet ribbons that hung vertically in rows on either side of the fireplace. She then sat opening a new batch that had arrived after she'd left for Canterbury. One from Uncle Serge in Paris. Just a plain white card embossed in gold with 'Joyeux Nöel et Bonne Année' – a bit dull, but then the French didn't care for Christmas the way the English did. One from Allie, one from Amelia and Josie. She inspected this very thoroughly, holding it with distaste. It was home-made, on thick drawing paper, torn, not cut straight around the edges, and showed an angel sitting in a tree with a trumpet. It was drawn in black with blue and yellow watercolour carelessly splashed over the robe and wings. She nearly threw it on the fire, but on second thoughts pinned the card right at the bottom of the ribbon, where it dangled unseen behind the log-basket, and she felt her eyes and nose fill with tears. Her whole life was becoming untidy, unravelling round the cuffs, and her beloveds were blowing away from her, like ten-pound notes in the wind.

Johnnie found her at teatime in the kitchen in the midst of an orgy of whisked egg whites, bowls of creams and custards spread out over the kitchen table, small saucepans of melting chocolate and of caramelizing sugar on the stove, dishes of toasted almonds and chopped candied peel on the worktops. There was a smell of vanilla in the air. He took a deep breath of it, and furtively nobbled a couple of almonds.

'Shall I make the tea, as you're busy? It all looks very scrumptious.'

'No! No! I'll do it! It's the ice-creams for Christmas. I've got to get everything done in advance.' She wiped her fingers distractedly on her skirt and rushed to take a saucepan off the stove, switched on the kettle and laid out a tea-tray, while continuing to dash back and forth between chocolate pan and eggs, whisking a bit here, blending a bit there, finding teaspoons and measuring tea into the pot with such speed that Johnnie felt queasy.

'Slow down, slow down! Let it all wait and come and have some tea.'

'I can't, I can't! There's so much to do. I'm nearly there.'

She combined several bowls and continued whisking the contents together as if driven by some alien force, splashing cream on to herself and all over the table. Johnnie took the tray and went off to the drawing room. The fire had gone out, and there were torn opened envelopes all over the floor. He looked for the newspaper and found only the front pages which were in the log-basket. She must have used today's paper for lighting the fire, he thought, uneasily, since such disasters did not normally occur.

'You've burnt the crossword,' he said when she eventually put in an appearance. 'And you've got custard on your chin.' He leant forward to chuck it away, but she shied back.

'So what have you been up to all day, apart from the ice-creams?' he asked, making an effort to try and draw her out.

'Christmas shopping,' she replied, almost curtly.

'That sounds like fun. Have you got everything now? I'm still waiting for those books we ordered for Henry.'

She did not reply, but sat cradling her teacup and staring at him suspiciously.

'You didn't eat the pigeon casserole.'

'No, I didn't have time to get back. I had a sandwich at the Woolpack.'

She could surely not be cross because he hadn't come back for lunch, when she hadn't even been there herself?

He shrugged and gave up; her edginess came as a shock after the over-eager desire to please which she had displayed during the last few days, and baffled him. Most unsettling. He wondered if it might be the wrong time of the month, but had never detected much change in her behaviour at these times before, apart from an irrational desire to scrub the kitchen floor herself, when she could perfectly well leave it to Rosy. Perhaps everything would calm down a bit when Edmund came down for the weekend, she was more relaxed when he was about. He had no Christmas shopping to do, having always left everything to her, apart from her own present of course, and that was in hand. When he had dropped in on Amelia that morning she had shown him the gold waiting to be transformed, and promised to have it ready by next week. He definitely still felt the same way about her – but was happy enough with the way things were, for the time being. Although she was neither encouraging nor dismissive, he enjoyed spending a few minutes with her, an hour here, once a week, once a fortnight, it didn't matter. He knew he would succeed in the end. The possibility of something more satisfying developing was enjoyable in itself; he was a hopeful traveller and was taking pleasure in the scenery en route.

However Xenia travelled badly. She was in any case a static person, deeply planted in her marriage and all that entailed – the children, who were ceasing to be children, the big house and its garden. She was frightened of venturing outside it. She was at this moment a sealed and overturned beehive of buzzing worries. Her energies had been perhaps unimaginatively directed at times, but who but a truly creative person could have summoned up an image of a burning, passionate affair out of such a gentle and well-behaved flirtation? Who could have been so mistrustful in the face of such minuscule evidence? Her intellect had been stunted because she suffered from an anorexia of the brain, refusing to allow it to be fed, nervous of the ridicule which she was certain would follow her admissions of ignorance, refusing to take an interest in any but the most superficial of arguments.

The brooding clouds which had hung over the Marsh all day began to shift as a northeasterly wind rose up, rustling the sedges and rattling the elder twigs. Lights were appearing along with the evening stars in the darkening dampness. They sparkled in the necklace of villages hung around the ancient inner shoreline, shone out singly in the empty expanse below. People were returning from work, putting on their kettles, lighting their fires, preparing their teas. Herds were milked, chickens and geese locked up against mink and fox, curtains were drawn, televisions switched on. Amelia shivered at the sudden change of temperature as she emerged from her warm workshop. Between the willows she could see the dumpy illuminated caterpillar that was the Marsh train riding along the causeway across the flatness, on its way to Hastings. She went to the washing line and felt the still-wet socks and sheets, and left them to take their chances in the wind, gliding back over the damp grass into the cottage. Josie would be home soon, so she busied herself with tidying up and washing dishes, having left all the housework till after she had completed her day's schedule of sawing, soldering and polishing. The hair dryer lay on one of the worktops and she switched it on, blow-dusting the row of glasses that sat on top of the cupboards, thinking that that alone was worth a mention in a slut's handbook. She had been relieved that Johnnie had not stayed long enough to become a pressing presence. He had seemed quite happy just watching her, and she was glad of this since she was so acutely physically lonely at times that a move in her direction would have been hard to repel.

Her sitting room was low-ceilinged, a small square room which had been the kitchen when the house was built, and in it she and Josie had put all their favourite things from their old house, so that it was full to bursting with unlikely objects and bright colours – a snug cave in which to lurk during the winter months. A wallful of books, arranged by subject or category, the dividing lines between biography and history, modern novels and anthropology, travel and gardening being drawn by a stuffed owl, a *famille verte* teapot, a box of Kleenex, a copper lustre jug, Amelia's silver christening mug and a deed-box with a broken lock. It was easier, when asked the whereabouts of the *Dictionary of Quotations*, to shout out 'Beside the cotton-reel box!' than 'Second shelf on the right-hand side, about halfway along.' There were pictures on the walls not taken up with the giant fireplace and the window: an early nineteenth-century naive portrait of a child in a low-cut white dress and a coral necklace, a painting of Amelia's of a girl riding a zebra, an architectural study of the interior of St Eanswith's church, a print of an Edward Lear landscape of the Lebanon mountains. All were framed identically in plain broad gold.

The walls were painted a soft pumpkin colour and the floor was covered by a large scarlet, blue and golden-green kelim. The curtains, cut down from the size needed to curtain the huge windows of the old house, were of faded thundercloud-blue velvet, sewn round the borders with a pattern of pearl buttons. On her desk, Amelia kept three brass globes, inscribed with intersecting lines and Arabic script – parts of an astronomical device of some sort, she had been told. She and Josie professed to believe they had magical properties, touching them when fate had been tempted, as people touch wood. They were also dented in places where Josie had once played bowls with them on the lawn when she was six. When she sat at her desk, Amelia used Nick's grandfather's country Chippendale chair, of walnut with a tapestry seat, and she placed her feet on a Stony George – a brown pottery hot-water bottle which she remembered using as a child before her mother had introduced the rubber variety. They had been gratefully discarded then, since they slipped out of the bed at night with a crash, waking up not only the user but the rest of the household.

The coal was kept in a green-painted fire bucket and the wood in an old copper boiler – polished to mirror status, reflecting the patterns of the kelim in its pink-gold silken surface. There were two scarlet painted wooden chairs on either side of the tip-up mahogany breakfast table where Josie sat and did her homework in the evenings, and Amelia drew or sewed. They had decided to put all their best things into one room since scattering them about the house had given such a meagre effect, Amelia having sold or farmed out so many of their other possessions. There was another small room on the ground floor, apart from the sitting room and kitchen, but in the winter it was very dark, and there were damp-stains on the walls, and both of them felt uneasy in there. It would once have been the parlour, with a bright fire burning in the grate and polished chairs for receiving visitors, but now they had filled it with packing cases and empty boxes and things broken but waiting to be mended when there was time to do so.

Amelia tidied up the newspapers and books, straightened the rug, ran a duster over the table and returned to the kitchen to make the tea. The cat lay on its back by the stove, its fluffy stomach exposed, daring her to tickle it. She stood and rubbed it absent-mindedly with her foot, rereading a letter from the bank. She was overdrawn, and would she kindly deposit enough funds immediately to cover the discrepancy. They were, she noticed with considerable annoyance, charging her twenty pounds for the privilege of being informed of this. She would have to telephone them and have a little shout, since she had two days before paid in a cheque which should see them into the New Year. And there was the money coming from Johnnie for the bracelet for his wife. She was still not sure whether the commission had come because he felt sorry for her, or because it was intended as a guilt-assuaging device for Xenia. But the poor man was not really guilty of anything. But then, she remembered, grinning, she had known what was on his mind. At school they had been taught that an evil thought was almost as bad as the sin itself, and she wondered if his conscience was quite clear. The cat yawned monstrously, showing all its dangerous needle fangs, and Amelia remembered the agonies of some of the girls at school when writing out a list of their sins for confession, for, in spite of it being an Anglican convent, they had all been made to attend confession the day before their confirmations. She had herself spent at least half an hour on her list, decided that she would hold everyone up in a queue if she went through them all and scrubbed out at least half her misdemeanours and laxities, not waiting for absolution. Was uprooting carrots in the convent vegetable patch gluttony or theft? She'd spent an anxious night worrying that she might have caught a disease from the pond water in which she had rinsed off the mud. And was sitting behind the curtains in the hall window seat secretly reading yet another banned book slothful, or was it something worse? Children had such an easy time of it now that most of the seven deadly sins had been transformed into matters of personal choice or 'rights', the majority of them being actively encouraged as a means of self-expression.

She heard Josie's footsteps running up the path, and the cat leapt to its feet in fright as the girl hurtled through the door, throwing her bag to the floor and asking all at once if tea was ready and was the man with the long hair and the deerhound actually living near here?

'Yes, to the first,' said Amelia, 'and I don't know what you're talking about to the second.'

'Well, it's a beautiful shaggy dog, and the man has long hair, plaited down the back like in the eighteenth century, tied with black ribbon – a queue I think it's called, and I've seen him twice before, walking past at the weekend. I saw him again just now as I got off the bus.'

'Darling Jo, calm down and pour the tea – have a bun.'

'OK, but he is *gorgeous*! How does one get to meet people like that?'

'Well, I suppose you could stand at the gate, and smile sweetly at him as he passes, or you could try dropping your handkerchief, or pretending you are lost . . .'

'No! Seriously!'

'You could ask at the Post Office . . . Do you mean to say that Ruffles hasn't found out who he is?'

'I did ask her, but she hasn't a clue. She lives even more out in the sticks than we do – she'd not seen him at all. But she's on the look-out now.'

'What's happened to Mikey? I thought *he* was man of the moment?'

'I did use to think he had this interesting mouth, and he has got a motorbike,' said Josie, eating her second bun and putting a second spoonful of sugar in her tea, 'but he'll be off to university in September, doing engineering, so it's not worth getting involved, is it? Oh well, I suppose I shall have to start going for walks as well. When does it start to get lighter in the evenings?'

'After the twenty-second, I think, that's the solstice. But winter's only just begun.'

'I can't wait for the summer then, all those long evenings after school, sitting out in the garden. I *loathe* the winter. I seem to spend all my time waiting for buses and lifts and freezing to death.'

'You could try wearing a coat.'

'But my coat is so awful.'

'I'm sorry, darling. It'll just have to do this year.'

Josie leant against the stove, then held on to the rail and bobbed up and down in a series of cursory pliés.

'Are my thighs getting fat, do you think?'

'No, they look the same as they did yesterday to me,' said Amelia, seriously inspecting them. 'What shall we have for supper, do you think?'

'I'll make it tonight. We could have a beautiful omelette and finish up all those bantam eggs. The woman at the farmshop says they've gone off lay now, and there won't be any more till it starts getting lighter. And I could do an apple crumble? School lunch was totally disgusting today – what they call curry, only it's sweet with horrid fat sultanas in it, like rabbit droppings.'

Amelia was pleased with the offer, and went back to the sitting room to read, until it was time for the six o'clock news. Josie went upstairs to change, and play a tape that had been lent to her. 'Liquid lady . . . shady lady . . . all I need is you . . . ooo . . .' she warbled, throwing her school skirt into the corner and putting on leggings and two pairs of socks. 'Admit it Sadie . . . you know deep down, you wan' it too . . . oo.' She stood by her window, opened it a crack and lit a cigarette, puffing the smoke out into the dark. There was no hedge in front of the house and she had a clear view of the lane, so she would surely see him, even in the darkness, as he walked back with his dog.

Mikey's motorbike was a serious attraction, the answer to getting out and about when marooned on the Marsh without a driving licence. But the young man with the plaited hair, a bit old hat, perhaps, but what a perfect face, and what long legs. Probably a bit pretentious. But he'd had a wonderful leather jacket, and his jeans were a good cut . . . She finished the cigarette and opened the window further, flinging it as far away as she could.

'Direct hit!' called out a voice, and a shadowy figure waved at her, walking past without slowing down. She nearly leapt out of her skin. Well, that was one way of making contact. She'd scored a hit with the butt, but he wouldn't be able to see her in the dark. She closed the window softly and went downstairs to start her homework.

Amelia was kneeling on a cushion by the fire, her book on her lap, a favoured reading position. She had taken Geoffrey of Monmouth's *History of the Kings of Britain* from where it had been resting beside the stuffed owl, and was now deep into the story of King Lier and his daughters.

'Mum?' Amelia did not appear to hear. 'Mum? Amelia!'

Amelia started and looked up anxiously, her hair in her eyes. Josie had had to resort to her Christian name in an effort to attract her attention. Shock tactics were needed when she was immersed in a book, when she went into a semi-conscious state and appeared to be oblivious of everything else.

'Sorry, what is it?'

'Do you still think about Dad a lot?'

'Not a lot . . . just regularly. I've got over the stage of thinking of things I want to tell him. It's more when I'm reminded of things we did together.'

'He *was* ill, wasn't he?'

'If you mean he wouldn't have left us if he hadn't been

ill, I don't know. There were some things he couldn't face – like loss of face itself.'

'It isn't hereditary, is it? Like cystic fibrosis?'

'Darling! Of course it isn't. He was going through a very bad time in his life, and he just couldn't cope.'

'He left us to cope, though, didn't he? Do you think he thought of that?'

'No, I don't think he did. What he did, he did on the spur of the moment.'

Amelia could never be sure if she was answering truthfully. She did not know if he had planned it. And if he had – for how long? He had been inscrutable, those last few weeks, as if he was gradually disengaging himself from them. But had that been intentional? She did not know, or want to know any more. But she understood that Josie still needed to talk about her father, and it was her job to listen, to reassure where possible, and field the questions as honestly as she could.

The relationship between father and daughter had been regularly punctuated by skirmishes, but just as Amelia had been inclined to think that one more sniper's bullet would ensure all-out war, they had suddenly resumed their normal protective father/loving daughter roles and Amelia, who had initially intervened and tried to keep the peace, realized that the bickering, teasing and snapping was more often than not initiated by Josie as if she were a cat sharpening her claws on a tree trunk – and that these sharp rows were somehow necessary to both her and her father, and that they both enjoyed the process.

Josie seemed satisfied for the moment and started on her essay on gang warfare in sixteenth-century Florence, writing furiously for a minute or two, then sighing and running her fingers through her hair and twisting the little gold sleepers round and round in her earlobes. Amelia read another few pages. Geoffrey's Lier had a far more honourable demise than Shakespeare's Lear; in this version Cordelia too was dealt a better hand, becoming Queen of Britain before eventually being imprisoned by her nephews and killing herself out of grief at the loss of her kingdom. Amelia wondered why Shakespeare had changed the story, at least as far as Cordelia was concerned. Things were becoming confusing again, with lists of kings with unlikely names rampaging across the pages – Cunedagius, Rivallo, Gurgustius, Sisillius and Jago.

'Mum?'

This time Amelia was more alert, her interest in Geoffrey of Monmouth waning.

'If Dad hadn't killed himself – would you and he still be together?'

'God help me!' thought Amelia, then aloud, 'I can't possibly know. I suppose that it is possible not, but, on the other hand, I think we probably would be.'

'That's very evasive. What does it mean?'

'It means that *I* never considered leaving your father before he died.'

'Ah.'

'What exactly is worrying you, Josie?'

'I'm not worried. There's no point in worrying about something that has already happened, is there? It's just that it is a year and a half now, and I still don't understand what went wrong.'

'Neither do I. Nick used to get muddled himself, some-times.'

'We will manage, won't we?'

'Yes, we will. We've managed so far. Things can only get better.'

That was tempting fate with a vengeance. She suppressed the urge to leap up and touch the golden globes on the desk.

'Do you get lonely, Mum?'

'Yes. But I've got you with me and that helps a lot. I've also got good friends.'

'I won't be here forever.'

'I know that,' said Amelia, sliding her wedding ring up and down on her finger. She must have lost weight, it was quite loose.

'I'll go and start the supper now,' said Josie, who had written no more than one paragraph. 'Crumble first, and get that in the oven. Then the omelette. Are there any chives left, or have they been frosted?'

'No, I've got some under a cloche. And thyme, I like fresh thyme in omelettes.' Amelia laid down her book and stretched. On the one hand she was glad that Josie wanted to get at the truth and not construct an arbour of glorification around her father. History woven into myth, embroidered with fairy tale and fantasy, a pattern of Chinese whispers based on an already misinterpreted and misunderstood story.

'Only two or three more hours to get through,' thought Amelia, 'then I can go to bed and lie safe.' She would drift as usual, plotting the likely course of their futures, working out stratagems for improving things, and having her usual daydreams of fame and fortune, and more recently and urgently, sex.

That night Josie awoke from a nightmare in which she had been standing at the bottom of a Martello-like tower, only it was taller, seeming to stretch up into the air forever, and her mother had called out to her from the top window, before throwing herself out, falling in slow motion like a dummy in a film, cartwheeling through the air before crashing limply to the ground at her feet. She went weeping into Amelia's room, feeling urgently for her in the bed in the dark to make sure she was still there.

'Sweetheart, don't, don't cry so. You are safe. Get into

bed with me.' Amelia held her close, rocking her like a baby, and Josie eventually slept. But Amelia did not. In her mind's eye, her brain was a small shining globe, and thoughts moved through it as drifting dead leaves, from top to bottom, slowly and gracefully side-slipping as she tried to catch them. At other times the thoughts flew past fast across the space, from left to right, like swallows, and were as difficult to trap as the leaves. Her memory had become very selective after Nick's death, refusing to file anything that did not refer to some immediate need or activity. It was not so much that things were not retained, but that her retrieval system failed her when it came to finding the right file. She tried to recall her own father who had died when she was three – and could only summon up the itchy feel of his tweed jacket on her bare legs as he held her in his arms, and the stale male tobacco smell.

When Nick had died, she had woken up into a nightmare, not awoken from one; having, she thought, dreamed her way through life till then, through men, husband, work, baby, never really aware of happiness until the moment was past, whereas the unhappinesses had always been in the present tense. Josie, only seventeen, had everything to come. But what was 'everything'? She hoped that the nightmares would eventually cease. Josie had not told her what she had dreamt, but Amelia could imagine it to have been traumatic enough.

After Josie left for school the next morning, looking fresh and pink, Amelia went outside to collect the washing, hollow-eyed and paler than usual. The clothes had frozen stiff, making them impossible to fold up. The air was very still and the cold crept like corrosion up her nostrils and into her brain. The warmer, damper lull in the weather had been brief. A cotton nightdress gave a creaking warning of intent to shatter like a pane of glass as she tried to manoeuvre it into a more manageable shape. 'Men are launching probes into outer space and I still have to do the washing by hand. What I need is a mangle, not the Internet.' She carried the unwieldy pile into the house, where everything stood up straight on the floor, empty ghost shapes of jeans, socks and board-like pillowcases, refusing all attempts to bend them over the towel rail. The technological world had passed her by.

However she could afford a Christmas tree and would drop in at the farm shop to order one for next week – Josie would spend hours refurbishing the tatty little collection that had survived from Amelia's childhood, mending the hangers on the coloured glass balls, restringing little circles of beads. She put her gloves on, picked up the axe from behind the door and went out to split the logs. Her least favourite task, particularly in this cold, since she was always frightened that she might injure herself in a moment's inattention, but it was quite satisfying watching the wood cleave neatly down the middle, then again, making four out of one, filling the barrow steadily, but she was out of breath, unfit. She must give up smoking.

'Would you like some help with that?' said a voice from behind the threadbare hedge. She nearly sliced her foot off, and called out nervously, 'Who's that?', unable to see clearly through the scrappy hawthorn and privet. The figure moved down and came in through the lower gate, a tall young man with a deerhound in tow. Amelia could not immediately see if his hair was in a pigtail but she suspected it was, there not being so very many deerhounds kept on Romney Marsh.

'I'm Will Redding, Mrs Redding's grandson, from the house by the bridge,' he explained, holding out his hand.

Amelia relaxed her grip on the axe, and held out hers. 'I'm Amelia Sailor.'

'I know. I met a friend of yours, Mary Beaton, Dr Beaton.'

Amelia was thinking that she would love someone to take over the log-splitting, but couldn't really afford to pay anyone to do what she could do for herself, if she put her mind to it, but he saw the doubt on her face and said quickly, 'When I said "help", I really meant it.' He held out his hand for the axe, and grinned most engagingly. 'If you hold Cosima for me, I'll get it done in no time at all.'

So she relinquished the axe; angels did not appear too frequently on the Marsh, and this young man had every appearance of one, so she put faith before suspicion and went to put on the kettle, taking Cosima with her. The cat spat and hissed a great deal as Cosima lay like a heraldic hound before the stove. The sun came out, bright but mean on heat, and Will worked fast, splitting up two barrow-loads and filling the copper for her before coming indoors and having the coffee. She found out that he was house-sitting for his grandmother who was in hospital, that he had a degree in environmental sciences but had been unable to find a job since graduating last summer, and was now working part-time at a local garden centre.

'I spend more time selling garden ornaments, upmarket gnomes in fake stone, and goldfish than in dealing with plants. It's very dull.'

She sympathized with him, thinking what a vast improvement he was on poor Mikey. Thanking him, she invited him to drop in for a drink next time, when Josie would be at home.

On Friday afternoon Johnnie and Xenia set out to collect Rupert from school and attend the carol service. Xenia was wearing the red jacket with silver buttons, and Johnnie thought she looked pretty good. She had renewed her bright smile with scarlet lipstick and was wearing her strong, 'I'm-in-control' expression. They found Rupert in a state of lyrical excitement, leaping about his dormitory like a ten-year-old.

'Where's your friend Foxy?' asked Xenia, noticing that the bed next to Rupert's was already stripped down, and all signs of him removed. 'I've got your grown-out-of jacket here for him.'

Rupert assumed a serious look. 'I'm afraid he won't need it now.'

'What do you mean? I told his mother I'd hand it over at the end of term.'

'He's been given the heave-ho. He left yesterday.'

'No! But why?'

'He got drunk and climbed up the Christmas tree in the Buttermarket, but he fell off, and brought all the lights and things down with him.'

'Well, I'm not surprised he's been expelled then. I suppose the school had to pay for them to be replaced? You weren't involved in this, I hope?'

'Me? Never! If I'd climbed up the tree I wouldn't have fallen off.' Xenia and Johnnie shot glances at each other, but carried on with getting their son's trunk and other bits and pieces into the car, before walking together through the precincts to the Cathedral, taking the narrow little passage, so hideously haunted, known as The Dark Entry.

It was quite astonishing, thought Johnnie, how the pupils, in their stiffly formal uniforms of winged collars and black jackets with striped Victorian shop-assistant trousers or skirts, managed to look so wildly unhomogeneous when grouped together. Rupert had left his parents and joined a gangling, shuffling, bulging, wriggling mass, drifting untidily into their seats in the nave. Generation upon generation upon generation had been educated there, first by monks, then by priests, and now, for the most part, by laity.

The lights were extinguished and silence fell, the congregation ceasing their rustling and whispering. A cool, clear boy's voice soared out of the darkness, sending shivers down spines.

> 'In the bleak mid-winter.
> Frosty wind made moan . . .'

Christina Rossetti's ice-like words floated above their heads as if bringing the weather indoors with them, chilling those snugly seated in the warm interior. Then a single candle was lit, followed by others as the service of nine lessons and carols commenced, and the soloist was joined by the choir and the other participants, with increasing volume and enthusiasm as the service progressed, till the sounds filled the high golden vaulted spaces above with exultant joy, rattling the stained glass.

'Joy at being let out of school,' thought Johnnie cynically, able to smell the suppressed anarchic excitement amongst the pupils, the restless thrumming of energy as they sang their hearts out. Glorious descants climbed up out of reach into the Bell Harry Tower, surely stirring the bones of the Black Prince lying dustily beneath his gilded effigy and accoutrements in the Trinity chapel.

Then, almost too soon for Johnnie, but not soon enough for the pupils, it was all over. The choir and priests processed and the congregation rose to its feet, smiling self-consciously with emotion, twitching scarves, buttoning up overcoats, searching for gloves. Allie Snodland sat two rows back from Xenia and Johnnie and barged her way forwards as they passed down the aisle, pouncing on them.

'Hello! Xen, Johnnie!' she exclaimed enthusiastically, beaming, with much uplifting of eyebrows and enquiring looks at Xenia, as if to say, 'And how is the old man behaving?' Her own husband, a small and bumptious man whom Johnnie loathed, dressed in an overlarge and important navy-blue cashmere overcoat, clapped him on the shoulder, as high as he could reach, and started to talk loudly, before they had even emerged from the Cathedral, about a forthcoming skiing holiday with his family.

'What, not going this year? What a shame!' He and Allie and the boys were off straight after Christmas for two weeks, he babbled on and on, till Johnnie, a polite smile fixed to his lips and the carols still echoing beautifully in his ears, felt like smiting him.

Once they were outside he caught Allie subjecting him to a fond but considering look, which he did not understand. Damn the woman, he thought, recovering Rupert from the crowd. They greeted other acquaintances, admired the floodlit exterior of the Cathedral, had a quick word with Rupert's housemaster to ensure that he hadn't been involved in the Christmas-tree affair in the town and were assured that he hadn't. Back to the car, hurrying now as it was too cold to stand around any longer and Xenia was worried that they wouldn't be back by the time Edmund arrived. Johnnie asked her what on earth was up with Allie, staring at him like that, as if she was almost sorry for him.

'Nothing that I know of,' replied Xenia, guiltily, making a drama out of adjusting her seat, trying to avert further questions.

'Does she know something I don't?'

'When's Henry coming?' interrupted Rupert, saving Xenia from replying.

'On Monday, after lunch,' she said to Rupert, a little pink in the face, and glad of the dark.

Edmund's car gave a choking whine, and died, as it had on occasion recently, so, cursing, he retrieved his bag and headed for the tube, too impatient to fiddle about waiting for garage mechanics to turn up. At Charing Cross there was a train due to leave in five minutes and he fumed at the ticket office queue and then dashed across the concourse, scattering commuters and backpackers, flinging himself on to the train. He was lucky to find a seat and collapsed into it breathing heavily. An unpropitious start to the end of the Mimi affair, for that is how he now saw it, having last night taken a deliberately pessimistic view of the whole thing, and in an effort not to tempt fate had forced himself to believe that a) he would find that Mimi Taylor had gone away to Africa on holiday, or b) if she had not done a) would turn out to be a scraggy witch in a gingerbread house who would invite him in and keep him there forever. The Marianne occasion had alarmed him.

He was sitting next to a young man in an enormous Puffa jacket which took up more than his share of space and whose headphones gave out a continuous tsikety-tsikety noise. 'I hope he goes deaf before he's twenty-five,' thought Edmund irritably, shuffling his bag beneath his knees and wondering why the train had not started. His opposite neighbour was a bosomy woman in a tight bright blue suit and a lacy white shirt, which gaped between the buttons whenever she moved, exposing little leaf-shaped expanses of some pink undergarment. She wore quantities of gold jewellery: a teddy bear brooch on her jacket, a watch chain around her plump creased neck from which dangled a gold sovereign, gate bracelets on each wrist and several large rings. She bent to get her *Evening Standard* from a shiny black shopping bag at her feet, also withdrawing, after a scuffle, a tube of very strong mints. Still not started; he'd sprinted for nothing. He read the headlines of her newspaper which announced that Royal Secrets had been Stolen. He was astonished to find that there there were any left to steal and turned his attention to her neighbour. A man in a dark blue suit, with a red tie and hornrimmed spectacles, sat with his legs crossed and an appreciable amount of white, hairless leg showing above his black sock. He was doing the *Daily Telegraph* crossword with such velocity that Edmund suspected him of having cheated and peeked at someone else's answers during the day in order to impress people on the journey home. Edmund guessed he was an accountant and that he would get out of the train at Sevenoaks.

Across the aisle a girl with a haversack and suntan turned the pages of a paperback novel, the cover of which showed a mystical-looking woman rising from a fog, dressed in a sort of Iron-age bra and holding a sword aloft. The title, *The Aeons of Irima*, was emblazoned in large gilt letters, suggesting that yet another English graduate had taken a deep breath and gone severely downmarket. The woman in bright blue spent a great amount of time trying to unwrap her packet of mints, dropping small pieces of silver foil into her lap, then opening her mouth exaggeratedly wide to pop one in, flashing a gold tooth as she did so.

The train started with a jerk, and rumbled out of the station, over the Hungerford Bridge and the glittering Thames, wheels squealing on the tracks. A ticket collector came and went, an attendant with a trolley passed up and down and the woman opposite went on eating mints. Edmund, having exhausted the possibilities of his fellow-passengers, and not having brought a book with him, since he had expected to be driving down, dozed. He woke with a start at a station – peering out into the dark he could see it was Sevenoaks, and the crossword maniac had put on his coat and left. Halfway there. Mrs Minty was opening another packet. Her newspaper was now folded on the empty seat beside her. Edmund asked her if he might borrow it, and read first the book reviews, then the theatre reviews, then Brian Sewell opening another can of pretentious worms, gradually crushing them one by one under a gleefully sadistic foot. City pages, sport, and then the train was pulling into Parden, and Mrs Minty stood up, showering the floor with a snowstorm of silver paper, fighting her way into a yellow macintosh, smoothing on pink gloves.

Edmund had to change trains here, and catch the old diesel Marsh train. It was sitting waiting, engine chugging comfortably, when he eventually found the right platform. He had successfully stopped himself from thinking about Mimi since leaving London, but now, avoiding the seat with chewing gum on it and flopping down by the mud-streaked window, he was struggling. He could still see in his head the photograph of the girl in the hat, the face hidden. The heating didn't seem to be working, but the trip was only fifteen minutes or so. An old man, malodorous in a filthy black coat tied round the waist with bailer twine, sat nearby, muttering and clasping a sack. An elderly couple handed each other biscuits and played children's pass-the-time games. 'Now, let's do stations ending in A. You start.' 'Victoria' – 'Vindolanda' – 'I'm sure there isn't a station at Vindolanda' – 'Well, let's go on to B, then.' 'Widdicomb' – 'I think that has an E on the end – give me another choccy biccy.'

Edmund thought how neat and cosy they were and the woman crossed her ankles in their sensible visiting-London shoes and smiled at him timidly, a sort of half-smile, meant to engender fellow-traveller feeling more than conversation. Edmund felt that if he turned round sharply he would catch sight of Lewis Carroll's Sheep, knitting in the corner.

The train mumbled its way across the dark fields and little bridges, depositing him at the dark and unmanned Eeldyke Halt, where he went in search of a telephone. There was no answer from the farm, so he presumed they must still be on their way back from Canterbury. There were a couple of sheep in the weatherboarded waiting room on the platform, so he didn't fancy hanging around in there. It did cross his mind that they might wander on to the track, but there was no one to inform, and he wasn't going to chase them out. They looked contented enough where they were. No one else had got off the train with him, and he stood in the dark outside the disused Victorian station building, the icy wind whipping round his face and scouring the tarmac of the small car park. There seemed no point in waiting there and the Eeldyke Inn wasn't far up the road, so he set off on foot.

Having made contact with the farm, Edmund slid gratefully on to one of the chairs beside the coal fire, the seats of which had been buffed into conker-like glossiness by five generations of behinds. Seth was polishing glasses behind the marble bar and one or two groups of customers were in quiet conversation about manifolds and gaskets in the candlelit back room, a pleasant hum of sound rather than the Sunday-lunchtime cacophony. An outsize scarlet amaryllis stood on the bar, its two massive velvety flowers pointing in opposite directions like secret botanical listening devices. Tomorrow, somehow, he would have to give Xenia the slip and go to find Mimi. He'd asked Seth the whereabouts of Jarvis Cottage, and it was less than a mile along the road. He was very close, but he needed time to psych himself up, to prepare for disappointment. He tried out the plausibility of various sets of excuses. 'I really need to go for a walk on my own – business problems to sort out.' That sounded unlikely. He could however say he was going to spend the morning investigating Marsh churches? That would ensure that neither Xenia nor Rupert would insist on accompanying him. But he had no car – he would have to borrow one.

A gust of wind caught the door out of Johnnie's hand as he entered, banging it against the wall.

'Hello, sorry to keep you waiting. I think I might join you in a pint. I always like to get away while Rupert is being debriefed at the end of term.' He turned to Seth. 'What's good this evening?'

'Marshadder,' said Seth, 'the Norseman's Whore isn't ready yet – too lively. Shot the bung out this afternoon – look at the ceiling.' He pointed at the sticky hop-encrusted spray across the ceiling above his head.

'Right then, Marshadder it is.'

Johnnie sat on the other side of the fire and, leaning forwards, said quietly: 'I think I should warn you that Xenia's a bit on edge at the moment. Not quite herself. See if you can't try to cheer her up a bit, could you?'

'Is she in a rage with you? Another attack of the green-eyed monsters?'

'She's got absolutely nothing to be in a rage about,' said Johnnie gloomily. 'I've not done a damned thing. Anyway, some of the time it's the opposite. She's being over-solicitous, over-zealously wifely – I find it quite frightening.'

'Well, she must think you've done something – to her, that's always been the same thing as being guilty. Thank God she's not a JP.'

'Lucky says he's finding it hard to get on with his work because she's forever tracking him down and asking where I am. Says he daren't have a pee behind a hedge in case she's watching.'

'What about . . .' Edmund lowered his voice still further '. . . Amelia?'

'What about her?' Johnnie snapped defensively. 'I've told you already, I just like her occasional company, that's all. She's an interesting woman.'

'Yes, she is, isn't she? Did I tell you I bumped into her in London, by chance, a while ago? I bought her a sandwich.'

Johnnie felt Edmund was treading on his toes a little, and looked about, intending to get off the subject of Amelia as fast as possible. He spotted his copy of the *Ingoldsby Legends* on the shelf next to the bar.

'May I take this back please, Seth? I think it was left for me?'

Seth, in a lull now that he had served Johnnie and no one else appeared to need attention, was back in his seat, dozing.

'You needn't say "please" to *me* about it,' he said, without looking up. 'I didn't put it there, and I'm not going to take it away.'

Edmund felt this sounded very familiar, but couldn't place it for a moment. 'Nothing going on then?' he said to Johnnie, grinning. 'Amelia seemed rather interested in the *Ingoldsby Legends*.'

'I'm not satisfied that that is what Xenia is really going on about,' said Johnnie. 'It's all so unlike her. Banging doors, silences, and then the next minute dreadful fake jollity and vast meals. I simply don't know what she's going to do next.'

'You've really tried to get to the bottom of it?'

'Of course I have. But she looks at me as if I were Vlad the Impaler and says, "Absolutely nothing" in the sort of dead level voice that means there is absolutely everything.'

'Well, I think she is worried about Amelia – perhaps you could try appearing as reassuringly faithful as possible? I know she can be infuriating but she's obviously in distress about something.' Edmund finished his pint. It was so pleasantly warm in the pub and the place had an air of sanctuary about it of which he felt that Johnnie had more reason to be eager to take advantage than he had.

They returned to delicious smells in the hall, and Rupert's half-unpacked trunk on the floor, with Xenia rushing up and down stairs with armfuls of shirts and pants. Rupert was helping in a desultory sort of way, removing the odd book, or boot, and leaving them on the stairs.

'Uncle Eddie! Great to see you!' He rushed across to the door and stopped short of giving Edmund a hug, being fourteen now, so they shook hands and Edmund teased him about the pin-up stuck to the inside lid of the trunk, gave him a lottery ticket and propelled him into the kitchen to help his mother prepare the supper trays, for they were to eat by the fire in the drawing room. Edmund searched for signs of stress in Xenia, but found none, though she did look a bit tired. Supper was hot game pie, with a salad and potatoes, followed by bottled Victoria plums and cream. Rupert put on a childish voice, difficult since he was at the stage where it scooped up and down the scale with a surprising range of growls and squeaks, counting out his plum stones: 'Tinker, Tailor, Soldier, Sailor – Crackhead, Surfer, Dipstick, Brief!'

'Darling, do try and grow up,' said Xenia, piling up the plates.

'It's not something that one *can* try to do. It'll just happen.'

'We need to have a talk soon, about what you think you might like to do when you leave school,' said Johnnie, who had at last been reading his report and was not impressed.

'Oh Lordie! Lordie! I've not even taken my GCSEs yet! Give a man a chance.'

Rupert turned to Edmund, hoping to change the topic.

'Fancy a game of chess?'

'No, I'm a bit off chess at the moment.'

'Well, cribbage then?'

'Cribbage would be fine,' said Edmund, glad of something to keep himself occupied.

Xenia went off to finish the unpacking and Johnnie sat reading the newspaper, listening to *The Magic Flute*, and covertly watching Edmund and his younger son where they sat on the hearthrug, dealing out cards and manufacturing pegs from broken matches. Rupert resembled his uncle, with the same oval face and small dent in his chin, the same slightly upslanting eyes and thick dark hair. But one could see Rupert would be taller, like himself and Xenia, by the length of the thighbones and the half-grown gangliness of the arms.

'Aha! Two for doing it!'

'Ten.'

'Fifteen for two.'

'Twenty-one.'

'Twenty-six.'

'Twenty-eight.'

'Thirty-one for two.'

'Six.'

'Twelve – that's two for a pair and one for finishing!'

'That's pretty expert pegging!' said Edmund, counting out his hand.

Outside in the hall Xenia picked up the final pile of clothes and, spotting a book on the table, placed it on top, intending to take it upstairs with her and put it in the spare-room bookcase. The book slipped off with a thud, landing on one of its leather-edged corners, spilling out a piece of paper. She stooped to pick it up, and saw 'Many Thanks – very enjoyable – Amelia' written across it.

Proof, proof, she had proof! To Xenia, in her present state of mind, sharing books was, as Edmund had pointed out to Johnnie, tantamount to sharing a bed. She pushed the note back in the book with a shudder of distaste, and leaving it on the table, stamped upstairs, stiff with wrath. She sat on Rupert's bed for a while, suppressing her rage, recovering her poise. There must be no scenes, particularly not now Rupert was back. But she would speak to Edmund, find out if he knew anything and enlist his support. She put away the last pile of underwear and went back downstairs, banging shut the lid of the trunk with its offensive picture sealed inside till next term.

9

Breakfast next morning was unusually disorganized, with Johnnie getting up and down to answer the telephone and shouting up the stairs to Rupert to stop mucking about with his guitar and come downstairs at once, since his bacon and eggs were getting cold. Xenia shoved piles of Rupert's muddy sports clothes into the washing machine while mechanically feeding bread into the toaster, making twice as much as was needed. Rupert, when he appeared, started pleading to be taken in to Tenterden to do his Christmas shopping.

'I've really got to do it all today. I don't want to waste time trailing around shopping once Henry's here. Can't we just pop in quickly this morning? I've got my list and the money saved up and everything. I hate shopping – it'd be great to get it all done at once.'

'But I'm so busy this morning!' said Xenia, reluctant to leave Johnnie and Edmund on their own. 'We can't leave poor Uncle Edmund kicking his heels alone. I'm sure he doesn't want to come shopping.'

Johnnie said that he had to go out and check the sheep, and Edmund was welcome to come with him.

Edmund saw his chance and took it. 'Oh, don't worry about me. I thought I might take one of the bikes and go and visit a few churches. Need some fresh air after being stuck in the shop all week.'

The combination of bicycle and churches did it. Xenia acquiesced and so, that sorted, she went to get ready for Tenterden, and Edmund sneaked upstairs to get his precious carrier bag.

There was no sign of Johnnie after Xenia and Rupert had left, so Edmund pulled Henry's old bike out of the shed by the barns, pumped up the tyres, and set off, weaving about uncertainly for a few minutes until he got his balance. It was a long time since he'd ridden a bicycle. It was sunny, but the wind was still fiercely cold and he stopped to tie his scarf round his mouth. A pair of swans climbed the bank of the Royal Military Canal, stood there for a second before turning themselves into the wind and, after two short steps, launched themselves into the air, swinging low over the road in front of him, their powerful wings making a curious skweeching sound as they gained height and flew, line-astern, across the fields, their necks stiff and straight as sticks ahead of them. The sun caught them as they wheeled about and turned inland, breathtakingly white against the dark clouds on the horizon. In spite of a pre-dentist churning sensation in his stomach, Edmund enjoyed the actual riding, feeling his muscles stretching as they propelled him along, the air rushing past, the immense open spaces and vast skies around him. He felt freer out here, away from the hills and copses surrounding the farm, and a million miles away from the claustrophobic overhanging cliff faces of the London buildings.

The house, when he found it, was square, with dirty white weatherboarding, sitting close to the narrow road which divided the Romney from the Walland Marshes, slightly raised up on a bank, part of the old Rhee wall – the ancient sea defences. There was a blue painted gate with 'Jarvis Cottage' in chipped white plastic screwed-on letters. He knocked on the front door. After a second or two a voice called out: 'Use the back door. This one's been nailed up!' and then 'Who is it?', but he had already gone round to the lower gate, pushing his bicycle awkwardly through, and letting it fall to the grass.

His heart was thumping as he heard footsteps coming to open the back door, so that by the time it was opened he felt almost breathless with excitement.

'Mimi Taylor?' he started. 'I've brought you some papers . . .' but he was stopped in mid-sentence by the sight of Amelia Sailor, who stood there, smiling at him, pleased to see him.

'But Edmund, how lovely to see you again so soon!'

He was thunderstruck, and quite unable to leap the barrier of the names.

'But I'm looking for Mimi Taylor – does she live here too?'

'Mimi Sailor, if you like. Yes, that's me. I just don't get called that much any more. I dropped it.' She was staring at him, since he had gone quite white. 'Nick didn't like it – he thought it sounded fluffy.'

'Mimi Anderson?' He was blundering.

'Yes, that's my maiden name. Whatever *is* the matter?'

He stood there with his hair on end from the wind, his face registering mild shock – perhaps he had made a mistake and hadn't been looking for her after all, she thought, or perhaps I have soot all over my face, or my skirt's rucked up? Perhaps someone has changed my name without permission?

'Oh, I'm so sorry. Can I come in? It's very cold stand-ing here.'

He followed her weakly into the low kitchen, where she stood with her back to the stove, leaning against its warmth.

'I'll try to explain. I just wasn't expecting to see *you*, but

I *am* pleased to see you, that it *is* you I've been looking for.' She was slim-waisted and upright in her long black skirt. He could not take his eyes off her, but held out the bag.

'These are yours, I think. Amelia, I am sorry. I must look a complete fool . . .' She did not stop him. 'Look, it's like this. Some time ago Xenia bought a trunk in an auction. I found these papers in it and I've spent weeks trying to find the owner, only there was so little to go on. Only M.A. Anderson, on an exercise book. I've even been up to Norfolk to try to trace her, you, I mean.' She was looking at him strangely, still not sure what on earth he was talking about. The woman he had practically fallen in love with on the strength of a few edited scraps of autobiography stood in front of him; the woman who had put such a gleam in Johnnie's eye. Oh God. Johnnie!

'Shall we go into the sitting room, and sit down? Then you can start again.' She led the way down a narrow passage and he followed her, twice as aware now as he had been in London, when she'd been bundled up in her old corduroy coat, of the long neck, the shiny gold hair, the slightnesses and roundnesses. She was, oh joy, shorter than he was!

He started again.

'My sister wanted to throw all the things in the trunk away. It's an old elm seaman's chest. But I found out who put the chest into auction. It was Helen Strood's niece, Marianne.'

At last a beam of recognition flitted across her face.

'Helen! Of course! She took my chest up with her the last time I saw her, and lots of boxes of books and things. I had to move to a much smaller place, and there wasn't room for so many things. I'd got into a terrible muddle, packing, and she came for the weekend and helped sort me out. It was chaotic. She took it to Norfolk with her. But I spoke to her, about three months ago. And I've sent her a Christmas card, and why has she sold the chest? I was coming up to collect it in the spring.'

Edmund had clean forgotten that he might also be the bringer of bad news. He felt suddenly as a policeman must feel at the door of a stranger, a destroyer of peace. He took a deep breath.

'Helen died in a car crash, in the autumn. Her niece put it in the paper. I'm so sorry you didn't find out till now.' He could see the shock in the dark eyes before she turned away from him.

'Helen. I've known Helen since I was a small child. She's my oldest friend.'

Edmund wanted to go to her, to comfort her, but did not move.

'We didn't meet so very often, but we always kept in touch. I would have rung her on Christmas Day. We are both alone, you see.' She pulled a handkerchief out of her pocket and blew her nose. 'It's such a shock. I can't believe she's *dead*? She was one of those people who are always there, you know? You can rely on them to feed the cat, criticize one's work, rock the baby, stir the jam, make you laugh when you're in a moody . . . I can't believe I didn't know she'd died. Why didn't the niece tell me?'

'Marianne, the niece, gave me her address book. I started ringing everyone in it, but only got as far as F – if only I'd looked a little further.' He got the book out of his pocket, and looked under S. There it was, Amelia Sailor, but the address was different, although still on the Marsh. 'A Mr Fuller had bought some of your books – he had a book with M.A. Anderson written in it, and the Flower House address in Kettleham. So we went up there to try and find someone who knew you. In the end there was your Christmas card, with this address.'

'But what was in the chest? I can't *remember* where I put

anything. All my bits and pieces are farmed out to so many places, boxes, bits of furniture . . .'

Edmund held out the bag again, and this time she took it, carrying it over to the window and up-ending it on the table. She stared at the contents transfixed, before diving for the two Jiffy bags.

'Oh my God! My diary things!'

She swung back to him, her turn to look white and bewildered. 'I can't take all this in. Helen is dead. And somehow you have all my private papers?' Tears started to run down her cheeks and Edmund went up to her and put his arm round her shoulders.

'I'm . . . I'm so, so sorry. I didn't think it would be like this. I kept telling myself it'd go wrong, rebound on me, so as not to be disappointed. I mean, I forgot you wouldn't know about Helen's death, or of course you wouldn't have sent her a card. But I just can't believe it's you . . . the child in Lebanon . . .' He stopped, too late.

'So you've read these? You've read everything?'

The white was transfused with an angry red, affronted, embarrassed.

'I had to read them to find out who they belonged to. I am sorry . . .' The word now had meaning to it. He was, deeply, sorry. 'I haven't shown them to anyone else.'

'I should hope not!' She was angry now, furious with herself for being so careless as to have left them in the chest in the first place, furious that Helen, whom she had loved dearly, should have just vanished into thin air, the grave, limbo, hell, heaven, wherever she had gone, furious at being *left*, again.

To Edmund all this was both better and worse than he had imagined. He had been searching for a woman whom it turned out he already knew and had begun to like a great deal. But he had doubly distressed her by being an inept idiot and rushing round to her, forgetting about the wretched Helen. He should have telephoned her first, after all. But the name . . . Taylor. Tinker, Tailor, Soldier, Sailor. The old vicar must have been deaf and got it written down wrong. Even he, now he realized how slow he had been, should have made the connection between Mimi and Amelia Sailor, or at least tried it out.

Amelia had moved away and was staring out at the road. A young man with a large dog walked past, and waved, but she did not acknowledge him. Time stood still for so long it grew mould. He didn't want to leave her in such a state, not without explaining how he'd loved what she had written, how fascinated he'd been by these glimpses into her life, how fiercely he was interested in her. Amelia wanted him to go now, at once.

'Please – I want to go and tell Josie about this.'

'Josie?'

'My daughter – please go now. Please,' she said, her voice thickened with tears.

Edmund could not do other than leave at once. He rode the bicycle back to the farm, making slow and wavering progress against the wind, his eyes watering, bereft. The encounter had taken ten minutes and had seemed to take ten hours. Where did he go from this dismally low point? He pedalled on, tormenting himself till, off the flat lands and facing the struggle uphill, he had to dismount and push.

Having done some food-shopping in Tenterden, Mary Beaton drove past him on her way to drop off some things she'd been commissioned to buy for Amelia, planning to go on to put in a couple of hours' paperwork at the surgery. She glimpsed the handsome small face as she passed and wondered if it was just the cold or the steepness of the hill which had caused such a set, grim, thundercloud expression.

'Dear Amelia, what is the matter?' she cried as the door was opened and Amelia's tear-streaked face presented itself, and instead of merely handing over the sausages which Amelia had asked for, came in and held her hand, retreating with her to the moulting carpet with the cat, holding on to her and listening.

'And that's not all,' said Amelia, tears springing out again, 'I was so dreadful to him. He'd read the papers, you see. Diaries and things to try and find out who I was, he said.'

'Well, I suppose that's true. Wouldn't you have read them, if you'd been him?'

'Well, I suppose I might. It's just the thought that someone I don't know, well, don't really know, knows about me. My private past.' She got up. 'I may seem hysterical, but Helen's dead, and that's all that matters. So many deaths, and I'm still alive. I wish I could have gone to her funeral.'

'Where's Josie?'

'She's gone upstairs – a bit upset too. Helen was great with her. She was such a splendid talker and never took account of age. I expect she's left everything to her unsatisfactory niece, and the niece just flogged everything off. She couldn't have known that the chest wasn't hers to sell. I only met her once, the niece, a few years ago. She was one of those people who doesn't really understand anything – takes one literally all the time, if she took it in at all. A dull, closed, little person. I felt there was something trapped inside, like a pinched nerve. I should write to her, shouldn't I?'

'I've got to get going,' said Mary. 'Look, I'll see you tonight at the carol service, if you still feel like going. Then how about us going to the pub afterwards and having a drink to her memory, together. I can collect you, and drive you home.'

'All right. Thanks for the comforting. I seem to always be asking people for comfort recently. My turn next.'

'See you.'

''Bye.'

Amelia stopped sniffing, and took the papers upstairs to put them away, popping into Josie's room to give her a cuddle.

She remembered winter nights, sitting with the old typewriter, reading the old diaries, cataloguing and clearing up the already distant earlier life. The diaries had petered out not long after she had met Nick. She had been content then, and busy, but it was strange that one should so rarely rush to record the happy moments, but spend hours scribbling down the miseries. She would miss Helen badly. They had always been aware of each other as they went through their different lives, often crossing letters, and telephoning when the other was thinking about them.

She stood by the window, picking up sheet after sheet till she found a short letter from Helen, written when they were in their late twenties and, being both about their own business, had not seen each other for some time.

Dearest Mimi

I've been very bad recently and not got in touch with anyone – having been wickedly and totally absorbed in the new life with Derry. I say 'new life', since everything has changed so dramatically, although I'm still living in the same place. My recent past seems like mouldy cheese, a pile of dirty washing in the corner, like a stuffy doctor's waiting room full of sniffles and sprained ankles and anxieties. Now all at once, I wake up singing, cured.

Derry is there when I go off to work, and I *know* he will be there when I return. I'm certain you will love him. He's not unlike that man we once met at Salthouse, do you remember? The writer on the beach? We talk, we argue, confirm, deny, assent, tell tall stories and laugh a lot. And the sex is utterly wonderful. I can't believe my luck. I had just settled down to be the archetypal English mistress, gradually becoming dottier and more eccentric as time passed. Well, I probably will continue to do so, but Derry will be there to control the excesses and gently guide me into buying the right jeans. I do miss you on that account! As well, of course, on other accounts, such as the time we got drunk together and quite out of order, when my parents went to London for the weekend and left us in charge of the house.

So there we are. Our spare room is ready and waiting for your visit. It's mustard-coloured (the dingy French variety, not Colman's). It is a mistake. And I thought it would look so pretty with the green and yellow curtains. I need your clear and generous hand with colour, so you must come before I turn the house into a dun-coloured Slough of Despond. Could you come for Easter? Derry's book will be finished by then, he swears on the Bible, and we can all rattle about the countryside visiting old haunts. My mother says she's looking forward to seeing you again very much.

All my love,
Helen.

Amelia slipped the letter back, and read another piece, by her erstwhile self, wondering why, with her intelligence, her brightness of vision, Helen should have been taken in by such a shit.

It's happened – what we, and by now Helen herself – had come to expect. Derry has pushed off and left her. We agreed the first time we met him that there was more than a trace of hubris in his character, and although I could never think of one single reason for disliking him, and indeed, always enjoyed his company, there was always a tiny reservation there, like a small weed in an otherwise immaculate border. It's easy to say this with hindsight, I know. His third novel was very badly reviewed, more badly probably than it deserved, and he seemed to blame Helen for it. At least that's what she thinks now she's functioning again. She was quite literally prostrated with shock when she first rang to tell me. I tried to enjoy reading the book when it came out, out of loyalty to Helen, but it's very, very patchy. So dense in some places, so incredibly thin in others, particularly when the first-person narrative comes to the fore. The person he invented comes across with a kind of narrow cruelty which he cannot have intended, from what I could make of the plot, and this made a nonsense of the chain of events. I never did like first-person novels, and there are patches in it which are almost certainly Helen's work. They stand out to me because I know her so well, and are, ironically, the only ones with any colour any sense of what kind of light there was, what temperature. Derry describes the physical features of places and people, their height and width and depth, but one is left with a curious formlessness, like trying to imagine the height of hills from the contours of a map. Out of perspective, no idea what time of day. I didn't notice this so much in his first book, which was an ironical autobiographical faction of the twenty-year-old Derry, and which was deservedly popular, carrying on at a great pace. The second book was good too, although he started with what appeared to be serious sociological intent, and then, thank God, got carried away by his own clever narrative, rather like Dickens in *Hard Times* (although not, obviously, in that class!)

Dearest Helen, thought Amelia. So many years of happiness measured out, then snip. Along comes Atropos with her shears. Is death easier to cope with, if life is seen as a preordained length of thread? One then need not ask, 'Why?' only, 'How long is your piece of string?'

She decided to go back to work for an hour or so, to cook the lunch, take Josie over to Ruffles for the afternoon, then go to the village carol service in the evening. She thought of Edmund's stricken face. Keep going. There is no alternative.

Edmund spent the rest of the morning lying on the spare bed amidst the lacy trimmings, reading. It took his mind off the mess he had made of his visit to Amelia. He should have – why hadn't he – why did he? He was reading a chapter of Robert Graves' *The White Goddess* which was sufficiently wordy and esoteric to make him concentrate very hard. He often used reading as a mind-cleaning exercise, knowing that he might be able, after a couple of hours, to rise up refreshed and clear-headed enough to face life in undimmed Technicolor. He was reading of the importance of proleptic thought in the creative process – the ability to leap over the methodological obstacles and come to a correct result, so often unobtainable by plodding through all the reasonable processes. Nowadays it would be called lateral thinking, he supposed, but it seemed an apt, if excessive, description of what he needed to do. He needed a new vision of Mimi, and in securing it would find he had circumvented the difficulties caused by his unwelcome intrusion. He'd had all the wrong ideas about her, having gained from her writings a picture of a woman needing some sort of help, his help. She had seemed at times to be floating, unsecured, and he had assumed that she needed an anchor . . . His ploy of distancing himself from Amelia by reading had not worked. It was apparent to him that it was he who was searching for the anchor of loving and needing to be loved, not Amelia. Well, he would just have to take himself to Amelia and try somehow to make amends. He got up, put away *The White Goddess* and caught his foot in the lace hem of the counterpane. Downstairs he could hear sounds indicating the return of the Christmas shoppers, and Johnnie's voice, rumbling in the kitchen.

Rupert whizzed past him on the stairs with a bag under his arm. 'Mission accomplished! Sorry, uncle Eddie.' He punched the air with his arm and disappeared into his room, locking the door against pryers. For his mother he had bought a Sabatier vegetable knife. For his father a novel by Derry Johnson, since he had seen copies of two other books by the same author in the drawing-room bookshelves and assumed that he was a favoured writer. For Edmund he had bought a bright green cup and saucer, breakfast size, from Webb's. He'd stayed in Edmund's flat on occasions after cinema or theatre visits and half-term treats, and thought the place needed cheering up, hating the stained beigeness of everything. Henry's present was a small shiny stone lion, about three inches high, which he'd discovered in an antique shop, whose chipped paw had allowed him to feel justified in bargaining the price down till the stall-holder had taken pity on him and let him have it for two pounds. Its face had a seriously silly, domestic-pussy expression, which had greatly appealed to him. Grandmama wasn't coming over from France this Christmas, so he didn't have to get her a present, and neither of his cousins were coming either, so he didn't have to deal with them. Cards would do. Very satisfied with his morning's work he put the presents in his shirt drawer and picked up his guitar.

Edmund spent the afternoon reading, and being interrupted by Xenia, who kept on asking him whether he fancied roast pork or lamb for Sunday lunch, whether he'd visited the Eeldyke church on his rounds that morning, since that was the church in the group of parishes which was holding this year's carol service, and whether he'd seen any more of Mary Portley-Tall over the last few weeks. Was he quite warm enough in this cold weather, she wondered, he could always have another duvet if need be?

He knew that reading near Xenia was like a red rag to a bull and put his book down.

'Xenia. Tell me. What's wrong?'

'Nothing, absolutely nothing.'

Edmund identified the same flat tone that Johnnie had detected.

'It doesn't sound like it.'

'There is nothing, absolutely nothing wrong.'

She felt there was no way she could put her feelings into words without sounding silly, although she had intended to tell Edmund about the book and the note.

'That's all right, then.'

He should have prised and poked, like Allie. She was expecting him to try harder and was annoyed by his lack of persistence.

'Shall I help you make the tea? Or you put your feet up, and let me do it anyway?' he asked.

'No, no. I've got things to do in the kitchen anyway. You make road-menders' tea.'

'OK.' He returned to his book, despairing of her. She felt he should have insisted.

That evening, wrapped up like Michelin men against the wind and the temperature inside the church, they entered via a treacherously slippery brick path, clutching at gravestones as they slithered backwards and sideways in the dark up the steep incline to the door, for the church had been built on a low mound rising up out of the Marsh. The interior was harshly lit and the air was arctic, feeling several degrees colder inside than it was outside. It had been individualistically decorated with a huge bowl of holly, pointily sparkling beside the pile of carol sheets; an arrangement of battered mauve chrysanthemums with Japanese pretensions stood on the font, skewered into an unlikely mossy log. Pretty little bouquets of berried ivy and some silver-leaved plant hung at the end of each pew and a vast florist's bunch stood handsomely to the side of the altar.

They took their seats modestly at the back, this not being their regular church and not wishing to take the familiar accustomed pews of those amongst the congregation who were regulars. The congregation had indeed been artifically boosted that evening, even allowing for the cheerful nature of the service. Phylly and Seth sat two rows ahead of them, surrounded by their family, glowing happily as they turned and welcomed those of their customers whom they had corralled into coming. These took up at least five pews, the would-be drinkers knowing that the pub would not open until the service was over and landlord and wife returned with the keys. The remainder of the worshippers were the local farming families and the few retired people who lived in the area, wedged solidly, like fudge, into their box-pews. Edmund read the printed sheet which had been handed to him at the door by a churchwarden, 'Worship Occasion for Advent with Carols', noting that the priest was now called a 'Leader'. When the 'Leader' appeared, he led in such a low voice that few could hear him, the densely packed people in their thick coats sopping up his voice like a sponge. The harmonium wheezed sadly as a white-faced old man, with whiter hair, pedalled ponderously. He seemed only able to play in time with his pedalling, so all the carols were taken at the same dead-march tempo.

The second carol was unknown to anyone, and after a few brave tries they all subsided into guilty silence, but there was an air of shy bonhomie as they lit their little candles in their cardboard drip-guards and Edmund feared for the safety of the lacquered hair of the woman in front as Rupert, struggling with the order of service and the printed carol sheet, wavered about, dropping little splatters of candlegrease all over himself and Edmund. During a quiet moment in the prayers, a hissing, burbling sound emanated from the vestry as an electric tea-urn was switched on. Edmund, head down, peered sideways, noticing an eighteenth-century lead plaque on the wall, commemorating the name of the plumber who carried out the releading of the roof, with 'all his jolly men', now all laid to rest in the mounded earth outside.

When the service ended everyone milled about drinking steaming tea and coffee and eating mince pies. Edmund wandered over to inspect the plaque in more detail, brushing against Amelia. She was with her daughter, he easily guessed, a taller, teenage look-alike of great potential beauty.

'I'm sorry . . .' they said together.

He took her hand.

She said, 'I was rude to you.'

'I upset you . . .' he said, wanting to talk to her urgently, but privately. He made do with asking if he could call on her tomorrow morning. He had not meant to sound so formal. Her face showed astonishment, then a smile came to her lips, flickering through her face like a leaf catching fire. What was it Charlie had called her? Incandescent. Not bad, for Charlie, who usually had a more *louche* vocabulary. She had liked the feel of his hand – cool, smooth, encompassing. That was all right then. She said she had a little work to do, but, equally with great politeness, that she would be delighted to break off for a while, say at eleven o'clock?

Had he been wearing a hat, he would have swept it from his head and bowed, but he had none, and so nodded agreement eagerly, retreating as Mary Beaton came up and stuck an arm through Amelia's.

'Coming for a drink now that an assignation has been made?'

'You were listening?'

'Couldn't help it. So sweet. Why didn't you ask him to join us for a drink?'

'No, he's with his family. I don't want to make things awkward for him.'

'Quite right. Stay in a stew all evening. Come on, both of you.' They followed Seth, who was rattling his keys suggestively, and joined the impatient queue which had formed outside the door of the pub.

'You do flash about,' said Mary.

'What *do* you mean?'

'First Johnnie, now Mr Edmund. No, I promise I'm joking!'

'You'd better be! You know Johnnie was never a serious proposition. I got an incredibly frosty look from his wife earlier on. If I'd shown any interest at all, he'd have run a mile.'

'I bet he wouldn't have.'

'What will you have to drink?' asked Amelia, laughing for the first time that day.

'In Helen's memory? I'll have a half of Bateman's, please.'

Josie wandered off with her drink to join some friends, and Amelia and Mary sat at a little round table in the back room, out of the reach of some dangerously inaccurate darts players.

'Now, tell me about Helen, since this is her wake. What did you do together, as children?'

'When we lived in Suffolk, we used to make a mixture of flour, sugar and water in a cup, and sit in an apple tree eating it with our fingers. We thought it was manna.'

'Drink up. Go on.'

'We used to go to the beach at Southwold – Helen's parents had a little beach hut there. It was shingle, by the town, but if you walked up to the left it was sandy – funny orange-yellow sand, and we'd walk miles, with no one ever worrying about us, or so it seemed, but I suppose we were actually under someone's eye. We pretended we were angels, with white bath towels hanging from our shoulders, tucked into the straps of our bathing costumes. Helen once found this huge piece of carnelian – that orange-red clear semi-precious stone? I was very jealous because I never seemed to find any. There was a shop in the town that sold carnelian jewellery, and I can remember being told that it was the same thing as Helen had found, and what was even worse – I stole it from her when we went to bed that night, and hid it in my sponge bag, but I felt so guilty that I got up early next morning and put it back. I hadn't slept a wink all night.'

'Then what?'

Amelia knocked back her whiskey, and went and got another one.

'It was pretty much an enchanted childhood, but it all changed. Georges Fleury turned up and I went to live in Beirut with him and my mother. Beirut's not a bit like Southwold.'

'No, I don't imagine it is. So did you and Helen keep in touch? How?'

'When we were six and seven, our mothers used to write for us. Then we started on our own, and kept it up two or three times a year. I saw her every other year, though, because my mother used to bring me back with her to England for a holiday – and Helen and I just took up where we had left off last time. Helen grew a lot taller than I did. She had the most wonderful elegant model's figure you can imagine by the time she was in her teens. But she was completely and utterly useless at showing it off. She just didn't care about how she looked at all, which was refreshing and infuriating at the same time.'

'Hold on – I'll just get one more half.' When Mary came back, Amelia made her promise to stop her if she got boring and started to ramble. 'Rambling, that's a lovely word, isn't it? Ambling with intent . . . intent to steal roses? It's the only thing I've ever stolen, apart from the carnelian. Helen and I stole them because we wanted to put them on Helen's dog's grave. They were apricot-coloured roses, and grew in Chesney Grove's garden. We went in with the scissors at six in the morning, a commando raid, and took five of them, one for each year of the dog's life.'

'What had it died of?'

'A surfeit of ice-cream.'

'No, really?'

'Yep, it was all Helen's fault. He was a very small dog.'

'Did you get caught?' asked Mary, imagining a cairn terrier rolling in agonies on the ground, stuffed to death with Walls' sixpenny tubs of vanilla ice-cream.

'I never got caught. But I often get guilty and confess.'

'Didn't Nick catch you?'

Amelia picked up the switch in meaning without pausing.

'No. I can truthfully say that I caught him. I chased and entrapped him. I was very determined. It was a mistake, looking back from here.'

'I got caught twice,' admitted Mary. 'They seemed so . . . possible? Now I know they were dreadful mistakes. I'm wiser now, and do the chasing myself, and I only chase men who are impossible. It makes life much easier. I can't really concentrate on work and look after a family, although I know lots of people who do. The trouble is I'd end up doing everything at half-strength, rather than one thing well. It's like these frantic women who give dinner parties of almost Victorian proportions, serving three-or four-course meals as if they were trying to keep up to the standards of their grandparents, only without the resources or the servants. And they do it after having been at work all day, or if they've got children they've been wrestling with recalcitrant toddlers all afternoon, making sure the silver's all polished and there are no dog hairs on the sofa and their fat husbands, who've probably already had huge business lunches, sit back and don't lift a finger to help except open the wine. The food is always all wrong, too ambitious, and the standard of conversation is appalling. I have to fight off sleep.'

'Come on! Not every one round here is that formal!'

'A lot of them are. It's like living in the eighteenth century.'

'There are times when I'd quite like to live in the eighteenth century. Look at this place, things have barely changed here at all.'

'Well, *we* wouldn't be in here then, sitting and drinking whiskey and beer. No, I love my life the way it is. Now.'

Ragged carol singing was going on at the crowded bar, and Phylly and her family were working hard. Some customers had wandered in carrying musical instruments and settled themselves down, tuning and wheezing and tweeting. Then they struck up 'The Holly and the Ivy', being joined by singers of varying degrees of tunefulness.

'To go back to the possibles and the impossibles,' said Amelia, 'I think, I know, that I married someone totally impossible out of wilfulness. I've had months and months of a strange sort of peace, like when the wind drops after a gale. But in spite of being able to get on with my work, I don't enjoy being alone. I miss being able to rush and tell someone about things, or show them what I've made, and listening to someone else talking, instead of to the endless voices in my own head. Josie is good company, but it's not the same. Do you mind being alone in the evenings?'

'Who said anything about being alone? I manage, but most of the time I'm too exhausted to care.'

'I think we ought to go soon.'

They sat and listened to the music for a while – things were hotting up and Irish drum and tin whistle were in concert with concertina and banjo.

'The reminiscing does good, I suppose,' said Amelia, picking the gutterings off a candle. 'And I love this place too. You never know what you're going to find or hear next. I've heard conversations that started off with raising goslings and ended up with the Big Bang theory. Anyway, thanks for the company – I was just hit hard, at a bad moment.'

Mary deposited Amelia and Josie back at their cottage, and then returned herself to her two-up, two-down red-brick farmworker's house in the middle of a field near Fingle. She locked the door behind her, took off her boots and turned off the light. She mounted the creaking stairs, pulling off her sweater, and met with some resistance as she tried to open her bedroom door, then it suddenly gave and she found herself facing Cosima in the dark, her tail waving thinly in greeting.

'Hello,' said a voice from the darkened bed. 'You've been ages so I thought I'd warm things up for you.'

'Will! You rat! You frightened the wits out of me. How did you get here, I didn't see your Gran's car?'

'Bicycled, with Cosima running beside me. But I'm not in the least tired.'

On Sunday morning, Edmund again found himself thinking of means of escaping the house without anyone knowing his business. Succour came in the form of an advertisement in the parish magazine for a charity booksale in Rye, which started at ten thirty.

'I think I might pop in to Rye, to have a look at this,' he said, waving the magazine under Xenia's nose. Then, 'But of course, I can't. I didn't bring the car.'

'Don't be silly – you can take the estate,' said Xenia.

Edmund thanked her without a shred of guilt. But Johnnie didn't seem to need a hand with anything, and Xenia was busy with pre-Christmas cooking. He wasn't quite sure why he had been invited down again so near to Christmas – she hadn't seemed about to unburden herself of anything of great import. He drove around a few lanes, killing time, reminding himself that to Amelia, however much she seemed like an old friend to him, he was a virtual stranger. Outside Jarvis Cottage he paused to take in the garden, where a few ancient apple-trees, leaning with the prevailing wind from the southwest, an overgrown raspberry patch and vegetable plot took up the north side, and a tangle of old farm machinery, rusted, forsaken harrows and trailers covered a large part of the south. Her workshed stood between the two and he found her still there, about to start a delicate bit of soldering.

'May I watch?'

'Of course, only don't distract me. If you stand there, you'll be able to see, but be out of my light.' She smiled up at him. 'I hope you don't mind? I really need to get this finished.'

She held the slim crescent of yellow gold in one hand and applied first borax flux, with a tiny paintbrush, and then little sequins of gold solder to the upper surface. She wedged the bangle upright between two charcoal blocks and lifted the already intricately formed lacing of gold, fingers very steady, and placed it on top. Then with the flux and the paintbrush she applied more solder and tiny beads of white gold into the pattern, holding her breath.

'Please God, it'll take all at once.' She lit her burner, and then her blowtorch from it, and glanced up at him. 'This is the make-or-break part of it.' She took a deep breath and, putting the rubber tubing from the blowtorch into her mouth, blew steadily and produced a large rosy flame from the nozzle, gently and evenly warming up the two component pieces. Then another deep breath, and Edmund was amazed at how long she could take in expelling it. She regulated the flame to a harder fiercer burn, concentrating it on the applied design, passing it up and down over the surfaces, till, magically, the solder suddenly ran brightly all at once and the top settled minutely down on the bottom.

'Alleluia!'

Edmund realized he had been holding his breath in agony in case something went wrong. She poked gently at it, testing it with a needle file, but seemed satisfied that it was all firm and now the two parts had become one.

'But it looks so dark. Does all that dinginess polish off?' asked Edmund.

'Patience. Wait a minute and you'll see.' She picked up the bangle, still hot, with tweezers, and dropped it with a little hiss into a deep dish of water which had a bluish tinge to it. 'That's hydrochloric acid solution. It cleans off the flux. I just leave it for a moment or two.' She leant back and wriggled her shoulders. 'Thank goodness that's done. Johnnie is supposed to be collecting it on Tuesday or Wednesday.'

She took the bangle out, rinsed and dried it and took it over to her electric polisher. Edmund felt quite dizzy, fascinated by the hot smells and her delicate skill, even more fascinated by the closeness of her. She held it under whirring brushes, tilting it this way and that, using a strange block of pink polish, then changed the brushes for a soft cotton mop-like thing. It started to gleam and he watched her intent, totally absorbed face, streaked here and there with carbon from the charcoal blocks, her beautiful filthy hands.

'May I see?'

She slipped it on to her wrist and held it out for him to look at. Her wrists were chicken-bone slim.

'It's very, very beautiful. Can I hold it, or will it spoil the polish?' It was still warm and surprisingly heavy, the raised and encrusted pattern had an ancient, wild and surging form – alive and moving – Celtic, Edmund thought, yet far from the tight and formalized knotted patterns he thought of as Celtic. 'The Mimi Anderson I was looking for was an artist, a painter,' he said.

'I changed horses when I was about twenty-three or four. I found this very satisfying, and more fruitful, in the financial sense. I love to work in the round; I did a bit of sculpture first, but that needed huge workspaces and I didn't have the money to rent them. So I started doing this. It's quite like sculpture, in a way, only in miniature.'

He transferred his attention from the lovely thing back to her, seeing that she was pleased with the close attention he had given to both the process and the result.

She held out her hand for it. 'I need to take it indoors with me, I have to sit and look at it, make sure I still like it!'

'But it's for Xenia?'

'Yes, but I have to like it too.'

'She'll think it's wonderful, it's so elegant.'

They were again in her gloriously parrot-coloured sitting room, which he had been too preoccupied to notice much on the previous visit.

'I wanted to apologize for the way I broke the news of Helen's death yesterday. It was thoughtless of me – I didn't mean to shock you. I was just so intent on finding you that I forgot that you wouldn't know, that I would have to explain what happened first. I was immersed in my own idea of what Mimi would be like and was a bit stunned when I found out she was you.' He drew a deep breath. 'Although, you see, I did want to see *you* again, anyway. I would have come sooner or later, and perhaps would have found out who you were, in time.'

'I have to admit that I hoped you would come too. You seem to have been very assiduous in your detective work.'

'I'm sorry I read your things. I felt sure that there would be a key there, somewhere. But you covered up your tracks very carefully indeed when you were writing. Not an address, not a name anywhere, nothing I could latch on to. Why *were* you so secretive?'

'I wasn't aware that I was being. I think that's just the way I function.'

'I can see now how you must have felt about the intrusion, invasion more like, of your life. I just wanted to beg you not to execute the messenger.'

She laughed. 'I dare say I can live with it. It was just embarrassing, that's all.'

'I wasn't some prurient peeping-tom, you know. I just enjoyed reading about you.'

'But you still don't know me, not very much more than I know you. Even if you have read everything.'

'I didn't actually read it all. I found you before I'd finished.'

'Did you tell Johnnie about this? I mean did you tell him you were looking for someone called M. A. Anderson?'

'Yes, I did, right at the beginning, but he didn't seem very interested. Why?'

'He would have known,' she said slowly. 'He knew Amelia Sailor was Mimi Anderson – look. Here's my business card. He had one of these when he ordered the bracelet.' Edmund took the little printed card and read: M. A. Anderson – jeweller, Jarvis Cottage, Eeldyke, Romney Marsh, Kent, and a telephone number. 'He's also seen the painting in the kitchen – that's actually signed Mimi Anderson. I think he's been rather unkind in not telling you.'

Edmund suddenly felt quite angry with Johnnie. The old bastard, he thought, the old dog-in-the-manger. He'd mentioned both names to Johnnie, now he came to think about it – he must have known. He said in a rush, 'I think he's been rather underhand with me. I think he may have thought he could keep quiet and keep you all to himself. Look, I would like to see you again, very much.' Steady, he thought, steady, don't rush.

'I think we'd better leave it at that, for the moment,' she said.

'For the moment, then.' He was staring at her too hard, and she had broken away, looking down at her feet, very still in her warm cave, surrounded by her books and odd-ities.

'I'm going back to London tonight, but I'll be down again at Christmas, and staying till the New Year.' He tensed himself up, preparing to put his foot in his mouth. 'Johnnie . . . ?'

She saw his drift immediately and tried to tell the truth, as she'd tried to do with Josie.

'I like him. It started as a friendship, and although I knew there was a bit more on his side, I did try not to flirt with him, or give him any reason to think there would be anything else. I was pleased to have some intelligent company, and flattered to have his attention, that's all. I hope he doesn't take it any more seriously than that. If you're speaking on your sister's behalf, she doesn't have a thing to worry about.' She was blushing.

'It's absolutely none of my business, but she's a very jealous woman, that's all, and I think she may have got the wrong end of the stick; actually I think she's swallowed the stick.'

'Oh dear. Can you reassure her?'

'I'll try. Meanwhile, can I telephone you? We could meet over Christmas.'

'I'd like that. But I've been invited to drinks there on Boxing Day, Josie too. Won't I see you then?'

Yes, he thought, but it'll be mayhem. And Xenia has asked you for the wrong reasons – I wouldn't presume to know what her reasons are, but they are bound to be the wrong ones. Aloud he said, 'I'll see you then – and I will ring before.'

'Goodbye, Edmund.'

She watched him from the window as he left – a neat small figure, coat swinging, a seemingly happier man. He turned and on the spur of the moment, seeing her watching, blew her a kiss. She notched him down a point as a romantic idiot, but felt a minute but distinct contraction of muscles somewhere deep inside herself – a tiny detonation of excitement. Now there was a truly possible man, clear-cut, simple in his dealings.

Edmund saw that he could not embarrass Johnnie by making him aware that his obstructiveness had been discovered. It had been understandable, given his undeclared interest in Amelia. He couldn't be blamed for trying to keep her to himself. However, having found Amelia, Edmund wasn't going to let Johnnie in on the secret, wanting to keep her privately in his head for a while longer. She'd been friendly, in a carefully controlled way. She'd accepted his apology, accepted further contact. What more could he ask for at this stage? The framework was there; he could work on it. He sang the rest of the way back to the farm. 'In dulce jubilo . . . o . . . o . . . o, Now sing with hearts aglo . . . o . . . o . . . ow.'

Johnnie was at the back door, unloading a barrow-load of logs. 'You were very quick. Nothing there to tempt you?'

Edmund had forgotten he was supposed to be at a booksale in Rye, and hastily explained that it had been a bit of a waste of time – nothing there but rubbish, but added that it was always worthwhile checking these things out.

He changed, putting on an old jacket of Johnnie's, and accompanied him in the Land Rover to feed the sheep, perching on the back with the hay bales. He was quite fond of the sheep, liking their patient, letter-box-slit eyes, and the oily smell of their fleeces. The wind dropped and a weak sun shone along their fluffy backs. He cut the twine with his penknife, splitting the bales into smaller book-like sections, teasing it up and scattering it to the sheep following behind as they drove along. It was good to be doing something practical, better than sitting worrying about how to proceed with Amelia. Phase one had been completed. Phase two was to convince her of his suitability as a second mate. He jerked nervously as the import of this thought hit him, nearly losing his balance as the Land Rover bumped back across the fields. 'Yes! Yes!' said alter ego, disconcerting him by being so positive and not slapping him down in its normal denigrating fashion. 'But,' it continued in a whisper, 'take it very, very easy. *Festina lente*. Don't hurry her – she is self-contained, perhaps a little stubborn . . . caution is essential.' He leapt off the back of the Land Rover to open a gate, getting back into the cab with Johnnie.

'I tried to get something out of Xenia. Not a sausage. As she says, "absolutely nothing". But I think it *is* Amelia she's worried about.'

'Thanks for trying,' said Johnnie. 'I'll take your advice and become her shadow over Christmas.'

Edmund nodded his head encouragingly.

Back in London that evening, Edmund was greeted by the usual tired smell as soon as he opened the door. The little pile of pages, the first two chapters of his book, sat reproachfully on the table, gathering London dust. He reread his description of the leading female character – his anti-heroine – and started to rewrite it in his head, transforming the tall dark woman into someone small, whose red-gold hair was curiously at odds with the deeply dark eyes. Amelia's eyes were not black, but a rich peat-colour, but he found to his dismay that any attempt to summon up her features dissolved each time he focused on a particular point, the nose, the chin, the jawline of the remembered image. Abruptly he closed the typewriter and shovelled the manuscript into a drawer.

Edmund was seriously worried about losing Amelia by being too pressing and kept himself from telephoning her during the week. The bookshop was furiously busy in the run-up to Christmas, which stopped him brooding on modes of approach. Tom Treasure was promoted to front-of-house, after his fingernails had been inspected, and Charlie and Edmund arranged to shut up shop from lunchtime on Christmas Eve till January the third. Charlie was looking forward to Christmas, having been invited down to stay with friends in Rye, and in his imagination had built up a brightly coloured glossy tourist-brochure image of blazing log fires and copious food, ancient beamed inns and dark cobbled streets. Tom was returning to his family in Cornwall, and was simply looking forward to sleeping a great deal. He was working full-time in the shop till Thursday, and then he was off, out of the hell-hole of his shared flat in Manor Park, out of the bookshop, out of university. He had sworn not to open a single book during his holiday, whether Russian or English, and had no intention of touching his essay on progressive thought in late Tsarist Russia either.

On Tuesday afternoon Edmund returned from a brief lunchtime respite of pint and sandwich and was just about to re-enter the shop when he caught a glimpse through the window of someone inside talking to Charlie. This caused him a flutter of anxiety. It was Marianne who leant against Charlie's desk, apparently writing out a cheque. He thought it most unlikely that she was buying a book, but what else could she be doing? Had she come to see him, or Charlie? Various pieces of possible unwelcome news flittered through his mind and he turned fast and walked up the street, pulling his ear nervously and bumping into ambling tourists. He had told Charlie a bowdlerized version of his trip to Norfolk, and had not informed him of his success in tracing Mimi. Wondering edgily what Marianne was up to but deciding reluctantly he had to brave it, he returned to the shop. She was still there, leaning her narrow little hips up against the counter and laughing. She turned as he came in, and gave him a look which he interpreted with relief, as much as one could interpret such an enigmatic expression, as non-dangerous. She looked considerably more animated than she had at any time on their snowbound excursion together, and Charlie's face was lit up like a neon sign, a flashing advertisement for over-stimulated hormones.

Edmund prayed that he had not been the subject of their conversation and put on what he felt was a welcoming grin.

'Hello, Edmund!' she said, returning his smile. 'Have you found your lady yet?'

'Almost – I really am hot on the trail now.'

She may have seen through his smile to the underlying anxiety, for she shot him another pacifying glance, which he hoped desperately he had correctly decoded and that she wasn't about to let any cats out of bags. He was sweating slightly.

'Oh, good. Well, I must get back to work,' she said. ''Bye, Charlie.'

''Bye, Marianne. I'll pick you up at seven thirty,' said Charlie, looking indecently pleased with himself.

She nodded coolly to Edmund, picked up the shop's little purple carrier bag containing her purchase and left, standing aside for a woman who was unsuccessfully pulling at the wrong side of the door, and who seemed to be mouthing things to Edmund through the glass. Marianne opened the door for her and Xenia almost fell through into the shop.

'Good heavens, Xenia! *Quelle surprise*! Have you been lunching?' asked Edmund.

'I should say I have been lunching. Yes, it's Good-Heavens-Xenia! Smudgie and I have had a wunnerful lunch at Wildfire's and now I'm . . . I'm on my way to Charing Cross, but it seems to have moved.' Her voice, deep and booming, had a more than detectable slur to it, her legs were those of a newborn foal, struggling and straggling to its feet for the very first time. She put her bag heavily down on Charlie's desk and let fall several expensive-looking carrier bags.

'Why Charlie, how immaculate you look!' She leant across towards him in a slightly alarming manner, as if about to proposition him. 'I do hope wicked Edmund isn't working you too hard?' she said, in a voice both arch and patronizing. Xenia had never quite managed to remember that Charlie and Edmund were equal partners, in spite of the age difference, and she had on the two previous occasions she had met Charlie insisted on treating him as a minion, embarrassing both of them. She is definitely drunk, thought Edmund, wondering what other unbidden visitors were going to emerge to torment him that afternoon. He raised his eyebrows apologetically at Charlie, who was retreating timidly beneath Xenia's onslaught.

'Xenia, you must be exhausted with all that shopping,' he suggested. 'Have a chair, and let Tom go and get you a cup of coffee.' Customers were staring at Xenia with interest.

'How kind, darling. Yes, I would like to sit down. I feel a little strange.'

Edmund commissioned Tom to fetch black coffee from the sandwich shop and tried to elicit from Xenia the time of her train, praying that it would be soon.

'Three forty-five, I think. I'm not sure. I think I'd rather stay here and chat to gorgeous Charlie. But I really wanted to tell you something . . . what was it? Oh, yes. Mummy's changed her mind again. She *is* coming for Christmas, arriving on Friday. I do like that dark green jacket, Edmund. You look quite tidy for once. She only let me know this morning. Isn't that typical of her? Such a nuisance. Where's the coffee?' She let out an enormous, Channel-Tunnel sized yawn. Edmund dealt quickly with a customer, glancing at her nervously, wishing her voice wasn't quite so loud.

'How did you get here, from Wildfire's?'

'In a cab, of course! Why are you whispering?'

Tom returned with the coffee. He had guessed correctly that a plastic beaker would not be quite the thing for Xenia, and had bullied the café assistant into letting him take out a cup and saucer.

'Now Xenia, drink your coffee and then I'm going to walk you down to Charing Cross. I'm sure the fresh air will clear your head.'

'And what are you doing for Christmas, Charlie?' She dropped the plastic spoon, slopping her coffee into the saucer as she bent to retrieve it.

'I'm going to stay with friends, in your part of the world, in Rye. That's on the edge of Romney Marsh, isn't it?' Charlie looked happier now that she was ensconced further away from him.

'Oh, what fun! I do wish *I* could go and stay with friends for Christmas. But we are giving a little lunchtime drunks party on Boxing Day. Why don't you come, and bring these friends? *Do*! Twelve o'clock. I'll give you the address.'

She scrabbled in her bag and produced a Harvey Nichols till receipt and a red lacquered fountain pen. Concentrating very hard, her tongue poking out like a child's, she wrote on her knee, digging the pen through the thin paper at intervals and making little splodges of ink on the skirt of her pink wool suit.

'There you are! We'll look forward to seeing you, won't we, Edmund?' She stood up uncertainly, cascading gloves and pink silk scarf to the floor.

'Perhaps we ought to go for that train?'

Edmund escorted her to the station as a constable steers an arrested suspect, wheeling her in and out of the crowds, waiting patiently while she bought a copy of *The Big Issue* under the impression that it was a bumper copy of *Harpers & Queen*, and almost man-handling her across the road at the lights at the bottom of the Strand, his hand firmly clutching her elbow. He got her into her carriage and folded her up into a seat.

'Now listen. You must not go to sleep and miss your station. Where did you leave the car? Parden or Eeldyke?'

'Eeldyke. It was Eeldyke.' She looked at him heavily, unhappily, as the high began to slide away from her.

'Good. Now I'll telephone Johnnie and get him to meet you. You really mustn't drive in that condition. I'll be down on Friday, and help you deal with Maman.'

Xenia leant back against the blue plush of the seat, and closed her eyes. He patted her hand, made sure she had her ticket, and left her, concerned. At least she had something to read. He raced back to the shop.

'Sorry to leave you in the lurch. I've never, ever, seen Xenia even remotely tiddly before, let alone pissed like that. I'll just phone Johnnie and get him to meet her.'

'What did she say she'd been doing?' said Charlie. 'Having a girls' lunch? It's obviously more fun than my lunches. What do you suppose they talk about?'

'Haven't you ever sat next door to a table full of Xenias lunching? They screech a lot, and cut each other to bits, very slowly, in tiny, carefully placed snips. It's very cleverly done, and then some of them tell dirty stories just loud enough to embarrass the waiters. Not that Xenia would join in that part of it, or even realize it was going on. She's astonishingly innocent.'

'Sounds a bit more sophisticated than throwing bread rolls, anyway. Do you think she meant the invitation?'

'I'm sure she did. I'm sorry she speaks to you as if you were ten.'

'I don't take offence that easily,' said Charlie.

'I saw you've made a hit with Marianne. What on earth did she buy?'

'Barbara Comyns – *The Vet's Daughter*. Yes, I think I've really cracked it this time – she's really easy to talk to.'

Edmund wisely shut up. He had been allowably flustered by both these visits, hating his private life running headlong into his business one.

He found it hard to concentrate. The flow of customers had eased and he needed to do some Christmas shopping. He had arranged to meet Hatty and Jerome at the bookshop at five thirty, for an exchange of presents, and intended to take them out for a drink and supper before they returned with him to stay the night at the flat. He squared it with Charlie, and then put his coat on again and braved the heaving mass of humanity moving up and down Regent Street in a multi-lingual, multi-coloured, chattering, moaning Mexican wave. His present-buying so far had been haphazard and eclectic, and this afternoon he found it difficult to remember who had been bought what. He saw several things he would like to give Amelia, and knew he could not. The most he could give her without seeming over-enthusiastic would be a book, but he was attracted variously by a tight green velvet jacket, then a fat little teapot with graceful spout and handle in turquoise blue, a red silk petticoat-thing, and an antique silver spoon, with bright-cut decoration, and the initials AM still softly visible through two hundred years of fervent polishing. He couldn't really afford any of them, which was lucky. He still had Hatty and Rupert's presents unsolved. Hatty he bought a bright green silk *choli*, the little short-waisted blouse that Indian women wear beneath their saris. It semeed cold and flimsy beneath his fingers, but the weather would change, summer would come and meanwhile she could wear it to go dancing.

Rupert? He'd forgotten the fourteenth birthday, and needed to make up. He recalled the pop poster on Rupert's wall. The Dark Entry, that was it. He pushed his way through the crowds; over-excited children, pulled along with their silvery-red helium balloons wobbling above them, wailing with tiredness and a surfeit of chicken nuggets, exotic-looking teenagers, with such quantities of makeup on their little faces as to look like refugees from a Kabuki theatre experience. Bewildered men, their arms stretched to new lengths by the weight of their purchases, trailing hopelessly after their frantic-eyed women, who appeared hellbent on doing just one more shop. The traffic was nearly static as he crossed the road beneath the gaudy street decorations, aiming for a ticket agency. He made enquiries and was immediately relieved to find that they *had* heard of The Dark Entry, indeed they had, and that the band was playing the Brixton Academy on January the seventh. He calculated that Rupert wouldn't have gone back to school by then, and found that the band were not so well known as to command ferociously high ticket prices, so he bought two. Rupert would undoubtedly have a friend he'd like to take with him. It was ten past five, time he went back to the shop.

He was pleased with himself at having solved everything so quickly. He passed a hot-chestnut seller as he turned into Leicester Square, and sniffed the evocative winter smell appreciatively. He was tempted, but he needed to do one or two things before the children arrived and hurried on up the street.

A roaring wind passed him, flipping him up with it – and then his eardrums exploded with sound and he could hear nothing more for an instant. He appeared to be on his hands and knees on the pavement, with half-cooked chestnuts rolling about him. Did hot-chestnut stalls explode? There was a strange silence. Was he deaf? Then, as he knelt there, still clutching the bag which contained Hatty's present, it started to rain, or so he thought at first, feeling warm drops on his hands. It was raining red and, confused, he looked up at the sky. Winded, he leant forwards and struggled to his feet. Slowly, slowly, sounds were filtering in: tinkling glass, the sound of bus and cab engines running, voices . . . and screaming. Upright now, and still facing the way he had been travelling, in slow motion, he put one foot in front of the other, but he seemed to be planting his steps in jelly. So slow. A pinkish mist filled his eyes, and something warm was dribbling down his neck. He knew the way. He turned the corner, crossed Charing Cross Road, plod, plod, plod, seeking markers for his progress. There was the lunchtime pub, there was the sandwich shop. People were staring at him, standing at their shop doors and leaning out of office windows. They loomed up at him, excited, frightened, shocked, offering help. He pushed the door open and saw Charlie's face, white with fear. He collapsed untidily into a heap on the floor. Safe.

They said he could go home, so Hatty and Jerome took him back in a cab, having first checked that he had enough money in his pockets to do so, since they had spent all theirs shopping. An exaggeratedly large bandage was wound about his head, shading his eyes so that to see properly he had to hold his chin up like a guardsman beneath a bearskin. What was under these dressings was not quite clear, but he had been told that he had lost the tip of his right ear, and had stitches put in a cut on the back of his head. He had been very lucky, he was told. They were superficial cuts caused by flying glass. Edmund was grateful that he did not have a television. He had no wish to see the carnage that had taken place behind him that afternoon. Jerome told him that miraculously no one had been killed, but that twenty people had been injured by the bomb, mostly by flying glass, and that the police were incredulous it had not been worse. He wondered what had happened to the chestnut vendor, and then turned his mind away from the thought, unable to cope with it.

Jerome went out and got a takeaway from an Indian restaurant and they sat close together on the sofa, eating it. He felt incredibly high, now that he knew what had happened. His children were pressed close to him, feeding him comfort. Hatty made a lot of phone calls, but Edmund stopped her before she rang her grandmother in France. He didn't want her worried when there was so little wrong with him. His ear hurt, but the only thing he could remember with any accuracy was the sight of the half-roasted chestnuts, rolling about him on the cold grey pavement. Charlie telephoned to see how he was and to tell him not come in next morning.

'No. I will. I'm all right, really I am. A bit euphoric. Hatty says that's post-shock syndrome, relief at being alive. I didn't see any of it, it all happened behind me, and I didn't look back. I'm being fed quantities of chapatis and rogan josh, and whiskey and sympathy, by the children. Thank you for mopping me up. Is the floor ruined . . . ?' 'Shut up,' said Charlie. 'Go to bed and get some rest.' His voice was constricted by an emotion curiously akin to that of a mother finding her child safe after losing it in a department store. 'OK. I'll see you in the morning, if you must. But Tom and I *can* manage, you know. I expect it'll be a quiet day.'

When he had time to think, taking full advantage of his children's loving concern, and sitting propped up in bed with extra pillows, a cup of tea steaming in his hand, there seemed nothing to think about. He had been lucky. He had escaped being killed by a bomb. End of story. Tomorrow his ear wouldn't hurt. Life was sometimes in very bad taste. Things would be calmer in the country.

He lay in bed next morning later than usual. Only the possibility of Jerome getting into the bathroom first and becoming immovable forced him up to bathe and shave. It was tricky shaving with the ridiculous mono-earmuff of bandage stuck to the side of his head. He edged cautiously round it with the razor, wincing as he passed over the spreading bruise on his jaw. He had no recollection of having hit it on anything when he'd been blown over. Drying his face, he fell naturally to wondering what kind of man could resort to murder for the sake of an idea, but he knew that all men could. But only those inflexible enough to invest their action with a kind of divine right, would. Then there were those who believed that they always had God on their side. This led him to think unfairly of Xenia, whose unfounded certainties dismissed any form of rational discussion. He had believed both Johnnie's and Amelia's refutations, but Xenia's fears were obviously quite real to her, and therefore needed attention paid to them . . . He hoped she would be so busy over Christmas with the family all present that she would have no time to brood. He was going to look monumentally silly, with all this bandaging. Perhaps he would be able to take it off for Christmas lunch? He'd been told to go to his local surgery for the dressing to be changed and to have the stitches out later, but he wanted to look under the bandage and find out how much ear he had lost. The nurse had said 'a bit' of ear, but how much was a bit? He'd made a weak joke about having to wear his earrings on the other side, but had been thinking that if he'd known it was missing he would have searched for it amongst the chestnuts and taken it with him to hospital so they could sew it back on again. He telephoned the hospital where they had taken the casualties and enquired about the chestnut man – and was told he was comfortable.

The only other ill-effect he had was a sensation of being slightly outside his own body, as though he were standing beside himself – this was so strong at times that he glanced aside to see what he looked like and got that unfamiliar side-view of oneself that occurs in triple mirrors on dressing tables.

When he got to work he was amused and pleased by Charlie's fussing and Tom's awed glances.

'You must admit,' said Tom, 'it must take guts to just carry on walking back to work in that state, as if nothing had happened.'

Charlie, who was lovingly unpacking a blue leatherbound set of Trollope, admiring the clean gilt-edged pages, agreed.

'But I don't think he knew what he was doing. He seemed a bit confused. The bookshop is his safe haven – his home, almost. Getting back here was probably an instinctive reaction.'

At about the time the bomb had gone off in London, Johnnie had left to collect Xenia from the five fifteen train. It was dark, and the train was late. He sat there in the Land Rover, fuming and worrying. Edmund had given him the briefest of explanations, that Xenia was tired, and verging on the emotional, and should be met. He couldn't believe that she had got drunk. It seemed so very unlikely. But then all her actions had seemed unlikely, recently. However, he knew that having her mother around would put her on her mettle; he was himself looking forward to seeing Sofia again. The red lights on the level crossing started flashing and bleeping and the gates went down, indicating that at last something was happening, so he went on to the platform, scanning the lighted windows as the train came past, looking for Xenia. He saw her nodding in a corner, and opened the carriage door.

'Xenia, wake up! You're at Eeldyke!' He had to shout.

She jerked awake and stared at him, her face crumpled and vague.

'Come on! Pass me those bags. That's it. Out you come.'

Xenia emerged, peering into the dark in a tentative manner, swaying slightly.

'I stayed awake till Parden, then after I changed trains I just couldn't keep my eyes open any longer. I'm sure I brought the car this morning. Why have you come to meet me?'

'Because I had a phone call from your brother who seemed not a little worried about you. What have you been up to?' He heaved her up into the Land Rover with her shopping, having first cleared the seat of mud and a few stray sheep-feed pellets.

'Oh, just Harvey Nichols, and then Peter Jones, and then lunch with Smudgie. Then I went to Edmund's shop. I can't think why he phoned you. I'm perfectly all right.'

'Have you got your mother a present? That was the reason you went up in the first place.'

'I seem to have bought quite a lot of things. I can't remember if any of them were presents. I think I may have eaten something bad at the restaurant. I felt most peculiar when I got to Edmund's.'

'Not too much drink at lunchtime perhaps?'

'I never drink too much. I only had a couple of glasses of wine.'

'If you say so.'

*　　*　　*

The sun set before four o'clock and Amelia and Josie sat on the kelim rug in the sitting room, curtains drawn and lights on, surrounded by old scraps of pink, scarlet and yellow material, cutting little strips of this and that, to which they attached old beads with gold thread. The cat, her dark tabby markings resembling nothing so much as a sleeping python, not stripes, but whorls and circles of creamy grey amongst the black, dozed by the hearth, occasionally putting out a paw and patting a piece which had taken her particular fancy. Amelia had her bead box beside her, filled with the remnants of generations of broken necklaces. Here was Bristol glass, mock jade, amber and shining, deadly black jet. Here also were the remains of a child's plastic daisy necklace, gold-speckled glass from Venice and rosy-pink quartz from China.

They had considered their box of old tree decorations and sadly decided enough was enough – they had been repaired beyond repairing, a fresh start was required – and put them away again, unwilling to consign the lot to the dustbin. They had instead decided to make a votive tree, such as one sees in eastern countries, with strips of cloth tied to the branches, left there by supplicants as reminders to the resident saint of that particular place of their prayers and expectations. So instead of buying a tree, Amelia had taken a saw and hacked a dead branch from an apple tree and stuck it in the earth-filled green coal bucket.

Amelia hoped that Edmund would telephone and gave an involuntary little jump each time it rang, but it was always for Josie, her friends arranging an end-of-term meeting of the tribes. She found her own reactions irritating. Here she sat, a mature woman, nervously twitching, waiting for a phone call she wasn't even sure she wanted. Had she always vacillated like this? Vacillation implied there were choices to be made, but what choices had she ever made? As a child they had been made for her; then on growing up she had caught Nick's butterfly attention and it was she who had instigated their living together, their eventual marriage. But had there been a choice? How could one make a choice when one was so desperately infatuated that the steps she had taken had seemed completely inevitable, without alternatives?

She cut three strips of red cotton, sewed three blue glass beads to the ends and handed them to Josie to tie on to the twiggy makeshift tree. This time she should let someone else do the choosing, should the occasion arise, her previous 'choice' having been so unsound. Edmund Yearne had the look of someone 'possible', just as Nick had had 'impossible' written all over his forehead. Perhaps she should, with no further ado, let loose and throw herself in Edmund's general direction, hoping with all her will that he would be inclined to catch her before she fell. But would it be best, perhaps, to just wait and see what he would do? Passivity was not in her nature, but she could cultivate it.

'Pass the scissors,' said Josie, who snipped off a piece of gold thread. 'There, that looks simply amazing!' It did indeed. They were astonished at their own cleverness, and picked up the tattered flame-coloured remnants, put away the beads and went into the kitchen to make tea.

Later that evening, when they were preparing for bed, and making hot-water bottles, Amelia asked Josie what she thought of Edmund Yearne.

'Edmund Yearne? Yearne's an odd surname, isn't it? Yes, lovely little man, in a middle-aged sort of way.'

'Oh, damnation with faint praise. Didn't you think he was rather good-looking?' she asked hopefully, screwing up the stopper to Josie's bottle.

'Oh yes. And he'd left his Zimmer frame at home.'

'You rude little biscuit!'

'Well, you know what I mean. He's got wonderful old-fashioned manners, hasn't he? I thought he looked a bit like a badger, I mean determined, solid, rootling about – looking for someone to play with?'

Amelia had to chuckle. 'You *are* unromantic. Yes, though, I think you are right about the badger.'

'Does this mean you're looking for someone to play with?' asked Josie.

'Well, I suppose I might be. Would you mind?'

'No, I don't think so . . . but you wouldn't go off with someone I absolutely loathed, would you?'

'No. If you absolutely hated them, I'd be bound to think there was something crucially wrong with them that I hadn't spotted.'

'I'm off to bed now,' said Josie.

'Goodnight, my darling. I think the tree's turned out most surprising. Quite magical, don't you think?'

'Yes. It was a good idea. Perhaps some saint will listen to our prayers.'

'What are you praying for? Passing your A levels? The attention of Will Redding?'

'Not a chance – winning the lottery. 'Night, Mum. And you don't look a day over thirty.'

Amelia cheerfully threw an oven glove at her.

When she got to bed, Amelia sat up with an old tartan blanket round her shoulders, listening to the news. She heard about the terrorist bomb in London which had exploded near Leicester Square. Amongst the injured was a chestnut seller who was still in hospital but was said to be comfortable. He had apparently escaped serious injury by chasing after a youth who had stolen a bag of chestnuts, just before the bomb went off, but staff at the hospital said he did not intend to press charges.

'And so, horror strikes the streets again,' said the newscaster, his voice heavy with the seriousness of the news item, 'and the people of London, happily going about their

Christmas shopping, are subjected to yet another outrage. A Sinn Fein spokesman said this evening that the injuries caused were regretted and talks will continue in Dublin tomorrow . . .'

Amelia wondered what 'comfortable' meant, in hospital parlance. Was it meant to indicate a lack of pain? The word 'pain', she had noticed, was very rarely mentioned amongst the medical fraternity. She had been asked, when giving birth, whether she felt any 'discomfort', and she had hit the nurse with her useless gas-and-air mask. And sworn at her, but apparently such behaviour was not uncommon, except in films where women puff and groan a little and then give sweet Madonna-like smiles, while their 'birth-partners' leap around as exultant as if they had done it themselves. She herself felt that the fathers involved should be a million miles away from any childbirth. There are some things one should do in private and that was definitely one of them. Having fought so hard to get rid of male dominance in the field of obstetrics, all these wretched women were doing was letting them back in on the scene to try to take over again. One should not be asked to produce a work of art with people leaping around yelling advice. Her mind was off on a ramble.

The paraffin stove was flickering. The comforting, little circle of blue flame was sending out warning yellow flashes that indicated it was getting low on oil. The image of the roast chestnut man, lying cut and damaged in hospital, kept returning. She got reluctantly out of bed to turn off the stove and thought, 'He hasn't phoned yet. But I will see him on Boxing Day in any case.' She saw herself in the long-mirrored wardrobe, huddled in her blanket, a tear in the hem of her nightdress where she'd caught it on a bramble while chasing sheep out of the garden. She also wore a pair of thick red arctic fishermen's socks. Not a very enticing sight. Her reflection was foxed and misty and there was not enough light to see her face clearly, but she already knew about the wrinkles, tiny creeping furrows by her eyes, the softening of the chin, which had once been so severely pointed. But her body, that wasn't too bad at all. Nothing seemed to have drooped the last time she'd been warm enough to stand still and look at it, except that her breasts seemed to get further apart each year, as if they were trying to escape under her armpits. She laughed, and did not care. Her hair showed only the slightest signs of grey and she had very few stretch marks. She was lucky. She jumped back into bed and turned off the bedside light, lying there in the rustling dark, thinking about Edmund.

A fox barked destructively beneath the window and she heard it with pleasure, for she was warm and snug in bed. The sound of the fox's unearthly harsh yelps gradually decreased as it went on its way, down across the silent moonlit fields, where it sniffed about Phylly's locked chicken shed and had to make do with remembrance of meals past.

11

At mid-afternoon on Christmas Eve, Sofia Yearne arrived at the farm, waiting in the car for Johnnie to come round and open the door for her, emerging in her grey fur coat with a flourish of still-graceful legs. Her hair, Xenia noticed, as she and the boys came out to help with her luggage, was dyed a new strong russet colour which it had never been before she had gone grey.

'My darling – 'ow wonderful it is to be 'ere again. Careful with that! It is the presents. *Mon Dieu*! 'Ow cold it is 'ere. I 'ope you 'ave the central 'eating on full, Xenia? Give me a kiss, Rupert. 'Enry, 'ow *wonderful* you look! *Très branché*. I adore the purple shirt.'

Xenia growled inwardly. She had spent half an hour trying to get 'Enry out of the purple shirt and into something less obtrusive. She had also been severely annoyed by the length of his hair when he had returned from university and now it was tied back in a short thick ponytail; she had told him that he looked like a barman.

'I must go upstairs and change. Xenia, darling, come with me and tell me everything.' She put her hand on Xenia's shoulder; being, if anything, slightly taller than her daughter once, she had not lost much height with age. 'My sweet – you look a little tired. I 'ope this is not too much for you, all this entertaining. I promise to be very good, and not annoy you at all.' She swept up the stairs with them all in tow, struggling with the luggage. Xenia stayed to help her unpack, unzipping little bags, hanging up dresses.

'Ah, such a pretty room. I am always so comfortable 'ere. And do you still 'ave all those naughty books?'

'What naughty books?' Xenia paused with a skirt and hanger in her hand, perplexed.

'Oh, you know, the little shelf of pornographic ones – quite amusing, I thought, to 'ave them there, to entertain your guests.' She took off her coat and threw it on the bed, and patted her outrageous hair, piled up on her head like an Edwardian dowager's. She unstrapped a suitcase and commenced pulling things out, leaving Xenia to study the bookcase in a puzzled fashion.

'These, do you mean?' asked Xenia, picking out a copy entitled *Les femmes s'amusent* by someone called only 'Victorine', and *O . . .*' I never noticed them before. But surely, not pornographic?' She had turned a gentle pink, trying to remember who had stayed in the room since her mother was last visiting, almost a year ago. Edmund, of course, but who else? Would they have noticed them? She opened the first one at random and read: 'Clothilde lifted her great spreading skirts up to her naked waist, and lowered herself voraciously onto . . .' 'Oh, Mummy!' She banged the covers together. 'How did these get here? Rupert could have found them.'

'I'm sure 'e 'as,' said her mother, busy putting out little bottles of creams and lotions on to the dressing table.

'But it's disgusting. I won't have them in the house. Why didn't you tell me when you were last here?'

'Because it never occurred to me that you did not know what was in your own bookshelves. They 'ave been there for a long time. I expect it was a kind thought of Johnnie's. Such a thoughtful man!'

The pink cheeks turned fuchsia. Her mother had succeeded in wrong-footing her, however unintentionally, in the first five minutes of her visit. It had to be Johnnie who had put them there, imagined them well-hidden from her. But it was possible they had been left behind by poor Edmund, or a guest. Surely not Edmund?

She gulped and helped Sofia, who seemed to have brought a great quantity of clothes for such a short visit. She would take the books downstairs and burn them on a bonfire when her mother had gone. And how could *she* read such things, at her age?

Sofia changed into a long grey velvet skirt, the hem encrusted with embroidered acanthus leaves, and a matching cashmere sweater. Her bangles and bracelets clinked on her thin wrists, seven gold on her right arm and seven silver on her left.

'*Bon*. Now I am ready. Let's go and have a look at your magnificent tree. When will Edmund be 'ere? I am looking forward to my tea, so much.'

Xenia was almost numb with annoyance, but had forgotten that she had to break the news of Edmund's mishap.

'There is something we have to tell you,' she said, as she followed her mother down the stairs. 'He'll be here soon and we didn't want you to have a shock.'

'Shock?' Sofia swung round on the stairs, an enquiring look on her face, which gradually turned to fright as Xenia hesitated.

'It's poor Edmund. He's had an accident. Only superficial cuts, but a lot of bandages, apparently.'

'*Comment*? Bandages? *Tell* me. What has happened to my boy?'

'Darling, there really is nothing to get steamed up about. He's quite safe. There was a bomb in London this week, and he got caught in the blast. But he says, truly, there is nothing the matter with him except a few little cuts. He's driving down. He'll be here quite soon.'

'But why wasn't I told when it 'appened?' Sofia's variably accented English suddenly became clearer and sharper, Xenia noticed, thinking, of course, this is going to be all my fault. She tried to lay the blame where it should have lain. 'Edmund told me not to fuss you with it. Come on, let's go and look at the tree.'

Sofia turned and carried on downstairs, a little hurt. She adored Edmund, could not bear to think of anything dreadful happening to him; he had had more than his share of unhappinesses in his life. She turned again to Xenia, stopping so suddenly that Xenia almost fell over her.

'Is it 'is face? I couldn't bear it for 'im. 'E 'as, you both 'ave, such beautiful faces.' So many aspirated H's were beyond her.

'No, it's just the back of his head, and his ear.'

Sofia recovered herself a little, admired the tree enormously and gradually settled down in the drawing room with the boys while Xenia went to prepare tea-trays, set out an apple cake and warm mince pies. She was still upset by the books, dirty books, in her house. She had indeed been unnaturally innocent at school, had married young and had led such a sheltered life since then that even the most lightly erotic works would have seemed to her grossly indecent. Her ignorance and prudishness, quite a novelty to Johnnie in the sixties, had amused him at first, then had merely become something which he had to accept that he could not alter. She did not want to know. Her friends found her naivety hilarious, but suspected that it had to be simulated; after all, no one could be quite that ignorant – or could they? In any case, it was a great laugh.

She filled the milk jug, put the kettle on the hob and wondered miserably whether Johnnie had lent such books to Amelia. She felt quite sick at the thought of it. The dreadful Amelia would shortly be coming to her house, at her invitation, and she could not, without letting Johnnie know that she knew all about their nasty little goings on, stop her coming. She returned to the drawing room, asking the boys to go and make a start on decorating the hall.

'The holly's in the kitchen, by the back hall. Where's Johnnie?'

'Gone off to move sheep from Home Field to Hilly Foxes. He's taken Meg and Flit, he won't be long. It's getting dark.'

''Enry 'as been telling me all about this exotic Manchester – I never imagined it to be so exciting,' said Sofia, leaning back on the Kaffe Fassett needlepoint cushions which Xenia had spent an inordinate amount of time stitching on winter evenings, carefully following the intricate pattern of greeny-blue cabbage leaves. She was very proud of them, and would have done more of the same pattern, only Johnnie, fearing his drawing room was being turned into a vegetable patch, had suggested she did something different next time, butterflies perhaps, and she had not been able to find a pattern for these.

Out of habit, Edmund drew up at the back door and sat in the car for a moment or two, needing to compose himself. The house was a dark block, the chimney belching out grey-blue woodsmoke against the darkening navy-blue sky. The lights were on, making an asymmetrical pattern of yellow lit panes against the bulk of the walls. He had tried to restrain himself from fantasizing, from imagining what would, what might, transpire at his next meeting with Amelia. He had been honest with himself about the success of their last meeting. She had said 'for the moment'. Well, that moment was over now, and another was about to begin. Another moment that he might very well have not been alive to see. He was intolerably impatient for more of her company, greedy for her to the point where he felt he could not sustain the formalities of family – the greeting and the hugging – the friendly Uncle Edmund and dutiful son performances – for his mind was so set on one thing that any amount of time not spent with her had become almost unendurable. But endure it he must. He must give her time, not let his head gallop ahead of their tenuous relationship. He planned to sneak off and use the farm office phone to call her as soon as he decently could.

There was a great deal of yelling and shouting going on in the kitchen when he came in through the back hall, hanging up his coat and hat on the old wooden pegs, patting the poor old dog, wondering why it had never been dignified with a proper name, like Horatio or Beowulf. The house had leapt into life as it had every Christmas since the first farm house had been built in the 1600s. He suspected it of hoarding a vast essence-of-Christmas breath of woodsmoke, stuffing and Chanel No 5 and exhaling it, year after year, on Christmas Eve, in great gusts of nostalgia. The smell of hot mince pies floated in the air above the heads of his nephews, who raced howling like small children, bellowing with laughter and mock rage, round and round the kitchen table, leaping over chair seats and knocking apples and clementines from the huge bowl on the dresser. Henry became entangled in the pile of holly by the back door, slipped and crashed full-length to the tiled floor at Edmund's feet. He did indeed, as Jerome said, look different. But it was, surely, a fairly surface difference; a thinner, paler Henry, who seemed however to be fit enough and in cracking good humour.

'Oh shit! Uncle Eddie! My word, you do look sick! Are you OK, really OK?' He got to his feet and gave Edmund a bear hug. 'Sorry about the chaos. This little turd just shoved some holly up my shirt and patted it. I was trying to get my own back. I think I've got an instant tattoo. Look!' He lifted his shirt and there on the white flat stomach was a small prickling of red spots.

'Rupert! What a miserable trick. Where are the parents?'

'Drawing room. Gran's holding court. We just came out to get the holly done in the hall. Shall I take your bag up for you? You're in the yellow bedroom. Gran's got the wifty lacy one.'

'Yes please. I'd better go and pay my respects to Gran.'

'But you haven't told us about the bomb!' said Rupert. 'Was it horrendous? Did you go in an ambulance? Have you lost your ear completely?'

'No. I haven't. Only a little piece. I've had a peep under the bandages and it's got stitches in it, which itch. It looks more dramatic than it is.'

He went off, closely shadowed by Rupert.

Sofia was still seated on the sofa. Her face, no stranger to the plastic surgeon, had a wide-eyed innocent look, but her expression conveyed not only unlikely youth, but concerned motherliness. She rose up and advanced, clanking her bangles, across the carpet, bending to kiss him.

'Darling boy! I 'ave been in a positive fever about you since Xenia told me what 'ad 'appened. I 'eard about the bomb when I was still in France, of course, but one 'ears about so many.' She put a finger lightly to his cheek. 'Such a shocking bruise! But I can 'ardly see you under all that dirty bandage. I shall 'elp you remove it after tea. I spoke with Hatty on the telephone and she tells me you walked all the way to the shop after it had happened. Crazy boy! What were you doing in Regent Street? Is Liberty's still there? That would be an 'orror, to lose Liberty's.'

She sat down again, pulling him with her and held on tight to his hand.

'*Maman*, Liberty's is quite safe. The bomb was in Leicester Square and caught me on my way back to the shop. Now let's forget all about it. I know I look very silly, and I'd love you to help change the dressing this evening. How was your trip?'

'Oh, dreadful. So many awful people and those seats are so close together, no room for one's legs.' She stretched hers, drawing attention to their great length.

'But, I sat next to this charming undertaker, and I'm 'ere now, and not at all tired.'

'I think you mean underwriter, *Maman*?'

'Perhaps. 'e 'ad something to do with Lloyds.'

'Then he's probably an undertaker as well.'

Xenia sat in her little chair by the fireside, looking tense and watchful, while Johnnie sat relaxed and benevolent opposite her. Edmund admired the great dish of silver foliage and orange-berried gladwyn before she drew his attention to it, trying to gain a few brownie points to heighten his stock with her, ready for the moment when she found out about him and Amelia. He adroitly manoeuvred the conversation round to his mother's garden at Nîmes, admired her skirt, asked her what she'd been reading recently and whether she'd seen any good films, and then moved on to her disgraceful neighbours, the Déligondes. He behaved exactly as a good son should, and she expanded with delight and approval and regaled everyone with the doings of the Déligondes' niece, Ségoulène, who had rushed off and married a Belgian footballer.

'She is of course *enceinte*. Marie-Ange is hysterical with rage and Georges is speechless. I mean to say, a Belgian!' Being a Belgian was far worse to her than being a footballer. Rupert and Henry arrived with the tea, and Sofia bit into one of Xenia's mince pies with uninhibited relish. 'Now that, that is delicious. All the way over on the plane I was dreaming of your mincy pies, Xenia darling. I look forward to Christmas so much.'

Xenia relaxed a little. It was hard to be cross with such a genuinely appreciative woman, although she was still on her guard against further embarrassments. After tea, Edmund made his excuses and said he had to go and wrap up presents, borrowed some scissors and ribbon and disappeared. He sneaked across the hall to the office next to the kitchen, shutting the door behind him and picking up the phone. He dialled the number at the bottom of the Christmas card Amelia had sent Helen. It rang for a long time, but when she answered she sounded as if she was laughing with her mouth full.

'Hello? So sorry, let me swallow this piece of toast. There, that's better.'

'Amelia?'

'Sure is! Danged cat has jest run off with the lairst biscuit. I'm so sorry – Josie and I have been watching *Stagecoach* on Mary Beaton's televison, and can't stop riding shotgun.' She paused. 'That is Edmund, isn't it?'

'Yes, it is.' He stopped, realizing that he would have to explain at some stage about the bandages. He was going to look ridiculous, confronting her in this lot; perhaps it would be better to take them off, and hope that the ear didn't look too repellent and she wouldn't notice at first the narrow shaven strip at the back of his head. But she was still laughing, so he thought he'd leave it till later. She had a lovely deep amused chuckle. Josie was screeching in the background.

'We are a bit out of order, I'm afraid. Mary had a bottle of damson wine and we've drunk it all in one go. It's fearfully strong, and I can't remember how we got back here.'

'I rang to wish you Happy Christmas, and to make sure you weren't going to chicken out of coming over on Boxing Day. I really *need* to see you, Amelia. But I can't get away. I'm going to be wrapped tightly in a silken cocoon of party games and food until then.'

'I'll be coming, and Josie too, I expect. I'm going to be very brave and meet your fierce sister face to face.'

'She's not very fierce at the moment. My mother is over from France and it takes all Xenia's energies to keep one step ahead.'

Amelia had calmed down now, and was telling Josie to keep quiet or go away and stop listening in.

'Edmund?' Her voice sounded softer, less jokey. 'I'm looking forward to seeing you again, I really am.'

'So am I. Very much. I was expecting you to be different, to put me off. I've been thinking about you a lot. I was scared of being pushy.'

'I've been hoping you would ring, ever since you left.'

He put the receiver down quietly and peered out of the room. The hall was empty. He tiptoed upstairs and wrapped up his presents. Then, facing the dressing chest mirror, he gingerly unwound the bandage round his head in order to inspect the damage properly. The ear muff came away with it, and there was the ear, looking rather red, but with neat stitching across the bottom like a tiny zip-fastener. He bore a faint resemblance to a farm animal that had had its ear clipped for identification purposes, but he didn't care. She *wanted* to see him. He ran downstairs again carrying the packages and set them about the base of the tree.

In the drawing room Sofia was beating Rupert at Spite and Malice, which game she had taught Edmund and Xenia when they were children. Later on that evening, after a light supper, they all trooped out to Midnight Mass, returning with wrinkles ironed out and light hearts – except for Xenia, whose interior being remained deeply creased.

Christmas morning dawned icy-white, a thick hoar frost decorating every twig of every hunchbacked hawthorn tree, every blade of dead brown grass, and clinging to the backs of the sheep in the fields, the tips of their creamy yellow fleeces shining with an unearthly whiteness. It was stone quiet – the wind had dropped, no traffic moved along the lanes, no birds sang, no beasts dared open their mouths.

Amelia sat up reluctantly. The rising sun shone watery pink through the gap in her curtains and the frost ferns on the inside of the window. It was a red sun, so deep a red that there was little brightness to it. Amelia felt the weight of one of her scarlet woollen socks, bulging and knobbly, stuffed to bursting point, across the bottom of the bed. Josie had made her a stocking! She got out of bed and lit the stove and crossed the landing to Josie's room, her feet wary against splinters in the rough floorboards.

'Darling, are you awake? I've found your stocking! Why don't you come and open it with me. It's no fun opening presents on one's own.'

'Mmnnh.' Josie's head appeared from beneath the mounded blankets.

'Come on!' repeated Amelia impatiently. 'It's Christmas morning. I've got presents for you too, and it's getting late. I'll go and make us some tea and bring it up so we can have it in bed while we're unpacking the goodies.' She disappeared again, and Josie padded across to the other room, while Amelia in a flurry of quite childlike excitement stoked the stove, boiled a kettle and fed the cat the unlovely mixture of fat from pork chops, gravy and mince that was its Christmas treat. She put half a dozen chocolate digestives on the tray, stuck a spring of holly in the teapot spout and whisked upstairs again.

'Oh bliss! I love chocolate first thing in the morning.' Josie munched, watching Amelia start to explore the contents of the stocking. Out first was a ball of purple string, then a chocolate heart wrapped in pink tinfoil, a clementine and three walnuts whose shells had been painted gold. Then a bottle of calendula handcream, a tiny phial of scent, L'Air du Temps, of the type given away as samples. A metre of green velvet ribbon, a yellow sugar mouse with almond ears and string tail, a fat orange candle, and a box of Black Russian cigarettes. Then a brass thimble, a fine-point drawing pen, three 2B pencils and a tube of cerulean oil paint. Finally there was a pair of green socks, printed with Persian carnations.

'Josie! I haven't had a stocking since I was six. It's the best thing you could have given me – I love it to death!' She gave her daughter a kiss. 'Move over, the cat wants to get in on the act. I've got to reach under the bed for your presents.'

She pulled out a large squashy package done up in newspaper with large red Urgent stickers all over it, and a little scarlet box tied up with gold thread. The squashy package contained Josie's velvet hat – The Velvet Hat. She squeaked appreciatively and put it on – her unbrushed hair sticking out at angles beneath it, the resemblance to the Mad Hatter being emphasized by the fact that Amelia had written out a ticket to stick in the hatband, which read 10/-6.

'I love it. I love it. I love it! Thank you, Mum. Now what's this?' Inside the red box was a pair of of gold earrings fashioned as tiny daisy plants, with cabochon amethysts as centres for the flowers. Josie adored these too and tried them on immediately. She stared at herself in the hand mirror Amelia produced, very, very pleased with what she saw.

Downstairs they breakfasted on fried potatoes and bacon and snarling black coffee with loads of sugar. There was ice on a mug of water left overnight in the sink. Josie lit the fire in the sitting room, and Amelia filled all the stoves and trimmed their wicks. Mary telephoned.

'This is an imposition, but I have a feeling you wouldn't mind being imposed upon today. Will Redding, who says he knows you, is at a complete loose end after he's visited his granny in hospital this morning. I found out he was going to be on his own all the rest of the day. If I bring extra pud and more wine, could he come and have Christmas lunch with you as well? He's very charming.'

'Yes, I've met him. Of course you can bring him,' then suddenly suspicious, laughing, 'He's there with you now, isn't he?'

'Well, yes. He's just about to take the dog out for a walk. But you are a pig! You've guessed!' She became serious. 'You must not tell a soul, though. You aren't having any other visitors, are you? He's not my patient of course, so that's all right, but I don't want any wagging tongues.'

'Of course, I'll be silent as the grave. Josie will have her nose put out of joint a bit. She rather fancies Master Will.'

'So does the entire female population of Romney Marsh. But they're all too late. I've got him, for the moment anyway. It isn't serious though, the age difference is mind-bogglingly awful. Meanwhile, I'm ecstatic'

'We'll see you both at one o'clock then. The goose will easily do four people. I'm just about to start cooking.'

Amelia felt a pinch, just a pinch, of envy which she could not quite suppress, but she made stuffing, scrubbed and cut up the potatoes, putting them on the stove to parboil, thinking of Edmund and wondering what tomorrow would bring. Josie, still in her hat, fished out a jar of redcurrant jelly and then a pot of Amelia's garlic, ginger and plum chutney.

'Would this be good with goose, do you think?'

'It's good with anything. Let's get the table laid, and the goose in the oven and go out for a walk round the fields at the back, while it's still sunny.'

She had a pair of green candles which looked pretty in the old faience candlesticks with chipped feet. In the drawer where she kept her drying-up cloths, butter muslin and greaseproof paper, she had waiting a set of thick white damask table napkins which she brought out for the occasion. Josie polished the glasses till they sparkled and they then set off, wrapped in as many clothes as possible, to enjoy the Marsh at its most magical, just to get a feel of the day, Amelia said. The white fields stretched ahead, glittering. A jack snipe flew up, and Josie ran ahead, crossing a ditch in a great balletic leap, her legs flying out fore and aft so she appeared to float for a second.

'I just had to do that. I suddenly have a surfeit of optimism.'

'Good, so do I.'

But it was too cold to stay out long.

'I'd like some more coffee, and I'd like to have one of my decadent ciggies. Let's get back,' suggested Amelia, whose nose had gone blue. Their mood was verging on the euphoric, and even the discovery of a dead fox by the hedge did not dampen it.

'How sad! But he's very handsome, isn't he?' Josie said, examining the sleek tawny fur, admiring the pointed mask. They knew it would be impossible to bury him, the ground being too hard to dig. Best to leave him to the crows and other carrion eaters. Amelia supposed he must have been hit by a car.

'Come on. Leave him now. I've got to go and turn the goose over and the sitting room fire'll go out if we aren't quick.'

Josie got up from her stooping position over the fox. She had been feeling his thick coarse fur which, ruffled by the slight breeze, gave an appearance of fluttering life.

'The wind's changed, gone round to the east. There's cloud coming up over there. Perhaps it will snow?'

'So there is. I don't want to be snowed in but a little sprinkling would be quite acceptable, on Christmas Day! Winter seems to have set in dreadfully early this year. Come *on*, Hat!'

The house had warmed up nicely while they were out,

and the smell of roasting goose wafted about the kitchen, to which was added the smell of Amelia's Russian tobacco and a little dash of the scent which had been in the stocking. The potatoes went into the oven, along with stuffing balls and small sausages and bacon. They opened a bottle of wine and toasted each other as they waited for their guests.

'Here's to us, and absent friends.'

'Here's to us!'

'Who's like us?'

'Damn few!'

'This is so much better than last Christmas, when we were living in that horrid little shack of a cottage in Fingle, and we were both so sad,' said Amelia, thinking that Josie had not seemed too unhinged by the fact that Mary Beaton had got there first with Will Redding, had seemed to think it quite a giggle. Josie had in fact been seriously pissed off for at least ten minutes, but she admired Mary's panache and although she had been surprised that anyone over thirty-five could possibly be attractive to someone of Will's age, 'wasted' on her, she thought, and although Mary did look very young for her age and rode a motorbike, she would have to rethink things.

There was a furious rat-tatting at the door, shrieks and shouts of 'Happy Christmas! Happy Christmas! Look, here you are Amelia, this bag's full of South African white and this is the Australian red, and here, tarara! is the pudding! Will, where did you put the beer? Oh, I see, in the middle of the floor.' Mary took the tinfoil off a green Wedgwood leaf dish and there was a miraculous, dome-shaped pudding, dark brown and dangerous, with cartoon icing dripping from the top and a sprig of holly stuck in it.

'It's ounces and ounces of bitter chocolate, butter and chestnut purée with oranges and a glass of brandy. It'll kill us all!' said Mary, satisfied with the applause it produced.

The final preparations for the Great Feast gathered momentum. Potatoes were turned, goose basted, wine was drunk and Will proved to be a sturdy butler. They ate slowly, with the greatest satisfaction, gales of laughter and Party Poppers, their pastel streamers trailing from the beams of the ceiling, startling spiders and deafening death-watch beetles. The remnants of Will and Mary's home-made crackers littered the floor; these had been a great success, having a horticultural theme, their ends tied with green garden string, their contents green paper hats and brightly coloured packets of seeds. Mary had handwritten the jokes on slips of pink paper, all strongly agricultural in flavour, and all quite unsuitable for children.

Afterwards they collapsed in a heap in the sitting room, Mary and Will lying flat out on the floor in front of the fire, devastated by the combination of goose and chocolate. By common consent they remained comatose for a while, before Amelia and Mary bestirred themselves sufficiently to go into the kitchen and try to make some order amongst the wreckage. Amelia tackled the worst of the washing-up, thinking that if she had to wait much longer to see Edmund she'd go spare. When Johnnie had called to collect the bracelet he had suggested that Edmund might like to meet Mary, that she had been invited to drinks too, with the object of introducing them. She relayed this piece of information to Mary while potting up the goose fat and giving the carcase to the cat outside in the garden.

'Good God! It *is* the eighteenth century. I told you so. Serious match-making, no less. Anyway, Mrs Sailor, I do believe the gentleman in question is spoken for, is he not?'

'I think indeed he might be, Mrs Beaton.'

'What, no indecision? No demurral? No blushes? I do believe you've cracked it!' She threw the drying-up cloth into the air. 'Now let's go and play cards or something. I'm on call from midnight on, so I can't have anything more to drink. Then we could all go back to my place for tea, I've got this silly film on video that Will wants to watch, called *Beetlejuice*, and Josie'll like it too. It's a mocky-rocky horror film.'

The rest of the afternoon passed lazily, with cards and a manic version of vingt-et-un, for which, there not being enough matches in the house to use as chips, Amelia had produced a packet of sultanas. Josie would have won had she not eaten all her winnings as fast as they came in.

'Right, let's go and watch the film, and I can drive you back afterwards,' said Mary, heaving Will to his feet. She had been pleased that Josie had accepted the situation, and that she had not appeared too alluring in her velvet hat. It was dark now, and as they opened the back door the first few flakes of snow drifted into the kitchen.

Amelia watched the film in a happy haze, tipsy enough to find it excruciatingly funny and to stop her wondering how Edmund was faring with his family. But the snow was settling fast, and they had eventually to drag themselves out of the warmth and head for home. It being Christmas Day, no gritters had been out on the roads. There was no traffic at all.

'Goodnight, dearest Mary. Thanks for bringing us home. Take care of yourself, with Will, I mean. Don't get hurt,' Amelia whispered as they hugged on the doorstep.

'I won't, I'm a tough old boot. But he is lovely, isn't he?'

'Yes, very beautiful, and almost unnaturally thoughtful for someone his age. I liked the way he helped you into your coat, and made sure you'd got sacks and a spade in the car, as if we were in the Grampians. I hope the snow doesn't stop us going to the Whitbys' tomorrow.'

At the Whitbys', the day had passed in a fashion so well-ordered as to be regimentally boring. Christmas breakfast was at nine o'clock on the dot, with Sofia grumbling in a dressing gown of supremely sumptuous terracotta-coloured velvet. She had at least managed to refuse to get dressed for the occasion. Xenia had the order of the day pinned to the wall. At ten thirty, everyone was to get ready for church. At a quarter to eleven, they would leave for church, after the geese had been put in the oven. At twelve fifteen they would return to the house and have drinks in the drawing room. There was a general rebellion led by Henry and Rupert about going to church, since they had attended Midnight Mass the night before.

'But, we never, ever, go to both. It's ridiculous!' said Rupert.

'No, not again!' said Henry. 'We'll have to sit through the vicar's Christmas sermon. It's the same one, every year. Listen, I can tell you how it starts. 'When I was a little, little boy, I lived in a small, small ever-so-poor-and-humble house, next door to a great big enormous manor . . .' I think the text is 'Blessed are the meek for they shall inherit the earth,' but he isn't meek at all. In fact he's got the most rampant chip on his shoulder about the people in the great, big enormous manor.'

'I don't think chips can be rampant,' said Rupert pedantically. 'I think chips should be huge, or heavy, or marble, perhaps.'

'I quite agree with you,' said Johnnie. 'It *has* been the same sermon for the last three years. I think he imagines he's communicating with the children in the congregation, but he only succeeds in patronizing them and infuriating everyone else. I'll give you three to one it's the same sermon this year. Any takers?'

Xenia was looking dangerous. She had planned that they would all go to church, and go they all would.

Sofia took the bet, and put a pound coin on the hall table in token of her sincerity. Xenia glared at them all as if they were recalcitrant children, and Johnnie decided a bit of mollification was needed and frowned at the boys and his mother-in-law, warning them of a serious rupture if they did not do as they were told. So they went, and sat through the first part of the service with mounting hilarity, breathlessly waiting as the heavy vicar mounted the rickety pulpit and leant forward to speak.

'Blessed are the meek . . . Now when I was a little, little boy . . .'

Rupert bent double and had to be pushed down by Edmund on to the dusty floor of the box-pew, out of sight of the rest of the congregation, muffled. To judge from their reaction, there had been gambling in other houses that morning. Edmund swore he saw money change hands.

Sofia looked annoyed. 'So I lose my pound,' she whispered to Johnnie. ''Ow could 'e do it again? Is it to tease us?'

'Shsh!' said Xenia, but Johnnie was smiling and shaking his head in exasperation.

Edmund's thoughts drifted off once the sermon had started and the excitement was over. It had been the only excitement of the morning, since Xenia had stuck rigidly to their parents' rule of Christmas presents not being opened until teatime. It had been there on the timetable, he had noticed. One o'clock, lunch. Five o'clock, tea and present-opening. Followed by drinks at six, supper at eight, and she had even put 'Eleven o'clock – *bed*', underlining it as though it were the most important item of the day. Perhaps it was for her. Glancing at Johnnie, who was in a depressed state of sleepiness, his head propped up so that he appeared to be listening to the vicar, he wondered how they got on in bed. It had crossed his mind before that things had not been as smooth as they might have been between Xenia and Johnnie, long before her present bout of insecurity and jealousy-provoked fits of sulking. But it must be very difficult, being married to someone with Xenia's temperament.

Although it was to a great extent her own fault, he loved and felt sympathy for her as she sat there, neat and apparently attentive, watching the vicar's fat chins wobbling loosely as he proclaimed his childhood meekness. Xenia's timetable was only an aide-memoire, interspersed with cooking reminders such as 'make cheese straws' and 'poach salmon'; it was a rather touching testimony to how much she cared that things should run smoothly; but surely she had gone completely over the top now, forcing everyone to come to church. Their mother was in any case Russian Orthodox, in so far as she was anything, and had been severely put out at being frogmarched to church like a child. They were all being treated like children so that she could keep to her blessed timetable. Was she in fact becoming slightly deranged? He could not see Amelia anywhere, although his eyes had passed up and down the pews ahead of him and he had even twisted round during the numerous risings and fallings as the service wended its way through the unfamiliar intricacies of Rite Z, or was it W, or even Y? It certainly wasn't the prayer-book order of service and seemed uncommonly lumpen in its vocabulary. He had not really expected to see Amelia – she had not struck him as being a church-goer. He had no religious beliefs himself, since having them seemed to entail, amongst other things, a belief that mankind was somehow able to swing events in its own favour through supernatural means and this appeared to him to be patently untrue. Neither had he seen any signs of meekness leading to anything other than the meek being trampled underfoot. 'For they shall inherit the earth.' He could understand that better if it had said 'for they shall inherit heaven'. Xenia was the least meek person he had ever come across.

The vicar was drawing his sermon ponderously to a close,

having wondrously lost the thread of his argument. Someone should do something to stabilize the pulpit, thought
Edmund, or the meek would soon be flat on his face
on the gravestones of past local worthies, who were also
unlikely to have been very meek, judging by the size and
beauty of their monuments. He supposed that going to
church provided people with ritual, and that ritual gave
people time to order their thoughts and concentrate on
things other than their own immediate needs. Which was
why there had been so much uproar when the forms of
services and wording had been changed, leaving everyone flustered and lost, and denied exactly that peace and
certainty which they had come to partake in and enjoy.
He could not really understand it. Here they all sat, like
members of a club at an annual general meeting (and
he disliked both clubs and committee meetings), waiting
for the chairman to proceed to the part of the agenda
which listed any other business. The incongruous Calor Gas
heaters hissed sibilantly in the background. Great fidgeting
was taking place.

'In the name of the Father, and of the Son and of the
Holy Spirit . . .' It was finished at last, and they rose to sing
again, feet ice-cold, fingers stiff.

Lunch was wonderfully cooked, amazingly all eaten up;
wine flowed, and any attempts at discussion of anything
was headed off by Xenia, who even stalled her mother
in mid-sentence, just as she was vehemently refuting
Johnnie's comment that Britain would quite likely become
a republic soon.

'I think that very, very *un*likely,' Sofia was saying. 'What
on earth would the British 'ave to talk about? It is in the
interests of the media to sustain . . .'

'Johnnie!' said Xenia, suddenly and loudly, 'have you
wound up the hall clock?'

'Good God! Xenia!' said Johnnie, exasperated. 'Have you been reading *Tristram Shandy*?'

'No. I just wanted to know if you'd wound up the clock. Is *Tristram Shandy* one of those revolting books you keep in the spare bedroom?'

There was a long silence.

Johnnie at last made sense of what she'd said, and looked helplessly at Edmund, who, unable to stop himself, gave an embarrassed and guilty grin. Henry said he didn't see how anyone could plough through all of *Tristram Shandy* and that none of it matched up to its first page. Rupert said he hadn't seen *Tristram Shandy* in the bookcase last time he'd been looking for something exciting to read, and then Xenia banged down her fork and, leaving her Christmas pudding, the table and her family, stalked out of the room.

Sofia also rose, as if to go after her, but Johnnie told her to please sit down. They would finish the meal.

'I don't see why we should have our conversation censored, do you? I'm bloody well not going to have everybody's Christmas spoilt by her autocratic behaviour. Now, Sofia, what were you saying?'

Of course it was impossible to continue the conversation, and they all made excuses for Xenia. How tired she had seemed, and overwrought by little things.

'I've finished now,' said Sofia. 'I'll make the coffee and take it through, and the boys will clear the table and stack the dishwasher, yes? Good. I'll just go and find Xenia. She needs a little calming, per'aps.'

Edmund doubted her ability to calm instead of inflame and offered to go instead, but Sofia insisted. She wished to get to the bottom of things, she said. Something must have caused this '*petite crise*'.

She returned with the coffee, saying that Xenia was fine, and would be down shortly, but she looked a little thoughtfully at Johnnie.

Xenia did reappear in time for tea, which Sofia and Edmund prepared. She had her unseeing smile on her face, said she was sorry she'd had to go and lie down, perhaps she had been a little tired. It was time to open the presents. A fire had been lit in the hall and they sat around it, the boys ferrying presents to their owners. The tree sparkled prettily in the corner. Edmund was the happy recipient of a navy-blue cashmere sweater from Johnnie and Xenia, which was a good thing, since the navy-blue cashmere sweater they had given him last year had worn out. He was terribly pleased with Rupert's green cup and saucer and looked up to thank him, but intercepted Johnnie's anxious hopefulness as Xenia unwrapped the gold paper from a little box and took out from its little burrow of scarlet tissue the bracelet.

'Here, let me slip it on for you,' said Johnnie, 'your wrist fits sideways through the gap – see? Like this.'

'Johnnie . . . I . . . it's gorgeous.' She seemed taken aback.

'I had it made specially for you,' said Johnnie proudly. She looked back at him, mercifully appeased and happy with it, he thought, and gave him a kiss on the cheek.

She showed it round to them all, and Edmund feigned surprise and admiration. It gave him a strange feeling to see it after having watched its construction and knowing the delicacy of the process. Now it rested on Xenia's arm as if it had always been there. Sofia was most intrigued by it, and kept asking Johnnie where he had commissioned it, but he was jokingly evasive.

'But the workmanship is exquisite, and such a strong design.'

She was quite envious. It would have made a nice addition to her own collection, but she knew it was too good to be worn as one of a group and needed to be seen on its own.

'Thanks! Thanks, Uncle Eddie. You're a magician!' Rupert waved the tickets about. 'Look, Henry! The Dark Entry!'

Henry had been unimpressed by the music of the band when he'd been at school, but had been friendly with its members and was now very interested indeed having discovered that knowing them personally had a certain cachet at university amongst the cognoscenti of such music. He hoped Rupert would give the spare ticket to him.

Xenia was both pleased and worried by her present. She could see it was unusual, special in some way she did not understand, and checked the hallmarks, gratified by everyone else's raptures. It did look good on her wrist, fitting snugly, the mysterious design gleaming up at her; she would not normally have worn such an obviously modern piece, preferring things to be less conspicuous. But it was heavy, solid gold. Gold – gilt – guilt. The words unfortunately dripped through her mind in sequence. Could it be a guilt present? It was quite out of the ordinary for Johnnie to give her jewellery: he had bought her rings when the boys had been born, but nothing since. Why now suddenly ignore her modest Christmas list and spend so much money? She spoiled her own pleasure in the gift by starting another agonizing tallying up of the signs of unfaithfulness, but meanwhile checking her list, poaching the salmon, making mayonnaise and counting the little pastry cases ready for tomorrow's party.

The snow was not thick enough to hinder them from getting to the party, so after breakfast Amelia and Josie set about their clothes; Josie pressing black jeans and picking the odd cat hair off the black jersey which Amelia had lent her. She would naturally wear the black hat, making a neat minimalist outfit to which she would, unfortunately, have to add the boots she wore to school.

Amelia was in a slight panic, at a loss to know what to wear, knowing what she would like to look like, but so financially strictured had she been recently that she hadn't bought anything new for over a year. She pulled from her cupboard a creased little green velvet jacket, a bit tight round the upper arms, but worn without another layer beneath, it would just fit. She expected the Whitbys' house would be well heated. Steaming the velvet over the kettle worked magic, and she shook out the creases, thinking that Edmund, whose attitude to dress had seemed casual to the point of negligence, would surely not be too critical. The coral skirt which came from Barnardo's in Parden would smarten it up considerably but she was anxious in case the previous owner of the skirt would be at the party and recognize it. Shoes! She hadn't thought of shoes. Josie watched her shuffling through the hoard at the bottom of the cupboard and pounced.

'What about those? They're so old-fashioned they've come in again. They'd look just right with that length of skirt and they're exactly the same colour as the jacket.'

'But the heels!' wailed Amelia. 'They're so scuffed – but I suppose I could paint them. Would they dry in time, do you think?'

'Of course they will. Use thick poster paint and spray them with fixative.'

'Brilliant. I'll go and do that now.'

After half an hour's fiddling she'd got the right shade and painted them, leaving them to dry on the stove. She washed and dried her hair, snipping a few loose ends and blow-drying it till it sat thick and wavy about her face. Then with great care, the paint appearing dry, she sprayed the heels of the old shoes with a can of matt artwork fixative; it smelt a bit gluey, like lighter fuel, but that would soon evaporate. They looked pretty good, she thought, as she slipped her feet into them. The snow would surely ruin the paintwork so she would have to carry them, go in Wellington boots till reaching the front door and then change quickly.

Josie put on her gold daisy earrings and made up her pointy little face. Since Will was temporarily unavailable she was in search of a replacement fantasy man and intended to stand out in the crowd – surely not all the guests would be geriatrics? The earrings looked cool. She might be able to get a commission for her mother. She took one final look in her mirror and saw the beginnings of a zit on her chin, panicked and applied more foundation over it but with any luck it wouldn't come to a head till the evening.

She went and stood in the door of her mother's room, a fashionable waif, posing and waiting for approval, while checking out her mother's makeup.

'Do your eyes properly, won't you?'

'Why, don't I usually?' Amelia asked, thinking that she looked perfectly all right as she was.

'No, you don't usually bother. Go on. Eyeshadow, that greeny-gold one. Pencil, mascara. The lot. If you've got it – flaunt it.'

'Bossy cow. All right, here goes. But won't I look a bit overcooked for lunchtime?'

'No. It'll look perfect,' said Josie, exasperated.

She watched as Amelia bent towards her mirror again, and did as she was told. She really looks quite startlingly good, thought Josie, with satisfaction.

'I'll go and scrape the snow off the windscreen. We ought to be going, soon. It's midday.'

'Right, I'm ready as I can be.'

Amelia nipped into the sitting room and gave the Arabian brass globes a quick polish. 'Come on! Come on! Some good fortune needed here. I want to like him, but I'm frightened of being disappointed. And I don't want to do any catching. I want to leave it to him. And I *don't* want another quick affair.'

She did not notice that her shoes left little reversed horse-shoe prints of green across the floor as she left the room.

They had to drive very slowly, as the roads were worse than she'd anticipated. They leant forwards, willing the car up the slope, thankful not to meet anyone coming down as it was quite narrow. The Whitbys' house was not visible from the road and the lovely cream-painted lines of the eighteenth-century front surprised them both when they came upon it suddenly. There was a muddle of cars and banks of snow in the drive, Johnnie having brought round the tractor with its snow plough earlier in the morning and attempted to clear as much space as possible. Amelia managed to park where she felt there was no opportunity of being boxed in, in case she needed to make a quick getaway should things turn out to be too much for them.

'Oh look! Two Rollers! I didn't know it would be this grand. I thought Johnnie Whitby was just an ordinary farmer, like Ruffles' Dad,' said Josie.

'He is just an ordinary farmer. But they know all sorts of people, so you mustn't be put off. You look absolutely fine,' she added, divining the source of the panic in Josie's voice. She left her old coat in the car and smiled with a confidence she did not possess as an elegant couple arrived behind them, just as she was leaning up against the doorway, changing out of her Wellingtons and into her painted shoes on the doorstep.

They went together into the hall with its huge blazing fire and the hubbub of talking and laughter coming from the drawing room. Already the gathering was spilling out into the hall where Rosy Pressing and her daughter stood in charge of the drinks, wearing black dresses and with beaming pudgy faces. She liked a good 'do', did Rosy, and she summoned up a certain frenetic energy for the occasion which was lacking when she went about her usual work in the house. Amelia smiled at her, having seen her in the village shop on numerous occasions, and Rosy smiled back in a conspiratorial manner, poured them both brimming glasses of hot punch and leant forward to say: 'You'll find Mr Johnnie in the drawing room.'

But Amelia wasn't looking for Johnnie.

Josie momentarily shrank back behind Amelia as they stood in the doorway. The noise was intimidating as forty-odd people with no inhibitions about the sound of their own voices brayed information at each other.

Edmund had been fielding sympathetic questions about the state of his ear and was lurking in the drawing room. Xenia had been popping in and out of her kitchen, anxiously scanning the new arrivals for signs of the great whore of Babylon, and getting her glass refilled by Rosy. Her trips in and out had become less frequent now she was embarked on getting the hot food ready, Edmund noticed. He also was vigilant for Amelia, but it is doubtful if it was the same person they were expecting. Sofia had been talking to a supremely uninteresting lawyer with a passion for rhododendrons.

'When we first moved here from Surrey,' he said, drawling condescendingly as if he had now reached Ultima Thule and found it wanting, 'I was appalled to find that so few people grew them. But I have, with great difficulty, and quantities of peat and acidifiers, induced them to grow.'

'But that is very cruel of you. They will never be 'appy 'ere. They will always be poor, struggling things in this alien soil.'

She caught sight of a woman with red-gold hair, standing wavering by the door, noticed the searching look on her face. A small woman, but with style, in spite of being a little down-at-heel, with dignity, looking for someone. Behind her was a tall girl in black from head to foot, unmistakably a daughter. She saw the scanning gaze flash into a smile, the dark eyes widening at first with pleasure, and then she put her hand to her mouth and the pleasure turned to concern. Sofia turned swiftly to see the object of the look.

'But, that is what I so enjoy, *making* them grow. You don't like rhododendrons, I can see,' said the man, trying to get her attention again.

But that attention was on Edmund, pushing his way through the guests with more haste than care, apologizing to left and right as he nudged hot punch on to the carpet and trod on patent leather toes.

'I think they are very beautiful, in Surrey. Per'aps you should return there where you will 'ave more success. It is sadistic to try to grow them 'ere.'

Edmund was taking the woman's hand, bending forward to kiss her on both cheeks, and greeting the daughter.

He was standing there, still holding her hand, making a charming exhibition of himself.

Well! she thought. At last he is interested in someone. I must meet her in a moment or two.

The rhododendron man seemed taken aback. Sadism was not something of which he was used to being accused, neither did he see how it applied to a plant lover, which he fervently believed himself to be. He tried again. 'My other great interest is bonsai.'

'Then you are definitely a torturer, a foot-binder!'

She smiled sweetly at him, and he discovered at last that he was being teased. He was wrong.

'You will excuse me, I think my son-in-law needs to speak to me.' She turned away and swished off in her soft silk skirt, leaving him feeling culpable of some unknown crime.

'Johnnie? Excuse me a moment – who is that – the pretty woman to whom Edmund is so obviously attached?' She nodded her head in the direction of the doorway. Over the heads of the crowd Johnnie saw Amelia talking earnestly to Edmund, who was bent towards her, trying to hear over the football match roar that was developing now in the hall as well as the drawing room. What did Sofia mean by 'attached'? Had Edmund found out who she was, at last? He looked hard and long at his brother-in-law's body, bent, now his attention had been drawn to it, protectively, proprietorially, over Amelia. They certainly looked better acquainted than he would like and a small seed of jealousy germinated, but he contrived to crush it.

He turned back to Sofia. 'Her name is Amelia Sailor.'

'But, my dearest Johnnie, your wife is convinced that *you* are 'aving an affair with 'er! She told me yesterday, after a lot of trouble. I did not believe 'er, and now I see I was right to disbelieve.'

'Keep your voice down, Sofia! Yes, you were right to disbelieve. For once and all, I have *not* had an affair with her.' He had lowered his voice and speaking directly into her scented ear.

'Why not, then?'

He stared at her. Was she suggesting that he should have? She was Xenia's mother, for goodness' sake.

'Because of Xenia, of course.'

'It is precisely because of Xenia that I asked. I know you 'ave a difficult time with 'er, you are good to 'er, but she is very, very *difficile*.'

'Sofia, I can't stand here talking about this in public. Someone will hear.'

'I don't see 'ow. I can 'ardly 'ear you myself. But take me over now, and present me.'

Reluctantly and slowly, Johnnie got his wits together and made a path through for her.

'Hello, Amelia, and Josie. How good to see you both. Did you have much trouble getting through the snow? Sofia, may I introduce Amelia Sailor and her daughter Josie? Amelia, this is Madame Sofia Yearne, Edmund's mother.'

Sofia's eyes were sharp and enquiring, alight with an almost gloating interest.

'*Maman*, Amelia speaks excellent French, so you may give up the struggle for a little while, and relax.' This was unfair of Edmund, since Sofia had no trouble with English, nor indeed with Italian or Russian, but she was delighted to hear that Amelia was bilingual, although as the conversation progressed, she found it hard to place the slight accent.

Edmund braced himself to explain to Sofia the tale of his discovery of Amelia, since Johnnie had so meanly kept his secret. He described his difficulties with such pathos, his discovery – almost as if she were a new continent – that she lived only a few miles away with such delight that Sofia was enchanted. Johnnie tried not to grind his teeth.

'But this is really a most extraordinary story – that you

should 'ave been so close, 'ad lunch with 'er and not suspected. You 'ave been very slow, Edmund!'

I'd have been a lot quicker, thought Edmund, if old Lothario here had come clean.

Sofia was searching Amelia's face, for signs of affection returned, and was almost satisfied. They need time together – then all will be well, she was thinking.

Henry passed by with a tray of little choux buns filled with crème fraîche and caviar, and was waylaid by Edmund.

'Henry, dear Henry. This is Josie Sailor. She says she remembers you from reel-parties when you were children.'

Henry stared at Josie with dawning recognition, but he was rather short on gallantry.

'I should say I do. You used to lie on the floor and see if the boys who were wearing kilts had anything on underneath!'

'Henry!' said Johnnie, growling at his elder son's lack of tact.

However Josie did not even blush. 'Well, yes. I remember. But I was only ten, and very curious.'

Henry thought she was considerably more interesting now than she had been then, but wasn't going to show it, just yet.

'I've got to get round with these. Would you like one before I go and throw them to the starving elephants?'

'Yes, please.' She took one and popped it in neatly between her painted lips.

'I'll catch you later on, when I've done the duties.'

She nodded as coolly as she could, thinking that he looked quite promising.

To save her from an imminent interrogation from his mother, Edmund asked Amelia if the necklace she was wearing was one of her own, one she'd made, explaining to Sofia that she was a talented jeweller and had made the bracelet which Johnnie had given to Xenia.

'Yes, it is one of mine. You like it?'

'I think it's lovely, but I've just been talking to someone who is looking for something original as a twenty-first birthday present for his daughter. I have a feeling he'd be tempted by something like that. Come and meet him. His name is Gavin Wallace and he's an astronomer. You come too, Josie. He's one of these people who has enthusiasm for so many things he's always interesting.' He shepherded them away, leaving Sofia and Johnnie feeling, for different reasons, like cats who have had their recently caught and as yet unplayed-with mice removed from them.

Gavin Wallace was an ascetic-faced man in his fifties, wearing a fashionably cut plum-coloured jacket with an extravagantly embroidered waistcoat, which delighted Amelia, since it was embroidered with the constellations in silver, with a border of silver flowers which would have done credit to the Tailor of Gloucester's mouse assistants. He examined the necklace with care, enquiring about the casting of the small acorns, eggs and birds with which it was hung, asked for her card and said he was sure they could come to an understanding. She was immensely relieved she had been optimistic enough to bring the cards. The room was becoming overstuffed and hot, upholstered with soft wool Jaeger suits, navy twill blazers, hand-tailored grey flannel, country tweeds, Laura Ashley velvets and unfortunately amusing Christmas-present silk ties. Rupert zig-zagged through carrying a jug of punch, and paused beside them.

'Would you like a refill?'

'Yes, please. You must be Edmund's other nephew?' said Amelia.

'Yes, I'm Rupert. How did you guess?' He filled her glass solicitously.

'I think you look rather like him. Did you have a good Christmas? Lots of interesting presents?'

'Oh yes, but the best was Uncle Eddie's. He came up with tickets for The Dark Entry. That's a brilliant band who used to be at school with my brother. I've met them all, of course, when they were in the sixth form.'

'Heavens! How exciting! So I can tell my friends I've had my glass filled by someone who knows Kieran Gaffikin, can I?'

Rupert looked at her with admiration. Josie became further interested in Henry.

'Not many people know that,' Rupert said, meaning that not many people her age knew that.

'Josie likes them too, that's how I know.' Rupert looked at Josie and was smitten. Here was the perfect person to take to the concert. She was older than him of course, but then some girls liked younger men. He'd have to think about it since there was Foxy to be considered, languishing at home in disgrace in Sussex, in need of cheering up.

Charlie Parrott appeared at Edmund's elbow.

'We made it! The roads are appalling – it's taken us an hour to get here from Rye.' Edmund stared in disbelief at his companion. Marianne had returned to haunt him again. She looked stunning, in tight black trousers and a soft jade-green leather jacket. She put her hand on Charlie's arm, and it occurred to Edmund that perhaps she was as nervous of him disclosing something untoward as he was of her. He managed a brotherly smile, introduced them to Amelia and Josie and Gavin Wallace. By common consent they all moved out to the less crowded hall and Edmund led the new arrivals to Rosy Pressing who was dispensing drink at high speed and managing to keep an eye on everyone and everything, storing it all up for a later recounting at the village shop, her face positively twitching with interest.

'Thank you Rosy, now give me a jug of punch and I'll take it round,' said Edmund, glancing about for someone to whom he could introduce Marianne and Charlie. He rejected old Major Snargate and Allie Snodland, who were discussing the iniquities of the Parden Planning Department and then lit on Ted Spirit, the science-fiction writer who was now deep in conversation with Sofia.

'*Maman*, you have met Charlie before, and this is his friend Marianne who was so helpful to me when I was looking for Amelia.' He turned to Marianne. 'You may have seen the television adaptation of the book, *Troic and Zilda*?'

Delayed by the snow, but undeterrred by their search for what they knew would be a good party, people were still arriving. Battalions of boots lined the walls of the hall, melting snow making little puddles of water on the flags. Regiments of coats were flung across the banisters, empty glasses lined the windowsills. He hated to leave Amelia for a second, but felt bound to do some more handing round of food and clearing of glasses. Light-minded, confused by the chaotic choreography of introductions and the noise, he headed for the kitchen to collect a tray. He hadn't set eyes on Xenia since the first guests had arrived, but he found her in the kitchen, dragging a tray of salmon patties out of the oven, hair limp and dress decorated with a spray of mayonnaise up the sleeve. He would have to let her meet Amelia soon – hoping that his explanation would take the heat off Johnnie.

'Just rounding up a few glasses for you, Xenia. Rosy's running low. Shall I take that food out for you, and put it in the hall? Rupert and Henry are doing a grand job waitering.'

'Rupert may be, but Henry's disappeared upstairs with a girl in a stupid black hat.'

'Oh, Josie Sailor.'

She looked flushed and her eyes were a little unfocused.

'Why don't you go and enjoy your party, Xenia? It's going so well. I'll get someone to come and take over here.'

'No, no! I've got to finish the hot food. And Rosy's brought me in a glass of wine.'

'That's punch, Xenia, not wine. It's Johnnie's maxi-strength brew.'

'I am not drunk – that's what you're saying, isn't it. You think I'm drunk?'

'Don't shout at me, Xenia! I merely said to watch it. It's very strong.'

Edmund took a dish of patties and returned in search of Amelia, whom he found talking to Mary Beaton, standing beneath the Millais portrait of Johnnie's great-grandfather, a bewhiskered young Victorian gentleman leaning against the gate to Hilly Foxes field, a bunch of primroses in his hand and a delicate, adoring spaniel at his feet in the green, green grass. *When* was he ever going to get a chance to talk to her alone?

Johnnie passed him.

'Where is Xenia? She should be out here with her guests. Some people are starting to leave and she's hardly even said hello to anyone. Why can't she just leave the damned food on the tables so that people can help themselves. I told her to get in caterers, but she will *insist* on doing it all herself.' He disappeared into the kitchen.

Sofia detached herself from an elderly judge who was ranting on about poisoning rats.

'No good at all. They're super-rats now. Doesn't have any effect on them.'

She followed Johnnie, meaning to offer a hand. She'd never heard so many ridiculous conversations in her life and thought she might get a minute's peace in the kitchen. Amelia introduced Mary to Edmund.

'Oh, but I remember you very well. You are the motor-biking GP who arrived at the Eeldyke pub just as Johnnie and I were leaving. Have you been working over Christmas, or did you manage a decent break?'

'I was on call from midnight last night till just now. Not too bad, really. One attack of indigestion, which the family took to be a heart attack, one broken ankle caused by someone falling off a table, or so he said. One genuine heart attack, but I managed to get the air ambulance helicopter in for him. And one croupy baby. Considering the appalling weather it was quite quiet.'

Edmund's eyes were straying to Amelia while Mary spoke. She was laughing at something Charlie had said, throwing her head back so that the necklace tinkled round her throat. Her skin was very pale as it disappeared into the deep V-shape of the front of the jacket. It was just as well he had not bought her the one he'd seen in London – a pretty coincidence that she had chosen to wear just what he would have chosen for her.

'You've known Amelia for a long time?' he asked Mary.

'At least four years. She was my first patient when I joined the practice, and we've been good friends ever since. She's been through a rough time since Nick committed suicide,' Mary said in a lowered voice, as if warning him not to muck her about any further. He wanted to ask what Nick had been like, why she thought he'd done such a thing, but Amelia was too close, and he could ask her himself, much later, if there was a later. They were interrupted by Allie Snodland who boomed into them, almost pinning Amelia to the wall.

'Mimi, darling! How are *you*?' she emphasized the last word as if Amelia, who was looking trapped, had already enquired about her own health. She was one of the people whom Amelia had known before Nick died, and who had drifted away on the tide of omission afterwards, and Amelia did not much care for her and her delving curranty eyes.

'I'm not contagious anymore, if that's what you mean,' Amelia said, hearing her own belligerent voice with astonishment. The punch must have been stronger than she'd thought. Allie did not know how to take this and was momentarily aware that she was being attacked, but was saved by Sofia's appearance.

'I've come to find an 'elper, Edmund. Xenia is a bit tired, but she will not stop putting things in the oven. I tell 'er everyone 'as 'ad enough to eat. She will not listen to me.'

'I'll come and help', said Amelia, thinking this would be as good a moment as any to set about dispelling Xenia's preconceptions about her.

'Me too', said Mary. Edmund took Marianne's arm. 'Come on, Charlie, come and meet Nigel Hogarth.' Nigel was the local celebrity, an actor steadily in work, a patient, gentle person with a scarred cheek and pitted skin who specialized in playing unpleasant thugs. Charlie followed. He had been impressed by the beautiful house and had spotted a set of George Vertue's 1830s *Picturesque Beauties of Great Britain* in the drawing room, which he rather hankered after.

By the time Edmund got back Sofia had taken Amelia and Mary into the kitchen, and he galloped off to protect her, leaving Allie with the rhododendron man who had resurfaced, searching for a fellow fanatic to enthuse with. He'd met his match in Allie, who shared the same level of intense passion, for azaleas, and could bore for England on the subject. A few people were beginning to leave, worried by the prospect of further snow, and were saying goodbye to a harassed-looking Johnnie who hurried back to the kitchen ahead of Edmund.

The beautiful painted cupboards hung open, there was water on the floor, and eggshells, and a large piece of fruit cake on which someone had put their foot. Johnnie had hold of Xenia's arm and was pleading with her to sit down for a moment. Xenia's eyes focused on Amelia and narrowed.

'Xenia,' said Edmund hurriedly, 'this is Mimi, the person whom I've been searching for all these weeks.' He was trying to throw her off the scent, and wondered why he so often thought of Xenia as some kind of dog. Allie appeared behind him.

'Hello, Xen. Where have you been hiding yourself? I told you in Canterbury, remember . . . this is Mimi Anderson . . .'

'I know perfectly well who she is,' Xenia said, venomously, her eyes snake-like, and Edmund hastily took Amelia's arm as if to emphasize the connection between her and himself, not Johnnie. Raucous male laughter came from the hall. Haw, Haw! HAW! Xenia took in the gesture, and snarled, 'I suppose you and your daughter will try to seduce Rupert next?'

'Xenia!' Edmund said, appalled. 'Don't be unpleasant and idiotic! We've just come to help – to give you a break.' Johnnie was looking stricken, Sofia quite shocked.

'I *know*! I know who she is, and I know what she's up to. She's trying ruin my life. Take everyone away from me! She's had Johnnie and now she's taken Edmund.' She was clenching the table top, her knuckles white. 'Her little tart of a daughter has gone off somewhere with Henry!'

Amelia, inspired by the punch, waded in. 'That's utter balls! You're completely off the mark and totally offensive! I wouldn't have come if it hadn't been for Edmund, and *only* Edmund.' Then, thinking desperately that there might be other reasons for the onslaught, 'Didn't you like the bracelet?'

Xenia looked at her wrist, where it shone gracefully, as if she had never seen it before. 'What has the bracelet to do with you?'

Sofia interrupted. 'Johnnie commissioned it from 'er. For you, specially. Didn't 'e tell you?' This was so untimely as to be seriously late.

'You did what?' Xenia screamed at Johnnie. 'You mean *you* made this . . . this . . . ?' she shrieked at Amelia. She scrabbled at the bracelet, trying to drag it off, succeeded and flung it to the floor, where it rolled beneath the kitchen table, clanging to a halt encircling a mislaid hard-boiled quail's egg. Allie couldn't wait to go and tell someone that the Whitby's were having an almighty row and headed for the hall, missing seeing Xenia picking up Rupert's present, the Sabatier vegetable knife, and lunging at Johnnie with it. Johnnie sidestepped smartly and made a grab for her arm but missed. The knife sliced across Amelia's collarbone, chinking harshly on her silver necklace. Sofia shrieked, leapt forward and captured the flailing arm and slapped her daughter hard across the face. In Edmund's eyes it happened simultaneously in slow motion and at high speed. So fast, like running, running to stay in the same place; Xenia was the Red Queen, gone horribly wrong and murderous. He flung his arms around Amelia, who was clutching the wound, blood welling up between her fingers.

'Oh Christ! Amelia! Someone stop her before she does any more damage!'

But Xenia had already dropped the knife and Mary stepped calmly into the middle of this little tragedy, took a quick look at Amelia's cut, tore some paper towels from the wall and told Amelia to hold them tight against it. She then looked at Xenia, limp and sobbing, still pinioned by her mother.

'I'd get her out of here and up to bed,' she said in a light conversational tone, as if discussing the removal of an overtired toddler who had outstayed its welcome with the grown-ups. Johnnie scooped her up, and staggered with her to the back staircase, just off the rear hall, but the old dog, convinced that Johnnie was about to do something unspeakable to the only person who had taken any notice of him over the past few weeks, and perhaps confused by old age and the smell of human blood, barred his way, growling, and as Johnnie tried to push him away with his foot, fastened his toothless jaws firmly round Johnnie's ankle.

'Get this bloody animal off me!' shouted Johnnie, shaking his leg and banging Xenia's head against the wall as he tried to climb the old staircase. No one took any notice and Mary went outside to fetch her bag, shutting the main door to the kitchen, a trifle too late, since the screaming and shouting had silenced the nearby guffawing guests who were now being given a blow-by-blow account of the scene by Allie. Rosy Pressing was looking wildly excited. The noise level abated in time with the spread of the news that all was not well with the Whitbys. Sofia was looking a lot older.

'Amelia, my dear Amelia. Sit down here. So lucky your friend is a doctor. Does it 'urt very much?'

'No. Yes. I don't know. I feel silly. I know it wasn't aimed at me.'

Edmund sat beside her at the cluttered and sticky kitchen table, holding her against him. This is nice, she thought, suddenly feeling sleepy.

'I'm a fool,' said Edmund to Sofia. 'I should never have let Amelia anywhere near her. None of us realized that she was getting into such a state. Not just today, but for weeks. It's been building up. There seems to be a lot of blood. Where *is* Mary? Do you think we need an ambulance?'

'Right, first things first.' Mary reappeared. 'I've told everyone that Xenia has been taken ill, and that it's snowing hard enough to warrant them all thinking about getting home. It is two thirty, and they've all had their money's worth. Why don't Edmund and Mrs Yearne go and join them and do the goodbyes and how-delightful-it's-been-to-see-you-agains, while I get on with this?'

Sofia left, but Edmund stayed put, not wanting to leave her until he'd found out the extent of the damage. Mary mopped up efficiently and Edmund felt slightly faint, which he hadn't when it had been his own blood last week.

'Look, it's not very deep at all. You've got a charmed life.

It could have been your throat. It's glanced off the necklace, very lucky. I'll stitch it, I think. OK?'

'I've never had stitches before.'

'I'll be so quick. I promise. I'm excellent at embroidery.'

Amelia knew this to be untrue, but laughed weakly at the old joke.

'What's happened?' Josie appeared at the door and took in the group by the table and let out a melodramatic shriek. 'Oh Mum, Mum! What's happened?'

'Nothing darling, a little accident with a kitchen knife – I'm fine. Mary's dealing with it. Make us all some coffee, would you sweetheart?'

Charlie also appeared, but hastily withdrew when he saw Mary bending over Amelia, preparing to stitch the cut. Edmund was about to explain to Josie what had happened, but this was harder than expected. 'My sister has just stabbed your mother' sounded a bit sensationalistic. Perhaps he should leave it to Amelia, whose explanation had seemed sufficient for Josie.

'I think I'll go and rescue Charlie and Marianne. Don't move. I'll be back in a minute or two.'

Sofia was in the hall doing her duty. 'Goodbye. Drive carefully, won't you? So sorry Xenia 'as 'ad to retire. Gastric flu, we think. Goodbye.' She improvised unwisely, not considering that the guests might be alarmed, having consumed quantities of Xenia's home-prepared food.

'Well, well. There seems to have been a bit of an explosion, I hear?' said Charlie, who had been collared by Allie.

'A bit worse than that. My sister completely lost control of herself and tried to stab her husband, only she got Amelia instead, but mercifully it isn't too serious.' Edmund found that his hands were trembling.

'God! It's all very Russian and emotional, isn't it? Is she really all right?'

'Yes. But we are feeling a bit shaky. Look, it would be

best if you and Marianne left now, if you see what I mean. There's a wonderful little pub about four miles down the road, if you fancy taking your chances in the snow. The Eeldyke Inn. I'll tell you all about it in the New Year. By the way, how was your Christmas with the friends in Rye?'

Charlie looked a bit evasive. 'Not quite what I'd thought it would be, actually. The farmhouse is a building site, unfinished, and Chris and Philomena are at each other's throats every five minutes; babies crying, untrained dogs all over the place.' He grinned. 'This all seems very civilized by comparison. I'll be quite glad to get back to London. I find the country overstimulating. Come on, Marianne, stop eating all the leftovers.'

Marianne gave Edmund a kiss. 'Perhaps you will get snowed in, tonight?' she said demurely. Edmund watched her leave holding on to Charlie's arm, then bending to pick up a handful of snow and threatening to rub it in his face. They seemed very friendly indeed, and he wondered what magic Marianne had wrought on Charlie. There was clearly nothing he needed to worry about on that score.

Ted Spirit was leaving too, and saw Marianne getting into Charlie's car. 'Lovely girl, that. So interested in my work. She reads a lot of my kind of thing. She thought the TV series based on *Troic and Zilda* wasn't quite up to the book.'

Major Snargate had joined forces with the judge, who was still on the topic of rats. 'You need one of my daughter's Jack Russells. Splendid little chaps! Kill them off faster than they can breed.'

'Yes. But I still think sitting there, waiting for them in the shed with the old rat gun is more fun.'

Allie had been refused leave to visit Xenia, even for a little minute, and had left in a huff with her confused husband. Rosy Pressing and daughter were rushing about the drawing room, setting it all to rights. Rosy had not caught the gist of the row since she had been in the drawing room at the time handing round a plate of miniature chocolate éclairs, but she knew something tremendous was up.

Edmund raced back to Amelia, who was sitting calmly, almost as if nothing had happened, talking to Henry and Josie. From upstairs they could hear Rupert playing his guitar.

'I think I should drive you home now. It seems best to leave Sofia and Johnnie to sort out Xenia. It's about time Johnnie looked after her.'

Mary was packing up her bag, sipping coffee. She picked up a blood-stained tea-towel and threw it in the dustbin. Already the kitchen was being returned to its former *House and Garden* immaculacy. The crumbled fruit cake and egg-shells had been swept up, the floor seemed to have been washed, the table cleared.

'Yes. I would like to go home. Josie's supposed to be going to Ruffles' tonight. But I don't think she can, if the snow keeps up, and anyway, I'll have to leave my car here.'

'I could take her. Is it far away?'

'No, only a couple of miles. Come on, Josie. Edmund is going to drive us home.'

Josie lingered with Henry after the others had gone out into the hall. 'No one will tell me quite what happened. It's ridiculous.'

'I don't know either, but I think Mum got rather drunk. She's never done that before,' said Henry,

'Oh, mine often does; well, not drunk, exactly, but definitely tiddled. We have quite a laugh sometimes. But I don't understand how she managed to cut herself.'

'I didn't know she had.'

'She's got this gash on her shoulder. I watched Mary put stitches in, she was incredibly neat. Do you think your brother would sell us his Dark Entry tickets?'

'Not a hope in hell, not an ant's chance in a Grand Prix.'

'Rupert said he heard your parents having a row.'

'Just don't know how to behave, do they?'

'I'd better go. Your uncle's giving us a lift home. He seems very keen on Mum, doesn't he?'

'Your mother's very attractive for someone her age. Perhaps they'll get it together? I'll call you, and let you know what I can find out.'

'Great, see you then.'

Edmund saw the little green hoofprints on the hall floor where Amelia's shoes had come into contact with damp patches from the melted snow. He wondered what they were – leprechauns? Once the final guests had departed and the Pressing duo were vacuuming the drawing room carpet, Sofia disappeared upstairs to see her daughter. The hall looked desolate in spite of the Christmas tree, the fire having burned right down; a serving dish with three little salmon patties sat on the white tablecloth amidst the empty glasses and punchbowl. There were several pairs of boots left behind by the front door. When Amelia changed into hers, Edmund was delighted to see the cause of the green footprints and by the time they had been joined by Josie they were laughing about the shoes, trying to cover up the awfulness of the scene in the kitchen.

13 ∫

Having been extremely drunk, Xenia slept heavily for some hours, watched over alternately by Sofia and Johnnie, both of whom were deservedly wrestling with a certain amount of guilt. Sofia felt guilty because mothers are always prone to, but Johnnie was visited by this irritant emotion not primarily because of his failure to understand the depth of his wife's distress, but because he had, by default, obstructed Edmund and Amelia's meeting. Xenia had not been the only victim of her own jealousy – Johnnie had suffered too, and could not get it out of his head that given more time, he could have overcome Amelia's scruples had not his wretched brother-in-law marched round his Maginot Line of silence and invaded his territory. That his wife had attempted to stab him had been a most horrible surprise and he was greatly shaken by it, although he was not displeased by the uncharacteristic show of her feelings for him. He could see that he had to renounce all thoughts of Amelia. Edmund had gone off with her, and had not returned.

Sofia busied herself with organizing the household and minimizing Xenia's explosion. She paid Rosy and her daughter and sent Henry off to drive them home. She brought Xenia coffee when she eventually woke up at seven o'clock and, disapproving of allowing people to shirk responsibility, gently told her the details, in case she had forgotten what had happened, and sat with her while she cried. She also noticed that Edmund had not returned, and was pleased. He was better out of the way and in any case, she and Johnnie could manage Xenia till they could see if any further action was required. She knew of a good nursing home in East Sussex that dealt in just such cases. A couple of weeks' total rest and Johnnie's constant attendance would do wonders for her, and then Johnnie should take her away on holiday for a bit.

Meanwhile Josie had wisely decided not to enquire any further into the incident although she was fairly convinced that things were being kept from her. As soon as they had reached Jarvis Cottage she rushed to telephone Ruffles, her mind now on other things.

'You're off the hook!' she said to Edmund, grinning. 'Ruffles' Dad has a four-wheel drive Jeep-type thing, and he's going to come over and collect me. You will be all right now, Mum?'

'Perfectly, darling. But *please* put some warm clothes on and take a blanket with you.'

After the warmth and space of the farm, the cottage seemed icy and cramped. Edmund made Amelia sit on the sofa and put her feet up, but she was hyped up and restless, watching him relight the fire, mentally measuring the pleasing ratio of width of shoulder to narrowness of hip as he knelt by the hearth at work with the bellows. She hoped that Josie would be fetched soon before he decided to try to get back to the farm, hoped that he wouldn't leave at all and remembered that having him sitting firmly beside her in the Whitbys' dishevelled designer kitchen had been very pleasant indeed. He had felt both frightened and angry for her then – she'd smelt it overriding his own particular male smell, which she'd found decidedly attractive.

'I don't feel comfortable like this,' she said. 'I want to wash and change into something warmer. The jacket is ruined anyway – look, the material's cut on the collar, and it's got bloodstains on it. Perhaps wearing green *is* unlucky.'

Edmund sat back on his heels. 'I was wearing a green jacket too, when the bomb went off. I think it's more likely to be a fortunate colour, since we've both survived. Hatty took mine to the cleaners who think they can restore it.' He got up, put his hand up to his ear out of habit, and then let it drop back. 'Do you know – I wanted to buy you a green velvet jacket I saw in London, as a Christmas present?'

She went upstairs, leaving him to stoke the fire and watch the snow, falling steadily now. It would soon be dark again. A red Jeep-type thing drew up outside, and hooted. He could see a man in a flat cap at the wheel, blowing on his hands, and a girl sitting beside him, who waved. Josie found her mother wriggling awkwardly into a thick jersey, green again, to flout fate, wincing a little.

'Can you manage? Does it hurt?'

'No, I'm fine. I really am. You go off, and ring me tomorrow.'

Josie gave her a hug and disappeared, clattering down the narrow staircase. She poked her head round the door to say goodbye to Edmund.

'I'm off now. I know you want to be alone with her. You'll take care of her, won't you?' Her voice had a trace of a giggle in it, a little teasing. 'What a couple of old crocks! Both of you all stitched up. Bye, then!'

'Goodbye, Josie,' said Edmund, thinking what a dear, wicked person she was, glad that she could happily trot off and pursue her own ends. She barely knew the Whitbys, was uninterested in their domestic dramas except in the fact that it had somehow affected her mother, whom she could now see was unharmed.

Over the last few days Edmund had been so concentrated on his growing desire for Amelia that the sudden violent disruption of the afternoon had shocked and disconcerted him far more than his narrow escape in London. He was, however, still thinking that he must hold back and give her a chance to get to know him, though she had not seemed uncomfortable with him holding on to her in the kitchen. He didn't believe he'd ever feel comfortable in that kitchen again.

'I was thinking,' said Amelia, coming back into the sitting room, 'that I seem to attract violence, or rather that it follows me about. Not necessarily violence done to me, I don't mean that, although that has happened once or twice, but that violent things seem to happen around me too often.'

Edmund recalled that she had witnessed an assassination as a child, and shivered. 'That doesn't mean it always will,' he said comfortingly. 'Things change, all the time. This might be the last occasion.'

'Yes, I suppose there is a chance of that. So, here we are, both alive. Are you very worried about your sister?'

'To be truthful, I'm more worried about you. I think Xenia will get better, now she's let off steam – only that is a trivial way to think of what she did – I think she probably needs professional help, but I doubt she'd agree to that. Poor Johnnie. Perhaps we ought to do graffiti on all the walls round the farm . . . 'Johnnie Whitby is almost innocent, OK?' I don't know anything about nervous breakdowns – they don't run in the family – and she's only been drunk once recently to my knowledge. But she's always been a very buttoned-up, strait-laced sort of person, constipated by her own precision, forever trying to keep tabs on everyone, organizing them, bossing. No one can keep up to her standards. I think she felt she had lost control of us all, and so lost control of herself.'

'Will your mother be able to help? I thought she was wonderfully funny.'

'Funny?'

'Yes, didn't you hear her telling everyone as they left that Xenia had been taken ill with gastro-enteritis? Then she got bored with saying gastro-enteritis and told the last two to leave, the two old boys who were bent on exterminating rats, that Xenia had conjunctivitis.'

'I expect they all left worried that they were going to catch something. But my mother is one of the people who Xenia has never been able to control. They don't get on at all. When my father died, Xenia moved in on her, ordering her to do this and that, sell her house, come and live with her and Johnnie. Sofia escaped to France as fast as she could. She visits us all at Christmas and we all go over to see her whenever we want. The children love going to stay with her, but I haven't been able to go as often as I'd like. She has a wonderful brother, Uncle Serge, who lives in Paris. I always drop in to see him when I do get over. He lives in their parents' old flat and he's an expert on icons and on pre-revolutionary Russian art.'

'What an interesting family you have. I've only got Josie now, and Aunt Margaret in Galloway. And there's Nick's mother, who still blames me for his death. I honestly don't think I had anything to do with his death. I suppose you've heard the story from Johnnie, of what happened?'

'Only partially, as I've come to expect from Johnnie. All I know is that he killed himself. Do you know why?'

'I think it was just as he said in his note. Boredom. He was frustrated by failure and bored with responsibility. I hate to admit this, because of Josie, and such things can run in families, can't they? But it became clear to me about five years into our marriage that he was mentally ill at times. Nothing you could put a name to, no syndromes, just depression of a peculiar sort. When one is married to a depressive, one tends to think that one is to blame for their depression a lot of the time, and they of course don't try to put one right, the opposite in fact. There were good times, of course, but it's getting harder and harder to remember them. In the same way that you've only just realized there was something wrong with Xenia, it took me ages to pin down Nick's problem. You've made your sister sound like an emotional terrorist.'

'Poor Xenia. But that *is* what she is. Do you know she practically forced us to go to church yesterday? In spite of us all having been to Midnight Mass the night before, to please her. None of us is religious by nature, and I can't seem to get on with the present Church of England at all – it seems to have become an uninspiring sort of club.'

'I went to the carol service because I thought you might be there. That's using it as a club, isn't it? But I like the marking of the seasonal changes, old pagan festivals dressed up as something else. I think they're more important than people think. But I must admit I've never fitted in to any clubs. A bit like Groucho Marx, you know?'

'That you don't want to belong to the sort of club that would let you become one of its members? Yes, I know what you mean. I found out after my wife Sylvestra had left that I had left a club I didn't even know I belonged to. Within a year the other members were all frenziedly matchmaking, desperate to get me to rejoin, as if I'd be subversive if I didn't, or else they didn't know what else to do with me.'

Edmund didn't feel that the conversation should be taking this turn at all, but seemed unable to stop himself.

'Why did you break up – can I ask?' Amelia had been about to ask if stabbing was a genetic trait in his family, but stopped just in time, but not before Edmund had divined what was on her mind.

'It wasn't violence on my part, I promise you,' he said, alarmed. 'Sylvestra left me because she had fallen in love with someone else. Which means that she had fallen out of love with me before she met him, I suppose, or she wouldn't have been looking, would she? She did have one or two flings before, but I didn't think they were serious. This one was and I stupidly didn't take too much notice until too late. People often ask if one has got *over* an event such as a divorce or a death. I don't see how one can get *over* it. The word has the wrong spatial connotations, don't you think?'

'You could always try going round instead. I got round Nick's death in the end, although at the time the event itself had taken on the proportions of Ben Nevis. I refused to take the blame, and had to work very hard, and Josie being there helped too.' Amelia felt the dressing over the cut on her collarbone and looked straight at Edmund, seeing how anxious and tense he was. 'There is a difference, you know, between over and round. Over implies an effort, uphill. Through is the same, tunnelling in the dark. But round, well that's just by-passing, circling, bending the rules a little. I don't want to, can't, I mean, forget life with Nick, nor what he did. But I don't have to let it take part in the present.'

'Since I found your papers I've thought about Sylvestra less and less. This is the first time I've thought about her since I last saw you.'

'You've come round then? Am I that diverting?'

'I think I have. And yes, you are.'

'What would you like for supper?' she said.

'I don't know what you've got. Something childish, I think. Scrambled eggs on toast? Eggy bread?'

'What the hell's eggy bread?'

'Shall I show you? I'm beginning to feel quite warm now, and very hungry. Have you got any jam, or marmalade?'

They went into the kitchen together. Outside in the dark, Edmund's car had all but disappeared. Snow had come in under the ill-fitting door in a little white drift, unmelting on the brick floor, like caster sugar. He took the loaf of bread she gave him and cut four thick slices, beat up three eggs in a wide blue china bowl and added a little milk and a pinch of salt. He had a frown of concentration on his face, his thick eyebrows drawn together. 'Now, see. You put the slices to soak in the bowl. They have to be really sodden, all the way through. Keep on turning them, top to the bottom. Then you get a large bit of butter. Butter, butter, where's the butter? Ah, I've got it. Big frying pan? Got that too. Then you get the butter hot, as if you were about to make an omelette, and you throw in the bread . . .'

The delicious smell, the sizzling sound. Amelia suddenly felt quite faint.

'Now, turn them over. Can I put my arms round you again, while the other side cooks?' He'd forgotten his resolution and reached round her waist from behind her, held her close, rocking her from side to side as she turned the bread.

'I'm not hurting your shoulder, am I?' he asked, anxiously.

'No. It's no worse than a cut finger. I think this is done.'

'Then quick! Plates and jam and sugar! It's called *pain perdu.*'

Amelia found that eating eggy bread with a man she now knew she fancied to death was an extraordinarily sensuous experience. She licked her jammy fingers, and Edmund, watching her with pleasure, thought she resembled nothing so much as an Abyssinian cat, completely unselfconscious, at peace with itself regardless of the havoc it had unwittingly caused around it. A cat returned from a fray, safe by its own fireside. She smiled up at him, clasping her arms round her knees, wondering what he looked like beneath the dark jacket and white shirt, with the tie askew.

'You must be cold, in your party clothes. I'll find you something warmer to wear.' He was cold, in spite of the fire. He'd been accustomed to Xenia's over-heated house, and was out of the habit of layering clothes just because it was winter. 'And I'm going to telephone Mary, to thank her. Back in a minute.' She disappeared again, leaving him wondering what to do, or what not to do.

Mary was unsympathetic to Xenia's predicament. 'She deserves an Oscar. I've never seen such melodrama, pure *Grand Guignol*.'

'Yes. The farcical elements didn't go unnoticed. But perhaps she hasn't had a lot of practice at throwing tantrums and didn't know how far to go.'

'She's gone quite far enough for the rest of her life. But are you OK? Is Mr Yearne looking after your interests?'

'I'm fine. He's just cooked me a delicious tea. And my "interests" are still untouched. But what about Xenia?'

'I've had a chat with her own GP, which I can't go into, obviously. You're not pressing charges, are you?'

'Good God, no! She meant to get Johnnie, not me,' said Amelia, appalled. 'Anyway,' she continued, 'I just wanted to thank you for looking after me again. I was quite scared you'd do blanket stitch, but I've just looked at it in the mirror and it looks very neat. I've put some marigold on it.'

'You and your herbal horrors! No, I know it's a good natural antiseptic.'

'It does make things heal up quicker. I don't want a huge scar. It used to be used by optimistic young women in an effort to restore their virginity. Did you know that?'

'No, it's a bit of information I failed to pick up in medical school. Sadly it's a bit late for both of us, isn't it?'

When Amelia had put the phone down, she scratched a little hole in the developing frost on the window with her fingernail, and tried to peer out. Still snowing. She ran upstairs again, to fetch a heavy grey fisherman's jersey for Edmund and returned to the pumpkin-coloured sitting room to find him going through her bookshelves, intrigued by the collection. He'd picked out Dorothy Hartley's *Food in England* and was leafing through it, wondering if the way to a woman's heart was through her stomach.

'I loved the *pain perdu*. What else can you do?' she asked.

Edmund thought he'd only thought the words: 'I'd love to make love to you, but not yet. We're both too shaken.'

Amelia laughed. 'All right then. I am a bit shaken. That's why I keep getting up and down.'

'What do you mean?'

'I mean, all right, not yet.' She hesitated and then laughed again at him. 'You didn't realize you had spoken aloud, did you?'

'I didn't!'

'You did. I heard you quite clearly.'

'Could I stay the night?' He looked doubtful, cautious.

'You could hardly do anything else, I think. The wind's getting up and the snow does drift here so badly.' As she spoke the wind was conjured to give a warning howl in the wide chimney. 'But you can't sleep down here. The fire will go out and you'll get hypothermia.'

Edmund's self-imposed restraint and Amelia's growing impatience passed each other in the street without recognition, then light dawned and they turned and waved.

'We could then, at least, keep each other warm?' he asked.

'I think that would be very practical.' She looked closely at him and saw that he was still very white. 'I believe you're more shocked than I am by all this.'

'I've been frightened half to death by the thought of losing you. And I think the bomb business has caught up with me. I keep thinking I can see myself out of the corner of my eye.'

'I can see you full on. You look like a man who's seen a ghost.'

'Come to me, then. I need you.'

And because it was he who had asked, chosen, she came and lay beside him on the sofa and they became inextricably involved, happily and painfully entangled, and quite desperate for somewhere more comfortable.

'You go up first, the fire's lit up there. I've got to lock the door.'

'Who do you expect to come, on a night like this?'

'You're right, I expect it would be rather difficult for anyone. We'll go together.' And in spite of the cold, the tangle of heavy bedding and not being able to take off their clothes without getting frostbite, and in spite of the bruises and stitches, they made love for a very long time, without once repeating themselves, tasting, testing and treating each other ecstatically, with infinite care and patience, till they fell into a pleasure-saturated state of sedation. The paraffin stove made a tiny fluttering sound and threw its little patterned light on to the uneven, bulging plaster ceiling. The wind moaned, as if saddened by the cessation of activity. Amelia slid her hand up Edmund's chest beneath his shirt, running along the sharp line of fur, and fell asleep to dream of badgers. Edmund dreamed of sitting naked on a beach with Amelia, in hot sunshine, eating, feeding her fingers of eggy bread, but she turned into a yellow cat and ran off with her tail in the air. He chased her all round the island, for that is where they were, but she was always a yard ahead of him.

'Edmund!'

'Mm.'

'Edmund!' The voice had more urgency to it this time, but was laughing.

'What's 'a matter?'

'You're holding on to me so tight I can't breathe.'

'I thought you'd run away.'

'Oh no, not me.'

He released her, reluctantly, slowly opening his eyes and staring at her in the semi-dark, eyes heavy-lidded. She stared back, the peat-brown eyes huge, pupils wide.

'Good morning, dearest man.'

'Where are you going?' She was sliding away from him, slipping out of bed. She stood there, wearing only her green jersey. He glimpsed the white roundness of her behind before she wrapped herself in a dressing gown.

'I have to go and feed the cat. I'll make some tea.'

'Bugger the cat. Come back.' He'd felt a twitch, a surge of renewed desire. 'But it can't be morning. I've only just fallen asleep.'

But she went after planting a kiss on his mouth. 'Keep my side of the bed warm too.'

He heard her footsteps on the creaking wooden stairs and the click of the inner kitchen door, her voice softly greeting the cat, clanking metallic sounds as she riddled the stove and poured in more coal. Then he heard her gasp.

'Edmund!'

He stuck his nose out of the bedclothes, feeling the bite of the air.

'Edmund,' she called out again. 'We're competely snowed in! It's halfway up the windows.' Edmund groaned and got out of bed but couldn't find his trousers, nor his socks. He dragged a blanket off the bed and wrapped himself up in it. This seemed awfully familiar. It was an odd coincidence that within a space of a couple of weeks, and after over a year's abstinence, he had made love to two different women while snowed in – but there was no comparison between them, between the two events, apart from the damned snow. His mind was full of last night, although he now considered it lucky that he didn't have chilblains on his private parts. He scraped ineffectually at the window. The ice was thick, but he eventually made an area large enough to look through. But there was nothing to see. Thousands of acres of snow, with just the odd black bush peering through it. The road, which he knew to be beneath the window on that side of the house, had disappeared. He stumped back to bed across the plank floor. He felt a sock, then another, then retrieved Amelia's tights and knickers, and his tie which looked as if someone had tied a reef knot in it. Amelia came upstairs with two mugs of tea and a can of paraffin. She filled the stove, and got back into bed with him, making him gasp as her icy legs touched his.

'I'll warm up in a second,' she said.

'Let me warm you up.' He stroked the bright hair, twisting his fingers into it and kissing her cold ear. Then he put his cup down, felt under the bedclothes and ran his hands up and down her thighs, warming them.

'Do you realize we've screwed each other silly and not even seen each other's bodies?' she said. 'Like a Victorian couple with all those voluminous nightshirts and dresses.'

'Well you're not seeing any more of mine till spring. You shouldn't have to live like this. It's like the Middle Ages.'

'I'm tough, and I got used to the cold when we lived in the other house. We couldn't afford to heat that either, it was too big. We used to wear our coats indoors, and two or three pairs of socks. I'm afraid I often go to bed in all my clothes. But this is exceptionally bad. It doesn't snow down here all that often – and it's certainly colder than I can ever remember. I don't see how we can get out at all. It's still quite dark downstairs because the windows are blocked up with snow.'

'Don't talk so much – is that nice?'

'Yes.'

'And this?'

'Even better. I suppose we could get out of the sitting-room window, that's on the other side of the house.'

'Who wants to get out? I'm sure there are bits of you that I haven't touched yet.' Edmund didn't feel it was an appropriate time to discuss means of escape.

They emerged breathlessly some time later, pink-faced and tousled and utterly happy.

'We didn't do that last night,' he said, looking a little surprised.

'I forgot to tell you how much I like it, but you do need to shave.'

'I didn't bring a razor. I didn't think I was going to be able to stay.'

'That was silly of you.'

'You don't understand, I was so scared of moving too fast and putting you off – you seemed so cool and self-contained, and you were very angry that I'd read your papers, if you remember. I felt so guilty.'

'Poor lamb. I did like you at once, really. I just didn't want to do any of the running at all. Just in case I'd made a mistake again.'

'And you think you haven't?'

'I don't think I have. No.'

At midday they got up and shared a bath.

'You could try shaving with this. I promise I've only used it once for my legs.' They'd warmed the bathroom first with one of the ubiquitous paraffin stoves, and she lay in the soapy water dreaming a little while he tried to remove the dark stubble. He turned away from the foggy mirror and watched her intently, savouring the ins and outs of her body, the breasts quite round and full, the small dark nipples, the light dusting of freckles on arms and shoulders, the ugly cut on her collarbone, even that he found attractive.

'You are beautiful, you know.'

She sat up self-consciously, splashing the wall, and began scrubbing her feet with a nailbrush, turning suddenly and giving him her set-afire smile. 'You don't mind the stretch-marks, then?'

Edmund couldn't see any. She rose, flicking water from her hands, and bent to show him, a little staggered row of pale silver streaks, just above the golden public hair.

'No, I don't mind them at all, so long as you don't mind me missing a bit of my ear?'

'Poor mutilated thing!' She reached out and put her arms round his neck as she stepped out of the bath. 'What I like about you is you're so three-dimensional – some men are sort of flat, have no depth to them. You are columnar, strong. Considering the amount of time you must spend poring over books.'

'Books are incredibly heavy and I spend more time heaving them about in boxes than poring over them.'

The room was full of steam, little runnels of water coursing down the inside of the windows coagulated and froze. They dressed quickly and greedily breakfasted on thick rashers of green back bacon and black coffee before attempting an escape from the house – the only exit being through the sitting room window. Edmund climbed out and passed logs back through to Amelia till the copper was filled and the dampest ones were stacked at either end of the large hearth, enough to feed a fire for at least three days. They lay in front of it, lazily talking, reading a little and since no one was going to be able to drive anywhere for the foreseeable future, drank two bottles of wine which had been unaccountably left over from the Christmas feast. The telephone was out of order, but Amelia did not worry about Josie since she would probably be warmer where she was. They heard on the local radio that large swathes of Kent were cut off but didn't greatly care, and lay snug, talking and talking.

'Tell me more of your marriage to Nick. You never wrote about him.'

'No, I didn't. In the early days it seemed that to commit

it to paper would destroy it. Later I was quite unable to be truthful any more, in case he read it and was hurt. We all expected too much from marriage. The romantic novels that girls read in those days, still do as far as I know, concentrate on the hunt, the banquet and then tail off. They never told us how indigestible marriage can be sometimes. I can only say that there were times when I was so bitterly disappointed that I couldn't bear it, and I'm sure he must have felt the same. We did both try, of course, to make things better, but we never managed to coincide in our efforts.' Amelia rolled over and propped herself up on a cushion.

'Tell me about Sylvestra.'

'The trouble there was that I only believed what I wanted to believe. I couldn't imagine that she was unhappy. It's easier to see now that I rushed her into it – marriage, I mean. I thought her emotional outbursts were just the way women were and didn't understand their reality. She needed excitement and admiration all the time. I just accepted her rages as part of our life together without trying to forestall them by behaving differently.'

'There won't be any real reason for us to have to do things differently, will there? We can go on just as we are – take it in turns to visit each other, have our cake, slice after slice and when that's finished, bake up another.'

'I think this is the first time in my life that I've dared to admit that I'm happy now, this minute.'

'Could I prick the bubble of your euphoria, just for a moment, and ask you to relinquish a little more of the rug. I've got one cold ear.'

'Happily.'

Edmund lay beside her in the dark that night, fully thawed out and thinking that middle-age could have the edge on youth in some respects, for one's optimism was by then tamed to sensible proportions and any delights that came one's way were seen as a glorious bonus rather than as rights. He turned to Amelia to see if she had any thoughts on the matter of rights, but she was sound asleep, breathing gently and regularly, her ivory-white face tucked into his neck. Breathing . . . The room smelt of paraffin warmth, of clean sheets and saltily of sex.

Two days later, when the roads had been cleared, Johnnie sat with Sofia in the pinkish teatime light of the drawing room, discussing Xenia's immediate needs. They had agreed, with her doctor's approval, that she should go to a nursing home for a couple of weeks, where she wouldn't be perpetually thinking of things which needed doing, and could have a proper rest, following which, Johnnie would take her for a holiday. Xenia, in a semi-sedated state, had vaguely agreed to the proposal. She was now standing on the landing in her nightdress, wondering if it were lunchtime or suppertime, staring at the crooked picture of the almshouses in the snow, unable to remember when or where she had bought it, while downstairs, Sofia was rising from amongst the cabbage-embroidered cushions, drawing a vast red cashmere shawl around her shoulders and saying: 'Well, that's settled then. I shall go and make arrangements for us to visit tomorrow to check whether it is suitable for 'er. It is a semi-religious institution. I 'ope she will like that.'

Xenia heard Sofia's footsteps in the hall, heard the tinkling of the bracelets as she dialled and her voice, muffled as if she were at a great distance.

''Allo? Is that St Cecilia's Retreat?'

Xenia's head began miraculously to clear. She knew that Johnnie was downstairs, planning a holiday for them both. She knew that Edmund had gone to be with Amelia. That, strangely, didn't seem to matter any more in the slightest.

She could see in her mind's eye the group of faces frozen round the kitchen table on the day of the party, shocked. With a slightly crooked smile she straightened the painting. She expected that they would all take her more seriously from now on.

PAINTING OUT OSCAR

The sight of you is good for sore eyes.

Jonathan Swift,
A Complete Collection of Polite and Ingenious Conversation
(dialogue 1) 1738

Chapter One

An ivory face framed with sallow hair pressed close to the window and watched the morning. Mrs Lewis passed most of her long days just watching. Her eyes merely recorded, her brain filing the images to no great purpose since she rarely wondered about what she saw or imagined about what she had not. Even comparisons were an effort for her.

A white car pulled up outside the cottage next door and she was startled by the rare description that fluttered through her vacancy: that the car resembled an upturned bathtub.

The occupants of the car were the next-door neighbour Oscar Mitty and an unknown woman in a red jacket and they appeared to argue briefly before Oscar climbed from the car, dressed in the weather-beaten black leathers he wore for riding his motorbike. Mrs Lewis had heard him leave on the bike earlier that morning, not long after his wife had gone to work. He now strode up the damp brick path in the fine spring drizzle and out of her field of vision, a roll of plastic bin bags beneath his arm. She heard him let himself in and the door slam. The unknown woman stayed at the wheel of the car, pulling the rear-view mirror into a more convenient position for fluffing up her dark hair with her fingertips.

The woman was the only moving object in view so Mrs Lewis sipped instant coffee from a Charles and Diana mug and continued to watch. She was unsure how this piece of commemorative pottery had come into her ownership. On the mornings when she was conscious enough to notice its poor design, she intended to donate it to the Help the Aged shop but a fog came down upon her before she ever managed to get it outside the door and so it continued in her possession. A white cat joined her at the windowsill, staring with her. The woman in the car tapped her fingers on the wheel, perhaps with impatience or to music which Mrs Lewis could not hear, bent forward to retrieve something from the floor, leant her head back on the headrest and stretched her arms, shifting about irritably.

Half an hour elapsed before Mrs Lewis heard the latch click and she saw Oscar return down the path, laden with bags. The woman leapt out to help him, supervising the loading into the boot. They were hurrying, maladroitly knocking into each other, silent and eager to be gone. Oscar Mitty cracked his head on the hatch and stopped to rub his scalp, ruffling the straight blond hair, now rat's-tailed by the soft rain. The woman reached up to kiss him, but caught sight of the vigilant face framed between the threadbare curtain linings at the window of the larger house, thought better of it and glowered. She drove off fast, leaving Oscar to fetch more cardboard boxes from the house. He loaded these into his own car and then he too drove away. Mrs Lewis sighed. Their houses were at the bottom of a dead-end lane, on the outskirts of the small town of Bellhurst; it was unlikely there would be more movement till lunch time when Beatrice Mitty returned home.

Seen through the faulty panes of the kitchen window, the blackbird on the bird table outside appeared to four-year-old Seb as a monstrous, distorted fairground raven. Letting out a histrionic shriek, he threw himself beneath the table. Bea put down her pencil, exasperated; the free Friday afternoons away from the job at the Bellhurst Bookshop were sacrosanct and she'd hoped to salvage a morsel of that particular afternoon by drawing Seb. He'd been still for precious few seconds since his mother Agnes Spring, needing time for research into her psyche with a healer, had importunately deposited him on Bea, preventing her from getting on with the small painting she had in progress.

Bea, coming up to thirty-one, had no children of her own and was neither particularly regretful nor overjoyed by the fact, finding children very much as she found adults: interesting, loveable, cantankerous or boring and treated them accordingly, making few allowances for age. Seb was an energetic and intelligent child possessed of all these characteristics, displaying them in dizzying rotation, but his beautiful oval face, surrounded by chestnut curls, was disfigured by a perpetual expression of fury. Bea discerned real fear in the howls and came down to his level on the floor to give him a comforting hug and determine the cause of the uproar.

'Look! Look!' He pointed a shaking finger at the window. She followed the line of his eye, saw the distorted bird behind the wavering surface of the old glass and patiently explained to him what the problem was and how it came about.

'If you stand on the table, you'll be able to see through the top of the window, where the glass is new, that it's just any ordinary blackbird.'

Clutching her hand as he did so, an exaggerated expression of fear on his face, he ducked up and down, making the bird alternately shrink and swell till he was satisfied that she was right.

During the course of that afternoon, Agnes having left him at one o'clock and it was now nearly four, Bea had entertained Seb with painting, stories and letting him help her prepare a lamb stew for Oscar's supper. She had coated his hands with gouache and helped him make white hand prints in the centre of the black squares of the chequerboard floor tiles. It had the pleasing effect, not wasted on Seb, of a small person having

3

walked on his hands from the door to the sink. The drizzle having stopped she then suggested he came with her to the end of the garden so they could hang out the washing and perhaps see a squirrel or two on the way.

'No!' he'd shouted vehemently, 'I'm frightened of squirrels! I get nightmares if I see squirrels!'

'Well, what shall we do then?'

'If you'd knowed I was coming, you'd have got me a video, wouldn't you?'

'No, I wouldn't have. The video machine is broken.'

Seb, having denied himself a tantrum so far that day, now threw a whopper.

'I'm 'sterical, I'm 'sterical!' he screamed, 'I *need* a video! I want *Dan Vard and the Children of Doom!*'

Bea weathered this by pretending exaggerated horror, as if watching a melodrama, impressed by the stage effects but ultimately dispassionate, knowing she could bring down the curtain when sufficiently stimulated. However, she was a kindly and quite patient person and having got him to giggle, made a house beneath the table as a distraction, draping it with a tartan blanket secured by a dictionary and a heavy cooking pot to provide some dark privacy for him. He played there for a while with a green rubber snake, hissing and snarling gutturally as he circled with it in an intricate Celtic lacework pattern, first clockwise then widdershins round each table leg. It was then that he had suddenly spotted the bird outside on the bird table and the screams began again.

Once comforted, Seb feigned exhaustion and curled up in front of the stove on the rush mat, apparently asleep. Bea had seized the moment and commenced a drawing. Seb was small for his age and with his eyes shut unrealistically tightly, he had looked almost feminine.

'Not one of the lads,' she thought as she explored the satisfying curve of his cheek, the roundness of his arm with a 3B pencil. She was reminded of her younger brother Patrick at the same age and the miseries of sharing a bedroom with him. Once, having stolen one of her precious drawing books of strange cartoon-like happenings, Patrick had scribbled a large 'P' in red wax crayon in the centre of each page. She could hear in her mind's ear his howls and recall his raspberry-coloured face as he shook the chair on which she had stood on tiptoe, punishing him for his misdeed by posting all his Lego pieces out of the bedroom window. The sense of outrage at the desecration was still faintly present more than twenty years later.

Theirs had been a childhood of constant disruptions as their father, Tom Kerepol, who had lost an eye in an accident in the Navy, sought to earn a post-naval living. They had accompanied him unwillingly among alien corn, moaning up silver ladders and groaning down unpromising snaky paths. He had worn a black eyepatch since the accident and the children saw him as a thinner but still hopelessly unreliable Captain Pugwash.

Bea had found the frequent upheavals of house moving deeply worrying. Melting away from the disordered rooms with which she had only recently become familiar, hating their denuded windows and wading knee-deep through scrumpled newspapers, she sought refuge in garden shed or attic where she sat on the floor and drew anything that came to hand, becoming absorbed in the fatly ridiculous curves of elderly teapot or the metallic intricacies of egg whisk. Brown-overalled men tramped past, her mother called distractedly for her to come and look after Patrick, and her father sang continuously – Zarastro's 'O Isis und Osiris' from the *Magic Flute*, nursery rhymes, the 'Ballad of Lucy Jordan' and 'Sweet Lass of Richmond Hill'. She ignored them all till it was time to close the door behind them and follow the van.

Memories of the family's earlier homes were defined by the bedrooms and whether or not she'd been forced to share them with Patrick: the first, a square attic in London, its window fitted with nursery bars from which she had gnawed all the chipped cream paint; the last the large dark room in the ancient

Canterbury house with a tilting, oak-planked floor down which marbles rolled into inaccessibility beneath the chest of drawers. There, aged ten, she had poked imploring letters through the cracks in the floorboards, addressed to her private, imaginary female deity Freda, pleading that she wouldn't have to share a room with Patrick again. Freda occupied the place taken in other children's lives by their teddy bears or their best friends. Bea had given up making best friends since they always stayed behind when she was moved on. The prayers to Freda had been answered almost immediately, for they moved yet again to a larger house with an ample amount of bedrooms, twice more in fact, before Bea had reached fourteen.

Her mother's Aunt Maude Cadwell then died ... it was a family dominated by aunts of several generations and in Bea's dreams, Aunt Maude's bulging greyish-ginger appearance had become confused with the large tan-coloured pigskin bag she habitually carried, bulging with leaflets and the agendas of feminist meetings. It was the feminism which decided her on leaving her nieces a sum of money and one house each from an eccentric portfolio of properties haphazardly sprinkled about Kent. The less fortunate male relations received a shelf of books each from her library to remember her by.

Jane Kerepol had come off slightly better than her sisters Nest and Isla. Aunt Maude had been worried by her marriage to such a particularly impecunious and erratic naval officer and her inheritance was a tall weather-boarded house in the High Street of Bellhurst. The ground floor was taken up by a rambling and chronically untidy ironmonger's shop and the garden was divided into two, half being taken up by a yard where lawn mowers were serviced and water butts, garden seats and a dispiriting collection of garden ornaments — sad grey concrete cats and lugubrious toads — were sold. In the half of the garden which went with the three-storey living quarters there was a quince tree, gloriously covered that afternoon when they first saw it, with furred, citrus yellow, bullet-hard fruit.

Here Jane Kerepol had at last assumed authority, as Aunt Maude had hoped she would. Jane had been extraordinarily patient with their wandering, penury-with-prospects existence but had at last become concerned by her offspring's continuously disrupted education. (Bea's confusion over the chronology of the Celtic, Roman, Saxon and Viking invasions of Britain and which of them had worn horned helmets had begun to irritate Tom.) Flushed with ownership and with a substantial improvement to her private bank balance, she felt it high time she called the tune.

'You can do what you like, Tom, but I'm going to live here with the children. This is the last move I ever intend to make.'

So they had moved out of a smelly chicken farm near Canterbury and into trim little Bellhurst. When the lease on the ironmonger's shop had run out some months later and old Jeremiah Hoad the ironmonger had retired, the family were not entirely surprised when Tom Kerepol announced his intention to buy up the remaining stock and continue the business. He had been distressed by the surreal arrangements of the store rooms and shop windows where moulting doormats and quivers of broom handles hobnobbed with seed trays containing incontinent bags of cat litter, mousetraps, gimlets and hatchets. He set about with naval precision to remove the extraneous without disturbing the charm and order was achieved. Although he had not been expected to stick at it, the business prospered when, at Jane's instigation, he started to sell French enamelled cooking pots and shining kitchen knives. Upstairs, the kitchen windows were perpetually steamed up by simmering cauldrons of plum chutney and quince cheese and Jane was happy, writing cookery articles for magazines aimed at the new young country-dwellers who had poured out of London in the eighties looking for farmhouses to do up and space to breed. Tom was possessed of a fine baritone voice and joined both the church and local amateur choirs, sang his heart out and encouraged his children to do the same.

Patrick and Bea's relationship grew less scratchy as they matured; he found her to be a reliable confidante and she discovered in him a variety of loopy humour which wonderfully defused the bouts of overintensity that so used to puzzle her mother. They escaped the incessant busyness upstairs by heading for the store rooms where, happily inhaling the delectable atmosphere of tarred string and paraffin, they played cribbage on an upturned packing case or went to the workshop where Patrick tinkered with a derelict lawn mower and Bea drew studies of Patrick tinkering.

Patrick was soon packed off to board while Bea attended the extant grammar school in the town, her seventh school, and after a while, discerning no imminent lapse in her father's enthusiasm for his new trade, decided this time they might possibly be staying put and cautiously bothered to make friends, the first of whom had been Agnes.

When they were younger, Bea had found the relationship a little claustrophobic. Agnes had found it difficult to accept diversification in friendships and had been apt to sulk possessively if Bea invited other people along on their jaunts up to London to shop in Camden Market or the cinema. There had been childish ruffles: Agnes had not turned up to Bea's fifteenth birthday party. She'd been unable to decide what to wear and had sat on the floor of the bathroom at home, damp with self-pitying tears. It never occurred to her that her non-arrival at the party mattered as much to Bea as it did to herself and that Bea would be hurt. Out of pique at a tactless remark of Bea's, she had let the cat out of the bag about underage drinking at one of the local pubs, with the result that both of them were put under a severe curfew; she'd also stolen Bea's first mascara and a tape of the Wonderstuff. Consequences were not her strong point.

So they had picked and poked at each other's half-fledged selves, then huddled close together again for comfort and somehow the rows smoothed themselves over, their relationship swinging from the ecstatic to the petulant and back again throughout their schooldays, continuing on the same footing even now.

They made an odd, contrary pair: Agnes with inky black hair, slate grey eyes and the demeanour of a wayward china doll, was small and giggle-prone, a clothes-twitcher, a fidget. Bea was tallish and fair, that's how she saw herself, no more. She was unhappy about her feet (too big) and sad about the nose (not straight) but had the common sense to realise that the sum of the whole was generally not unpleasing. To others, her enviably slim, high-breasted figure resembled a gilded gothic effigy, or maybe a cathedral saint stepped down recently from its niche. The narrow nose, only a trifle long and due to an accident with a hockey stick, just very slightly crooked, had the effect of emphasising the strong regularity of the rest of her features. The clear blue gaze was considering, amused, sometimes apt to narrow in deep isolating concentration but just as frequently widened into sudden all-embracing eiderdowns of laughter. Beneath the apparent dreamy self-containment ran a deep rift of artfully concealed timidity and a will, which whenever put to the test, proved to be of iron.

Agnes had swirled off gleefully to London for a course in design and illustration. She'd married in her third year, and then after a short time, unmarried. Seb had arrived eighteen months later, cramping her style somewhat; finding it impossible to make ends meet as a single mother/freelance illustrator, she had been forced into an ignominious return to her mother and a year or so before, she and Bea had resumed their edgy friendship.

Agnes seemed unchanged, still attractive, flirty and untidy, still balancing chronic unreliability with apparent good humour and spontaneity and whose sexuality was all she thought she had to offer to the world. After a hectic bout of activity with the available local talent, during the course of which she caused two fights and a suicide bid, she surprised everyone by a further attempt at domesticity and mystifyingly married plain Phil Spring, works manager of the small ironworks owned by Bea's husband, Oscar.

Bea put her pencil down and yawned. Seb had woken up and disappeared beneath the table again, muttering dark things to himself. He was aware of the closeness of Bea's long, black Lycra-covered legs invading his private space and was intrigued by the shoeless feet, the tiny hole showing white flesh at the side of the rounded black calf. Forgetting that the legs were attached to a sentient being somewhere up above he was overcome by an urgent need to sink his teeth, experimentally, into the ankle. Bea shrieked and was jerked most painfully into the present.

'You little beast, Seb! How would you like it if I bit you that hard?' Wondering what the hell had happened to Agnes, she limped exaggeratedly across to the radio, fiddling till she found a Mozart concerto, hoping that flute and harp would soothe both herself and the little savage sulking silently in embarrassment beneath the table, aware that he had gone too far but unable to apologise. The back door crashed open and Agnes blew into the kitchen with a blast of cold air, her skirts all prancy-pouncy and apologies flying from her lips like confetti but with less substance.

'So calm in here, Bea! I'm parched with so much talking. Are you making tea? Such an interesting session with Ludmilla.' She threw a couple of plastic carriers and a shoulder bag down in the middle of the table, as if claiming territory, and rubbed her hands. 'I've been regressing. You should try it sometime. Do you know, I never realised what an unhappy childhood I had – but you're looking a bit boot-faced – I really am sorry I was so long. Where's Seb?'

'Under the table. If I'm boot-faced it's because he's bitten my ankle.' Bea stuck her foot up on the table and stretching the patch of tights around the offending area, indignantly pointed out a little semicircle of baby tooth marks. 'Should I get a tetanus injection, do you think? Does he do that sort of thing often?'

Agnes looked mortified for no more than a second, then became defiant.

'Well, yes, he did bite someone at nursery school, but it was pure frustration, you see. He had such a difficult birth and is so very intelligent, but he can't always explain what he needs.'

'He needs a good smack.'

Agnes ignored this and sipped her tea. 'Ludmilla wants me to take him to her for a session. She thinks she ought to meet him.'

There were times when Bea found it hard to take Agnes seriously and she now had an unguarded attack of censoriousness.

'Agnes! I'm sure he's forgotten being born by now . . . and do you think you should muddle children up with those sorts of people? Has she any qualifications, this Ludmilla?'

'She doesn't need qualifications – she's psychic!'

'That's what I mean. Oh, never mind! Perhaps one *can* remember one's birth – I used to get nightmares when I had a temperature, of trying to get out of the inside of this very tightly wound ball of red knitting wool. Have a biscuit?' Bea's voice had an edge of impatience to it which Agnes picked up immediately.

'But you don't understand! You're calm and ordered, and *evaluating*! I'm so muddled all the time. Don't be ratty with me – you sound just like Phil!' Seb emerged from his hiding place and she picked him up and hauled him onto her lap, smoothing the curls and twitching the collar out of his jumper. He snuggled into her, casting petulant sideways glances at Bea from beneath his frowning eyebrows.

'No, I'm not ratty, Agnes. It's just that I don't think other people are much good at helping unravel oneself; I feel it's something that's got to be done alone. Does Ludmilla charge a lot?'

'Only twenty pounds a session.'

'Good grief! That sounds rather expensive just to be told you had an unhappy childhood. Couldn't you remember on your own whether you had an unhappy childhood or not? I can remember nearly everything about mine.'

'Lucky old you! I have great voids in my memory. I can't remember why I married Phil. All I'm doing is trying to get some of *your* order into *my* life. I had a double session actually, then I had to buy a new bra in Parden. Look! Matching knicks as well!' She produced a tiny handful of crunchy black lace and wafted it about. 'But you did get time to do some drawing, I see. I know you like to sit and draw.' She rarely saw any of the secretive Bea's work and peering critically at the sketch book, open at the firm and unfaltering outlines of the drawing of Seb asleep on the floor, felt forced to acknowledge the truth: 'Oh Bea! It's so very, very good! I still don't understand why you didn't come to art school with me, when you'd got the place and everything. Couldn't you have waited to marry Oscar till afterwards? It seems such a waste.'

Bea considered this while making a fresh pot of tea. She was unsure why she had spun off the track so suddenly but had an inkling that it was due to lack of confidence. She'd had a shy resistance to being taught and from the beginning the art lessons at the various schools she had attended had seemed a form of sadism. At primary school she had been required to paint pictures with titles such as 'A Windy Day' or 'My Family' on vast sheets of coloured paper, with big stiff brushes in the garish poster paints supposedly beloved by children but which to her were anathema. Wistfully wishing the subject could have been 'In the Hall of the Demon King', she used to fold the intimidating sheet into a more manageable size, eventually producing with great trouble some small drawing in the corner. Pig-headed obstinacy and sheer ability were eventually harnessed to produce the required portfolio of work to gain a place at art school.

But then she met Oscar. Beautiful, amiable Oscar. Oscar who

had come to visit Tom in the shop one morning with a new range of iron door fittings copied from eighteenth-century originals. Bea, luminous, lissom and seventeen, had entered the shop as they were discussing prices and had been violently smitten. Oscar, then aged twenty-two, self-confident and charming and already showing signs of the good businessman he was to become, had similarly been attracted. He had an agreeably childish streak in him and she had enjoyed this and besottedly mothered him, long past the time when he should have grown up.

They had, Bea eventually came to admit, been attracted like Narcissus, look to look, in love with being in love and also revelling in the attention they received as a pretty couple riding about the countryside on Oscar's motorbike, a princess and her matching child-knight errant. Tom had been alarmed by Bea's sudden awakening and the sight of her searching her mother's cupboards for unwanted pots and pans rang warning bells. Informed by an excited Jane of their intention to marry, he had been disappointed and gruff.

'Oh God! I always knew it was pointless educating women!'

They had married the autumn after Bea had at least taken her A levels – Art, English and History – that much she had conceded to her unhappy father, but once the excitement of getting married was over, she appeared to her family to have happily gone to sleep. She continued to paint and draw in private, never sure that what she achieved had any point other than her own satisfaction, but rather expecting that one day everything would fall into place. What she did was a habit of consuming interest, a near-obsessive necessity. Oscar was encouraging about her abilities in the early days, although he initially found it disturbing that she had any serious interests other than himself. His own mother had not been so distracted. He had jealously watched the perimeter of the area of what she called her 'work', looking for a gap through which to pour himself. When he found that she wouldn't even try to exhibit or sell anything, he began to lose interest, unable to understand that she was either shy of the opinions of other people, or uninterested in them and that to her the drawings and paintings were never more than preparatory work.

Agnes, catching the delicate bay-leaf-and-garlic waft from the lamb stew simmering in Bea's oven, remembered that she had forgotten to buy the sausages for Phil's supper and setting Seb on his feet rather abruptly, downed her second cup of tea in a hurry. Seb set up a howl. He had enjoyed the afternoon spent manipulating Bea's attention and he had to be manhandled into the child seat in Agnes's scraped red Citroën.

'I wish I had a pair of handcuffs!' his mother moaned, dodging a flailing foot as she attempted to strap him in. 'Leg-irons, even. 'Bye, dearest Bea, and thanks a million for looking after him. I honestly don't know what I'd do without you.'

Once the turbulent pair had departed, the kitchen assumed a disappointed air, as if a party had been cancelled at short notice. Bea cursed herself for mean-spiritedness in having wished to be by herself that afternoon. She really rather enjoyed the friction that Agnes's visits caused and clearing away the pencils and paper, she felt a prickle of guilt at her earlier snappiness.

She hovered over the table and picked at the succulent pot plant in its centre, sharply digging a fingernail into one of its fleshy leaves, leaving a little crescent tattoo which would survive for years. She was thinking about Agnes's phrase 'calm and ordered'. If she was, it was due to a massive effort of will, not a natural instinct, it being something of a battle to keep things running smoothly in order to fit in the drawing. She couldn't tap her disturbing visual imagination unless at least one room in the house was in perfect order and if Oscar was about and unoccupied, he wouldn't stand for her shutting herself away for long. She was amazed at his ingenuity in finding new methods of disruption, never realising she been made to believe over the years that she was at fault in wanting to continue painting.

She pulled down the yellow blinds and laid the table for their supper, using the remaining plates of her Great Aunt Maude's green-and-black Art Deco dinner service and placing a fat green glass bowl of primroses in the centre. It was Friday night, when she and Oscar usually ate early before going out for a drink at a local wine bar or in the summer rode off on Oscar's old motorbike to some more distant place to meet friends and chat. Black oily hand prints in the kitchen and pieces of engine soaking in petrol in the washing-up bowl were tolerable inconveniences, fair exchange for the few hours of peace she gained in which to paint while he took the bike to pieces in the garden. The friends who shared his interest in the more elegant older machines, the classic Triumphs, Nortons and BSAs, were scornful of the gross, modern Japanese bikes, snobbishly calling them 'fitted-kitchens'.

Bea checked the stew and opened a bottle of white wine, poured out a glassful and carried it upstairs with her. Their house, Fleming Cottage, on the outer edge of Bellhurst, was a two-up, two-down with a bathroom added downstairs, but the rooms were quite large and she had made it very comfortable, revelling in its permanence.

The bedroom seemed unnaturally tidy. She had left before Oscar that morning, leaving him humped beneath the bedclothes mumbling that he didn't have to be in at work till ten. Bea grinned to see that the bed had been made and that there was no sign of dirty socks or shirts. Was it possible that he had discovered the true use of the laundry basket after all these years? She changed her paint-smeared jersey for a short blue-green sweater – she liked strong, bright colours – dabbed foundation on a small spot on her chin and made up her eyes, light-heartedly humming 'Waltzing Matilda', one of her father's favourites. She brushed her shoulder-length hair and twisted it up into a blonde tortoiseshell clip, turning her head this way and that and deciding that her nose looked less crooked from three-quarters right before returning to the kitchen still humming happily, to read and wait.

Immersed in Angela Carter's *The Bloody Chamber*, Bea did not at first notice that it was getting late. She enjoyed reading almost as much as drawing but as a child had found it difficult to progress from fairy stories with their 'and so she married the prince' endings to seek more sophisticated denouements. Why should 'lived happily ever after' be considered a cop-out? Surely the suspension of disbelief was the whole point of fiction? Anyway, it stood to reason that happy endings occurred in reality with the same frequency as sad ones, didn't it? Oscar read mainly SAS memoirs whose covers all depicted the same black chin-jutting silhouette of a man behind whom a flash of lightning lit up a scene of destruction. He would quite happily have bought a copy of *Barchester Towers* had it had an explosion on the cover.

Oscar was usually home by seven-thirty and it was now eight-fifteen. He might be held up at the ironworks, or the smithy as he liked to call it, though it had expanded way beyond being just a smithy since he had taken it over. By nine-thirty a narrow cinch of unease settled around her waist, tightening gradually till at ten o'clock she telephoned Agnes and enquired whether Phil knew if Oscar was held up somewhere.

'Phil says Oscar booked himself out of the office all day today,' said Agnes. 'He's probably gone to visit a client in London and forgotten to tell you.' She paused and relayed another message from Phil. 'He hasn't been in all day. Apparently he often visits clients on Fridays.'

'Does he? I didn't know.' But then Bea heard what she thought was Oscar's bike humming along the lane. 'Panic over! He's coming now. Agnes, I'm sorry I was so bad-tempered this afternoon.'

'Oh, don't think about it! You were rather controlled under the circumstances! See you soon, Bea. 'Bye.'

The anxiety dissipated, she hurried to put on the stew again, heard strangely uncertain footsteps coming up the path followed by a fumbling sound at the door and before she could get there to open it, the squeak and flop of something being thrust through the letter box. The letter, with 'Bea' scrawled on the envelope, lay on the coconut matting of the passage. She flung open the door and called out 'Oscar! Oscar?' but the rider was already astride the bike and off into the dark.

Back in the kitchen, heart thumping and wondering why she had not noticed that neither his car nor his bike had been outside the house when she returned from work at lunch time, she laid the letter down on the table in the place she had laid for Oscar's supper, lining up its upper and lower edges with the grain of the wood and the sides with the knife and fork and staring at it transfixed, as if expecting it to open itself. She knocked back another glass of wine then, fumble-fingered, ripped open the envelope.

'Dearest Bea, I know this is the cowardly way out, but ...' Her eyes blurred and odd words leapt out like jeering sprites from the bramble-patch of writing: sorry, selfishness, children, art, Andrea. Art? He had always patronisingly referred to her drawing as 'your *Art*', with a capital A, as if it were a tiresome hobby. The letter was half diatribe against herself, half *mea culpa*, and ran on, and on. Selfishness? It seemed unclear whether he referred to her or himself. She was disbelieving and indignant. Had she not spent the early years of their marriage working for him, helping as best she could with his new but wavering enterprise? And later the tedious years in the book shop to provide a backup to his fluctuating income? They had never spoken of children, that she could recall. At least he had never, in any way, indicated that he wanted any or that they should address the situation and she had always felt relieved, knowing that he wouldn't have been able to cope with competing for her attention with a baby. As for herself, she'd been frightened of the idea – frightened that she would never again have a moment to herself in which to paint. Yes, she supposed that amounted to selfishness. Andrea? It appeared he had left her for someone called Andrea. She combed her mind for Andreas but could only think of one. 'Andreary Bullshit', the name she and Agnes had coined for the suffocatingly over-feminine woman for whom Oscar had made a pair of wrought-iron gates. Agnes had designed them, with elegant greyhound forms loping across the tops, and she, Oscar, Phil and Agnes, had gone over to Sussex together to see them hung in place at the entrance to Andrea Bullingden's rambling Victorian house. 'Actually,' Andrea had announced in her strange, falling little voice, 'it's not Victorian, it's William the Fourth.' Andrea Bullingden, who had totally ignored Agnes's part in the work and who had lavished praise and cow eyes on Oscar. Andrea who had left them drinking mugs of tea in the kitchen while she led away Oscar, by the arm, to inspect a further small gate she wished to replace. They had got bored waiting and nosed into the cupboards, finding in one of them a neatly stacked green glass wall of empty gin bottles.

Bea's first reaction, after the shock, was the uncorking of several years' worth of vintage rage which until that moment she had been unaware had been stored in her cellar. It seethed about her till she felt imminent suffocation. She picked up the fork from Oscar's place at the table and jabbed it through all three sheets of the letter with such force that she pinned it to the kitchen table; she clasped the rage tight and would not let it go again. The air began to fill with greasy smoke as the stew scorched, but she drank another glass of wine before turning off the gas and opening the window. She cleared the table, putting away Oscar's untouched knife and methodically tidying the kitchen. She took the shed key down from its place above the door and went outside, carrying the burnt and cooling stew pot.

In the shed lay a wooden tool chest which had belonged to Oscar's father. She switched on the light, lifted its lid and with difficulty shook the dead, stiffening stew onto the gleaming, greased and lovingly cared-for contents. Small gobbets of burnt meat stuck to the saw teeth and the handles of the graded sets of screwdrivers. Thick and glutinous tomato dripped into the motor of the electric drill. Caramelised carrot and barley clung about the interior, bejewelling the tobacco tins of nails and screws. The dusty light bulb popped and in the darkness Bea shut the lid, locked up the shed and returned down the garden path, sobbing.

'After revenge, what is there?' she wondered, and went to bed where the tears came faster; loss, hurt, regret, self-pity, but, oddly enough, no despair, merely a terrible sense of time wasted. 'What has happened to Bea?' she imagined people asking in the months to come. 'Oh, she's bravely soldiering on alone,' she heard the answer. 'I will *not* bravely soldier on alone. I will not become a cliché. I will not be just another discarded wife,' she promised herself, through clenched teeth. She had accepted the fact, if not the reasons of his going, with a strange rapidity.

By the early hours of the morning she slept, a little, and dreamt in chasing clouds of colours and shapes, that she was part of a prayer meeting, evangelical in mode, out on a shingle beach. She wore, as did the other worshippers, a white sailcloth robe which billowed stiffly about her.

'Allelujah!' they all cried, raising their arms to the hot blue sky. 'Allelujah!' Out of the lapping waves arose her own particular goddess, wearing a straw hat trimmed with poppies and cornflowers, resembling a garden statue of a nubile nymph with folds of muslin carved discreetly about her hips.

'What is my name?' called the goddess and it seemed to Bea that she was being personally addressed, so she replied:

'Freda. Your name is Freda!'

The goddess grinned, showing sharp stone teeth and sank back beneath the water, her hat floating off, twirling round and round in the scummy foam.

Oscar lolled exhausted on the large leather sofa, his boots off, his pale blond hair being fondly smoothed by Andrea of the man-drowning eyes. The room about him, Andrea's drawing room, was decorated in film director chic. Each item in it was large, but spare and singular. Space echoed about a wooden horse placed by the long windows, a fairground relic whose hectic colouring had been tastefully burnished back to leave a ghostly pink, green and blue-stained grain. The heavy coffee table, carved and silver-leafed, was placed just too far from the sofa to be of use in serving coffee. Pale polished floors shuddered away from contact with Oscar's cast-off leather jacket. The dark green walls were almost hidden behind gargantuan paintings in distressed gilt frames; poor, old copies of indifferent seventeenth-century paintings, perhaps even copies of copies, in which Brobdingnagian nymphs lumbered through their painted woodland, heavy brocade draperies floating impossibly lightly about the flaking acres of their flat, cracked and uncleaned flesh. Andrea's ex-husband, a film producer, had, she mournfully complained, '. . . left her with all the tat.' Oscar was past taking notice of the decor, was in any case more familiar with the blue-and-white striped silk tent that was Andrea's bedroom upstairs.

All day he had been in an agony of fluctuating guilt and excitement. After Bea's departure for work that morning he had biked over to Andrea's house near Battle, returning in her car to collect his possessions and refused, out of some misplaced delicacy which Andrea did not pretend to understand, to let her come inside and help. Bewildered by his own decision to leave Bea, he felt half penitentially that her home should not be violated by Andrea's presence in it, however brief; he was unused to complicated emotions and his feeling that Andrea should not come inside made him angry and confused.

His life with Bea, all twelve years of it, had been so stable, so still. She had made so few demands on him that he had at times felt perhaps it was because she had thought him incapable of fulfilling them. It was this general tolerance that had annoyed him most. He'd tidied the bed and just to show her that he was capable of it, unthinkingly rammed his dirty socks, pants and yesterday's shirt into the laundry basket. All that he was certain of at that moment was his inability to resist Andrea.

One last look and out he came, seen by no one except the pale, incurious eyes of Mrs Lewis at the window of the house next door. They had driven back to Sussex in their respective cars, heading, for the time being, in the same emotional direction.

It wasn't until later in the afternoon that Oscar had become so unflatteringly silent, white-faced and haunted that Andrea had had to tease out of him that he had as yet made no attempt to tell Bea either that he was having an affair or that he intended to leave her. Becoming whimperingly tearful, she insisted that he should do it at once and he had eventually ridden off into the evening's slight drizzle to do the impossible deed.

'You've done the right thing. You know you've done the right thing,' she whispered in his ear, 'for you and me. How brave you were to go and tell her now. How did she take it? Was she hysterical?' She rubbed his cheek with hers, painfully entangling her dangling silver earring with his small gold one, not knowing that he had floundered, panicked and instead of telling Bea in person, had gone to his office desk in the ironworks to write the lame and infamous letter, trying desperately to dredge up slights and injuries he knew he had not felt at the time, to find faults in her that he had never previously imagined were important. He knew, as he lay on the sofa with Andrea, that he had behaved appallingly, but also, rather smugly, that he could not on that particular day have done otherwise. He turned to Andrea's drooping eyelids, inhaled her civet scent and sank, choking only weakly, to the bottom of the well.

Chapter Two

It was April Fools' Day, in the early pearl of the morning with the sun not yet risen when Bea awoke. Nauseous with tiredness, eyes gummed together with rubbery sleep and dried tears, her vision was hazy but her mind painfully clear. She washed her face and opening the window, flung Oscar's blue, duck-shaped sponge as far as she could into the back garden. She dressed in the first garment that came to hand out of the wardrobe – a long scarlet evening dress, a plain tube of stretchy satin that she had last worn for their tenth-wedding-anniversary dinner in London. She draped an old gardening jacket across her shoulders; its pockets held bits of string and crumbs of earth, a half-empty packet of perpetual spinach seed and one of the ubiquitous bits of broken blue-and-white china that litter old gardens, which she'd saved because there was a transfer print of a pheasant's head on it.

Downstairs, barefoot, she put on the kettle and set about washing the floor on her hands and knees, expunging with vigour yesterday's splash of stew, a smear of jam and Seb's hopeful white hand prints. Yesterday was March, today was April. Ritually dressed, she ritualised the unnecessary housework in order to pass through the time, hoping to hold disorder at arm's length. Naming the months, the days, the hours and minutes would keep everything in proportion. It was now a quarter to seven and moving with slow dignity she emptied the bucket down the sink and ceremoniously made tea. She did not care for China tea, but the occasion demanded it. She ate a knobbly Lincoln biscuit while staring blankly out through the undulating glass to the garden, childishly scraping the moulded nodules off the top of the biscuit with her teeth.

The sun was up now. The stealthy frosts had started to retreat northwards like vandals on the run and the sprouting tips of shallots and the young leaves of pink fir-apple potatoes were bursting through their earthy pie-crust in the vegetable patch. Out of habit she wandered outside to inspect them, kneeling to loosen a minute feathery seedling from beneath a cramping stone and gently pushing it upright to face its future. 'I don't want to be here to help them,' she muttered. 'I don't want to hoe, water or weed the sodding things and I don't want to harvest them on my own.' It was impossible to stay here, waiting. She'd been waiting for years. It was time to leave for another place, time for something quite different.

Mrs Lewis opened her back door with a rattle and enfolded in a stook of shawls and dressing gowns, tapped hesitantly with a spoon against a tin plate, calling her cat in a faded voice which lacked any sense of urgency:

'Here, Pig. Pig. Piggy.'

The white cat arose from his spot beneath Bea's yew tree, stretched his smooth front legs, then his fat, fluffed-up hams, yawned and gathering speed, cleared the fence in one bound. Mrs Lewis saw Bea in her scarlet dress, but if she was surprised at the choice of clothes for dawn gardening, her impassive face did not show it.

'A very nice morning, Mrs Mitty,' she called formally, feeling that since their eyes had met she ought to speak to her neighbour. Bea forced the muscles of her face to produce a spasm of a smile and managed a careless wave of the hand. Mrs Lewis's appearance was as normal; untidy but not unkempt, scrubbed out rather than unclean. A small cloud passed over, abruptly switching off the yellow sun.

Indoors the clock ticked out the morning and Bea commenced a frenzied cleaning, blocking out all thoughts of Oscar's whereabouts, of his disloyalty, of his indigestible letter which still lay skewered to the table. Only ideas of the future were allowed to percolate through the sieve of practicalities and these she developed furiously. While polishing lime-encrusted taps, wiping old fly spots from windowsills and even dusting Oscar's empty desk, a plan began to form, inspired in part by the night's disordered dreaming.

At ten o'clock she telephoned her mother's younger sister, Nest, who ran a plant nursery and who had inherited, as her share of old Aunt Maude's will, a small Victorian villa near the coast, just outside the town of Fingle.

'Hello? Nest's Nursery here. Could you speak up a bit, the line seems very faint.'

'Aunt Nest? It's Bea. I need to ask you something, a favour. I'm surrounded by mega-catastrophe.'

There was a pause at the other end.

'Is that an herbaceous perennial?' enquired Nest cautiously, finding it hard to imagine that anyone should telephone her about any other subject.

'No! Aunt Nest!' Bea tried to raise her voice, but her throat contracted and cold sweat gathered on her neck at the thought of all the explaining she would have to undertake over the next few days. 'I said "catastrophe". Oscar's left me. I can't, don't want to stay here in this house. I wondered if you had rented out the Fingle house this year? If you haven't, do you think I might? I'd pay proper rent, of course.'

Nest's response was generous and immediate.

'Darling Bea! How dreadful! The sod! The unspeakable bugger!' Nest curbed herself. 'Oh my poor love! Of course you can have it. It's quite empty. It's usually advertised in the birdwatching magazine in February, but we had the deep snow then and fearful frosts and my mind was taken off it, trying to keep all the greenhouse heaters going. I only remembered yesterday, as a matter of fact. It's free for as long as you want it. I could take some time off at lunch, and take you there to have a look, to see what needs to be got in?'

Alone among the family, Nest had never been concerned or impatient with Bea's lengthy nursing of her draughtsmanship and apparent lack of progress in the art field. If the child was slow to make use of her undoubted talent, then it was because she was not yet ready to do so. She had no doubts that Bea would one day astonish them all. She was reminded rather bitterly that her own husband Ivor had left her some years before, unwilling to compete for her attention with pots of *Meconopsis horridula* and *Polemonium carneum*. Bea, to Nest, was a sleeping princess, put to sleep not by the prick of a spindle but by that prick of an Oscar. Her mind shot off tangentially, exploring the possibility of the spindle being a phallic symbol – she had attended university in an era when any object longer than it was wide was granted this doubtful Freudian smear. Perhaps the princess had encountered something nasty in the attic which had enforced her being locked away for a time ... say nine months? A gestation period of one hundred years seemed a little excessive; she needed to re-read the story in all its versions ...

'Aunt Nest? Are you still there?'

'Yes, Bea darling. I do so hate to think of you on your own at a time like this. You've told Jane, of course?'

'Not yet, but I will have to very soon. I need to borrow her car.' She was aware this sounded as if this was the sole reason for informing her mother and that her voice was tired and diminished. 'Oscar has taken ours as well as the motorbike. If I can borrow the car, I'll be over at lunch time.'

'*Au revoir* then, dearest.'

Bea slipped a long green mackintosh over the red dress and walked the half mile into the centre of Bellhurst where, shaking a little with shock at the simplicity of the start of the enterprise, she withdrew £4,000 from their joint building society account, leaving behind £15.90. 'Not enough for him to take bitch

Andreary out to dinner,' she thought, pocketing the cheque and heading with some trepidation for T. Kerepol, Ironmongers.

The remainder of the morning was filled with expressions of indignant solicitude and fist-shaking, exotic naval threats from her father peppered with offers 'to go and sort the bastard out', viciously strong coffee, hugging, general bewilderment and mud-slinging from her mother. This left Bea comforted and encouraged since it was very much the way things had forever been expressed at home, where sound and fury often took the place of significance. It was her own disaster and it would be dealt with in her own reflexive way but she felt like a dead weight on wheels, spinning off after Oscar's violent shove. 'Mum would have been happier if I'd been hysterical,' she reflected sombrely as, exhausted by their emotion, she left in the borrowed car for her aunt's house. 'She never could cope with anyone trying to contain their feelings.'

Nest stood at the end of a long glasshouse, bending over a bench repotting cuttings of a particularly dark mauve-flowered *Abutilon vitifolium*, easing them gently into larger pots and firming them down with long bony fingers. Beside her was a half-eaten ham sandwich, lightly peppered with dark specks of compost, and a half-empty glass of white wine in which a small insect floundered in its death throes. Nest, not unlike Bea in features and slim but shorter, looked up and her sharp violet-blue eyes (better than Elizabeth Taylor's, she'd been told in her youth) softened as she took in the dishevelled and woebegone appearance of her niece. She at once gave her a muddy hug but Bea felt that she would be unable to survive much more hugging and drifted unhappily up and down the central concrete path while Nest dealt with the last pot, drained the wine, and finished up her horticultural sandwich.

'There, now that's done. Shall I get Blue to get you something to eat?'

27

Bea thought of Blue's perpetually soil-filled fingernails and declined the offer.

'I'm not really hungry. I did eat breakfast and I've had a gallon or so of Mum's coffee.' She forced her voice into a conversational tone as her Aunt rinsed her hands beneath a standpipe and wiped them on her faded pink shirt, 'How is Blue?'

Blue, dark and earthy, was Nest's lover. It was accepted that he was a good few years younger than Nest. He had relinquished his earlier job as a shepherd in order to look after her, deciding that there was little difference in the jobs. He could just as well see that she ate proper meals, didn't get footrot and had her hair shorn occasionally as he could deal with a flock of sheep. Sheep also were fussed at being interrupted about their business to be dosed, dipped and clipped. He had discovered to his delight that Nest had surprisingly catholic views on sexual matters and they suited each other very well indeed, sharing also a love of fairy stories, which Nest would read to him at night after supper. He called her, affectionately, Cuckoo.

'Blue,' answered Nest fondly, 'is pricing-up pots of *Perovskia* and has quite got over his bronchitis. I'll just go round the back and tell him we're off, but we mustn't take too long ... I've got a new girl – Lucinda – on her own at the till this lunch time. She seems to be rather too chatty and is trying to gain recruits for some ecological group she's involved with. I found it quite riveting but I hope she doesn't start on the customers.'

Bea followed her, threading through the narrow paths around gravel beds tightly packed with container plants, past handwritten signs illuminating the prices, virtues and vices of the stock. The entire front garden was taken up in this way and on busy days in spring, such as today, Nest had found it necessary to introduce a one-way system round the maze to prevent the more ardent plant collectors from overflowing into the beds. Nest ignored her own warning signs and strode ruthlessly through the browsers, leaving Bea awkwardly leaping across roundabouts of ferns in her wake, dodging bamboo stakes and oncoming traffic.

Nest's house and nursery garden were on the high ground of land that some hundreds of years past had been an island but which was now merely trammelled by a tamed river and various dykes, sewers and channels. Bea's spirits lifted as they drove off in Nest's yellow van down a lane running with rivulets of water, its deeply cut banks singing with primroses. She glimpsed the expanse of marsh lying below them and the varying greens of the fields of wheat, rape and grazing dotted with sheep and lambs. The road dropped sharply down to the levels, heading for the coast and Fingle where they stopped briefly to satisfy Nest's sudden need of a Mars bar.

Driving out the other side of Fingle and taking a narrow pot-holed track across pebble-strewn fields barely coated with grass, they came first to a group of bungalows, then after half a mile of emptiness, to a small brown farmhouse, its window frames painted alternately red and yellow and surrounded by rotting sheds of corrugated iron and rusting machinery.

'That's Rumm's Farm,' Nest informed her. 'Jerry Rumm lives there. He's a nice old boy and will happily help you out if you have any difficulties. It was his grandfather who built the house I've now got, for his second wife who thought she was a cut above him, but Jerry's father hated it, sold it off and moved back into the old one. His father also refused to have electricity put in when Aunt Maude bought the new house and had it installed. The line goes right past his farm, but he wouldn't pay the extra to bring it in. Jerry has a generator. Here we are.'

A few hundred yards further still stood Nest's surprising white Victorian villa. Bearing no relation whatsoever to its surroundings, it resembled a child's drawing of a house: a weather-beaten central blue door with a square window on either side and two more symmetrically placed above, a slate roof and single central chimney from which one expected to see issuing a curling of woodsmoke. A wooden board propped against the stone wall was inscribed in dribbled green paint, 'Little Rumm'.

Bea got out of the van and stood in the scrubby, square walled garden, taking in the windswept tamarisk bushes, the pink rusting child's bicycle abandoned by a previous summer's tenants. A line of pylons, grey against the spring-blue sky, loped bleakly across the flatness, but the sky itself seemingly came down to one's feet in every direction, a broad and sweeping compensation for the lack of what most people would have called an attractive landscape and an agoraphobic's nightmare. 'As near as one can get to flying while staying earthbound,' thought Bea, gazing up at the white streak behind a toy silver airliner thousands of feet up. The area was short on trees of any height and even the telegraph poles leant drunkenly with the prevailing south-westerly wind. While she stood and stared about, suddenly alarmed by the thought of being here on her own, Nest was wrestling with the door handle.

'It seems to have jammed. I shall have to put the boot in,' said Nest, standing back to give it a hefty blow with her stout, mud-encrusted boot.

It swung open unwillingly on the third kick and Bea followed her aunt into the hall. A long, sparsely furnished sitting room lay on one side, white, rush-matted and sunny, with a pile of dusty bus timetables, local newspapers and badly folded footpath maps on the window seat. A collection of large grey-and-white pebbles stood along the upper shelf of an ornate Art Nouveau iron fireplace, along with odd bits of seaside flotsam, a gull's feather, and sea-smoothed fragments of green bottle. Cockle shells and empty sweet wrappers filled a glass bowl on the gate-legged table. On the other side of the hall there was a smaller room with the kitchen lurking dimly behind it. Nest's ideas of what was necessary for a holiday let seemed a bit odd. Bea pulled open a drawer in the mildewed post-war utility dresser and discovered eight miscellaneous corkscrews, a tin-opener, an apostle teaspoon and a lot of silverfish.

'Don't worry,' said Nest, briskly shooting up the kitchen blind and flooding the room with startling light. 'I take out all the small bits and bobs when it's empty in the winter.'

'Can I bring some of my own things?' asked Bea hopefully, hating the stained and matted rag-rug on the floor and the blackened aluminium saucepans hanging above the stove. There was grubby cream paint on the walls and a lot of chipped grey Formica.

'Of course you can. Anything you like. It's all got a bit tatty, I suppose. But quite suitable for bird-watchers.' Bea, wondering at what degree of discomfort the house would become unsuitable for the poor bird-watchers, gave a watery giggle.

Upstairs the sunniness and comparative modernity of the bathroom were cheering as was the stark but comfortable bedroom with a large iron, brass-knobbed bedstead, its castors sunk into the floorboards as if it had stood there for ever. The feeling of permanence was comforting.

'This room has a good light,' said Nest opening the other door off the landing. It gave into a square white room, with two windows hung with floor-length striped black-and-white curtains, rough pine floorboards painted black and a bed covered with a red counterpane. White wardrobe, white chair and a white painted dressing table. 'It'll do very well as a studio for you – that is, I'm presuming that the plan is to come here to paint, not sit and keen? If you *are* going to paint, then I won't charge you any rent.' She stared at her niece, the violet eyes challenging.

A room with a sense of purpose, Bea thought, standing at the sash window and staring out across the pancake land to Fingle where the church's peg-tiled roof lay long and low among the houses, like a lizard warming itself in the spring sunshine.

'No, no keening,' she agreed, turning back to re-examine the space. 'I'll work and then there won't be time to mope. And anyway, I'm more enraged than sad.' There'd been a sickening little knot in her stomach which had untied a little as Nest spoke; not having been quite aware of the idea of coming here to paint till Nest so confidently put it into words, that of course was what she'd do and this was where she would do it, living through all the mess as one lives through lunch, cutting one's toenails or any other necessity. It would end. Eventually another set of circumstances would take over, something would be achieved here and Nest's generosity was a wonderful bonus. Bea's imagination began to fly.

Outside again, the practicalities of electricity and gas bottles dealt with, the necessity of a mobile phone insisted on, Nest sat down on a low brick wall in the garden and lit a cigarette.

'I'd like to come and live here myself one day, when I've made enough money to retire. There are days when I ache to get away from all the lush and feathery greenery inland. It's so dry and hard here. Wind-blown clean and so little mud. It's quite surprising what'll grow. I'll look out some seeds for you to brighten up the garden during the summer. There's a well-sheltered spot out at the back.' Nest leant sideways and picked some young leaflets from a thorny stem, crumpling them between her fingers and holding them out for Bea to sniff. 'What does that remind you of?'

Bea obediently sniffed. 'It smells of apples! Granny Smiths in particular, slightly fake – an apple scented bubble bath or something. What is it?'

'I'm not a rose-fancier myself and the flowers are insignificant, bright pink and very tiny, but it was growing here when I came. I'm not sure what it is . . . *Rosa eglanteria*, or a *villosa* seedling perhaps? The scent is twice as strong as any I've ever come across before or since. It smells even stronger when it rains. I can't remember the name of the rose on the wall, either. Lady something . . . but there's a nice old horticultural joke about it – it's a difficult rose to please and they say it's lousy in bed but great up against the wall.' Nest watched Bea snort with laughter and nodded approvingly, chuckled herself and put out her cigarette half finished, hiding the butt beneath a stone and stood up, eager to get back to work.

Bea could smell the invisible sea behind the high-banked shingle of the sea wall in the distance, see the black silhouettes of a man and a prancing dog moving along its top, heading for the great wen of the nuclear power station. She was grateful for the pause in the day's frenetic movement and could have sat there for a while longer.

'We must get going,' urged Nest, 'much as I'd like to go for a walk. Blue and I'll pop down tomorrow evening with the things you'll need, clean sheets and blankets and such. When do you want to come over here?'

Bea gulped, breathless with the speed with which things were falling into place while Oscar's side of the bed was still virtually warm. She found it difficult to think about him, the unpalatable *fact* that he had gone off with someone else, like one of those gelatine capsules of cod-liver oil which disgustingly burst in the mouth before one can swallow them down. It was his failure to tell her in person that had been more devastating than the actual departure.

'I thought next Friday? I've got things to settle, things I need to buy.'

'Fine. You take these keys; I've got others. I must say I envy your capacity for putting aside the irrelevant,' said Nest, glancing at the tense little face beside her as they sat in the van and remembering the child's unbending determination once she had put her mind to marrying Oscar. 'It means you're thinking extremely straight, in spite of what's just happened.'

'How do you mean?'

'Well, for the time being at least, your errant Oscar is an irrelevance. You seem to be accepting without any argument that he's gone? Perhaps he was a hindrance to your creativity, which, by the way, I also envy.'

'I am still operating on reflex,' Bea admitted. She tried to turn the conversation away from her aunt's blunt and worrying percipience. 'You're creative too. You're a gardener.'

'No, I'm a manufacturer,' said Nest, forcing the gear stick

into reverse and jerking backwards in the first manoeuvre of a six-point turn. 'I produce plants for gardeners to use in *their* creations. Like a paint-maker grinding colours for artists to use. Only gardening is such a variable thing.' She grunted as she scraped the garden wall. 'There's no exact formula as there is with paints ...' Nest took the turn out into the main road too fast, straightening up with difficulty, barely pausing in her talk but Bea's mind was elsewhere, thinking about Oscar, absently nodding her head to Nest's lecture on the differences between gardening and painting but hearing none of it. 'I should be sadder, madder, badder about it all. Why do I feel so ... so little?'

'... However talented one is one can't rely on one's materials in the way you can predict what will be squeezed out of a tube of Winsor and Newton's Cadmium Red,' continued Nest, slowing behind a Land-Rover and trembling trailer-full of nervous sheep. Bea clutched at the dashboard, shutting her eyes as her Aunt, at last managing to find second gear, overtook the sheep on a blind corner.

'Damn Blue,' said Nest, 'I always have trouble with it after he's been driving it. How are Jane and Tom taking all this?'

'Mum and Dad seem to think I'm bent on suicide,' Bea said, 'at least that seems to be the only way Mum can imagine how I feel.'

'And you're definitely not?'

'No ... I'm angry,' then sadly, 'It hasn't really sunk in, I suppose, what his leaving means. Perhaps he thought things had ground to a halt between us and I didn't notice ... there weren't any signs that he was having an affair.'

'No not-quite-hidden incriminating photographs in his sock drawer? No unexplained phone calls, or unknown knickers in his pocket? How very unpredictable of him. If men are having an affair, they seem unconsciously to want to let one know about it.' Nest spoke from experience. 'But perhaps it's not unconscious?

'There was nothing, but I wasn't looking for anything, you see. I'm not a jealous person. I was quite happy, being at the book shop and painting in my spare time and supposed Oscar was happy too. He never said anything to the contrary and I always thought we got on so well. I thought he loved me. I certainly loved ...' she paused uncomfortably unfinished, knowing that what she had been about to say was possibly not as true as she'd imagined it to be.

Bea's predicament and her apparently extraordinary fortitude were remarked on by relatives and friends during the following week. Agnes remained agog at the suddenness of it all and came hurrying the next week to the Kerepols, full of aggravating sympathy, to help Bea sort out some belongings from her old bedroom in the attic. Later, as they sat with coffee at the Kerepols' overcrowded kitchen table, the day before Bea's planned move, Agnes was at first a little overawed by her air of furious calm and was inclined to mournful personal reminiscing which Bea found more tolerable than the continual regurgitation of the reasons for and the events leading up to the Flight of Oscar, which was all she'd heard for the past few days.

'I used to love coming here in the days before I went to London. It was so much more comfortable than at home. Here it didn't matter where you left your coat, or where you put down your tea cup.'

'You were lucky to find a space to put down anything. It was always so cluttered.' Bea remembered the contrast between Agnes's mother's house and her own very well; Agnes's mother smoked cigars and was an interior decorator. Every year a new look was ruthlessly imposed; Agnes would return from school to find her friendly green velvet curtains had been changed for sophisticated, crisp grey-and-white *toile de Jouy*, or that her paintings had been taken down from the walls and hidden behind the wardrobe because they didn't accord with the current look. This unnerving chopping and changing had had a dire effect on Agnes and she had taken to secreting precious possessions in boxes, bringing them to a sympathetic Bea for safety in case they were to be the objects of the next ransacking of her bedroom.

'Do you remember Minimalism,' demanded Agnes, 'where one daren't leave even a hairbrush anywhere or the entire effect was spoilt?'

Bea nodded and gave a small sigh. It all seemed impossibly long ago, another life.

'There didn't seem to be any space to actually live in,' carried on Agnes. 'I once caught her scooping up that pink-and-green nylon satchel I had, do you remember, from the kitchen table and hiding it in the cupboard under the sink. She said it looked out of place.' She groaned theatrically. 'It was a relief when "Decaying Country Gentry" came in and she went off and bought some broken fishing rods and a box of old riding boots in a sale, because she thought they looked good in the hall. It was OK to be untidy then, as long as it was the right kind of untidiness. You know, antique patchwork flung carelessly across a chair was all right, but tartan Doc Martens left on the stairs were a no-no. Your mother achieved it without even trying so mine used to come and take notes to see how it ought to look. She never quite got the hang of it – it had to be explained to her that it wasn't something you could arrange convincingly, more something that grew organically.'

'I always wondered,' said Bea slowly, 'if she might have been trying to control you by causing as much uncertainty as possible.' She wished Agnes would shut up.

Agnes looked startled, then dubious. 'Yes, I suppose it's possible – although I'm sure she wasn't aware she was doing it. Anyway, her current craze is *still* feng shui. She shudders whenever she comes into our house – last week she wouldn't come past the door and said she wasn't feeling strong enough to cope with all the negative aspects.'

Agnes then returned to worry at the subject which Bea had hoped had been laid aside: Oscar, and her own imminent removal.

'You and Oscar always seemed to me to be the perfect pair – I was jealous of you. He's so stunningly attractive, so interested in everything.' Here Bea wondered briefly if they were talking about the same Oscar, but Agnes flew on. 'It's hard to believe he's gone off to that cow-woman with the mooing voice. She had a bad skin, I thought, as if she might have had bad spots in her teens and I thought her legs were a little short.' Agnes's porcelain skin had never known the indignities of acne, but she was on less solid ground with legs.

'You won't shut yourself away completely, will you? I can come and visit, can't I?' Agnes sounded plaintive.

'Of course you can come. Fingle's not abroad.'

'But it won't be the same, not being able to pop in to see you at the book shop, or meeting you at lunch time for a glass of wine and a moan. What did they say when you gave in your notice?'

'Bill thought I was being overdramatic. He told me he'd keep the job open for me so that I could come back when my forty days in the wilderness were up. He's going to get someone in temporarily, imagining that Oscar and I have just had a little tiff, as he put it. I couldn't explain to him that I hadn't even been given the chance to have a tiff ...' There was a tickling at the back of her nose and a prickling in her eyes. 'I don't want to be thinking about it. I want to be "doing".'

She leant her chin on her hand and drew circles in a splash of coffee on the table. Things had been achieved at such high speed over the past few days that there blessedly had been no time to think: a fourth-hand pick-up truck had been bought, ancient and rattling, but with six-months' MOT and a good starter. Stretchers and canvas had been ordered from London, entailing a drive up there to collect them and to replenish stocks of paints, wrestling all the way with the unfamiliar mechanical foibles of the truck. Then there had been the selective packing up of belongings loved or needed in the self-imposed exile.

The artists' suppliers, which she had visited on Agnes's advice, had lifted her spirits. There had been a magical feel to the premises just off the Holloway Road, a dusty cave guarded by an amicable dragon, filled with the tantalising jewel-sheen of tubes of oil paints, water-colours and gouaches in colour order, the very names of which induced a delinquent chemical hunger. The ultramarine, cobalt, cerulean, monestial, Prussian and indigo, the alizarin crimsons and scarlet lakes, the cadmium reds, chrome oranges and yellows, the earthy ochres and Havannah lakes. Passing up and down the collections of shining coloured crayons and dusty rainbows of pastels in their black pigeon holes, Bea, like a child in a sweet shop, almost salivated at the satisfying sight but put herself on a diet and bought only what was strictly needed.

She looked up and saw Agnes was staring at her, head on one side, a speculative jackdaw.

'Do you think *I* should open up communications, make some sort of effort to speak to him?' Bea asked, dipping her finger in the cold coffee and adding a few dots to the pattern she had made.

'I think you should at least give it a try,' Agnes replied, self-conscious at giving advice, the reasons for and advisability of which she was uncertain, to the Bea who had never previously seemed in need of any, 'you won't be happy if you don't. Till death do you part and all that. Personally, I'd never, ever speak to him again.'

Bea did not answer. Agnes had not read that self-pitying letter and there were a large number of people in the south-east of England whom Agnes no longer spoke to. From the store rooms beneath the kitchen came the sound of Tom singing.

Agnes felt that Bea had retreated deep inside her head and was unreachable. Both of them dissolved into tears; Bea because she was exhausted and Agnes because it seemed, well, suitable to keep Bea company in her sorrows.

Tom Kerepol mounted the stairs with heavy tread, still singing:

> *'Dies irae, dies illa,*
> *Solvet saeclum in favilla . . .'*

He wanted to find out what had happened to the cup of coffee he had been promised earlier, but broke off, embarrassed and alarmed by the two lachrymose women and uncertain how to proceed. It hurt him dreadfully to see Bea cry. When she was small he'd made her laugh by waggling his false tooth but he could no longer very well try that, since being deserted by one's husband was a bit more serious than a grazed knee. He adjusted his eyepatch, cleared his throat and looked around hopefully for Jane before remembering she had gone to London that morning to consult a specialist in eighteenth-century handwriting, seeking help in the decipherment of the Cadwell family commonplace book which had resurfaced after a miraculous escape from a garden bonfire. Jane hoped to have it printed in tandem with a quantity of pictures and updated versions of the receipts plus a copious commentary of her own.

'As if there was a need for more cookery books,' Tom thought, looking balefully at the stuffed bookshelves around the kitchen. 'If she thinks I'm going to put up with folksy food while she experiments, she'd better think again.' The month before he had broken a tooth on a candied violet during the testing of a range of mediaeval marchpanes and scented custards.

Bea solved his emotional inadequacies by regaining control of herself, going to the stove and pouring the coffee. Tom imagined that crying was not such a bad thing for her; didn't Jane always swear that it made her feel better? Best not to say anything.

* * *

Agnes sat that evening with arms crossed, warming her feet on the fender at the coal fire, which wasn't burning as well as it might since the cinders hadn't been raked out for several days.

The only sounds were the occasional footsteps along the narrow Cuckold's Lane as people passed close by the sitting room window on their way to the fish and chip shop. As gentrification had taken its stultifying grasp on the town and the business rates rose inexorably higher, the fish and chip shop had been moved from Bellhurst High Street into their mediaeval alley. There was little natural daylight in the sitting room because of the oppressive closeness of the overhanging jetties of the opposite houses and there was only a small courtyard out at the back for Seb to play in. She envied Bea's flowerbeds and vegetable patch at the back, with only the fields behind her and the ineffectual and uncomplaining Mrs Lewis next door.

Initially guiltily aroused by Bea's predicament, her spirits had plummeted, for other rather selfish reasons, on hearing of Bea's planned emigration. It was, however, most interesting to her that Oscar was on the loose again, even if temporarily he was holed up with Andreary. But his timing had been poor. If Oscar had left Bea for anyone, Agnes felt it should have been her; she'd delighted in flirting with Oscar at parties when Bea was in the kitchen, had always been certain that her attraction was reciprocated and that she knew how to manage him better than Bea did; she was able to compose her features into a wonderfully fascinated expression as he spoke and yet be thinking of something else entirely – an effect Bea had never mastered – and he used to flash her understanding, commiserating looks when Phil decided autocratically that it was time that they went home.

Seb had gone to sleep at an unusually early hour, exhausted by his acts of terrorism at nursery school and in the unaccustomed quiet she contemplated the viruses of marriage, her own as much as Bea's, without finding any remedies. The bacteria of boredom were beginning to multiply. She was prone to sudden bouts of dissatisfaction and these had led her into a circular therapy syndrome, a peripheral exploration for answers, employing practitioners of fringe alternatives about whom she was ecstatic, briefly, until a crisis of a different colour fell upon her. She often switched treatments before she could possibly have had time to find out the positive or negative effects of the previous one.

Agnes yearned for a soul mate, frequently imagining she'd found this quality in some man or other but when eventually disappointed, never realised she'd wilfully confused intellectual compatibility with physical attraction, continually overestimating the former in order to put the latter in a more attractive setting. Thinking of Phil, she started to describe him to herself, to see if she still fancied him. Five feet ten, wide shouldered and strong. Large feet and rough hands with fingernails so stout that he broke scissors trying to cut them. His face was pleasantly cast and surrounded disquieting eyes, one hazel, one clear green. The small, neat nose had once been broken playing rugger and was now a little flattened ... Hair fair and thick, prone to curl. A chipped front tooth. Cheeks pink, freckled ... an adult but still boyish version of Just William, which had made the idea of sleeping with him seem oddly illicit; after a year the charm of this had worn away and she could no longer convince herself that it had been an adequate reason for marrying him, but he'd seemed to want to look after her and Seb and opportunities like that didn't come along too often. She liked boyish faces. Bea's brother Patrick's, for instance. He'd had the same look when at fifteen and she was eighteen, she had joyfully seduced him in a prickly field of barley and then again, she smiled smugly at the memory, on several more comfortable occasions before the summer holidays ended; it had been difficult to get him to understand that it was their secret and that being under age, he must not under any circumstances tell his family. Patrick was in the Navy now and they hadn't met for several years.

When Phil had come home that evening Agnes had been busy catching up on the work she should have done that afternoon instead of comforting Bea – another set of illustrations for the children's *Charlie Chooch* series. There had been no signs of preparations being made for anything in the kitchen so Phil had volunteered himself to fetch a fish supper, which annoyed him a little since he was tired out.

He now strode back in purposefully and went straight to the kitchen, ostentatiously rustling paper and clattering plates and she hurried to the drawing desk at the end of the room, switching off the Anglepoise, guiltily tidying paints and swishing brushes in the dirty paint water. She cleared a place to eat at the dining table among the thick grey strata of accumulated newspapers and magazines before Phil returned to the sitting room with two warmed plates of plaice and chips decorated with half a lemon.

As they ate, Bea's troubles were naturally uppermost in their conversation. Phil indignantly denied that he had known that anything was afoot although Oscar's secretary Sheila had mentioned that there had been a flurry of calls for Oscar from Mrs Bullingden recently, but they'd both innocently assumed that these concerned the garden gates that were being made for her.

'Bea says she never noticed anything about his behaviour to warn her either. But then, she *wouldn't* notice. She didn't notice any of the others. She's intolerably vague. I'm sure Oscar found it irritating.' Agnes polished off the last chip and sucked her fingers.

'Not half as vague as you,' replied Phil, good-naturedly surveying the innocent doll's face. 'I'm starving when I get home from the ironworks.'

Phil's green eye was disconcerting; it appeared to a sometimes unquiet soul to interrogate, to criticise, even if its owner hadn't intended to do so.

'But it's all a bit *sad*, isn't it?' she demanded. 'I always thought

Oscar was the perfect husband, so tolerant.' She reached out and stole one of Phil's chips and added with light sarcasm: 'She *always* had his supper on the table like a good little slave.'

'God! You do wolf your food down. Do you mean sad that he's left her, or sad that you misjudged him? In any case, I definitely don't understand him. I'd die for a woman who had supper waiting for me.' Phil hastily reached out, put his arm round her waist and tickled her ribs. 'Don't glare at me. I was only teasing – I know you've been busy working too. Can't we drop the Mitty scandal and get on with our own lives? The Koreans I told you about? They're bringing the architect for the new offices in the City over tomorrow and there should be a commission coming through.'

'Any chance of design work for me? I really enjoyed doing those gates for Andreary Bullshit although,' she added loyally, 'now I wish they'd clang shut on her neck and decapitate her.'

'If there's a chance available I'll make sure you get a crack at it. You didn't get enough praise for the Bullingden gates.'

'The money more than made up for the lack of praise. Anyway, I've got some title illustrations to do next week for a new glossy gardening magazine. Very upmarket. Lots of little green watering cans and hanks of raffia. That'll make a welcome break. It's more satisfying doing that type of work than yomping through these repetitive *Charlie Chooch* books. If I have to draw his smug little face again, I'll be sick. I'm just praying that the author doesn't take it into his head to do a fourth series.'

'You invented his face in the first place. That's the reason they're so successful.' Phil went over to the fireplace and rattled the poker half-heartedly among the smouldering coals, setting himself down with a sigh of tiredness on a sagging, knobbly chair whose cover consisted of an overambitious patchwork of cobbled-together pieces of Indian bedspread.

'Any danger you might make some coffee?' he asked, unlacing his boots, levering them off against the edge of the iron fender and wriggling his toes in their red socks in relief at being home, fed and safe from the worrying world outside.

Things had been difficult enough this week, trying to lay the flying sneers and rumours at work. It would have been better if Oscar had come in and carried on as if nothing had happened. Not having himself found Andrea Bullingden particularly attractive, he was puzzled by the man's behaviour; Andrea, he'd thought, was a sly, catty woman, the type who rub themselves up against one, pleading all manner of hardships while their whiskers quiver with acquisitiveness and challenge. He was fond of Bea ... the beautiful, faithful Bea. Agnes had told him once, with amazement, that she didn't think Bea had ever even looked at another man since meeting Oscar.

He'd first seen her almost dancing down the street, mouthing the words of a song on a Walkman plugged into her neatly-modelled little ears, but there was something about her that gave the impression of a girl merely paying lip service to the common concerns of her age group. She couldn't have been much more than sixteen then and he had for some time fantasised about her. There'd been glimpses of her at pubs and parties that year where, with an attractive otherworldliness, she had appeared to be thinking of something other than what was going on around her but he had been too shy to approach. By the time he'd gained enough courage to ask her out, it was too late; the bolder Oscar had scored a bullseye. Now that he had Agnes, he thought of Bea only occasionally ... but still experienced a little jolt of unrequited love every single time he saw her. He was distressed for her and disgusted with Oscar, but talking about it would achieve nothing. He was too tired that evening to have an opinion and shut his eyes for a moment, waking an hour and a half later to find that the fire had gone out, that a cup of coffee stood cold on the fender and that Agnes had gone up to bed without him.

Chapter Three

During the weekend Bea swept away the accumulated dusty clutter of Little Rumm's previous tenants – she would find her own shells, stones and feathers for different aesthetic and sentimental reasons. The acts of cleaning away the house's winter mildew, of nesting and rearranging only partially dimmed the sense of loneliness. She squirted the last remaining drops of a bottle of Poême on the backboards of the wardrobe to mask the mustiness and snuffed appreciatively before unpacking the single suitcase of clothes. The precious collection of blue glass was displayed on little shelves hastily fitted-up across a narrow window at the side of the sitting room. Now the early morning sun glittered through Bristol finger bowls, a turquoise wine glass and a Victorian sapphire poison bottle, throwing a stained-glass pattern across the rush matting. Books were on the bookshelves, a monograph on the paintings of Samuel Palmer and her grandmother's copy of *Grimm's Fairytales* among them, and *Gulliver's Travels* which she'd always meant to read but never managed. The painting room upstairs was cleared for action and waiting, like a person meeting an unknown visitor off a train. Anything was possible.

The immediate area around the house was treeless and the need for kindling for the fire drove her further afield to search the ness for driftwood, driving back into Fingle and out again on the road to the point with its lighthouses, shacks and bungalows. These were dwarfed, even the massive disused brick lighthouse, by the elephantine outlines of the nuclear power stations squatting in gross intimacy together beside the sea. She found them so invasive a feature that it was strangely possible to ignore them – in the way in which it is possible to ignore distant atrocities – by simply suspending belief in the evidence of eyes and ears.

She'd been to the area before as a child, when she and Patrick had climbed the echoing white interior of the old lighthouse and stood beside the polished latticed glass containing its giant lamps, staring out over the windswept shingle ridges scattered with broom. A ghostly grey tanker sailed far out past the point, almost hidden in soft mist. Jane was a vertigo sufferer and had leant stiff as a doll against their toy car far below while the children sickeningly waved and screamed from above. Half way down the lighthouse stairs, on a window ledge, they'd seen a kestrel's nest; it had been one of those days when Bea had caught and held a feeling of buoyant happiness, right there at the moment rather than looking backwards and remembering it at bedtime.

The fishing boats perched on top of the shingle bank were tough, squat shapes against the sky, their upper outlines a confusion of ropes, wires, aerials and quivers of flapping black and red marker flags, the purposes of which were unknown to Bea. They loomed above her as she walked along below the deeply shelving shore towards the lifeboat station; her pockets were full of rattling cockle shells and a canvas bag of driftwood was on her shoulder. The wind was in her ears and salt on her lips and the night before, the third at Little Rumm, she had at last slept well, unstirred by dreams. Nest had been right; life was cleaner and simpler out here and the untidy limbo of the week before was at least physically behind her.

As Bea scaled the bank, moving crabwise up the steep incline of shifting stones to the flat-topped storm beach above, a tractor came into view, nosing a fishing boat down to the sea. There was a steady-paced activity as men moved back and forth with planks, rotating them from behind the boat's transporter to place them beneath the wheels at the front, inching it across the gentle slope from where it would undoubtedly tilt and slide smoothly into the high water. The boat was new and blue, its paint unstained and its cabin shiny white. Although it was only eight o'clock in the morning, several groups of interested spectators stood placidly about with loose children and joyful mongrels galloping dangerously about among them. It dawned on Bea that she was witnessing the launch of a virgin fishing boat and being secretly a little superstitious, felt in need of good omens. This looked like a most auspicious one and she squatted down optimistically in a dip in the shingle to get out of the wind and watch the technicalities.

It became fast apparent that the launch was not proceeding according to the rule book. The boat became stuck fast with its conveyor's wheels pressing ever deeper into the shingle, the weight too great for the straining sea tractor to shift forwards. The prospective skipper, navy sweatered and rubber booted, stood on the deck leaning over the rail, his grey hair flapping in the breeze as he engaged in strained discussions with the launchers below.

Bea took out her pencil and pocket-book and drew, leaning her back into the bag of lumpy driftwood, absorbed by the tubby boat and awesome rotundity of a new arrival, a white-bearded man also in navy sweater, who carried red-and-green flags beneath his arm and who gesticulated towards the lifeboat house as if indicating that help would soon be at hand. A very tall, energetic-looking man with a short thick plait of red hair hanging down the back of a faded green jersey was consulting with two dark, deep-chested men with hefty forearms who ambled off to fetch more planks to place beneath the wheels. Erik the Red, she thought, swiftly sketching him in, and Castor and Pollux.

The sky grew dreary and a spatter of rain forced her to put away the sketch pad and patiently wait but in spite of this it seemed to Bea miraculous to be away from Bellhurst and the claustrophobic book shop and out of reach of those people who *would* keep wringing their hands, unkindly reminding her of the fact that she had been deserted.

After a while, as the watchers were beginning to disperse disappointedly, the lifeboat made a swift entrance stage left, and shot down its ramp past the stationary fishing boat, slapping satisfactorily into the grey-green water and bringing fresh orange, blue and scarlet drama to the scene. The launchers were re-animated and rushed about attaching a turquoise nylon line to the transporter; the lifeboat with its yellow-oilskinned crew moved further out and at a signal from the fat flagman, went engines full ahead into the slight swell. The rope drew taut but still the boat stayed put. The signaller waved the red flag vigorously, and then frantically the green. Bea got up from her hollow and crept closer to watch. It was beginning to drizzle in earnest.

Nothing budged although the lifeboat was straining ahead again and pungent blue smoke from its roaring engine was floating out across the water. At that moment Bea, perhaps hearing a change of pitch in the singing sound from the vibrating rope, had a flashing premonition of danger and stepped back, tripping on an abandoned plastic fish box. Erik the Red leapt back too, yelling a warning as the towrope snapped apart and flew like a striking snake, whip-lashing backwards towards the fishing boat and missed slicing into Bea only by inches.

There were some red faces about, pinked by embarrassment and the freshening wind but Erik the Red turned white-faced to Bea as if she had no place there at all and was in some way to blame for their mortification and in a surly fashion, gave her a hand up.

'You all right?' he asked, kicking the fish box out of the way.

'I'm fine,' she bent to take off her boot which seemed to have collected half the beach inside it when she fell, 'I shouldn't have got so close.'

'No. There are problems enough without looking out for sightseers.' To Bea's English ears the tenseness of voice and the faint Ulster accent instantly brought to mind TV news interviews with other recalcitrant and self-justifying men and she momentarily stiffened; but by now she felt quite desperate for them to succeed with the launch and asked timidly if they were going to try again.

'Once more, perhaps,' then seeing her genuine interest, his voice softened and became less churlish. 'The water's getting too low. We'll get a new line attached but if they can't make it this time, we'll have to leave it till next high tide, this evening.' Perhaps feeling he had explained enough, he smiled briefly, turned his back on her and with a squaring of broad shoulders went back to his mates.

She found the shoulder-squaring amusing, rather poignant, a male reminder that she had come perilously close to getting in the way of men's work and shamingly witnessed its failure. There were other women among the quiet onlookers, wives and girlfriends perhaps; one of them in white high-heeled shoes and black leggings, the visible bare skin between the two unattractively blue with cold. She tottered when she moved, inappropriate feet sinking deep in the stones and forcing her to clutch, helpless and tittering, at the leather-jacketed arm of the patient man beside her.

Bea rather weepily wished she hadn't turned the launch into an augury for herself and when the final attempt also came to nothing, moved off to carry the driftwood back to the pick-up, deeply disappointed. Erik the Red turned from his rope-coiling or whatever it was he was doing and waved as she left, and she raised a hand only tentatively to acknowledge it.

'I must not waste working time,' she muttered to herself, stumbling along on the wet and slippery sleepers of what looked like old railway track, before remembering that her hours were no longer circumscribed. She would like to have seen the boat on the water, but perhaps they would be able to get it afloat tonight.

Back in the house, she laid out the kindling to dry by the fireplace and went up to the painting room with a cup of strong coffee to stand in the middle of the floor, day-dreaming for a moment, vividly imagining the room overflowing with paintings, zooming in on them in turn, inspecting aspects, details, shapes, colours. Then she laid out the components and started to assemble the stretchers for two canvases, larger than anything she had so far attempted or indeed had room for before. She measured, cut and tacked on the canvas and primed it. Nest was right too about this room; it had a positive, workman-like air about it and with the red-sheeted divan bed pushed up against the far wall and the white-painted wardrobe shifted into a corner, was spacious. Intending that the first attempt at such a scale would be a trial run, she primed a large piece of hardboard. There was a play on the radio, set in urban Yorkshire, but it was heavy-handed amusement with an irritating overload of surrealist touches of the '. . . me wife's mother went off with an entomologist who had a deep regard for kippers . . .' variety. She switched stations and with Berlioz's *Symphonie Fantastique* as background, roughed out on paper the picture loitering in her brain.

The morning passed and suddenly starving she foraged for a bowl of tinned pea-and-ham soup and a couple of squashed fly biscuits. The sunshine came and went. Isolated, coping, working. Contentment hovered shyly above but although aware of its presence she refused to allow it to settle before setting down the outlines of her theme.

By mid afternoon the blank white surface of the hardboard was dry; the great space was sufficiently daunting to make her pause, inhaling deeply as if about to leap over rather than paint on it. There had never seemed to be enough time before – it had always been measured by Oscar's needs. Now it all appeared delightfully open-ended and she could carry on painting till circumstances dictated otherwise. She took off her watch and laid it face down on the chair and began, jabbing at first anxiously with the brush, only to be stopped when the light began to fade and it was urgently time for more food.

The composition was in soft grey outline, with some sky blocked in and trial patches of colour, more or less as she had seen it in the dream. A group of robed figures stood on a beach, their arms raised and behind them the fishing boat was being towed out to sea by a large wading figure of the goddess Freda, draperies tucked up above the knee and on her head the poppy and cornflower-trimmed hat. Bea grinned the first grin she had grinned since Oscar had left and started to clean the paintbrushes, humming again. Unburdened or unblessed by children, unless you counted Oscar, she'd squandered the years. She *could* have gone to art school, or even university, *could* have started painting properly years before. Well, she was going to make up for it now. Was it conceivable that the rage and hurt felt at the manner of his leaving were already undergoing transformation, into something like relief? She was too tired that evening to think of going back to watch the second attempt to launch the boat and after supper, lay on the lumpy sofa beside the crackling blue-flamed driftwood fire and started on *Gulliver's Travels*, falling asleep at page four and dreaming. 'You must paint on these,' said an overseer, handing her a blank perforated sheet of second-class stamps; however when she returned with pictures of the fishing boat painted neatly on each stamp, he snorted and tore them up, saying 'Not nearly big enough! Try some first-class ones. They use a better class of glue for those.'

Two days later the first visitor arrived. A solicitous mother stood beaming on the doorstep with a bulging carrier bag in one hand and a bunch of narcissi in the other.

'Beatrice! Darling! You didn't telephone to say everything was all right as you promised! You don't mind me coming unannounced, do you? Look, I've brought some vegetables and two goose eggs and a bottle of wine. Oh, and a sharp knife! Nest wouldn't know the importance of a sharp knife for cooking. I thought we could have a little lunch and a drink together? I couldn't bear to think of you being lonely and miserable.'

Bea had been working confidently since seven o'clock that morning and having just eaten a large cheese-and-onion sandwich, was both touched and irritated by the assumptions that she was miserable and couldn't be anywhere else but in.

'I haven't had time to be miserable,' she tried to reassure. 'I'm trying to put it off and there hasn't been time to be lonely either, I promise you,' and added, uselessly, 'Please, you mustn't worry about me.'

A visit from one or other of her parents had been inevitable, but she had hoped they might have allowed her a week to herself first. A routine was still being established. No longer having to fight for time, the concept of total freedom was troubling; doing what she wanted, when she wanted, didn't come easily. There was a need for some type of framework to the days and having been freed so abruptly from the self-imposed domestic courtyard, she was constructing a much longer and more interesting perimeter to pace.

Tom had already seen the inside of the house when he'd helped Bea move in but Jane had been worried by the vagueness of his description of its comforts or possible lack of them and couldn't restrain herself from hurtling over as soon as she had got rid of ancient Uncle Perry whose arrival on a long-promised stay she'd been unable to avert.

She strode into Bea's kitchen and arranged the flowers in a child's tin seaside bucket which she found beneath the sink and looked about, recognising various vital items imported from her daughter's kitchen but in the main the dreadful inadequacies of the catering arrangements were confirmed. She whipped out a red notebook and scribbled down 'colander, grater, chopping board'. Bea heard her rattling swiftly through the drawers and smiled. Jane had been in the forefront of a generation of relatively impoverished upper-class women whose own mothers' helplessness when faced with the loss of their cooks during the war and whose hopeless struggles with limited and poor-quality ingredients had led their daughters to pray that there might be more interesting things to eat than potato-and-onion pie. Jane had loathed the way the lead shot clattered out on to the plate as the thin rabbit stew gravy was served, the indigestibly undercooked potatoes and the monotony of the brown, pink or white packet cornflower puddings. In her teens she discovered Elizabeth David and had taken over the family's feeding, at least during the school holidays. There had been unkind rumours among the family that her father's early death had been induced by gorging himself on her chocolate pie. It was in the house at Bellhurst that she'd written her first cookery article on the delights of rediscovered suety puddings such as Humpy Locktooth, Figgy Hoggin and Flabby John.

Bea had inherited her mother's talent for cooking, when it was necessary, but not the obsessional approach. Having already eaten a sandwich, she refused to be moved on the subject of lunch, but happily opened the wine and made her mother a deep yellow and thickly frothy goose-egg omelette, under unnecessary shouted instruction from the sitting room.

Jane, suddenly unsure how to start on the substance of the visit, nudged with her foot at the books which lay on the floor by the fire.

'What's this you're reading? *Gulliver's Travels*? And what's this – what a horrible title!' She picked up the Angela Carter. Its cover was curled and its pages were stained. Bea had been reading it in the bath the night before and had dozed off, to wake with a jerk as her head and the book slid beneath the soapy water. She'd tried to dry it out in front of the fire but it was seriously spoiled and smelt of Badedas.

'Adult versions of fairy stories, Mum,' Bea said. 'You wouldn't care for them.'

'Yes, I can see. Not about my sort of people,' Jane happily agreed and Bea smothered a giggle. Jane would have dismissed *Crime and Punishment* or *Nana* in the same fashion, seldom having time for more than cookery books and when consulting these, marking errors of method, punctuation or typography in fine red pen in the margins. In one book by an over-celebrated television cook, she'd indignantly scrawled across a recipe for stuffed courgettes: 'Tastes like sea-slug stuffed with sick.' Patrick had once unfairly remarked that she was the sort of literal-minded woman who might check love letters for temperature and quantities.

'Now,' said Jane brightly, having eaten the omelette fast without more than a surprised 'Not bad at all!' and, having firmly re-corked the wine bottle although Bea would have liked another glass, 'you must tell me what your plans are. You haven't told me anything at all about what you intend to do about the cottage, or what you are going to do about Oscar.'

'Firstly, I've changed the locks, so Oscar can't take Andreary there, although I can't imagine he would, really. I'm sure he's safely tucked up in her mansion. I just couldn't bear the thought of her looking at my things. The cottage is being looked after by Mrs Lewis – she's got a key but won't tell Oscar. I was a bit worried about asking at first, since she appears half witted at times, but she seemed pleased to be asked and said it wouldn't be any trouble. She'll send on any post for me, and all the bills to Oscar. Anything valuable I've put for safe keeping in my old room at home, as you know. I don't see that there's anything else to worry about, is there?' Pleased with her own practicality, she looked hopefully at her mother to see if she was satisfied.

'But who's going to mow the lawn? And finances? You *must* get in touch with a solicitor'. Jane wailed. 'And what about Oscar?' The poor child was being most impractical.

'What about him?' said Bea edgily, removing her mother's plate and trying to evade things by taking it out to the kitchen.

'Don't wander off like that, and don't be difficult.' Jane got up and followed her, protesting. 'You can't let things slide, like this. You *must* get in touch with him, for money, till things are sorted out. How long do you propose to stay here in this isolated shack?'

'I don't see why *I* have to get in touch with *him*. I need to be isolated, to work things out on my own. And this is not a shack. It's got everything one could possibly need and I mean to stay here for the moment ...' How long could one extend a moment? Why was it so hard to accept the look of distress on her mother's face? '... Indefinitely. As long as Nest will let me. As long as the money will last.'

'I see.' Jane excelled at sounding just slightly hurt and she stared at her daughter's smooth, still insolently young and closed, self-protective face. 'Golden' was the word that jumped into her mind whenever she saw her daughter and a clear image of the new-born Bea slid before her eyes; nervously holding the child for the first time, she'd feverishly searched the squashed pink face for resemblances and signals. The fragile head with its still encrusted strands of hair had nuzzled sideways then raised a near-invisible and cynical eyebrow in a miniature query, as if to wonder whether she had been deposited with the right parent. Jane had just then caught that look as Bea was speaking. She had turned out to be an attractive but wilful child, a little oddball, difficult for Jane to fathom. Although she had had her doubts about the advisability of such a youthful marriage, she had breathed a cautious sigh of relief when Bea was safely ensconced in her cottage with Oscar and had been secretly amazed that Bea had settled down so peacefully for so long.

'Well, let's talk about something else then, as you're obviously going to be intransigent. Patrick is home on leave for three days in July so I hope you'll come out of your cocoon of self-containment and see him?'

'Of course I will.' Impatiently. July was a long way off. 'He's written to me with the dates.' It would be a pleasant relief to see the still unmarried Patrick whose leaves seemed to be less often spent at home; he at least would not lob unreturnable questions at her all the time.

'And what do you do with yourself all day?' Jane asked, rather desperately, feeling herself unfairly being forced into the role of interfering mother yet unable to resist the pressure, and the pleasure.

'But I'm working of course. Painting.' She misjudged Jane's tenacity if she thought that any mention of art would send her off on another track. Jane felt called upon to ask, as eagerly as she could manage, if she could see and Bea prevaricated, knowing that although her mother might be wonderfully adventurous in the area of taste buds, had a good sense of colour and three-dimensional form, she was bizarrely inadequately equipped in the two-dimensional visual sense, being slow to unravel the subject from the lines of a drawing and finding any distortions hopelessly puzzling and tedious. Bea had once been reduced to asking her, when she'd expressed a lack of understanding on being confronted with one of the simplest of figurative paintings, whether if it had been a plate of food, she would have been tempted to eat it? Her mother, forced to pretend to study it in depth, had replied that it seemed to be a bit heavy on the cabbage side.

'Not yet. It won't be finished for ages, the thing I'm working on. But I will show it to you, and the other things I've planned, if they work out all right,' and she added, 'I'm quite all right, you know. I will keep in touch. I'm not going to become an anchoress.' And more desperately, seeing Jane's expression of forlorn concern, almost as if *she* had been the one to have been deserted, 'I was thinking of going out for a drink, to try a pub in Fingle.' This was a faux pas. Jane's mouth tightened, the tiny lines above the top lip deepening. Her mother had imagined her to be pining, felt that she *should* be pining and had needed to be able to console her.

The visit ended. Gathered up in Jane's arms and fiercely hugged once more, Bea wished she had been less childishly defensive, but that involved comforting the would-be comforter and she hadn't the strength for it and she so very much wanted to get back to work.

'Well, you *must* be careful. I seem to remember hearing Nest saying the pubs were rather rough. I hate you being sequestered out here. Anything might happen. You must keep the door bolted at all times, particularly when you're working upstairs. Anyway, I must sally forth, although I've no idea how one sallies – where does that expression come from? It sounds as if it should be used for gays coming out, doesn't it? I have to run through a Turkey *à la Normande* and a honey ice cream for an article and it's your father's final rehearsal of the Verdi *Requiem* tonight. He'll need feeding up beforehand.'

Bea expressed a hope that all would go smoothly with the Verdi, and remembered to ask whether the commonplace book had proved to be interesting.

'Oh, yes! Very, very interesting. I'm certain there's going to be money in it. There's an awful lot of tiresome research to be done first but I'm getting the hang of it at last.'

Bea kissed her good-bye and waved from the doorstep then taking the bucket of narcissi with her, she skipped upstairs to try to catch the painting unawares, to see it as it might be seen for the first time and check that the composition was really working out as she hoped, before she had been interrupted.

She gave it a stern stare, stepping back to the opposite wall for a better view, then mixing the colours on a dinner plate, began to fill in the schematic head of the figure on the boat with Jane's face, ruefully remembering a childhood episode when she had shown her mother a drawing of an acrobat perched on the back of a donkey.

Jane had been leaning up against the kitchen dresser, writing business letters. She rarely sat to do anything and even sewed standing by the window.

'That's a lovely drawing,' Jane had said absently after giving it the merest glance. 'What book did you copy it from?'

'I didn't copy it,' Bea answered, puzzled and annoyed, 'not from a book. I thought it.' She'd removed the drawing and later that afternoon presented Jane with another one, in bright crayons. Her mother was now scribbling in a notebook with a marbled cover, standing by the stove while keeping an eye on a chicken carcase boiling in the stockpot.

'Oh God!' she'd said, putting down the pen and staring hard. Even to her it had been a recognisable portrait of Patrick in his scarlet-and-black striped Dennis the Menace jersey, apparently being eaten alive by chickens. Quite gory. 'Darling! It's quite horrible!' Then hastily: 'Whatever gave you such an idea?' She had looked anxiously down at Bea's narrow, obstinate little face beneath the fair pudding basin haircut. Bea did not know where her ideas came from. She deliberated.

'I thought this one too, in my own head. You couldn't say I copied it.'

'No, I can see now that you didn't. I'm sorry that I thought you had copied the other one. I'm sure they're both very good drawings indeed. Poor Patrick though. I wouldn't show it to him – it would give him dreadful dreams.'

'I don't mean it to happen, or anything like that,' Bea had said anxiously. 'I just thought it.'

Bea was too young still and had lived too continuously close to her parents seriously to have examined her relationship with them.

Oscar sat uncomfortably at the bar that evening, waiting for Phil. The new trousers which Andrea had bought him were too tight around his waist. Was it possible that in spite of all the worry he could have put on weight in the two weeks he'd spent with Andrea? The atmosphere at work had become miasmic with disapproval since he'd gone to live with her and hoping to clear the air, he'd invited Phil to come for a drink to discuss events in general. Sheila had been casting him basilisk glances from behind the screen of her word processor and he was certain he'd heard the foreman Ernie Fletcher call him a prat behind his back when the Koreans were being shown round the works. There had been a resentful silence from Phil, which had to be broken.

He'd cautiously returned to Fleming Cottage, early in the evening a week after his decampment, steeling himself to cope with a distraught and hysterical Bea and unreasonably, he could see now, expecting to be able to make her understand how deeply sorry he was that he had let her down by falling in love with someone else. Knowing her normal rationality he had not expected a major campaign and imagined that they would be able, not all at once of course but gently, in time, to come to an understanding and make sensible arrangements about their possessions and the future.

He had encountered only Mrs Lewis, who had trailed him like a pale slug up the path while ineptly explaining that Bea had gone away. He was angered to find that the front door lock had been changed. However he had the spare key to the tool shed on his key-ring and opened that up, intending to remove the chainsaw.

Inside he had been assaulted by a powerful smell of decomposition. Snuffing about like a dog in the dark, his heart pounding with foreboding, he eventually traced it, throwing open the lid of the tool chest and staring in disbelief at the encrusted tools inside and the ruined electric drill. It looked to him as if someone had been voluminously sick into the chest and it dawned that he didn't know Bea at all, had been unable to imagine how she might behave, and that it was possible that things were not going to be so simple to finalise as he'd hoped.

The sun had set and he peered through a window into the darkening kitchen. All was neat and tidy apart from the fork piercing the pages of a letter on the table. He knew even at a distance that it *was* his letter. He felt foolish and turned sharply away, straight into the wretched Mrs Lewis standing silently just behind him.

Unable to get any sense out of her, he'd apprehensively tried Tom on the telephone but had received an emotional and imaginatively abusive ear-bashing, Tom refusing to tell him if Bea was in the house and only grudgingly agreeing to pass on messages. Oscar thought she must be staying with her parents though, since first Phil then Agnes had denied knowledge of her whereabouts. Andrea had suggested frostily that morning that it would be best to write to her to organise a discussion about the separation with a solicitor at hand and he was now inclined to agree with her.

It had been foolish not to have foreseen that there might be some partisanship among his acquaintances and staff. It appeared that Bea had taken time off work at the book shop and disappeared and no one was prepared to tell him where she was hiding, which seemed to him unnecessarily obstructive since he wasn't a wife-batterer or anything like that, merely ... he paused to think for the first time what he was in other people's eyes ... an adulterer, a deserter, a prat? He found it hard to acknowledge that he was any of those things, particularly after spending time with Andrea who thought him a gleaming white knight, her rescuer from solitary confinement in the country. But it wasn't as if he and Bea had children to worry about – in fact if they had had children ... he tried to justify himself and failed. Andrea had a child, a little boy now at preparatory school, and perhaps, in the not too distant future, he might have one of his own too.

Where the hell was Phil? He'd chosen the Eeldyke Inn particularly as being remote enough from the town to make it unlikely that he would encounter any more baleful stares or knowing whispers. It was a quiet old place with no music, but the landlord didn't seem inclined to make conversation and the only other customers, a middle-aged man and woman laughing and chattering in the corner by the window, seemed more than content with their own company. Quickly glancing in their direction he saw that the woman was pretty, in fact she was very attractive but although all her bits seemed still in the right places, she was obviously quite old, at least fifty.

He wished he had Andrea with him, although this was hardly the sort of place she'd be used to. Judging by the reception he'd had so far, it would take time before they would be able to be seen in Bellhurst together but people surely had other things to think about and it would all soon be forgotten?

He began to feel sleepy. Although it was a warm, wet evening, willow logs snapped and sparkled on the fire. The clock on the wall suddenly struck the half hour, making him jump. The door flew open and six or seven men came in, stamping their mud-spattered seven-league boots and shaking out work-stained raggedy jackets, for it had started to rain heavily. They were obviously regular customers. Noisily pulling out stools and chairs and teasing the landlord, they settled near to Oscar, taking up a great deal of room with elbows and splayed out legs, setting up a wide and intangibly fenced area about them. Oscar read the proprietorial signs and moved along the bar. There was much passing about of tobacco pouches, borrowing of Rizlas and careless slopping of pints of real ale. They appeared to be celebrating something for they were impossibly jolly. After a while one of them leant over the bar and in a penetrating stage whisper, offered to sell the landlord something.

'Here, Seth, fancy a bit of wild boar? Got a nice leg out in back of the van.' Seth looked interested and stopped polishing the glasses.

'Phylly's partial to a nice bit of pig, wild or not.' He whispered back. 'Where did you shoot it?'

'Cade's Wood. Charlie and I split it down the middle, so to speak. Come outside and have a look.'

Seth disappeared into the wet dark outside and re-appeared a little later with a grin on his face and a large bundle loosely wrapped in dirty sacking which he carried out through the back room and into his private quarters. The pub began to fill up, but still no sign of Phil. Oscar studied the wall behind the boar-seller's head. It was covered in notices, some handwritten offering washing machines or lurcher pups for sale, others small posters advising the advent of past point-to-point races or sponsored beard-shaving for Balkan orphans. There was also a pink poster, computer-written by someone with such an eclectic eye for typography that it took him some while to decipher, advertising 'Dwyle Flunking on Easter Monday at the Eeldyke Inn. 3 p.m.' Whatever dwyle-flunking was, it had already taken place.

The wild-boar man slipped over to the couple in the corner, had words with them and the woman got up eagerly and followed him outside with a backward conspiratorial smile at her companion, so glowing that Oscar felt quite lonely. They obviously fancied a nice bit of boar as well.

Phil slammed through the door, obviously in a foul mood and Oscar nervously bought him a pint.

'This is a hell of a long way to come for a drink, it's pouring out there and I still haven't caught up with my sleep after your little flit for freedom – you might have left it till we'd got the fire-backs order out.' Phil sat down heavily on the stool beside Oscar. 'Ernie was off work that week with a bruised foot and I've done my back in helping load up the lorry.' Phil sank a third of the pint and waited, aggressively. 'Come on. Spit it out.'

'Look, I know you – everyone – thinks I'm a bastard to have left Bea so suddenly like that. I've tried to get in touch with her to apologise but she's gone to ground somewhere.'

'Apologise?' Phil, recalling again how obsessed he'd been with Bea all those years ago, suddenly felt a flush of pure anger.

'I wouldn't have thought you could round off ten – twelve is it? – years of marriage with just an apology.'

'No, of course it isn't possible. But there are things about our marriage that you don't know about. She's never treated me as if ... as if I were an adult. More as if I were her child. And we haven't got any children ...' he added, very lamely.

'The sperm count a bit low, is it?' said Phil, nastily.

'Um ... No ... why should it be?' Oscar shrugged his shoulders carelessly. 'It's Bea. Women's problems, odd periods, that sort of thing. But she never seemed interested enough to get checked over by a doctor.' It had not occurred to Oscar that it might in any way be his problem. But if it had occurred to Bea ... and she had not said anything ... 'Anyway, she'd be useless with babies – they'd probably have to make their own bottles while she carried on daubing away. Bugger everything! I know there's no excuse, Phil. I just fancied Andrea rotten, I fell for her. End of story.' Oscar's handsome face bore an expression of self-conscious complacency. Phil loathed his straight nose and even white teeth.

'Being honest doesn't help either,' he said slowly. 'Open, but still amoral. What about Bea?'

'She's still young; she'll get over it and she can have Fleming Cottage.'

Phil stood up, and hit him.

Chapter Four

Agnes stared moodily down from a bedroom window into the damp little yard where Seb stood in a puddle in his socks, bumping a toy car up and down in a tray of double daisies. After yelling at him she clumped grumpily downstairs, dreary with the lack of stimulating happenings in her current domestic life. Perhaps it was time she visited Bea and poached a share of hers? Her rampageous London days sparkled still in her memory; she was wasting away, drowning in small-town mundanity. The idea of having a chat with Bea was instantly cheering – she at least had managed to kick Bellhurst in the behind and get away – quite romantic really and besides there was one morsel of news she could justifiably impart; Phil's bruised hand had not gone unnoticed. She had been accustomed in the past to people fighting over her and although to have her husband punching Oscar on Bea's behalf wasn't exactly ego-boosting, it was at least an event and she was aching to see where Bea had secreted herself. Bea's mobile seemed to be permanently switched off but undeterred Agnes abandoned work for the morning and set out with Seb, knowing it was only about fifteen miles away but with only the haziest idea of how to get to the house. Bea had described its appearance in detail but on leaving Fingle Agnes took several wrong turnings before happening on the right God-forsaken, unmarked track.

Drawn away from her work by the need to cope with maniacal clankings inside Nest's diluvial washing machine, Bea had mopped up the floor for the second time that morning and then discovered a snail trying to force an entry into the bread bin. A further search and some tracking on hands and knees of viscid trails discovered a veritable gastropod's doss-house beneath the piece of slate covering the outside drain so she fetched a bucket and piled in all the snails, intending at first to fling them over a far corner of a foreign field.

'I wonder if *all* snails are edible?' she thought, pausing with the bucket and leaning on the wall at the front, enjoying the piercing brilliance of the spring morning. Earlier that day there had been brief visitations of dark squalls flashing across the windows of the painting room. There had been an unimpeded view of the whole dazzling one hundred and eighty degrees of rainbow, the arc framing a thunderous sky above the miraculously sunlit line of orange and yellow thumb prints – polled willows decorating the dykes in the distance. Pots of gold doubtless lay buried at both ends.

Her relationship with the new surroundings had grown ever warmer with the weather. In the first damp days of the move there she'd walked disconsolately across the fields around the house and the air had pressed crushingly on her skull. Now with the heat of the sun striking through her shirt, the deep, clear sky appeared to draw her up into itself, breathe and suck her own breath in and out and cause a sense of giddy levitation.

Another noise was competing with the muffled but now despairing clattering of the washing machine. Agnes's car was proceeding erratically up the track to the house, diapasons of tuneful twanging emanating from its suspension as it bounced along, swerving to avoid the pot-holes. Bea sighed, abandoned the bucket of snails and thoughts of garlic butter and hurried to welcome Agnes and also Seb, who glowered in the back. Releasing himself from the imprisoning car seat he rushed for the pink bicycle, leaving Bea to show Agnes round the house.

Agnes was near speechless with envy.

'But Bea, it's magic!' How fortunate Bea was with all this space to herself and how interesting she'd made it, bringing the yellow sitting room curtains from Fleming Cottage and the favourite little soft blue armchair sitting in the sun by the window. The room had a cool, uncluttered look that was very different from the cushioned cosiness of Fleming Cottage and the walls reflected back the sunlight in a myriad of different shades of grey and translucent creams. A neat stack of bleached driftwood lay beside the fireplace log basket and the fire itself was already laid against the evening chills. Bea had the knack for that sort of thing, apparently effortlessly turning the most unpromising place into something that looked suitable to be photographed for *Country Living*. She looked amazingly good too in spite of the recent emotional upheaval: hair clean and windblown, no bags beneath the long, cool blue eyes. How like Bea to turn a disaster into a asset.

'I tried to phone you but you must have switched it off,' said Agnes as they sat in peace on the warm stone steps in the sunshine and drank coffee. 'Anyway, you might have put me off if I telephoned first.' She bent forward to roll up the bottoms of her jeans and kick off her shoes, offering up pale legs and grubby feet to the ultraviolet rays.

'I would have called you, quite soon, anyway,' said Bea. 'I tried to explain to Mum that I didn't intend to become a recluse, but she doesn't believe it. She seems to have given my phone number to almost everyone. It never stops ringing. I have to turn it off sometimes to get any peace. She's always been able to work with seventy thousand people around her all demanding different things and not turn a hair. I don't think she understands at all what I'm doing here.'

'What *are* you doing here?'

'I'm working. I've never worked so hard. It started out as a means of blocking out things but already there's more to it. It's what's been put off since I was eighteen – a score that needs to be settled. I owe it to Aunt Nest, too, not to disappoint her and waste the time here.' She paused and cleared her throat, tried to sound matter-of-fact but came across rather dryly; not surprisingly it had not been entirely possible to expunge thoughts of Oscar and Andreary from her mind. 'Anyway, a change of scene seemed sensible. The least of it is that it's extremely embarrassing, being dumped.'

Agnes hesitated, chewing her fingernails, then said: 'Talking of settling scores, Phil met Oscar the other evening, after work. I think they had a bit of a barney. I mean, I *know* they had a row. Phil hit him.'

'God! Whatever for?'

'Don't be naïve, Bea. Phil always had the softest of soft spots for you. You must've known? No? Well, he did. Phil thought, afterwards, that he would have to leave his job. However, Oscar seems to have taken it on the chin.' She giggled and Bea could hear the relief in her voice. 'They were both thrown out of the pub and the fact of them both being ejected seemed to have brought out a smidgen of male fellow feeling. Cleared the air a bit. I expect Oscar was hoping to be punished, secretly. Now Phil's landed him one, he'll feel his conscience salved, a little anyway.'

Bea gave a snort of disbelief. 'You think Phil's hitting him makes Oscar feel less guilty about what he did to me? What sad dogs men are.' She found her hand shaking a little as she raised her mug to her lips, which had suddenly become tight and dry. 'Don't worry about the job, though. Oscar's usually pretty practical. He couldn't do without Phil, not at the moment certainly.'

'Would you go back to him if he left Andrea and came home?'

Bea shook her head. 'No. Absolutely not. Well, yes, I suppose it's possible. But not yet, certainly. I haven't thought it through. First I've got to see if the painting works out. But he won't come back. I'm sure of that.' She got up from the steps and stood with her head down and hands tucked defensively into her armpits, thinking that a little time spent away from the painting wouldn't do any harm, but she wasn't going to spend it discussing Oscar, having him and the so-recent past dragged out to this pleasantly anonymous place, polluting it by forcing her to think, undermining the too rapidly acquired disregard for the future.

Perhaps because inlanders automatically think of going to the coast as an occasion for a picnic, Agnes had happily stopped off at a supermarket and bought food on the way: a selection of fine-cut salamis, *pain rustique*, a decadent treacle tart and an odoriferous goat's cheese.

'Let's take the food you've brought out to the sandy beach,' Bea suggested. 'It's so warm today and Seb would love it. It's too far to walk from here but we could go in the pick-up to save your car's poor springs?'

'That sounds perfect. What's in that bucket?' Agnes peered in and drew back in disgust. 'Whatever are you doing with those?'

'I thought they might be nice, cooked properly. I think you have to feed them lettuce, or bran, perhaps, to clean them out in case they've eaten hemlock in the night, and put on a lid to stop them escaping. I was going to telephone Mum and ask her how to cook them.' She saw Agnes's wrinkled nose. 'You could stay and have some for tea.'

'How repellent! Don't tease. You've gone native already. I bet the locals eat frogs?'

'No, I don't think so, but they could if they wanted.' Bea laughed. 'Aunt Nest says the frogs make a terrible noise as the nights get warmer.' She poked some air holes in tinfoil and sealed up the bucket. 'Right, let's be off.'

As they got to the top of the narrow track a blue van came along the road from the left and paused as if about to turn in. The driver was the red-haired man she had met a few days before, Erik the Red. The track was too narrow for two and he smiled in recognition, making a graceful gesture as if to ask them to pull out first and she waved back a thank-you.

'And *who* was that?' asked Agnes, craning round, goggling.

'I don't know his name. I just watched him launching a fishing boat a few days back. I suppose he's a fisherman.'

'He's rather yummy-looking, isn't he, for a red-haired man and in spite of the pigtail?' It appeared to Agnes that there was life after death on the marsh.

Seb enjoyed the beach, wildly. They sat with their backs against a wooden groyne out of the breeze and Bea, having dodged further enquiries about her state of mind, when questioned about her painting, explained some of her doubts.

'Do you remember the malevolent Mrs Morgan, who taught us in fourth year?'

'Of course. It was free-expression time and she hated you because you refused to express yourself. She used to have it in for me too, for the opposite reason.'

'It was having the means of expression forced on me that I didn't care for. Anyway, I'm doing the kind of thing that she would have simply hated. She once asked me which artist I liked most at the moment, and I said Stanley Spencer, at the moment, and she said in her most spiteful voice that that was just what she would have expected. "Your work is so idiosyncratic, Beatrice,"' Bea mimicked. 'I've been a bit haunted by it ever since.'

Agnes thought she shouldn't worry about that now. 'I think its all the rage. Think how successful whatsisname, Damian Dewhurst the artful butcher is – if those displays of surgical dissection and ambitious pickling weren't idiosyncratic, I don't know what was – perhaps he became unhealthily interested in the contents of all those disgusting bottles they have on biology lab windowsills, at school – *Seb! Seb!* You're not to paddle in the sea on your own . . . Come back where I can see you. Look there's a lovely shallow pool just by the end of the groyne – Do you remember when we went to see that silly sheep? Pass me a bit more of that salami, would you? The one with curly edges?'

'Here you are. I thought you'd become a vegetarian? Yes, I do remember. Was it important to him that it was a *pickled* sheep, rather than a stuffed one, do you think? It was too clean by half compared to any sheep that I've since met round here.'

'I'm a vegetarian four days a week, except for bacon at breakfast. I visited a food therapist the other day who said people of my blood group shouldn't eat meat more than three times a week, and then it should only be game. I couldn't afford to eat pheasant for breakfast though.' Agnes chuckled. 'Yes, wasn't it a clean sheep! Bum hand-washed in Dreft, and the way its fleece stood out about the body in the liquid, as if it had been electrocuted.'

'. . . And we couldn't afford the catalogue to see if there were any clues as to how we were supposed to think about it. Perhaps he meant to insinuate it's cruel to eat fluffy food. The only thing it made me think of at the time was Nelson's body being brought back to England on board ship, preserved in rum.' Bea took a bite of salami sandwich and watched Seb for a minute as he filled his little plastic beaker with sea water and tasted it. 'Talking of fluffy food . . . you could always eat rabbit . . . that's game and very cheap. Jerry Rumm told me about a game dealer who sells them, dressed and everything, for one pound apiece.'

'I hate rabbit.' Agnes cut another thick slice of bread. 'I suppose what you were getting at is rather like those "artists' statements" one sees pinned up beside the pictures in art galleries,' she said, folding the last of the salami into a monster doorstep sandwich, 'you get dragged back to the perpetrator as if it was them that was the artwork.'

'But does it matter?' persisted Bea, 'I do wish I'd been to art school, then I'd know if I was talking nonsense or not.'

Agnes snorted with laughter. 'I don't think you missed much on that score. I found most of it great nonsense. The fine art lot were always rather precious.' She lay flat out and patted her stomach. 'I've eaten too much, as usual. I'll have to have a rest before the treacle tart.'

Although she was genuinely pleased to see Agnes, and the sound of the incoming sea rustling in over the sand was very soporific, Bea began to feel a certain amount of angst at the time slipping away and after a while, a feeling of longing for the safety of the painting room came over her. She was relieved when it clouded over and a niggling wind reminded them it was still only April. They suffered the usual screeching from Seb when they decided to leave, Agnes holding him under one arm and trying to push him into the cab head first, while he clung to the doorframe. Eventually they achieved it but then Bea felt she couldn't drive till he'd calmed down. He was throwing his arms about and thrashing, kicking the dashboard and, by now desperate to get on with her work, Bea lost her temper and smacked his knee, just hard enough for him to take notice.

'You've damaged me! You've damaged me!' he screamed.

'Well, you shouldn't have damaged the dashboard!' She held out a sizeable piece of broken plastic. 'I'm sorry, Agnes, but I must get on.' Seb stopped screaming and looked at his mother in surprise, having expected support, but Agnes looked straight ahead, trying not to laugh. 'Oh well, whatever does the trick,' she said, settling back comfortably. She'd enjoyed the outing.

Agnes had to stop at the supermarket on the way back to Bellhurst. During her raid on its shelves earlier that day she'd again forgotten poor Phil's supper. With Seb sitting in the trolley she went and had a look at the frozen game; there were imported rabbits there, miserable skinny little things in plastic wrappings priced at two pounds seventy-five each. She was looking at them doubtfully when someone tapped her on the shoulder.

'Hello, Agnes!'

Mary Dunnock, a friend from school days, stood behind her with three of her children clinging stickily to the trolley, their faces gaudily smeared with orange ice-lolly. Seb immediately crossed his eyes and stuck his tongue out at them and made the youngest howl. Mary herself looked annoyingly trim and un-marked either by lolly or the wearinesses of motherhood.

'Hello, Mary. Just look at the price of these rabbits! My game dealer sells much better ones for only a pound each.'

'Ssh! You'll frighten the children. They think all rabbits are called Benjamin Bunny and can talk.' She lowered her own voice. 'I heard that Oscar Mitty's done a runner – it can't be true?'

Agnes had no sympathy with anthropomorphism but replaced the frozen bunny hastily. 'It is, I'm afraid. I've just been to see poor Bea – she's in a dreadful state and gone into hiding. Oscar ran off with a Sussex cow from somewhere near Battle, Andrea Bullingden. Isn't it sad, after such a long marriage?'

'How extraordinary!' Mary patted the howler on the head, none too gently and looked at Agnes, curiosity laced with suspicion. Mary's husband had once confessed to a passing affair with Agnes some years before she had married him and he had told her some strange stories. She could never quite understand why Agnes and Bea appeared so friendly but put it down to the attraction of a goody-two-shoes for a reprobate and vice versa.

'I've met Andrea. Actually, I met her when I had that little trouble and had to go for a short stay at Saint Cecilia's Rest Home-cum-clinic, at Hatton Hoo, if you remember? Andrea was being detoxed.' She raised her hand and rapidly made the delicate repeated unscrewing motion before her mouth generally used to indicate a drink problem. 'She said it was her fourth time. I thought she was rather charming but her husband had left her because of it so perhaps Oscar won't stick it out very long either.'

Agnes stared back at Mary, noting with satisfaction the rather large pores in her nose but greedy for further information and remembering the massive kitchen in the 'William the IVth' house, remembered also the stash of gin bottles in the cupboard.

'Isn't she cured this time?'

'I don't know, we didn't meet again. She used to get supplies of miniature vodkas smuggled in, so probably not. Well, I must get on. I've got to collect the baby from my mother's, and we've got eight for dinner tonight. I'll call on Bea myself soon.'

After Agnes had left Little Rumm, Bea hurriedly hung up the abandoned washing and went back to work. Messianic wafts of scent from her mother's narcissi hung in the air above the lower notes of paint and white spirit. It was hard to get into a rhythm knowing that all too soon the light would begin to fade, expecting any minute that there might be another interruption but she made good progress during what was left of the afternoon and after clearing up, decided to brave a Fingle pub, have a glass of cider and a bowl of chips, watch the world go by and stop trying to make sense of her present mode of existence. Being on a voyage of discovery and constantly having to return to port and report progress, which was what it felt like when people called, destroyed her concentration for hours afterwards but she was ashamed of her tetchiness with Seb. 'I mustn't be so quick-tempered,' she thought, scrubbing yellow paint from her nails, 'I'm lucky that Agnes cares, and everyone else. But it's such a paradoxical situation . . . I've got to be alone to work, but can't help feeling lonely. Perhaps it would be better to get in first and arrange the visits, in the evenings, then they would come when I was pleased to see them and they would go away happy.' At least Agnes had stopped suffocating her with sympathy and advice. Bea had never found it easy to receive either gracefully.

There was a tinny, crackling sound in the kitchen coming from the snail bucket left by the sink. A mass escape had been effected but two or three had become institutionalised and were rattling about on the underside of the tinfoil, as if trampolining in reverse. It was nearly eight o'clock by the time they'd all been recaptured and saying farewell to the impractical idea of a solitary snail-*fest* she tipped them up outside again, whereupon they slick-footed it back to their previous crannies.

She changed into a freshly-ironed blue shirt, clean trousers and, as it was still cold in the evenings, a black quilted cotton jacket. She glanced at herself in the mirror and lifted her chin, wiping the frown lines from her forehead. Once seated behind the steering wheel however, confidence began to ebb and she fought an impulse to run back into the house.

'Perhaps I only exist on paper,' she thought uncomfortably, 'like a novel. I'm nothing more than the sum of my paintings; but Going Out should restore a measure of reality – it'll be quiet and boring – but I will have been Out. I'll feel less like a statistic.' On the front seat of the pick-up was a plastic bag full of the shells and smelly weed that Seb had wanted to take home. There was also a dear little pair of wet and sandy red socks rolled up and hidden in the bottom. They could be dropped in on Agnes on Saturday when visiting Bookshop Bill, Mrs Lewis and making pre-emptive calls on Tom and Jane. 'Stop prevaricating, get going. You *will* get used to being uncoupled.' She started up the truck.

The Bell and Hatchet had a strong nautical theme, was crowded with brass binnacles, bells, rudders and ships' wheels, the walls hidden by browning photographs of gnarled fishermen in sou'westers, posing by their boats, hauling on ropes and doing embroidery. Blue was perched on a stool against the wall, round the corner of the L-shaped bar, drinking with his friend Nut and talking about that wide range of things which men discuss in bars. Their conversation did not dwell on their work or private lives in any detail, but covered the fact that the rust on Nut's van was sufficient to stop it getting through its MOT and which of them should go out fishing on Sunday afternoon with Big John, since there was only room for one more in the boat. Nest's great approval of the rabbit terrine Blue had made for her the night before was mentioned, as was Nut's useful discovery on the beach of a small wooden table, drifted up in the spring tide last night, relatively undamaged and complete with drawer. They went from beaches to the sea, from sea to sailing ships, from ships to triremes and ancient Greece. Their conversation sometimes veered in unlikely directions.

'What was this golden fleece, d'you reckon, that Jason went out after?' enquired Blue.

'Ah. There's a theory it might be the way the Greeks used to pan for gold. Weight sheep fleeces down on the river bed with stones, then take them up after a couple of days and find the little bits of gold caught up in the fleece along with the silt. It sounds possible.' Nut enjoyed Blue's discursiveness and Blue liked the way Nut told him interesting things, without ever putting on the appearance of being surprised by his ignorance. Though virtually illiterate, Blue was highly intelligent and like many illiterates, had an amazing memory.

'I see. Very clever. It was a good story. All them brazen bulls and dragon's teeth.'

'Is that what you've been reading with Nest?' Although Nut had known Blue for the best part of a year and they got on famously, he had not yet met Nest, and would very much like to.

'Yes – *Tanglewood Tales*, the book's called. I didn't know they were Greeks though. She's teaching me poetry too,' he said, proudly. 'She says I often speak poetically. What *are* iambics?'

'What was it you just said, when you asked about Jason just now? "What *was* this *golden fleece* . . ." Speaking of golden, the girl that's just walked in . . . she's the one I told you about, that I met on the beach.'

'Ah! And that's the one I told you about too. Nest's niece, Bea. We'll go over in a while and I'll introduce you. But go careful. She's been a bit upset recently. What a racket – things seem to be getting a bit rough round the other side. Yes, her husband walked out on her and she's come down to live in Nest's place, to get away from everyone. Hey, it's getting way out of order over there . . .'

It was dark and what little room was left seemed to Bea to be taken up by couples, chomping fish, chips and peas, or pies, or indeterminate pieces of something in orange breadcrumbs with floppy lettuce. She sidled up to the bar, bought a cider, ordered chips and finding an inconspicuous small table in a corner, began to watch. Being tall, fair and on her own, she had not gone unnoticed.

The customers at the bar seemed to fall into two groups: one, a noisy bunch of young men with aggressive haircuts and manners, were clustered round the end of the bar nearest to her, and another group round the corner of the L, who seemed to be mostly locals.

The division between the two groups was not only marked by the geography of the bar; their clothes as well as their behaviour and motley collection of regional accents set the young men apart. Apparently celebrating a birthday, they were spruced up, well-shaved and wearing fairly uniform, pointedly casual trousers with loose pastel-coloured shirts and polished loafers, not trainers or boots. The locals that she could see from her corner appeared scruffier, but were quietly sober and watchful.

Bea sensed a mounting, muttering irritation with the celebrators emanating from a grey-haired man and wife sitting at the next table. The man, dressed in several shades of brown, was of the opinion that squaddies shouldn't be allowed in while there were decent people eating. His wife, in a silver-sequinned T-shirt and black jersey tracksuit trousers worn with high heeled red sandals kept repeating, 'Go on, Les! They're only young once.' There were cheers as one of the boys spilled a pint of lager down himself. As he wavered through the bar on his way to the gents he spotted Bea and her heart sank as he lurched over to her table. Oh no, not over here! Please not over here.

'What 'ave we 'ere? A spot of loveliness in with all the grey shit.' He stared, unfocused but heavily meaningful, at the man in brown, then put his hands on Bea's table and leant over to her, rocking slightly and slopping her drink. He was not bad-looking, Bea thought, but rather short and about to be sick at any minute. She leant as far back into the corner as possible.

'Gi' us a kiss then, sweet'art.'

'Perhaps another time,' said Bea, smiling at him in a placatory way, hoping to defuse him, her clear-cut and well-educated voice echoing unfortunately in her own ears. He swung unsteadily round to his mates, seeking reassurance.

'I'm not drunk, am I?' Then back to Bea, suddenly vicious, 'No need to get upset, you little slapper . . . just passing the time of day.' His breath was noisome with beer and curry.

Bea was saved from further annoyance by the delivery of the bowl of chips by a woman of considerable breadth and height.

'Push off now, and leave the young lady alone.' She towered over him, and Bea also stood up, adding further height to the confrontation. She was suddenly angrily prepared to douse him in cider if he didn't leave her alone. He only came up to her shoulder.

'Oooh! Young lady, is it? You watch it, Pete!' jeered his friends, 'They're bigger than you!'

Pete's bravado was overcome by his need to get to the lavatory fast and he disappeared. The waitress looked at Bea apologetically:

'Don't worry. They're all mouth, this lot,' and she disappeared. Bea sat down and started to pick at the chips. The atmosphere was getting a little tense. Sequins leant over and patted her knee consolingly. 'That's right. Don't worry, dear. We'll keep them in order.'

At that moment Pete re-appeared, and in passing, removed Sequins' plate of chicken nuggets from before her and carrying it high up in the air, danced towards the bar, shouting,

'She's too fat already. She don't need these!'

Sequins sat back, her plump thighs splayed out on the Dralon-covered bench, her jaw agape, knife and fork poised uselessly in mid-air. Her brown-trousered husband leapt to his feet and set off, bent on rescuing his wife's supper. No easy matter, since the plate was being passed around from man to man above his head while he leapt and grabbed ineffectually, a piggy-in-the-middle, a rainstorm of peas cascading on his head. The group of locals put down their pints and moved in. The landlord behind the bar was frantically telephoning.

Then they were instantly brawling and Sequins' remaining chicken and chips were ground into the worn floral carpet. The juke box was playing 'Love Me Tender, Love me Do' from its golden oldie section but as Elvis faded and Brown was decked, it switched to pre-selected jungle music. Sequins started to squeal in short breathless bursts. A tiny grey-faced old woman in a bright pink nylon shell-suit stood by the flashing fruit machine, unconcernedly poking money into it and nudging buttons. Bea shrank disbelieving back into the darkness of her corner, wondering how to escape and was considering diving under the very inadequate cover of the table. She heard for the first time in her life the agonising crunch of fist against cheekbone, and thought miserably of Phil and Oscar. People were trying to leave through a side door, but it appeared to be locked. A beer mug flew across the room.

'Come on. Move. This way!' Erik the Red urgently put a hand on her arm and hauled her to her feet. 'Come *on!* The red-caps'll be here in a minute.' He ducked as a bunch of plastic daffodils, still wedged in their vase, sailed past him and shattered on the wall. He almost dragged her through the door marked Toilets just as a whistle blew and the front door burst open. There was a frenzied barking and a sudden lessening of the din but also the sound of a pumping cascade of coins as the old lady in pink won the jackpot.

There was a long stone passage lying behind both bar and

kitchens and she followed Erik out into a dark and greasy backyard.

'You *must* have been hungry,' he said, grinning with no trace now of his previous surliness. She was still carrying the half-empty bowl of chips.

'I hadn't finished my drink either.'

'Well, we'll have to get you another one then, won't we?' said another voice behind her, and there was a dishevelled Blue, his shirt hanging out, sucking his knuckles. He had an attractive gap between his front teeth when he smiled, and looked remarkably pleased with himself. Bea knew why Nest found him so compelling. 'The police have taken the dogs in to sort them out. They only bite squaddies – they can smell their aftershave. I don't think Nest'd approve of you being in the Bell and Hatchet.' He wrung his wrist as if to re-arrange the bones in his hand. 'We'll take you somewhere a bit quieter, if you'd like? Bugger! I've left me jacket behind in the bar – I'll just pop back into the kitchens and get Susie to fetch it out.' He disappeared again.

'But where do they come from, the squaddies?' Bea offered the Viking a chip and together they finished them, leaving the bowl on the doorstep where a fat, blue-chinned member of the kitchen staff in a stained white apron was leaning against the door jamb, unconcernedly rolling up a cigarette.

'There's army firing ranges not far away. Didn't you know? You've not noticed the MoD signs? There's only occasionally a bit of a bother. It used to be a good pub before the brewery changed its name, tarted it up, and put in a manager.'

Bea had never before seen grown men fighting. The build up to the affair and the subsequent violence had been both subtly fascinating and frightening – it was all a long way from evening drinks parties on the neatly mown lawns of Bellhurst. She asked him if he thought the fighting had been territorial or punitive.

'A bit of both, I expect. Protective even, for poor Lally's supper. But the fact that a woman on her own, a friend of Blue's, was being bothered might have had something to do with it!' He was scrutinising her, now so close, with an eye for the fine detail of her face. The so-almost-straight nose. Eyes like delphiniums. A couple of tiny lines at one corner of the mouth, as if she often smiled lopsidedly, up one side more than the other.

'But how did they know so quickly, the locals, that Blue knows me?'

'The people round here are very private about their own doings but not so pernickety about outsiders and aren't above a good gossip. I'm an outsider too. You can probably tell by the accent? It's known that you've moved into Little Rumm and there is a bit of speculation about it.'

Bea digested this somewhat uneasily while covertly listening for the colour in the voice beneath the Northern Irish accent, and found it a pleasantly crunchy chestnut brown.

Blue reappeared, wriggling into a patched army-surplus combat jacket. It had been the locals, not the soldiers, who had been wearing the odd piece of army uniform.

They were escorting her through an alleyway out into a small square green and over to another less threatening drinking place. Bea, heart still pumping with adrenalin, was much comforted by Blue's presence and more than a little interested in the now friendly Erik striding along beside her in his flapping ancient Dryzabone waterproof.

'I spotted you earlier and would have come over anyway, before the trouble started,' said Blue, standing back for her at the door, 'but Nut said he'd met you already and fetched you away while I sorted the one in the blue shirt.'

She turned to Nut. 'Nut? That can't be your real name?' It couldn't, of course, have been Erik the Red.

'Francis Nutmeg,' said the re-baptised Erik, somewhat defensively. He wandered off to fetch their drinks and she noticed Blue's expression had passed from smug to positively demure.

'Here we are there then, Blue – none but the brave

deserve the beer. How's your knuckles? Bea, your cider.' Nut folded himself up on the chair opposite her and grinned a companionable, even, white-toothed grin

'What happened to the fishing boat?' she asked. 'Was it launched eventually?'

'Oh yes. That night. A bit more drama to the story though. Shall I tell you about it? Well, its engine, a reconditioned engine, mind you, cut out on the way along to Rye, and there was a stiffish onshore wind. They got it tied up snug up against a wreck marker and had to radio for help, so the lifeboat had to be launched again, for real this time, to tow them into harbour.' Nut chuckled unmaliciously at the skipper's continuing misfortunes, pulled tobacco from his pocket and started to roll a cigarette, fingers deftly tidying the brown threads into the skinny white roll of fine paper.

'It seems,' said Bea, 'to be rather a reluctant boat.' She noticed that in the lapel of his long coat there was a little loop of very pale green ribbon fastened with a pin, like the red Aids ribbons or the pink ones for breast cancer, or the bright green for Sinn Fein. Curious, she asked him what cause it represented.

'That? Lettuce Awareness Week.'

'No, be serious! What is it for?'

'I haven't a clue. I got caught by a pretty girl outside the Boots in Parden. She had a tray of them, so I gave her twenty pence and she pinned one on. I must admit I can't remember what the charity was. Where were you off to this morning?'

'Taking a friend and her little boy down to the beach for a picnic. And where were you going, down the little track?'

'On a visit to Jerry Rumm.'

There was an exceptional something about Nut's cheek-bones. High and sharply jutting, they gave his face, which when resting had a certain fine severity of line, an attractive, almost elfin look. Concerned that she was staring too obviously she turned to her drink and pondered the source of the attraction. Too obsessed with Oscar's face for so many years, she truthfully hadn't often had fancies for other men, nor had she ever slept with anyone apart from him. She imagined now, probably rightly, that she was the only person among her contemporaries with such a limited sexual history and wondered what it might be like with someone else; with Nut, for instance?

Sex with Oscar had been, at first, a curious journey inside herself. It had taken time to discover what destination was intended and though there had been moments when she spotted it in the distance and swam desperately towards it, each time it seemed if not a mirage, then further off. She had put down the descriptions of sex in the teen magazines to fanciful imaginations, although she'd discovered from them what innovations to their private rituals kept Oscar happy and although vaguely disappointed, she settled for that level of pleasurable fun she had attained. There had been times when Oscar had quite suddenly gone off sex for two or three months and she'd felt lonely and crossly deprived. Then gradually things had picked up and he too tried unfamiliar things, but she was still aware that something vital was eluding her. There was something finicky, she now realised, about his delicate lovemaking. She had no idea how to discuss it. The large and immediate presence of Nut across the table had aroused pink-inducing thoughts of further research but she was interrupted in mid-blush by the sound of a siren.

'Do you think someone was seriously hurt?' she asked, thinking the wailing might be an ambulance.

'Doubt it,' said Blue, 'but here's more Bell and Hatchet evacuees. What's the score, John?'

'The birthday boys have all been carted off in a truck and the police are taking a statement from Lally. They've sent an ambulance for her Les. He's got a plastic daffodil embedded in his left buttock. The manager's trying to keep things low key and is offering everyone free drinks.' John was undoubtedly one of the two dark brothers Bea had seen at the beach talking to Erik/Nut and was now accompanied by a girl in tiny black top and jeans decorated with a red splash of tomato ketchup down one leg.

'This,' said Blue, with a vague introductory gesture in Bea's direction,' is my Nest's niece, Bea Mitty.'

'Pleased to meet you, Bea,' said John, 'This is Lucinda. She works for Nest.' Lucinda smiled rather fetchingly at Nut, more curiously at Bea and sat down beside her on the bench, dabbing at the ketchup with a paper napkin. She looked a bit young to be going out with John, who had greying sideburns, the promising beginnings of a paunch and monstrous blurred red and blue tattoos from wrist to elbow, and as far as Bea could see, more starting just above the neck of his T-shirt and working downwards. He asked Lucinda hopefully whether she hadn't been just a bit scared back at the Bell and Hatchet. She replied she hadn't been, but it had all happened so fast, hadn't it, and she did think it was a shame whoever it was had had their birthday spoilt, 'you're all as bad as pikies ... it was only a bit of fun, taking Lally's plate; I'm sure they'd have given it back, given the chance, and just look at the mess on my jeans ... someone shoved me and I sat right in Ernie Thompson's supper ... I only got them in the market on Thursday ... they were ever so cheap ...' she turned to Bea, 'Have you found the clothes stall between the man with the urns and flowerpots and the old girl with the cheeses and the wraparound Indian skirts? Those flowerpots are good value too, much cheaper than the ones your Auntie sells ... you look just like her, doesn't she, Blue?' She rambled on unchecked, till Nut caught Bea's eye – she'd been trying not to laugh – and smiled.

'Time I was off. I'll see you, John, and Blue.' He nodded pleasantly to Lucinda who nodded back without ceasing the flow of chat and then he bent down and asked Bea, very quietly close to her ear, where her car was parked and if she would care to be escorted back to it? Bea, having finished her drink, did rather. She certainly couldn't face much more of the loquacious Lucinda, nor did she want another drink. Blue looked up at her with a gap-toothed grin of irritating benediction.

'See you soon, Bea.'

A police car was leaving as they turned into the street where stood the infamous Bell and Hatchet; they could hear sounds of sweeping and the tinkle of broken glass being emptied into bins as they passed the closed doors. It was starting to drizzle.

'Is this yours? It's held together with baler twine! It's worse than mine!' He held the loose-hinged door for her while she climbed up into the cab. 'I'll see you around then?' he said, standing back with his hands in his deep pockets.

'I expect so,' she said, 'and thanks, for hauling me out of that mess,' and seeing from his expression that he was just about to say something else, waited.

'Would you like to come out for a drink with me one day?' He looked momentarily uncertain of himself.

She was also uncertain, but found the idea of saying untruthfully, 'No, thank you' quite impossible.

'I'd like to, yes. But not here, though? Not at the Bell and Hatchet?'

'Lord, no. Plenty of better places, round and about. I'll call for you, where you're staying. How about this Saturday, at eight?' Pin-heads of fine rain glistened in the street light on the caped shoulders of his coat and in the red hair. The street was now empty and silent.

Bea smiled; it was twelve years since she'd been asked out on a date. 'I'll see you, then,' she said, starting up the engine.

Nut watched the truck's tail lights till it turned the corner and then exhaled deeply. He'd been holding his breath, rooted to the spot, with knowledge in his leaves and branches. He hunched his shoulders as the rain became heavier and a sudden wind got up, drifting the spray across the road in the light of the single street lamp as he walked, softly whistling, to the blue van and sat inside rolling another cigarette. 'Jesus,' he said, aloud, 'I think that might be my woman.' He was a great optimist.

Nut had discovered early in his teens that he was attractive to a good section of the female population and had, at first, been terrified. Though his good fortune had been impressed upon him by envious friends who'd noticed that within fifteen minutes of him walking in to the JCR at Liverpool (where he was reading geography) that over half of the females present had gravitated down to his end of the bar, he'd gradually realised that those who could abide red hair in the first place, which certainly wasn't all of them, were very definitely overinterested and he'd had to unhook a few of them from his shirt like burdock seeds and rein in the ebullient, sociable nature. Friends had put it down to an unfair share of pheromones and found his reluctance to take advantage of the unlikely allure quite incomprehensible. Eventually he'd begun to enjoy himself, but carefully, learning to sift very politely through the women who were unaware why they stood so close that they almost drowned in his drink.

Twice he'd made mistakes and been seriously outplayed. Pretty, impatient, loquacious Mel, Mel the raven-haired Australian social anthropologist. They had not intended their relationship at university to become permanent and it had initially, on his part, been a means of holding off the hordes, but through a growing and genuine affection they'd stayed together for four years, until she decided she wanted a child, became pregnant, changed her mind and had an abortion all in three months and all without, for once, telling him a word of it. On discovering the scrunched-up antenatal card while searching desperately in her pocket for some small change to pay the milkman, he'd been gobsmacked by the unnecessary duplicity.

Nut leant his head on his arms on the steering wheel, remembering how it had been the secrecy which had been unhinging, since he wouldn't have tried to impede her, whatever she'd decided. He had not known that feelings could change with such drastic, tearing swiftness; tenderness to repulsion in minutes. Unbeknownst to him she'd been offered a well-funded job in Finland studying some social foible of the Lapps, who had surely already been seriously studied from every possible angle till they were in a state of nervous self-consciousness. She admitted that was at least part of the reason for aborting the baby (perhaps a baby daughter? – he'd thought about it a lot). It seemed incredible that he'd lost his child for the sake of some poxy, magic mushroom-munching Father Christmases, all tinkling bells and red-and-blue skirts. It hadn't made sense; he'd happily have looked after and loved it while she was charming shamans or researching the impact of TV on little Lapps.

Mel had also spent time in the States and been convinced that being Irish in England, he was a badly treated underdog and she would keep fighting his corner for him when there was no need. He'd explained about dual nationality, told her how she of all people should know how mixed and mongrelled the inhabitants of the British Isles were, but she'd sigh and look at him and say 'But, Fraz, I know that deep down inside you're culturally Irish. You must find it difficult, living in the land of past oppressors.' Well, perhaps she was right about the Irishness; it is the earliest years which count and still, after seventeen years here, the English picked up on his accent. However, whenever he went over to visit his Uncle Charlie, it was always commented a little mockingly, that he was 'quite the Englishman now'. He wasn't one thing or the other, sod it, and it was the English father who'd had red hair, but he was comfortable with being an inhabitant of the British Isles – he felt no urgent need to belong or conform to any particular ethnic group. Geographer was his nationality, and religion, well, that was merely one way of making sense of the world, but it was not his way.

There had been a period of globe-trotting after the separation from Mel, supporting himself by arranging temporary teaching posts along the way in Hong Kong and Singapore and after a brief stint in Sydney, returning to Europe for a glorious six months rounding the rim of the Mediterranean from Morocco to Spain, stopping for longer than was strictly necessary in Turkey where he'd met the ethereal, silent Annie and returned to England with her. It was during this odyssey that he regained his child's eye for landscape, had seen once more the emotional content of the earth rather than its physical consituents, taken pleasure in the shape of a hill without immediately analysing its provenance.

Happily indigent, he and Annie had shared cramped flats in a variety of places while he completed his PhD but his constant absences due to the nature of his work eventually irked her and she had given up on him while he was only half way through, embarked on a circumnavigation of the world with an over-charming and equally silent Swede. Not broken-hearted for long, more briefly melancholic, he'd nevertheless played hard to get till coming South, where there had naturally been the occasional hunting forays and once after a party, unfortunately, Lucinda. Sadly there'd been no one who'd held his interest for long and anyway, he'd been kept busy in his particular palaeogeographical bent, for the Siegfried McKay-Tart Trust's grand survey of the marsh.

But Bea. There was a rare grace and a deliciously gullible, half-bewildered innocence about her, a little out of keeping with her age, perhaps, but hers was surely an unusually gorgeous body. On one of their recent evenings out together at the Eeldyke Inn Blue had described Bea, unoriginally but with a dreamy sigh, as heaven on long legs and a bit shy. Certainly there was a great deal more to her than the legs and she was not shy but he had gained the impression of tension behind the eyes, a sense of purpose. He sensed competition.

Ironically it had been footloose Annie who had told him that he didn't take life seriously enough. He took work seriously though and thoroughly enjoyed it, but life – too short, too long, too unpredictable. When did you examine it? Give it an MOT? At what period did you begin to feel this is a life I'm living – I'd better poke about in it a bit and see if it's still pink inside, or getting burnt on top? If you're unaware of its beginning, how to judge the moment to take stock? The years had zipped past, but then, that was the payment for enjoying yourself. He was thirty-four. He felt the need for a different pace and a change in direction. Now Bea; he re-explored her golden oval face which disconcertingly faded as he thought about it, and what she'd said and the sound of the clear, bell-metal voice . . .

There was a firm tap-tap on the window. He nearly leapt out of his skin and glancing up saw through the rivulets of rain on the glass, the face of a constable peering in suspiciously. He swatted away the sensation of instant but unnecessary guilt.

'Are you all right there?'

'Yes. I wasn't asleep. I was thinking,' and seeing the doubt in the man's eyes, 'I'm not over the limit, I'm not smoking crack. I'm just thinking.'

'Might I see your licence please?'

He felt in his inside jacket pocket and produced it.

'*Doctor* Francis Nutmeg?'

'Yes, that's me.'

'Thank you, sir. Sorry to have bothered you. Mind how you go. Good night.'

Chapter Five

Bea sat outside Fleming Cottage, rain drumming on the roof of the truck and dripping through a gap in the windscreen seal, splattering her knee. Postponing the moment of entering her own house, she decided to visit Mrs Lewis first. She threw her green mac over her head and made a dash for it, shaking herself like a Saluki on the doorstep and ringing the bell. There was a lengthy pause followed by scuffling from inside as Mrs Lewis unchained, unbolted and finally escaped from her jail. Standing there clad in a long, drooping cardigan she blinked in the gloom as if confronted by a bright light. The cardigan was parrot green, with scarlet buttons. Bea had never seen her wear anything but grey before and the originality of her dress was astonishing.

'Hello, Mrs Lewis. I came to thank you and see if it was still all right, if you minded carrying on seeing that everything's OK next door?'

'Come in, dear.' said Mrs Lewis, surprisingly. 'You seem very wet.' She stood aside to let Bea in. 'Everything is quite in order next door. I've checked it every morning and every night. Here's your post.' Her voice retained its thick crackled glaze but there was something definitely different about Mrs Lewis, an awareness, almost a cheeriness that was difficult to comprehend. The faded grey-blue eyes, instead of sliding down and to one side now looked straight into Bea's, alert, pleading even? The semi-catatonic trance that had prevailed ever since Bea and Oscar had moved in next door seemed to have lifted; certainly so many sentences had never crossed her lips during their previous encounters.

Bea followed Mrs Lewis, for the first time, into the drawing room and was again surprised. It was a faded place but the colours had lightened into an exquisitely soft fruitiness. Palest lemon cushions lay on a sofa now unevenly bleached by the sun to pomegranate pinky cream. The curtains were of aged apricot and lime-green stripes, long since stripped of their chintzy glaze, the only patterned fabric in the room. Everything else was plain; the carpet a plain ripe melon, the worn armchair by the window plain grape-purple tweed. Even in the gloomy light it was a delicious fruit salad of a room.

'Would you care for some coffee?'

Bea nodded, speechless. On the walls hung black ink drawings in grey frames with yellow mounts and it was these that attracted Bea like magnets while Mrs Lewis rattled in the kitchen. A young man in a striped Breton jersey and rolled-up trousers lounged laughing on a stone wall, surrounded by fruit and fish. Another in boots, corduroys and waistcoat leant upon a spade, surveying a trophy of vegetables. They looked familiar to Bea – there was a similarity to the frontispieces of one or two of her mother's library of cookery books. There were others to do with food and cooking and a water-colour of derelict machinery in a farmyard by Eric Ravilious. The style of the room – the teak coffee table with its tapering pin-like legs stuck out at angles, the shapes of the jugs on the wide windowsill and the asymmetrical yellow fruit bowl on the side table – was the unchanged, unadulterated late nineteen-fifties. Agnes's mother, now on a new retro tack, would at present give her front teeth for the things in this room.

Mrs Lewis returned, moving steadily and with little sign of her previous shakiness, carrying bi-coloured cups of coffee, pink on the outside and green on the inside, on a smoky glass tray. She sat stiffly down by the window in the grape-coloured chair, gesturing Bea over to the sofa.

'Now tell me, how are you getting along?' Two direct questions in five minutes. Having decided not to dissemble when she'd asked for Mrs Lewis's help in keeping an eye on the cottage, and having told her briefly the facts of what had happened, Bea now found herself summing up.

'I've settled in very well. I'm ... I'm painting a lot. I was scared of being lonely, but I'm getting used to it. And people keep coming to visit. It's different.'

'Yes. People your age, so young, you need changes now and then, I expect. Although I don't mean for a moment that the sort of change you have undergone was in any way the sort you needed.' Mrs Lewis paused, her veined hands clasping and unclasping in her lap. 'I've seen your husband.' Her eyes gleamed briefly and Bea detected a little flicker of malice in the pale eyes now fixed on her again. 'He came to get a chainsaw. But I *didn't* tell him I had the new keys to the house, so he couldn't get in. Was that the right thing to do?' Her face had a hint of colour to the cheeks and Bea saw she was very pleased to be participating, however peripherally, in an undercover operation.

How sad it was that she had not made more strenuous attempts to be friendly in the years gone by, but Mrs Lewis then had appeared inert, dementedly dull and unresponsive; but this was not the room of someone dull, however long ago it had been arranged.

'Yes, you did the right thing. If he wants to get in touch with me he can, via my parents. I can't face speaking to him directly, at least, not yet ... That water-colour ... it's very interesting isn't it? The arrangement of the machinery shapes into a believable order and the clean hills behind, so round and fat? Are those the South Downs, do you know ...? I've only ever seen his work in the Imperial War Museum. We went there on a school trip once, years ago ...' Bea halted since further signs of animation were flowering on Mrs Lewis's face.

'That was my mother's. She was at the Royal College of Art with Ravilious,' Mrs Lewis's eyes, so nearly always cast aside or down when she was speaking, now looked with hope straight into Bea's, 'and the John Mintons as well. I hope you won't be cross with me ... I found a sketch book of yours, on your kitchen windowsill when I went inside to check, and had a little peep.' She cleared her throat and sipped at her coffee, peering shyly up at Bea over the rim of the cup. 'They were beautiful drawings, quite exceptional. I saw you often, drawing in the garden ... I wanted to see what you were doing, but couldn't make myself ask. Silly of me, I know.'

'Why did you feel you couldn't ask?'

'Because ... I ... I get frightened of people. Not all the time – just on and off. But since you came round, and asked me to look after the house, I felt I could talk to you, perhaps. But it was too late. You were leaving. And you were so distressed. I think it was the coming in contact with your distress that made me stop.'

'Stop what?' asked Bea, her sense of sins of omission nearly reducing her to tears.

'Stop taking the pills – I've been taking them for such an age – they'd become a habit you see. They stopped me thinking, and that was very pleasant, easy. I took sleeping pills, too. For quite a while after stopping them, I felt rather ill, been tempted back, but I've been feeling so much better over the last three days. I wanted to apologise to you, for being such a bad neighbour.'

'It's us, we who've been such bad neighbours, Mrs Lewis.'

It was extraordinary, she explained to Agnes later on that morning after she had cursorily visited her own cottage, which had a moribund air and seemed already to belong to the past, quite extraordinary how one could see Mrs Lewis returning to life, stretching her cramped faculties like a cat let out of a basket. '... and the black-and-white illustrations on the walls were John Mintons, and she had her mother's paintings upstairs, and her own – amazing still lives of fungi. Her name is Geraldine and she's been suffering from depression, on tranquillisers and Mogadon since her husband died. I think it's criminal, locking up a woman's personality for all those years. I feel so guilty. We, I, *could* have helped her before, at least we could have tried. If *only* I'd known.'

Agnes looked at her doubtfully. Bea rarely sounded so impassioned; how was it that she managed to unearth such interesting people in such unpromising surroundings? She appeared to be growing wings since moving and seemed to be getting to grips with life without Oscar rather too fast. Her cheerfulness was out of place. Having asked Bea if she would like to meet Phil and herself for a meal out that night and been told that no, she couldn't as she was being taken out for a drink by a fisherman, Agnes could see that her own caring role might be short lived. She had imagined herself as the loyal friend providing interesting succour for the grieving, lonely Bea and finding she was not needed for the part, well it put her out, just a bit. One relies on one's friends to need one now and then.

'Tell me more about this Nut, then.'

'There's not much to tell. I don't know him yet. But he seems very pleasant and pulled me out of the pub when there was a fight.' It was quite enjoyable, teasing Agnes.

'Fight? What fight? Tell me about it!' Agnes squawked, gratifyingly agog and Bea obliged, ending up irritatingly with '... so, anyway, he asked me out for a drink. I'm finding it quite exciting living on my own. What does he look like? But you saw him in the blue van, just as we were pulling out of our lane, do you remember? That one. He's big and rangy, a good six foot four, and has astounding bones. I badly want to draw him.'

'So you're going round picking up fishermen as models then?'

'Of course not. Actually I don't think he is a fisherman, but it's nice to find some tottie on the marsh. I've got to be going. Here's Seb's shell collection and his little pair of socks. I've washed them. I'm sorry the shells are a bit noisome; something must have died in one of them.'

Agnes was quite stunned by Bea's insouciance and was left feeling unreasonably acid, taking it out on Phil when he came home with the food shopping.

It had been a carefully produced show of bravado. Bea had been determined to give Agnes no space to start Oscar-ing, almost as if she were mourning his loss herself. By the time she got to the Bellhurst supermarket, she was feeling very nervous indeed of being alone with Francis Nutmeg. Although Blue knew him, and she had some trust in Blue, it had occurred to her that perhaps Blue had had an ulterior motive in sending him over to rescue her. Perhaps they had even discussed her as they sat out of sight round the bend of the bar? She watched a tall man and woman in well-bred jeans and identical Guernsey sweaters meet by the kitchen towels; they both wore spectacles which clashed like stags locking antlers as they kissed, totally unself-consciously, once, twice, thrice. They seemed so pleased to see each other that Bea felt a little pang of envy. Then she bumped into Phil in the Pet and Baby-food aisle.

'Hello Bea,' said Phil, awkwardly. There was an unnatural expression, combining complicity and guilt, on his normally guileless schoolboy face. '... Agnes says you're bearing up well, under the circumstances. I am so sorry ...'

'Does she? Well, yes, I hope I am.' Tensely.

'If there's anything I can do for you, you know, chopping firewood or lifting anything heavy?' The startling green eye looked wistfully at her.

She wanted to tell him, but did not, that there was a faint crust of breakfast egg yolk gilding his upper lip. He was a kind man, Phil. This, however, was the man who had thumped her husband. How rough everyone seemed to be becoming; she hoped Nut didn't go in for that sort of thing.

'That's sweet of you, Phil, but there are logs there already, a great heap of them, cherry and apple, piled up against the wall and I shouldn't think I'll be needing fires for much longer. But thank you, for offering.'

She must get back to the marsh as fast as possible; it was too exposed in the supermarket and she was dreading running into other acquaintances. They made their farewells, locked the wheels of their shopping trolleys, sorted themselves out, flustered and apologising and said good-bye again. She got as far as Fingle before remembering she'd forgotten to buy a chicken.

The rain clouds had passed over and there was a carrion crow in the garden, tearing with its horny beak at the sodden remains of a rabbit. It flew off as Bea heaved her shopping up the path to the blue door and she side-tracked across the damp garden with the bag of food, to stand and stare curiously down at the little corpse. It had died of myxomatosis, blind, its eyelids grossly swollen and weeping. The crow watched her from the field, pacing up and down like a shoulder-padded, small-town crook, waiting to resume its meal. With revulsion gagging her throat, she gingerly picked up the rabbit by a hind leg and flung it over the wall towards the crow, who flapped upwards a foot or two then pounced again on its interrupted lunch.

She went in and washed her hands, deciding not to eat anything. The sight of the diseased rabbit had been off-putting. Upstairs in the painting room, she watched the bird from the window; it had now been joined by two other circling undertakers, their black plumage dull even in the brief bursts of afternoon sunshine. She stood drawing them while thinking about the revelation of Mrs Lewis that morning and about the possibly revelatory meeting with Nut that evening. This was flustering but she calmed herself by adding a crow to the prow of the fishing boat in the painting before restlessly returning to the wet garden to draw. The child's bicycle still lay, dying, where Seb had left it half-crushing a rosemary bush. One of the pedals had fallen off and the leprous chrome was peeling from the handlebars. She was saved from becoming further oppressed by the obviousness of the image of decay by Nest's arrival bearing gifts of chocolate biscuits and little brown envelopes of seed.

'Hello, my darling! Am I interrupting anything? You look very gothic sitting on the wall. May I show you where the windproof patch is? We should scatter these seeds about, now.'

Bea looked curiously at the labels on the packets, hand-written in Nest's awesomely irregular writing and read them aloud, rolling the words around in her mouth: 'Opium, single, dk. purple/scarlet fringe. *Papaver rhoeas*, claret and smoked pink doubles ... Opium, v. double, dusty-mauve ...' Smoked pink doubles sounded exciting, like a salmon sandwich. Nest's 'should' emphatically signified 'must'. Now was the time, so now they would do it.

'All right, Aunt Nest. Let's find this windproof patch.'

When they returned to the front of the house, seeds sown and carrying mugs of tea and biscuits, to sit damply on cushions on the steps, one of the carrion crows was sitting on the handlebars of the bicycle. He did not fly away but sat there beady-eyed, patiently waiting for something. Nest ate the chocolate off the top of a biscuit and threw it the remains, remarking that he seemed too tame for his own good.

'Perhaps he's someone's pet?' suggested Bea. 'What about the farm back down the track. Perhaps it's Jerry Rumm's.'

'Not very likely — most farmers are convinced that crows peck out lambs' eyes while they're still alive and I wouldn't put it past them. Jeremiah Rumm would be more likely to shoot it.' Nest finished her tea, and got up to go. 'Right, I must get back at once. The nursery's open all day tomorrow as well.'

'I met your Lucinda the other night, in a pub.'

'Blue said. I bet she gave you earache. She doesn't draw breath, does she? I have to rescue customers from her sometimes, standing there with heavy pots in their hands, their eyes glazing over while she tells them about what she wore to last year's New Year's Eve party at the Alcatraz in Parden. But she's gentle with the plants, seems to know quite a bit and is resolutely cheerful. She's still nagging me to join that ecological movement she's involved with, but I haven't really got the time for anything formalised like that. It all sounds a bit strange and I couldn't get from her who exactly the organisers of this group are. I might pop along to one of their meetings but I'll stick to writing letters to the papers, I think. Glad you're getting out and about, though. See you soon, my sweet.'

Nest swung nimbly up into the yellow van and rattled off, leaving Bea even more restless and wondering what to do to fill in the time – it was impossible to concentrate on painting with the evening's outing hanging over her head. She thought of ringing Blue to get Nut's phone number, calling him to say she didn't feel well, or perhaps hide upstairs and leave a note on the door saying she'd unavoidably had to go out to look after a sick granny, but knew she couldn't.

'For goodness' sake,' she told herself, 'stop making such a big deal out of going out for a drink! Other women do it every day, I believe. We'll have a beer, tell each other lies about ourselves, rub noses and then he'll bring me home. There's no need to get involved. The fact that I *think* it's going to be so difficult probably means it'll be perfectly easy. It'll be a positive step – good to have a friend in the area. I won't change my clothes – I'll go as I am. This is me. Take it or leave it.'

At seven o'clock she bathed and washed her hair, spending some time at the mirror plucking her eyebrows before changing into a thick cotton, indigo blue skirt, long and narrow and a matching long-sleeved top. She thought she looked too dressy, changed back into her jeans, then almost weeping with annoyance, back into the skirt again, cursing her neurotic indecision. *Had* Blue suggested to Nut that he take her out to cheer her up? She didn't need cheering up; she wanted to work without these nagging interruptions. What had Blue said about her, if anything? 'Go on, Nut! have a crack at the ice-maiden . . . ?' She could hear the round Kentish intonation of Blue's voice in her head, imagine the suggestive grin . . . one couldn't go out with someone attached to such a ridiculous name. However, when Francis Nutmeg rat-tatted firmly on the door at eight o'clock, out she went.

He had been leaning gracefully against the garden wall, resting back on his elbows, the great long legs encased in black trousers. The sun was setting behind the fiery head and he wore a black shirt and dark jacket which emphasised the eerie paleness of his skin. If she had been in the mood to allow herself to consider such a thing, she would have fallen for him on the spot. His startled appraisement of her as she came through the front door was first pleasing, then annoying and he smiled broadly, which was annoying then pleasing since he had a smile that started deep under the skin and fairly zipped across his face, around the short, straight, sharp nose and up along the wondrous cheekbones.

Bea awoke to a mighty noise, and fell out of bed. On hands and knees, head throbbing with thunder, she peered about in the gloom and found she was still fully dressed and had not been in bed, but lying on it. There was a flash of lightning, pink, another rip of thunder and she crawled shakily back onto the bed and clutched the duvet round her. With mouth parched, her head a football being kicked about the room, she fumbled for the bedside glass of water and knocked back the dusty contents. What time was it? What day? Why did she feel so ill? Oscar was good at tea and hot-water bottles. Why wasn't he looking after her? She had been dreaming that patches of gelatinous green mosses and liverwort had been growing round her hairline and peering frantically at her reflection in a dark, spotted mirror, had been trying to pull them off, but as fast as the green pads and cushions were peeled away they grew back again.

Wincing at each movement, she put fragile feet to the floor and stood, swaying. There was paracetamol somewhere, but where, where was she? Little Rumm, that much came back to her. She must be ill, have typhoid, yellow fever or marsh ague . . . what had happened yesterday? Bill at the bookshop, parents, Mrs Lewis, Agnes . . . not in that order but it was a start. Nest with her poppy seeds in the afternoon . . . she opened a drawer of the dressing table, found the pills and tottered to the bathroom, downing two with great throat-stretching gulps of water. In the mirror the face was white, eyes ringed with black and what at first she took for shaming bruises on her neck turned out to be stains from the indigo dye of her shirt. She was grateful however, that the expected creeping growth of moss around her face was not a reality.

The thunder still grumbled and it was the sky itself which was bruise-purple, the light an angry bronze. The sound of a fire engine in the distance brought to mind a previous evening, of a fight, of Blue, and of Nut and she sank down on the damp bath mat on the floor with a moan of mortification. She must have become ill and he had brought her home. She stood up again and holding both temples tight in case they flew apart, returned to the bedroom at the front and looked down into the lane. The pick-up was there, and so was Nut's dark blue van; a carrion crow, *the* crow, was lurching up and down, sliding on the roof's wet surface. There was a lumpen burden on her head. Remember, remember.

First they'd gone to friends of Nut's who'd lived, where? A place called Rhee? No, it was Eeldyke. She remembered the lettering on a signpost. But where was Nut now? At least she had not woken with him in her bed. Asleep on the sofa downstairs? There was no sound of a soul about the house. It was all too much effort and she returned to bed, slithering down beneath the bedclothes feeling pitifully grim and dozing fitfully, the noise of the circling storm and occasional monsoon-like downpours invading her unconsciousness.

She regained her senses two hours later and feeling infinitely better though still amnesiac, had a bath. The door of the painting room was half-open and still towelling her hair, she went fearfully in to check on the painting.

Nut lay asleep on the bed, an alien presence sprawled out in a patch of watery sunlight, still fully dressed in black but with the flaming hair unplaited, wildly at odds with the half-covering, crumpled scarlet poppy sheet. A starkly uninhabited dark jacket hung over the chair, empty sleeves still echoing the curve of his arms. She tiptoed forward and felt the warmth rising up from the long, unstrung-puppet body, caught the definitive male scent and the beer and tobacco of the night before.

A feeling of wicked power overcame her, a smirking Delilah examining Samson as he slept and itching for the scissors, or the paintbrush? A stealthy professionalism insinuated itself: 'Why not? I've done things I can't remember. Perhaps said things I shouldn't have? I shall steal a portrait without him knowing and get my own back. How stupid it is to be so seduced by the shape of a cheekbone. Just bone, that's all it is, a form caused by a gene. *Mere* bone, like bones from the butchers.'

Nut woke later to the sound of a paintbrush tinkling against a glass of water and found Bea sitting nearby in the sunlight on a white chair, frowning in concentration over the drawing board on her knees, a black water-colour box in hand. Dressed in a small green jersey and long skirt, with bare feet, pretty feet, tucked up on the rung of the chair, she sat there with clean gold hair swinging round her face, quietly considering what she'd done. He stared, unsure whether he were awake or not. That had been quite a session, last night. She'd seemed so cool when he first met her, but had turned out to be surprising, talkative and funny, although the drink didn't seem to have agreed with her.

They had hilariously broken all the pub taboos with religion, sex and politics, continuing with manifestations and miracles and their own belief in them or lack of it. She'd said that she didn't understand why Jesus's turning water into wine was a miracle, since if Jesus was divine and it was accepted that God could perform miracles, what was miraculous about His son being able to do them as well? Or words to that effect. But then, becoming gradually more irrational as the evening progressed, answered herself that she supposed that if you wanted proof that Jesus was divine, then the fact that he performed miracles would be that proof and that was the whole point, and whether or not miracles could actually occur was not the point and did he like monkey nuts or dry-roasted peanuts because she was about to buy some?

Confused, but interesting that someone with no ascertainable religious background had even thought about it. But then the most unlikely things seemed interesting when drink was being taken. He smiled and stretched.

Bea looked up intently, straight into his open eyes, jumped nervously and dropped her paintbrush, hastily getting up to lean the board face to the wall. There were dark shadows beneath her eyes and a small smudge of scarlet lake beside the upper lip, as though she'd been caught out eating some rare forbidden fruit. It would have looked almost charming on someone less good-looking but on her it was delightfully risible.

All Sunday afternoon Bea spurned her headache and worked furiously on the boat picture while running over the events of the night before as they had been amplified by Nut and touched up, here and there, by recollections of her own. Sitting at first a little edgily together over toast and tea in the sitting room that morning, he'd obligingly filled in the voids.

It appeared that they had called on friends of his, Amelia and Edmund. They were considerably older than himself; Amelia, a pretty, gregarious woman in her forties, was a jeweller and Edmund a book-dealer. Bea regained a clear memory of a soft yellow lamplit room, with shelves of books and a bottle of wine, or two.

From there they had all visited a nearby pub and with a flash of recognition, Bea saw the four of them sitting talking round a candle-lit table in a low-ceilinged room. They'd played a game of darts and she'd felt more at ease. It had turned out Nut was neither a fisherman nor a professional boat-launcher and had only been helping out a friend at the launch for fun. He was engaged in some long-term scientific research project on the area. Geographical, or was it geological? She remembered geomorphology. She had imagined geographers to wear brogues and khaki jerseys with leather patches on the shoulders as had the geography master at school but things had obviously moved on since then. After the departure of Edmund and Amelia, whatever conversations had taken place alone with Nut had sunk down into the dark and spongy peat-bed level of her mind.

'Then what happened?' Bea asked anxiously, resigned to hearing that she'd pranced on a table with a rose between her teeth, although all she could recall was talking too much. It was humiliating enough to know that Nut had had to search in her pocket for the key and carry her indoors flopped over his shoulder. It was important to find out the precise degree of her imbecility so she could be properly repentant. Mercifully he hadn't so far shown a propensity to mockery.

Nut, thickly waterproofing another slice of toast with butter before spreading it with Jane's runny raspberry jam, had been teasingly comforting.

'We just talked. I think we covered most of the usual subjects last night: overpopulation, the murder in Rhee, the greenhouse effect, the Four Horsemen of the Apocalypse and when they might be calling.' He paused, the muscles in his jaw smoothly working beneath the skin as he munched his toast. 'Then we hit some of the high spots: the creative impulse, muses, visions. By the way, who's Freda?' He stared at her with long, clear sea-water eyes, emphatic eyebrows lifted enquiringly, as expressive and illustrative as a pair of Italian hands.

'I can't explain. Not now, it would take too long. And what happened then?'

'You hadn't had a great deal to drink, but the cider at the Eeldyke Inn is very strong, been known to make big men cry. I should have warned you off it; you were squinting a bit, like a Siamese cat.'

She laughed uneasily and recalling retreating and advancing out-of-focus candle flames, wandering planets in the dark back room of the pub, again insisted, 'What next?' Politely factual, he told her. She'd stood up and thrown some more darts, with startling accuracy, more than she'd shown when they were playing Edmund and Amelia, suddenly unburdened herself of the last few weeks' worth of fears and humiliations, punctuating sentences with enviable and previously unattainable double and treble twenties. A lifetime's private insecurities had been dumped in his lap and she'd been as angry with him for listening as if he had been eavesdropping.

She covered her scarlet face with her hands but Nut gently removed them, denied it had been boring, said he knew she was under a lot of stress and reassured her that before the volcanic eruption, she'd been excellent company, asking him his views on this and that, what his work was and telling him about her mother the single-minded cook and her one-eyed naval father, singing in the ironmonger's shop. He left out the bit about the miracles.

'You muttered that you shouldn't be out drinking, you should be at home working and told me that you were painting a picture about letting go of childhood. I'm glad you told me what it was about. I'd never have guessed when I saw it this morning. Then you passed out with your head in a dish of peanut shells and fag ends. I brought you home and sat with you for a while, in case you were sick. It was late so I dossed down in the first bed I found. I didn't know I was in your holy of holies.'

'You must think me a complete idiot.'

'Why should I think any such thing?' He embarked on yet another slice of toast. 'May I have some more tea? And am I allowed to be pedantic when you're feeling rough? I once looked up idiot in the dictionary, probably because someone had called me one. It comes from the Greek *idiotes* which means a person who doesn't hold any public position and who has no professional knowledge. I know, before you leap at me, that just because an idiot is defined as such a type of person, it doesn't follow that all persons of that type are idiots, but it's a tad ironic, isn't it? I mean, think of the vast amount of people with professional knowledge in public positions who appear to be the most complete idiots, in the English sense of the word. Particularly politicians.'

'Yes, but I suppose it's their being elected or promoted by us idiots that has something to do with it. Oh God! My head does ache.'

'Did you mind me looking at your painting before you'd finished it?'

'Yes. No. I'm realising it's ridiculous to mind. I would be more confident if I'd been to art school. It's my own fault that I didn't go. I'm neither communicating anything nor amusing anyone with it all hidden. Sooner or later one must find out if anyone else can understand it, or cares.'

'I look forward to your first exhibition then.'

'Unimaginable! I'm terrified of people laughing, in the wrong sort of way.'

'So is everybody else. What I saw looked as if it should be on someone's wall, being admired. I liked it a lot. You're an arch-imaginist. Why is the term "exhibitionist" so derogatory, do you think? Someone who makes an embarrassing public scene, rather than just a person who exhibits their work? Is it English false modesty, perhaps?' He stared at her, interested in her predicament. 'Would it be that, that's worrying to you?'

'I don't know that it is, quite. I've a confession to make.'

'Go on. Confess.'

'I painted you, when you were asleep.'

'Oh shit! How scary. I wondered what you were doing. Can I see?'

'I can't very well refuse, after what I've said, can I?'

'No, you certainly can't. No one's painted me before and I think I'm entitled to see it.' He sat back, still munching, and although teasing, he was deeply intrigued.

'OK.'

She fetched it, still taped to its board and he sat and stared at it, dumbfounded.

'Well?'

'It's quite extraordinary! I mean, I know I do look like that – would suppose that that's what I look like when asleep. But the likeness isn't the only thing, is it? It's the pattern of reds and blacks – the elbow of the black shirt on the red sheet makes one think of poppy petals. It's so immediate. Did you think of the poppy because of the colours that were there, or because of Morpheus?'

Bea let out a little shriek of delight. She'd thought it was fortuitous, the connections between the sleeping man and *Papaver somniferum* – the opium poppy, dreams and Morpheus the Son of Sleep.

'You're too clever by half! I just painted what was there, and had to work in a rush, in case you woke up, but I saw it was quite Elizabethan, emblematic. Although it *doesn't* mean anything. It just tied up so neatly.' Bea stared at her own work, the shapes and colours blurring, then it became the picture also of Flanders poppies, red blood and ripped white skin and her own skin goose pimpled; the hangover was still lurking.

'Now you've seen it, and like it, I suppose it doesn't have to be hidden away.' She propped it up above the fireplace.

'It still seems disturbing, that I didn't know you were doing it. A bit like a native who feels a portion of his soul is stolen each time a photograph is taken.' He leant back in his chair, long fingers laced across the flat stomach. 'Taking a likeness, portrait painters say, don't they? Photographers *take* your picture.'

'I'm sorry.' She reddened again, remembered the feeling of theft as she painted him. 'If the photographer had said, "I'm going to *make* your picture," then perhaps no one would have thought of losing a snippet of their soul. Can you imagine what it might be like, to be shown a shiny flat black-and-white something and be told, "that's you," when you've never ever seen yourself before? How could one interpret it?'

'That could be it, the making or taking. And the photograph, a magic drawing of some sort.' He smiled at her, the same knock-out smile. 'Well, thank you for the breakfast. I've got some work to catch up on this morning, or is it the afternoon? We'll be meeting again, quite soon, I hope?' He gave her a quick, almost furtive kiss on the cheek as they stood on the doorstep. Then the crow flew straight at him, and thinking it was about to attack she screeched as it flapped about his head, but it settled on his shoulder and quickly wiped its beak on his jacket sleeve. So, it was a pet. 'But he's been grown-up and free for over a year,' said Nut. 'This is only the third time I've seen him. He just turns up occasionally, where I happen to be. They're quite bright, crows, but it's odd he doesn't seem to have found a mate.'

'Has he got a name?'

'Yes. Budgie.'

Budgie could not be persuaded to leave him alone and Nut swung into his van and drove off with the bird still aboard his shoulder, chuntering absurdly into his ear and leaving her, almost breathless, on the doorstep.

Bea scratched at her finger. A rash had developed beneath the wedding ring. She removed it and saw a narrow circle of irritated pinkened skin above the knuckle. She put the ring down on the chair beside her watch and the mobile phone, cleaned a paintbrush with white spirit and started on another canvas.

'At least I understand now what the subject of the boat painting is ... it wasn't at all that clear when I started. I've got a new friend, I think. Thank God I wasn't sick. He wouldn't have been so friendly if he'd had to mop me up.' Bea felt tenuously bonded to the person who'd neither taken advantage of her drunken state nor appeared in the least disgusted by it. She now knew more about him: he'd been born in Dublin, of an English Catholic father with an over-romantic view of Ireland and the Irish, and an Irish Protestant mother. They'd gone North to Ulster when he was three, before moving again to live in England when he was sixteen; he lived in a house made from a converted railway carriage near the lighthouse and was a lovely cheerful man, and quite strangely beautiful. Apart from the weak moment on awakening that morning, Oscar had been absent from her thoughts for twenty-four hours, which she counted as a triumph. The physical separation had been a stone breaking in half, the mental more like pulling dough apart into two separate rounds. Her half at least was rising. She stood beside the bed where Nut had slept, and then sat down on it, leaning forwards to sniff the indented pillow, to try to catch the lingering smell of him. A single long red hair lay there. She picked it up and gently dropped it out of the window.

Chapter Six

'Yes, Major Higgins, we did manufacture the gates to open outwards, as you specified, not inwards. Yes, we did check them before they left the works. No, the circular pattern should be at the bottom, not the top.' Oscar leant back in his chair and kicked up savagely at the underside of his desk in frustration.

'Well, perhaps if you'd let us hang them ourselves as we suggested, rather than allowing your Bagshaw do it . . . No, no, I'm sure he's perfectly competent . . . May I suggest you do the following? Lift the gates off their posts and turn them upside down, are you with me? Then turn them back to front, keeping the pattern at the bottom. OK? Then reverse them, left to right and right to left, re-hang them and you'll find they then open outwards and close properly. Oh, good. Yes. Right. Good-bye, Major Higgins.'

He put the receiver back and let out a groan of annoyance before turning back to the paperwork before him, running his pen down a column of figures with a frown. But his instruction to Major Higgins – was he right? He retrieved a couple of empty cigarette packets from the wastepaper basket and drew on them in felt tip pen, L and R with a wavy line along their tops, marked on the sides where they sat upon their pivots and followed out his own instructions. Ridiculous, of course it worked. He was going insane.

'Whatever are you doing, Oscar?' Sheila had ceased to type and eyeing him curiously as he fiddled with the cigarette-packet puzzle, was obviously thinking the same thing.

'Nothing, nothing.' He threw the packets back into the basket and returned to the figures. During the month since he and Bea had parted Sheila had gradually eased off the overcoat of chilly disapproval. Things were back to normal now, everything going smoothly. She no longer passed over calls from Andrea with the words, 'It's that woman,' and had stopped accidentally slopping his coffee as she put it down on his desk.

That woman was being a little strange, he thought, ever since he'd suggested that once he'd got Bea sorted, the divorce in progress, they might think about having a child of their own. She'd shown every appearance of shock, her mouth falling open showing her tiny white teeth, then she'd screeched with laughter and told him she wasn't going to go through all that nonsense again. 'You can't be serious? Once was quite enough.' Hiding his dismay he laughed sycophantically and changed the subject. He'd bring it up again, when she'd had time to think about it sensibly. The telephone rang.

'It's Major Higgins again,' said Sheila.

Oscar picked up the phone and cleared his throat.

'Good morning again, Major Higgins. How can I help?'

This time Major Higgins had achieved the left gate on the left-hand side with the circles at the bottom, but the right gate was still the wrong way up. Oscar suddenly felt that this might be a wind-up.

'I think it would be best if I popped round to sort it out in person, don't you? No, no extra charge. I'll be there in fifteen minutes. See you then.' It was nearly lunch time in any case. What unfortunate regiment had had to suffer Major Higgins' ministrations?

He left the office and drove out the few miles to Major Higgins' residence, a tile-hung farmhouse, the front garden of which was colour-banded with pink and yellow tulips standing nervously to attention. He heaved the gates into their correct position with the hindrance of Bagshaw, an elderly man with a yellowing, droopy moustache and a near total absence of logic. Having ascertained that everyone was at last happy and politely refusing the glass of sherry offered, he drove back into the town to get some lunch. Andrea had become worried about his waistline and no longer provided bacon and egg breakfasts, so he had for the last week been resorting to compensatory meals at the Mummers where they served large helpings of sub-Mexican food. With rumbling stomach he was eagerly spooning up a plate of chilli when Agnes walked over and plonked herself down in front of him, a glass of wine in her hand and a strangely complicitous grin on her face.

'Hello, Oscar. Let yourself out of the cupboard then?'

He was pleased to see her since it signified a return to some sort of Bellhurst normality. She seemed friendly enough and was looking summery and sexy in short skirt and tight pink cotton jersey. A very tight pink cotton jersey. He automatically glanced down at his stomach, and tried to rein it in. It was extraordinary how women changed shape with the fashions, first all loose baggy things so that you couldn't tell what shape they were beneath but had to guess, now everything a size too small so that their shapes were thrust upon one. Their meeting might lay a few ghosts, but on the other hand . . . but she didn't look as if she was about to follow in her husband's lead and try to damage his face.

'Would you like to join me, have something to eat?'

'No, thanks. I just came out for a drink to celebrate finishing a piece of work. Why are you crying?'

The pub chef had incorrectly assumed a correlation between degrees of hotness and authenticity and having bitten on a whole incendiary chilli pod, Oscar's eyes were starting to fill with tears.

'Chilli. Too hot!' He self-consciously fanned his glowing face. 'I *am* pleased to see you – it's all been so difficult since the bust-up with Bea. I imagined you wouldn't be speaking to me? Phil still seems a bit touchy about it.'

'That's because he fancies Bea himself, didn't you know?'
Agnes's round grey eyes looked at him innocently and without
any ascertainable malice. 'So, how are things? How's life with the
cow-woman, Andreary?' Her tone was teasing, with no trace of
hostility, but he could hardly answer her without a self-defensive
touch of it in his.

'It's wonderful. And she's quite wonderful, a beautiful,
intelligent, self-confident woman. Everything's wonderful. If
you've come over to be rude about her, I wish you'd go away
again.' He took a more cautious mouthful of his meal.

'I'm sorry. I've heard different, that's all and you know how
much I love Bea.'

'Have you seen her at all? I am, contrary to what you think,
seriously worried about her. It was very distressing for me too,
after all this time together . . . but we have to sort out our affairs,
and she won't answer the solicitor's letter, or mine. All I got was a
message from Tom Kerepol saying that she was too preoccupied
at the moment to deal with it. I want to know what it is she's
preoccupied with, and *where* she is?'

Agnes sat back and wondered which information and how
much of it she should impart to cause maximum annoyance.

'She's doing very nicely.' she said, infuriatingly. 'She's
recovered from the appalling shock you gave her and having
a fling with a fisherman. She seems quite happy.' She watched
his reaction to her barbed reply, noticing the faintest shadow
of discontent on the so-fanciable face and the slightest yellow
tinge at the side of his nose, the faded remnant of a bruise. 'I just
don't understand why you couldn't just poke the cow-woman
and leave it at that, as you did when you had affairs before?'

Oscar looked stunned, for a second or two, then wisely chose
to ignore the last bit of her remark, deciding that it was beneath
his dignity to deny but wondering how the hell she knew.

'What do you mean, a fisherman? Where would she meet
a fisherman?'

'*I* don't know.' she said airily. 'Sitting weeping inconsolably on the bank of a river? Or knocking back double rums at an Inn called "The Jolly Roger"?'

He leant forward as she spoke, suddenly uncomfortably aware that he had had a sneaking thought when he left Bea, that his leaving her would cause her to think a great deal more about him than had his continuing presence. He was obviously wrong. It hurt him a little, to find that she'd recovered so rapidly. Agnes discerned an anxious interest. Perhaps Andreary didn't have quite such a hold on him as she'd thought but he'd hardly be likely to tell her if he'd discovered she was an alcoholic.

'I need to see her, really I do. There are all sorts of practical matters that need to be sorted out.' It was awkward and disturbing, not being in control of the situation ... of Bea.

'But you've only just left. I'll tell her, next time I see her, that you need to speak to her. But don't hold your breath — she *is* very busy.'

'That's what Tom said. But doing what, exactly?'

Now he sounded worried. Superb, she thought. The more he wonders about what Bea's up to, the less time he'll have for Andrea. First things first. Get him away from Andrea.

'She says just busy. Anyway, I must fly. I have to collect Seb at twelve-thirty, and look, it's a quarter to one!

She left, collecting a wolf-whistle on the way out which caused her to turn and smile at the perpetrator in a way more reminiscent of a cheeky sixteen-year-old than a woman of thirty, Feminism was drearily incomprehensible to Agnes and she found it more uplifting to the spirits to be whistled at than asked for her opinion on the judging of the Booker prize.

Oscar got out of the car, opened the elegant iron gates, *his* elegant iron gates, and was unwelcomed by Andrea's whippet Passe-Partout, who barked neurotically and nearly got itself squashed as he drove into the drive. It nipped at him as he got out again to close them and he fended it off gently with his foot, sure that Andrea would be watching from the drawing-room window, gin and tonic in hand, as she did most evenings. He was looking forward to a drink, and the pre-supper snacks of nuts and Kalamata olives she always set out. He looked forward to dinner and watching her as she ate, to being melted by the femininity of her movements as with a tiny, plump and almost inadequate hand she lifted the overburdened fork up to her open mouth ... Bea never needed help to open jars, or move a chair. Andrea's hands were beautifully shaped, with varnished nails, hands which he could imagine smoothing, touching ... Bea's hands were narrow, with tapering, spiky fingers of quite extraordinary length and strength, the thumbnails, and the thumbnails only, bitten. Exploratory hands that weren't reluctant to dabble in mud or gut a fish, hands that drew and drew, with a callus on the second finger of the left hand ... he stopped and pushed open the door to the drawing room and stared, jaw-dropped, at the sight of Andrea. He had become accustomed to her early evening dress of beautifully-cut slit tunics of some silky stuff over swishy skirt, in chestnut brown, chic grey or black, to her carefully tended face and hair, to her very eager kisses and seductive looks.

Andrea lay on her back on the sofa, her legs unattractively splayed out in some sort of exercise outfit of red and fluorescent pink-patterned leotard and orange leggings, which looked unfortunate on her pretty but slightly pear-shaped figure. Her mouth was indeed open, but she snored. An empty gin bottle and unemptied ashtray lay beside her on the giant silver-leafed coffee table and there was a dog's mess on the polished floorboards. She looked impossibly, dreadfully, ridiculous. There was no sign of either nuts or olives.

It was May Eve and Bea was out in the garden of Little Rumm, sitting on the wall, basking in the warm air and in the process of dissecting her situation in the safety of the copper sunset, forcing an admission that in her particular circumstances, being a deserted wife wasn't as miserable as expected. She could also admit freely now that over the last few years the marriage had rolled quietly and gently down the slope to a standstill although she had also made quite sure that this was what *she* believed, that she was not accepting it just because it was what Oscar wanted her to believe. At the very back of her mind was the uncomfortable feeling that things could be, ought to be mended should the chance arise, but it was unlikely that he would leave Andreary and anyway alongside it sat the thought that not in any way did she wish to return to life in a cottage in Bellhurst.

At night, however, still unused to sleeping alone, she lay wide awake in the early hours of the morning. She waited for the increasingly earlier dawns, listing the minutiae of night noises in order to prevent, or at least stave off, the uncontrollable remembrances of Oscar and fearful imaginings concerning the future which loomed up like threatening swans emerging from dark rivers, hissing warnings that she was too close to the water's edge, too close to them. She listened to the sudden dry rustling as a bird on the roof shook its feathers, the dripping tap in the kitchen, the creaking release of tension in a floorboard, a clatter as a fox investigated the rubbish bin followed by the sound of its tongue, rasping along the goffered sides of the tinfoil case of a chocolate cup-cake.

Had she ever done more than scrape at the surface of her life, been too insecure to dig any deeper? There had recently been a loosening of the snarled-up thinking, allowing an exploration of those few thoughts which were not connected with the painting in progress, or increasingly, worryingly, of Francis Nutmeg. It was too soon to get involved, would inevitably divert from her purpose of proving herself to be a painter. First paint the pictures, then . . .

Nut had put in an appearance a couple of days after the debacle of their evening together, arriving with a present as if to reassure her everything was fine. He placed a fossil, a sea-urchin type of thing in her hand, warm because it had been in his trouser pocket, with the delicate star-burst marking of tiny points where its spines had once grown still clearly visible. Nut was a magpie, laying a stolen trinket before a potential mate; she could feel him searching her face for signs of approval as she examined the fossil.

'It's so beautifully *almost* regular,' she examined it with care, turning it over and looking at the central depression, like a neat umbilicus, feeling the ancient shape with her fingertips, 'just these tiny differences in distance, as if they'd been caught grow-ing, fluid, that are so pleasing, aren't they? And sea-urchin shells look the same now, don't they? They've hardly changed a bit?'

'Not much.' Nut was thinking that the description she had given applied to her face just as well, so pleasing. 'A few hundred years ago there was a widespread belief that God made fossils, just as they are and scattered them about the earth to amuse us, like toys.'

'But that's a consoling idea and it must have been so easy to believe. How old would this be, how long since it was alive? Where did you find it?'

'I found it near Dover. They're common in chalk, so Cretaceous times, perhaps seventy million years ago at least?'

'There was a seventeenth-century bishop who believed he had got the age of the earth all sorted out by using the Old Testament, did you know? He counted all the begats, I suppose, and came to the conclusion that the world was created at nine o'clock in the morning on the twenty-sixth of October, four thousand and four BC. I remembered it because I liked the idea of someone with such utter faith in the Bible settling down at a desk by candlelight after a supper of toasted cheese one evening and working it all out, even if they were so horribly wrong. And it must have seemed a certainty to the un-educated, having been pronounced by a bishop.'

'It's been revised since then. It's more like three and a half to five billion years old.' Nut grinned. 'Yesterday's certainties — fairy tales today. You seem keen on certainties at the moment?'

'I'm still missing the ones I thought I had, yes. But fossils are certainties, even if people did once think they were toys. I'd like to find some for myself.' She put the fossil down in the centre of the table. 'It's eerie, to be handling something as old as that, unearthed from beneath all those layers of other life. Do you see time, I mean your own life, as layers one on top of the other, like blankets?'

'As chapters in a book, I think. Less digging. Personally I never seem to get past Chapter Three. And how are you enjoying *Gulliver's Travels*? He picked it up from the kitchen table and flipped through it, examining the illustrations intently. 'Lovely pictures!'

'They're lithographs by Edward Bawden. It's my father's copy. Have you ever read it?'

'I have not, but since we are having a most polite conversation, I know that it was Swift who wrote 'The sight of you is good for sore eyes.' He meant it as an example of a particularly well-used compliment, but I mean it particularly truthfully!'

It being endearingly given, she beamed at him. 'I'm finding Gulliver rather heavy going. It's difficult with satire, old, old satire and I'm not always certain what particular trait of the times he is making fun of, but one can feed off the invention and I've only fallen asleep reading it once. You weren't so chatty, that time we very first met.'

'No. It was rather early in the morning and I'll admit to a hangover and considerable embarrassment. Have you recovered now, from yours?'

She was very pleased with the present of the fossil but disconcertingly, since an interruption by him was very acceptable — did not count as an intrusion at all, Nut insisted that he didn't want to hinder her work and only stayed a few minutes more, just long enough to draw a neat sketch-map of exactly where his railway-carriage house was and to invite her to drop in on him sometime soon.

'I can see you're in the middle of something, there's paint on your ear and I've got a site-meeting in a field four miles away in fifteen minutes.' His eyebrows flicked upwards, anxiously. 'I've been to Nest's house; now it's your turn to visit Nut's nest.'

'I will. Is the crow still with you?'

'No. Budgie's buggered off again. He didn't seem to care for roast chicken, which was all I had to give him. It was corned beef that was always his favourite.' He touched her arm. 'I've got to go. I'll be late.' He'd turned and left so fast that if it hadn't been for the fossil and the map, his visit would have seemed an illusion.

An old estate car came lumbering up the track towards her, nearly grounding itself between the hardening ruts for it was heavily loaded with women. The car slowed down and then pulled up, the front passenger calling out of the window to ask for directions.

'Hi there! Sorry to interrupt your communications with the natural spirits, but could you tell me if we're on the right road for the power station?'

This seemed to Bea an odd request. The power station's Visitor Centre must be closed in the evenings. The five women, a mixed age group, had a semi-suppressed nervous excitement about them as if they were anticipating a party although Bea thought it a bizarre location for one. There was a grumbling chorus from the back seat. 'We thought you knew a special way, Emma.' 'I knew you'd get us effing lost.' 'After all, you're supposed to know the area.'

'This track just peters out near the shore,' said Bea, aware of five pairs of eyes trained upon her as she leant forwards to the enquirer, 'but you *could* park and walk along to it from there, it's less than a mile. If you want to drive right up close to it, you'd have to go back to Fingle and take the lower road. That'd be much easier.'

There was a discontented 'That's what I suggested, only no one would listen to me,' from the driver. Intrigued, Bea watched as they consulted urgently among themselves, three for the walk, the other two groaning that the shingle would be too tiring to walk on and that they would be late. The chastened navigator thanked Bea and said they would be late in any case, and may as well continue the way they'd come, that is, if Bea thought it would be safe to leave the car parked there?

'As long as you don't try to park it off the track and sink in stones. The only people who use the track are the men who fish from the beach at night. But no one's gone past this evening, so far.' There was more excited comment at this but the car bumped off in the direction of the shore, exhaust pipe scraping the infill of broken bricks. Bea felt sure she'd seen the driver before, but couldn't place her. The heavy dew was dampening her hair and was falling visibly in the half light, gleaming on the stones.

Frying two dabs for supper, making toast under the hissing grill, the odour of the bottled gas reminded her of camping stoves and tents on holiday in France and she chirruped a song as she flipped them over, anticipating the milky freshness of the dab's white buttered flesh, the crunchiness of the toast. Her eating times had become wildly erratic, but she bothered to make each meal a treat, however simple, and it was important to keep things simple, to save time, to get on with the job. After supper she sat in the little blue armchair by the open window in the dark, stomach pleasantly full but brain churning.

'How *do* I appear to other people? To Nut, for instance? I want to know. Can self-confidence only be achieved if one believes in one's own image of oneself, of one's physical and mental shape? Other people's perceptions of ourselves seem so drastically different from our own. Which view is real? Does Nut have a view of me? And if he does (surely he must have one – I do hope he has) does it coincide with mine at any point?

And the other way about. What did Oscar think I was, or am? How did I see Oscar? Perhaps we disappear in our own eyes, in a puff of smoke, when others refuse to see us as we think we are. Did Oscar see me at all, as anyone? He must have lost sight of the me he thought I was or he wouldn't have betrayed me like that. But betrayal's far too high-flown a word for what he's done. How long had he been seeing Andrea? Sneaky pig. I didn't think to betray him, did I? But perhaps the thought was there all the time waiting for me to think it. I bloody well should have thought it.'

She got up and restlessly started pacing up and down, worrying at the river of questions and then thinking up a few more.

'Is it only the totally self-confident people who are undisturbed by other people's views of themselves? Perhaps a lack of imagination is necessary for real self-confidence, or at least an ability to turn imagination off. In which case self-confidence can't always be the mega-blessing it's supposed to be, can it? Very imaginative people are so often secretive. They daren't court too many of other people's views of themselves, or their work, for fear of destruction; but one can't perform forever without an audience. No, I'm going mad and muddling imagination with sensitivity. Over-sensitivity is a symptom of an unhealthy interest in oneself,' she addressed herself severely, 'which is what you are very much in danger of.' A large house spider raced across the floor and she sat down on her chair again in a hurry with her feet tucked up.

'One can pretend, go on pretending past childhood. One can act out self-confidence – dash about saying "Take it or leave it, I don't care! I'm the greatest. In my view *this* is right." Lots of people must do that and have to live with knowing themselves to be con-artists. All that calm and ordered bit was pretended. I pretended being happy and contented so well that I believed myself. Did Oscar know it was a colossal porky? But was it pretended for him in the first place because I knew he wouldn't have liked the selfish cow inside? What a tortuous, shitty muddle!'

Not surprisingly having lost the train of thought she turned again to the window where her eye was caught by an orange flicker on the skyline, up on the shingle bank. Then another blossomed after it, and another, till there were five flames bobbing along the top at different heights towards the power station. The women in the car? With torches, firebrands? What could they be up to? It must be a beach party, but it shelved so sharply there was no beach to speak of at that point, even at low tide. Her curiosity was up but since there was no one there to make her feel shame faced about being nosy and overcome with a sudden sense of excitement, she slipped on a jacket and locked up the house, thinking she could drive round to the ness before they reached it, and find out. If it wasn't a party, never mind. It would be more bearable, being outside in the night.

The exterior darkness was less scary to Bea than the interior darkened rooms of houses, where perhaps memories of past events and people of unknown nastiness might have become trapped, concentrated and stored like stock cubes. Outside they were diluted and one could run amazingly fast, at least in the imagination, to escape from the murderers or lolloping corpses that chased one in dreams. It would, she thought, be poetic justice if murderers were plagued by the nightmares of their victims, forced into taking them on as punishment, to dream them as well as their own, every night, for ever.

As a child she had been convinced that to recall a nightmare during the day would mean that she would dream it again the next night and so forced herself into forgetfulness of the worst of them; those dreams where things touched became disgusting decaying messes, like rotting pumpkins that looked so firm but gave beneath the pressure of a finger to expose a softening mass of putrescent, pulpy flesh.

She shuddered and drove off down the track, nervously remembering her mother's story of being frightened when a child by the idea of German soldiers beneath her bed, lying there waiting to machine-gun her ankles as she crossed the room. Jane said she used to run upstairs to her bedroom door, burst it open and fling herself across the room in two great bounds, shouting to surprise them, and crash down on the bed, safe. She said Gran eventually took to coming upstairs with a broom at bedtime and rattling it about under the bed to prove there was nothing there. The soldiers in their hideous chamberpot helmets had gone away by morning so she could get *out* of bed quite safely in the daylight. It was just the getting *in* which caused problems.

It wasn't too late in the evening to take up Nut's invitation and drop in. The map was in her pocket now. Nut, chestnut, cobnut, hazelnut, ginger-nut, nutmeg Nut – all vegetable – perhaps he'd respond to Carrots instead? But it wouldn't suit, the hair not being curly carrotty orange; it was thick, smooth, wavy and a riotous maple-leaf red. A fox ran across in the headlights as she drove along the causewayed road between the deep gravel pits on either side. There was a second's flash of reflected light from its close-set petty-criminal eyes before it disappeared beneath the wire fencing to the left. Foxy-headed Nut. But his hair was brighter than a fox's fur.

Approaching the lighthouse and slowing down, she began to scan for signs of more torches, or a bonfire, and there it was, blazing out on the shingle. Pulling in and turning off the engine, she debated what to do. It was still some way off, she could walk a little closer, see what was going on. No one else seemed to be about. Although there was a spread-out settlement of small bungalows and weatherboarded houses along that stretch of road, they all seemed to be dark or empty or have their curtains tightly drawn.

There was an astonishing crowd around the bonfire, in long, red hooded cloaks and black masks, circling several circles deep and holding hands. They were singing and every now and then one of them threw back its hooded head and howled.

Bea thought it looked both creepy and atavistic, and serious fun and since one could hardly be accused of gate-crashing in a wide open space, wandered up closer to watch. A couple stood at the base of the new lighthouse's ammonite-like spiral ramp, the firelight catching the look of disbelief on their faces as the bobbing horde, now indulging in mass ululation, stamped their feet on the rattling pebbles. Bea tried to estimate their numbers, but gave up.

'Bea? This is very jolly, isn't it? I wish I'd brought my red cloak too,' said someone who had come up behind her. It was Nut's friend, the affable Edmund whom she'd met on that disgracing evening out with Nut, standing there stockily, smiling widely. 'Are you about to join them?'

Amelia also arrived, a little out of breath, and slipped her arm possessively through his.

'Hello, Bea! This looks just like a scene from John Masefield's *The Midnight Folk*, doesn't it, Edmund? Do you suppose they have broomsticks and will do a fly-past later on?' She turned back to Bea, fairly bubbling with amusement. 'This is how we first met, Edmund and I, at a bonfire. Not like this one though. That was only a pedestrian Guy Fawkes' night. A bacchanalia is much more exciting. Let's enjoy it before someone calls the police and spoils it all.' She grinned. 'I had an overwhelming urge to come out this evening and have some fish and chips at the pub up the road. We were going to call on Mr Nutmeg afterwards, but we've been deflected by the spectacle. I'm so glad Edmund was willing to indulge me, or I'd have missed it all. Oh look! They're breaking up and leading a procession up the road. Where are they going?'

'To the power station — I think it was some of them that passed my house and asked for directions earlier on, only they weren't dressed up then. Perhaps they're going to put a curse on it.'

'That sounds rather unwise. Anything might happen. Let's follow and see!' So they linked arms, with solid Edmund in the middle and followed in the dark.

Inside the floodlit perimeter fence, the buildings and their gleaming, steaming exterior pipework and bright lights became a science fiction stage set – a surreal Alphaville, or a Mayan temple besieged by a revolt of priestesses. The red-cloaked ones parted in a well-organised fashion and in two columns filed either side of the gate, as if to encircle the area. 'They're like ants out on a foray,' thought Bea, 'single-minded and programmed.' Chanting and holding long lengths of red ribbon between them they spaced themselves out widely. A group who stood apart from the encircling ones still brandished lighted torches and the air was heavy with the stink of paraffin. There was a glittering and clashing as a large number of them appeared to be handcuffing themselves to the fencing. Security guards were both outside and inside, remonstrating with them, but were being drowned out by chanting. Tiny dark faces appeared at the lighted windows above in the main building, peering down on the extraordinary theatrical performance below.

'What is it they're shouting?' asked Edmund, enraptured by the spectacle.

'I think it's "The Daughters of Nature invoke your departure," said Bea. Far away in the distance sirens were heard, and across the flatness from every inland direction, blue flashing lights could be seen approaching, converging on the site. There was now a growing group of silent, entranced spectators. The first police car drew up and disgorged three young constables who, advancing upon the tethered maenads, were stopped dead by a well-organised, one-handed ripping of Velcro fastenings and a casting aside of cloaks. The women who were being advanced upon stood abruptly naked in the flashing, flickering, reflected lights.

The policemen wavered, halted again and conferred, then backed off a little way to use their radios. More cars arrived, three fire engines and an ambulance or two. Bea now recognised the woman who'd asked the way earlier that evening – she worked in the Parden library. Her mask had slipped around her neck and her stiffly lacquered helmet of blonde hair and heavy make-up caused her startlingly well-built body to appear even more naked than it was already, like a Cranach nude in a hat and pearls. A van load of more senior officers drew up and megaphones were being deployed.

It was after midnight now and policewomen, one of them apparently quite overcome with giggles, advanced on the naked ones accompanied by helplessly smirking firemen with bolt-cutters. The policewomen tried to cover the nakedness while the firemen snipped; however as soon as one was freed from self-imprisonment, wrapped up and ushered away, others, still chanting, triumphantly disrobed themselves. A flashing of photographers rushed upon the scene, intent on getting pictures of police manhandling, but more particularly of tits. Two women still safe inside their cloaks, were handing out leaflets till a pair of constables tried to take them away and then the taller of the two let out a screech and tried to claw them back.

'I'm not disturbing the peace! I'm handing out leaflets – this is a religious movement. We're natural witches about our business. We're not damaging anything! It's you lot of pigs who are disturbing our peaceful demonstration of ... let go, will you ... our trust in nature ... our abhorrence of nuclear pollution ... Let go of my effing cloak! You tear it and I'll sue you for damages! It cost a lot of money that material, *and* I had to make it myself.' The voice was undoubtedly Lucinda's. The shorter of the two women became overheated and a policeman's cap went flying.

Some of the expanding crowd took Lucinda's side. 'Go on, let them go. They're not doing any harm!' She was firmly taken by the arm and led back towards the old lighthouse where a police van was parked, but she wriggled and abandoning the leaflets, in one eel-like movement fell out of the cloak. Finding himself clutching naked flesh, he let go, reluctantly but pink with embarrassment. The crowd hooted and cheered as Lucinda disappeared into the darkness, leaving her companion jumping up and down with fury. There was something familiar about her too. 'Bea, Bea! Tell them I'm only handing out leaflets!'

'Aunt Nest!' Bea leapt forward anticipating some sort of struggle but the policemen shrugged and gave in, returning to their more challenged companions at the gates and fruitlessly imploring the onlookers to go back home.

'Now I can die happy,' chortled Edmund, 'I've seen a streaking witch! It's most impressive, as demonstrations go.' He rescued one of the leaflets fluttering across the road and put it in his pocket to read later.

Aunt Nest was quivering with indignation and Bea was near hysterical with laughter. 'You weren't going to strip off too, were you, Aunt Nest?' she asked, wondering whether to introduce the witch-aunt to Edmund and Amelia who were impolitely staring at her with delighted incredulity.

'Good God, no! I'm only a lay-witch, and just for tonight, I think. There are limits to commitment. Look.' Aunt Nest, temper restored and now with her violet eyes sparkling through the eye-slits of her fetching mask, flashed open her cloak and Bea was reassured to see she was wearing extremely sensible long navy blue Damart underwear. Edmund appeared to be inconsolable.

'"Cast not a clout till May be out!"' Nest cried gaily. 'The twenty-somethings may think it's a warm night, but I think there's a distinct nip in the air. I'd better take Lucinda's cloak back to the car and see if I can find her. Here's a leaflet to read. I'll tell you all about it later on. I didn't think it would get quite so rough but I've never enjoyed myself so much!'

'Does Blue know?'

'Perish the thought! He'd have got far too emotional.'

Bea rather wished that she had been alone to see the demonstration; on reflection it was a bit embarrassing watching with other people whom she knew, let alone finding that one of them was her aunt.

'I don't want to spoil your fun, but I think you've probably seen enough pink bits,' said Amelia, taking Edmund's arm again, her face reflecting Bea's own quandary.

'But it was the navy-blue bits which were so devastating!' gurgled Edmund, 'However,' he appeared to be recovering himself, 'it is getting too late to see if we can find Nut, although I suspect he's out here somewhere – even if he was immersed in work he'd hardly fail to notice a Beltane bonfire on his doorstep. Were you on your way to see him, Bea?'

Bea admitted that she had intended to drop in on Nut. It was getting very late, or rather early, since now it was May Day, but he surely couldn't be asleep with all this racket going on. They were walking back to where they'd left their cars, occasionally overtaken by a fleeing witch, when she caught sight of him.

Nut stood at his ease with folded arms, leaning broad shoulders against a peeling wall emblazoned with the Trinity House coat of arms, chatting to a man in waders, down-filled jacket and a flat tweed cap.

'. . . there must have been over a hundred of them,' Nut was saying, '. . . or perhaps they came in covens, say thirteen thirteens? That's one hundred and sixty-nine little witches!'

'Some of them weren't too little, neither,' said the man, stubbing out his cigarette on the wall, 'a bit too much, straight after a big fish supper, all that flesh. Fair puts you off. Didn't know where to look. I wasn't going to come up off the beach, meself. Thought it was just a radioactive leak alarm and went on fishing, but George said he'd look after me line . . .'

'One of them was Lucinda,' said Bea to Nut, 'and another was my aunt Nest.'

'One of them was a bloke,' said the man who was unworried by the contingency of radioactive leaks. 'Surprised the lady constable a bit. Lucky the fireman had control of his cutters.' He shook his head in disbelief and ambled back to his fishing.

The amusement being over, more or less, Edmund and Amelia made their good-byes and Bea stood alone in the dark with Nut.

'Was it the witches you came to see, or did you intend to visit me at last?' he asked, arms still folded and a very slightly foxy smile on his face.

They crunched across the shingle to the house, avoiding broken lengths of rusty iron hawser and crushing the woodsage growing in the stones, releasing its antiseptic smell into the salty warmth of the night air. The house was rented from a woman who lived in Blackpool, he said, opening the door into a world so self-contained and so obviously suited to his own purposes that Bea initially felt quite out of place. He removed a pile of books from a small armchair, invited her to sit down and after flicking on a tape that he had been listening to previously, made tea. Kurt Weill's *The Threepenny Opera* unexpectedly welled out into the room. This Bea associated with evenings up in the attic bedroom at home, listening to 'Pirate Jenny' floating up the stairs as Tom played old vinyls of Georgia Brown, whose voice he adored, sometimes urging her to come down and sing with him, which she nearly always did.

They were in a narrow, dark green room with an arched ceiling, a reminder of the fact that it was once a railway carriage, with a tiny kitchen at one end and a black, dormant woodstove at the other. The walls were shelved and so tightly packed with books that they leaked out around the floor in puddles, then seeped up voraciously to cover every available surface.

Nut watched her while the kettle boiled, as she got up and prowled about, inquisitive and tense as a cat in new surroundings, exploring his Lilliputian territory. Beyond the kitchen a bedroom could be seen through the doorway. An extension with wide windows on the seaward side ran the length of the carriage and contained lavatory and shower room and formed what passed for a conservatory in which were fishing rods, tomato plants growing in Sainsbury's plastic carrier bags, waders and binoculars hanging from a hook. It was clean, and tidy in a way. Her eyes raked the room for signs of past or present female companionship and found nothing. There was a balance to the room, things were aligned, papers laid straight on the desk beside the computer, 'Palaeoenvironmental Investigation ... Rickards Flats ...' she glanced further down the page but it was too technical to be immediately interesting, seemingly to do with diatom counts, frustules, pollen analysis and inter-tidal mudflats of which she knew nothing. Maps, charts and a square of four framed drawings of delicately interlaced seaweed-like plants hung on the walls.

Nut brought out a tray with two mugs of tea and a half-eaten packet of ginger biscuits and as he leant forward she caught sight of his neck, the strength in it, the whiteness of it, and the red-gold hairs at the base of it seen through the open neck of the dark blue shirt. Her whole interior being suddenly shifted vertiginously downwards, a deep sinking feeling in her stomach and hips. Lustless for a considerable time, it was a sensation of extraordinary strength and most disconcerting. She turned quickly back to the pictures on the wall and desperately pretended to be studying them while listening to the insinuating 'Mack the Knife', fighting off the violently physical twinges in the loins department and trying to recover her internal dignity.

'I'm sorry. I'm being intolerably nosy,' she said, as the sensation fluttered and protesting, slowly died away. 'Did you do these?'

'No, that's Amelia's work.' He was looking at her, a sudden surmise had come to him and the slightest of tremors shook his hand as he passed over a mug. 'She comes down here to draw sometimes. That's how I met her. She was drawing seaweed, and I stopped to look, tried to chat her up on the spot, even. I must admit I thought she was pretty exciting. She held me off so elegantly. What do you think of them both?'

'Very friendly. They must have been married as long as my parents; they seem so definitely paired, twinned. I liked to see them walking off, arms round each other. Their happiness seemed almost tangible.' She wished she was like Amelia, so confident and happily garrulous.

'Ah, yes. But they're not married, and they've only been together for a year or two. Amelia's first husband died, committed suicide. Edmund's divorced.'

'Have they got children?'

'There's Amelia's daughter, Josie. She's a sunbeam girl, about nineteen, and just like her mother. She was there tonight, handing out leaflets too. I recognised her voice. I bet Amelia didn't know.'

'You seem to know them very well?'

'Yes, they've become good friends. You could see Amelia loved the to-do this evening. She's the grand-daughter of the writer Connaught Marvel, incidentally, and is a connoisseur of strange happenings. So, what's the story about your aunt? Aunt Nest?' The image he had gained from Blue was of an eccentric horticultural houri.

'Well, she told me Lucinda was trying to get her to join some eco-organisation, but I don't think she knew it was to do with witches. Or perhaps she found out and that's why she did join. It's the sort of thing that might appeal to her for a while. And dressing up is irresistible to her.' Bea was still in turmoil and her body was deeply disappointed. 'It's peculiar, this business of dressing up. I suppose it enables one to behave in a way one wouldn't if one started out the evening in a flowery frock.'

'What's dressing up? Have a soggy biscuit? No? It's hard to tell if people are dressed up for fun or for some more esoteric reason. Most of the people you see wearing sports clothes, they're dressing up, pretending to be sporty, imagining they've a chance of winning gold, if only . . . They've never played a game in their lives, look as if they'd have apoplexy if you asked them to run out and post a letter.'

'Don't they just? But that's fashion, not dressing up and what about judges and bishops wearing antique clothes to lend them dignity, and soldiers and police? Are their uniforms meant to inspire respect or to make sure they all recognise each other and do the right salutes?'

Nut laughed. 'I suspect uniforms came about when fights between tribes got so big they had trouble knowing who to hit. No problems if it's family versus family, but town against town would be difficult. If one side wore wolf-skin trousers and the others polecat, it would have made it easier.'

'I did really mean fancy dress, like tonight. The long red cloaks and masks, although in spite of the different shapes and sizes, the nakedness looked more like uniform than the cloaks.'

'I felt a bit embarrassed at first,' Nut said 'that I shouldn't be watching, not in the way that a man *would* watch. It was hard, trying not to leer. One can't help oneself thinking and sizing up, as it were. All those different coloured beavers. I did *try* to drag my eyes away and think of it as necessary exhibitionism! Was it necessary, though, to strip off like that, to make the point?'

'It was a wildly successful delaying tactic, wasn't it? You've got to risk ridicule, I suppose, to get the point across. Will they be charged with indecent exposure? I'm so glad Lucinda got away.'

'Lucinda likes taking her clothes off. That's what you'll have to do when you exhibit your work, in a way. Put your ideas naked before the public.'

'Yes, I suppose.' So, Lucinda liked stripping off, did she? Was he speaking from personal experience? The idea of it brought her sharply out of her hypnosis. 'Since you've now seen a picture, I'm less neurotic about it. It isn't so threatening. Tell me more about what it is *you* do, and do you have to wear a uniform to do it?'

'Oh God, where do I start? Well, I've been working for an archaeological trust for the past eighteen months, on the geographical part of an inter-disciplinary survey of the area. It was commissioned and funded by them when they were left a huge bequest by a dilettante patron, the late and unlikely Siegfried McKay-Tart from Vancouver. He believed his ancestors came from around here; but what seemed a very substantial sum is dwindling fast and my part in it is nearly over, for the time being anyway.'

'But if you're a geographer, and it's an archaeological set-up, so where do you fit in?'

'Simply or in detail?'

'Very simply, please.'

'The coastline and the marsh behind it are constantly in the process of change. We need to find out how it evolved, when it changed, where and why. That sort of thing. We can assess the presence and influence of man on the area from prehistoric times; find out when different parts of the marsh were inned, how changes in sea level and storms changed river courses, silted up harbours or destroyed what had once been prosperous ports. A little land lost at this point, some gained further along. There were Roman salt-workings here, small settlements on higher ground there ... it all ties in.' He stopped. 'Please, you're not bored? The most interesting thing to me about the job is the collaboration with the other specialist researchers, the palaeobotanists, the hydrologists, the historians, the archaeologists.' All the while he talked he was moving, a mercurial Nut, thrumming with energy, but he glanced anxiously at her. 'I just love it – the land is everything, poetry even, to me. Are you sure you don't think it's boring? Most people doze off if I tell them what I do. The only thing that gets them going is digging up buried treasure. One hint of precious metal and they're out causing havoc with their little detectors.'

'I'm not in the slightest bored. It's rare to meet someone so enthusiastic about what they do instead of moaning all the time. Do you have to do a great deal of writing, reports and things?'

'Well yes, there is, but I don't mind although I'd naturally prefer to be out of doors. I like putting the final full stop on a conclusion.' He waved his hand in the air with a flourish. 'A conclusion is the white rabbit being hauled out of a top hat.

Then everyone pokes and prods at it to see if it's real, worried that their pet theory might be discredited by it. The only trouble is the scientific vocabulary becomes a bit predictable and boring. I'd love to be able to use words like "angst" and "arriviste".'

'I've never had reason to use "arriviste" either! You are the most unlikely geographer! What happens when your work here is finished?

'When the money runs out, you mean? The work itself is almost unfinishable. I'm hoping to get a post at either London or Kent University. I should get to hear fairly soon whether I've got one or other of them.'

She watched him prowling about, picking up a postcard from the desk, moving the red Anglepoise lamp, tapping out a word on the computer keyboard, now carefully not looking at her. In spite of his size and the smallness of the space, he never brushed against anything. More and more she was attracted to what she saw, but was very, very wary.

He was thinking that he would need a butterfly net to catch this inconsistently timorous angel. But then angels were only messengers and didn't feel desire and that was what he'd for certain seen, flashing across her face for that one instant. How to make the leap from palaeobotany to bed?

'How brave are you?' he asked, moving behind her and suddenly laying just a finger lightly against her neck. She jerked involuntarily and slammed a foot on the brakes.

'Not as brave as that.'

'Please, stay. Stay with me.'

Bea had a brief tussle with physical instincts, and won. If he could be bold, she could, in competition, be at least resolute, and pathetically plead internal imbroglio.

'No, Nut ... Not now. I've got to go home, quite soon.' Why had she said that? How sad and unnecessary it sounded.

'All right, then,' he said, as lightly as he'd touched; you great fool! He cursed himself. Too soon, too soon.

Momentarily affronted, as when an offer or request is

gratefully retracted on receiving a first polite refusal, she was then relieved. He could have thought he'd ask because it was expected of him? To Bea, the obstinate waverer, her curt 'No, not now' meant: 'OK I'm attracted, and you know it, but there are other things in life just at the moment that seem so desperately pressing and I'm not interested in *just* sex at all, not without being involved and I'm not *allowed* to get tied up with you, or anyone. Not until this lot of paintings is finished. But when does one say that's enough for the moment? I can't go on for ever saying just one more painting, like Penelope weaving her everlasting tapestry. But I'd like to be able to say yes, and might perhaps, later on ... Shit, it's *frightening*. But I didn't expect to be understood at once. As what am I dressed up? A siren in sackcloth and ashes? And what's he? A fox in a rabbit's mask? I must go before he pretends to nibble and then takes a larger mouthful. It was insane to have come in the first place – I haven't escaped from Oscar so recently to be recaptured, even for a single night. But it wasn't an escape from Oscar, he escaped from me. I was jettisoned ...' Not unnaturally she couldn't bring herself to say a syllable of this aloud.

'Nut?'

'Yes, Bea?' He had been extremely patient with the long silence but still looked friendly, if somewhat resigned, leaning back against his desk as if waiting for her to speak again.

'You will see me again? Won't you?'

'Oh yes, if you'd like to, absolutely yes.' He sounded relieved, she thought.

'I would like. I can't say what I mean because it sounds trite – and I often don't know what I mean till after I've heard myself say it.'

'Don't say anything more then, if you're feeling unintelligible. Best to leave it, if you're needing certainties. I'm sorry I leapt over the fence.' He couldn't bear not to touch her again and put an arm round her shoulder and gave her a little squeeze. She felt a clear and definite physical kickback from the feel of the flesh, bone and muscle in his arm, and a second, echoing, craven ache.

'Come on, Bewildered Beatrice. I'll walk with you back to that rat-trap of a truck of yours.'

The smell of bonfire lingered in the little house and Nut clapped shut the bedroom window on the black velvet night, cursing himself again. But she'd taken it as her fault, the poor pigeon. Why was that? Well, he'd wait. He'd wait because she had a beautiful walk, swaying and gliding with an occasional stammer – a skip, a hiccup, like her speech – fluent then held up by a liquid giggle. He'd wait because she was flustered and still too recently bereaved by the marriage breakdown. But was she bereaved? He wondered about that. Things happened about her, she did not seem an instigator or a participant. Was her entire energy being saved for her work? Was she an introverted soloist? No, he was being unfair. But the urges to change, to progress, to defeat and to possess were as strong in Nut as in any man. He'd have to wait because there was nothing else he could do.

That night Nest, safely back at home, lay back in bed and gazed with immense affection at Blue as he haphazardly removed bits of clothing while weaving clumsily about the room, dropping a sock by the dressing table before picking up a bottle of scent and idly sniffing at it. 'Phew! Is that called Eau de Nil?' He discarded the other sock on the floor beneath the window and leant forward to stare at the stars as he clumsily unbuttoned his shirt, abandoning it by a chair, not on it, and the leather belt he wound absent-mindedly round one of the brass finials at the foot of the bed.

'Don't draw the curtains, Blue. I like to be able to see the sky when I wake up. You can see Cassiopeia, just above the weeping ash tree.'

'Where? I can't see nothing. Is that the one shaped like a W?'

'Yes. You can see it from here, from this angle.' He caught his foot in his trouser leg and staggered, falling across the bed, his face close to hers on the pillow. 'Ah, I've got it now, just above that branch that looks like an angel's wing.' He put his hand on her breast, and heaved himself up into a sitting position without letting go. 'What are you going to read to me tonight, my Cuckoo?'

'It's far too late. I'm sorry the meeting with the horticultural society went on so long. You shouldn't have waited up for me. Oh, all right. Don't look at me like that! How about Lamb's *Tales from Shakespear?* I think you'd like *The Winter's Tale* – but it's a bit complicated for someone who's drunk a bottle of Chenin Blanc and two double brandies. Do you think, by the way, that your friend Nut is interested in Bea?' She imagined Oscar to be well out of the picture, for surely he'd never come back to Bea now, but Nut could be a complication, a distraction to Bea's burgeoning talent. She'd not actually seen any of the dear girl's work yet, but last time she'd called there'd been a satisfying smell of oils drifting about the house, and the odd paint-stained finger which meant she was at least doing something.

'Might be. He'd not tell me if he was.' He sounded cautious.

'Keep an eye out for me, would you, to see if anything develops?'

'No, Nest, it's none of your business, is it? Naughty, nosy little Nest. Come on, let's have the lamb's tail story, then. If you don't start at once, I'll start on you.' So Nest commenced their strange game of literary foreplay, reading aloud while he leant up on one elbow, listening with his eyes closed and softly stroking her thigh.

Chapter Seven

Honey-scented seakale, then scarlet poppies and brilliant blue viper's bugloss rampaged across the shingle and insects in their thousands hummed, buzzed, bit and bumbled as Bea continued to explore in the few spare day time segments she grudgingly allowed herself.

The trips into the world outside the painting room were rewards for work completed but a tooth-achingly cold early evening swim from a deserted beach near the firing ranges proved more of an of an endurance test than a prize. Holly and foxgloves grew in these unpromising surroundings and freshwater lakes lay hidden among the scrub of goat willows, marred a little by an ugly scattering of rusting beer tins and plastic bottles jettisoned by the angling fraternity. In addition to the recent rubbish, the land was still blighted by concrete detritus from the Second World War, but it was hard to mind such things while larks sang overhead and on one duck-egg-blue-and-primrose morning she stood and painted from the vantage point of a ruined, tip-tilted concrete gun emplacement. She was ignored by an absent-minded looking heron standing as if tranced at the water's edge, but was kept amused by the abrupt illusionist vanishings and reappearances of grebes on the little lake.

Further inland, she uncovered the open grave of a skeletal horse-drawn carriage in a shallow dip and drew its unintelligible iron suspension parts, fanned out like rusting angels' wings among possessive thistles. Frogs flopped into dykes, always just ahead of her footsteps and at night they put up a froggy chorus as deafening as the cicadas in a Corsican pine forest.

Low-growing dog roses and ground hugging blackthorn wove themselves across the stones, splashed with bright pink centaury and white and yellow stonecrops. She sat contemplatively eating an apple on an old railway sleeper, unsuccessfully trying to distract herself from Nut-thoughts by searching at her feet for the minute plants which Nest had pointed out, the lemon yellow mouse-eared hawkweed and pink dove's foot cranesbill. Since the night of the witches she'd kept a half-Nelson on her emotions, in fact had swaddled them so tightly that they couldn't breathe, let alone wail in the middle of the night but she was delighted when Nut visited and guiltily thought about him afterwards when she was alone, mentally warming up her hands in his hair.

To save money on petrol, she acquired a maidenly upright bicycle from Jerry Rumm for a tenner and relearnt the skill one evening in the dusk with him standing by his gate shouting encouragement as she rattled up and down the dusty track, the bike stuck dangerously in the dried-out groove of a tractor rut. He shook his head disbelievingly but applauded as she rode past him over-confidently, yelling out: 'Look! Look! No hands!' Next day he came and pulled her out when she went, shrieking with laughter, headfirst into a bank of sedges and when she swerved and banged her knee on his gate post, he kindly brought her out a compress of witch-hazel. She re-painted the bicycle in scarlet and green stripes.

Jerry Rumm, shading his eyes when he saw it, commented that at least it was now pretty certain no one would dare to make off with it.

Back in the painting room, time was measured only by the

soft sounds of the brush on canvas, the sharp scraping of pocket knife on pencil and the steady encroachment of shapes across surfaces. Working four hours, five hours at a stretch, the number of new canvases lined up against the walls slowly multiplied as her imagination expanded and filled the painting room with whispering stories and silly jokes. She sang and whistled, adding to and consulting stacks of old sketchbooks, re-working and rearranging drawings, careful not to lose their immediacy.

Round about the beginning of June she arranged a seaside picnic for Mrs Lewis, a happily self-inflicted break in routine. It was showery in the morning and a little breezy, not the best of days for an outing, but warm enough as they drove out through the prettier lanes till forced to travel along the incoherent ribbon strip of coastal bungalows, hilariously deflected from their invasive unloveliness by the coyness of their nautical names: Halyards, Hispaniola, Scuppers, Bilges, Chip's Plaice and with touching irony, Sea View – this last built on land so low that even from the new loft-conversion windows the sea must have been teasingly hidden by the height of the sea wall across the road. Chalked signboards advertised Fresh Fish and Bait, two London cabs stood washed and polished on the forecourt of one and a dusty hearse was drawn up before another, its glass sides advertising a band, predictably The Overtakers.

It was the hearse which reminded Mrs Lewis that there was a church in the area which she'd always wished to visit; the church had an ossuary, the bones of which were already centuries old when disinterred some five hundred years before, when building work was in progress in the town. The mask-like skulls were prettily arranged, upturned brain-bowls in tiers in the wall arches of the crypt, along with a veritable hedge of femurs decorated here and there by the insertion of more skulls. Both Bea and Mrs Lewis found the effect matter-of-fact and calming rather than macabre and the curator pointed out that as one progressed along the ash-dry bone hedge, the skulls became more and more polished and rubbed, due to the visitors gradually becoming brave enough to give them a little caress as they progressed into the dark. Perhaps prepared for disgusted shrieks and overdramatic shudders and fearing for its safety, he doubtfully handed Bea a skull to hold, a child's skull, the eggshell lightness of which was infinitely touching, as were the yet unknitted plates of bone, the little molars still cusped, unworn by years of eating gritty, stone-ground bread.

The sky cleared and having done enough yoricking, they sat on a wall in the steeply sloping churchyard to eat their sandwiches, near the gravestone of Lionel Lukin, who '... was the first who built a lifeboat and was the original inventor of that Principle of Safety ...' A fat black cat made love to them, undoubtedly attracted by scents of tuna and hard-boiled egg.

'Now I wonder what your name is?' said Mrs Lewis, rubbing his broad chest and admiring his thunderous purrs and mighty whiskers.

'Morgue?' suggested Bea, still preoccupied with the rows of empty-eye sockets in the crypt and the thoughts and desires of those soft, long-gone brains and bodies, their impulses switched off and finally earthed.

They drove back along the coast before stopping for a walk and Mrs Lewis shared Bea's pleasure in the absence of prettiness in the landscape – 'How Ravilious would have loved the gravel-works!' She seemed to be advancing in unexpected hops and skips since their last meeting, shaking off the last traces of the tranquilliser zombie. They traipsed happily across the muddy shoreline, Bea slowing her pace to that of Mrs Lewis. Prehistoric-looking, reptilian cormorants sat on posts. Smart black-and-white oystercatchers sped with clockwork energy in parallel with their reflections along the fitfully gleaming sand, bobbing over ruched and pin-tucked ridges. Far out in the shallows a solitary shrimper in waders pushed his wide net across the outgoing tide.

'So, what have you been doing since we last met?' Bea asked, 'Are you still feeling better, off the pills?'

'Much, much better, though I still have the occasional shaky day, but it's easier to concentrate now, and I've ordered lots of books, and taken out subscriptions to some art magazines. I'm finding out what's been happening in that world, since I slid out of it.'

'What name did you use, when you were still painting?' asked Bea, bending over to retrieve first a razor shell, then a half-full discarded pink plastic lighter, which she shook and tried to flick into life, but the cog was stiff and rusting, so she put it in her pocket.

'Geraldine O'Brien, my maiden name. My husband, Richard, was a bit cross about that, after we married. But I pointed out that it would only confuse people to change it, since I'd already started to sell work under the name of O'Brien. What about you?'

'I've never even signed a picture. I've not tried to sell anything, so it hasn't been necessary but I'd use Bea Kerepol, I think. Not Mitty.'

'No, it sounds a woolly, fingernail-catching sort of name. Kerepol is unusual – is it Breton, or Cornish perhaps?'

'My great-grandfather came from Brittany, from somewhere near Saint Brieuc. He fell in love with an English governess and followed her back to England. It seemed to be a very happy marriage; he became a partner in a publishers and they had two sons and four daughters. In the old brown photographs we've got left, they're both always looking at each other and smiling. None of that stern, glassy, eyes-front look that you normally see in Edwardian photographs.'

'Photographs can lie, you know. I've photos of my husband and myself, grinning like maniacs.'

'And you didn't feel like grinning? You were unhappy, even then?'

Mrs Lewis halted and stood still, her hands deep in her

pockets, the skirts of her thin fawn raincoat flapping in the light breeze, a bleb of moisture on the tip of her nose. She lifted her chin and stared out to sea, meditating on an answer, appearing taller, straighter. She was changing before Bea's eyes from being Mrs Lewis into Geraldine O'Brien.

'I've only just started to think about it. I'd forgotten so much, intended to forget, I believe. I worshipped him to start with. But I think now he had a streak of cruelty, and was intolerably possessive. He wanted, it seemed at times, to *be* me.'

She stared at Bea, the pale eyes watering. 'He turned me against my family, one by one, destroyed my trust in them, and theirs in me. Then he started on my friends, little sneers here, unkind remarks there. I was very young when I married, very immature and something of a fool. He managed my career, dealt with the art dealers, commissions, everything. I was hardly allowed to meet anyone and I did so love people and parties. Then there was Simon Greensand.' She paused again. 'Forgive me, at my age time's short – I can't be bothered to wait for you to find out things. I have to tell you all at once, now.'

'Yes?' said Bea, captivated by the emergent tragedy, and a little flattered by the confidence of the older woman. 'Simon Greensand?'

'He had a gallery in Chelsea; was well thought of by the artists who showed there. I think he saw how it was with Richard and me. He refused to deal with Richard, only with me directly. The amount of work I was doing was dwindling steadily throughout the nineteen sixties, and had become a little unfashionable, being figurative, painterly. The young things, op, pop, bop and flop and the hard edge crowd were all the rage.' She laughed, a little bitterly. 'However he had clients who still liked the kind of work I did, and I was, had been, quite well known. Simon gave me a couple of shows, quite surprisingly successful, and Richard ... Richard made my life hellish after that.'

'What, jealous of your success or of Simon Greensand?'

'Of Simon certainly, but perhaps of both. I fell for Simon, although I must have been over forty, but he was married, very bourgeois and proper, with children, and though it was reciprocated, there was nothing we could honestly do ... It's a terrible mistake to force people against their grain. Richard slowly destroyed my confidence, accurately planting doubts like darts, and I felt I had no one else to turn to, to gainsay him. He wanted to be *the* magician in our lives, to control all the tricks. I was a fool.' She looked away again, and became distracted by the sight of a vast block of concrete which lay abandoned in the sea, with wreck-marker posts at each corner. 'What *is* that great incongruous lump doing there?'

'I've been told it's a piece of the Mulberry Harbour which slipped its towline, I suppose as it was being moved to France for the D Day landings. It was obviously too big to move again, once it had sunk. I don't understand how it floated at all, unless it was on some sort of giant barge. You can almost walk out to it at low tide. But do go on, you were telling me about your husband?'

'Ah, yes, my cautionary tale. I had what he called a nervous breakdown. That was in nineteen seventy. We stayed together but I didn't paint much again. He looked after me like a china doll, took over my sadness, even made it *his* so much that I felt I had no right to grieve over either Simon or my inability to paint. He suffocated me with forgiveness. I'm sorry – I'm a boring old woman.' She sniffed and smiled a watery smile at Bea. 'I've only unearthed all this myself so recently, not had time to rearrange it to make it sound less self-pitying, and I haven't blamed myself enough.' Her face drooped a little. 'I'm a little tired, Bea. Perhaps you should take me home.' She was distressingly returning to being Mrs Lewis.

'Of course, if you want. But wouldn't you care to come to my house first, and have some tea?'

Mrs Lewis considered for a moment, 'Yes, that *would* be wonderful, to go to someone else's house, although you mustn't think I've been entirely absent from such places for ever. There were days when I felt quite well, and even got as far as London. Although I couldn't always remember what I'd gone there *for*, when I got there, I seemed to have quite a nice time. I did notice things in my pill-addicted days! It was just hard to think, to decide what they meant.' She turned in step with Bea and they started the walk back. 'There is still a Greensand gallery, though not in Chelsea any more. It's moved to Savile Row, alongside the pinstripe and grey flannel.'

'And is it still run by your Simon Greensand?'

'I didn't ask. I did go up to see him, quite some time after Richard died and found the old gallery was now a boutique. I tracked down the new one eventually, but when I arrived it was so awe-inspiringly modern and spacious, I merely stood outside the door, too frightened to go in. Too old, and changed, you see.'

Refreshed by the experience of being driven somewhere new and by the form of transport, traces of the more animated Geraldine O'Brien confusingly reappeared on reaching Nest's house. 'A real doll's house. Out here in the middle of nowhere! Now, how extraordinary! The sort of house one visits in dreams.'

'It is, isn't it? Just like that. Only now I'm inside it, turning it inside out and dreaming in it, not of it. At first each time I came down the track, I felt that it might not be there and that I'd imagined it existed.'

Geraldine sat down on the little sofa, staring about her.

'I can see which bits of it are yours already and which were here before.'

'Which bits are mine?' asked Bea, returning with a tea-tray, unfortunately printed with cartoon Dalmatian puppies.

'Well, not that tray, for a start. How ugly it is, but one is not allowed to make judgements like that any more, is one? Now everything has to be equally valid so that no one gets hurt, ever? It must be a terrible shock to the poor young things, being told at art school that whatever work they produce is of *importance*, so they have nothing to kick against, then getting out into the world and finding that there are still some old-fashioned critics lurking in the corners, waiting to come out and nip their self-important little ankles. But I expect their self-confidence is so high they take no notice.' She sounded surprisingly malicious. 'But I'm going off on a tangent. What's yours? That bunch of the black-and-white feathers in the grey jug. Are they from magpies, or plovers? The scarlet mugs? The blue glass. The saffron yellow Indian cushion by that awful fireplace? I never could get to grips with Art Nouveau; it reminds me of my mother – all those plants rearing up and twisting about as if they'd been formally poisoned. Thank you, yes. I'd like some sugar. Now that is your work, the red man painting on the mantelshelf. You've made it look like an altar, with the candlestick, and all those shells. Is he worthy of it? Bring it over here and let me see?' Bea did so, biting her thumbnail and apprehensively scrutinising Geraldine's face for clues. She became alarmed at the prolonged silence.

Geraldine put her red mug down on the floor and stood up.

'May I see what else you've done, while you've been here?' She looked almost shaken but at least it didn't appear to be with disappointment. Bea hadn't realised her own need to hear approval. It *did* matter what Geraldine thought because she most obviously knew what she was talking about and it would be sensible at last to find out what. Twisted up inside with nerves, she led the way upstairs and showed her to the painting room.

Geraldine fairly danced about in her green socks, stooping over and moving smaller canvases, asking for help in turning around those facing the walls, propping one up on the seat of the white chair, muttering and grunting.

'Dear girl!' She swung around, her face alert and interested, ten, twenty years younger. Even her flaccid hair seemed to spring out and brighten. 'This has quite made my afternoon. I can't think what you've been *hiding* this away for, for so long. Your observation is acute and the technique is good, very good. You've developed your own iconography but it is really quite accessible and most original. I do think you should be able to do well ...' she beamed, 'Carry on, like this, and never let anyone tell you otherwise. Good heavens, is this really only two months' work? You must have been sweating blood.' She gasped for breath and sat down on the red-covered bed and clasped her hands together. 'It *is* exciting, seeing something fresh. I suppose that comes from your *not* having been trained with other people – they can all come out like little sausages. I gather the sausage machine at the moment is, on the whole, still churning out "conceptual", and the concept of horror is highly rated. I've been catching up, you see. Not that I ever lost touch entirely.'

Bea's worst fears were assuaged, but she still felt an awkwardness. She was outside, untouched by the unaccustomed flow of praise. Experiences at school, contrary to Mrs Lewis's beliefs, had taught her never to expect encomiums and she still gnawed doubtfully at a thumbnail.

'I needed an opinion, I can see that now, from someone who knew how to look and I'm so pleased you like them. Can we leave them, and finish tea?' The pictures were disturbing with all their fronts facing outwards into the room at once, an audience waiting for a play to start, rather than the reverse.

Once they were safely downstairs again, the now almost ebullient Geraldine continued chatting and asking questions.

'Tell me about this red-haired man so sound asleep across the paper. Is he a lover?' She was quite unabashed to ask the question and Bea curiously did not find it intrusive and laughed.

'No. Not yet; he's been held off till ... till I've got to grips with what I'm doing. But he may not wait that long. I'm sure he thinks I'm playing games with him, but I'm not. I can't just let go and jump in, somehow.'

'Remember my cautionary tale. It's so easy for misunderstandings to arise. Perhaps women artists shouldn't marry. Husbands so often either want your whole attention or swamp you with all theirs, which comes to the same thing. Either way it's impossibly difficult to concentrate, but I'm being flippant. It's never that simple.' Her pale eyes, now alight with interest and fixed on Bea, seemed to have assumed a deeper, greenish tint; they reminded Bea quite forcefully of Nut's and she felt a little spasm of longing. 'But no, *you* mustn't turn your back on loving,' said the paradoxical Geraldine, more gently for Bea had looked quite lost for a moment. Bea was compelled to change the subject.

'When you spoke of horror earlier on ... do you think it's because we've been brought up to see horror as an entertainment? She was thinking it out for the first time. 'It seems a perversion, an unclean fascination, but perhaps it's a *need*, or a way of preparing oneself?'

'Yes, I'm sure we've a need to rehearse our responses to fear at a distance, so that if it happens one knows one's lines. I think women particularly do that type of rehearsing, imagining terrible accidents to our husbands, running through our children's funerals, making ourselves quite ill with fear as a precaution against eventual loss. I was born between the wars, but obviously some of the generation on either side experienced unbelievably disgusting atrocities – no rehearsal, but for real. A very few of them were inebriated by the excitement and found peacetime impossibly dull, but most of them didn't care to talk about it; any bloodlust they may have had was quickly sated. Read Siegfried Sassoon, or Robert Graves.'

'I have read *Goodbye To All That*. I was appalled.'

'It *was* appalling. You must remember to stay appalled. Now, I should go home. I've taken up far too much of your precious time and it's been a great treat, seeing you and your work. You must come and have lunch with me soon; I could go into Parden by bus and get ready-made dishes from Marks and Spencer!'

'Mrs Lewis, Geraldine, I mean, how does one get started? How do I get someone to sell my pictures? I know I haven't enough work yet, to show anyone. But I do need to start thinking about what the next step is and it all seems so intimidating.'

'Let me think about it, my dear. I'm so out of touch with everyone but perhaps I can come up with a plan of action. I think it really is time I looked up some old acquaintances. From now on, I intend to grow old boldly.' This sounded like a threat.

Bea's confidence soared after Geraldine's visit. She continued to drive herself hard and there rarely seemed enough daylight. The dreamtime was over. She was fired up with an energy and a certainty only once before equalled in her unfortunate determination to marry Oscar. The painting had taken precedence over everything else and she was gaining more and more control, knowing the likely effect in advance of every patch of colour, of each line, of each brushstroke on the canvas.

It was clear that several themes were emerging. The marble Freda appeared in more pictures. In one she sat as decorously as her draperies would allow, on a bar stool in a recognisably gloomy Bell and Hatchet in conversation with Oscar and Agnes who loomed menacingly over her. She sported a nose ring and her plump stone arms had acquired graffiti: 'noli me tangere' round one upper arm as if tattooed, and 'man the lifeboats' round the other. There hadn't been quite enough space on the curving surface of the arm for the final four letters of either inscription. The other customers in the bar were the fishermen, watching with the wide-eyed horror of Fuseli phantoms as a pair of scarlet witches danced a tango. In another, Freda floated over the roof of Little Rumm, scattering a benediction of poppy petals over Mrs Lewis who sat in a deckchair in the garden beneath, reading a newspaper. The other works were mercifully less arcane.

But it wasn't easy. The major problem was the volume of interruptions. It seemed that in seeking seclusion she'd found a greater degree of popularity than she'd known when in circulation and felt unable to turn away the visitors who were intrigued by exaggerated stories of her lonely life spread around by Agnes and had travelled out to relieve the unhappy solitude.

In order to curtail the invasions she went visiting herself but found that the visited were all dying to see where she lived and promised to drop in soon, which quite defeated the object of *her* visits. Anyway she did enjoy company, even if guilty afterwards.

Three days after the picnic with Geraldine, Mary Dunnock arrived unannounced with her four children under seven, one of whom was immediately sick in the wastepaper basket. Mary, slim in her sensible denims and spotless white blouse, wandered about erratically after the children as they each in turn endeavoured to escape; Bea wondered how she kept herself so pristine while the children were so thoroughly encrusted with chocolate and marmalade. Mary continually broke off her conversation to answer their questions and demands and murmured discontentedly when she saw the red painting of Nut, that Bea was so lucky to have such talent and that she'd often thought herself how she would like to paint, given the time.

'Of course, it must be *easy* for you with no other worries,' she said, unblushingly, 'but then I'd no idea you were so talented. No, Megan, the top of the bottle unscrews *this* way. How do you get started, Bea? Do you drift about the marsh ... that's right, Harry, oh dear, you've spilt it ... waiting for inspiration to strike?'

Bea gritted her teeth at the implication that having talent was an unfair short cut, meant one did not have to sweat at it or frustratedly rip up days of work because it was crap. There were frequent occasions, unseen by other people, when things did go spectacularly wrong and she was either in a state of frenzy or of despair. However, Mary was a cheerful person and her visit was refreshing, particularly so since she did not deign to even mention Oscar.

The painting of Nut had not gone unnoticed by Nest who'd popped in with Blue and a bottle of wine one evening and towards the end of her second glass, she exhorted Bea to concentrate on the work in hand and not be distracted by pretty faces.

'And how are the Daughters of Nature, Aunt Nest?' Nest looked fiercely at Bea and indicated with a violent jerking of eyebrows and other physical hintings that she was to shut up in front of Blue.

'Oh, not very interesting,' she said dismissively and rather hurriedly. 'A lot of unsound eco-babble, with very little scientific backup. I told them they must have facts at their fingertips, facts up their noses and coming out of their ears if they want to get anywhere with officialdom.' Bea resisted asking her if she could borrow the red cloak.

Jane telephoned frequently, reminding her gently that she was lucky to have friends and relations so interested in her wellbeing, not to forget that she still had a family nor that Patrick would be home soon and that a publisher had been found for the Cadwell Commonplace Book, work on which was proceeding apace.

'Congratulations, Mum, I think you're a star. You'll probably outsell *Country Diary of an Edwardian Lady* and make millions in spin-offs. You can have Cadwell Egg Cosies, Cadwell Cooking Pots and Cadwell Lavatory Paper ... It isn't really going to be called that, though, is it? Don't you need something a bit snappier? Mum, I love seeing you and Dad. I love seeing everybody. I just wish they would ring first, or at least come in the evening.'

'If they do telephone, you keep putting them off. You must be more sociable, darling. You can't be throwing paint about all the time.'

But the interruptions increased. She thought they might as well make themselves useful and asked the visitors to sit for lightning water-colour sketches, shutting her ears if they were inclined to Oscar-speak, talking effects while thinking causes.

And there was Nut. She noticed that she never counted him as an interruption and even sought him out herself or came across him about his business on occasions. Even if she had not seen him for several days, the idea that he was working in his railway carriage or travelling about the marsh somewhere was enormously comforting. Her regard and liking for him steadily increased and they had reached a stage of warm but still wary, teasing companionship with a pleasant, almost exhilarating tension between them — unfinished business. But, as Nest said, he was an impediment to concentration and confused her devices and desires merely by knowing what they were. To Nut, she was increasingly a frustrating and tantalising enigma.

Out on a foray late one afternoon on the exotic bicycle, she was intrigued by the looming silhouette of a Tudor castle lurking apparently untouristed and inaccessible in the distance of the flat land and rode joltingly among the sheep along a grassy track, towards its crumbling, golden biscuit-coloured, sandstone walls. Sadly it was barred against her. She leant the bike against a wall and on walking round it seeking an entry, she came slap up against the solidity of Nut as she rounded a bastion, startling him and almost winding herself.

'What are you doing here?' she asked, rather rudely because her heart had jumped at the contact and continued to racket about after they disentangled themselves.

'I was supervising the collection of some core samples about two miles away and thought I'd walk over for a private viewing. Did you want to get inside? I've spotted a way.' He guided her round to the other side.

'The whole pleasure in this place,' he said, giving her a leg up to a gap where a grating had been at some time illicitly removed and giving her a friendly shove through it, 'is its emptiness. No car parks, none of that intrusive heritage stuff, signposting, payment booths and bookstalls. It's only recently been opened up on occasions in the late summer. It's too far for most people to bother to walk.' He squeezed his shoulders through and leapt down to join her in the sunlit dereliction.

They poked about, Bea bewitched by it in spite of its clearly having been in use for many years as a secret place for teenage drinking and other exploratory pastimes. In one area the odd crisp packet was pushed into a crevice and a drink can thrust into a rabbit hole, for it was a rabbits' paradise with ankle-wrenching burrows in the sandy rubble. 'I love Jim B. 1956' and the inevitable 'Chris is a wanker '92' were scored into the walls and a couple of used condoms lay limply among the weeds. A russet dragonfly large enough to qualify for helicopter status roared past, its copper and gold-spangled cellophane wings clattering harshly.

'And have you finished *Gulliver's Travels?*' asked Nut, presenting her with a jackdaw's feather.

'No. I'm still working at it. He's just jumped off the flying island, arrived in Lagado and met the old man who spent eight years trying to extract sunbeams from cucumbers. I was feeling a touch irritable at the time and thought that it was a good description of painting.'

'And why aren't you extracting sunbeams today?' he enquired, gazing at her as they sat together on a stone block in the honey-coloured light.

'One has to have a break sometimes! I weakly decided that it was too beautiful an afternoon to stay indoors any longer.'

'Weak isn't a word I'd ever use about you. You appear to have a most steely self-control.'

'What? Me? You must be joking. I'm the world's worst procrastinator. Anyway, the steely look can be put on in a flash – it stops people nagging. You make your eyebrows go straight across and stare at the spot between the person's eyes.'

'Go on, do it. Oh I see! Horribly intimidating!' He chortled with laughter and then leant back on his elbows, looking at her more seriously. 'Procrastinator, certainly. I'll go along with that but once you *have* made up your mind, you seem to stick to a decision like bubble gum to hair.'

'Is there by any chance a column of smoke in the distance? Do I guess what this is leading up to?'

'Oh, I hope so, Bea.' He leant over and put a hand behind

her head and turned it towards him, cool sea eyes sparkling with intent but she leapt up and dashed off, laughing a little nervously. 'Absolutely not, not here.'

'I only thought I might try for a kiss. Or have I got to ask your father for your hand first?'

'I'm still married. I won't ever get married again. Been there, done that.'

'So, it's "not now", then it's "not here". I'll be frightened to try again in case the next one's "not ever". I'll crumble into dust shortly. Then you'll be sorry.' He lay down on top of a narrow wall and folded his long hands together as if praying, a figure on a tomb, his face caught in a shaft of late afternoon gold, his lids closed. The image was chilling.

'No! Please, don't!' she cried out. 'You look like a knight crusader lying there. Didn't they have their legs crossed on their tombs to show they had been to the Holy Land? And shouldn't you have a little dog, or a lion at your feet? But it's definitely not "not ever". It's time I got back. I'm on the bike and it's quite a way from here.'

'Time?' said Nut, opening his eyes again and turning his head towards her. 'Time? Time's a bugger. *At* nine o'clock, *by* six o'clock, *before* next Tuesday, *after* tea, *only* a minute, *just* a second – this time, sometime never. How I hate having to work to other people's schedules! Time is for other people. You've got as much time as you need, honeybee. Just grab it.'

Bea laughed helplessly, since as he lay on the wall, she had become aware of the size of his feet.

'What huge boots, absolutely vast boots!'

He suddenly rolled off the wall and sat on the dusty ground, looking down at them with pride. 'Yes, they're pretty impressive, aren't they? Size thirteen.' He strengthened the Ulster accent. 'My mother said I'd the most beautiful big feet in the whole of County Down.' He looked up at her and held out a hand. 'Help me up. You are good at turning the subject. I tell you, your body and soul are made of stainless steel, just like a carving knife.

Pitiless woman, *Belle Dame sans Merci*, Iron Maiden ... Status Quo ... I have to try now and again, to keep my hand in. At least a hug, then, to keep me going, if I'm not allowed to make love to you.'

'Oh, all right!' Chuckling she hugged him and her knees let her down by nearly giving way.

He whispered in her ear – 'It's always the legs that go first. Me too – I know, you know,' he was reluctant to let go, having to keep close to her, 'I saw it in your face, the first time you came to my house. It was the most amazingly erotic expression, a stunning turn-on ...' He stopped and looked about him as if not quite sure where he was. 'Oh, well. Now getting out of here might be a bit more difficult than getting in ...'

She rode off across the nibbled grass on her bicycle, wobbling because he was watching and acutely feeling his longing looping after her like a lasso, rang the bell in recognition. She dreamed of him that night, striding across the green land with a great measuring stick in each hand, a chalk outline against grass, the Long Man of Wilmington, the Long Man of the Marsh.

During these weeks of early summer Agnes visited with a frequency that bordered on harassment. She was often short tempered and arrived unannounced or phoned at least twice a week to talk at length about her 'treatments' with Ludmilla, who was, it seemed, enjoying a longer period of favour than was usual. Arriving earlier one Thursday morning than Bea had expected, she walked straight into the house and started up the narrow stairs.

'Bea? Are you all right? What's that horrendous racket?'

Bea came out of the painting room, looking vague and preoccupied and preventing her from coming up any further, like a schoolchild shielding its work from a fellow pupil in case they copied the answers.

'Oh, the radio. Hold on a second, I'll turn it off.' She nipped back up again. 'I kept hoping it would get better,' she shouted out, 'but it hasn't. The composer talked about it first and said he wanted to create organised chaos, but I couldn't detect any attempts at organisation.'

'It sounds like a someone banging a cat with a carpet beater,' said Agnes, crossly, thwarted again in her attempts to get into Bea's painting room. 'Are you ready to come out to lunch?'

'I thought as it was still so early, you could perhaps sit for me for a few minutes?' Bea now had paintbox and water-colour book in hand.

Agnes grudgingly agreed. Sitting on the sunny steps where they now habitually sat for Bea's enforced counselling sessions and now rather astonishingly attempting to arrange a reconciliation, Agnes rumoured that Oscar was cooling off Andreary, harping tiresomely on the subject while Bea patiently sat paintbrush in hand, watching Seb destroying the wounded pink bicycle. He appeared to have forgiven her for the Battle of Slapped Knee and gave her a sly grin as he unscrewed part of the bicycle bell and tossed it over the wall.

Agnes was a lousy sitter and needed short breaks every five minutes, getting up and drifting about, looking and poking at things, leaping from subject to subject but, a symphonic nuisance, returning too frequently to her theme.

'He's been seen drinking on his own, in the evenings. I'm sure he's miserable and it's all gone wrong. Do you think your aunt would mind if I took this large flowerpot? I've got a pink geranium that needs a bigger home.'

'He often used to have a drink on his own, in the evenings, and no, I'm sure she wouldn't mind about the pot. Do come and sit down for me again, I've so nearly finished.'

'But Sheila said he was mournful,' said Agnes broodingly, first shaking out a root-bound, pot-shaped clump of stony earth which burst in an untidy dark smudge across the flagstones, before replacing herself on the steps again, with her legs in yet another position. Bea rearranged her.

'Tough titty! I'm glad he's suffering.'

'Why don't you come round to us for supper?' asked Agnes artfully. 'I could arrange for Oscar to drop in afterwards. Then you could meet on neutral ground? I could ask Ludmilla, too.'

'Are you mad? Don't you ever give up? It sounds horrific. I don't want, at the moment, Agnes, to meet Ludmilla on any terrain at all. Nor Oscar. I mean it. Nor, obviously, does he. He left me. I'm not saying never, but I'm serious about what I'm doing for once in my life. Now is not the time. You've changed your tune a bit, haven't you? And I'm thinking of pouring the paint water over your head, if you don't sit still! There's a lovely green reflection just along your jawbone and under your nose. If Oscar was having second thoughts, he'd tell me through the solicitors. Why don't you go round and cheer him up yourself, if you're convinced he's so depressed?'

'Well, actually ... I did go over one Saturday morning.'

'You did what?' Bea sharply raised an eyebrow.

'I just went to see them, him and Andrea, only she was out shopping, he said. Honestly Bea, he doesn't *look* happy. He pretended to be very jolly, but I could see through it.'

'Agnes, please! Just shut up! He's got no intention of coming back to me. He's still with her, isn't he? And I've just answered the last and bullying solicitor's letter written on his behalf, and sent a new key to the cottage. That was childish of me, getting the locks changed, I must admit. Anyway I've told the solicitor that he'll have to wait till I decide what to do about the cottage and things. It's all too soon.'

'It's over two months. I visited Ludmilla the other day, and told her all about it. She's so supportive. She thinks you're in deep grieving mode and need to rediscover your inner strengths.'

'Bugger Ludmilla and her modes. Why did you go to see him?' Bea asked aggressively. A lobotomy would be too minor an operation for Agnes.

'Just nosing about. He seemed quite pleased to see me. He

was wandering about the garden with a spanner in his hand, as if he was looking for something to unscrew, for a change. Why have you made my legs look so short?'

'Sit down, please? Partly it's because I've got too many long vertical lines already, and partly because, from this angle, they do look a trifle chubby. Aach!' A fly dragged its feet across a pink painted cheek.

'Oscar . . .'

Bea flicked a plantain head at her and abandoning the water-colour, got up from the mat where she'd been sitting. The more Agnes pushed Oscar at her, the more she felt inclined to go in the opposite direction. Agnes, however, was well pleased with the conversation. Seb gave a shrill scream of triumph as the bicycle chain broke and he pulled it off, waving it in the air and clouting himself around the cheek with it.

'I'll get him a flick knife for his fifth birthday, shall I?' Bea asked. 'Then he'll be all trained up for when teddy boys come back into fashion. Come on. The idea was to have sandwiches in the garden at the Eeldyke Inn, wasn't it? We'd better get going soon. I'm starting work again at two in the afternoon, without fail.'

'We're only late because you wanted to paint me. Fifteen minutes you said, and it's been half an hour. When can I see upstairs in your secret room? When can I meet the hunky Nutty?'

'When *I* know what I'm up to, and not making a fool of myself, that's the answer to both questions and it *has* only been fifteen minutes.' She hadn't told Agnes about Mrs Lewis's visit.

'You always were too worried about that. Unlike me, you never have made a fool of yourself in the past. Oh God! I do fancy a break from Phil. I've been quite faithful, you know, since we got married. That's nearly a year. He's really getting on my nerves at the moment — so critical, you wouldn't believe! Just because I'm having a break between jobs — well actually, I don't seem to have a job in the offing. I shall have to go and shake up my agent or do the rounds with a portfolio again. I hate that too. Showing all one's best work to some snotty art director, only to have him say 'We'll put you on file'. I hate being filed; I can imagine myself abandoned, sex-less, chocolate-less and wine-deprived, in some dark drawer for twenty years. Oh, poor Agnes. She does need some fun! You've always been too careful to have fun, Bea.' Bea wondered what she did with Seb, when she was out having fun. It must be difficult, being a baby-sitter short.

In the garden of the Eeldyke Inn they came across Nut poring over a notebook and a packet of monkey nuts, long legs in mega-boots stretched out along the bench in the sunshine with hens clucking and pock-pocking around him, searching for miscarried nuts. Bea wished strongly that they had chosen another pub, wanting to keep him to herself, particularly did not want him to be exposed to Agnes, not in the ranty-tanty mood she was in today.

He looked up, startled as Seb hurtled past him in hot pursuit of a cabbage white butterfly, straight through a flowerbed of scarlet and orange snapdragons, then he saw Bea and gave the beaming smile that so unnervingly disarmed her.

Agnes fielded the greeting and caught the little tremor in Bea as she responded. Had anyone ever smiled at her in such a way, she asked herself. No, truthfully, they had not; grievance settled round her head like an itchy blanket. She did not wait to be introduced but plumped herself down beside him, asked him to budge up a little and kicked off her shoes, wriggling her toes in the grass.

'Mm, that's nice and cool. Hello. I'm Agnes. You must be the famous Nut.'

Bea sat on the other side of the table and watched, at first fascinated, then gradually becoming more and more incredulous, embarrassed and suspicious as Agnes proceeded to complain of the sultry heat, blew down the front of her shirt and then tied the garment up in a knot above her midriff, exposing as much of herself as was possible to the sun and to Nut's rather bewildered gaze. She then talked across Bea, asking wincingly provocative questions, appearing deeply interested and laughing conspiratorially at the answers and generally behaving as if . . . as if what? The landlord came out with the sandwiches and asked Agnes if she wouldn't mind keeping control of her child. He had planted the snapdragons, he pointed out, for the pleasure of his customers, not to act as a playpen for hyperactive little boys. Agnes apologised prettily, said nothing to Seb, delicately picked at her ham sandwich and continued to expend a vast amount of energy on charming Nut. Annoyingly, he seemed to Bea to be quite amused. She shrank back from the conversation, trying not to sulk. The intended quiet snack lunch was brought to a noisy close by an attack on Seb by a cockerel who was mooching about with murder in his heart beneath some bushes and who had taken a dislike to Seb's scarlet shorts. Agnes did a good deal of screaming and flapping, during the course of which her shirt appeared to become both unbuttoned and untied and revealed the fact she wasn't wearing a bra. Nut averted his eyes and hastily grabbed the cockerel up by the legs, hefting it gently over the fence.

Driving back later, rather silently, Bea decided that Agnes had appeared much as she had when she was seventeen – using tactics not out of place in one of the old black-and-white classic films from the 1930s that appeared on TV in the afternoons. The bright repartee, the gales of laughter, the fake-scatty flirtatiousness and the occasional smoulder.

'So, what's he like in bed then?'

'Agnes! Mind your own business!'

'Aha! Don't tell me you haven't yet?'

'I keep telling you, I haven't got the strength to get involved at the moment.'

'Don't leave it too long. He'll get bored, go away and take up with someone more accommodating. He's enormously attractive. I've never met anyone with red hair that I fancied before.'

'You're not allowed to fancy him! We're . . . we're . . . (what were they?) Anyway, he won't go off.' She was hurt and panicked by the thought.

'They always do.'

Old rivalries had come back to mind and Bea thought, quite reasonably bitchily, that it appeared that in the greater number of cases it was the men Agnes *had* slept with who had always afterwards gone away. 'I will not rise to the bait,' she told herself. 'She's got an attack of the seductions – she used to have the odd try at Oscar now and then, like testing the twanginess of an elastic band, when she thought I wasn't looking – and sometimes when she knew I was. She's just practising. I just wish she wouldn't go over the top.' She was a little rattled.

'I've got seventy-five snapdragons in my pocket,' interrupted Seb the Destroyer.

A couple of days later, Oscar, finding Andrea in yet another of her of pre-supper alcoholic comas when he returned one afternoon early from work, sat shaking with indecision on the steps of the terrace in the still fierce sunshine, massaging the neck of the perpetually quivering whippet for whom he now felt nothing but sympathy and consideration.

'My God,' he thought, 'what a mess she's made of things.' 'Things' had been getting worse; most evenings Andrea awoke snivelling and moaning with a hangover at nine o'clock, and crashed about the kitchen attempting to make supper from increasingly unlikely ingredients – the preceding evening they had eaten flabby slices of ham rolled round cold spaghetti, with mango chutney dolloped erratically across the surface and sprinkled with some roughly chopped green stuff which she had taken for sorrel in the dark, but which being tough and chewy and lacking the acidity of sorrel, he eventually identified as dock leaves. It had been served with fried carrots and a bottle of Krug.

His erstwhile helpless passion had turned to present and powerful disgust and this afternoon he rebelled from carrying her upstairs to bed yet again. Sitting at her desk and sweating in the stuffy heat, he wrote another letter, left it on the silver table beside her as she snored away the rest of the afternoon and packed up most of his belongings. Regretfully he pushed the motorbike into the garage, to be collected at a later date, patted Passe-Partout commiseratingly and drove away through the wrought-iron gates and back to Bellhurst. He returned via the Mummers and stoked up on what passed for lasagne at that establishment: pasta interleaved with lunch time leftovers of chilli mince and beans, which left him feeling aggressive and near-nostalgic for one of Andrea's messes.

Mrs Lewis, or Agnes and if not them, Tom, would now have to give him Bea's address, although he quailed at the idea of asking Tom. He could not go on like this. It was a cock-up. He'd been misled, bewitched, and yearned to return to Bea's pastel calm rather than endure any more of Andrea's poster-paint hysterics. Andrea's ex-husband had cut her allowance since finding out that she had another man living with her. The dear little son to whom he'd looked forward to being a second father had some type of behavioural problem involving animals – at home for half-term, he'd been discovered in the kitchen dissecting a mole on the bread board; after being taken to the cinema in Hastings to see *Robin Hood*, the boy had tried to execute the whippet, hanging it from an apple tree with a length of clothes-line.

On leaving the pub he met a bright and cheerful Agnes hurrying towards him with a letter in her hand.

'Can't stop now, Oscar, I've left Seb on his own. Why don't you come and see me and Phil this evening before you go back to Battle? Any time after seven-thirty – I'll have Seb in bed by then!' And not waiting for an answer she dodged between the cars and ran across the road, dropped the letter in the postbox opposite and turned to wave before disappearing.

The freshly ground points and angles of the new key were stiff in the lock so Oscar jiggled it a little and it turned with an unwilling crunch. The hall smelt dusty and the rush matting squeaked dryly beneath his shoes. All seemed to be in order but once upstairs in the bedroom he detected a faint scent, of jasmine, or perhaps vanilla, at any rate a scent of Bea, hanging softly in the air.

There was an unopened pot of instant coffee on the shelf and some semi-solid brown sugar still in the chipped blue-and-white Spode bowl by the kettle. Bea would never have thrown it away, she was kind to cracked objects but they made him uneasy. He made a mugful of coffee and sat at the kitchen table staring remorsefully at the fading pages of his letter, still impaled by the murderous table fork. He casually tried to pull it out, but was surprised by the depth to which it had penetrated and had to stand and tug hard to remove it. The letter he scrumpled up and threw in the rubbish bin. He reckoned it to have been written under duress and didn't wish to be reminded of its sulphuric acid contents. He would go later to see Phil and Agnes, tell them the good news and he even briefly imagined basking in their approbation. It was time he had a word with Mrs Lewis, whom he imagined would be fairly easy to browbeat into revealing Bea's whereabouts.

He stared open-mouthed at her when she opened the door. In order to leave a free hand to tackle the locks, she held a paintbrush clenched in a grimace between her yellow teeth, and in the other hand was an old wooden artist's palette. Her pale face was enlivened by farcical red lipstick and her eyes were almost fierce. Her long body was encased in a paint-stained lab-technician's coat worn over a jazzy leopardskin print T-shirt. She removed the paintbrush from between her teeth.

'Ah, Oscar. What can I do for you?' Astonishingly self-assured and crisp.

'Mrs Lewis, it is vital I get hold of my wife, contact her, I mean. Would you please give me her address, at once.' Brusque and bullying.

'No.'

'What do you mean, no? I must get in touch. I've come back to her.' Even to Oscar, this sounded a little optimistic. He tried to be ingratiating. 'If I could just get to see her, I'm sure we could sort everything out.' It was ridiculous, pleading with her on the doorstep.

She thought so too, and invited him to come inside. The old-fashioned, scruffy drawing room was scented with cat, with top notes of turpentine. An easel stood beside the window of her sitting room and beside it a newspaper-covered table bore oily scraps of rag and an assortment of stained, ancient tubes of oil paint, the colours of which were unascertainable to the casual eye. On the windowsill, arranged beside a hideous purple Charles and Diana mug and an empty brown glass pill bottle, was the skull of some animal, the haunted hollows and powerful jaws of which were decidedly perturbing. She didn't ask him to sit down and he didn't like the unpromising tightness about her lips.

'You must apply to your father-in-law. She has not changed her instructions *not* to let you know where she is, and I have no intention of going against her wishes.'

The old witch, Oscar thought. She was enjoying this . . . it was amazing what a little bit of power would do to a woman. It was demeaning enough that she knew so much about his personal affairs. He tried again, forcing his features into an expression of open-eyed honesty, which merely made him look surprised.

'Mrs Lewis, I'm sure you would not want to stand in the way of a reconciliation. I *must* see her.'

'No, I wouldn't want to stop you getting together again. But it has to come from her. I presume you'd rather not speak to her father — it would be embarrassing for you. I'll pass on the message, tell her you have returned and want to make amends. but I think you may find that she has other ideas.'

'I think that's for me to find out, don't you?' He was getting angry. The leaden pasta was behaving belligerently in his stomach.

'Perhaps. I will pass on your message but she is occupied, and . . .' she looked at him pitilessly and added, without licence, 'she's very happy as she is.'

He'd heard this before and was unable to accept it, nor his failure to obtain what he wanted and he was stunned by the flow of decided opinions. He stared about the room helplessly and his eyes rested on the easel. Keep talking, he told himself, and perhaps she'll relent.

'I didn't know you painted.'

'Yes. But not for some time. I'm doing this in order to get my hand in again. A *vanitas* painting, to remind myself that time is short and how much of it I've already wasted.'

Not understanding what she was talking about, Oscar returned to the subject of Bea.

'What *is* she doing?'

Mrs Lewis ignored his question, but pointed to the skull and said; 'Bea lent me that, the badger's skull. A friend of hers found it, and boiled it up. But the teeth fell out and the jaw came apart in two, see here, where the join is?' She pointed again with her paintbrush to the gruesome object. 'She stuck it all back together again with Uhu but she may have got some of the teeth in the wrong places. It doesn't matter, of course; only a zoologist would know the difference.'

Oscar gaped at her, and she thought what a foolish man he was, though heart-rendingly good-looking. Bea must not be distracted from her painting. She would do everything in her power to stop it.

'I must tidy up now. The light's quite gone.' She was put out by this visit; she could have finished that little bit of ivory cream in the inside of the eye-socket if he had not come. 'The sun's setting. Thank you for letting me know you are back in the cottage.' She walked quickly out into the hall and opened the door, so Oscar had no option but to leave.

He drearily finished unpacking the car then wandered disconsolately about the garden for a while in the twilight, looking at the lush jungle that had been the vegetable patch. How quickly weeds took over, hid the traces of human effort. An untidy row of poppies had appeared, not yet flowering and struggling for air between the lanky potatoes and the spinach; mixing up flowers with the vegetables was a habit of Bea's that had always annoyed him. What were flowerbeds for? What to do, what to do? His stomach was still twingeing but the worst was over. Agnes held the key. When Agnes had visited him over in Sussex she had seemed to be sympathetic to his problems; surely she'd be prepared to part with Bea's address, now that he'd come home again and needed so badly to be forgiven.

It was a warm evening but the town's streets were now empty apart from a few early tourists wandering hand in hand round the ancient streets in the half-light, marvelling at the quaintness but wondering where the action was. The spell of settled hot weather had induced a small hotel in the High Street cautiously to place a few potted bay trees and white plastic chairs and tables outside on the pavement and a group of teenagers had commandeered these and were shrieking and laughing exaggeratedly, their noise echoing against the stolid Georgian brick frontages of the buildings. Oscar approached them feeling old. 'Ooh!' said a girl aged about fifteen, in a voice intended to be heard by the boy sitting opposite her, 'I fancy *him*,' and giggled. Oscar straightened up and held in his stomach as he walked past. 'Go on!' jeered another, sensing blood. 'He's old enough to be your Dad!' Oscar turned thankfully out of sight into Cuckold's Lane, and rang the doorbell of No 8.

'Oscar! How good to see you! I was feeling so bored. Do come in – I'm so sorry, but I forgot that Phil had arranged a drink with a couple of old school friends, a boys' night out.' Agnes was dressed in a small blue cotton dress with tiny straps, not much more than a petticoat and her hair was tied up in a pink towel-turban, dark curlicues escaping, dripping onto her brown shoulders. She led him through the kitchen and out on to the pocket-sized terrace where sat two chairs and a tiny table crowded with glass, half-full bottle of wine, an overflowing ashtray and a guttering candle in a jam jar.

'I was sitting out here, pretending I was in Madrid,' she said, putting a glass in front of him and pouring the wine. Oscar was incapable of the feat of the imagination required to transform a back yard in Bellhurst to a balcony in Spain and watched Agnes apprehensively as she tilted her chair back and leant against the scraggy jasmine that grew in a pot behind her.

She felt wonderfully powerful. Earlier on that evening when she'd gone to post an indignant letter demanding the overdue payment for the last of the *Charlie Chooch* artwork, she'd spotted his car standing outside the pub, its rear seat loaded with boxes covered by a pile of jackets on hangers. On a sudden hunch she had crossed the road, intending to go into the pub to see if he was there, but after having met him in the street had beetled back to the house, battling Seb to bed in a self-defeating hurry, waved goodbye to Phil, whose intended absence that evening she had not forgotten, washed her hair and changed her dress. She'd had to wait some time, but it had been worth it. He was there now, a captive lion before her and Bea could never say she had not pleaded his cause.

'Ssh.' She glanced up with an exaggerated grimace of mock dread and whispering, 'We must keep our voices down. Seb's bedroom window is just above us, and it's so hot I had to open it wide. I couldn't bear it if he woke up!' She removed the towel and shaking dark damp hair about her face, ran her fingers through it vigorously. There was a ripeness to Agnes that even in his distracted state Oscar found appealing.

'I've left Andrea,' he announced portentously.

'I wondered how long it would take for you to find out.'

'Find out what?'

'Ssh! That she's an alcoholic. When you first met her, she'd just come back from a drying-out session in a clinic. I met someone who'd been in the same clinic at the same time, only they were addicted to chocolate. It was Andrea's fourth time in there. That's why her husband pushed off.' Her look was open and sympathetic. 'I wouldn't bother, about Bea, if I were you. She's having a wonderful time.' Go carefully now, she thought, don't rub it in too much, just enough to have him feeling just a little indignant.

'But once she knows I've come home ... now things have changed, she'll see me, give me a chance to explain and try to make it up to her. I can't do that via solicitors.' He was trying to keep his voice down to a whisper. 'God, I feel so appallingly guilty – she must have been desperately miserable. Please, Agnes. Give me her phone number. That bloody Mrs Lewis refused point blank, only agreed to pass on a message. She seems to be a born-again artist, had some sort of awakening. I couldn't believe it was the same woman when she came to the door, all covered in oil paint and her face was all tarted up with bright red lipstick. She looked like an old ferret that had just gorged on a rabbit. I couldn't get through to her. Could you take a letter to Bea for me?'

'Of course I'll tell Bea. I can't give you her address – I promised. But don't, in any case, get your hopes up. She's been pretty adamant she doesn't want to see you again.' She leant forward and put her hand on his arm. 'Poor Oscar. She's become quite cool and unforgiving. Don't forget how well I know her. We were at school together, remember?' Agnes didn't remove her hand at once.

'You do understand, don't you? I simply can't break a confidence. It was a promise. But I'll see what I can do on your behalf. I promise that, too.' She gave his arm a tiny pat, beautifully timed, sensing the tense muscularity beneath the thin cotton of the shirt sleeve, and withdrew her hand slowly, so that it casually brushed his. Kind, sweet little person, he thought.

She's on my side. He felt a surge of optimism. Bea would surely listen to Agnes.

'I really am grateful, Agnes.'

'Mummy! Mummy? What are you doing? I've wet the bed.'

Seb leant out of the window above them, his face pale in the soft darkness and Agnes knocked over her glass.

Chapter Eight

'That was Mags on the phone. I'm just going to zap over and see her – I won't be long. Could you give Seb his supper, do you think?' Agnes stood before the glass by the front door, brushing her hair in smooth, unhurried strokes then bent over and shook it, ruffling it up again.

Phil watched her, intrigued by the apparently pointless ritual. Her eyes were very bright, even in the dark of the hall. 'OK. What's he to have for his supper? And what are we having? And why mess up your hair again just after you've brushed it?'

'Seb's having spag bol and an orange. I've already opened the tin and put it in the pan. I daresay you could manage to open an orange? We're having fish and chips, as we always do on Friday. I'll pick them up after I've seen Mags. And my hair is *meant* to look messed up.'

'Then why did you brush it in the first place?' He was really interested.

'For goodness' sake, Phil! I just wanted a different sort of mess, that's all.' She blew him a kiss, as if she didn't really know him. 'See you later.'

Phil padded back to the sitting room where Seb was sitting on the floor, close up to the television, watching a video. The room was stuffy. Phil made a few companionable noises, opened wide the window on to the street to let in some air, and settled down in the bulgy chair to read the newspaper. It seemed a very noisy video but he managed to concentrate until he heard terrible female screaming and looking up startled, saw Seb, fingers in ears, his head face down on a cushion. The screams came from a semi-nude woman being slowly and realistically chewed up by a giant beetle. He leapt up and turned it off.

'Calm down, Seb. There's a good chap. Whatever were you watching?' He cuddled the small tense body against his own broad shoulder and rocked him. The child was not much more than a baby – how dare Agnes let him see things like that? It was not surprising that he suffered nightmares. 'Look, we'll put on the old Disney one, *Bambi* is it?' He ejected the video and looked at the label on the box. It was rated for over-fifteens. Seb was now sobbing.

'But I don't want to watch *Bambi*. I want the other one back on. I liked it really, really I did.'

'Absolutely not. It's too old for you. Mummy must have got it by mistake.'

'I choosed it.'

'Then she can't have seen the label. Look. It says for people over fifteen and you're not five yet. I'll make your supper and then teach you how to play chess. How about that?' They were still engrossed in the game when Agnes returned.

'Good heavens! Why hasn't Daddy put you to bed? Phil, it's nine o'clock . . .' she stopped, realising she was about to shoot herself in the foot.

'Yes. It's nine o'clock. And he isn't in bed for a reason I'll tell you about after *you've* put him to bed. Let him finish the game first.' Seb, losing concentration with the interruption, was rushing a rook up and down the board, making car noises.

'He seems to have picked it up very quickly? Perhaps he'll be a grand master when he grows up.'

'You're a clever chap, aren't you Seb? He's had his supper, which is more than I have. Check.'

'Well hurry up, Seb darling. Why don't you cheat and then we'll get upstairs all the quicker?'

Phil looked up at her from the floor, the green eye piercing and she saw he was seriously angry. When she returned after putting Seb to bed, he was still fuming.

'So, where are the fish and chips you were going to bring back?'

'Oh shit! I forgot all about them. I . . . I had a bite at Mags's. But you could have gone to get them while I was putting Seb to bed, couldn't you? Mags and I were planning a trip to London, this weekend. There's an exhibition we both want to see at the Tate. That's why I was so long. Why don't you come too?' She was on safe ground here.

'No thanks. The last exhibition I saw with you was like an afternoon at playschool. If people want to put their navel fluff into little green bottles and label it "umbilical detritus – take two a day" that's fine. I just don't need to pay to see it. How could you be so careless with Seb's videos? Look what I found him watching.' He thrust the offensive object under her nose. His hand was shaking and his nose looked pinched.

'What's wrong with that?'

'It's a horror film, that's what. I think letting children watch that sort of thing amounts to child abuse.'

'Don't be ridiculous! Anyway, I didn't notice it was for over-fifteens. It's an awful mistake. I really enjoy being a bad mother. So, you don't want to come to the exhibition? Well, that's fine. I need to keep up with what's going on, get out of this dreary backwater occasionally.'

'I'm to look after Seb, I suppose?' He was furious.

'No, I rang Mum from Mags's. She says she'll have him for the whole weekend, so we thought we'd stay the night with an old art school friend of Mags's. Look, I'm sorry. I'll get the fish and chips now.'

'Don't bother, as you've already eaten. I'm going to the

Mummers. I need a drink. You seem to have drunk all the wine.'

That night they lay stiffly apart, avoiding each other's skin even in their sleep and were woken twice by Seb crying out with bad dreams; Agnes took Seb into bed between them, a useful barrier which made sleep easier for them all.

Bea was sweeping the painting-room floor, having a general tidy before starting on a fresh picture. It was near the end of June and she had got through her supplies of paint faster than intended. She checked the tubes of paint, noted down that more expensive cerulean blue was needed and thought how odd it was that Agnes hadn't been round for well over a week, nearly two in fact. As she contemplated the peace of the morning, the phone rang.

'I hope I'm not preventing the completion of another of your masterpieces,' said Agnes with an unusual sarcasm in her voice, 'but Seb has taken it into his head that he *must* visit the old lighthouse this morning. He's bored because there's no nursery school this week because both the play-leaders have mumps.' She sounded aggrieved. 'He's insisting you come too.'

'Heavens! I'm honoured. There's a sketch of a derelict boat, not far from the lighthouse, that I've not finished; if I came I could stay on afterwards and finish that.'

'Don't put yourself out. It's only a whim of Seb's.'

When Agnes arrived, she seemed distant and jumpy and was more than a little inclined to snap. Bea was not sure why she had bothered to come. 'She looks as if she hasn't been sleeping too well,' she thought, 'and it's odd how it always seems to be Agnes who determines how well we are going to get on on any particular occasion.' Bea collected her purse and outdoor painting bag and felt in her pocket for the keys. 'There are times when she seems able to manipulate me into a bad temper myself. Well I won't be, not today.'

They set off in their own transport as Agnes grumbled

she had to go back afterwards to lunch with her mother and didn't want to have to bring Bea all the way back to Little Rumm first.

It was a clear, hot day and Seb adored the lighthouse. Bea had never seen him so concentratedly delighted and felt his enthusiasm made up for Agnes's unnaturally crotchety and nervous behaviour. Bea pointed out a yellow light aeroplane looping the loop, the direction of his home far away inland behind the hills, the direction of France, the massive container ship in the distance barely moving across the crepe-paper sea.

'Look,' said Agnes, at last having got her breath back after all the stairs and ignoring the view, pointing down to the road, 'removal vans. See? Over there . . .'

'I see, in front of Nut's little house. But they're big enough to hold the house itself and he's not moving. I'd know and anyway he's away.' Far below a pair of black Levis hung stiffly abandoned on Nut's washing line and there was no sign of his blue truck. 'He's gone off for a few days to a conference in York. Three vans, and all those cars – perhaps it's a film crew?'

'How do you know he'd have told you? Are you sure it's a conference he's gone to? He might have gone off on a jolly with a beautiful scientist. He might even meet a sexy geographer there.'

'Of course I'm sure where he's gone to, Agnes. It's a conference on coastal erosion and he's giving a paper.'

'Sounds absolutely riveting. And are you still just good mates? Isn't he pining for a bit more? If you don't give him a break you'll lose him before you've even had him.'

'You said that last time too. He just isn't like that.' Ruffled, Bea turned round to Agnes and caught sight of a pouting bottom lip. She refused to be dampened down. 'He knows I'm still in chaos and need time. There are other sorts of relationships, you know.'

'It all sounds very vague to me – not what I'd call a very satisfactory relationship, without any sex. Ludmilla said my paths of sensory intelligence were all irritated due to lack of sex. Do you still think about Oscar?'

'Of course I do. But less and less. Irritated paths of sensory intelligence — isn't that just a fancy way of saying your nerves are on edge? Why don't you get her to cut the cackle and give you a good massage?' Bea had begun to wish she was somewhere else.

'I used to have massages sometimes, but when I rang up for one last month the receptionist said the aromatherapist I used to like so much had gone on an extended holiday to Dominica and she wasn't taking any more bookings for him, which is odd since I'm sure I saw him in The Body Shop in Parden soon after.' Agnes's tone was now markedly acid. 'I wouldn't bother to think about Oscar at all if I were you.'

'The last time I saw you, you were trying make me to feel sorry for him. What's up, Ag-bag?'

'Men,' she replied cryptically.

'Are you having trouble with Phil?'

'No, not more than usual.' Agnes sniffed and turned to start the long journey back to ground level.

They had a cup of tea in the little café nearby which was full of strangers. They were not the usual sightseers doing the round trip on the light railway from Hythe, but well-dressed-down London people who had pulled together two tables and sat with heads close in a group discussion, passing bits of paper about between them, noting things down on clipboards.

Agnes, who was introducing Seb to the thrills of rock cake dipped in tea, turned her chair a little so she could see them better, and they her. Seb dropped the second rock cake, in its entirety, into Bea's cup of tea.

'You're right, I think it is a film crew. I'll just go and get us some more tea,' said Agnes. 'Mine's got cake in it too, and I'll ask the woman at the counter if she knows what's happening.'

She returned and whispered loudly, 'It *is* a film, and they're starting today sometime.' She seemed to have had a swift change of mood and sat there uncomfortably sideways, her legs sliding out into the aisle between the tables with her skirt half way up her thighs, trying to hear what the film people were saying.

'Where's the tea?'

'Actually I forgot to get it. It's only a TV costume drama or something, called *Black Lace and Brandy*. Sounds like smuggling, doesn't it? An old-fashioned bodice-ripper of some sort? Perhaps I could get taken on as an extra? It's about time somebody paid me for the pleasure of ripping my bodice.'

'What's a bodice?' asked Seb, now biting open and squeezing little packets of salad cream that were placed temptingly, along with packets of brown sauce, in bowls on the Formica table.

'The top half of a woman's dress,' said Bea, attempting to fish out the disintegrating bun with a white plastic spike implement, intended to be used for stirring. It snapped beneath the sodden weight.

'Can I wear one? Why haven't I got any dresses?'

'Because boys don't wear them. Much. At the moment. Not unless they're dressing up.'

'I want to dress up. I want to wear a bodice. And I want knickers like Sylvie's got.' He giggled, unpleasantly knowingly, semi-aware even at four that there was something smutty-funny about women's underwear. 'Hers have lacy bits.'

'Who's Sylvie? One of your friends at nursery school?' asked Bea, fascinated.

'Yes! She showed me them! Why can't I have some like that?' He was now warming to his subject and half kneeling on his chair. His voice was piercing. He dragged a yellow plastic flower from the bunch sitting in a clean white yoghurt pot on the table, dismembered it and flung the petals into the air.

'Go on, Bea. Why can't he have some?' Agnes was proudly aware that the film people and the woman at the serving counter, had stopped to listen and was sure they were quite enraptured.

'Because you are a boy, and boys usually wear boys' knickers.

But if you ask Mummy,' she returned the ball to Agnes, 'I'm sure she'll buy you some, for dressing up perhaps.' She picked up the petals and tried to rearrange them on their green plastic stalk.

'Time to go home,' said Agnes firmly, 'or we'll be late for lunch with Granny.' She bent towards Seb hoping to avert the usual departure crisis. 'You can tell Granny all about climbing up inside the lighthouse, she'll love to hear about that.'

'No, she won't,' he protested, 'I'll tell her 'bout Sylvie's knickers. Ladies are more 'trested in that.'

'I'm sure she will be,' said Bea, helpless with laughter.

Agnes and Seb departed for their interesting lunch with Granny in Bellhurst and Bea fetched her khaki wide-awake hat and the canvas bag containing the tools of her trade from the truck, and set off for the boat.

The sun was high but there was a shady semi-derelict iron shed, open on the side facing the boat. Its roof was holed and it was half taken up with a skeletal and rusting Lister engine, pillaged for spare parts, and an ancient winch with the cable rusted solid, but there was room to rest against the small workbench and paint.

A fly discovered her and buzzed round her mouth annoyingly. She swiped it away. She ignored the sound of people walking nearby on the shingle, kept quiet and went on mixing colours, trying them out on a separate sheet, matching the many layered peelings of faded paintwork on the curving sweep of the boat's planked sides: scorched tangerine, jade green, flamingo pink.

'Pink, pink with a dab of yellow, salmon pink, peach silk Granny's knicker pink. Why should pink be a feminine colour? How long has it been a feminine colour? Which was the first scarlet-faced baby girl to be thrust into a pink bonnet? Which man first refused to wear pink underpants and vest? Who first felt silly in pink doublet and hose? And why does Seb want to wear Sylvie's knickers?' She supposed people not to be strictly male or female, only predominantly one or the other, most women having a few 'male' tendencies, and most men a few 'female' ones, without compromising their sex, since they wouldn't understand each other in any way at all if they did not.

The heat from the tin roof was drawing sweat from her palms. 'Odd though,' she mused, beginning to pack up her painting things, having finished the boat, 'how people who are without that sort of emotional cross-dressing in their being, the stereotypes from the extreme ends of the spectrum, are *the* most boring people on earth. The fatally "female" woman, from a traditional male point of view, with irrational and insatiable desires to both please and get things all her own way – one couldn't spend five minutes in her company without going mad with annoyance. Add a fluffy *pink* brain (I am, of course, thinking of Andreary) and it's hopeless trying to communicate with them, or the stereotype male, heavily muscled, dominant and unable to understand anything more emotionally complicated than a combustion engine. Baby-blue-brained. I wonder if stereotypes are attracted to stereotypes? Perhaps they are; then that would cancel out the boredom factor. They just wouldn't notice. Nature isn't bothered about people being bored, anyway, as long as they reproduce while they're being it.' Then she thought that Agnes seemed to be getting decidedly more pink-brained than she had been and perhaps the bad temper might be put down to volatile hormone levels, if hormones could be volatile. She imagined them more as moving upwards in a steady surge, whispering subtle innuendos along the way as they edged towards the brain to cram it full of unattainable and mind-bogglingly gymnastic demands. Her grasp of biology was weak. 'Time to stop. I'm going loony out here. Perhaps it's the heat.'

A wavering heat haze danced above the woodwork of the boat and the colours dried fast on the paper. She gulped down the last of the fresh water from the bottle and crunched off down to the shore to indulge in a cooling paddle. She hitched up her long skirt. It was very quiet and the sea was wonderfully calm, the waves barely rattling the gravel as they rolled back and forth, sucking softly at the larger stones, scouring gently between her toes and leaving trails of moonstone and opal bubbles on her skin. Turning to face inland, she was struck by the sloping expanse of gravel before her; a large canvas, just waiting to be marked.

Against the upper part of the steep angle she began to construct an eye; first a dark circle for a pupil, then the brown iris and this took a considerable time, since the brown stones were harder to find than most. Slithering about, using her green cotton skirt front as an apron for collecting stones for the white of the eye, then grey shading, then more dark for the outline, Bea was totally absorbed in her child's game and did not pause till the eye, like those painted on Mediterranean fishing boats, a four-foot long aversion of evil, guarded the shore. Exhausted by the effort, but determined to finish it she searched out one last white stone, and pushed it into the pupil whereupon the eye took on a wicked glint. The effect was intriguing, however short-lived; the next high tide would lap at least the lower lid, and probably erase it all. Her hands and forearms were a little pink with sunburn beneath their salty sparkle and she felt sleepy. Leaving the solitary and quizzical eye to stare out to sea, she headed back for the shady side of the boat, lay back against its wooden side, tilted the hat over her eyes and dozed.

'Excuse me for waking you, but would you mind moving a few yards back to that white marker over there? We're starting shooting, and although I don't think you'll be in view, we'd rather have the area clear for the next hour or so.' The polite voice came out of nowhere, out of the sun. Bea gazed up muzzily into a girl's dark face bending over her. 'I'm sorry,' the girl repeated, 'but I have to clear the area, get people out of shot.'

Bea yawned enormously, and staggered to her feet. 'What time is it, do you know?'

'Four o'clock. If you want to watch, there's a marker over there, if you stay the other side of it, you'll be OK.'

Things had been happening while she was asleep. A handful of sweating eighteenth-century soldiers, followed by a man on horseback wandered past her and two men in T-shirts, a large one whose extensive stomach bore the word 'Megabelly' across it, the other more sylph-like, with 'Minibum' printed on the back. From where she stood none of the shore itself was visible. The action must all be taking place below the shelf of shingle. She found a better vantage point out of the way, along the beach and settled down to watch.

A modern fishing boat came into view, towing a large wooden rowing boat behind it in which were actors dressed in period clothes. It was followed by a rubber boat filled with men in wet suits. One of the actors, a women in a dark-blue hooded cloak, leant over the side of the rowing boat and appeared to be being sick. This caused something of a hold up but the rowing boat was loosed, oars were raised and it was rowed ashore. There was suddenly shouting, megaphones and radios being used and a lot of rushing up and down the shingle. The scene appeared to be being filmed first from the sea where there was some passing back and forth of boats, of cutting engines and drifting about. The rowing boat was towed out a little way and then the oarsmen repeated their trip from sea to shore, less vigorously this time and the woman was sick again, which was obviously not allowed for in the script, since it caused a third performance. The oarsmen were quite definitely flagging. The attendant boats moved out of view and the scene was filmed from the beach. As the now exhausted oarsmen again leapt ashore to pull the boat up, the woman in the cloak was heaved out and set on her feet whereupon she immediately lay down and began to retch. She was made to sit, then stood up again, brought a glass of water brushed down and attended to by a frantic make-up girl.

Filming seemed to be a quite tedious process and not nearly as interesting as Bea'd expected it to be. She felt great sympathy for the seasick woman, but it all seemed to be taking forever. Her throat was dry and she was contemplating going home when the actress with re-pinked cheeks, having recovered herself sufficiently, weakly indicated that she was ready for another take. The filming started again and Bea didn't like to move past the marker. Just at that moment, a group of nuns in full flight, startlingly tall and closely followed by two men with camcorders came round the point at some speed. They wore shockingly bright pink habits and were shouting in deep voices and leaping balletically, paddling in the water and kicking up spray. The unfortunate man whom Bea took to be the director gave a wail of distress and squatted on the ground with his head between his hands. Having at first thought that the nuns were an intended post-modernist touch to the proceedings, it became apparent even to Bea that two separate films were in the process of being shot. There was further slithering about on the shingle and arguments between the less well-equipped pink nun faction and the bodice-rippers and a little temper and petty shoving.

The tide was steadily rising, eroding what little foreshore there was at that place, and the shadows were beginning to lengthen. Bea was thirsty and although she hadn't seen the soldiers and the man on the horse in action yet, it was time to leave. If they weren't actually shooting, she could avoid the markers and cut back across towards the pick-up. She overheard various bitter comments from the crew as she passed: 'Effing queens, they must have done it on purpose.' 'How's Marie-Christine? She going to throw up again, or wot?' 'The tide's coming in. Our Tel had better get a move on or the boat'll float off and the cast'll get drowned.' '. . . all I picked up was the sound of her ladyship vomiting.' 'She's never been in a boat before, didn't know she was going to be seasick.' 'Poor bitch. It's a flat calm. How can anyone feel seasick in that?'

Having settled the argument with the pink nuns, or monks, since they were definitely male, the director turned away and consulted with one of the crew. His voice hoarse with frustration, he called out to Bea.

'Hi there! Are you a local? I saw you in the café this morning. You don't happen to know when high tide is, do you?' He glanced reproachfully at the girl standing beside him, the one who had earlier on so politely woken Bea. 'We appear to have lost the tide tables and the phone link to the boats has packed up.' A tear rolled down the girl's cheek and dripped on her clipboard. The irritable speaker had a high, intelligent-looking forehead and a lot of thick brown hair and was dressed in khaki trousers and a crumpled cream linen jacket with bulging pockets that seemed too big for him; it was still quite hot and his sunburnt face was covered with a film of perspiration. Bea felt very sorry for them.

'It should be about five-thirty.'

'Oh Christ! It's nearly that now. Well, that does it then! We'll have to start again tomorrow. Go and get everything sorted, will you, Jane — and for God's sake, please stop weeping! I know it's not your fault.' He turned back to Bea, who still stood there, fair, slim and shyly intrigued; an apparition, a beautiful and somewhat scruffy sea goddess risen from the uncompromising English Channel, the hem of her trailing green cotton skirt tide-marked with salt. 'Thank you. Have you been watching? You won't believe what trouble we've been having.' He wiped his hands on a large green cotton handkerchief, then ran it round his face and neck. 'The first thing was that someone had drawn, built really, a massive great eye made of stones on the spot we'd marked out this morning for the landing.' He was staring with curiosity at Bea as he spoke. 'Of course we couldn't see it from this side, with the slope being so steep and it wasn't till the crew on the boat started shooting that it was spotted. Talk about the evil eye being cast in our direction!'

'That was me, I'm afraid. I did it earlier this afternoon. It took ages. I didn't know you were going to be filming at just that spot.'

'Good heavens, you might have warned us! Oh hell! It wasn't part of anything important was it, some project or something you were going to photograph? I'm afraid it's been destroyed. This was one of the few spots where we could film from the sea without getting anachronistic telegraph poles and houses in the shot. We had to catch the water level just right, in order to be able to pull the boat up.'

'Well, I didn't know that at the time. I only woke up when your production girl told me to move. Wouldn't it have been easier to film it on a sandy beach somewhere?'

'The script specified a steep shingle location and this was close to the others we had to use. You were asleep, on the beach?'

'Why not?'

'No reason at all, I suppose.' He rubbed his chin and held back a yawn. 'You wouldn't fancy a drink with some of us, I suppose, after we've packed up for the day. Do you know of a good pub, not too far away?' He sounded hopeful. In spite of his harrowing afternoon, he seemed still to have a certain amount of energy about him. 'We haven't discovered anywhere bearable in the area yet. We're all staying in Fingle, in various bed and breakfasts and a motel. It's always the way. By the time one's nosed out the best places it's time to be off somewhere else.' He thrust out his hand, 'Terence Moorbury.'

Terence Moorbury handed Bea an ominous glass of cider over the balding head of a moustachioed, wasted sixties' hippie slumped across the counter of the crowded bar of the Eeldyke Inn. The pub was already two-thirds full when she led in the film crew and the only available place to perch was on the sticky, glass-ringed mahogany lid of the piano. Terence took an appreciative gulp of his beer and smiled encouragingly at Bea whose eyes were wandering about the room, entranced by the shapes of the customers. Beer bellies bulged, breasts heaved, flesh tried to escape from clothing in all directions, or in some cases the opposite, where clothing hung limply on spindle shanks and flapped about narrow bony chests.

They had to shout to be heard above the engulfing waves of ten different conversations going on about them.

'How bizarre to meet up ... on the same floor at Queen Mary and Westfield ... do you remember? ... Well, I should try putting more oil into the mixture ... Hang Sok Joi got sent off for biting ... I'm not surprised, with a name like that it was surprising they let him on the pitch in the first place ... You were Cinematography and I was Social Sciences ... *endless* trouble with the gear box on that model ... Freedom from pregnancy, that's what we gained ... What do you call a dirty book for amphibians? ... the squirrel pie was wonderful, with toasted hazelnuts ... Frogsporn, ha, ha ... I can remember ploughing that field with horses ... No, the *pink* ones came from Kookai, these are from the Fingle PDSA ... George had a heart attack on one of the Countryside Marches and Auntie Meg inherited the lot and sold it to a developer ...'

'Tell me about *Black Lace and Brandy*.'

Terence looked puzzled. 'I'm sorry?'

'Isn't that the name of the film you're making?'

'Where did you get that from? It's *Patrick and Marguerite* we're filming, one of Connaught Marvel's nineteen-twenties' ghostie best-sellers. He's undergoing a revival at the moment, it seems.'

'Perhaps *Black Lace and Brandy* was what the pink nuns were filming,' said Bea, abashed at getting it wrong. 'I heard it second-hand from a friend who got it from the woman at the counter in the café this morning when we saw you all in there.'

'More likely *Black Lace and Randy*. In spite of the havoc they caused, it was very hard to keep a straight face.'

'I thought Connaught Marvel wrote travel books?'

'He did and they're wonderful, but he wrote these to finance his journeys abroad, hiding behind the nom-de-plume of A. C. Holliday. They're pretty good, I'm told, but I've only ever read this one, in the course of duty. This is for TV and an acquaintance of mine is working on a private life of Connaught Marvel, to go out nearer the time of showing but on a different channel. It's a pity I didn't find out about it earlier, we could have liaised.' He had to raise his voice still further to be heard above the prevailing racket.

'When's that going to be?'

'The end of January. A two-parter. Will you watch it?'

'I'll try to, although I haven't got a television at the moment and don't know where I'll be for the winter.'

'Why's that?'

She became evasive; friendly and approachable as he was, there didn't seem to be any need to give him the details of her current situation. 'I'm probably going to move and I'm not sure where to, yet.' At the other end of the piano a woman was complaining bitterly that she wasn't getting the same pay rise as a male member of staff in her company. 'I think it stinks! I thought we were supposed to have equal rights?' Terence glanced round at her then turned back to Bea with an encouraging smile, trying to draw her out.

'So, where do you stand, on equal rights? Have you got all you need?'

'Have I got enough of your sugar on my pancake, is that what you mean?' The cider had kicked in. She said it accusingly. 'Anyway, equality isn't the right word. I mean, it implies fair shares between two identical beings – we're as dissimilar as oranges and lemons.' She drew breath and caught a look of incredulous horror in the face of the underpaid woman behind Terence and grinned. He looked slightly taken aback himself.

'What I'm getting at is that we wanted for ourselves the rights men had, without realising that these rights were designed *by* men, *for* men, but now we've got them, it's as if we've been handed out men's clothes and are expected to be grateful. They don't fit. I'm thinking of returning some of mine and asking for a bigger size.'

He chuckled. 'What's the answer, then?'

'I don't think there is just one that won't make you choke with indignation at its apparent unfairness – how about the right to have a job, or children, or both and not be constantly criticised or financially penalised for whichever option we choose?' She gave a triumphant smile at the woman who had stopped talking to her friend and was listening warily, then she asked Terence if he could play the piano.

He could and did so without fussing that it was a little out of tune, beginning with a passable rendering of Fats Waller's 'I can't stand you 'cos your feet's too big'.

'Can you sing?' he asked, looking up with a grin and switching his playing confusingly to Kurt Weill.

'Yes,' she said at once, now fully unwound after her touchy morning with Agnes and unable to collect up any false modesty in time, since he was now playing 'Mack the Knife' and the coincidence was causing a strange recurrence of the physical agitation caused by Nut's closeness that other evening.

'You don't, by any strange stroke of luck, happen to know the words?' he asked, pushing back his hair and looking up at her hopefully.

'Yes,' she said again. It would be easy, there was a lot of noise and no one was really listening. This was something which she knew she was able to do and slightly better than him.

'Right then, off we go.'

Her voice was small, untrained, but warmly smoky and inviting and people nearby stopped talking to listen; Terence looked up, genuinely astonished.

'Good heavens! I thought you were a beach bum, or a wandering art student with a passion for rearranging the landscape. You could really do something with that voice.'

'I think I'd rather leave it as it is. Arranging the landscape is more interesting.'

He played a few more standards, then put down the lid and stood up.

'There's a party on Friday night, this Friday. Would you like to come?'

'Isn't this a party?'

'No, we can't stay long this evening. We've all got an early start tomorrow morning, to catch the water at the right height. I've been assured the weather forecast is good. We're going to dose Marie-Christine with anti-seasick pills with her coffee. So how about the party?'

The social life here was a definite improvement on that of Bellhurst. What a shame Nut was away.

'I'd love to come to a party. Where's it being held?'

'I'll give you the address, where is it, ah, here we are.' He pulled a large business card from his pocket and copied the address down, and Bea noticed with amusement the enormous black fountain pen he was using. Perhaps it was a sop to his ego, making up for a lack of inches, in height, she hoped for his sake; his other belongings, not just the jacket and pen, were perhaps also a size too large for him.

'Here you are. I hope you know where that is, because I don't — we're being taken by minibus, those that want to come of course. Some are heading back to the bright lights as fast as they can. We've been doing a lot of rural filming recently and it's beginning to get some of them down. The party's being given by the man who's doing the documentary on Connaught Marvel. It's a house-warming party and neatly coincides with the end of filming.'

The address, Blackshorne Court, Ragstone Street, St Rumwold-at-Cliffe, was written in larger than average schoolboy handwriting. She turned the card over: contrarily, 'Terence Moorbury, Mogalite Films' was printed in a neat minimalist format.

'I've met Connaught Marvel's grand-daughter. She lives somewhere near here. Do you think she'll be at the party? Saint Rumwold-at-Cliffe is about four miles away, that's all, along the inner edge of the marsh, on the top of the old cliff face. I've got footpath maps of that area at home; the house is probably marked on one of them. What time shall I come?'

'About nine-thirty? There's a band, and dancing. But on second thoughts, why don't we take you with us in the minibus? Then you can show us the way.'

Later that evening, occupied slightly dizzily in planning a painting of pink nuns dancing on the beach with Megabelly and Minibum, the telephone bleeped and an impossibly exigent Nest was there plunging about on the line.

'Darling, I'm worried about you. I felt I ought to warn you, you mustn't let anything, or anyone, come between you and your painting.'

Nest sounded breathless with urgency, but had in fact spent all week wondering how to broach the subject. Any hint of her protégée straying too far from the paintbrushes made her feel apprehensive and while they were potting up forty *Geranium* 'Kashmir White', Lucinda had dropped a little squib into one of her Molly Bloom monologues which had rattled her acute alarm system. '. . . Saw your Bea down at the beach a few days ago with Francis Nutmeg – he was helping her into a boat – one of the old derelicts pulled up on the shingle so they can't have been planning on sailing off to France, tee hee . . .'

'What are you talking about, Aunt Nest?'

'I'm talking about Blue's and your mutual friend. Nut, dear child. Nut. I've been thinking . . . Blue thinks, well I think he knows, he didn't actually say in so many words, that this Nut is seriously interested in you. I'm interfering, I know. But it would be out of the frying pan into the fire, wouldn't it, to get involved, if you are involved, with someone now you have your freedom? You shouldn't let anything come between you and your work.'

'Aunt Nest, I am not "involved", as you so politely call it.' She nearly shouted. It was intolerable that she should be discussed, that she should be told what to do, even if Nest did have a point ... 'Aunt Nest? Hello? Look, I'm in the middle of something ... in the middle of cleaning the oven.'

'That sounds very unlikely to me. No one else has ever bothered to clean it. Now I've made you cross. I'm sorry, darling. I shouldn't have rung up like this, poking my nose in.' Nest didn't sound remotely penitent. 'But do remember what I've said, won't you?' She paused and then repeated importantly, infuriatingly bossy, 'Your work must come first.'

'Good-bye, Aunt Nest.' Bea put the phone down, indignant and chewing a thumbnail. The strain of the workload under which she had put herself during the last weeks had been considerable and now she was being pushed further. Everyone was warning of involvement with someone they didn't even know and even Agnes had been discouraging, slotting uncomfortable ideas into her head. You could never tell; perhaps Nut did have a glamorous colleague with whom he was sharing the trip? Well, screw them all. It was ridiculous. She wasn't involved. Not yet. And she'd been working flat out while wading through friends and relatives, forcing herself into a spectator's role as other people came and went, had holidays and did interesting things. 'They're treating me like a teenager doing A Levels. I shall go to the ball. I will give dinner parties, get my eyebrows pierced even. No I won't – it sounds agonisingly painful but I will do what I damn well like. Too careful to have fun? Huh! I'll have some fun all right.'

Gently swearing, she stumped back up the staircase to the painting room and threw herself down on the scarlet bed, lying there her arms behind her head, worrying, whereupon a heat-seeking mosquito immediately homed in on her hot skin, searching for its blood meal.

As children, aged perhaps six and nine, she and Patrick had splatted mosquitoes lurking on the ceiling of one their bedrooms by the skilful aiming of tennis balls. It had been in the house near the river when their father was in his yacht-building phase.

The ceiling became decorated with a pin-chart of tiny splatters and they kept a pencilled scoreboard of the kills on the wall beside the light switch. Patrick had been most intrigued that the tiny splash of blood soaking in to the emulsioned ceiling after a direct hit was his own.

Aunt Nest could not be flattened with a tennis ball. Dear Nest had given the house for as long as it was needed. Nest, however importunate, wanted to be a part of what she was doing and it was owed to her not to be shut out. Bea rolled over on the bed and picked abstractedly at a piece of loose plaster. Something was missing; not the bland security of living with Oscar, so it was another something. Something was absent and she felt starving for it, as if having eaten a delicious but unfilling first course, she'd then been deprived of a chocolate pudding. It was, she had to admit, most probably sex. Other people went in for recreational sex. Agnes had, probably still did. But she couldn't contemplate allowing herself Nut, since he was a particular, special man, not until she'd painted herself out for the time being, till she was one hundred per cent certain that the growing ache for him wasn't caused by being on the rebound.

How very unpredictable and vaporous a thing a close friendship with a man was — one false move and it might brew up into something else entirely and what was there to be gained by it? An incubus munching away at one's edges, like the sea gnawing at the land, constantly eroding as it sought out a weakened place to seep or batter its way through … she laughed nervously. It was so still outside. Not a sound out there in the night. The moon was up and almost full and she got up and hung out of the window, listening and sniffing. There was the faint apple-waft from the rose, the smell of sheep, and saltiness. She could hear the sea murmuring in the distance but perhaps it was only the sound in her ears of her own blood flowing. Goose pimples prickled up her arms. 'I'm quite safe here; there's a solidity in the loneliness. Invulnerable, in my castle.' It was time to lock up the house and head for bed.

At about three in the morning the sound of revving engines, crashing gears, squealing brakes and voices woke her. Alert in a second, she peered out. Further up the lane, perhaps a hundred yards past Little Rumm, she could see the moonlight glinting on the roof of a car angled crossways and sharply downwards, as if it were half in the ditch, and another car was in the process of reversing. Automatically thinking there had been an accident, she was about to lean out of the window and call out offering help, when with a whoosh the crashed car was engulfed by flames, a figure ran across to the revving, waiting car and leapt into the passenger seat. It screeched back towards her with the doors hanging open, bouncing and crashing on the uneven track. There was a small explosion from the burning car as whatever petrol was left in the tank ignited. They were gone.

Jerry Rumm turned up on his bicycle before the police and fire brigade, come to check she was unharmed. A half brick had been hurled through the windscreen of his old Peugeot estate and he was puffing, his unshaven chin bristling with annoyance, the collar of a pink, blue-and-white-striped pyjama jacket flapping outside the neck of his green farm overalls.

'Joy-riders! My arse — excuse my French — criminals, that's what they are. Those lads come out from Parden in stolen cars and drive out here to disturb us, racing them up and down the lanes at night. They get low on petrol, dump the car in a dyke or set fire to it for kicks, see? Then they drive back to town in the other. It happens quite a bit here, in the summer. They chose the wrong lane here, didn't they just? No place for handbrake turns or racing. You all right, Mrs Mitty? You do look a bit shook up. You want to have a nice cup of tea and go back to bed.'

Alone again after a statement had been taken and the police had departed, she stood at the bedroom window, disturbed, listening again. An oystercatcher called mournfully, 'kee-eep, kee-eep.' All was quiet but the clean air was brutally contaminated with the stench of oily rubber smoke and petrol. Dawn was not far off.

Chapter Nine

On Friday morning Nut moved with practised caution about his hot and claustrophobic quarters beneath the eaves of the bed and breakfast in York, whistling as he sorted through papers. There had been a mix-up with the rooms at the University and not feeling much like socialising, having Bea seriously on his mind, he had been relieved to be sleeping out but he had not slept well. The guests in the room beneath had been up till late watching television and breathy, echoing voices accompanied by gunshots had penetrated the floorboards.

The landlady had looked doubtfully at him when he arrived, silently judging his height. Having expected a female Dr Frances Nutmeg she had him placed in the pretty rose-covered room in the attic of the house near the Shambles and not having any other rooms free, was forced to apologise for the shortness of the bed and the lack of height to the ceiling.

The centre of the awkward space was taken up by the splayed-out upper beams of a great king-post supporting the roof and by a forcemeat stuffing of unnecessary items intended to give a homelike air, things which tripped or bruised the occupant: fluffy green-and-pink bedside rugs – three; stools – two, their seats upholstered with needlepoint spaniels surrounded by white roses; ashtrays – three, two of them emblazoned with horned helmets and 'Welcome to Yorvik', the third decorated with shamrock leaves and with a model leprechaun seated, loathsomely perky, on the corner. An overhanging plethora of tiddly wrought-iron shelves bearing miniature jugs. A frilled glass vase of pansies and an electric copper kettle on a painted tin tray cluttered up the bedside table. A cut-glass bowl overflowing with infinitesimal packets of instant coffee and fiddly tublets of milk, designed to be opened only by the midget fingers of the repellent leprechaun.

Nut was not an urban man and was immensely pleased to be leaving. He preferred the fewness of things in the country to the many in the distracting jumble of cities with their itinerant populations of trooping tourists cluttering up the pavements. In what was left of the countryside, it seemed there was one person to look at at a time, to get to know, one particular dog or cat to befriend, house or barn to observe and the people and animals were proud of being well known and of their singularity. Joyfully tossing the majority of the papers, followed by his plastic name tag, into a painted tin waste-bin decorated with découpage carnations and chickens, he packed the remainder neatly in his briefcase.

He whistled while he shaved hunchbacked over the washbasin beneath the sloping roof, flushed away a faint tidemark of red whisker stubble, unplaited, combed and replaited his hair, stowed razor and toothbrush in his haversack and gave the room a cursory check for any remaining personal bits and pieces.

The little book on fossils which he had bought for Bea lay on the bedside table and he collapsed himself on the rumpled pink rose-printed polycotton sheets, as out of place as a large dog fox in a suburban flowerbed, and opened it, wondering what he should write as an inscription. He paused, then bravely wrote in a clear, italic hand: 'For beautiful, bewildered Bea — certainties to search for.' He stopped writing and crunched the end of the ballpoint pen between his tough white teeth, snapping the plastic, unsure whether to put 'with all my love' or just 'love from', and whether to call himself Nut, or Francie, which was what his parents called him, how he usually signed personal letters and which she didn't know about, or even plain Francis Nutmeg. He settled on 'with all my love, from Nut' and the date.

He'd been hopelessly distracted throughout the three-day conference by images of Bea, an enquiring gilt-bronze angel in indigo blue, untarnished by her husband's flit, who floated across his field of vision whenever his attention wandered from the current speaker. He'd felt so briefly close to her in the castle yard ... again he'd seen the thought fly through her mind, leapt to catch it as it raced through her body but he had again misjudged the opposing willpower. He didn't want to take temporary advantage of someone on the rebound, but what an everlasting ricochet it was turning out to be. He saw her, hopelessly romantically, both as a fugitive and as a gilded bullet with his name on it, always just grazing past when there he was with his tongue hanging out, shirt open and his chest waiting to receive the blow. He had been pursuing, mind, body and soul, as relentlessly and methodically as she single-mindedly pursued her painting and knew now that he was competing with a passion as serious as his own. Having reluctantly admitted to himself that he ought not to get in the way, he tucked the knowledge back on the shelf to re-read later when it was more convenient. He could not now do without her. Peace of mind depended on it.

He slipped the book into the rucksack and fastened the straps. Time to set off for London, breaking the journey back to Kent by having a meal and staying the night at the Nutmegs' tall terraced house in Lewisham. There was good news to impart; the offer of the university post which neatly dove-tailed with the end of his employment on the marsh. He was looking forward to seeing his plain-speaking mother and seeing her face crack into the smile which had the power to hoist the spirits of the sourest of personalities. She worked part-time for a wine importers and he wanted to collect two or three bottles of something special to set aside for an eventual celebration. The smaller the bubbles, she had told him, the better the quality of the champagne. She loved the job and living in London. What would she make of Bea? He could not imagine that his father wouldn't adore her too. The sight of her might stop him grumpily counting the days till retirement and getting back to Ireland. He didn't visit often enough in spite of living so close and it would be great to see them both again.

Now it was back to the marsh and back to tempting Bea. But who was tempting whom? Remembering once more the hot skin of her neck as he'd touched it, the frantic antelope agility with which she'd bounced away across the rubble at the castle, that one and only hug, he was once more incredulously impatient with the fleeting, tentative visits, the amicable wanderings about the marsh, like the young couples one still saw walking arm in arm round the stone-walled lanes at home in Ireland, trying to find a bit of peace away from the prying, giggling younger siblings. Courting, that's what it was, but why not? It was certainly an original idea. Was there a better way to get to know a person? He'd search her out again and again and *would*, eventually, take hold of the sheeny shoulders and melt her down. Metal, melting; wasn't it odd that all his images of her were metallic?

Contriving with a shiver to take a tougher grip on his imagination, he slipped on the rusty black jacket and once more thinking about the formation and deformation of the earth and its inhabitants, bent again to avoid cracking his head, bumped with bag and briefcase down the low twisting staircase, heading for the high-curving, vaulted Victorian elegance of York railway station and the intercity train to London.

The rebirthing of Geraldine O'Brien was not proceeding without its secondary labour pangs. On that same Friday morning she had started smoking again, comforting herself as she inhaled the first lung-heaving breath, that she did it merely as an aide-mémoire. She rummaged through the spring issue of *Modern Painters* in which she had spotted an advertisement for the Greensand Gallery and copied the telephone number onto a piece of card torn from the top of a tea-bag packet. She spent the remainder of that morning haunting the garden, flitting from plant to plant procrastinating, the piece of card so tensely clamped between her fingers that the numbers written on it became rubbed and faint. At last, going indoors, lighting a fifth cigarette and inhaling deeply, she sat down beside the telephone, only to delay things a little longer by opening that morning's post. There was only one missive, a promising fat envelope which disappointingly contained a thin booklet, with no covering letter, entitled *Pork Mince*. It seemed to contain, well, pork mince recipes. 'Why have I been sent this?' she wondered. 'Does someone think I look like a pork-mince eater? Does my address indicate I keep a black Berkshire pig secreted in the garden shed? How did a pork-mince seller get my address?' Like a goldfish bowl filled with tadpoles, her head had been swimming with small, developing black terrors, that Simon might have died, or had forgotten her, but the minced pork booklet made her smile. She threw it into the wastepaper basket and tapped out the digits, with a finger so tremulous that she had to re-dial twice.

'Simon Greensand Gallery,' said a young woman's voice, its American accent and languid tone so at variance with Geraldine's resurgent fright that it was oddly soothing. She could hear voices in the background and the echoing sound of someone walking heavily across a wooden floor in an open space. She forced the throttling quaver from her throat, sat up straight, stubbed out the cigarette and asked as casually as possible if she might speak to Simon Greensand himself.

'Simon! It's for you! the girl called out with what Geraldine felt to be a lack of deference, before she took in the fact that he was actually there. The languid voice returned to her as an afterthought: 'Who is this?'

'It's Geraldine O'Brien.' She restrained herself from explaining further who she was, or was not. There was a muffled exclamation as the information was relayed and further footsteps.

'Geraldine? Geraldine! What a most wonderful thing! How *are* you? *Where* are you?'

The conversation proceeded at first in jerks and tentative

tweakings of memories then settled to a steady exchange of facts, explanations, and delighted laughter. How stupidly easy it had been, after all. She was invited to London for lunch with Simon and his son and the son's wife tomorrow, that very Saturday, 1 July and she had accepted.

Crossing and recrossing the room in a daze, two things rose inconveniently in her mind as she passed the looking glass – hair and clothes. She telephoned Bea.

'... I'm in such a mess. But I have a few hours left in which to do something. Where do I start? What *should* I do, do you think?'

Bea could hear the indecisive agony in Geraldine's voice, imagining an older and down-at-heel self suddenly bravely rowing out from a rural backwater into the rushing mainstream; abandoning a juicy brushful of cadmium lemon, she rallied. She made a pleading phone call to Pauline, the hairdresser in Bellhurst who normally cut her own hair, managed to wangle an appointment for Geraldine at four o'clock that afternoon and galloped to the rescue.

Geraldine's lined, doubtful face, glazed between the diamond panes of the Wimple Coffee House, lightened as Bea, ready for an emergency shopping session and face flushed with enthusiasm, arrived to meet her as arranged three quarters of an hour later. Apart from the five charity shops, which were a last resort, there were only three clothes shops in Bellhurst. The first was male-oriented and contained merely heavy-duty farming clothes, moleskin trousers, ferretskin underwear and riding macs. There was improbable lingerie, pleated, printed silk dresses and pie-crust frilled blouses, not Geraldine at all, in the next; there being no time to drive all the way to Parden and desperate to discover something suitable they tried the boutique catering for the more fashion-conscious thirty-somethings. It was a hot and sultry day which made trying on clothes an ordeal for Geraldine, standing bony and vulnerable in her grubby white petticoat in the oven-like changing room. But Bea, taking the job seriously, guided her into a miraculously well-cut long black denim skirt with a decorous mid-shin slit that both suited and fitted Geraldine's tall body and a loose, saffron-yellow, Chinese-collared cotton jacket. Neither of these were expensive and while her lank and untidy hair was being transformed into a very becoming, straight silver-grey bob, Bea breathed easily again and hurried off to Boots to buy her a new lipstick as a present, a pale brownish rose-thorn pink. She was thrilled by the romantic aspects of the forthcoming lunch and much heartened by the sight of Geraldine in new clothes.

'I can't believe it was so easy. I won't be able to sleep tonight, I imagine, with excitement! I have so much to tell him. It's not too late for us to be friends. Did I tell you that his wife divorced him years ago and went to live in Venezuela?' Geraldine examined herself in the hand mirror with a touch of new found self-respect. 'I think I was pretty, once. I can't really remember. Thank you so much for the lipstick. I shall pitch the old gore-coloured one into the dustbin as soon as I get home!'

'I was wondering if you needed to borrow a little T-shirt or something to wear beneath the jacket?' Bea suggested as they left the hairdresser's and Geraldine was about to agree but suddenly changed her mind.

'No, dear Bea. I have just the thing at home, sleeveless black silk – old, but no one will see the little holes – I'll wear it back to front. Thank you for your help and time, and your quite extraordinary patience. I'd forgotten how to buy clothes and wouldn't have had the faintest idea what to do with my hair. I've interrupted your work long enough. You must trot off now and let me walk home and think about things. I'll ring you up and tell you how it went, as soon as I get back from London.' She leant forward and planted a grateful kiss on Bea's cheek.

Geraldine was thankful to have remembered Oscar's possible presence next door in time and turned Bea from the idea of escorting her home. It wouldn't do for her at all to discover the wretched husband had come back. If she had popped in to

Fleming Cottage to ferret out clothes she would have seen his belongings, might even have walked into him as he came back from work. What a dear girl she was! How could Oscar have left such a lovesome, toothsome, gladsome poppet? Then, wondering what it was that had made her use such antiquated adjectives in relation to Bea, she coaxed the skirt and jacket from the brilliant pink tissue paper and laid them out. The yellow jacket danced across the blue counterpane, a cut-out paper shape snipped by Matisse, and the flat black skirt bent at the knee in a reverence. With Piggy the cat's uncomprehending yellow gaze upon her, she took them up and tried them on again, struggling with the stiff new zip, the virgin buttonholes and twisted and turned before the long mirror, amazed at the sight. But she was not fooled – the apparently elegant old woman she saw was a weak, fumbling thing inside, with a heart as withered as her dried-apricot textured neck. It was sad when the clothes one wore became more interesting than what was inside them. There was a thread hanging from the sleeve of the jacket, and she nipped it off with her teeth. How badly finished modern clothes were, and how expensive. But she was not short of money, she reminded herself. She had spent nothing on herself for years.

It would of course be amusing, but also acutely painful, to meet Simon again after such a time but the central purpose of the visit was to tell him about Bea and see if he could be persuaded to offer her some help, even if only in the form of a second opinion, when she was ready for it. She hoped Bea would be pleased. She *had* asked for help in finding an outlet. Life was hard enough for artists and the offer of professional help, should it be forthcoming, was not to be swatted like some irritating midge. She carefully hung up the new jacket on an old padded silk hanger and laying the skirt across the back of her chair ready for the next day, went downstairs to pour herself a large Bloody Mary and went out into the front garden to inspect a rose.

*　　　*　　　*

Arriving earlier than expected on the Friday afternoon Patrick Kerepol had let himself into the house in the High Street with his old key and found it empty. His father was still busy with the ironmongery and his mother apparently out shopping for delicacies for the homecoming feast. He carried his bag up to his old room; the familiar smell of it grew elusively fainter with each leave and while retaining the trestle table, a green-painted bookcase full of his old books and a model pterodactyl still dangling dustily from a drawing pin in the ceiling, it had been reborn as his mother's office. Patrick shifted some papers on the table, searching for the name, *Agnes*, written several times in varying degrees of depth of desperation. He suffered a twinge of nostalgia on finding it, remembering the unlovely lust and fearsome longings of first love being swiftly followed by the pleasurably excruciating teenage pain of being jilted.

Assuring his father that he needed to stretch his legs after having been so cramped up on the train, he went out for a stroll in the late afternoon sunshine. Bellhurst High Street seemed to shrink in length and width each time he returned, the houses appeared to have become neater and smaller, the roses in the front gardens brighter and tighter. He was eager to visit his sister but understood from Tom that Jane wished for his undivided attention that evening and that they would probably not visit Bea in her hidey-hole until Saturday morning. He drank half a pint at the Mummers and then strolled up the narrow lane that led eventually to Bea's Cottage, partly to fill in time till Jane's return at six o'clock and partly because his legs just naturally led him there. How excessively tame it all was; how succulently green the neat front lawns, how glossy the front doors and windows.

Geraldine saw the tall young man ambling up the lane with his hands in his pockets and thought she had seen him before visiting Bea at some stage in the past. He smiled at her when he came level with the gate and as soon as he smiled she could see it must be the brother Patrick of whom Bea had spoken so fondly. She waved and spilled her drink.

'Mrs Lewis, isn't it? Hello.' He introduced himself. 'I'm back on leave and came out for a wander, killing time till the parents are back.' Having thought her to be a quiet recluse, he was a little surprised by the friendliness of the reception and the long cherry-printed cotton skirt.

'Well, why don't you come and kill a little more by having a drink with me? I've just spent the afternoon with your sister.'

He glanced across to Fleming Cottage. 'I'd love to. Bea wrote to me and said you were looking after the place. What's the news on that quarter?'

She bade him pick up a chair from the kitchen and bring it with him, leading him out to the back garden to sit in the thick shade of an apple tree beside the fence. She carefully lowered herself down onto the old steamer chair she set out each summer and leant back with a sigh of satisfaction.

'How good to be off my feet! I find shopping exhausting . . .' but before she could continue, they were disturbed by the slamming of the Mittys' back door and they heard raised voices. Oscar's they both recognised but the woman's, Geraldine thought, must be the woman he had gone off with, come back to beg him to return for they were indubitably arguing. Patrick recognised both voices and froze, looking agonised at Mrs Lewis and making as if to leave. She put a finger conspiratorially to her lips and hissed, 'Don't stand up, they'll see you!' and he obediently remained seated, feeling thoroughly uncomfortable.

'You're a shit, did you know that?' the woman said.

'For God's sake! The weekend was just a bit of fun. You said so yourself. I didn't know you were serious. It was entirely your idea.'

'Of course I was serious. I thought *you* were serious. You seemed pretty keen on it, too. We had a wonderful time, you know we did. We've always got on so well, anyway.'

'Yes, but that was it. It has to finish. You *know* it would be impossible to carry on like this, with Phil working for me. You never gave Bea my letter. I know you didn't. There were things in that letter that would have *made* her answer it.'

'I forgot to give it to her.'

'Bollocks! I bet you haven't even told her I've come back, either. Have you? *Have you?*' He was almost shouting. 'You're a deceitful little cat.'

'Talk about people in black houses calling glass pots! No, why the bloody hell should I have told her? She's much better off without you, I can see that now. You're a bastard and you're a louse in bed. No wonder Bea doesn't want you back!'

Geraldine was entirely riveted and Patrick entirely embarrassed. Geraldine thought the name of the woman he'd gone off with had been Andrea but couldn't remember and anyway it wasn't credible that she would be go-betweening for Oscar. She didn't care for the idea of eavesdropping but was determined to find out as much as possible on Bea's behalf. She smiled unashamedly and encouragingly at Patrick who became a trifle pink in the face as there came through the fence a screech of rage and the sound of someone getting their face slapped followed by a bit of grunting and squeaking as if there was a scuffle going on. Geraldine beckoned to him, took her chance and bending double, beetled back inside her house surprisingly speedily, drink slopping from her glass. He abandoned his vodka and reluctantly also hunched down and followed the bony print-clad behind across the grass. He had been listening to his brother-in-law fighting with Agnes and conflicting emotions washed about as he stood in Geraldine's kitchen while she dashed upstairs to see what was happening from the bedroom window.

Keeping her knees agonisingly bent, Geraldine poked her head above the sill. The woman was sitting on the grass crying angrily and Oscar was pacing up and down muttering and rubbing the back of his neck but she could no longer hear and didn't dare open the window. The girl got up and ran to the back door. She had seen that little person before, hundreds of times. It was Bea's friend Agnes, the one with the delinquent child, the one who wore her skirts so short you could see her knickers when she bent down to pick him up and her legs weren't quite up to the challenge either — a bit too short and plump around the thigh.

Geraldine had lost most of the Bloody Mary on the lawn and went downstairs again to pour another larger one and to inform the already enlightened and unhappy Patrick.

'Well, Patrick, that makes one or two things clearer, to me at least. Do you think Bea ought to be told? It might constitute interference, but this is not gossip. We both know what we heard quite clearly and there's no other interpretation one can put on it.' Geraldine thought it should at least make incredible any thoughts of Bea's reunification with the awful Oscar, if Bea had any lingering thoughts in that direction. Bea had mentioned Agnes occasionally, recently with a slightly guilty irritation. The girl was a two-timing egg-waster ... egg timer and two-waster ... the vodka was getting to her ... a two-timing time-waster. Bea deserved to be warned, but on the other hand, would the information upset her so much it put her off her stroke? It was not amusing to be the bearer of bad news, either.

'I didn't even know that Oscar had left the first woman, let alone started up something with Agnes,' said Patrick. 'What does Bea know about that?'

'Nothing, I imagine. I'm guilty of not letting her know that Oscar had returned to roost, but it was just as well, I see now. Are you going to tell her? She's in the middle of painting a most wonderful series of pictures and it would be sad if she were to be upset any further, just at the minute. However, I'm fairly sure she doesn't want to get back with him, so the effect of the news may be minimal. Except that it won't be too pleasing to find out that her friend has been mucking about with him. You must decide.'

Patrick's departure from Geraldine's house was delayed by the continuation of the altercation at Fleming Cottage. As he paused with Geraldine beneath the yellow roses at her front door, Oscar and Agnes burst out of theirs. Oscar seized Agnes, who appeared red in the face and hysterical, and shook her like a rat. Both appeared unaware of their rapt audience. Agnes expertly and sharply brought up a knee and caught Oscar in the goolies. Patrick winced, involuntarily sympathetic, imagining the excruciating pain of the impact. She raced down the path, leapt into an old red Citroën and roared off.

'Now really! Just what I would have expected of her,' said Geraldine, pretending to be shocked but chuckling with delight. 'Absolutely no manners whatsoever.'

'It's a bit exciting for Bellhurst, isn't it?' Patrick was bemused but the old lady seemed to have found it all rather invigorating. It was no time to wave to Oscar who, still oblivious of their presence, was on his knees holding on to the door jamb, clutching himself and swearing.

Patrick walked home puzzling over the various possible permutations of the scene. His adolescent love for Agnes had cooled to indulgent indifference many, many years ago and he'd gathered from Bea that Agnes was quite settled down with Phil Spring. He decided it could wait till he saw Bea the next day.

Bea had driven back to Little Rumm relieved by the success of the clothes-buying enterprise. She was determined to take a break, enjoy the party that night, forget advice, everything and everyone. She stood in front of the poppy water-colour gazing at the fanned out pre-Raphaelite red hair and without knowing she did so, ran hands through her own, mimicking the effect. In her mind's eye she again had her fingers in Nut's hair and shaking her head from side to side, she turned the painting face to the wall, ready for a few carefree hours on the outside.

It had proved impossible to work in a people-free vacuum as she'd expected when first arriving here. She'd been in such a tearing hurry, fearing that the money might run out before there was enough work got together. But what was enough? And got together for what purpose? She had not considered what might follow. Real difficulties would now begin and there was still the cottage to decide about and what would happen if Oscar did, or did not, return – but Oscar was no longer wanted, was he? She could no longer imagine that they could repair the damage. But should she try, if the occasion presented itself? Everyone should have a second chance. How would she earn a proper living once the money had run out? The bookshop wages were minimum, even if she were able to get the job back. She was untrained, useless, unemployable. She'd been a fool and would probably end up living at home again while taking evening classes in book-keeping or computer studies. Oh, Freda!

She put on an old Housemartins tape and danced about the room singing 'Happy-Hour Again' to drown out the panic-inducing practicality of her thoughts, to disassociate her mind from the swirling fog of worries and emotions. 'Too late, too late, too late,' she chanted, waving her arms about above her head. 'It's too late to stop now. Far, far, far too late! Party, party, party.' The course was set and she must find a new world and the price of an electricity bill.

Terence Moorbury was not quite able to believe his eyes when he jumped out of the bus that evening. It had halted, in order to have room to turn about, just short of Little Rumm Farm. The sun was setting overdramatically in a sumptuous whirl of orange rays and uplit clouds, turning the square white villa rose-pink, and casting himself a giant's long shadow across the turf where rose-gilded sheep, too many sheep and more sheep, quietly munched. It was not the outlandish flatness and impossibly romantic colouring of the scenery which stopped him in his tracks, he'd had quite enough of that during the last week, but the sight of the narrow column of the static woman in dark blue, standing outlined against the low horizon, apparently deep in conversation with a large black bird on her wrist. It was a painting by Odilon Redon.

'I'm not having that hen on board!' called out the driver. The place had been hard enough to find in spite of the instructions, the lane wasn't suitable for a tank, let alone his new minibus and he wasn't having a mucky bird travelling in it.

'I'm sure she's not going to bring it with her,' Terence called back and walked up to Bea who dragged her attention away from the bird and looked at him with rather vaguely as if not quite sure who he was.

'I don't know how to get him off my arm. He's very heavy. He's shat on my skirt, wiped his beak on my sleeve and if I stop scratching his neck, he tries to peck.' She spoke quietly and quickly, as if scared of hurting the bird's feelings.

'Well, what do you usually do, in order to get on with your life?'

'I don't usually *do* anything. It's never happened before. I mean, I've met him before, but he isn't my pet. I've not been instructed in getting rid of birds once they've outstayed their welcome. I'll try shaking my arm.'

Bea waved her arm about hopefully, but the crow hung on, rocking and balancing as if it was a game. Inside the bus the other members of the film crew hooted with merriment. Terence tried sharply clapping his hands but Budgie, who had arrived unexpectedly while Bea waited in the garden for her lift, struck out viciously, feinting at him with a fearsome meat-ripping beak and flapped and Bea let out a shriek as one of the great wings hit her on the nose.

'Suppose I come up from behind, and try to grab him? You could start scratching his neck again, to see if you can put him in a good mood,' Terence suggested, feeling rather ambivalent about this. He had never, that he could remember, touched a live bird. This one, he supposed it was a raven or something and obviously not a hen, seemed most unfrightened and was rather threatening. He advanced behind it and bravely grabbed, forcibly lifting the bird off, his hands cringing from the dry feel of dusty feathers, and jerkily launched him high into the air. A whoosh and flurry, a furious 'cra-ark, cra-ark' and the delinquent bird was airborne and circling with intent.

'Oh! thank you. What a relief – he was getting so heavy. Come in to the house.' He followed as she ran for cover and Budgie made a bombing run at him. Indoors, Bea scrubbed the mess from her skirt, examined her arms for scratches and then peered outside.

'I'm so sorry about this. I shouldn't have tried to get him to sit on my arm in the first place.' She looked at him again as if she couldn't quite remember why he was there. He wondered briefly if she was high on something. 'Of course, the bus is waiting. I'll try to distract him with a piece of bacon while we run for it. It seems all clear outside.' Their reappearance brought yells of encouragement and cries of 'Look behind you, look behind you!' from those on the bus, but Bea extravagantly tossed the rasher of best unsmoked back bacon to one side of the garden and they scrambled aboard the bus without any further attention from Budgie, who glided down from the roof of the house to inspect his danegeld.

Bea was flustered and pink. It wasn't quite the sort of impression she'd hoped to make.

'Well, tell us all about it. Is he a local crow, or has he just dropped in from the Underworld? Does he sit at the head of your bed and cry 'Nevermore!' at awkward moments to your lovers? *Hello*, is there anyone there or have you gone out to lunch?'

She jerked back to Terence who had passed his hands back and forth in front of her face.

'That was a raven that cried "Nevermore!" Budgie was hand-reared by a friend of mine and arrived while I was waiting for you. I stupidly thought it would be nice to see if I could get him to sit on my wrist, like a falcon – he was a bit reluctant at first. They've got such sharp toenails and very rough, hard feet. I scratched the back of his head which seemed to make him quite ecstatic, then he wouldn't leave. I'm sorry if I seem a bit distrait.'

'You looked like a sorceress with a familiar. Quite unearthly.'

'I suppose I must have done.' Terence was looking at her attentively. Finding him neither unpleasing nor wildly attractive, she felt easier in his company and relaxed, laughing a little. She hoped it didn't sound too false.

'How far did you say Blackshorne Court was, from here?' asked Terence, persevering.

'From here, about six miles, as the crow flies.'

'I hope to God he isn't flapping along behind us. There's something eerie about those birds. Harbingers of doom and confusion? Didn't the Vikings have a thing about crows?'

'Don't say things like that. You don't know how true that has been for me this evening.' Then suddenly she found she could not stop talking. 'Anyway, that was ravens again. Odin carried a pair about with him – Huginn and Munnin – Mind and Memory. It's just that all the crow family are scavengers, feed off dead things, road accidents and suchlike, that makes people think they are unlucky; that's why people salute magpies, to ward off the bad luck. Budgie doesn't seem to have brought dire happenings to the man who found him when he was a fledgling. I've never met anyone less doom-ridden and more cheerful.'

'I'm very ignorant about birds. That's the first one I've met socially. I was brought up in London and can only recognise pigeons, starlings and sparrows ... and swans and ducks, of course. I might even know a goose if I met one. Actually that's quite a good tally. I might even become a bird-watcher one day.'

Bea did not comment but tapped the driver on the shoulder, commanding, 'You need to turn right at the T junction just up here, and then first left after the Swan pub.' The driver, a Parden man, had earlier been reluctant to take directions. The minibus crossed a bridge over a dyke and carried on uphill, eventually coming to a halt at the junction. The driver pointed out exultantly that according to the signpost, St Rumwold-at-Cliffe was to the left, and seemed prepared to argue the point. He didn't like taking directions from women, he remarked aloud, since they never seemed to know left from right, waving wildly to one side while shouting out the other. He raised a cheap laugh among the other passengers.

'Ignore the signpost,' said Bea, firmly. 'It was blown round in a gale in the spring and no one's pushed it back. Ragstone Street is to the right, then first left.'

'You seem very confident. I thought you hadn't been here before?' asked Terence, peering out into the twilight dubiously.

'No,' whispered Bea, fearful of raising further irritation in the driver, 'but I memorised the way. I must admit I do get the words wrong when I'm poring over a map, just as the old misogynist in front complains. But once I've got the plan in my head, I never get lost, not even in all those mazy lanes we've come through. Look, there are the gates just up ahead.'

Ragstone Street, on the degraded cliff facing out over the marsh, was a Roman road. It petered out into a nettlesome farm track in a hamlet, in the centre of which stood Blackshorne Court, a miniature manor alternately augmented and destroyed over the ages so that now all that stood was the most ancient part, a tiny thirteenth-century chapel beside the central section of a Jacobean wing built of narrow red bricks, the old house from which it had sprung having been demolished by a Victorian coal merchant. They drove through the gates, past a lily-filled, semi-circular moat, in which a full and creamy rising moon was reflected. The sight caused the first murmurs of interest among the chattering crew, who craned their necks to see the top of the sole remaining turret behind which the moon sat fatly, as if pierced by the pinnacle and held captive atop like a crumpet on a toasting fork. The effect was decidedly magical and in near silence they disembarked among the other cars in the driveway and ascended the steps through a wide door, into a high-ceilinged, galleried hall, candlelit and already stuffed with guests.

Bea was herded through the throng towards their host by

the small and ever-attentive Terence, who had a firm grasp of her elbow and who began to remind her of a Border collie, a Ben, Pip, Bess, or Bel. The man, grey-haired although perhaps only in his late thirties, heron-tall and flaunting in a cream silk jacket, turned from the couple to whom he had been talking. Heron embraced sheepdog theatrically. 'Terence! How *won-der-ful!*' 'Justin! It's tremendous to see you again ... what a stunning place!' The couple to whom Justin had been speaking were Amelia and Edmund. Amelia let out a screech of surprise, 'Bea! How lovely!' and she was embraced by them both like a long-lost friend. Amelia was dressed in green, a sorceress's silver necklace round her neck, a thick hand-made chain hung like an old-fashioned charm bracelet with cast silver fish, shells and palms of seaweed, which chinked and tinkled when she moved. Justin released Terence from the bear hug.

'Now please introduce me to your *friend*, Terence.' He was staring down at Bea from his great height. 'Are you tired of being told you resemble Botticelli's Primavera, my dear? You are Simonetta Vespucci, to the life, and so appropriately dressed, in indigo blue.' Bea had not heard of Simonetta Vespucci; it sounded suspiciously like an Italian make of motorbike, but since it was obviously meant as a compliment, she was pleased by it. In the down-to-earth circles in which she had grown up, complimenting a pretty woman was considered to be not unlike taking beefburgers to McDonald's, it being assumed she must already know she was beautiful and therefore didn't need to have her head turned any further. She was about to thank the tall man and introduce herself but Terence spoke for her.

'This is Bea Kerepol, a painter. We've only recently met.'

Justin advanced upon her and bent to give her a light, almost butterfly-like brush on the cheek. 'Well, I'm very pleased you have come to the house-warming party. Now you must listen to *quite* an extraordinary story.' Justin's voice was resonant, and swooped up and down with unusual emphases upon unlikely words. It was perhaps a nervous tic of his, which distracted from the substance, scattering false clues about and making one wait for the unexpected pause or stress rather than hear what was said.

'I went to Edmund's beautiful *book shop* last autumn, when this *project* was still on the drawing-board, to enlist his help in collecting up Connaught Marvel's *out-of-print* oeuvres. We worked together for quite a while before, *lo* and behold! The most amazing coincidence – his partner, dear Amelia here, *is* Connaught Marvel's grand-daughter! She has been so helpful in telling me about his later life, and come up with some quite brilliant photographs of *him* and his mistress at their *farm* in Suffolk. I knew there was *a grand-daughter* of course, but had given up hope of tracing her,' he turned gracefully to Amelia, 'but it's your *story* my dear, why don't you tell this lovely Bea and pretty Terence all about it while I *discover* where all the *waiters* with the booze have hidden themselves. It's very trying having to do this all one one's own, when there *are* so many people I want to talk to.' He smiled benevolently at them and turned away, his eyes searching over the heads of the crowd for the errant waiters.

It transpired that Amelia's aunt, the wife of Connaught's son, had recently died gaga and intestate and the remaining copyright of his books had passed to Amelia. Only no one had told her of her aunt's death, the solicitors having been unable to trace her. Justin, whose researchers had only just managed to contact the aunt a few weeks before her death and found her sadly incomprehensible, was unable to get out of her the whereabouts of the niece, of whose existence Justin had been beginning to doubt. Then he had approached Edmund.

'And wonderful for Amelia that he did,' said Edmund, 'and as some of the A. C. Holliday novels are to be republished in paperback to coincide with the TV series and biography for the centenary of his birth, it's going to be financially rather pleasing. His travel books have often been reprinted before but Aunt Margaret seems to have had a stingy side and has been sitting on the royalties for years. Amelia and her daughter Josie are the old man's only living descendants.'

'Isn't *that* exciting?' said Justin reappearing with a wobbling trayfull of champagne, 'I was so happy to be the medium by which Amelia regained her rights. It is of course a fairy *story* and I felt quite smug to be the fairy godfather. So, on with the ball! The *music* in the marquee in the back courtyard should be starting up soon. I do hope you'll like the band, The Preachers. They specialise in Paul Butterfield-type Chicago blues, they tell me. Then by popular demand there's an Irish band for set-dancing or something; whatever it is I can't do it. I can only do Strip-the-Willow.'

He looked hopefully at Bea. 'I hope you enjoy dancing – I shall come and claim a shuffle and sway later on, but now I must go and prostitute myself by being charming to some rich businessmen and their wives whom I hope are going to be useful in relation to another project.' He gave an unlikely wink, the lid closing slowly like a blind over the penetrating bright blue eye then snapping up again and he stalked off. Affected and camp, but more intelligent than he let on, Bea decided.

'The last time we met Bea,' said Edmund, turning to Terence, 'was at an extraordinary midnight demonstration by a collective, no a coven, several covens of covens of witches down at the power station. We were all drawn there as if we'd been summoned. Quite odd really, but not without its farcical side. I expect Bea may have told you about it?'

'No, but that's also where we met. We were there for a couple of days shooting the final scenes of *Patrick and Marguerite*. We finished this morning, thankfully. The whole production has been dogged with troubles and we've all come up here to Justin's to let our hair down and relax. You say you met witches down there? Well, we became entangled with some rather raucous "nuns" in pink habits. That place seems to attract the bizarre. Have you read *Patrick and Marguerite* by any chance?'

'I have,' said Amelia, 'when I was about fourteen. I thought it was wildly romantic and quite frightening and totally missed the fact that it was a spoof.'

Terence looked puzzled, then awkward. 'What do you mean, a spoof?'

Bea was in need of the bathroom and excusing herself for a moment, left Terence to Amelia and headed for the wide staircase. Upstairs various dark doors opened off a wide corridor and she had to resort to testing them all to find the lavatory. The first opened on to a large bedroom where the lights were blazing, the walls hung with plain cream silk and was otherwise most unsybaritically bare, although what furnishings there were appeared to be in keeping with the period of the room. Her curious eye was trapped by a framed black-and-white photograph standing on a large oak table by the door; it was of a pussy-cat-faced woman with dark hair, looking as if she were about to open her mouth to complain and holding stiffly at a marked distance on her knee a very fat infant in long lacy christening robes. It was professionally done in the manner of royal photographs, the subjects posed on a vast sofa. Bea looked hard, twice to make certain, and then quickly shut the door again, heart pounding. The woman was unmistakably Andrea Bullingden.

'Are you searching for a bathroom, my dear?' said Justin, looming up behind her. 'It's the next one, on the left. I should have labelled them, I know, for the party. Are you all right? You look a little pale.'

'No, no, I'm fine. Thank you. I should have asked directions.'

When she reappeared, having recovered her calm, he was leaning on the banisters at the end of the passage by the staircase, apparently waiting for her, which she found rather embarrassing, but with an Edwardian courtesy he offered her his arm. She took it and they began the descent into the packed hall below.

'I can't resist walking downstairs with you like this in such a compromising fashion, although neither of us have been upstairs for long enough to have had a fuck.'

Bea became distinctly unamused and disengaged her arm.

'Oh God! I'm sorry, I didn't mean to upset you. I am a bit

pissed already, I fear. I do a lot of upsetting these days. Crude, bitter, horny old me.'

Bea stopped. He stopped too and looked down at her. The bright blue eyes were avuncular, apologetic.

'That photograph, on the table. Is that your wife?'

'*Was* my wife. I keep it so I can pull faces at her every morning. We were at last *divorced* this month – the party is not only a house-warming but an *un-marriage* party. We share my son fifty-fifty. A judgement of Solomon without the intelligent psychological insights.'

'My married name is Mitty. Is yours, your surname, Bullingden?'

'It is.'

'My husband Oscar left me, for your ex-wife.'

He did not speak for a moment, then put out a narrow, elegant hand and patted her cheek. 'How very nasty for *you* to have come upon her *face* to face like that! An unpleasant coincidence for you, but she is very attractive, on the surface, and it was quite likely that she would steal away *someone's* husband in the end. Whether she will be able to keep him long, I very much doubt. I also keep the photograph because it's the only one of my son as a baby, and it reminds me never, ever, to get married again. Yes, the name *tolls* a passing-bell in my head. Oscar Mitty, your husband. I remember seeing it on a solicitor's letter. How very strange.' He sighed. 'He does know, by now, that the hell-cat is an unredeemable alcoholic? I've spent a fortune, several fortunes, on getting her dried out. No, never mind all this. It's taking us an awful long time to come down these *stairs*. The band's getting going and Terence will be becoming fretful.'

'I only came tonight with Terence by coincidence,' she said, warming to Justin again as they came down the last flight of stairs into the great hall, 'and you won't mention this to the others, will you?' He shook his head understandingly. They rejoined Amelia and Edmund and the coincidental Terence. Amelia was laughing her head off and Terence was looking piqued.

'Well, it's hardly serious, is it?' Amelia was saying. 'At the end, when she's arriving by boat from France, to be reunited with her lover and they rush towards each other, knee deep in passion and shingle, and she is seasick in his lap on the beach.'

'That wasn't in the treatment, or the script! And when Marie-Christine Boulette, who's playing Marguerite, *was* actually physically seasick, we re-shot it, twice. We treated it as a straight ghost story; no one realised it was meant to be funny.' Terence sounded a little sulky, but began to see the silly side of it and rallied. 'Now I come to think of it, that bit where the ghost of her husband makes love to her in the French *auberge*, and she complains, in marvellously elliptical language, of having a cold fanny . . . what an opportunity wasted!'

'Poor Grandpapa! He'd have thought it hilarious, someone coming along and taking one of his jokey pot-boilers seriously. But it would have to be done straight in any case, in order to be funny – but it's a shame they've cut out the amusing bits.'

'I thought you said you'd read the book,' said Bea to Terence accusingly, delighted to have caught him out.

'Well, I didn't have time. Anyway, it's still a good story. Let's all go and listen to the band.' Justin had wandered off again to mingle. She could see him, head and shoulders above everyone else, moving through the crowd as if searching for someone.

The marquee was midnight blue and eccentrically fitted with circular panels of something transparent let into the roof round the central poles so that as one approached, beams of pale light from inside searched up into the sky. There was a sumptuous looking buffet laid out on miles of crisp white linen, the band was playing 'Blues with a Feelin'' and a great many very chic people were beginning to filter in and sit at the tables round the dance floor. The area was planted with flowerbeds of huge indigo-blue paper flowers. Bea became reckless, feckless and ready for any contingency, knocked back a third glass of champagne and took off for the dance floor, with Terence in sweaty pursuit.

Chapter Ten

Now small and riding coldly high, the moon cast a broad light across the waiting garden, light enough to guess the shade of pink of the newly opened apple-scented rose.

'Light enough to do some gardening,' she said aloud, fumbling the key into the lock.

'Moonlight gardening is out of the question,' said Terence firmly, behind her. 'What's that strange burnt smell?'

'Just a burnt-out car, up the track,' she said casually, then as if discussing a gas log fire, 'I love a good blaze, don't you?'

The minibus driver had first dropped the others in Fingle, apart from the obligatory missing member who had decided to take his chances with a pouting blond waiter and had disappeared just as they were leaving. The driver, complaining all the way, had then brought Bea home, accompanied by Terence, who had unexpectedly jumped out of the bus with her — just to say goodnight, she thought fuzzily, how sweet — but the bus had turned and driven away without him. Bea, happily full of poached salmon and bubbly, was unfazed and guessed that he just might have arranged this with the driver. Better to muck it up with a comparative stranger than with Nut, she thought, hazily irrational, better to have another breathing life in the house than be alone. She pushed open the door and let him follow her inside. Wild strangers had last night invaded her territory and she didn't want to sleep by herself.

She clattered the keys on the kitchen table and let out a cracking yawn, stretching long arms and witchy fingers up towards the ceiling and knocked the dangling lampshade, dislodging a dead moth. Terence's oak-apple brown, sheepdog eyes looked curiously inflamed at the sight of the red throat and white teeth, and he seized his chance and Bea about the waist. They tottered upstairs, Bea missing one step in three, and paused on the moonlit landing where she put her arms around his neck, sagging slightly at the knees. It was past two o'clock in the morning.

'Where to?' he asked, 'in here?' He put his hand out to the handle of the painting-room door, and she became alert, for a second.

'No, no! Not in there. This way.' He must not, they must not, sleep in the red bed. That was Nut's. She backed, still holding on to him and laughing, into the front bedroom, and they fell onto the bed.

'You do know what you're doing, don't you?' he asked, desperately trying to pull off his jacket with Bea still holding onto his neck.

''Course I do. Did you think I might scream "date rape" afterwards? I wish I could remember where I sowed the parsley,' she remarked incomprehensibly, laughed again and couldn't stop, and he was enveloped in the warmth of it and the salty taste of her skin and was immensely grateful for the lack of complication in the woman. Why couldn't it always be this simple?

She had not been able to stop herself from planning the next painting as he made love to her, or rather she'd made love to him. Only you couldn't really call it that. He had some funny ideas, which entailed her doing all the work. He was now tucked against her back, hotly asleep and snoring slightly, one hand still firmly anchored to the old iron bedrail with a long green silk scarf. Having slept for an hour or so she was wide awake again. It was difficult to sleep round the time of the full moon and even with the curtains so tightly drawn that not the finest needle of light penetrated, she felt its omnipresence, disconcertingly watchful, askance. 'So?' it seemed to query, 'SO?' and the O of the SO was itself. She had the strongest sensation of having made a very serious mistake.

A quarter to five in the morning. Moon-cooled air came in through the open window and she turned to look at the dark face deep in the crevasse between the pillows, sleep leaching sonorously out into the bedclothes. She crept from the bed, picked up jeans and shirt from the silvered chair beneath the window and tiptoed stealthily downstairs in the dawn. She would have to think of it as a practice run, inconsequential and yet again unsatisfying, even if in retrospect it had also been extremely funny. 'They say it's better to break a fast with a biscuit than a full meal,' she thought; her surmise about the giant fountain pen had been correct.

A blackbird fluted on the garden wall as she made a Marmite sandwich and a cup of coffee to chase away the cobweb wisps, taking great care not to rattle the kettle against the tap and to smother the clinks of knife against plate. There was no point in going back to bed now it was nearly light and further sleep would be impossible with the ridiculous Terence in her bed. Optimism seeped back into her with the first glimmers of sun to the east and she slowly drew the bolt, wincing at the scraping sound, slipping out into the garden with cup and sandwich. The flags were chill gravestones beneath her bare feet and she stood among the stock-still, tightly furled poppies by the wall, their dagged grey leaves thick with dew-bloom and filigree-trailed by little cream and brown humbug snails. One bud approached opening, flashing densely packed petals between the two halves of the splitting sepals. She stole a snail and held it on the warm palm of her hand, watching its painfully sensitive and tentative horns expanding, searching left and right, contracting from the harsh touch of a fingertip.

A magpie walked portentously across the field in white waistcoat and green-black tails, a self-conscious head waiter approaching to take an order in an empty restaurant. The air was milky soft, there was silence and mercifully no sign of Budgie. It would be beautiful down on the beach, but the noise of starting up the truck might waken Terence and it would be unkind, so early, and unforgivable to leave him to wake up alone with no means of transport. She would have to drive him back to Fingle after breakfast. It was Saturday, he was returning to London and that would be that. She left the morning to mind its own business and with rewarmed coffee and a humbug snail on a plate, to draw, slipped noiselessly upstairs to the painting room.

On that same Saturday morning, dressed in the new clothes, Geraldine nodded with satisfaction at the old-new self in the looking glass and then double-checked she had locked the back door, and that Piggy was shut outside and not in. Unused to being left alone for as much as a half day, he had taken to piddling in protest on the kitchen floor whenever she went out. Standing by the window, watching for the cab which would take her to Parden station and the train for London, she was soused in the unreality of the enterprise and checked again in her large black leather bag for the address of the gallery, although she had it by heart. In the bag were secreted two of Bea's sketch books, borrowed from the cottage before Oscar had returned, and Sylvia Plath's *Crossing the Water* to read on the journey. She thought it a flimsy lath-and-plaster name for such a turbulent poet, but guessed not much else might take her mind from the worry of seeing Simon Greensand again. It was a paperback bought just before she had started on the pills and had never read before her brain had turned to syllabub, unable then to concentrate for long enough to recall the beginning of a sentence before reaching its full stop.

She was catching an earlier train than was necessary in order to have time to look at shops and other galleries and not arrive in a hurry. She disliked to be fussed by arriving late. 'In Russian plays,' she reminded herself firmly, 'people all sit down for a moment before leaving on a journey, in order to gather their thoughts, remember if they've turned off the gas and to pray for a safe passage to wherever it is they're going. If I do the same, I will feel calmer and probably, as soon as I sit down, the cab will arrive – so it would be a good thing to do in any case.'

She sat in the middle of the faded sofa, bolt-upright so as not to crease the back of her jacket, bag on lap and neat feet together and immediately remembered she had not shut the bedroom window. By the time she was downstairs again, the driver was ringing the door bell.

The train itself was late in arriving at Charing Cross and was met by an outgoing rush of passengers on platform six, a group of poorly shepherded teenaged travellers were trying to enter the train before the incomers had left it; a kind young man, very tall and with red hair, gently held back with a long arm a shoving, baggy-trousered youth and smilingly offered her his hand as she descended. She was out of the station and into the Strand before remembering of whom he'd reminded her.

Simon was waiting in the sun at the door of the gallery as she approached, her heart fluttering. The once-loved, remembered shock of uncontrollable fair hair was now white, but still uncontrolled, and the inquisitive beaky nose was redder. Immaculate pale grey tailoring upholstered and retained a body that had thickened slightly but was not much changed. That, Geraldine noticed in spite of her interior agitation, was an extremely expensive suit. Simon had obviously done very well indeed.

Neither of them had clung to any illusions. Having recognised her immediately and apparently as undismayed by her ageing as she was by his, he beamed with pleasure as she walked slowly up to him. He took her hand and kissed her on both cheeks then drew her quite tenderly inside to meet the son James, one of the spoilt, beloved boys for whose sake he had sacrificed both their happinesses.

James was a gold-bespectacled version of his father, full-facedly prosperous and a little self-satisfied. He was dressed in a long black jacket and trousers and a collarless white shirt and Geraldine noticed premature little red spider veins crawling across his cheeks.

They lunched in a restaurant where one had to ring the doorbell to gain admittance, in the plain surroundings of a private eighteenth-century drawing room where the floorboards were bare and the service was neither obsequious nor patronising. It was pleasantly buzzing and the food was, to poor Geraldine, so much of a revelation that she definitely resented having to talk throughout the meal. She had only recently discovered pot-noodles and had been living on those for the last few days, being totally incapable of the mechanics of cookery.

Simon was explaining that he was now semi-retired, but that his opinion was still kindly sought and he still had command, courtesy of James, of one slot in the calendar of exhibitions. Geraldine pursued a piece of salmon dusted with parmesan and chopped rocket about her plate with the determination of someone who knew it was their last meal for a week. In November, Simon continued, he could put on a show of whomever he pleased. James looked proudly indulgent and poured more wine; his wife, May, half-English, half-Chinese, who had been waiting for them at the restaurant, was smiling with charmingly scrutable relief at the success of the reunion.

'Straight after your phone call I thought how a retrospective of your work would fit the bill. I did have a new young man booked, a bit of a wild card perhaps. Unfortunately he's taken a tumble off a motorbike and broken his wrist quite badly. He can't now complete the amount of work needed to make the show worthwhile. The poor fellow is so desperately disappointed. I've told him I'll keep the November slot open for him next year and perhaps we'll put one or two of his paintings in this year's group Christmas show, if James will allow it. Meanwhile, James agrees with me that your work would make a most intriguing show, stop-gap or not. What do you think?'

Geraldine, whose polished plate had now been replaced by a dish of succulent little rounds of venison with green beans, so fine they could pass through the eye of a needle, hauled her attention back to her host, put down her knife and fork and stared at Simon, eyes luminous with real food, wine and excitement. Was this a straightforward, genuine offer, or was it prompted by guilt? She did not care. Either would do.

'Simon! Where would we find all the work? I told you I virtually gave up after ... after Richard died. I've only just re-started and there are only about six presentable old works in the house.'

'And I also have four of my own, if you remember? I am still in contact with at least five other old patrons of yours. In fact I sat beneath one of your paintings at a dinner two weeks ago. There's also McNamara and Rob Gurgelfeldt in New York. As soon as you put the phone down yesterday, I started to think about this, and I've already been in touch with them and they think they can trace four or five more. Rob's coming over in September and could bring them with him. People like to lend their pictures – see their names up beside the artist's at the show. There are probably others I can contact if I go through our records. We have back sales invoices dating from the nineteen fifties,' he leant back and looked fondly at her, 'and your last solo show with us was in November, nineteen sixty-eight. I didn't have to look that up; I remembered it very well.'

'Your gallery is huge, two vast rooms, and most of my work is on the small side.' Geraldine thought it the perfect moment to broach the subject of Bea. She blotted her mouth with a thick linen napkin and sat up importantly.

'I have an idea to put to you which will entail you coming to me at Bellhurst and visiting a certain young woman, Bea Kerepol. She is my own discovery and I'm very proud of her. She was the reason I came off those wretched carnivorous, life-digesting tranquillisers – they should come with a government health warning.' She had a swig of Perrier and making an effort not to be side-tracked by her own regrets, recovered the thread, conscious that she was dangerously putting a label on Bea, that such a label might possibly deter as much as attract.

'Bea is a one-off. She has spent her life until now – she is thirty, I think – drawing and painting. Teaching herself to draw, teaching herself to paint. Her imagination is frightening and she doesn't know it but is astonishingly strong-minded. Her work is figurative, modern, funny and yet there is a neo-romantic undercurrent. Insofar as they belong in any particular type, I would suggest an unlikely parentage, by Stanley Spencer out of Leonora Carrington. You *have* to see them. Once you have, if your views concur with mine, then perhaps she could be approached to fill up the other room? You could then have my retrospective and her launching together? I don't know why I'm addressing myself only to you, Simon. James, she'll interest you too. Now, I've been rather underhand and stolen something from her to whet your appetites.' She bent down and from the black bag elatedly produced the two sketch-books. 'This one is what she was doing as a child. Look, it's dated. She would have been ten or eleven? It's quite extraordinary. And this one is last year's.' She passed the child's one to James and the other to Simon and managed at last to get a piece of the melting venison into her mouth. Oh, bliss!

'Go on and have a look. But when you come to see her, if you come, you must not under any circumstances mention these – she would be furious with me. Oh my goodness, this venison is just too delicious! I know I said she's quite tough but there's a tender plant behind the front of hawthorn hedging, apparently most tiresomely lacking in confidence in her own abilities. I thought it might be a form of attention-seeking at first, but now I believe it to be genuine reticence.'

Geraldine was enjoying herself, hearing her own confident sales pitch. All three of them had ceased to eat and were listening attentively. How much easier it is, she thought, to make men *really* listen when one is older and they are no longer distracted by one's face or body. James was leafing through, turning the book this way and that, showing his wife, intent and amused. Simon's jaw had dropped slightly. He was looking at a water-colour of Agnes sitting half-naked in the dappled shade of an apple tree drinking a gin and tonic, while overhead a massively suggestive boa constrictor coiled itself about the branches, watching. It was drawn from the viewpoint of just above the boa and was both ridiculous and suggestively tense.

'Normally we'd like to be sent slides first, and CVs,' said Simon, 'but under the circumstances, I think I'll come.'

'Me too,' said his son, adding carefully, 'but I'll leave the decision to you, Dad.' He knocked back his wine, refilled his glass and turned politely to Geraldine, knowing that his father's apparent altruism was usually based on sound judgement. 'I grew up with your paintings on our walls, Geraldine, and continue to love and admire them. I'll trust your judgement.' He thought Bea's juvenilia very interesting and although not quite his scene, the more recent sketch-book showed promise of considerable commercial potential; he thought it would be tasteless to mention the latter in front of another artist. May, delicately scenting the promise of getting first to an interesting discovery said she would like to make a visit to this Bea Kerepol.

'May,' said James, gobbling down his halibut, 'is a freelance arts journalist,' he raised his arm to attract the attention of a waiter and ordered another bottle of wine, 'which as you can imagine, can be discreetly useful to the gallery at times.'

Geraldine became hypnotised by the food as the meal progressed through walnut-and-ginger steamed puddings and cheeses and became quite silent till they returned to the gallery for coffee. She went with Simon to look through the racks of paintings of the gallery's stable of artists in the basement storeroom. One or two she did not comprehend at all, another made her cackle with laughter: 'Good God! Is that old fraud still at it?' More often she was most interested in what she saw, and thoughtful. It was always best to start at the top end of the market when selling something. Yes, she could see Bea Kerepol fitting in with these, outshining quite a few of them with honesty and ease. But then, she knew she was so very biased.

'So,' said the old man behind her, putting his hand on her arm as she eased a painting back into its upright stack, 'you've forgiven me?'

'There's nothing to forgive. You were right, in the long term, although I couldn't accept it then. You suffered from Bea's problem. Too nervous of other people's opinions, perhaps?'

'I didn't want to lose the boys. I couldn't have borne it.'

'No, it would have been an atrocious decision to have to make. I do understand, but I also want you to know, Simon, what happened to me after Richard found out about us. I was virtually imprisoned — trussed up with yards of his stringy insecurity. I didn't survive, or rather the painting did not survive it.'

'My dear Geraldine, I am so terribly sorry. I felt too guilty to contact you after Marjorie buggered off. I felt sure you wouldn't want to know. I was a coward.' There was a stricken look in his eyes but Geraldine, wiser and now feeling no more than a gentle affection, and some power, did not quite relent.

'Yes, you were. And so was I, later on. You owe me, perhaps, just a little more . . . I obviously won't press you about Bea if you are disappointed by her work, but I know I'm right. Anyway, I have too little of my own to sell, most of it will be on loan, and perhaps Bea might do even better than I think and ensure the gallery doesn't have a complete loss of income for a month! Simon, it *is* wonderful to see you again.'

✳   ✳   ✳

The breakfast, the full kippers-scrambled-egg-bacon and sausages of it, had been a bit much after the massive homecoming supper of the night before and Patrick sat back from the table and let his belt out a couple of holes. He had not dared give the food less than his whole attention. Ecstatic to see her beloved boy home again, Jane sat among the eggy breakfast plates and scattered yellow croissant crumbs and between demanding to know further details of the state of his health, love-life, teeth, career, plans and politics, was explaining to him the tribulations of rewriting an eighteenth-century cookery book. Tom had relapsed into silence. To him, the breakfast was imperfect without Bea. Tom wanted his family complete around him and wistfully asked Jane if she'd tried to call Bea to invite her over for breakfast.

'You know I did. Several times. But she'd switched the phone off again.' She turned to Patrick. 'I hope you can talk some sense into her when you see her, if she allows you anywhere near, that is. We worry so about her living in that damp hut of Nest's. She just daubs away all day and probably all night, quite alone.' Jane's voice rose a fraction, irritably. 'She's impatient with us if we visit. One can see her longing for us to leave as soon as we arrive. I think the shock has temporarily unhinged her – poor child. I hate to think of her grieving alone like that, unable to share her troubles.'

'I remember going there for a picnic in the garden with Aunt Nest when I was about thirteen. It wasn't a damp hut – rather a solid little house and very sunny. It must have been so difficult after Oscar left, quite desperate for her. She always hated sympathy because she always tends to think things are her own fault. It's hardly surprising she wants some time on her own.' Defensive of his sister, Patrick tilted back on his chair and reached for the phone on the dresser. Bea found it difficult to accept help and that had always frustrated Jane.

'I'll try her again myself. If it's switched off, we'll just go round unannounced, on the off-chance. You'll drive me over, won't you Dad? If she's not in we'll leave a note asking her to lunch and go for a walk on the beach.'

Bea's phone was still switched off.

'I *told* you so,' said Jane dramatically, pouring Patrick another cup of coffee. 'She could have become a Moonie and not told us. We only wanted to help her sort out the practical, legal side of her separation. We're having nettle soup and poached chicken for lunch.' Patrick chortled; Jane's vivid, strong-flavoured nettle soup delivered a blood-cleansing punch that usually brought Bea out in spots. He looked at his watch.

'It's half past ten already and she's an early riser.' He thanked his mother for the emperor's breakfast and gave her a kiss. 'Are you sure you won't come with us? No? You go on ahead then, Dad, I've just got to run upstairs for something.'

He delved in his suitcase among neatly folded shirts for the two-inch square miniature brown paper parcel, tied with cream thread and red sealing wax seals the diameter of a pencil. Buying the contents had taken three minutes but wrapping it had taken half an hour. With a fine-point pen he addressed it, in minute handwriting, 'To Mrs R. Crusoe, Nest's Hut.'

'Hello? Bea?'

The smell of burnt toast drifted through the open front door and Nut had knocked and entered without pausing, following his nose fast into the kitchen, so eager to see her, calling out as he came.

How rare she looked to Francis Nutmeg as she sat there in a long white cotton dress at the kitchen table, shining amid the matt sheets of grey Formica. There was alarm in her face, an unflattering astonishment as she looked up from the kitchen table, caught spreading butter on toast, her hand with the knife in midair, hair swinging round her face. At the table also sat a bare-footed man in a dishevelled state of unbuttoned unbrushedness, who also looked up at him, his features first registering an iced surprise, followed by the unmistakable creakings of antagonism.

There was silence in the room, encompassing perhaps five seconds – a long five seconds. Nut snapped it, not by speaking but by crashing the book on fossils down upon the table, so hard it rattled the china. A half-open poppy, broken off short and placed in a glass of water, dropped one of its iced-jade sepals with a soft plop and the shutter clicked, the still was taken. Swinging round on his heel – they felt the air moving as he turned – he strode out of the house, a red ruffling breeze that became a hurricane as he drove off down the track in the blue van.

Terence, relieved, picked up another piece of toast.

'Who was that?' He gave an uncertain little chuckle. 'He didn't look too pleased to see me.'

Bea was still staring after Nut, shocked.

'No.' She closed her eyes for a second. 'He wouldn't have been. Though, for all he knew you could have been my brother ...' Her cheeks were flaming. 'Oh God! It's this weekend that he's due on leave – I'd forgotten.' She still held the buttery knife in one hand and the toast in the other and was thinking rapidly what to do. She felt very bad indeed, powerless, roughly shaken in his wake.

'That was a friend of mine, a close friend ... he's been away these last few days.' She wished desperately he hadn't discovered her with Terence. But he had no reason to be quite so angry. Of course he had; she had led him to believe she might ... Terence curtly interrupted her.

'Oh, I see. I'm just an interim passion, am I?' Now he was annoyed.

'Who said anything about passion?' she snapped, swinging round on the unfortunate man and a nobbet of butter flew off the knife and landed in his coffee. He scooped it out with a spoon, eyebrows raised but his mouth stretched tight and turned a little down at the corners in a disappointed smile. He'd awoken that sunny morning in a mood of delighted optimism; now things were no longer as they had appeared, were drifting out of his control.

'You seemed quite certain about it last night.'

'That was last night,' then she added, with a hopefully disarming smile, 'Today we are . . . well, friends. Won't that do?'

'Oh, I see, just like you and the departed Viking. Well, I'm usually better friends with the women I don't sleep with. You're a lunatic, did you know that?' The skin on his face was taut, but then softened a fraction. 'OK. You've made a mistake. I don't think I have.' He stood up in an attempted graciousness, fighting back disappointment and tucking his shirt into his trousers. He looked small and disproportionately furious. He looked, she thought, as she fought back tears, exactly like Seb.

'I'll get the rest of my clothes and leave you in peace – but I'm not walking all the way back to Fingle. You'll have to drive me.'

'Of course I'll drive you. Please, please don't get cross, there's no need.' She was aware now that he was hurt. She had assumed that a one-night stand was what he'd been expecting and had not allowed for him wanting more than that. There was the sound of a vehicle drawing up outside and Terence became vigilant for a moment, half-expecting the return of Nut, armed this time not with a book on fossils but with a double-headed axe. Doors slammed and another male voice called out.

'Bea? Where are you?'

In burst a tall, sunburnt young man who swept past Terence and gathered up Bea in a hug so tight that she squeaked in protest. Another lover or the brother she'd mentioned? He was followed by yet another man, older, grey-haired with a black eye-patch. Brother, Terence decided, thankfully noting the physical resemblances, and Daddy. They were all too damned tall and the one-eyed old man was peering at him in a most unfriendly manner. Terence was marginalised, a member of an ethnic minority.

Bea sat down again, shakily putting aside her panic about Nut till she had dealt with poor Terence and her family. A blush was spreading. She tried to shift her mind from Nut's obvious distress at finding her breakfasting with someone else, deferred thinking of explanations and managed to introduce Terence to her relations, in what she hoped was neither an offhand nor too overtly affectionate way, telling them that she would be taking Terence back to Fingle fairly soon and that if they helped themselves to coffee, she would return in a moment.

'All right, Bea. Don't worry. Only mind how you go – the farmers round here seem to have a death wish – we were nearly forced into a dyke by a red-haired lunatic on the way here.' Tom glowered again at the discomfited Terence as if it was his fault.

Terence would have liked to re-shoot the morning and give it a different ending; that being impossible he wished to be rapidly removed from this increasingly undignified farce. He smiled tersely good-bye to brother and father, collected his jacket and shoes and followed the impossibly distanced Bea outside into the sunshine, vibrating with annoyance.

'Sorry about all that,' Bea said, inserting herself into the driver's seat of the truck, white skirt tucked up over brown knees, long brown hand wrestling with the gear stick, 'but I haven't seen Patrick for over six months. He's in the Navy, you see.'

Terence couldn't care less which branch of the armed forces her brother was in. He felt in his pocket for the little camera he always carried. He'd taken photographs of her dancing with Justin the night before, like two beautiful cranes circling each other, and of some of the paintings he had discovered in that other entrancing room full of dreams while she had been making breakfast. He had let his imagination run amok. He didn't want to drive to Fingle in silence and he wasn't going to give up, not yet. As if nothing had occurred between them and their peaceful post-party breakfast had not been rudely interrupted by a succession of giants, he forced a return to attentive politeness.

'You're quite a painter, aren't you?'

'You went into the painting room?' Her voice was not encouraging.

'And what did I see? Not what I expected, I admit. I expected tender little water-colours of sheep and barns, I don't know why. Nothing quite so feisty, or so magical. Where do you exhibit?'

'I haven't shown my work anywhere yet, although I've been painting for a long time, ever since I could hold a pencil or a paintbrush – look, this is no good. I'm sorry, so sorry. I'm a bit distraught. If I've led you up the garden path, I didn't mean to. Your friend Justin, my husband Oscar . . .' He looked startled so she hurried on, 'I found out last night that the woman who Oscar ran off with, Andrea, was Justin's ex-wife.'

'So it was revenge of some sort, your sleeping with me?

'No, it was hardly revenge,' she said tiredly, 'that all happened months ago. Finding out brought it all back, that's all. Then there were the car-burners the night before. I didn't want to be alone, needed to go to bed with you. I thought that was all you wanted?' She sounded genuinely puzzled.

Terence was unable to deny it, but also found that it was no longer the complete story. Having seized an opportunity last night, expecting to leave the next morning without any entangle-ment, he now contrarily wished to continue the relationship; but she seemed to hold all the cards and the Viking was certainly an impediment. He turned and stared at her profile as she drove, the gently rounded chin with the merest hint of a cleft in it and felt despair.

'You're unique. Quite unique. Thank you for last night.'

She drew up outside his lodgings. 'I am not an unicorn, really I am not,' she said imploringly, 'and I am sorry, I really am. If Nut hadn't turned up like that, and then my family, we'd have parted company without all this fuss, wouldn't we?'

He had to suppose that was the truth and wondered if it was

merely the Viking's appearance and violent departure that had unearthed his competitive spirit. She smelt of the honey she had eaten for breakfast and he was about to try to kiss her good-bye but a plump child in a tightly-stretched acid green T-shirt, wobbling up and down the pavement on rollerblades, seemed to be taking too keen an interest in them and put him off.

After Tom's departure, Bea and Patrick lurked in the thin shade of the tamarisk bushes and Bea, too hot, tired and miserable to protest, submitted to Patrick's tactfully intrusive interrogations. He steered the conversation away from his own doings and enquired casually about Terence. Lying flat on her back with a straw hat over her face, she gave muffled explanations of her feelings about Nut.

'And have you see much of Agnes since you've been here?'

'Have I seen Agnes! She practically lived here for a while, or so it felt. There were times when I thought she was going to ask if she and Seb could move in, but she's recently become oddly distant and rather bad-tempered. I haven't seen her a few days for which I am supremely thankful.'

'I witnessed a rather strange scene between her and Oscar yesterday evening, that's all. It was quite crudely embarrassing since I was having a drink with your Mrs Lewis in the back garden and they didn't know we were there. She's been having an affair with Oscar and they were rowing. She kneed him.'

'What?' Bea removed her hat. '*Agnes* and Oscar? *Oscar* and Agnes?' Bizarre, unthought-of things rushed into her mind. 'Did it look as if ... What *did* it look like?'

Patrick recounted the tender scene. 'You don't get that physical with someone, for no reason.' He looked at Bea anxiously. 'Oh God. She is impossible! She's just not happy unless she's mucking someone about or causing a scene. I never told you, anyone, but Agnes was my first.'

Bea sat up so suddenly she nearly ricked her neck.

'You are joking? When?'

'Well, I was fifteen. During the summer holidays, after O levels. I was desperately in love with her for at least six months, but after a couple of little notes from her when I went back to school in September, she lost interest. I was longing for the Christmas holidays but by then, she'd gone off with someone older than me. I was devastated!'

'Oh, Agnes!' Bea lay down, put the hat over her face again and laughed till she wept and Patrick patted her hand as the sun pierced the tightly woven straw in little prismatic pin-pricks, shifting and changing as she breathed, star-blurring as tears came into her eyes. She was overwhelmed by the gentle, brotherly concern.

'Poor, poor Patrick. I didn't mean to laugh. It's just that everything has come like three courses of a badly cooked dinner served all at once ... Do you know something? I don't give a damn about either of them any more. At least I now know that there's no *way* Oscar and I could make a go of it again. Agnes has been miserably underhand. It all suddenly makes sense. She's been forever keen to find out what my intentions were, should he come back. Perhaps he's been back for ages and lying low and Ag-bag just sank her little teeth into him. But I'm narrowing my interests for sanity's sake. Painting and Nut. Nut had no *right* to be so upset. We aren't lovers ... Although I think I love him ... I know I love him and he knows I know; it's just that I gave the impression that I didn't want to get involved with anyone at all, not sexually anyway, at the moment; he jumped to the right, wrong conclusion this morning.' She wailed. 'All I need at the moment is to paint – it's an imperative thing – but people won't let me alone and the motives for everything I do are beginning to be suspect even to me.'

'Can I look at your pictures?'

'Of course you can. Everyone else seems to have looked at them, whether they've been invited or not. Leave me here for a bit and go upstairs and see what you think, or is it think what you see? Although I don't know that I want to hear what you thought you saw, afterwards. I am dreadfully, dreadfully tired.'

She heard his grunt as he got to his feet and his footsteps receding across the flagstones towards the house. There was the distant roar of some antique lumbering hulk, bravely vibrating its way through the sky to a flypast at some far off Saturday airshow. The closer soft pulsing of Jerry Rumm's generator. The minute scraping of an insect beneath a leaf, just by her ear. A lark shouting its head off overhead. A penetrating whistling as shepherd directed dogs and the indignant baa'ing of newly shorn sheep a few fields away. The thud of explosives at the firing ranges. The creaking of swans as they flew overhead. Although blinded by the hat, she could see the swans in her mind's eye. 'How sad one should get used to seeing swans fly. It seems such a miracle they could get off the ground.'

Picking at a mosquito bite, she wondered if she could cope with a family lunch, for that had been the plan when Tom left them. Then, Agnes, who'd never shown signs of the sort of concentration required for serious plotting. Was there any man left in the Bellhurst area that Agnes hadn't had at one time or another? She liked to spread herself around generously, like Marmite on toast. She was a sportswoman who had 'stalk, catch and kill' in her vocabulary, but not 'keep' since her prey always turned out to be inedible. Then Nut's agonised, incredulous face returned to Bea and she began to chat to Freda as she had not done since she was a child distressed; a conversational prayer for guidance around the minds of men, as it had forever been.

'"From ghosties and ghoulies and long-leggitty beasties,"' said Patrick, '"and things that go bump in the night, Good Lord deliver us." What were you muttering about?'

'In confabulation with Freda, or me, since we are obviously the same thing, about Nut. I've started talking aloud to myself rather a lot.'

'My God! Is Freda still in residence? I thought you'd lost touch with her when you were ten.'

'She visits occasionally. I am not mad. I will not go mad. I have never been mad.'

'Of course you aren't. Won't. Weren't. I've made you something cool to drink. Look, orange juice and lots of ice. Your feet are getting sunburnt.'

'Well, what did you think of them?' She pushed off the hat and sat up, squinting in the brightness, strands of hair sticking damply to her forehead. She looked very forlorn.

'I thought you didn't care to know what I thought.'

'Well, I do care. Very much.'

'I'm a bit astounded still. They are so much bigger than anything you've done before. I think they're absolutely brilliant. I need time to think about them. This is what you've been building up to, ever since you were a child, isn't it? All this time you've been a thunderstorm brewing, and none of us noticed.' He sat down again beside her while she gratefully sipped the orange juice. 'I'm not joking when I say I'm stunned. They look so utterly different to what I'd imagined.'

'That's the second time someone has said that today. Do I look like an aged spinster indulging herself with water-colours of oast-houses and cherry blossom?' She sounded sharply cross.

'No. Not much.'

'Oh, good.' She made a decision at last. To attend a happy family lunch would be a torture, but it might enforce a temporary order among the thousand threads of Nut-anxiety, at least until the afternoon. A respite of sorts. Dealing with events. Doing them. Living them. Confrontations, arguments, assessments, assignations, encroachments, a thick, black molasses of impossibilities to be rendered into fine flowing golden syrup.

'I've left a little present on the chair in your painting room, something to while away your evening,' Patrick said later that morning as they were leaving for lunch in Bellhurst. 'Don't forget to go and look for it when you get back. Mum's going to be very relieved to find you haven't become an anchorite and she'd relax even further if you tell her what you told me about last night's amazing navy-blue party.'

'Yes, she understands parties.'

'But not much else, you mean?'

'I don't think that's fair, but at times it seems so. We expect too much from our parents, don't we? She works so hard. Anyway, I'll tell her *everything*; apart from Terence, obviously, and not about Agnes and Oscar, and you're not to tell her about Nut either, although it's possible that Nest has passed that one on already.'

'It's going to be a quiet lunch then.'

'I have to visit Nest after lunch. She's owed an apology since I was a bit cross on the telephone and she's been so excellent, allowing me stay at Little Rumm.'

'I thought Mum and Nest didn't see each other much.'

'They don't. Mum's always been jealous of Nest's education, and is secretly appalled by Blue, and Nest thinks Mum is bird-brained, which she isn't, and wasting her time with all this foodie thing. Fetishist, she calls it. Her food writing certainly seems to be bringing in the cash – I can't think the ironmongery makes enough to live on. They love and disapprove of each other, but you never know. I don't want Mum charging down here insisting on meeting Nut, particularly now he's evaporated.'

'He looked a bit steamed up as he passed us this morning. A fiery fellow, obviously. Come on. Let's get going, or we'll be late for lunch and it's your favourite thing. Nettle soup.'

'Ugh! We'll both wake up tomorrow morning covered in whiteheads.'

The fiery fellow was standing hands in pockets, cooling his heels in the English Channel. Pewter-coloured clouds were brewing far away to the west and the afternoon air was stifling. Nut's sweeping eyebrows were drawn fearsomely together as he proceeded through the useless litany common to those who have reacted incautiously to an unpleasant surprise. Had he been sensible he would have waited to be introduced, at least found out the identity and intent of the stranger and then he would not now be suffering. Shit, shit, shit! Was it Bea or himself who had transgressed? It *could* have been her brother sitting at the table — she'd mentioned a naval brother; but he hadn't the look of a brother, so short and dark, but then it was possible. Anything was possible and it was the anything that frightened him. His expectations had obscured the facts. The sea was nagging at the bottoms of his rolled-up jeans and he kicked at the water hopelessly. He was hatless and the sunlight's flicker on the water gave him the beginning of a headache and began pitilessly to scorch the bridge of his nose. His eyes suddenly filled with ridiculous tears and he stood facing out to sea, struggling unsuccessfully to contain them; after a while he became interested in the phenomenon of their steady drip from cheek into the sea: salt to salt, water to water. Disgustedly he dragged his great waterlogged feet out of the shallows and set off home.

On arriving at the railway carriage, as hot inside as a biscuit tin left in the sun, he tried to work for the rest of the afternoon, reassessing the findings, both sedimentological and microfaunal, for the supposed course of a tidal inlet. He laid out photocopies of ancient maps and plotted routes but his mind was elsewhere, fretting and hoping Bea might ring, but she did not. He tried to call her to apologise but there was no answer. There was no reason for her to explain herself and he was miserable and sick to the stomach in the way of a small boy who has broken a longed-for Christmas present within five minutes of unwrapping it.

Switching on the radio he caught the tail end of a severe weather warning on the local station. A freaky hundred mile-wide front of thunderstorms was fast approaching from the south-west with high winds and heavy rain imminent. The radio was crackling furiously. Better batten down. He saved the afternoon's pathetic vacillations on the computer and unplugged it, fetched a tin bucket to place beneath a persistent leak in roof of the lean-to conservatory, went outside again to wind up the windows of the van and stood astonished, watching the approaching storm. The sky faded from metallic cobalt to an eerie liverish yellow, lit by flashes of lightning of a dangerous electric blue. The landscape of sunny sand-coloured shingle turned to olive green as the clouds piled up, boiling black. A wave of hot air tumbled over him, vacuuming up dancing bits of litter. As the glaring sun was engulfed the first great raindrops slapped across his face. He stood there till his shirt was sodden, daring the lightning to strike him, then went indoors and lay flat on the bed, listening to the rising wind and the creakings of the flimsy house. Whatever strength the storm reached, it would not be sufficient to match his mood.

Struggling with the key, hair blown into blinding seaweed tangles and soaked in the short dash from the truck to her house, Bea burst in and fought the door shut against the wind. She retrieved the fossil book from the kitchen table and stumbled upstairs, dripping white dress dark against her skin, to find dry clothes and search for Patrick's present. Once dried and sitting safe on the bed in the painting room, she admired its meticulous wrapping and with a penknife carefully slipped beneath the tiny seals — she was reluctant to break them — unwrapped it and stared at the contents in her lap: a minuscule tinfoil package of cannabis, a packet of Rizlas and a pinch or two of tobacco. She let out a screech of laughter. Dear, dear Patrick. It was too dark to work, although only five o'clock, and the power was off. The storm seemed to be growing in strength and there was nothing else to do. It might stop her crying over Nut.

With clumsy fingers she heated then crumbled a piece of resin, as she had watched Oscar do in the days before they had grown out of it, had less and less time to spare. She rolled up a little spliff and lay smoking and smiling idiotically, pictures forming and dissolving on the canvas of the cracked white ceiling, as uncatchable as drifting petals. Her body sank heavily into the scarlet sheet as she analysed the depths of each tearing crack of thunder, followed the dwindling, rumbling timbre into the distance till the storm abated some two hours later. The wind blew an oboe-like note through the letter box. At one time she considered the addition of a circular patch of viridian to the two-thirds-finished picture leant against the wall, but mercifully became aware in time that perception of colour, perspective and her rationality were still quite hopelessly distorted. She turned to the fossil book and became visually entangled in the segments of a trilobite, enjoying the tranquillity of a non-functional brain.

At seven-thirty the storm blew itself out and yawning, she sat up, not quite able to dismiss the idea that she had been wasting time. The problems were still there – but were they really problems? Problems emerged or rose up, challenges were thrown down. Nut had thrown down the little book on the table at breakfast, that morning which now seemed so far away as to be over the horizon. She could no longer defer the knowledge of being not in control and deeply to blame.

In the newest painting, Freda had sprouted wide, carved and painted wings and loomed across the sky; she had put on weight and appeared to be moving at some speed, a vast and streamlined angel above a little group of people on the ground all looking up and pointing. Better not work on it tonight, but tomorrow she must get on with it. No work done since lunch time yesterday. Geraldine. Geraldine O'Brien's London lunch! What had transpired as the two elderly lovers met again? Her foot crunched unpleasantly on something on the floorboards as she went to fetch the unloved mobile phone and switched it on. It bleeped instantly.

'Please, Freda, let it be Nut. It must be Nut!' flashed through her head, but Geraldine had connected with her previous thought. Rapidly dragging ragged thoughts together, her own voice sounding like a ponderous echo in her skull, she enquired:

'So, how did it go? Was he bowled over by the splendour of your Chinese yellow jacket?'

Geraldine chuckled — a new laugh.

'He did admire it, and yes, it all went well, very well in fact. I've just got in, and what a storm that was, so exhilarating driving through it from Parden in the cab! But I'll save the details of the lunch for a minute, there's something I want to sort out first. The thing is that Simon is coming to lunch with me in a couple of weeks. His son is coming too, and perhaps the son's wife, who is a journalist. That's the sixteenth of July, Sunday, I think. Now take a deep breath and don't immediately panic and start thinking up excuses.' Bea had stiffened automatically, and then did as she was bid and uncurled. 'I want to bring them to your house,' continued Geraldine firmly, 'perhaps for tea, so you can show them your paintings. Simon wants to see them. Now, transport. They are coming by train, since the son, James, appears to have had his driving licence taken away and his wife doesn't drive at all. Simon refuses to drive more than ten miles. They're getting a taxi at Parden. You'd have to come and fetch us from Bellhurst and drive us back here afterwards? Please Bea, you must not pass up this opportunity out of misplaced shyness.'

'Oh! Yes!' Bea was astounded by the simplicity of agreeing and the resulting sense of euphoria.

'Yes?' Oh, I am so relieved. Well done, my dear. I know how difficult you find it. You won't regret it, whatever happens, I promise you. Astoundingly, I've been offered a show myself, a retrospective! But he is a very rich man, and very kind, and can afford to indulge himself occasionally. Now, shall I tell you how it went, the lunch?'

*　　*　　*

Bea went back to the bed, still with the phone clenched in her hand. She could no longer telephone Agnes and give her the good news, nor could she get through to Nut. On the floor was the squashed shell of the humbug snail. The heightened introspection brought on by the cannabis caused her to wonder if it was a warning, that the snail was a future self squashed by fate for being too adventurous in new places or whether it was a sign that the drawing in of horns leads one unsafely to nowhere, and she silently began to shake with hopeless giggles. Of course it all meant nothing of the sort, nothing at all. It was a meaningless accident, except for the unfortunate snail. The storm had passed on its way along the coast and the evening sun was patterning the wall with pink light.

She spent the rest of that tiresomely revelatory evening moving pictures needlessly about, worrying at them, shifting them into groups, fretfully rearranging them into further sub-divisions. She inspected her face for signs of emergent nettle spots then went outside to the cooled, wet garden and desultorily weeded goose-grass seedlings from between the flagstones. She ate a carrot. In between she repeatedly tried to raise Nut on the telephone, making little bargains with Fate/Freda of the 'if he answers then I'll do all the washing by hand for the rest of my life' variety, but she eventually dozed off on the red bed before it was quite dark, evading thoughts of Simon Greensand's impending visit, angry with herself for having stamped on Terence's feelings, since she liked him, futilely wondering *why* Agnes had gone after Oscar behind her back, despairing that she had damaged for ever her relationship with Nut.

If she couldn't see Nut she would see no one else and come what may, the angel picture must be completed during the next two weeks.

Chapter Eleven

Agnes Spring was unused to things going so embarrassingly wrong. She had allowed herself to think of Oscar as an escape route but chutzpah and flamboyance had both deserted her in the three days since the confrontation with him; however the indignity of the outcome had been a little reduced each time she recalled the satisfying, invigorating feeling of the *slap* as the palm of her hand connected with his face and his look of shock as the knee had driven home. She had come to believe, as she frequently did, that it was she who had come off best in the encounter.

The delicate little black eyebrows were twitched together across the china-doll face and the grey eyes were still a couple of tones deeper with discontent. She sat in a huddle over the drawing board, tussling with a further commission for the grand gardening magazine who had accepted her previous page-headings with an unflattering lack of appreciation. This was a delicate rococo water-colour of misty blues and sepias to illustrate an article on garden furniture. A chinoiserie summer house with matching benches and pergola with a drift of wisteria tumbling down elegant steps. To punish them for their lack of interest, and late payment, she was bloody-mindedly painting in a tiny garden gnome, peeing fully-frontal into an antique watering can, just to the side of the summerhouse, melding in nicely with the climbing plants. 'I bet a hundred to one that they don't notice it. It'll be interesting to see if I can get away with a gnome and a penis in such a precious mag.' She laid her brush down and shaking back her hair, half closed her eyes and inspected her work. 'Too good for them.' This effrontery gave rise to a resurgence of good humour and she gleefully set about making out the invoice.

If Oscar was out of the question, she was most definitely out for a good time. It had, after all, been quite ludicrously simple to overcome his pretended eagerness to get back to Bea and he'd rolled over on his back like a pussy cat. Not much of a challenge after all. The really hard work had gone into it when he was still with Andreary. At first he'd seemed so very interested in her dreadful life with Phil, the lack of mental stimulation, of understanding and of her need for appreciation and excitement. It was incomprehensible to her why he should want to break it up after their weekend away and she had felt used and put upon. At least Bea didn't know about it and there was no way she would find out. Oscar wouldn't tell her, that at least was certain. Why was it Bea seemed to collect all the attention without ever actually *doing* anything?

She looked at her watch. Two o'clock. Her mother had collected Seb from nursery school and was baby-sitting him all afternoon so that she could finish her work. Well, it was finished now so she could go out and buy a new pair of sandals, or go and visit Mary, or Mags. Or ... she might drive over and see if the most interesting Nut was at home. They'd got along so well when they'd met that Bea had got pleasingly near to being annoyed. Well, she deserved a little competition. Bea and Nut weren't exactly together, an item, were they? In fact Bea showed a strong disinclination to get any closer to him; trust Bea to go one better and find someone with the full complement of green eyes. To Agnes their relationship was inexplicable and she had felt waspish towards Bea since being manoeuvred away from seeing the paintings. What strange imaginings were being concocted up there in that painting room week after week and why shouldn't she see them? Bea suddenly appeared to her like a sailing boat on a pond, forever gracefully circling. She had the sudden urge to call up a storm and sink her.

Nut, returning from a trip to Canterbury, saw Agnes from the road as he parked his van. She was peering through the window of his house, nose close up to the glass and shading her eye with her hand. He could not for a second place her and was momentarily annoyed by the peering.

'Hello, Nut, remember me? We met at the Eeldyke Inn a few weeks ago? Bea told me where you lived and as I was down here doing some drawing – I am an artist too, you know – I thought I'd drop by. I was sure I heard a noise inside, that someone was in.'

Nut was perplexed. What could he do but ask her in for a cup of tea?

'So, have you seen Bea today at all?' he asked hopefully.

'Oh, no. I hate to bother her when I know she's working so hard. She takes her work so seriously – no time for anyone else! I haven't seen her for ages.' He put the kettle on and unpacked his briefcase and Agnes sat down heavily on the crisp pages of a report that he had printed out that morning and leaning back in the chair, beamed at him.

'Could I ask you to move for a moment, while I rescue those papers?'

She didn't actually get up, but mischievously wriggled aside so he had to put his hand beneath her to remove them, was forced to touch the warm flesh of the plump thigh.

'So where do you live then, Agnes?'

'In Bellhurst – that's where Bea and I met – we were at school together. But she's changed so much, you wouldn't believe, since her husband left her.'

'Have you met her brother? The one in the Navy? Patrick,

is it?' He was looking at her with what she interpreted as rapt interest.

'Good Lord, yes! We're very old friends. But we don't see him often.'

'So he's not on leave, paying a visit at the moment? I thought she mentioned something about him coming this month.'

'Oh, well I wouldn't know. She never tells me anything any more . . .' she insinuated deep regret, 'I'd love to see him again. We had quite a thing going when we were teenagers.' Again, a touch of delicate sadness crept into her voice. 'I think Bea tries to keep him away from me, when he's on leave. She broke it up in the first place, you know. I think she was a little jealous. They look so alike, almost twinnish. Almost unhealthily close.'

She watched him voraciously as he made the mugs of tea. She had never had sex with a redhead.

She stayed and chatted for too long till Nut, tired and miserable, made 'I have some work to do' noises and she left, threatening to make a return visit one day when he wasn't so tied up.

So, it had not been Bea's brother, sitting at the table.

In the late afternoon of the following Tuesday, Bea put the final touches to the angel painting and lay flat down on the floorboards and cried with relief. She was mentally worn out but there was something she could do about it. She washed her hair and rinsed it in a tea made from chamomile flowers. She made up her eyes and with a water-colour of a fat ewe and lamb in a little folder as a present and every hope in the world, she set out to make amends.

The crude juxtaposition of Nut and Agnes was to Bea's eyes so unexpected that for a second her vision fogged. When she looked again it was still there, only this time instead of frantic movement there was a stillness. The front door had been ajar. As she had stood uncertainly in the doorway she had seen straight down the tunnel centre of the railway carriage, through the kitchen, into the bedroom and there was Agnes, wrestling with Nut on the bed. Nut's cry, 'Bea! Help!' sounded to her as an admission of guilt on being discovered rather than the cry for assistance that it was.

With a shout of near murderous hate, Bea flew towards them and dragging Agnes to her feet by her hair, knocked her sideways with a left hook. She then turned and fled. As she got in through her own safe front door in a moither of misery, Agnes's mother phoned.

'Ah, Bea dear. How are you? Agnes is with you, isn't she? Can I speak to her please? It's just that Seb has been violently sick and I wondered when she was coming home.'

Bea's anger was terrible.

'No, you can't speak to Agnes. She isn't here and hasn't been here at all. At the moment she is screwing somebody. My somebody, my man. I hope she burns in hell!'

Later Geraldine telephoned.

'I just wondered how the work was going, Bea. Bea, Bea? Dear girl, whatever is the matter?' Bea was sobbing heartbreakingly down the line; all self-restraint had vanished with that blow to Agnes's face and out came the sad story.

'That girl's a malicious little bitch, but *ce n'est pas le fin du monde*! Why don't you ask your Aunt Nest if she'll come over to keep you company. I think, for once, that you don't want to be alone? Or you could come and stay with me for the night? I've got some wonderful blue vodka.'

'I don't think I could drive, Geraldine. I'm all shaky. But you're right. I don't want to be alone and I will ring Nest. The angel painting is finished. I'm all geared up for the Greensands' visit next Sunday, really I am.'

'Good. That sounds nice and positive. Now ring Nest.'

*　　*　　*

Blue dropped Nest at Little Rumm at eight o'clock and told her to give Bea his love since he couldn't come in because he had to visit a man about a fishing trip and would pick up Nest later.

Nest poured her unhappy niece a glass of burgundy, in fact several glasses of burgundy, for she had been certain that it would be a two-bottle occasion and had come prepared, together with a chunk of duck-liver pâté and a packet of oatcakes. She was deeply worried but also pleased that Bea had so unusually confided in her. She listened, sitting with Bea on the front steps in the twilight till they were driven indoors by midges and then listened some more, sitting by candlelight since there was a power cut caused, the electricity board said, by a swan flying into a power cable. She was unusually quiet, only interjecting the occasional word of comfort but when Bea had eventually dried up and was looking across the table at her somewhat muzzily, she tightly clasped Bea's shaking hands and admitted she was partly to blame.

'I've pushed and nagged you, Bea. I am so sorry. And this Geraldine friend of yours, she has too, hasn't she? And you've been driving yourself in order to escape from the past, so determined to succeed and worrying about what the gallery people will think of the paintings? And this Nut fellow – he's been after you too? Oh poor darling – you must have felt quite hounded! But you really do love him, do you?'

'I'm afraid I do. Absolutely. Oh, Nest! If I hadn't been so sanctimonious about my work, none of this would have happened ... And whatever possessed me to go to bed with Terence?'

'Darling, don't get things so out of proportion! That's a very minor misdemeanour, surely?'

'Then, I'm supposed to take finding him screwing Agnes as a minor misdemeanour ...? I can't ... I can't! Particularly because it was Agnes.'

'You are certain you didn't misinterpret it?'

'How do you misinterpret finding someone astride the man you love, in the process of removing her dress? She didn't have anything on underneath, either. And her bottom's all flabby.'

'Did you hit her very hard?' Nest looked a bit worried.

'Not as hard as I meant to. She sort of jerked backwards. And my hand only hurts a little.'

'Bea, I can't believe I'm sitting here discussing you and violence in the same breath!'

'It seems to be all over the place — everyone knocking about everyone else. I think I just picked it up, like a verruca. I felt, felt sort of *diminished*, afterwards. I think we've all gone mad. I will recover, won't I?' In the flickering, moth-infested candlelight Nest stared across at Bea's face with its pathetic shadows beneath the eyes. 'I don't believe she knows how beautiful she is,' thought Nest. 'None of us, certainly, has ever told her. She has no more defences, no more energy and needs calm, to be loved and cosseted. She needs the wretched Nutmeg ...' An extraordinary thought crossed Nest's mind and once implanted, refused to be removed. She was all for trying things out. And if the ridiculous little plot that was burgeoning in her mind didn't work, she would have to send in the heavies, Blue in particular, to speak to Nut.

She was unaware at that moment that Blue was half heaving, half supporting a drunken and near speechless Nut back across the shingle to his house. He held up the great height of the staggering man and somehow or other got him into the house and managed to roll him on to his bed and remove his boots.

'Goo' man, Blue. I'm uspshet. My girl's uspshet too. My fault. Fuckin' muddle. It's all shite. Don't know what to do ... Hrmph. She'sh a goo' ... She'sh a dangerous hitter. Southpaw.'

Nest interrogated Blue later that night about Nut.

'So he says it was accidental — that she jumped on him? Hm.

I've heard that before, sometime, still . . . You must tell him that he's not to bother Bea for the next few days – if they see each other now, they'll only fight. The dust needs to settle. She's seriously overwrought and needs lots of rest. I have a plan.'

'I can't tell him what to do, Cuckoo! We don't talk about our private lives.' Nest looked eerily like Bea, but the expression was not one he'd ever seen on Bea's face. Crafty.

'You will ring him tomorrow when he's sober and tell him,' continued Nest. 'What *do* you talk about during those hours drinking then, if you don't talk private lives? Just evade the gaskets and mackerel for once and tell him. As I said I have a plan.' She was on the telephone to unknown acquaintances for a long time, till Blue called from the top of the stairs, was he never going to get his story that night?

On Wednesday evening two women came to call on Bea. They introduced themselves as friends of Nest's and said they had a proposition to put to her. Thinking it was something to do with painting, she invited them in and there still remaining half a bottle of burgundy on the dresser in the kitchen, glumly offered them a drink. There was something covert about their attitude which reminded her of something, but in spite of being in a highly suggestible state of mind, she was completely taken aback by what they had to say and just sat there looking at them with her mouth open. They smiled charmingly, further explained that they believed the unnecessary stress caused by modern living was a form of psychic pollution and were prepared to help, and waited patiently.

What could rational, well-educated Nest have been thinking of? Why had Nest told these complete strangers, these two members of an apparently elect inner circle of the Daughters of Nature, about her private life? But they hadn't mentioned what they knew at all, they had merely said they understood she was in trouble. It was all so completely removed from her adult existence that she had to force her mind back to childhood, to the discovery of Freda, before she could comprehend what it was they were about. Then, past rational argument, she thought, 'What the hell! Why not? My life is in ruins. It can't make it any worse.'

The elder of the two women produced a mobile phone and spoke to someone, very briefly. 'Bell? It's on. And not a minute too soon. Yes. Very, very strained and unhappy. No, only a little resistant. We'll see you shortly.' 'What very up-to-date witches they are,' thought Bea, 'and how practical.'

They seated Bea in her favourite blue chair in the centre of the room facing the fireplace. They drew the yellow curtains, lit candles on either side of Nut's portrait and lit one in an old blue enamel chamberstick and placed it on a stool before her where it guttered in the draw from the chimney. They turned off the phone and checked that all the light switches were off and were generally so thorough in their efforts to ensure that they would not be interrupted that she had to stifle the urge to giggle hysterically and twiddle her thumbs. Whatever had she let herself in for? It was monstrously ridiculous. But she would co-operate.

There was a soft tap-tappit on the door and one of the women crossed to the little hall and Bea could hear muttering, like someone negotiating with carol singers, then: 'Yes, we're all in place. Off you go.' It was like having an operation, Bea thought. 'Any minute now they'll approach with hypodermics and offer me a pre-med.'

The two women locked back and front doors and instructed her to watch the candle flame and think only of her dearest wish. 'Just like a fairy story,' thought Bea, 'only they're short-changing me. I should have three dearest wishes.' Resigned to making a fool of herself and remembering Nest's motto 'Try everything once, except murder and incest,' she submitted. It was all so weirdly commonplace, so excitingly banal.

They took up positions standing behind her chair which at

first felt uncomfortable, since she'd rather have liked to keep an eye on them. Outside in the warm dark a soft chanting began, so soft that she was unsure if she was imagining it and strained to hear. It rose and fell and her invigilators seemed to slink gradually away into the background, the whole dark room slowly sinking away from the chair and she was suspended in space and could not take her eyes away for one second from the aching brightness of the candle flame for fear of falling, nor turn her cheeks away from its heat. Her dearest wish was definitely Nut.

She awoke the next morning with a crick in her neck and with the sunlight pouring in through the window behind the collection of blue glass bottles and bowls. She stretched cautiously and blew out the candle. Something fell to the floor from her lap. It was Nut's fossil sea-urchin. She had fallen asleep, evidently, while the women were still there and they had gone away disappointed at her lack of appreciation. Well, no harm was done and she did feel very clear-headed and comfortable for someone who'd slept the night in a chair. Her hair was a bird's nest, there was a wine stain on her T-shirt and her skirt had a spatter of candle grease across the front.

She couldn't remember the women's faces at all, other than that they had been heavily made up, like stage make-up, mask-like faces now she came to think of it and that their voices had been soft, reasonable and insistent. Even that small amount of recall seemed to fade as the morning drew on and she got on with washing clothes. The washing machine had long since expired and as she scrubbed the collar of a white shirt with a nail-brush she remembered someone saying, at some stage last night: 'Allow three clear days.' The events of the night before didn't hold her thoughts for long. She'd gone along with it to please Nest – knew only that she had not dreamt it, had been in some fashion hypnotised, that painting was for the time being finished, that she had survived and was now quick and awake. She opened the back door and took the washing out to the sunshine.

There were spots of candle wax on the paving stones and the long feathery grasses around the door had been trodden down.

Had she blown out a candle when she woke up? How could it have stayed alight all that time? In spite of the brightness of the day, a shiver ran down her spine.

On the morning of the Greensand visit she pottered about the misty garden in her nightdress, refreshed and wakeful with a piece of toast and honey in her hand, inspecting the poppies. She had been sleeping well since Candle-Wednesday, curled up cat-like and dead to the world with her tail around her nose.

The morning promised heat. The smaller flowers, the strange greyish violets, soft dusty pinks and whites of the *Papaver rhoeas*, were flowering now. Very pretty, she thought, but they couldn't compete with the *paeoniflorums*, blackberry purple with tightly scrunched petals doubled and quadrupled around the powdery cream anthers. A decadent *fin de siècle* rustling petticoat of a flower. There were other lovely marvels in the mixture which she and Nest had sown together; in particular a singleton, a wicked looking plant fit for a sorcerer, a sinister mediaeval popinjay. The petals were perfect cockleshells of purple pleated silk, darkening to black at the base, flame scarlet towards the dagged and snipped fringing of the upper edge. She went indoors again to fetch paintbox and water-colour paper.

The painting room was prepared for the aliens' landing that afternoon and, over-tidied, looked uncomfortable. The paintings still stood with their faces to the wall except the latest one since sections of the paint were still tacky, particularly round Freda's head. Freda was no longer a stone figure about the face and upper body; a blushing hint of blood was running in the marble veins and her enigmatic lips were a definitely predatory pink. Bea cast a considering eye around the room; a stack of preparatory drawings and a pile of water-colours were laid out upon the bed. She had no idea at all what

Simon Greensand might be like, could not picture Geraldine's reluctant lover.

'Well, there it all is — can't change anything. But I can think "take it or leave it" now. After driving them back to Bellhurst, I might just have to go Nut-gathering. I can't take-or-leave him. Whatever he was up to with Agnes — pretty obvious what he was up to, actually — it couldn't have been serious. I know it was just revenge for finding me with Terence. The distress, my distress, was deserved. It matches his. Every time I think of him, there's this mewling in my stomach, demanding to be fed. Someone's got to make the first move and if we don't meet soon, I'll wither away.' After all the past agonising, she was surprisingly certain that he would want to see her.

Outside again and sitting on a kitchen chair painting the popinjay flower, she found her hand was trembling slightly and she had to get up again, walk about, shaking it to loosen the wrist. Jerry Rumm, ambling past the house on his snorting, rusty tractor, caught a startling glimpse from his high seat of a phantom woman in white, walking up and down wringing her hands in distress; but the ghost turned and waved at him and he saw it was Bea in her nightie, waved back and drove on, an unlikely grin spreading the sombre foldings of his dark weather-beaten face. That was quite some strange party she'd had round there on Wednesday night.

By mid morning, Bea, on her seventh painted poppy, decided it was time to get dressed and start preparing for the afternoon's ordeal. She put on black jeans and T-shirt and the long-abandoned watch; her wedding ring still lay half-hidden, embedded in the rush seat of the chair on which it had been discarded months before. No, it was not an ordeal, more of an examination. Think, she told herself, of taking an exam. You know the syllabus, you've an inkling of the questions; for goodness sake, be more positive. She began to work out an explanation, moulding it into a manageable formulaic sentence, trying to sound as if she knew what she was doing. 'I'm working on a series on growing up,' sounds inane, she thought as she scrubbed out the lavatory. She was thirty-one in a couple of weeks. 'Rites of Passage' sounded a little more intelligent and feasible and was not far from the truth. Shaking a rush mat outside the back door, she thought that there was a new rite of passage now, slotting into life between the births, marriages and deaths – divorce. A second leaving of home and certainties. She wondered why the Church of England, now it more or less accepted divorce and in some cases even remarried divorced people, or at least blessed their unions, had not jumped on the bandwagon and instituted some sort of memorial un-blessing service to mark divorces. The participants could wear scarlet and black clothes, perhaps with bows of sackcloth to signify remorse. 'I, Beatrice Jane, renounce thee, Oscar George, from this day forward . . .' The idea was really quite attractive. Guests might even be invited to jump forwards at the appropriate moment and declare impediments to their being put asunder. The congregation could hopefully sing 'Abide with Me'. There was another painting there, somewhere.

She had truly meant her marriage vows when they had married that windy autumn afternoon in Bellhurst parish church. She had wanted to get married in a registry office, but Oscar's family had been scandalised at the idea (his uncle being a vicar) and she wished to keep them happy. It didn't matter much to her where the ceremony took place or under whose auspices, civil or religious. Vows were vows. The reception had been held in a flapping red-and-white striped marquee, on the lawn of the house belonging to the organist, adjacent to the church. Agnes had danced on a table. She had made a small painting of Agnes's dancing. The idea of divorce had always been distasteful – but she could not stay tied forever to someone who wasn't there. Time to cut the legal string, or even the ribbon – like opening a new supermarket, pull the cord unveiling both a memorial and the future. When tunnel-visioned by a sense of besotted rightness and very young, she had been utterly convinced that

Oscar was the only man she'd ever love. Wrong, but she had weathered the disappointment rather well; it would soon be time to speak to Oscar but now it was time to eat.

A tap on the door disturbed her as she was breaking an egg into the pan.

Nut stood there, but a strange Nut. She became cold as ice with fright and it took a heart-thumping second or two to focus on the nature of the change. He'd cut his hair and relieved from the weight of the scraped back plait, it surged out round his head in a simmering halo painted by William Blake.

'Hello,' he said, his face pinched with anxiety. He held out a hand tentatively, to take hers, or just to touch? 'If I'm not welcome now, tell me at once.'

'Your hair!' she squeaked. It was hacked off roughly, at just below ear-level.

'I've come to apologise for bursting in like that the other morning, and for what you think you saw the other day.'

'There's no need, really. I understand you wanted to get back at me . . . But your hair . . .' She at last took the outstretched hand in both of hers.

'I didn't want to get back at you, not at all. It was, you see, I'd come to think, then, that we . . .'

'Stop! *Why* have you cut your hair off?'

'Don't you like it shorter? I'm sorry I jumped to conclusions – it was, is, none of my business . . . Agnes . . .'

'But why? I . . . I loved it long.'

'It was none of my business who you choose to break-fast with.'

'I'd rather have been breakfasting with you,' she admitted.

'Ah ha! So why didn't you wait . . .'

'As you said, it's not your business.'

'But I want it to be.'

She knew he knew. 'Well, I'm sorry. I was breakfasting with a friend who stayed the night. He left that morning. We won't meet again. End of story.' Not a lie, but thrifty cut-work. 'Your turn.' Her eyes gleamed sapphire at him.

'Agnes attacked me. I am not joking. It was the second time she'd been round. She came for tea the first time and for me the second, it appeared. Perhaps I didn't give her enough biscuits first time around. I was nearly suffocating by the time you got there. I'd given up and thought my days were numbered. Didn't you hear me call for help? The hair will grow again, you know.' His eyes were brilliant with release. 'I went to the bedroom to fetch a notebook and she followed and jumped on me as I bent over to get the book from the other side of the bed. You know how small that room is. Mind you, I don't know how long I'd have been able to resist — she's very strong and a few minutes later it might have been a different story.' True, but embroidered with silk thread.

Bea hooted at the image of a man of Nut's size unable to subdue the sexual onslaught of tiny Agnes and a warm relief flushed through her. It would be all right. 'We won't talk about breakfasts any more, or Agnes again, ever. I don't want to know. Who cut your hair?'

He had intended to tell her it was self-inflicted but decided ruefully on the shaming truth. 'I'm afraid we'll have to talk Agnes again. It can only have been her.'

Bea gaped at him and anger rose up in her throat.

'How, how could she? Without your knowing?'

'She flounced off pretty quickly after you interrupted her attempt on my virtue. I remember seeing a little wallet left on the desk, beside where she'd sat in the living room. Everything got exaggerated in my head and looked blacker and blacker and I'm afraid I got a bit pissed with Blue that evening and he couldn't lock the door behind him when he left; he had to put me to bed. I had my hair when I went to the pub and when I got back at about ten o'clock. In the morning, no hair, no wallet and the dressmaking scissors I'd borrowed from Millie next door, to cut up a map, they weren't where I'd left them on the desk either, but were on the front step. It wasn't Blue, that's certain and I couldn't even stand up, let alone wield a pair of shears. Perhaps she wanted it as a trophy. She's probably tied it to the radio aerial of her car.' He ran an exploratory hand over his hair, still missing the weight of it. 'What are you doing for lunch?' He didn't look too worried about the hair but Bea was still furious.

'Oh Nut! I'm so sorry. It must have been her – she did it once before, at school. She's unbelievable, a monster. You could sue her for assault! Was it a little red wallet, with a flower on it? Would you like me to re-cut it? It looks a bit raggedy.'

'Oh please, Bea, yes, and yes, it had a daisy on it. It's a bit weird though, to think she was wandering around in my house when I was asleep. She must have been hanging around down there, out on the shingle all evening, then, waiting? Is she mad? What does she do with that tiresome child, when she's out on the razzle? What is that awful smell?'

'Oh shit! My egg!'

The offensive smell of scorching albumen was dire enough for Bea to agree to go for a pint of prawns a little later and she threw open all the windows, explaining the impending invasion of Geraldine and the gallery people. There had been no destructive arguments, no recriminations. She was being offered a meal, a respite, a hand and knew it was not deserved.

'You're very cool about this deputation of art dealers,' said Nut, who appeared to have somehow sneaked an arm across her shoulders and it was all she could do not to bury her head in his chest. 'Are you not frightened any more?' He was sunnily smug with the outcome of the foray. Earlier that morning he'd ingenuously come to believe that the change in his appearance might just be beneficial, give him a few seconds' advantage in a conversation with her, a shock tactic to stop her from slamming the door in his face which was a contingency that he'd been unable to get out of his head. They were talking again and that was all that mattered.

'No, not scared at all anymore.' said Bea. 'There's no point. A bit worried perhaps, but I'm dying to ring up Nest and tell her all about it once it's over, even if it goes badly. She's good at mending people who've been carelessly dropped, or who've chipped themselves . . . What did you do all this time?' she asked, gently removing his arm and searching for a comb, taking the scissors from the red wicker sewing basket on the windowsill.

'I'm afraid I moped a bit, but there was a lot of work to do and I polished off an article for an extremely prestigious journal in between mopes. I'm not usually so forthcoming about my emotions, you know. By the way, the gentleman who calculated the age of the earth from the Bible – his name was James Ussher and he was the Archbishop of Armagh. What did you do?'

'I worked. I've not seen anyone since I saw you. Except Nest that night, and,' she stopped for a second but decided to tell, even if he laughed, 'some rather odd women who came to see me. Nest sent the Comforters Division of the Daughters of Nature round to hex me out of my miseries after I'd come upon you and Agnes – I'd got everything out of focus, I think. She was worried.'

'You mean you consulted *witches*! You are joking? No, you're not. Am *I* enchanted then? You haven't put the black spot in Agnes's hand have you? You don't *believe* in all that stuff, surely? Did they arrive on ecologically sound electrically-driven broomsticks, come in red cloaks? What did they do with you?'

'No, they were just two ordinary women in ordinary clothes, with extraordinary presence. All they did was light candles and sing me to sleep, I think. It was odd.' Just how odd, she could not explain. 'They locked the doors and shut the windows. It was very hot. They didn't seem to mind I wasn't taking it seriously. They were very persuasive. Someone ought to employ them selling double-glazing. There were more of them, I think, circling outside the house, chanting, sort of, in harmony . . . I can't remember anything more. I was terribly tired and never saw them go. I knew you'd laugh.'

'So they didn't ask you to whip out your chequebook and make a huge donation?'

'No. They just came, sang, and left. I woke up feeling much better and with the painting all done for the moment, I spent the last three days just doing blissfully mundane things, like cleaning the windows, making a skirt and lying in the shade with a book. I've even finished *Gulliver's Travels*.'

'Is that the skirt? It's very pretty. Did you know you could see through it, against the light? Can you cook and sing and spin as well? You are extraordinary. A lunatic. You think you brought me over here by witchcraft? It wasn't you that cut my hair? I'm joking, I'm joking.'

'Oh, Nut! No. I was going to come over to you myself. Isn't it funny, I'm sure they said it would take three days.'

'Blue told me, from Nest, that I was to keep away for three days, under threat of bastinado. It's all the power of suggestion.'

She fetched a wheelback kitchen chair and seated him on it outside in the sun, threw a blue-and-white checked tea towel about his shoulders and started to snip and shape around the bent and vulnerable neck. She'd often barbered Oscar's hair; pale, straight, slippery hair. Nut's hair sprang forcefully from his head, glossy, alive and slightly curling, each lock a trail of sparks between her fingers. A tiny far-fetched thought came uncomfortably to her concerning the whereabouts of Nut's thick plait. Something to do with red cloaks. No, it was too silly. It *must* have been Agnes.

'There – head up – don't fidget, the blades are close to your ear – that's better. A bit choirboy for someone of your great age, but that's what your hair seems to want to do.' Snip, snip.

'I'll trust you.' The smile was devastating as he peered slyly up at her and she caught the briefest glimpse of the ten-year-old Francis Nutmeg.

'Well, you shouldn't.' Snip, snip. 'Are you a Catholic or a Proddy?'

'Neither. Well, I suppose I'm a Catholic. I was baptised one, but after first communion my father lost interest and my mother took over. At one point they gave me the choice but I couldn't bear to offend either of them. Primary school was Catholic, Secondary was Protestant. I got bullied at both which makes for atheism. That's all there is to it. Now, you'll tell me about Freda?'

'Freda is a concatenation. There's a word for one of your Conclusions! It happened when we were visiting Canterbury, to see my mother's Aunt Maude when I was five or six and went into the cathedral and saw the Saint Eustace wall paintings – or rather copies of them. I was never taught to say bed-time prayers and I'd barely been into a church then, let alone a High Anglican cathedral smelling of incense. Then we went down into the crypt to the Chapel of Our Lady Undercroft where there is a ceiling painted with a starry pattern and a gilded bronze statue of the Virgin and Child, and candles, and a very heavy sense of mystery, of depth, both mental and physical, deep down in the bowels of the earth. That was before the days when it became overcrowded with giggling Japanese and screeching French teenagers on coach tours. I was allowed to light a candle and make a wish or say a prayer, whatever you will. It all seemed immensely powerful. The candles, I could feel the heat from the candles . . . Then we went back and had tea in the garden with Great Aunt Maude. She left this house to Aunt Nest – move your head a little this way, there, almost finished – she had a statue in the garden, a Ceres, with a garland of wheat and a cornucopia. It was pretty. The statue became wonderfully confused with the Virgin Mary I'd seen in the Cathedral. I asked Aunt Maude what the statue's name was and she said Freda. So that was it. For years all desires and secrets and a certain amount of adoration were bestowed on a transmogrified female deity. It was a naturally occurring religious urge, albeit pagan. So, there it is.'

'I've heard of children having imaginary friends and pets, but never one with a tame goddess. As a child I had a magic bone.'

'Tell me? What were its powers?' Snip.

'It was a cow's leg bone I found in a field. I cut a Viking pattern on it; it was more of a wishing bone – I wish that Kevin McGee would fall in the lake and drown himself – I wish that Siobhan O'Brien would hold my hand, that sort of thing. It didn't actually work, of course. I buried it when we left Ireland thinking it would be nice for someone else to find. I'd stopped loving it when I was ten but it hung around in my bedroom for a while, breathing out irrationality. Have you finished, now?' He did not mention the small sister who in spite of all the bone-wishing, had died of meningitis when she was five.

The sudden, unexpected but wished-for, easy intimacy of holding his head between her hands was overwhelming, and she became contrarily crisp and matter-of-fact.

'We'll have to make it an early lunch. I have to be at Geraldine's at three. You know, I think her hair was red too, when she was young, though I imagine it to have been more fine-cut orange marmalade, not such depth of colour as yours.' She finished the personal journey round his face and neck, softly blew away the feathered clumps and tufts that decorated his shoulders.

They went to the Bell and Hatchet for lunch and sat outside at a table in the hazy sunshine, ate and covertly watched each other eating. Nut's appetite, which had all but deserted him during the past week, vigorously returned. He rolled his shirt sleeves up and set to, snapping off the prawns' pink heads, and without removing the shells and legs crunched up the bodies with relish, devouring not only his own lettuce and bread and butter, but seeing she hadn't touched hers, with permission ate most of that as well. He watched her lingering over her share, squeezing a little pool of lemon juice onto her plate, frowningly de-whiskering and peeling them with extraordinary spiky fingers, examining the little segmented bodies and dipping them in lemon before popping them into her mouth. She looked preoccupied in spite of what she'd said about not being scared, as if a child's pre-school fear still lurked inside her. She watched his hands busy with the food, the long curving line from point of elbow to wrist bone and was suddenly aghast at having to leave him that afternoon.

'What's the matter, Queen Bea?'

She tried to drag herself back to the business fast approaching. 'I'm trying not to worry. Little worries, but they refuse to drown. They never give one quite enough lemon, do they?' Then, becoming obscure, 'Do you think trilobites were edible?'

'What can I do? Come with you, perhaps? Lighten up, my love, it'll soon be done with. I'm still hungry.' Grinning, with fishy fingers held out, 'Can I give you a crustacean kiss?'

A camper van cruised by, engorged with disorientated, gawping Belgian tourists. Big-boned Susie came out to collect their plates, chuckled and retreated. A dusty collie who had previously been asleep in the shade of the newspaper shop doorway ambled over to investigate who was eating whom. Somewhere, in a back garden close by, throaty chickens clucked and murmured thoughtfully. His breath blew through her like a breeze in a flute.

'Have we time to go back to ...'

'No, we haven't. I *must* leave in ten minutes.'

'What a strong woman you are! But you're right as usual, I suspect. It'd be a shame to rush things. You'll call me, as soon as it's all over, whatever happens? No, don't call. Come round to me? I'll have a fatted calf ready, although God knows where I'll find one, on a Sunday.' His eyes had narrowed into green slits in the sunlight and she leant her hopeful, prawn-filled person against his shoulder, knew she was sinking deeper and deeper in and couldn't bear to leave. It was nearly time to give in — abandon Freda, take on the Promethean Nut.

'I will. I'll be there between seven and eight. Would you like me to hang a flag from the car, black or white to signal disaster or success as I drive down the road?'

'Yes. I'll be waiting.'

They had to stand up together, all of a single piece, propping each other up and unable to let go.

'I must go, now.'

'Yes, you mustn't be late. Let go my arm then.'

'You let go first.'

'There. I think I'd better sit here a little while behind the table till there's a sign of subsidence.'

She glanced at him furtively, and then drowned him with warm and wicked laughter.

Chapter Twelve

Bea parked out of habit outside her house rather than Geraldine's. Neither Oscar's car nor his bike were in evidence. The strip of grass that ran alongside the brick path had been mown, but the flowerbed beneath the sitting-room window was knee-high with weeds through which poked two or three stunted cornflowers, the sole survivors of seeds sown in March. When she returned the Greensands later that afternoon and if he still did not appear to be in residence, she'd go inside, make decisions. She hung back a minute or two, hugging the memory of Nut's parting embrace, before swinging down from the pick-up, pushing hot hair back from her face and opening Geraldine's creaking iron gate. She strode up the path, appearing as bold as brass to Geraldine, watching for her from the open sitting-room window.

'The door's open, Bea. Come in, my pet, come in!'

In spite of the heat Geraldine had resumed the green cardigan, but emphasised the parrot theme with an orange silk scarf and the new black skirt. She looked dazed.

'I've been being interviewed, Bea, and I didn't even know it was happening!' Her eyes were wide and she sounded as if she had expected a tooth extraction, but had been pleasantly surprised by the skill of the dentist.

The guests turned, expectant and inquisitive as Bea walked in. Her eyes had trouble for a second adjusting to the shade after the brightness of the light outside, the room being all reflected greens from the trees and shrubs beside the window, a sub-marine flickering dancing across the faces of Simon and his son as they put down their coffee cups, got to their feet and extended hands; Simon's was cool and dry-papery, his son's slightly moist and over-firm, his face flushed and he was brandy-breathed. The daughter-in-law, May, a chic small person in black trousers and blue denim shirt, had a near-circular face, the features as neatly painted on the surface as a pattern on a plate. Her smile was small, confined, and her Chinese eyes were sharp and noticing. Bea automatically felt lumbering and large. Beside May on the worn pomegranate sofa was a professional-looking camera, discarded film boxes and a black file. She saw Bea's glance.

'We have been photographing the reluctant Geraldine. I like to take my own pictures to illustrate the profiles. I'm proposing to do an article on her for a magazine.'

'A review you mean, of the retrospective in November?'

'No, I write biographical pieces rather than reviews, although it will obviously contain an appreciation of her work. This is a pre-show piece, an appetiser, to remind those who've not seen her paintings for some time and to inform those who have never seen them. I have been interviewing her over lunch.' She sounded very business-like.

Geraldine closed the window firmly. 'Now, I think it's time we made a move, don't you? I have blankets and cushions, Bea, for the men to sit on in the back.' They had arrived as instructed, very much townies dressed for the country. James had had visions of struggling through deep mud and rushes and wore a khaki bush shirt and trousers tucked into expensive-looking, stout new walking boots. Bea wondered if Geraldine's and Simon's intertwining past had been unearthed during May's interviewing, and what James thought about it.

There was only the faintest smell of burnt egg still hanging about when she led them in to Little Rumm. Simon and James were windblown breathless after their jolting up the track, and speechless with amazement that anyone could live alone in such a desolate place. James was regretting the half-full glass of brandy he'd left at Geraldine's.

'Shall I take you up now, to see the paintings?' asked Bea, eager to get the thing over with. During the drive, in order to turn aside Fate's beady eye, she'd managed to convince herself they'd hate them.

'By all means,' said Simon, recovered from his hellish shaking. He had brushed the worst of the dust from his trousers and was even now rehearsing the telling of the ordeal to his London friends. 'Lead on. Are you coming too, Geraldine?'

'No, there won't be room up there. I'll put on Bea's hat and go and sit in the garden while you contemplate and rummage.' Geraldine was as tense as Bea.

It had been a useful idea, turning the other paintings to the wall. As the Greensands entered the sunny white room, they were faced, undistracted, by the angel picture.

'Wow!' said the perspiring James, who darted forwards, past discomforts forgotten. Simon was silent for a while, then said merely, 'Right! Now let's see the others, one by one.' They spent an hour in the painting room in the heat of the afternoon, questioning, examining, considering. They delved among the sketches and water-colours, asked ever more apparently irrelevant questions till Bea felt ready to explode with nervous tension. Moon-faced Mini-May was moving silently but obtrusively about in her tiny black espadrilles, taking photographs of her talking to James, of her with one of the paintings and again alone by the window. Bea was not expecting an unqualified approval but her mouth had gone dry with apprehension.

Simon produced a red notebook and a pen, and said: 'Now let's see, there are four of the "Freda" paintings completed, and those three large preparatory sketches which are very interesting, worth framing up and showing in their own right. Of course you have the rest of the summer to work? Good, then we'll have another look later and select a few more, say in late September? I'd also like the four smaller oils, particularly the one of the wedding. Could you bring it out again and put it on the chair, there?' This was the painting crowded with figures in a dark marquee, their faces blurred with movement, all except one of whom were leaning suffocatingly in towards the tall central mound of bride, groom and cake. The light was diffused through red striped canvas walls, but came strongly through the opening in the tent, shining on the flaunting exception who was Agnes, dancing on a table.

'Mm. Yes. Yes.' He went and stood by the window, considering as he stared out over the shimmering fields for what seemed like aeons.

'Well, shall we go downstairs, and start organising things? I will of course be writing to you to confirm the details, but Geraldine says you haven't shown before, so I expect there are things you'd like to discuss?'

James and May were still sorting through the water-colours, putting some aside. Bea was witlessly staring at Simon.

'Is something the matter, my dear?'

'No, I mean, I don't know. Have you just offered me a show?'

He looked quizzically at her, then threw back his dishevelled mane of white hair and laughed. Having at first thought him a bit wimpish, Bea began to like him.

'I think I have,' he said, and held out his crisp hand again, to shake on the deal.

They drank tea out of Nest's thick bird-watcher's cups and made lists, wrote notes, discussed which paintings needed to be framed and how, prices (which Bea, starry-eyed, thought veered into the realms of fantasy but she was brought sharply back to earth by taking in the fact that the Gallery's commission was fifty per cent) and Geraldine, quite beside herself with delight, wouldn't stop chattering.

'I told her, you know, but she wouldn't believe me. Bea,

where's the painting of your sleeping friend? Has Simon seen it? James, don't you think that the one of the Freda-angel is otherwordly? And that dark water-colour portrait of her father outside the ironmonger's shop window with the sun setting, isn't it exciting? I do love water-colours used like that, full strength. You'll need a photograph, Bea, of yourself, for the exhibition card, won't she, Simon?'

'May's taken care of that while we were upstairs. Now, Bea. I need a brief autobiography, since you have no relevant CV. I think its important to include some of the smaller water-colours too, since they appear to be studies for the larger paintings.'

'I *am* dreaming this,' thought Bea, pink with embarrassment at the approval and little warning bells jangling guiltily as she began to discover the rare pleasure in being approved of. 'There must be some mistake. I mustn't float away on a cloud. This is happening because of Geraldine – he wants so badly to indulge her,' she started to write out the requested list of titles, sizes and mediums used, 'but I must get them out of here; they're driving me insane.'

Chattering and even squabbling a little they were manoeuvred back into the truck. Bea drove back again to Bellhurst silently bubbling with joy and almost beside herself with excitement. She was intent now on the next move and was muttering a Monopoly mantra: 'Pass GO, Collect £200, grab your get-out-of-jail free card and get back to Nut.'

Oscar's car, she noticed, had acquired a new dent. It was parked outside the cottage, which seemed so normal that it was a second or two before it dawned upon her. The day was filled with sticky complications. She might have to face him. A shadow crossed the glorious afternoon. Involuntarily she checked the time, five-thirty. No, not now, she couldn't. It would spoil everything.

Geraldine almost danced up the path, forcing Simon to bend stiffly and sniff the chocolate-scented *Cosmos* and insisting that Bea come in with them to have a sherry, collect the badger's skull and see the painting of it. Bea agreed, needing time to think. What would it be like to see Oscar after three months apart? Knowing that he had also had a fling with Agnes? Disquieted, she followed them in to collect the skull, politely refused a drink, truthfully admired the painting, and thanking Simon gratefully for his time and the offer, said good-byes and promised a London visit soon to see the gallery and the space which would be hers. She hugged Geraldine in gratefulness and backed out into the garden, waving. Geraldine threw open the sitting-room window and leant out, orange silk scarf catching on the yellow rose bush, calling out:

'You see, it wasn't impossible, was it?' She disentangled the scarf with an impatient jerk. 'Good-bye, my dear, and watch out! I've become a boldy oldie!'

There was the summer smell of grass cuttings, of some sweet lemony scented rose which covered the dead apple tree in the garden. She was startled by the opening of the front door of Fleming Cottage and the incautious appearance of Agnes, hand in hand with Oscar. At that point Bea was hidden from their view by the apple tree. Her inclination was to run for the truck and get the hell out of it but it was the hand in hand bit which floored her. Stunned, she stared as they came down the path. Agnes halted as she noticed Bea's truck first, then let out a squawk of panic as she saw Bea herself, standing both indignant and irresolute on the path of the house next door. Agnes skidded on the bricks in her pretty sandals and dropped her little bag. Oscar, in the middle of a sentence, went scarlet, then paled, pale as his hair, which Bea noticed had been cut much shorter. He was wearing a pink shirt which she hadn't seen before and was considerably plumper. Her heart lurched in such a violent fashion that she felt herself turn sick and shaky. Their own shocked surprise made things suddenly quite clear to her. They had been laughing. So, he had forgiven Agnes for kicking him in the balls. They had made up their differences. Nut, Nut had definitely been to Agnes what Terence had so deftly described as an interim passion.

To their great discomfort Bea now laughed, all the way
on jelly legs, a long way — a mile at least it seemed — from
Geraldine's front garden to the truck. She climbed up into
the hot cab, still grinning viciously, placed the badger's skull
carefully on the meltingly hot plastic seat beside her, and started
up the engine. Agnes was instantly at the window, saying things
at first placatory, then, as usual, defiant. '. . . but you didn't want
him, you said you didn't . . .'

'Piss off, you cow!' shouted Bea suddenly, making Agnes
jump. She put the truck into reverse and shouted some more.
It felt pretty good, shouting. 'I don't give a damn about Oscar.
Oscar's second-hand, third-hand, junk-shop stuff. I don't care
now how many little slappers he stuffs. You knew he'd left
Andreary, had come back, and didn't tell me because you wanted
him yourself! You've always been after him. Am I right? It's you
having a go at Nut that I care about, more than anything. How
could you? How could you cut off his lovely hair?'

She stopped and stared straight into Agnes's shocked wet-
slate eyes, noticing the small bruise on the cheekbone, and saw
that Nut's suspicions were proven. Then she spoke more quietly,
although it was still audible to Oscar. 'How much did you enjoy
making me look a fool? Not much — it must have been too easy.
Did you ever think at all? What the fuck did you think you
were doing? You terrified the wits out of Nut and nearly ruined
our lives.' She jerked backwards in the truck, regained control of
herself and executed a perfect three-point turn. Then she leant
out of the window and said to Oscar, still whitely gaping at the
gate: 'You've got obscenely fat.' Agnes, crying now and suddenly
impassioned, called out, 'Well at least I can give Oscar what he
wants! I'm pregnant, Bea, I'm pregnant!'

'Poor old Oscar,' called out Bea, 'I didn't know you had it
in you! I'll give you sixteen to one it's not yours.'

The Greensands, their taxi to the station due at six,
were crowded round Geraldine's window unashamedly watching
and listening, fascinated. They now gave her a round of

applause. She waved cheerily to them and roared off. Geraldine would explain.

Agnes's eyes were brimming as she and Oscar hurriedly retreated to the cottage for shelter and recriminations. She thought she heard Mrs Lewis's husky, mocking laughter as the heel of her sandal detached itself and flapped awkwardly as they scurried back up the path to shut the door again behind them. There was a lot of explaining to do and Agnes wasn't sure her imagination was up to it. She had tried to seduce Nut out of sheer devilry. It had just seemed an interesting idea at the time. She could see now his alarm, his intended rejection ... No, of course he wouldn't have rejected her, it was only that Bea had burst in and he'd felt guilty. Oh well, that was just a little mistake, now she had Oscar back in line. Fight. She would fight for Oscar, and the pretty cottage and garden. She'd gone to the doctors pretty smartly though, when she was two weeks late and it had taken a panicky few days patching up with Oscar, but Bea might now have screwed up that a bit ...

Oscar paced up and down in the sitting room, wonderingly running through the convolutions of the scene. Bea had looked amazing, just slightly tanned and shiningly healthy, hair much longer. He was wondering how to cope without Phil at the ironworks – he had never forgotten that blow to the nose. The weekend with Agnes in London and the few odd evenings afterwards had been a spur-of-the-moment thing; he'd left the practicalities of it to her, never imagining she would actually be able to extricate herself from her family for a whole weekend and had been a little nervous when she'd phoned to say it was all arranged. Despondently alone after the debacle of Andrea and in the face of Bea's apparent indifference, there had been Agnes panting for him, most flatteringly adoring. His efforts to break off the affair had caused an appalling scene. Yet today, today she'd brought him the test results from the surgery and he was so exhilarated by the idea of a child that he'd almost forgotten about Phil, almost forgotten how she'd cheated on him by not delivering his letter; it sounded as though it would have had little effect anyway . . .

'It's going to be a real bore to have to find someone else at such short notice,' he said, a little petulantly.

'What do you mean, find someone else?' She was staring at him, horror-struck. He hadn't thought she could be so daft.

'Don't be ridiculous Agnes. Phil and I can't go on working together after this. He'll resign. When are you going to tell him? Who is Nut? And who's collecting Seb from your mother's?'

'Poor, poor Phil,' thought Bea. She was driving automatically, thinking furiously. 'Agnes always lets people down.' It had been a shock, to see them holding hands like children. That's what they were, children, in which case they deserved each other and should get on famously. Bitch-child Agnes.

The heat was shimmering on the road, causing wavering watery mirages on the hot tarmac ahead. The marsh was smothered in a hovering heat haze and fields of wheat, just turned to dusty gold, hemmed her in on either side, bowing as she rattled past unseeing.

'I just wish that if she was so unhappy with Phil, she could have bothered to look a little further for a replacement. Replacements.' Bea corrected herself. 'Right on her own doorstep. How lazy. Oh hell! It doesn't matter how it came about. I knew, I knew the whole thing was over between us, before Oscar even left, and wouldn't let myself believe it. But why, why did she go for Nut? Just for fun, to see if she could pull him? Or did she really want to hurt me? Why? I must have done something to get up her nose so badly. And there's poor, monstrous little Seb, who thinks Phil is his Daddy. Will she drag him off to live with Oscar, or stay and battle it out with Phil? Which would be worse for him?'

By now she'd reached the track without remembering having driven there at all. Time to celebrate with Nut. The saga of Nut, and the paintings (she had a feeling it would be a saga and not a fairy story – there'd been quite enough fairy stories) had just begun. She'd be so bold even Geraldine would be shocked.

Bea indulged in a ritual bath to cleanse away the day, ex-husband, ex-friend and the sweat of fear of unknown people. She lay there twiddling toes and chin on chest, looked down her own length, thinking how funny her breasts looked from that angle, rising up out of the deep steamy water like white islands with small coral castles on the top. She shaved her legs and sang a snatch of 'Pirate Jenny', thinking serious sex with Nut and knowing that even if it were no better than with Oscar or poor Terence, she would still want him. Oscar had been a destination, a full stop, when she was seventeen. Nut was a destiny she'd been trying to dodge. One must keep trying. The bath water swirled away with all her stale young past, as if sucked down by a thirsty biographer.

Dressed in the now fading indigo skirt and shirt and digging hurriedly about in a drawer, she found a white halter-neck top that Agnes had once lent her and went outside to fix it to the bent and useless aerial of the truck: a white flag of success. She was startled by a strange hiss from the back and went round to investigate. Geraldine, in her concern for Simon's aged behind, had kindly placed a folded tartan rug on the floor of the truck just behind the cab, and on it was now encamped a white farmyard goose.

There was no end to these birds! Had someone put it there in the half hour or so she'd been indoors? She suspected a Nut joke and walked cautiously round the house to make sure no one was hiding. Perhaps it was injured. She couldn't go to Nut's place accompanied by a goose! Letting the tailboard down and hitching up her skirt, she climbed up but it resisted shooing and arched its neck, put its weaving head down level with the floor and hissed again, the mad blue eyes warning. She bravely put her arms around its body and tried pinning the suddenly thrashing wings to its sides, making a quick grab for the snaking neck but it hissed more ferociously than ever, jabbed and nipped her with its horny orange beak and she lost her nerve and jumped out in a hurry and re-fixed the tailboard. It stared at her, ruffling its snowy feathers. It obviously thought the rug was a nest. It was seven o'clock and Nut would have started his vigil. Since he had a way with birds, he could damn well deal with it! She fetched a blanket and slung it over the vituperative bird which thus extinguished, fell immediately silent.

Broad-shouldered, whippet-hipped, Francis Nutmeg leant against a telegraph pole at the side of the empty road, long hand shading eyes against the slanting sun, watching for her as she slowly approached along the pot-holed tarmac. His house was ready, tidied and scrubbed, flowers in a milk jug, food cooking in the oven. He spotted the white pennant, waved ecstatically and punched the air, leapt to open the cab door and handed her down.

'There! I nearly didn't bother to look, I was so certain it would be white not black. I'm quite relieved. If it had been black I thought you might want me to throw myself in the sea like King Aegeus.' She was almost smothered by his hot embrace and struggled loose, still perturbed by the problem of the truck's cargo.

'Nut, there's a goose in the back of the truck!'

He looked startled. 'But you shouldn't have bothered, my Bea. I have a little leg of lamb roasting in the oven! And the best of new potatoes, all waxy and yellow ...'

'No, not to eat! The goose is alive, and terribly cross. It won't get out and I don't know how it got there.'

Nut also walked round the back, swung aboard athletically, and removed the blanket. There was a further frenzied hissing.

He jumped down again. His way with birds did not apparently extend to domesticated members of the *Anserinae* family and besides, his mind was on other things.

'Come on, we've better things to do than worry about mad geese. We'll leave it alone and perhaps it'll take itself off.'

'Perhaps it's going to lay an egg?'

'Too late in the year. Now let's *leave* it.'

'Yes, of course. Do you think she might like a bowl of water?'

'We'll bring one out later.' Dear God, he was thinking, am I never going to have her whole attention? She became aware that she had all his and took his arm, distancing herself from goose, and the whole hot cauldron of the day.

Nut produced a bottle of champagne with a flourish from the midget fridge in the kitchen and picking up a couple of glasses, led her through the sunroom out to the wooden deck where he'd placed two chairs and laid a white cloth on a sea-bleached wooden table.

'It seemed a pity to waste another fine evening and supper won't be ready for half an hour. Now sit down, just there, at a proper distance from me, so I can look at you while you tell the story.'

She recounted the stages of the afternoon, the Greensands' offer, Geraldine's overexcitement, but deleted Oscar and Agnes from the script. His eyes never left her face but for once she wasn't self-conscious, her own being similarly engaged. While she spoke and sipped the champagne, children called to each other in the distance, pastel washing flapped on the next door railway-carriage's line, a black-and-white collie dog picked its way across the shingle, a stick in its mouth and a long shadow in front of it. Gulls cruised past, the early evening sun shining through their transparent wing-tip feathers. The power station hummed in the background and the lamb sizzled in the oven. An unlikely and ridiculous place in which to be drinking champagne; but no such place exists.

'It's a beautiful soft evening, isn't it? You've got the sun in your eyes. Turn around a bit, and I'll go and carve.'

The lamb was pink and tender, the potatoes just as he said they would be and he'd tossed up a sharp green salad with dandelion leaves and borage flowers. His legs were firmly clamped on either side of hers as they ate, as if to prevent her from escaping. He could cook. It was definitely love.

'In this light, you look as if you'd been lightly coated all over with cream,' he said, stroking her shoulder and seeing in the half-veiled blue eyes staring at him in the early twilight an expression combining delighted surprise, smugness and not a little cunning, a lottery winner at last. He reached forward and with a cool hand stroked back the tangle of hair from her forehead. Her entire interior from scalp to toes had been transformed to honey.

'That's what it feels like. I didn't know it could be like that,' she stammered, a little shy of what she was about to say. 'I mean I knew it could be better, if I could get there, but I never did, quite, before.'

'You're joking!' He sat up, disbelieving, shocked. 'You *never* had an orgasm?'

'No, I'm *not* joking! And no, not like now.'

'But you were with your husband ... how long?'

'Twelve years.'

'What a good thing you're shot of him! Oh Bea, what a waste, and what fun! And it's barely dark. The whole night's ahead of us. I think there's some cream in the fridge.'

'And how did you sleep, Bountiful Bea?'

'Oh! pretty well, considering ...' She rolled over lazily, insolently exultant eyes peering at him through tangled hair. She was back inside her skin – a comfortable skin – warm, loved, melted. 'We used to play a game with our grandmother, Patrick and I, called 'I love my love with an A ...'

'Because they're anxious, awkward, argumentative, amorous, agnostic, archaic,' he rattled them out, ticking them off on his fingers and then found more '... amicable, amusing, arrogant, aggravating, anatomically perfect ... Yes, I played that in the waiting room before the dentist ... Where are you off to? Oh I see. Here, wrap this about you. We're not like you, living in the wilderness, we have neighbours here and I don't see why they should get the benefit of the sight of you through a window when I've had to wait so long.'

He knelt up on the bed and wrapped a length of blue-and-green printed cotton around her as she stood, rolling over the top like a sarong.

'There, that's my dressing gown. I didn't think myself a jealous man till That Morning. Now I'm disgustingly jealous and hate to let you out of my sight. But I will, though. I was quite fearful that you would disappear last night, between the roast lamb and the bedroom. I'll trust you not to dissolve into a pool of sea water or slip off with a seal while I make us tea?'

'I wasn't jealous either, till That Afternoon,' she called out. Almost loth to wash away the night, Bea stood turning herself beneath the shower then dried with Nut's green towel, surveying the extent of his personal things lying there in the prismed sunlight from the patterned frosted glass, and greedily knew that even his belongings were now a part of her. The green toothbrush and black razor lying on the edge of the basin, the twisted toothpaste tube squeezed from the middle and wearing a collar of dried paste (they wouldn't have rows about that, at least, she thought, grinning, an offender herself). She even sniffed the soap and felt a personal fondness for his balding shaving brush. Already missing his presence, she tied the sarong about her again, went and stood in the doorway of the little dark kitchen, watching his dark shape framed against the brightness of the tiny window, unable to get enough of looking at him, destroyed by the tall grace of his body, completely and utterly at ease with it and for once, with her own.

'*You* don't seem worried that the neighbours might walk past the windows?'

'They could only see me from the waist up.'

'Nut! We've forgotten the goose! She might be lying there, dead in the back of the truck!' She leapt for the door, stopping long enough to slip her feet into Nut's Herculean boots and shuffle clumsily across the hot shingle to the roadway. Nut followed, swearing, struggling into his trousers as he hurried after her. An old boy passing on a bicycle wobbled lethally across the road. Was he witnessing an attack? Should he pedal furiously for the nearest telephone box? But he knew Nut by sight and remembering the night of the witches, decided that nudity was now the fashion in the area and pedalled on, glancing back, shaking his head and clucking as he saw that the hopping, red haired chap had now managed to get both legs into his jeans and now decently buttoned up, was tentatively barefooting after the girl. He'd not catch her at that speed anyway and the girl was turning about, calling to him, from the back of a truck. Nothing to worry about, though from what he'd seen, you'd need a fire extinguisher to put that man out once he was taken with a passion. That was flaming red hair, and no mistake.

'Nut, she's gone! Do you think someone stole her, or that she went off on her own?'

'I guess she managed by herself. I've stepped in a goose turd. Perhaps she's a sea-going bird.'

'I was quite looking forward to keeping a goose.'

'Never mind. Can I have my boots back, please? I think I've trodden on some broken glass as well. I'll give you a piggy-back.' He bent and she mounted, clutching at the slithering sarong. 'Hey up, off we go. I was thinking of taking the morning off. You don't have a pressing reason for going back to Little Rumm, do you?'

'No. Of course I'm carrying on with the painting, but the

pressure's over. It's been a little bit like being on a pilgrimage, a static pilgrimage, more of a retreat perhaps.'

'Then here's a cockleshell for you to prove it. You'll have to sew that on your hatband, like the pilgrims to Santiago de Compostella.' He stooped to pick it up and she shrieked and clung, almost catapulted over his head. She slid down from his back at the door.

'What's this bird's-nest stuff on the ground here?' She bent to examine a mound of tangled, reddish threads weaving through a ground-hugging, wind-dwarfed clump of broom.

'That's dodder. It's parasitic, like mistletoe. Its leaves are too small to see, but look, it's got minute pink flowers dotted about it.' He crouched down to show her. The expanse of naked shoulders, the bloom on the fair skin, the slim line of the spine, dividing the two sets of muscles, diving below the back of the old salt-water-stained black jeans had a marvellously erotic effect; she became supremely uninterested at that moment in either the goose or little pink flowers.

Half an hour later they heard the overfamiliar sounds of a police car but did not allow it to interrupt them.

They were unaware then that Agnes, having found that Oscar was a little too interested in the paternity of her forth-coming child to be comfortable, had driven down to the sea, bought a ticket for visiting the old lighthouse and was now at the top of it, clutching at the railing and threatening to dash herself to the ground below if Oscar refused to believe her. She was rather cross about having to buy a ticket, since she felt that attempted suicide was one of those missions that should have made her eligible for at least some sort of discount, if not free entry. Oscar was sent for and panted up the one hundred and sixty-nine steps in a sweating, panic-driven fury, the policewoman attending the emergency having been unsympathetic both to his pleas of innocence and his rather querulous and vague shouts to Agnes from the safety of the ground. Out of embarrassment and genuine fear for her safety, he promised all manner of things which he later would have preferred to forget, and took her back to Fleming Cottage.

A couple of days later, when things had calmed down a little and Bea and Nut could support the idea of sharing a moment of their Olympian hours together with mere mortals, Bea rang first Geraldine and then Nest, who responded exultantly to the news of the promised exhibition.

'Darling! I always knew you'd pull it off! What an excitement though, a London show straight off! Can Blue and I come and see at last what you've been up to?'

'Of course you can, Aunt Nest. That's why I'm telephoning, to thank you for all your help, particularly the curiously sedative couple of occult envoys, who worked so well. How about a celebratory supper at Little Rumm, Thursday night? Geraldine's coming. I knew about it on Sunday, but made myself wait for written confirmation, in case it was just a nice dream. It came this morning. There's something else. I want you to meet Nut. He's very eager to meet you.' Nut stood behind her, his sharp nose buried in her neck, stroking a shoulder, sliding his other hand around her hip and downwards, distracting.

Nest's pride in the rightness of her convictions knew no bounds – she was the instigator, a thaumaturge, a Svengali! She raced off to find Blue and discovered him in the little office behind the long greenhouse, his feet on the desk, reading a tattered copy of *Memoirs of a Midget*. A muddy finger was passing slowly along the lines and his lips were moving. That was another of her successes, having taught him to read.

One late August morning Oscar stood impatiently in the drought-stricken front garden of Fleming Cottage, waiting for Bea to put in an appearance. It was an unbearably sticky day and both weeds and herbaceous plants had suffered that summer – the flowerbeds were a tangled mane of fawn and tawny seedpods and cracks had appeared in the dried-out little patch of lawn.

The agent's sign in the dusty hedge now had SOLD slapped across it and in two days' time the new owners would move in. It was over.

Bea drew up in her truck. It was the apocalyptic day when they met to split the remainder of their possessions; they had already discussed settlements at the end of July and The Divorce was now on its stealthy journey. She imagined it passing through letter boxes and across solicitors' desks, in and out of IN and OUT trays, being tapped out on word-processors, dated, sealed, stamped, preserved, laminated, set in concrete and tied up in pink ribbon.

She looked very good, Oscar thought unguardedly as the blooming, polished Bea approached up the brick path, a little plumper and smoother in neat black jeans and T-shirt, smiling pleasantly (she could not help smiling since she was, as everyone had been telling him for some time now, perfectly happy), her thick hair twisted up into a large golden knot, striped further by the sun and escaping wildly in all directions.

'Isn't it a relief it's gone so quickly?' she said, nodding at the agent's board. 'Shall we go in and start at once? It needn't take long. I know what's yours – you know what's mine. We could toss a coin for the rest.'

He followed her. She had a little heart-shaped patch of sweat between her shoulder-blades. He was unable quite to believe that he had lost forever that lithe body. But it had happened. He had made it happen. And now he had Agnes, and his child to come although he still had doubts. They sorted through the remaining books: SAS and motorcycle manuals in one box, everything else in the other.

'The baby's due in March,' he said casually, evaluating the depth of the circular ripples of thought floating out across her face.

'Jolly good for you!' she said, as if he'd scored a century in a school cricket First XI, smiling up at him, brow shining. She brushed a dangling piece of hair aside and carried on packing.

'That's my school Bible, the Coleridge and the Penguins and the Revision notes on *Othello*, that's your *Fungus the Bogeyman* – is the RHS *Vegetable Gardening* yours or mine? Yours? OK. Shall we do the china next?' She could be discomfited by nothing.

On the kitchen table was a box of odds and ends which Agnes had brought with her only a few weeks before, on the sadly ill-founded assumption that she and Seb would be moving permanently into Fleming Cottage with Oscar. Oscar was unable to raise the amount needed to buy Bea out without borrowing exorbitantly and so the cottage had to be sold; they were now domiciled, or rather incarcerated, in a rented flat on the far side of Bellhurst, with no garden at all for poor Seb to play in.

Bea began piling china out on to the table. 'Look, I remember these plates came from your mother . . . and these are mine, Aunt Maude's. I'm sure there were *two* vegetable dishes?' She looked up, querying.

'Seb . . .' began Oscar, but Bea swiftly interrupted him.

'Say no more. And this pile is wedding presents. Oscar, do pay attention or we'll never be finished. You pack these away in your box. Have you got a coin in your pocket? Right, give it to me. Heads or tails for the silver saltcellars. Heads? Tails. I seem to have got them. Now you spin it and I call for the toast-rack. Actually I don't want it anyway. Now for the teaspoons . . .' here her voice trembled. She had not expected to have to take charge so completely, while Oscar stayed mum, staring desperately at her, his throat working. Her lack of sentimentality had always thrown him.

'Oscar?'

'Yes?' His voice, diminished to no more than a croak, came from miles away.

'We can't change anything, now. I don't want to, never really wanted to, I'm afraid. I told you, even if Agnes and Geraldine had passed on your messages, it would have been far too late. I don't feel any animosity towards either of them for not doing so, since I might have felt I ought to give it another try,' she looked squarely at him, at the fair hair sticking to his forehead in the heat, 'and I know now that it would have been utterly wrong for both of us, and it's very miserable of you to try and make *me* feel guilty. It's quite obviously your turn to look after Agnes. Everybody else has tried it and failed.'

Oscar swallowed, did as he was told and they spun and spun the twopenny piece till the things had all been fairly divided and tucked away in their respective boxes.

Civilised to the last, together they carried out and packed into the truck the small amount of furniture and boxes. Neither of them desired the bed. The curtains and rush matting went with the house.

'How will you manage on your own, at the other end?'

'I have Nut, waiting to help.' She looked at him a trifle anxiously. 'We're getting married, after the show in November.'

Oscar looked sharply at her. 'What show?'

'Of course. You haven't been told. I'm being given a show at the Greensand Gallery in London. Geraldine has one half of the gallery for a retrospective and I get the other.'

Oscar felt dazed. Bea reached out a hand and put it on his upper arm to balance herself and leant forwards from a distance, planting a cool kiss on his cheek. Oscar sensed the chasm between their bodies with an interior sob of self-pity.

'I'm going in to see Geraldine now. We'll be in touch. 'Bye.' She half turned, then came back to him. 'Is Agnes at the flat this afternoon?' Oscar, looking down and playing with his key ring, said she probably was.

'What's the flat like?'

'Not too bad. It looks out over an orchard – it's quite pretty. But they're cutting it down soon to build executive homes.'

Poor Agnes, Bea thought. She'd love an 'executive home'.

Geraldine O'Brien, painting *molto furioso* in her sitting room, on glancing up from her easel saw them by the truck, standing so very much apart and gave an almost vulpine grin and waved, a little wildly, as Bea came up to the door. The pointer measuring her state of mind over the course of the summer had gone from 'deep sleep', passed 'calm' at some speed, and was now quivering nervously somewhere between 'excitable' and 'manic'.

'Won't you be glad when this hot spell is over? I can't wait for one of those cool mornings, when one can see all the spiders' webs laid out in the grass covered in dew, and smell decay. I'm old and decaying and now take an even greater interest in the process. It's nearly mushroom time. You do look wonderful. Are you pregnant yet?' She vigorously cleaned a brush and looked at Bea with interest.

'Oh, I shouldn't think so for a moment.'

'So, it's all sorted out is it, Bea? There were no confrontations about who has the salt spoon and who the saltcellar? Well done! Now what do you think of this picture? Hold on a minute, I've some iced coffee ready in the kitchen. You must be parched after all the emotionals.'

Bea watched her with affectionate amusement as she spun about the kitchen, fussing through the drawers for spoons and hunting among the geraniums on the windowsill for sugar. She was moving very fast these days. Bea wondered if perhaps she been prescribed tranquillisers for other reasons than distress, had been a little overexcitable even before her breakdown.

'There's no hurry, Geraldine!'

'No, of course not. I seem to be whizzing about these days. There's still so much to do before this exhibition. Now, there we are. Come into the sitting room and tell me what you think.'

The painting was of flowers – just the flowers, no stalks or leaves, and they were crushed together to cover the entire small canvas; loosely painted in some areas, more sharply focused in others, glowing, slightly sinister. Roses, their faded silk velvet petals insect-nibbled. Bent-petalled daisies, dying lilies, withered irises ... from a distance it was a pretty Victorian posy – from close-up, something else entirely. Bea wanted it quite badly.

'It's incredibly decadent. I love it.'

'The idea came from all those unfortunate flowers dying in the sun in their silvery paper pokes; cut, chopped and suffocated when the Princess of Wales died. I'm planning to paint rotting pumpkins in the winter. The moulds that grow on them are stunning. Putrescence can be so intensely colourful. Simon's coming down again next week to have his final pick and to see which of our new ones can fit in, so he can get the catalogue printed, I suppose. Are you excited? I am. No stage-fright at all. See?' She held out a remarkably unsteady hand.

'Bea, do you never have periods?' Nut leant up on an elbow, a mug of tea in his hand, watching Bea speculatively as she lay reading one of the multifarious sections of the welter of Sunday newspapers, cosily propped up on the pillows in the bedroom at Little Rumm. Bea was startled and glanced at him slightly apprehensively.

'Oh, yes, occasionally. Normally only about three or four times a year ... I thought it was great, getting off so lightly ... is that what you're on about? I did warn you there's little chance of me becoming pregnant.'

'And why didn't you find out what was wrong? Didn't you want children?'

'Nut, I lived in dreamtime, then. Nothing mattered much except keeping Oscar at bay and as happy as possible so there was time to draw. I wasn't bothered since I never felt anything was wrong. The idea of intervention was frightening.'

She folded up the newspaper in a great untidy rustling mess and ruffled about searching for the colour magazine, then looked up at him again, anxiously. 'Do you mind about not having children? Because if you do, I'll find out if it can be solved, immediately.' She sighed. 'Now Agnes is in pod, it looks as if it probably was my fault, all along.' She put the paper down and looked at the foxy length of him, his cheek pushed up with his fist and the sea-water eye above it narrowed, shining like a pale green tourmaline.

'No, I'm easy. You get your career going. It would be nice to have a daughter though, don't you think? I'd like to have a copy of you, if at all.'

Nut could imagine, almost touch, a little giggling thing, golden or red-haired, in a green cotton dress, running up and down the sand while he chased her, caught her and lifted her up close to his heart. The vision was clear enough to be quite disturbing. His eyebrows were twitched together for an instant and a shadow lay across his face.

'I just wondered,' he continued, carefully picking his words, 'if you might perhaps be pregnant and were hiding it from me till you were certain sure. You'd tell me, wouldn't you, if you were? You've got rounder all over, more curvy. Your behind is sumptuous. A juicy-lucy bum.' He left it at that most wisely, and cowered since she was threatening to beat him to a pulp with the rolled-up lifestyle section.

'I'd know if I was pregnant! One feels sick in the morning, and goes off coffee, all that sort of thing. I feel absolutely wonderful and I've loads of energy.'

Three weeks later, driving back from Parden Station after a visit to the Greensands in London, Bea's eyes became unfocused, and she was forced to pull up sharply in a field gateway. With singing-ringing noises in her ears and the sickening sensation of being whirled away down a darkening circular corridor, she fainted. She did not know for how long but on coming round, she had to sit there for a while attempting to regain her equilibrium before shakily continuing on her way back to Nut's house.

She told him about the incident, but because she now felt infinitely better and wonderfully hungry, she made light of it. Nut was cooking smoked sprats for supper and she went down to the shore, feeling suddenly that she needed to be alone for a few minutes. She stood invoking Freda while the cooling September sea made little hissing rushes at her feet and dashed against her shins and along with it came the certainty that she too was pregnant.

She was astonished and a little piqued that it could have happened without her knowing, but this soon gave way to an absolute and tense excitement. Apart from the fact that there was the faintest but agonising possibility that the child might be Terence Moorbury's. Terence had been true to form and taken Extra Large precautions, which she seemed to remember had not been entirely satisfactory. She'd been so certain of her infertility. The child *must* be, *was*, Nut's. This conviction took quite a while to take root, but in the short term she achieved it. The companion seedling fear was temporarily crushed.

The fact was later confirmed and the surprised and congratulatory doctor mentioned spontaneous ovulation as a possibility. Hmph! she thought. If any spontaneous ovulation had occurred, it had definitely not been procured by Terence's doings. During the following months, she never confessed the fear to Nut; her whole being was caught up in the experience of being both impregnable in the mental sense and pregnant in the physical.

If Nut briefly remembered the stranger at the breakfast table he had put the thought aside, preferring to indulge the euphoria waiting in the wings. It was a memory he did not mention to Bea, willing himself to be convinced by the strength of her own apparent certainty. Women, he told himself, firmly disregarding all past biological evidence, know these things. He still did not know if she had slept with Terence or not and no longer cared. He was happy to see Bea apparently so very contented and in his eyes she was as hopelessly seductive and interesting as before; the minutely thickening waist, the swelling breasts made her resemble more and more some secretive renaissance beauty. He was a brave man and a loving man and decided to bite the bullet and not enquire any further — he was besotted and would in any case have taken her on with an army of other men's children.

Geraldine was already at the gallery when Nut arrived with Bea for the private view. Bea could see her through the glass door, wearing a green silk jacket that they'd bought together in Canterbury. She was talking to Amelia and Edmund, gesticulating with her glass of wine as was now her wont, erratically. A niggling November wind nipped their cheeks as they lingered together outside in the London street, looking in at the brightly lit interior and the early-comers wandering about with catalogues in hand, examining the pictures. In the window on the right side of the central plate-glass door hung one of Geraldine's darkly glowing paintings of vegetable decomposition, suspended by invisible nylon thread, and on the left side hung Bea's wedding painting, likewise suspended in mid air. The names Bea Kerepol and Geraldine O'Brien were displayed on the glass window in three inch high white letters.

'Take a deep breath, Bea,' said Nut, sensing her sudden panic, taking hold of her hand and squeezing it before pushing open the door and holding it for her to pass through from the dark evening into the warm, light interior. Once in he stood protectively behind her for a moment, hands comfortingly on her shoulders before propelling her forward. 'Go on, my darling, it's you they want to meet. I can look after myself.'

The strange thing was that she felt completely disassociated from the paintings. 'Good heavens! Did I do that?' was the only thought that occurred as she travelled with Simon round the wall space, admiring how they had been displayed and trying not to notice parts of them which could have been handled better. The rooms filled up rapidly and she was soon whirled away from friendly well-known faces to be introduced to (and interviewed by) terrifying potential clients. Phil came, solid, strong and bitter but so obviously pleased to see her that her heart went out to him.

'I miss Seb dreadfully and I never thought I would. I keep finding little toy cars under cushions. She lets me take him to the playground, now and then ...'

Mary Dunnock arrived with her husband and only two of their offspring, followed by Justin Bullingden who already appeared to know four fifths of the other guests.

'Ah Bea! Before I go and look at the pictures, Terence asked me to give you this.' He handed her an envelope which contained a blown-up photograph of the eye she had made from stones on the beach that unpropitious day in the summer. It had been taken by a crew member on board the boat. On the back was tactfully written: 'Heard about the show from Justin. Congratulations and hope it's a sell-out. Terence' Justin stooped and whispered in her ear. 'He says to tell you he has no hard feelings and sent the picture for good luck.' The reminder of Terence sent an unwelcome frisson to her stomach but she was instantly distracted by the arrival of Aunt Nest, stunning in violet velvet, with an astonishingly washed and manicured Blue.

Nut moved about the rooms on his own while Bea was being busied about, eavesdropping on the private viewers' reactions to her pictures with growing pride, wondering how it was that a person so susceptible to fears and forebodings had achieved work of such astounding self-confidence. He discovered Jane standing predictably bemused before the boat-launching picture.

'*What* is this about? I'm afraid I don't understand it at all. Why is that giantess pulling those people out to sea in a boat? And who are all these robed people, waving? Is it a nursery rhyme? And what does it mean?'

'I wouldn't worry about what it means, Mrs Kerepol. You know Bea. Always abstruse ... That girl is putting a red sticker on its label. Does that mean it's been bought, do you suppose?'

'How exciting. Why do you think they want it?' Nut looked

again at the now familiar picture; Bea, softening in her attitude
to the past summer's incursions by family and friends, had
been altering various parts of it since he'd first seen it in
the painting room. In the prow of the boat standing like a
pair of smug figureheads were himself and Bea. The robed
figures were Jane and Tom, Oscar, Agnes, and others whom
he did not recognise, including, he'd been told, the art teacher
from Bellhurst Grammar. Bea'd explained that it appeared less
intolerant for her and him to be seen sailing away helped by
Freda. To have her parents and acquaintances apparently dragged
out and possibly dumped at sea would not be conducive to
family stability, however much that had been the prickly original
intention. Mercifully Jane had not identified herself.

'Have you seen the portrait of your husband, Mrs Kerepol?'

'Yes, but it doesn't look in the least bit like him, does it? So
very dark-skinned and with all those pinky splotches down the
side of his face. Makes him look as if he had a skin disease.'

Tom had found his portrait and was most impressed with
the finished article. He spent some time standing close by it,
hoping someone would remark on the likeness; it was hard not
to, with the eyepatch so satisfyingly identifying the subject. He
was bursting with pleasure in his daughter's achievement and
indulged in mutual congratulations with Nest.

Blue sauntered about and finally made himself known to
James's secretary who, proving susceptible to both his particular
brand of rough-trade charm and the gap between his front teeth,
briefly disappeared with him downstairs into the stock room to
demonstrate the difference between an etching and a lithograph.

Nut was detailed by James Greensand to ensure that
Geraldine did not hit the bottle and become uncontrollable.

'I'd be so grateful if you could go and engage her in a bit
of banter for a while, make sure she eats some nibbly things,'
pleaded James, refilling Nut's glass. 'I don't want to stop her
enjoying herself, but if you could just keep her down for another
half hour, then it doesn't matter if she kicks off her shoes and

dances a can-can like any other nineteen-fifties bohemian. I must say Bea's being most helpfully lucid this evening. I'd thought that she was something of a shy flower but she's quite overpowered Mrs Gurgelfeldt – the one over there, the old American leather lady all in black, yes, that one with the grey number two haircut – it was like witnessing a confrontation between a seraph and a bat. Oh! Goodie! I can hear the rustle of a chequebook.'

Bea was sweating after her encounter with Mrs Gurgelfeldt, and had hidden in a corner of the gallery where she encountered Patrick bending to look at a set of four early charcoal drawings which had been included in a little section showing the development of her work. These drawings had been done at the age of sixteen and were of Patrick mending a lawn mower.

'I've bought that one, Bea. I thought it ought to stay in the family!'

'Then I'll give you its companion piece as a present.'

'Which one is that?'

'Oh, it isn't here. It's back at home. It's of you at about the same age, smoking secretly behind the hornbeam hedge in that field we used to go to, to get away from all the cooking, if you remember. We used to sit in the wet grass coughing, with clouds of blue smoke drifting up, thinking how adult we were.'

'Of course I remember. You are absolutely grown up now, aren't you, Bea? This show sort of puts the seal on it. Professional. Are you all right? You look a bit over-rosy.'

The room was very warm, and smelly – to Bea's oversensitive nose a synthetic cacophony of the competing scents, a bouillabaisse of the talcum powders, soaps and aftershaves of the well-groomed private viewers. It was a shame, Bea thought, that they didn't co-ordinate themselves before leaving home, that the particular smell to be worn should be printed on the invitation – 'Gardenia tonight, please' or, 'Only Ylang-Ylang will gain you admittance' and already she longed for a salty sniff of sea. She murmured to Patrick that she was fine and was fanning herself with an exhibition card when Simon came up to her and whispered, 'Go and take a peep in the other room. You'll see red stickers on three of the big Freda paintings, and several of the little ones. You're doing really well ... that piece by May in the *Daily Telegraph* about you and Geraldine aroused a lot of interest. We're very pleased. You look a bit pink – are you all right?'

Preoccupied, Bea was staring at Simon as if she had not heard. A delicate but self-important fluttering sensation had just run across her interior like a mouse, making her gasp and clutch at her stomach. She was wearing a long lace jacket which hid any hint of bulge beneath her straight dress; very few people had been let in on the secret.

'Now you've gone quite white,' said Patrick anxiously, 'are you all right?'

'No, yes, I'm ... I'm absolutely stunned, Simon. Where's Nut? Have you seen him? I've got to tell him at once.' He was standing by the drinks table, his arm firmly clasping Geraldine's while telling Amelia a tall story, making them both rock with laughter.

'Nut, just a second, I must speak to you,' she whispered and drew him away, quivering with excitement.

'Are you sure? It's quickened?' Eager and solicitous, he slipped his arm round her waist, spreading fingers out over her stomach. 'I can't feel a thing.'

'No, it came and went so quickly – but I'm certain.'

He was grinning like a Cheshire cat, but she felt a mixture of thrill and fear. Closer, closer came the time. Five months more and it would all be clear. There was nothing to worry about. Of course it was Nut's. He looked wonderfully elegant that evening, in a new dark blue jacket and cream shirt. She loved him so fiercely she felt almost sick, a physical manifestation that Oscar had never managed to engender.

The evening wore on and on and the small talk grazed past her ears like bullets but as she was never sure if it was Geraldine's or her own work which was the target or something else entirely, she took little notice, but continued to shake hands and smile.

'... A secular spirituality ... perverse degeneration ... Peter's girl is doing very well at Leeds ... inspiring ... magical ... nine hundred pounds ... prostate trouble ... I must say, Geraldine's aged incredibly ... How much was it? Speak up m'dear, I'm deafened by this racket ... What? No, Caroline's had hers lifted, twice, *and* implants ... wind-tunnel effect ... that one has a tenderness and an authority ... wildly idiosyncratic ... Carla's very good at ball-room dancing – she did a lot of it in Zimbabwe ... what draughtsmanship, so rare in the young ... it was Henrietta who kept the de Kooning.'

'Right, Bea. Are you feeling all right? Have you done your duty and chatted up all the customers? Might we go to supper soon? Geraldine's sold her three new pictures and just tipped back another drink. She's trying to entice James into taking her on to some pub called the French, in Soho, with a lot of old reprobates who've come along to support her! One of her old haunts apparently. Was she really a shy old lady when you first met her? She's not now, is she? She's just felt my bum and Simon's hiding in the other room in case she tells everyone they once were lovers.'

'Did she tell you that?' Bea asked.

'She did, and told Amelia and Edmund who, incidentally, have just bought one of your mad water-colours of fat angels eating poppies. And your Heron Man, Justin. He's bought two drawings.'

'Oh, that *is* flattering! I still can't quite believe it's all happened. It *wouldn't* have happened without my three lifeboats: Nest, Geraldine and you. We should be allowed to go now, it's nearly nine and it was supposed to end at eight and I'm starving again. Should we stay and help Simon with Geraldine, perhaps? She's staying the night with him.'

'Jesus! No! Let's leave him to it. They've got years' worth of making-up to do.'

'Right, I'll just go and say good-bye and thanks to Geraldine and Simon and then round up the family.'

Chapter Twelve and A Half

Bea had at first been reluctant, then cautiously agreed as Agnes pleaded and they met, still with suspicions on Bea's part, at the recreation ground in Bellhurst on a June afternoon. Seb, released from primary school, hung upside down by his knees from a climbing frame and hooted like an owl. Sitting on the bench beneath the fresh green leaves of a lime tree, they inspected the wriggling contents of each other's baby-baskets.

Agnes peered at Bea's fairy changeling lying there in the dappled shade. It appeared to grin at her, delicate little wrists and minute hands circling and waving as if enticing, wreaking enchantments.

'What have you called her?'

'Freda Mary.'

'Good lord! That sounds a bit heavy. Sort of Lawrentian. Freda! Is it a family name?'

'No, it just came to me. It means peace – which of course was asking for trouble.'

'Well, at least there aren't any doubts about whose it is. I've never seen a baby with so much red hair.'

Bea glanced nervously at her, as if expecting her to produce some scissors, and did not mention that her great Aunt Maude had been a red head, as her mother had pointed out loudly in the hospital, in front of Nut. She hastily turned to inspect

Agnes's little boy, bending over him for an uncomfortably long space of time and when she looked up, she could barely keep a straight face.

'God! Agnes! But the chances of this happening are astronomical. I didn't think it was something that could be inherited?'

The kitten blue mist had faded from the baby's eyes and Bea had seen that the blond, plump, rose-cheeked William's eyes were of different colours: one slate, one green. Agnes looked away into the distance, disconsolate.

'Well, it's happened, astronomical or not. Oscar noticed, went all white and quiet and after muttering about deceit and other things I won't go into, has left. I got a letter this morning from his solicitor, demanding blood tests.'

'This is Phil's son, then? Have you told him?'

'It looks like it, doesn't it?' Agnes replied crossly; little lines were beginning to etch themselves about her mouth. 'I can't think how it happened. I must have been drunk. And he was three weeks earlier than expected. Just as well, he weighed nine and a half pounds. Anyway, even if it's just a freak chance and the tests prove whose it isn't, I don't want to go back to either of them. Oscar's a pompous prat and Phil's a sanctimonious grouch. And Seb's being horrid to William. As soon as my back's turned he pinches him.'

'Agnes, he's probably terribly jealous, poor lamb. And as far as Seb's concerned, Phil is his father. Phil would be devastated if he knew this one might be his.'

'It's not fair, Bea.' Agnes's voice wobbled. 'Why does everything always go wrong for me and right for you?'

Unfathomable, except by Freda.

Waiting for Lindsay
MOIRA FORSYTH

On a hot July day, Lindsay Mathieson, confident, careless and thirteen years old, walks up the beach where she has played all her life, around the rocks and out of sight. She leaves behind her two younger brothers, and her cousins Annie and Alistair. She does not come back.

Thirty years later, the rest of them are still coping with the consequences of events on that fateful day. Each has to deal with a child – or the absence of a child; with the emotions express – or inexpressible; with silences that are as eloquent as words. Gradually they are drawn back to the High House, where as cousins they played on that sunny beach. Here they must come to terms not just with the past, but with their own fallibility and an uncertain future.

Moira Forsyth is a poet and short story writer and has contributed to several prestigious anthologies such as: *After the Watergaw, New Scottish Writing* and *New Writing Scotland*. She was awarded a Scottish Arts Council Writer's Bursary in 1996.

∫

SCEPTRE

Under Construction
PAMELA JOHNSON

Everyone says it's crazy: renovating a dilapidated house in North London is no job for a young widow with teenage daughters. But it's three years since Greg died, Amy needs a new start. A team of builders tears the house apart around her. As they rebuild it, Amy develops an intimacy with Conor the Irish joiner. Where in her new life can she accommodate a relationship with a married man, father of four young children?

Conor and Amy can exist only in the pockets of time and space they slip into, unnoticed: London cafés, windswept Dungeness, the West coast of Ireland, and the infinite space of Amy's imagination. In reconstructing her life, Amy treads a fine line between creating something and destroying it.

This poetic first novel explores the intimate spaces one woman constructs as she recovers herself.

'Irresistibly readable, with a striking storyline. Pamela Johnson writes with great feeling and wit'
HELEN DUNMORE

'The slow, yet dizzying slide into love makes for a compelling read'
JAMES FRIEL

∫

SCEPTRE

Deep Blue Silence
PAMELA JOHNSON

Maddie is haunted by silence that surrounds her mother.

Silence. We came to depend upon it, an extra element. Vital as air.

As an artist, Maddie explores the silence without using words. She begins to make work for a major exhibition but is distracted; she may be pregnant. Maddie discovers she too can be secretive. As the new work progresses, pieced together from fragments of broken glass, Maddie delves into a silence spanning three generations.

'Compelling reading . . . The novel looks at the complex sources of inspiration that inspire new work.' *Crafts Magazine*

'An elegant novel about a woman obsessed with a secret past and how art can be made from the stuff of ordinary lives. Maddie, an artist living in London is on the brink of success. She is working on an installation using family glass that was broken by her mother, Faith, in a shocking incident twenty years earlier. The story is buried in silence and, as Maddie works, she begins to unravel her mother's past.' *Belfast Telegraph*

'Johnson's compelling second novel explores the corrosive effects of family secrets and the results as the past is finally made visible . . . Very well written and immensely readable.' *Wigan Evening Post*

SCEPTRE

STEVIE MORGAN

DELPHINIUM BLUES

Of course I knew he was shagging someone the moment I found the Queen's Greatest Hits cassette in his car, amongst the usual ones by Howling Dog Shannon and Stinkin' Feet Brown.

Jess is just about to discover that the marriage she thought made in heaven turns out to have been knocked up from spare parts in a back room of hell. When her husband of fifteen years takes off to do Personal Growth and Advanced Shagging with a red-haired twenty-something, Jess is left with two grief-stricken children, a vast mortgage on the rural idyll and nothing on her CV but cake crumbs.

No wonder her first instinct is to smash plates, stop eating and spend whole days face down on the kitchen floor. Not for long. Starting with painting her bedroom pink and buying a pair of purple stilettos, Jess reinvents herself. And with a little help from her friends, discovers there is life after divorce.

A FLAME PAPERBACK

STEVIE MORGAN

FLY AWAY PETER

Even though it is five years since Peter died, Myfanwy still has memories of their time together playing constantly in her head. By choice, she leads a solitary life in their beach cabin on the Welsh coast, her only social contact with cousin Idris and his large and exhuberant family. Myfanwy is not unhappy – more emotionally numb.

Until the arrival of David . . .

David's determined efforts to seduce Myfanwy are foiled initially with comic effect, but do eventually succeed. Both are stuck in their pasts. Both must let go to be able to start again, and through each other they do. Through David, Myfanwy finds the strength to say 'Fly away Peter' and seize her own life with vitality and vigour.

A FLAME PAPERBACK

LIBBY PURVES

MORE LIVES THAN ONE

A generous hearted novel of modern family life

Kit Milcourt – impatient, quirky, idealistic and brilliant – has been a climber, diver in exotic waters and affluent young city banker. Now, because of his beloved Anna, he is a teacher. Glumly mediocre Sandmarsh High School, reeling under assaults from Inspectors and its own unpromising pupils, is hard put to contain his maverick ideas. Year Seven, on the other hand, love them. Only the soothing presence of Anna keeps the peace.

But Anna can't guard her erratic husband on the school trip: instead a far darker, more malevolent staffroom presence crosses Europe and discovers what Kit has secretly planned for the children amid the dim alleys of winter Venice. But children are unpredictable too, and things move rapidly beyond both teachers' control.

Between farce and tragedy the resulting events swiftly change Kit's and Anna's lives in unthinkable ways, strain a great love to the limit and open a dark chasm into the past.

A FLAME PAPERBACK

LIBBY PURVES

REGATTA

Anansi, child of council care and parental carelessness, is cast up for the summer in a Suffolk town, between sea and muddy river. Her hosts' complacency and her own demons drive her to torpedo its peace with a well-timed revelation about what she saw in the old Martello Tower. The results are comic, catastrophic and cathartic for Anansi, for cosy Sheila and her peevish husband Simon, for his lover, and the whole summer community around them. An atmospheric adventure story about childhood, courage and reconciliation.

A FLAME PAPERBACK

A selection of other books from
Hodder & Stoughton

Waiting for Linsay	Moira Forsyth	0 340 750014	£6.99	☐
Under Construction	Pamela Johnson	0 340 71798X	£6.99	☐
Deep Blue Silence	Pamela Johnson	0 340 718005	£7.99	☐
Delphinium Blues	Stevie Morgan	0 340 718021	£6.99	☐
Fly Away Peter	Stevie Morgan	0 340 718048	£6.99	☐
More Lives Than One	Libby Purves	0 340 680431	£6.99	☐
Regatta	Libby Purves	0 340 718811	£6.99	☐

All Sceptre books are available from your local bookshop or newsagent, or can be ordered direct from the publisher. Just tick the titles you want and fill in the form below. Prices and availability subject to change without notice.

Hodder & Stoughton Books, Cash Sales Department, Bookpoint, 39 Milton Park, Abingdon, OXON, OX14 4TD, UK. E-mail address: order@bookpoint.co.uk. If you have a credit card you may order by telephone – (01235) 400414.

Please enclose a cheque or postal order made payable to Bookpoint Ltd to the value of the cover price and allow the following for postage and packing:
UK & BFPO – £1.00 for the first book, 50p for the second book, and 30p for each additional book ordered up to a maximum charge of £3.00.
OVERSEAS & EIRE – £2.00 for the first book, £1.00 for the second book, and 50p for each additional book

Name _____

Address _____

_____

_____

If you would prefer to pay by credit card, please complete:
Please debit my Visa/Access/Diner's Card/American Express (delete as applicable) card no:

Signature _____

Expiry Date _____

If you would NOT like to receive further information on our products please tick the box. ☐